Katie Price x

Make My Wish Come True

CENTURY

Published by Century, 2014

2 4 6 8 10 9 7 5 3 1

Copyright © Katie Price, 2014

First published in Great Britain in 2014 by
Century
Random House, 20 Vauxhall Bridge Road,
London SW1V 2SA

www.randomhouse.co.uk

Addresses for companies within The Random House Group Limited can
be found at: www.randomhouse.co.uk/offices.htm

The Random House Group Limited Reg. No. 954009

A CIP catalogue record for this book
is available from the British Library

Hardback ISBN 9781780893471
Trade paperback ISBN 9781780893488

The Random House Group Limited supports the Forest Stewardship
Council® (FSC®), the leading international forest-certification organisation.
Our books carrying the FSC label are printed on FSC®-certified paper.
FSC is the only forest-certification scheme endorsed by the
leading environmental organisations, including Greenpeace.
Our paper procurement policy can be found at:
www.rbooks.co.uk/environment

Printed and bound by CPI Group (UK) Ltd, Croydon, CR0 4YY

Make My
Wish Come
True

Then

As sunlight streamed through the kitchen window, Storm Saunders paused midway through basting the turkey and allowed the warmth to wash over her. She couldn't remember the last time the sun had put in an appearance on Christmas morning – perhaps it was the sign of a perfect day ahead for them.

It was only mid-morning but she had been up for hours, wrapping last-minute gifts, putting finishing touches to the tree, preparing the lunch and hastily getting rid of the mince pie left for Santa – all before her younger brother Bailey and sister Lexie got up.

Still, it had been worth it. The kids had loved the second-hand toys and games she had saved for, and her mother Sally had been impressed with the perfume set. As for Storm, her brother and sister had treated her to a lovely new pair of woolly gloves that were soft as snow. Spotting

them on the worktop, she absentmindedly stroked them. She always felt the cold and was touched the kids had remembered that. After she had pushed the turkey back into the oven, she flicked on the kettle and reached on top of the breadbin for her bumper edition of *Vida!* magazine. Peering at the kitchen clock, she saw there was just enough time for her to catch up on some celebrity gossip. Bliss!

'Enjoying a well-earned rest, love?' said Sally, walking into the kitchen.

'Something like that,' replied Storm, unable to tear her eyes from the magazine. 'I've got about twenty minutes before I have to put the spuds on.'

'Why don't you let me do that?' her mother suggested. 'Go out and play with Bailey and Lexie. They're dying to show off the new scooter that you bought them.'

Storm looked up from her magazine in surprise. Usually Sally didn't get out of bed until lunchtime. Perhaps the sun outside really was a promise of change.

'If you're sure?' Storm grinned, eager for the chance to spend some time with the kids. 'I'll take them to the park for an hour.'

'Don't rush back,' Sally replied, shooing Storm away as she reached for the apron hanging behind the kitchen door. 'I can manage here.'

Storm walked along the hallway's threadbare floral carpet, calling to her brother and sister, 'Kids, get your coats on. We're going to the park.' Hearing the sudden scramble of Bailey and Lexie running down the stairs, she couldn't help smiling. Christmas really could be a magical time of year.

Reaching for their hands, Storm shouted goodbye to her mother and together the three of them walked out into the cold morning air. They were halfway down the road when Storm realised she'd forgotten her gloves. 'You guys wait here for just two seconds and I'll be right back,' she told them, racing towards the house.

But passing the kitchen window, Storm stood rooted to the spot as she took in the sight of Sally adding a very generous measure of whisky to her cup of tea. Storm's eyes brimmed with tears as she watched her mother sip her drink and smile. To any bystander this would just look like a busy mum enjoying a drink on Christmas morning. But Storm knew the truth of it – since her father Alan had passed away four years ago, her mother had become an alcoholic, constantly looking for ways to sneak a drink whenever she could.

Looking at her mother now, filling her mug with more whisky, Storm felt like kicking herself. How could she have been so stupid as to hope for a happy Christmas? Leaving the gloves, she stuffed her hands in her pockets as she ran back towards the kids, she realised that for her there was no such thing.

Chapter One

Storm raced into her flat and began tearing off her clothes before the door had even banged shut.

As a journalist for Brighton's *Daily Post* she'd spent the past three hours covering what could only be described as the world's most boring planning meeting, and was now running seriously late for her one and only swanky Christmas party

'Can you get me a wine?' she shouted to Dermot, her boyfriend. 'I'm gagging! The meeting ran over.'

'You're the one who looks like you've been run over,' a voice bantered from the living room.

Storm spun round and saw her friend Carly, taking the piss as always. Perched on the battered IKEA sofa, smiling her trademark toothy grin, she waved a bottle of supermarket champagne in the air. The best medicine! Dumping her bag on the floor, Storm realised one of the reasons why she and Carly were best mates.

'You're a mind reader, I've had a shitty day,' she complained to her friend.

'I'd ask you to tell me all about it, but before he went out Dermot said you were covering some council thing. I think the details might kill the party spirit.'

Fair point. Watching her friend fill her glass, Storm admired Carly's outfit. At a little over five foot Carly was sensitive about her height, but she was an absolute stunner. Tonight she was dressed in a black and coral shift dress, skyscraper black heels and a chunky metal necklace. With her long blonde hair effortlessly piled on top of her head and secured with diamante pins, she looked gorgeous.

'Do you ever have an off day?' Storm asked, hugging her friend.

'Can't afford too, babe, image is everything!' As a stylist Carly never walked out of the door looking less than one hundred per cent perfect. Luckily for Storm, Carly's job meant that she could usually lend her cash-strapped pal a bit of bling, and had even been known to 'lose' the odd designer dress Storm's way. Tonight, one of Carly's clients had invited her to the biggest party in town and Storm was her plus one.

Just as well. Being a journalist for the local rag wasn't exactly what you'd call glamorous. In fact, weekly planning meetings, neighbourhood watch groups and prize marrow contests were not at all what Storm had imagined when she'd left college seven years ago with dreams of becoming a showbiz journalist. Back then she'd imagined she'd be hanging out at Cameron Diaz's birthday party one day and shopping for Jimmy Choos with Cat Deeley the next.

Instead, despite hundreds of applications to magazines and newspapers across the UK, Storm had landed a job as a reporter for Brighton's *Daily Post*. The salary was so lean, the only designer lining her wardrobe was George at Asda – talk about a reality check.

She was well aware of how she measured up against her glamorous friend. Her hands were covered in biro and as for the unflattering purple blouse she'd thrown on that morning, she had a horrible feeling it reeked of stale garlic thanks to last night's takeaway. She kicked herself – she should have squirted on that extra bit of perfume before leaving the office.

As Storm reached for a glass and took her first grateful glug, the sound of the doorbell killed her party vibe.

'What now?' she grumbled, hurrying down the stairs.

Opening the door, she came face to face with Sally, who was clutching a pair of straightening irons as if her life depended on it. 'You left these behind when you styled my hair last week.' Her mother smiled and kissed Storm on the cheek. 'I thought you might need them for tonight.'

'Oh, you're a lifesaver, I'd forgotten all about them,' she said gratefully.

'No problem. Do you need any help getting ready?'

'Not really, Sal, but why don't you come on up for a cuppa and say hi to Carly?'

As Storm shut the front door she saw a cloud briefly pass over her mother's face. It wasn't lost on Storm how much Sally wanted to be called Mum, but even though she'd been clean almost nine years now Storm still found it difficult to forgive her for everything she'd put her children through.

Nobody had been happier than Storm when her mother had finally admitted she had a drink problem and went to Alcoholics Anonymous. Now she had sorted herself out and built a new life for herself away from drink. She worked part-time at a nearby supermarket and had made many friends while working on the checkout there. She liked to play bingo on nights out with them. But these days she insisted family came first.

'I've got to be there for my kids,' Sally always said.

Storm knew her mother meant well, but now that Storm had reached the age of twenty-five this show of maternal devotion was too little, too late. As far as Storm was concerned, Sally was never going to be anything more than a kind, well-meaning relative she had to keep an eye on. Nearing the top of the stairs, Storm was grateful to see Carly was already boiling the kettle. Storm could have kissed her – her bestie was always one step ahead when it came to Sally.

'Thought I heard voices. How are you, Sal? I haven't seen you for ages.'

As Carly gave Sally a warm hug, Storm wished she could be more like her friend, who seemed to find it easy to act naturally in every circumstance.

'Oh, Carly, it's wonderful to see you, love. You look fab.'

Graciously, Carly did a little twirl in the kitchen, showing off her new dress.

'Do you mind if I leave you both to it? I've got to ransack my wardrobe for something clean to wear,' Storm told them.

Carly grinned, handing her a carrier bag. 'You need to

chill, babe, it's all taken care of. Now, get your arse in gear and get that on so we can enjoy a girlie night out.'

Reaching inside the bag, Storm gasped as she pulled out a midnight blue mini-dress studded with crystals. It was obviously designer and God knows how much it cost. More than she'd make in a year, if not two. Turning the soft material over in her hands, she smiled in delight. 'It's gorgeous, thanks.'

Carly poured herself another glass of champagne, and shrugged. 'No biggie. Just don't spill anything on it, that one is not on permanent loan!'

Emerging from the shower with her wet hair wrapped in a towel, Storm quickly did her make-up. When she wasn't wearing a suit, she stuck to her uniform of skinny jeans, jumpers and a slick of lip gloss. But tonight she had a feeling her usual mango lip butter wouldn't cut it.

Considering the contents of her make-up bag, Storm decided to go for a classic smoky eye with lots of sultry black kohl and a nude lip gloss to give her a super sexy pout. After blow drying her long hair she reached for the dress, teaming it with a pair of tan stilettos and a matching clutch. Storm felt like a different person. Peering at her reflection in the full-length mirror, she hardly recognised herself. There was no denying the dress was a brilliant fit. It showed off her long, slender legs and hugged her in all the right places, but it was so short it barely covered her arse! Feeling self-conscious, she tugged it down.

'You sure I don't look mutton in this?'

'Don't be stupid,' said Carly firmly. 'Storm, quite

honestly, if I had your legs I probably wouldn't even bother wearing a skirt at all.'

'Carly's right, Stormy. You look beautiful. A far cry from when you were a teen and barely knew one end of a mascara wand from the other,' Sally teased her.

Yes, because make-up was the last thing I had time for when I was so busy taking care of you and being mum to your other two kids, Storm thought furiously.

She had never forgotten how, when she was still coping with the shock of her dad's death, she'd been cruelly teased by the kids at school. Tall and skinny, with pale skin and thick black hair, she'd become a target for the bullies. But over the years Storm had blossomed and was now a knockout with her high cheekbones, taut stomach, clear porcelain skin and deep green eyes. As for the long black hair she'd always hated, it now hung in natural face-framing waves, highlighting her perfect features.

Outside Carly hailed two cabs, one to take Sally home and another for Storm and herself. By half-past nine the two women had reached the seafront restaurant and were more than ready for a good time.

Nico's had opened a month ago and already had an achingly long waiting list. The celebrity chef, known for his brooding Italian good looks, not to mention his Latin temper, was famed for cooking up hip fusion food with a Mediterranean twist. With a primetime TV show and Michelin-starred restaurants in London, Hampshire and now Brighton, Nico had been catapulted into A-list stardom over the last year. When Carly had insisted Storm should join her at his Christmas party, she didn't even need

to check her diary to see if she was free – she was there! When she'd pressed her mate for details of who exactly was on the guest list, Carly had reeled off an impressive list of names that included several actors, reality stars and TV presenters, as well as a string of premiership footballers and WAGs.

Spotting a stack of paps waiting by the red carpet, Storm clambered out of the cab with as much grace as possible in what she felt could only be described as a pussy pelmet. Linking her arm through Carly's, she felt a stab of excitement as they sashayed up the red carpet together.

'How posh is this?' Storm exclaimed.

The restaurant looked stunning. The huge white sash windows were lit with gold hurricane lamps and matching candles. At the entrance stood two enormous pillars, decked in billowing gold drapes. As for the red carpet itself, understated was not the look the party planners had gone for, as a glittering gold yarn with the restaurant's name was woven into the luxe red pile. The whole place screamed glamour – and the security guards dressed in black suits and crisp white shirts added an extra frisson to the general excitement of it all.

Watching the latest TV star glide up the carpet towards the paps, Storm felt a flash of irritation. A journalist just out of her teens stuck a microphone into the star's face and asked which designer she was wearing. How had a young reporter got so lucky?

Sensing trouble, Carly quickly pulled Storm towards the restaurant's entrance and gave their names to the girl in charge of the guest list.

'Have a night off,' whispered Carly. 'You're beautiful, talented, and one day you'll get your big break without sleeping your way to the top like that skank probably did!'

Typical Carly. She always knew just what to say to cheer her up. Storm was seriously impressed to find that inside the restaurant had even more of the wow factor. Greeted by a waiter dressed in black tie, she grabbed a glass of champagne and took a sip. Bliss! Usually the only Christmas do she managed was the office party, where everyone indulged in overcooked turkey and a slab of Arctic Roll at the local pub. Her editor Ron always guzzled way too much whisky and tried to pull Lucy from advertising.

Now Storm drank it all in. Here were the rich and famous, dressed from head to toe in couture. As they sipped free-flowing champagne and feasted on delicate canapés, the sultry voice of Emeli Sandé pumped through the sound system. In one corner stood a huge Christmas tree, lavishly decorated in gold and black, and in another a small gold and black stage had been set up for superstar singers to perform on later. Peering around the corner, Storm was delighted to see a group of elves inside a massive gingerbread house, helping guests make their very own delicious miniature versions – this party really was the bollocks!

'Thanks so much for inviting me, babe.'

'Any time!' Carly smiled as she scanned the room, looking for anyone she might know – it didn't take long.

Weaving her way through the crowds with Storm following close behind, she patted the shoulder of a man dressed in skinny black jeans and a fitted blazer. He

whipped around and his face broke into an excited smile as he saw Carly. 'OMG, you look fab!' he said, air kissing her on both cheeks before she introduced him to Storm.

'That dress looks like it was made for you – damn, girl, you look fierce.'

Storm smiled. Jez was clearly a sweetheart. She'd heard all about him from Carly, as they often worked together when she styled magazine shoots, but Storm had never had the pleasure of meeting him until now. She knew Jez was a hairdresser, gay, married to Rufus and total BFFs with Brighton royalty Angel Summer and Liberty Evans, the Hollywood actress who flitted between the States and the south coast with her artist fiancé Cory Richardson.

'Thanks! You're totally rocking that Tom Ford,' Storm replied.

'Oh, I'd like to do more than rock Tom Ford,' sighed Jez theatrically. 'With those brooding eyes, he is *gorgeous!*'

'And what am I . . . chopped liver!' mocked the good-looking man standing next to him.

Jez smiled fondly at his husband Rufus. 'Darling, you know I only have eyes for you, but Tom's on my allowed list! Besides, I said I'd totes forgive you an indiscretion with Michael Fassbender. But enough about me. What do you do, Storm?'

'Oh, Storm's a news— ' cut in Carly.

'Don't say it!' she interrupted, putting a hand in front of Carly's face. 'Tonight I'm anything but a local newspaper hack. I'm having a night off, like you said.'

'Ooh, be an air stewardess!' exclaimed Jez. 'With those

legs you could easily pass for a trolley dolly, doling out chicken or fish in first class.'

Storm giggled. 'Knowing my luck, I'd end up dropping it in their laps so often I'd be bumped straight back to economy, but it's definitely different.'

'And what about you?' Jez turned to Carly. 'The spray tan you had earlier really sets off that divine little coral number. Wearing it for anyone in particular tonight?'

'Pah! I'm off men, remember?'

'Darling, can I be honest? I know you caught your ex with his hand in the cookie jar, but they're not all the same, I promise.'

That's putting it mildly, thought Storm. A year ago, Carly had been loved up and planning the wedding of the century to Paul, a music promoter. With his open, friendly face and thinning hair, Paul wasn't the best-looking bloke Storm had ever seen but he adored Carly.

They'd been together five years when he'd proposed on a beach in the Maldives with a whopping two-carat diamond engagement ring. And although Storm would never admit this in a million years, from the moment Paul had slipped that ring on her finger, Carly became a bit of a Bridezilla. In fact, she got so wound up about everything that she made herself ill and fainted at work. Jez sent her home, making her promise she'd do nothing more than put her feet up for the rest of the day.

But when Carly walked through the door, she found Paul with another woman in their bed. Poor Carly was broken-hearted. To add insult to injury, Paul then threw her out of the flat he owned, telling her that the slapper

he'd been screwing was moving in instead. Bastard! Storm could have killed him.

Thanks to Jez, who had once dated an estate agent, Carly found a gorgeous new flat overlooking the sea. After selling the ring, she had enough money for a deposit and could rebuild her life.

Now she was doing much better, but Storm knew her friend was still fragile. She hadn't been on a date since the split.

'Listen, I know the hottest straight man with seriously ripped abs,' continued Jez.

Rufus rolled his eyes. 'Don't ask how he knows that.'

'Yes, well, I might have tried to show him the error of his ways by convincing him he was wasted as a heterosexual, but he wasn't having it. Anyway, you know what they say . . . when you fall off a horse, you have to get right back on. And I think he'd be the perfect stud to get you back in the saddle!'

'Yeah, come on, live a little. We're at a party, there must be someone here you fancy,' Storm coaxed her friend.

'Thanks, guys, but no.'

Storm reached for a canapé from a passing waiter's tray and took a hungry bite. 'If you don't get some action soon, you're in danger of becoming a virgin again, and you know how bad it was popping your cherry first time around!'

'Cheers for that, but seriously I'm in no mood to find Mr Right or even Mr Right Now.'

'What about Mrs Right? Jez twinkled. 'If you fancy a complete change of scene, I know a gorgeous American lesbian who insists on a Brazilian, if you know what I

mean.'

'We all know what you mean!' laughed Carly. 'And, no, leave me alone, all of you! I don't want a man, or a woman, or even a Rampant Rabbit! All I want is another drink.'

With that, Carly left her pals to gossip and went in search of more champagne.

By half-past ten the party was in full swing. Scanning the now crowded restaurant, Storm caught sight of Carly by the Christmas tree, being chatted up by a very handsome man. Tall, mixed-race, with broad shoulders and dressed in designer jeans and a navy V-neck jumper, he was gorgeous. Storm looked again. Hang on. That was only Dillon Adams, Chelsea's newest player. Way to go, Carly!

Storm smiled. It was about time Carly listened to her. She couldn't avoid men for ever. And this one was seriously hot – maybe Carly was in for a little Christmas bonus. God knows, she deserved it. But taking a closer look, Storm realised Dillon wasn't chatting Carly up. Instead he seemed to be having a go at her. With his face bent over hers and a mean look in his eyes, Dillon appeared menacing. As for Carly, she looked defeated with her eyes cast down and her mouth set in a grim line. Storm knew tears would start flowing any minute.

Tosser! Who the fuck did this two-bit footballer think he was, upsetting her friend? She drained her drink, banged down the empty glass on the nearest table and threw her shoulders back, ready to give the scumbag a piece of her mind. She didn't see the man heading towards her, carrying a very large glass of red wine. As Storm stepped

straight into his path they collided, wine spilling all over his pristine white shirt.

'*Per l'amor di Dio!* Try looking where you're going,' the man snarled.

Storm was horrified. 'I'm so, so sorry. Let me help clean you up.'

Reaching into her clutch for the packet of tissues she always carried, she feebly started patting at the stranger's chest. But it was no use, she was only making the stain worse. Aghast, she looked up into his seething eyes. What she saw took her breath away – he was fit! Taller than her, with olive skin and black hair that was greying at the temples, he was seriously her type.

'Just leave it,' the stranger hissed, gripping her wrist.

His touch sent a jolt of electricity through Storm. Looking into his chocolate brown eyes, she knew he'd felt it too. Dropping her hand as if it had scalded him he stepped back, their eyes still locked. As Storm's pulse raced the man eventually looked away, breaking the spell. His fierce expression softened.

Taking a deep breath, he looked down at his shiny Italian loafers before returning his gaze to Storm. 'I'm sorry. I overreacted, it's just a shirt, and I shouldn't have lost my temper like that . . .?'

'This is Storm, she's an air stewardess,' chimed in Jez, who had very suddenly appeared at his new friend's side. Elbowing Storm out of the way, he thrust his hand towards the stranger and babbled on. 'She's just as clumsy in first class, so she's back in economy from next week. Let me just say, hand on heart, Nico, those lobster canapés were

to die for.'

Storm looked again at the man quietly steaming in front of her. Of course – Nico Alvise! Some showbiz journalist she would make if she couldn't even recognise the man throwing the party. Storm wanted the ground to swallow her up there and then. Had she really just slopped wine all over the hottest chef in the country?

Must have been those razor-sharp cheekbones that distracted me, she thought as she ran her eyes appreciatively over his face and what appeared to be some very solid pecs. Shit! What was the matter with her? She had a boyfriend at home!

As Jez prattled on Storm saw a smartly dressed young woman scurry over to Nico to hand him a fresh white shirt. He murmured his thanks and turned back to Storm, bending down to kiss her cheek.

'My apologies again for losing my temper. Please enjoy the rest of the party. *Ciao, bella.*'

Speechless, Storm watched him walk away, already unbuttoning his sodden shirt. Jez nudged her sharply in the ribs.

'What a silver fox! He's even better in real life than he is on the telly. What I wouldn't give . . .'

'Adding him to your list, are you?' she laughed.

'I'm tempted. He's like a younger George Clooney, and you know Clooney never goes out of style.'

'Forget it. My husband wouldn't have time to get through his existing list, never mind start adding to it,' Rufus added, joining them.

'That's what you think. I'm a young man in my prime,

I'll have you know,' protested Jez. As he kissed Rufus firmly on the lips, Storm was finally able to rescue her friend.

It didn't take long to find her. Sitting alone at the bar in a black velvet tub chair, Carly was steadily working her way through another glass of champagne. It looked like she was definitely drinking to forget, Storm thought, as she slid into the chair next to hers.

'Everything all right?'

'Yeah, fine,' Carly slurred.

Storm grimaced. 'Don't give me that, babe. You know I can see right through your bullshit. How do you know Dillon Adams and why was he giving you grief?'

'No reason,' muttered Carly, pretending Storm didn't know her better than she knew herself.

Wordlessly Storm waited. She reached for another glass of champagne. She knew Carly would talk eventually. 'I've done something really stupid,' her friend admitted.

'What? Convinced a bitchy client to buy a mini-dress when they've got legs like tree trunks?' Storm teased her.

Carly shook her head. Putting her hand over her eyes, she started weeping.

'If only it were that simple.'

For the second time that night, Storm reached into her clutch for a tissue. This time she pressed it into her best friend's hand and put her arm around Carly's heaving shoulders.

'Bollocks!' Carly sniffed back tears. 'It took me hours to do my make-up tonight.'

'Yeah, and you'll have to go to the loos and spend hours doing it all over again unless you want to look like Marilyn

Manson.' Storm smiled. 'Now tell me what is going on?'

'Promise me you won't tell anyone?'

'Do you really have to ask that?' Storm fired back.

The girls had been through hell and high water together over the years and had been the keeper of more of each other's secrets than either of them cared to remember.

'You know I worked on a shoot for that football magazine the other week?' Carly sighed.

Storm nodded. Carly often styled models for the covers of glossy monthlies, but when a friend of hers fell ill at the last minute, she'd agreed to step in and style a handful of premiership players for a football mag.

'Yeah, you said it went really well.'

'It was brilliant. Afterwards one of the players wanted to talk to me about helping his sister find an outfit for her twenty-first birthday party, so we went to Nobu together and afterwards to The Sanderson for cocktails.'

'And?'

Carly didn't miss a beat. 'It was fab. I had the sea bass and one too many dirty Martinis.'

At the mention of food, Storm looked fleetingly around her. Everybody was now busy devouring the blinis which were being handed out. Storm's tummy grumbled appreciatively. The two canapés she'd eaten earlier hadn't touched the sides. Especially as all she'd had time for at lunch was a bag of Quavers and a can of Diet Coke. Now she was starving and predictably the booze was going straight to her head.

'But what about the outfit?' she urged.

Carly shifted uncomfortably in her chair. She'd forgotten

why Storm was such a good journalist. She was like a dog with a bone and always managed to get people to talk, not satisfied until she'd heard every last detail.

'That's the thing, we never actually got around to deciding on an outfit.' Carly laughed. 'I mean, we discussed it obviously, but after The Sanderson he was a bit tired, and so was I, so we . . .'

Storm squealed and clapped her hands in delight. 'You shagged him, didn't you? No wonder you didn't want to meet anyone tonight. Come on, I want all the gory details, and I mean *all*. Who is he? Are you going to see him again?'

Taking another sip of champagne, Carly drummed her fingers on the chair's armrest and avoided meeting her friend's eye.

Storm was confused. This was brilliant news. No wonder Carly didn't want to pull if she'd already met someone. So why the secrecy? This was something to celebrate! There was no reason for her suddenly to start being weird unless . . .

'He's married, isn't he?' Storm asked quietly.

Nodding her head, Carly slumped back in her chair. Storm did her best to hide her shock. Carly was the last person in the world she would have expected to do this. Storm thought back to all the late nights she'd shared with Carly drinking tequila after Paul had betrayed her. She'd lost count of all the conversations they'd had then, insisting they'd never sleep with a married man. That it was a total deal breaker. That you should always think about the wife or girlfriend at home waiting for her man.

'Please don't look at me like that, Storm, I didn't set out

to do this. I feel terrible about it.'

'So what happened?' she asked gently.

Carly didn't answer for what felt like an age. 'I don't know. I don't know if it was because I hadn't been touched in what felt like for ever, because I was lonely, because I wanted to feel loved and special for a change, because I was sick of being on my own . . . or even just because it felt like a good idea at the time.'

'Who is he?'

'I'd rather not say.'

'You've come this far, you might as well tell me everything.'

Carly hesitated then she said, 'Aston Booth.'

Storm flinched. Aston Booth wasn't just married, he had three kids and another on the way. Like Dillon, he played for Chelsea and England. Together with his wife Tanya he was always in the press, plugging his charity that helped disadvantaged kids across the world. Storm had thought he was different from a lot of footballers. He seemed a kind, decent, devoted family man, still madly in love with his childhood sweetheart. While other players were constantly in the press after bedding lap dancers, Aston never was. In fact, Storm was sure he had been in the papers the other day, talking about how he couldn't wait to be a dad again. Apparently he wanted a football team all of his own.

There could very well be a football team out there with his name already on it, thought Storm wryly. She suddenly felt nauseous and wasn't entirely sure it was down to lack of food. As for Carly, she looked beaten. Storm knew kicking her while she was down wasn't the answer. She'd suffered

21

enough for one night.

'So how was he?' she asked, lightening the mood.

'OK,' Carly replied. 'Not brilliant, but definitely not the worst. He seemed a bit out of practice, shall we say?'

Storm giggled. 'And was it weird, being with someone else?'

Carly shrugged. 'Yeah, but it was nice. I took a photo of us together . . . look.'

Fishing out her phone, Carly showed her friend a selfie of her with Aston, who seemed completely absorbed in kissing Carly's neck. They looked like a typical couple, young and in love.

'Afterwards wasn't great,' Carly admitted as she put her phone away. 'He couldn't get out of the hotel quick enough. I thought he might at least stick around for breakfast.'

Storm said nothing. What else was Carly expecting? Hearts and flowers? He had a wife and kids to get back to, for God's sake.

'So what did his team mate want?'

'To warn me off going to the press.'

'As if you'd do something like that!' exclaimed Storm, loyal to the core. 'That is totally out of order, branding you as some cheap slut who needs to sell her soul for a couple of quid.'

It was not OK for some lowlife footballer to diss her best friend. Cheeky bastard!

'That's what I said, but Dillon told me there'd be trouble if I even thought about it. He said he'd make sure my career ended in tatters if I talked to the papers.'

Storm shook with rage as she scanned the room looking

for Dillon. He'd gone too far and she was about to tell him just how much of a tosser she thought he was. But he seemed to have disappeared. Getting to her feet, Storm suddenly sobered up. She realised it might be a blessing in disguise if he'd gone home after all. That wanker had ruined enough of their night. It was time to draw a line under all this.

'Let's party,' she said, reaching for Carly's hand.

The rest of the night passed in a blur as the girls drank too much champagne and ate too little. Thankfully, Storm didn't see Nico for the rest of the night and they both danced like mad as the DJ played hit after hit.

But if anyone was really going for it it was Jez, who prided himself on an outrageous Dirty Dancing routine.

With his pelvic thrusts and perfectly timed moves, he gathered quite a crowd of onlookers, including Storm and Carly who joined Rufus to show their support.

'What's got into him?' Carly asked.

'He filled in for one of the hairdressers on *Strictly* the other week,' Rufus explained. 'Since then he's convinced he's Craig Revel Horwood.'

'He looks more like Darcey Bussell, with that woman over there trying to pick him up,' Carly laughed.

Amazed, Storm saw a large woman try to lift Jez off the floor. Obviously pissed, it looked like she was trying to reinvent Patrick Swayze's famous move, but Jez was having none of it.

'Get off me!' he hissed, shaking himself free.

Back in solo performance, he was keen to step things

23

up a gear. It didn't take long. He soon had his audience's full attention as he grabbed hold of a counter-height table packed with drinks and began bumping and grinding against it as if his life depended on it. As the crowd whooped and cheered, he executed some further ambitious moves that included the splits and an eye-watering high kick.

Sadly for him, disaster struck when one turn too many brought the table and drinks crashing to the floor. Jez was lying on the ground, his blazer and skinny jeans soaked in champagne. Rufus rushed to his aid, leaving Storm, Carly and the crowd howling with laughter.

As Rufus pulled the table off Jez, he got to his feet and hobbled towards the girls. 'It's not bloody funny! I could have drowned in all that booze, you witches. In fact, it's a miracle I'm alive at all.'

'You've survived, but your street cred definitely hasn't,' Carly giggled.

Still shaking with laughter, they watched Jez limp towards a taxi. Deciding nothing was going to top that, the girls called it a night.

Chapter Two

The following morning Storm woke to find that drummers had moved into her brain. Gasping for water, she reached for the glass she always kept on her nightstand and gulped down the liquid gratefully.

'Oh, God! My mouth feels as dry as a pair of grubby Havaianas,' she groaned.

'So just how scuttered were you last night?' murmured Dermot, snaking his hand around her waist.

'You don't want to know.'

Leaning against the headboard, Storm reflected on the night before. On the whole, it had been brilliant. She and Carly had partied hard, and the place had been wall-to-wall with celebs. Star-struck at first, Storm had felt shy, but after a few glasses of champagne she'd loosened up. She'd spent a lot of time talking to a couple of the *Made in Chelsea* girls, who turned out to be really sweet. It was exactly the sort of event she'd have expected to cover if she'd ever made it as a showbiz journalist. But the chances

of that happening now seemed even slimmer after she'd embarrassed herself by spilling wine all over last night's host.

Willing away the humiliation, Storm turned her head face down into the pillow. She wouldn't be invited back after showing herself up in front of Nico like that.

Dermot chuckled as he pulled her closer. 'What did you do this time?'

'Can't talk about it. Too embarrassing.'

He trailed his fingertips across her shoulders. 'Sure, I bet I can get you to open up.'

She didn't know if it was his soft Irish lilt, or just the fact that she was too knackered to resist, but Storm found herself melting into his featherlight kisses.

'Knew I could get you to talk,' he whispered. Easing her cotton nightshirt over her head, he gazed lustfully at her.

Afterwards they sank back gratefully against the mattress, the duvet tangled around their legs. Dermot propped himself up on one elbow and said, 'So tell all, darling, how was the *craic* last night?'

'Brilliant.'

'And your man Nico?'

At the mention of his name, Storm shuddered.

'Let's just say, I let the host know exactly who I was.'

A smile played over Dermot's lips. He knew what that meant. In the two years he'd been going out with Storm, he'd seen many times at first hand just how clumsy she could be. She'd dropped countless cups of tea and coffee, and broken more than her fair share of mirrors. The first time she'd invited him round to her place for dinner

26

had become legendary. Storm had proudly told him she had cooked a Spanish chicken stew from scratch, but as she carried the casserole dish from kitchen to table she somehow ended up dropping the entire thing on the floor.

She had been furious with herself as she and Dermot scraped bits of chicken and tomato off the carpet. But he thought it was sweet and after they'd cleaned up the mess had treated her to a pizza around the corner, promising never to mention the incident again. Privately, Dermot nicknamed his girlfriend Calamity, but valuing his knackers as he did this was something he kept to himself. He always reckoned there was a reason why Alan and Sally had had the foresight to call their elder daughter Storm.

'And how was Carly? Did she pull anyone?'

Storm sighed as she thought about her best friend's latest disaster. There was nobody who deserved a chance of happiness more than Carly did. No doubt she was feeling rough in more ways than one after last night. Storm looked at her boyfriend, wondering just how much to tell him.

They'd met when Dermot had joined the paper as chief reporter just over two years ago, and Storm had never forgot the first moment they saw each other. With his sandy blond hair, square shoulders, piercing blue eyes and cool exterior, she'd fancied him straight away – and it seemed the feeling was mutual. Making a beeline for her cluttered desk, Dermot Whelan skipped the small talk and asked her out for a drink that night.

'Are you always this forward?' Storm demanded.

Dermot grinned cheekily, his broad Irish brogue already

making her melt. 'No, but when I see something I want, I go for it.'

Since they'd been together, Dermot had seemed to have become as fond of Storm's friend Carly as she had of him. Besides, they were a partnership, they didn't keep secrets from each other.

'OK, I'll tell you about it. But promise not to tell another soul?'

'Scout's honour,' Dermot replied, raising his right hand to his forehead and giving her the traditional salute.

Storm grinned. 'Do you even have the Scouts in Ireland?'

'Sure we do. I might have been thrown out for smoking on my first day, but I still made the promise.'

'And broke it too!' she shot back.

'Just tell me! Or do I have to make you?'

As Storm squealed in delight, Dermot pinned her wrists to the bed. Trailing a row of kisses across her already erect nipples, he left her in no doubt of the pleasure that lay ahead . . .

Over breakfast in their sunny kitchen overlooking the sea, Storm popped a couple of Paracetamol. After pouring herself a second cup of coffee, she mopped up the pool of tomato ketchup on her plate with the remains of her bacon sandwich and flicked through her guilty pleasure – *Vida!* magazine. She'd been addicted to it since she was a kid. When she'd been taking care of Sally and the kids, it was her one luxury. Back then it had provided a release from the drudgery of her everyday life and Storm had adored poring over the pages of glamorous celebrities and reading

about their lives. It was almost as if she could pretend that she was there too, transported to another world that wasn't filled with drunk mothers and dead fathers. She couldn't stop fantasising about what it would be like to live in an exciting world filled with celebrities and parties, where your biggest worry was what you'd wear or how you'd style your hair.

Even though she was grown up now, she still loved the mag as much as she ever did and dreamed of working for the title one day. Reaching the back page, Storm was delighted to realise her headache had nearly gone. But then two rounds of sex first thing in the morning always made things better.

Storm smirked to herself. Should be available on prescription.

Looking around, she sighed contentedly. This room never failed to put a smile on her face. It was bright, with tall ceilings and windows overlooking the sea. She and Dermot had spent an entire weekend painting it a cheery yellow when they'd first moved in. Or rather, she and Carly had painted it. Dermot had been too busy working, apparently, and hadn't done much. It was the first time Storm had realised he would always put his career before her.

Setting a plate of toast and Marmite on the table, Dermot interrupted Storm's daydreams by taking a noisy bite.

'Do you have to?' Storm groaned. 'My headache was just beginning to go.'

'Forget about your headache,' he replied, spitting toast

crumbs everywhere. 'No more keeping me in suspense. What's going on with Carly?'

Where to start? Storm pushed the coffee cup away from her and looked him squarely in the eye. 'She shagged a married footballer the other week.'

Dermot's eyes were out on stalks. 'No way!'

'I know, I couldn't believe it myself when she told me.' Storm sighed.

'Bloody hell! I didn't think Carly was like that.'

'She's not,' Storm said firmly.

'But Carly's gorgeous, she could have her pick of blokes,' Dermot continued, ignoring Storm. 'Why on earth would she drop her standards and shag a footballer? And who is the lucky bastard?'

'Aston Booth.'

Crumbs flew across the table. 'Shit. Aston Booth! His wife's well fit, and didn't he just win Celebrity Dad of the Year or some bollocks?'

'Apparently,' Storm said sarcastically. 'Obviously not a lot of research goes into these awards.'

'Is she sure it was him? Not being funny, Stormy, but it wouldn't be the first time a bloke had pretended to be someone they weren't to get a woman into bed,' Dermot pointed out.

Storm reached into her work bag and pulled out a mobile.

'Somehow I ended up with Carly's phone last night. Look, she took a selfie of them together.' As she showed Dermot the picture, Storm carried on talking.

'You know, I'm worried about her. This team mate of

30

Aston's was at the party, warning her off going to the press.'

'Like she'd ever do that.'

'I know, but the scumbag made her cry, I'm worried it'll send her right back to rock bottom again.'

'Carly will be fine, she's been through a lot worse than this, and that Aston fella will have moved on to some other yoke now,' Dermot reasoned as he finished his toast and stood up to dump his plate and Storm's in the kitchen sink.

'True,' she agreed. 'But . . .'

'But nothing,' Dermot said firmly. 'Lookit, in a way it sounds as though she's back to normal, if she's finally slept with someone else.'

Storm paused. She hadn't thought of it like that. Perhaps in a funny way this was progress. Maybe now Carly had got that awkward first shag out of the way she'd feel ready to meet a nice bloke.

'You off to work in a minute?' Dermot asked, interrupting her thoughts.

'Yeah, got last night's exciting meeting to write up and I'm already running late.' Storm yawned. 'I'm going to need coffee intravenously if I'm to get through today. Plus I want to drop Carly's phone off on my way there and check she's OK, so I'd better get my skates on.'

Leaving her phone on the table, Storm rushed out of the room, leaving Dermot staring thoughtfully at her phone, a sly smile on his face.

Fifteen minutes later, Storm was ready to go.

'I'm not in until eleven so I'll see you at the office.' Dermot said, giving her a swift kiss on the cheek.

31

'OK, babes. Love you.' Grabbing her phone and bag, she ran out of the door.

Stopping at Carly's flat on her way to work, Storm couldn't help noticing how down her friend seemed. Despite the fact they'd had a brilliant night out, the whole Aston Booth saga was obviously upsetting her. And who could blame her? As if she needed another man to make her feel like crap. Storm felt bad she couldn't stay, but Ron would kill her if she took a sickie.

As soon as she got into the office Storm called Carly, just to make sure she wasn't sobbing into her pillow, but there was no answer, she must have gone back to bed. Slumping down at her desk with a sigh, wishing she could be asleep as well, Storm turned on her computer and was surprised to see an email from Miles Elliot, editor of the *Herald*, a national Sunday tabloid where she'd been doing some freelance work recently.

Strange. He'd never contacted her directly before, always leaving one of his minions to do that. Curious, she clicked it open and, as she read, all thoughts of Carly and her problems left Storm's mind.

I've been impressed with the work you've done for us in the last few weeks. The interview with the young widow was brilliant, and you seem to have a talent for getting people to talk to you. So I'd like to offer you a position on the showbiz desk effective immediately.

Storm was stunned. She knew Miles had been pleased with the widow's story which she'd brought in, but the last

thing she would ever have expected from him was a job offer. And not just any job! It was the one she'd always dreamed of. Staring at the screen, she checked the email. Was this some kind of joke? Quickly she punched Miles's number into her phone and was put straight through to his secretary, who happily confirmed that Miles wanted her to start as soon as possible but wasn't available to talk to her today. She just needed to email a response.

Putting the phone down, still Storm couldn't believe it. This was the opportunity of a lifetime – and covering showbiz too. Wow! Dreams really did come true. That left her just the small matter of Dermot to deal with. He'd been after a job at the *Herald* for as long as she'd known him, and she wasn't sure how he'd take this news. Perhaps it would be better to wait until she saw him in person. She had a horrible feeling he wouldn't be pleased. Storm bit her lip; she had no idea how to handle this situation.

She glanced around the office, desperate to talk to someone, but couldn't speak to anyone at work, not until she'd seen Dermot. Grabbing her phone again, she dialled Carly, waiting impatiently for her friend to pick up. But there was no reply. Throwing her phone on her desk in frustration, Storm read the email again, still not quite believing that her dreams were starting to come true.

After that the office was unusually busy for a Friday and Storm's phone wouldn't stop ringing, but though she tried to concentrate all she could think about was Miles's email, awaiting her response. Feeling sick from a mixture of excitement and her hangover, Storm couldn't take it any more. If she didn't talk to someone she'd go mad. Bolting

down two flights of stairs to the ladies and locking the cubicle door, she called Carly, only to hear her voicemail again.

'Babe, call me! It's urgent!'

Aargh! She needed her best friend more than ever. Where was Carly?

Sitting on the toilet seat, Storm thought about how her life was about to change. Not only would she finally be doing what she'd dreamed about, but she'd have many more nights out like last night — champagne, dancing, celebrities, and fit chefs . . . what more could she want? But despite it all, she was scared. Would Dermot stick with her or would their relationship founder? And she hated leaving Carly when she seemed so down . . .

As if on cue her phone rang – Carly. Finally!

'What's up, babes? You sounded frantic.'

About to blurt out her news, Storm paused. Carly sounded croaky, as if she'd been crying. Maybe it could wait a bit. 'I was worried about you. You seemed sad this morning, are you OK?'

'Sorry. Monster hangover so I went back to bed after I saw you and slept it off.'

Storm felt a pang of envy. She'd have given her right arm for a lie in. Then again, she thought, blushing as she remembered the passionate sex she and Dermot had enjoyed that morning, waking early definitely had its advantages.

'So how are you feeling after last night?' Storm asked her.

Carly hesitated then said, 'I'm all right. I mean, I'm

34

still upset about what happened, but the way I look at it, we're all human, and we all make mistakes. I never have and never would go to the press, so I've nothing to worry about.'

'I'd just hate that wanker who threatened you last night to think his tactics worked,' Storm sighed.

'Yeah, well, he's a tosser, just like Aston. I've decided to forget about them both, chalk it up to experience and concentrate on single men only from now on.'

'Good for you, babe. He's definitely not worth it,' Storm replied, excited to hear her friend talk about future boyfriends. 'We'll soon find you a nice hot bloke, I promise. Anyway, listen, can I come round after work? I need to talk to you.'

'Why? What's up?'

Hearing someone come into the ladies, Storm dropped her voice to a whisper.

'Listen, I can't talk now, I've got to get back to work – I'll call you later, OK?'

Back at her desk after lunch, Storm flipped through her notepad. Scanning her notes, she wasn't surprised to find her scribbles were just as dull as the council meeting she'd been to the day before. God, how could she concentrate on this? She felt a bubble of excitement swell inside her. Soon she'd be writing up interviews with film stars. No more trying to make town parking issues interesting! Throwing the pad on to her desk, she looked up and spotted her editor walking briskly her way.

Shit! She was supposed to have finished this story an hour ago. He was going to have a right go at her. She may

35

be about to leave, but she didn't want to leave anyone in the lurch. Sitting up straight, Storm stared ahead at her computer screen and pretended to be typing.

'Storm, where's Dermot?' asked Ron, getting straight to the point.

'Dunno . . . at his desk?'

Craning her neck over towards Dermot's cubicle, Storm expected to see his sandy curls peeping over the top of the divider. But there was nobody there. He must have popped out.

'Don't get clever with me,' Ron shot back at her.

'At lunch then?' she suggested brightly.

Ron Jones wasn't a patient man. An old school cockney with a reputation for taking no prisoners, he prided himself on slicing through bullshit like butter. Now it was Storm's turn to know he meant business.

'To take a lunch break he'd have to turn up for work in the first place, and nobody's seen him all day. Now, I'm asking you nicely. Where is he?'

'Um . . . maybe he's got wind of a scoop?' Storm suggested nervously. 'You know what he's like.'

'What sort of a story stops him answering his phone?' Ron snapped, bringing his fist down hard on Storm's desk, making her jump. 'I bloody well need him here. There's a crisis over at the town hall and I want my chief reporter to cover it. Find him!' he snapped before storming back to his office.

Storm looked down at her keyboard and tried to make sense of what Ron had just said. Dermot didn't have a day off. In fact, he'd said he'd catch up with her at the office.

She'd been expecting to see him any minute. Where the hell was he?

Reaching for her phone, she dialled Dermot's number but it just rang and rang. She tried again, but this time the call went straight to voicemail. What was happening?

Anxiously she called Carly, who answered on the first ring.

'Random question, but I don't suppose you've seen Dermot this morning?'

'No. Why the panic?'

Quickly, Storm explained.

'I wouldn't worry, babes. He's probably just gone to a meeting and forgotten to tell anyone.'

Ending the call, Storm realised Carly was right. But ten minutes later she was back in panic mode. What if Dermot wasn't in a meeting? What if he was lying in a ditch somewhere hurt? She couldn't stand it any more. Punching in the numbers of the fire and police press officers, Storm asked if there'd been any accidents that morning.

'Nothing serious, Storm, why do you want to know?' the police press officer asked.

'No reason, Mike. Just can't find Dermot.'

'He'll be fine, Storm, he's probably chasing some story – he'd wrestle an alligator if it meant he'd get a scoop.'

Storm hung up, knowing Mike was right. When she had first started dating Dermot she'd been impressed by his focus on reaching the big time. He fancied himself as the next Piers Morgan and often covered the weekend graveyard shift on the *Herald*.

Dermot's commitment to work was admirable, but it meant that Storm was often only at the back of his mind. He routinely forgot her birthday and their anniversary, and thought nothing of standing her up if he had a story to cover. Often Storm went for days without seeing him, which was why she'd started working freelance at the *Herald* herself.

If you can't beat them, join them, she'd thought when she'd emailed Miles Elliot, begging for a chance. It wasn't showbiz as yet, but she was gaining quite a reputation for herself as a reporter who could be trusted with a difficult interview.

One of the other *Herald* journalists had said that what set her apart was the fact that she cared about people, and made them feel as though they were chatting with a mate rather than an unfeeling journalist.

'I could do with picking up some tips from you,' Dermot commented after Storm had managed to persuade a young widow all the nationals had wanted to talk to, to give her an exclusive interview. She'd been proud of that piece, and the young woman had written her a note afterwards thanking her for being so sensitive. 'It's not a science, Dermot. I'm just interested in other people.' *Unlike you,* she'd thought to herself then. And now she couldn't help wondering whether this job offer would be the end of their relationship. God, where was he? She couldn't bear not knowing. But that was typical of Dermot. He always treated her as some sort of afterthought. Deep down she knew she deserved better. But damn it! She didn't know if it was the fact he was so focused on work, or just so

irresistibly hot in bed, that meant she just didn't have the heart to dump him.

It was a murky, grey day and as Storm peered out of the window on to the street below, she realised this wasn't the first or last time Dermot would behave so irresponsibly. Watching a toddler having a massive tantrum with his mother, crying at the top of his lungs that he wanted to go home, Storm knew just how he felt. Because even though she'd just been offered the job of her dreams, until she knew Dermot was all right, she couldn't feel happy about it.

One thing was for sure: she couldn't sit here for the rest of the day worrying about her boyfriend. There was only one thing for it. Reaching for her bag and coat, she walked towards the exit, determined to find him. Just as she put her hand on the door she saw Ron surface from his office.

'Where the bloody hell's that planning story, Storm?' he bawled.

'Five minutes, Ron,' she promised.

Sighing, she slipped off her coat and returned to her computer.

Dermot sat on the tube with his head buried in a free newspaper. He'd just got to the middle of a story about a cat rescuing a dog when the doors jerked open at Wapping. Tossing the paper on to the seat next to his, he stepped off the train and headed towards daylight. Anxiously he checked his watch. Half-past one. Brilliant. Just enough time to grab some coffee and a sandwich.

Turning right out of the station, he walked for a couple

of minutes before pushing open the door to his favourite greasy spoon. 'Tuna melt and a flat white, please, darlin',' he said to the woman behind the counter.

'Coming right up.' The waitress beamed at him.

As he walked over to his usual window table, he took a deep breath and tried to relax before he saw Sabrina Anderson. With her hard as nails exterior, violet-blue eyes and long blonde hair, she was his ideal woman. He'd fancied her from the moment they'd bumped into each other in this very café twelve months ago. When he'd rung her this morning and told her he had something special for her, she'd played it typically cool.

'Trust me, this is going to be the biggest and best Christmas present you've ever had,' he cajoled her.

'Yeah, yeah,' she replied, playfully.

'Seriously. You'll be screaming my name in ecstasy by the time I've finished,' he teased.

'Just tell me what it is.'

'I can't say on the phone, but you won't be disappointed. Promise.'

'Meet me at two, usual place.'

Now, as he waited for his food, he pulled out his mobile and grimaced. Shit! Ten missed calls. Four from his editor and six from Storm.

'That's not a happy face,' said the waitress, bringing his coffee. 'Everything OK?'

'Fine,' Dermot replied. 'Just a bit of woman trouble, nothing I can't handle.'

He was setting his phone on the table when it rang again – Storm. For fuck's sake! Couldn't the girl take a hint? He

was busy. She was the last person he wanted to talk to right now. And his editor wasn't far behind. If Dermot had to speak to either of them, he wasn't sure he'd have the balls to carry out his plan and play hookey with Sabrina.

Switching his phone to silent, he decided to deal with the consequences later. This was something he'd been looking forward to for a long time. He was going to enjoy every second of it. Sabrina walked in on the dot of two and sashayed over to his table, dressed in a slim-fitting black trouser suit. Dermot's eyes roamed appreciatively over her body. Her arse looked incredible.

'Good to see you,' he said as she sat down opposite him.

Touching his arm, Sabrina beamed, showing off a row of perfect white teeth. 'So what's this amazing Christmas present?'

Dermot took a deep breath. 'Aston Booth's cheated on his wife.'

Sabrina said nothing, leaving him on tenterhooks. Hadn't she heard him properly?

'Photos?' she asked finally, not mincing her words.

'Yeah, including one of him with the girl he shagged.'

Dermot reached for his bag, pulled out the snaps of Carly and pushed them across the Formica-topped table.

As Sabrina flicked through them he thought about his busy morning. While Storm was in the bathroom he'd sped into action. First he'd forwarded the photo on Carly's phone to his own. Then, when Storm had gone to work, he'd printed it out, along with some other pictures he'd found of Carly over the years, which were stored on Storm's laptop. After a quick shower he'd dressed in his

work suit and walked to the station. He had to admit he'd felt slightly guilty about stitching up Storm's friend, but not enough to change his mind. Chances like this didn't come along twice.

'Pretty girl,' said Sabrina. 'Well done, Dermot. I knew you had it in you. I take it you've got time to talk this through with the chief?'

Dermot felt like punching the air with happiness. Instead he nodded and stood up. After he'd opened the door for Sabrina, they crossed the road. Dermot savoured the moment. Here he was, with Sabrina Anderson, the *Herald*'s news editor, about to walk into the national newspaper's headquarters and meet the editor. Finally, Dermot Whelan was making his name.

Chapter Three

Glancing around the now empty office, Storm reached for her desk phone and punched in Dermot's number for the last time. It was almost 10 p.m. and she'd long-since worn out the battery on her mobile. As the call went predictably straight to voicemail, Storm flung the receiver back into the cradle in frustration and let out a loud scream. Bloody Dermot!

Icy fear gripped her heart as she tried desperately not to let her imagination go into overdrive. About three months after she'd got together with Dermot, she'd caught him snogging a colleague in the stationery cupboard. It was laughable really, a cliché situation, and Dermot had sworn blind it hadn't meant anything. They hadn't been going out for long then so, after making him grovel for a good couple of weeks, she'd forgiven him on the understanding that it was never to happen again. But despite forgiving him, Storm had never quite forgotten his betrayal. Now, whenever he was out late or working overtime, she always

felt a flash of insecurity and distrust. Was he really where he said he was?

Then there was the other option – that something truly awful had happened to him, just like it had to her dad. An image of Alan's smiling face flooded into her mind then and she felt her eyes start to water. There wasn't a day that went by when she didn't miss him.

Storm had been a real Daddy's girl, and the apple of her father's eye. On Alan's precious weekends off they used to stroll down to the pier first thing in the morning, where they'd eat fresh hot doughnuts from the stand at the front. They'd chat, laugh, and if the weather was good Alan would teach her how to skim stones over the sea. It had been their special time together, and Storm missed those mornings with her father as much now as she had just after his death.

Alan had been thirty-nine when he'd passed away. Sudden Adult Death Syndrome, the doctors had said, and after his funeral Sally had gone to pieces so it was Storm who had sorted through all her dad's belongings and decided what to keep and what to give to charity. The one thing she couldn't part with was his gold watch. He'd bought it with his first wage packet when he was eighteen, and had worn it every day. He said it brought him luck because if he hadn't gone into the jeweller's to buy it, he never would have met Sally, who'd been working behind the counter. Storm hadn't been able to part with it after his death, and carried it with her everywhere. Pulling the watch from her pocket now, she rested it on her desk and stroked the face. The action never failed to comfort her, as

did a cup of tea with the one person she could always rely on. She needed to see Carly.

'Get that down you,' her friend said, handing Storm a mug of hot sweet tea.

'Thanks, babe.' Taking the mug, she curled up on Carly's huge grey sofa and glanced at the TV. *The Graham Norton Show* was on – she could do with a bit of light relief.

'Still no word then?' Carly asked.

Storm shook her head.

'The bastard!' Carly fumed. 'I could kill Dermot for this.'

Storm said nothing. She was well used to Carly's outbursts when it came to Dermot. Her friend had made no secret of the fact she thought he was a great bloke but a shit boyfriend, something she'd worked out when she'd temporarily moved in with Storm and Dermot following her break-up with Paul.

Over the years Storm and Carly had been through more than their fair share of ups and downs. When Storm's dad had died, Carly had been a huge support. A shoulder to cry on at school, not to mention a complete rock at the funeral. It was Carly's hand Storm had clung to as she sprinkled earth on to her dad's coffin while it was lowered into the ground.

Then, later, Carly made sure Storm ate lunch every day and frequently insisted she came over for a well-deserved night off. Not only that, Carly had thought nothing of spending weekends at Storm's house rather than out on the town, to help her friend babysit the kids and put her

mum to bed when she was too drunk to make it up the stairs.

To Carly, Storm was a hero. It was amazing how she'd found the time to excel in her GCSEs, go to college *and* take care of her family. As for Storm, she was as devoted to Carly as she was to Bailey and Lexie. Although Carly had pretty much led a charmed life, she was the first to admit she'd struggled at school. She was by no means thick, but when it came to hitting the books, Carly preferred to spend a night in watching *Friends*, gossiping about boys, painting her nails and flicking through fashion magazines, rather than concentrate on her studies.

As a result she was always in trouble with teachers, who took great pleasure in dishing out detentions while telling Carly to remove her bright red nail polish and mascara.

Watching them pick her friend apart time and time again had left Storm fuming. She had always stood up to them in class, telling them to leave Carly alone and pick on someone else. Unsurprisingly the girls often both ended up in lunchtime detention, but the fact that Storm would put herself out like that had touched Carly and they had always remained close.

'Do you want me to call him?' Carly asked now, reaching for her phone.

Storm shook her head.

'It's pointless. When Dermot gets a story in his head, he forgets about everything else. Anyway, there's something else I've got to tell you. Miles Elliot offered me a job today.'

Carly's eyebrows rose. 'What! Why didn't you say? Doing what? Where? When do you start?'

46

Carly was so excited, Storm almost forgot her misery over Dermot. 'As soon as possible. Apparently there's a job going on the showbiz desk and he thinks I would be perfect for it.'

'Wow, babe! That's so brilliant! I couldn't be prouder,' Carly told her, leaping off the sofa to hug her friend.

'I know. I can't believe it,' Storm replied. 'It's everything I've ever wanted.'

'And everything you deserve,' Carly pointed out loyally. 'I take it you haven't told Dermot yet?'

Storm shook her head. 'And that's the thing . . . I've no idea how he's going to take it. Dermot's further up the career ladder than me and he's supposed to be the big rising star, not me.'

'Don't be daft, Storm,' Carly said. 'You're very talented, which is why Miles offered you this job. Dermot will be fine about it, and if he isn't, well, he'll have me to deal with. Now, you're welcome to stay here tonight if you want? That sofabed's pretty comfy.'

'Thanks, babe, but I'll go home.' Storm smiled gratefully at her. 'At least that way I'll be ready to kneecap the fecker when he finally puts in an appearance!'

Dermot lit the final candle and smiled as he surveyed the living room. The whole atmosphere screamed romance. As well as lining the flat with what looked like hundreds of tea lights, he'd arranged a huge bouquet of Storm's favourite flowers, red and white roses, on the kitchen table and put two bottles of champagne on ice. Then, to really sweeten the deal, he'd placed a small Tiffany box containing a silver bangle in the centre of the table.

Dermot wasn't a complete idiot, he knew he owed Storm one hell of an apology when she got home. But try as he might, he couldn't help grinning as he thought about how well that afternoon had gone. The moment he'd walked into Miles Elliot's office, he'd had the *Herald* editor eating out of the palm of his hand.

They'd bantered, joked and laughed, and Miles had been seriously impressed when Dermot revealed he'd got photographs to prove his story.

'You've done very well,' he said admiringly as he leafed through the stack of snaps Dermot had brought with him. 'Do I need to ask if you've done anything illegal?'

'Well, I didn't hack anyone's phone, if that's what you mean?' Dermot bantered.

'Good. And these photos are proof enough if we can't get either Aston or this girl to talk . . . unless you can help us out there too?'

Dermot shifted in his leather chair and sipped thoughtfully on his flat white. He knew if he even approached Carly about doing an interview he'd get a swift kick in the nuts, and Storm wouldn't be far behind her.

'She's my girlfriend's best mate,' he admitted. 'Might not be that easy.'

Miles scratched his chin thoughtfully. 'It's a good story, and I appreciate you bringing it straight to us rather than going to anyone else. Anything we can do to make the situation easier at home?'

Dermot couldn't believe his ears. Instinctively he knew he had to look out for Storm. He wasn't a complete bastard – she deserved something out of all this.

'Well, I don't suppose you've got any jobs going here, have you?' he asked.

'What did you have in mind?'

'A job for me, and something for Storm, my girlfriend. She's been working in features for the last few Saturdays.'

Miles chuckled. 'I know exactly who Storm is. She's a very good reporter and in fact I offered her a job first thing this morning.'

Dermot was surprised. It had taken him months to get the editor even to look at him; now suddenly Miles was telling him he was not only aware of Dermot's girlfriend but had also offered her a job. This wasn't supposed to be how it went. Dermot was the talented one, not Storm. Everyone at the *Post* was always telling him how brilliant he was. There had to be a mistake.

Miles gave him an amused look, and changed the subject. 'You remind me of a younger version of myself. When I was your age, there were no lengths I wouldn't go to for a story. We always need reporters like that here.'

Dermot smiled a lazy smile. Now that was more like it, and no more than he deserved after the hassle he'd gone through.

'So what do I get in return for the story?'

'How about I offer you a six-month contract as a news reporter? That way you and your girlfriend can move up here to London together, which will keep everything sweet at home. As a staffer Storm can use the company flat in Clapham till she can sort herself something else out, so you could move in there together. Last thing I want is to split up the Romeo and Juliet of journalism.'

49

'Has Storm got a six-month contract too?'

'No. I've offered her a permanent position. With her interviewing skills, I reckon she can get us some great stories.'

Dermot's heart beat faster. Was this guy serious? Storm was nothing without him. *He* was the one with the talent – Storm was just some chancer who'd managed to make a widow tell her sob story. Dermot should have been the one to have a crack at her . . . anyone could have done it. Still, he wasn't about to look a gift horse in the mouth. Getting to his feet, he pumped the editor's hand furiously. 'You don't have to worry about that, Miles. I can promise you, Storm and I will do you proud. When do we start?'

Feeling exhausted, Storm walked towards her front door with all the fight knocked out of her. As soon as she got in she planned on doing nothing more than collapsing in bed without even bothering to remove her make-up.

But nearing her home she was amazed to see the flat lit up like a Christmas tree. Thank God! Dermot was home.

'Where the hell have you been?' she yelled, bursting through the front door and straight into the living room. Stopping short, she couldn't believe what she was seeing. Dermot was standing nervously by the window, looking tired and dishevelled. On the kitchen table stood a champagne bucket with what looked like two bottles wedged firmly in ice, while next to it stood the biggest bouquet of red and white roses Storm had ever seen and nestling between them was a small robin egg blue box.

50

'What's all this?'

'For you, gorgeous,' replied Dermot, walking over to her and handing her a glass of fizz. 'We're celebrating.'

But her relief at seeing him quickly turned to anger, and Storm threw her glass of champers all over him. 'You might be celebrating, I've been worried out of my mind all day, you bastard!'

As liquid dripped off his forehead, Dermot hung his head and did his best to cover his anger with a semblance of shame. 'I'm sorry, babe, I was busy on a job in London and my phone ran out of juice.'

'You've been totally out of order,' Storm fumed. 'I was terrified you were lying dead in a ditch somewhere. And as if that wasn't bad enough, I've had to put up with Ron bollocking me all day because he couldn't get hold of you either.'

Dermot stepped closer to Storm. He needed her onside, and quickly. It was stupid not to have taken her calls, but if he'd spoken to her before his meeting there was a chance he might have pulled out. It was time for him to play his ace card. 'I'm really sorry, Storm, but the truth is, I've been spending the day sorting out our future.'

'What do you mean?' she snapped.

'What would you say if I told you that I'd landed a job as a news reporter at the *Herald*?'

'I'd say you were being a selfish dick,' Storm fired back. She was still fuming. The bloody cheek of him! And after she'd spent all day defending him to Ron. Enough was enough.

'That hurts, pet, especially since I know Miles has

51

offered you a position too. When were you going to tell me about that? Or did you want to make me suffer first?'

'Well, if you'd bothered to call me, I could have told you hours ago. You might have noticed I left a few messages on your phone?' she said sarcastically.

'So I assume you're taking it?' Dermot said, ignoring her accusation.

'I'd like to, yes,' she said quietly. 'This is my dream, Dermot. And now you've been offered a chance to work for Miles too, we can go to London together – it's perfect for us both.'

'I know, darlin'.' Dermot smiled at her. 'I'm just messing with you. I'm not mad, I would have done the same thing, and you're right . . . we can be together now, which is the only thing that matters.'

Storm breathed a sigh of relief. 'So tell me how it all happened?'

'Miles rang out of the blue this morning and asked me to come straight in,' Dermot explained. 'He said he'd been so impressed with my work recently, he wanted to offer me a full-time job.'

'So we both got offered jobs out of the blue this morning? Just like that?' Storm asked, incredulous.

'Just like that. So am I forgiven?' he said, nuzzling her neck once more.

'Just this once,' she teased, flinging her arms around him.

The following morning, Storm woke to the sounds of swearing in the kitchen. Blearily peering at the alarm clock, she was amazed to see she'd slept in until a record 11 a.m.

'You OK, babe?' she croaked.

'Fine. Just burned my hand on the coffee pot . . . don't move a muscle!' he called back.

Hoisting herself upright and sinking her head back against the pillows, Storm was delighted to see Dermot carrying in a tray loaded with toast and coffee.

'Am I still dreaming? Breakfast in bed. What have I done to deserve this?' she squealed.

'Thought it was more than justified after everything I put you through yesterday.' Dermot was outdoing himself with all this thoughtfulness. How had she got so lucky? She had her dream job and a boyfriend that gave her a Tiffany bangle and made her breakfast in bed. Reaching for a hot buttery slice of toast, Storm could hardly contain her excitement.

Taking a bite of toast, she pictured herself sashaying into a posh London hotel room, interviewing Jennifer Lawrence about her latest blockbuster. The interview would go so well, she fantasised, Jennifer would lean over and slip her personal mobile number into Storm's hand, insisting they paint the town red the next time she was in London.

Storm spilled hot coffee over the bed sheets and snapped back to reality.

'I couldn't speak to Miles yesterday, did he mention when he wanted us to start?' she asked.

'Next Monday.'

'That's ten days before Christmas!' she replied, horrified. 'We can't do that.'

Dermot said nothing. His raised eyebrow told Storm all she needed to know – they had to.

'Well, I suppose we only have to give a week's notice at work. And we can live in the *Herald*'s company flat in Clapham until we find somewhere of our own.'

'Exactly,' Dermot agreed. 'Aren't you excited?'

Storm grinned. 'What do you think?' The thought of no more council meetings or bollockings off Ron was like a dream come true.

'So have you told Carly your big news yet?' Dermot asked, nicking the last slice of toast.

Storm nodded as she shook the crumbs from her nightshirt on to the plate. Swinging her legs out of bed, she stood up and stretched. 'I told her about my job offer but she doesn't know you've got one too. Thought I might pop over to hers now and tell her the big news.'

'Brilliant idea. I've got a bit of work to do while you nip out. Then we could go for a celebration meal tonight at the Italian around the corner, if you fancy?'

Walking around to Dermot's side of the bed, Storm kissed him passionately on the mouth.

'Bloody hell, babe, you look like you ran a marathon to get here,' Carly laughed, spotting Storm's bright red cheeks as she opened the front door.

It was true. The moment Storm had jumped out of bed she'd wanted to get over to Carly's as quickly as possible. After pulling on her trademark grey skinny jeans and navy jumper, she'd gathered her hair into a high ponytail and raced over to her friend's flat just a few streets away.

'I've got some brilliant news,' Storm panted. 'Dermot's

been offered a job on the *Herald* as well. It means we can go together!'

'OMG! For real?'

'Totes for real,' Storm squealed as she clutched her friend excitedly by the elbows and together they jumped up and down, shrieking in delight. Bolting upstairs to Carly's kitchen, Storm reached into the fridge and pulled out the emergency bottle of champagne she always kept for special occasions.

'Sod tea,' Carly agreed. 'News like this deserves a real drink. Now . . . tell me all the details.'

Storm explained how a couple of positions had opened up at the paper that Miles thought they would be perfect for. 'Although I don't know why he insisted on interviewing Dermot when he just offered a job to me straight away,' she said. 'He emailed this morning with my contract and to congratulate me on my new position. Apparently he thinks I have unique skills, which the paper can benefit from. And all this without even giving me an interview!'

'Oh, yeah! I hope it's just your writing skills he's talking about.' Carly raised an eyebrow suggestively.

'Carly!' Storm giggled, throwing a cushion at her friend.

'Kidding! Seriously, Stormy, congratulations. If anyone deserves this chance, it's you.'

'Thanks, babe. It's just all so sudden, I can't quite believe it.'

It hit Storm then that she wouldn't just be leaving her job at the *Post* behind but also her hometown and Carly. Overcome with the emotion of it all, tears blurred Storm's

eyes. Waving her hands in front of her face to stem the flow, it was only a matter of time before she set Carly off.

'What the hell am I going to do without you?' Storm exclaimed.

'I'm going to miss you so much,' Carly wailed. 'Even though we can still see each other in London, it won't be the same!'

After a full on tear-fest the girls stretched out on Carly's sofa with a family-sized bar of Dairy Milk each and watched their favourite movie, *The Notebook*. There was something about Ryan Gosling that always put a smile on their faces.

'I'm so full,' Storm moaned after devouring the entire bar.

'Me too,' added Carly. 'I hope you don't want any help packing today.'

'Nah, Dermot's given me the afternoon off. Besides, I want to know how you're doing.'

So far the girls had stayed off the topic of Carly's fling, but Storm was keen to know what her friend was thinking now.

'I'll live. I just can't believe how stupid I've been, sleeping with a married man.'

'It takes two to tango, you know.'

'I know. I just can't stop thinking about Aston's wife,' Carly said quietly. 'She didn't even enter my head before . . . what is wrong with me?'

Carly looked so fed up, Storm's heart ached for her.

'I just wanted to pretend I was in some bubble where me and Aston would live happily ever after.'

'Is that why you took that selfie?'

'Yeah. I've deleted it now. I feel sick at how badly I let everyone down. I wish I could say sorry to Tanya.'

'You've got to stop punishing yourself, babe. Anyway, sod being in a romantic bubble with Aston – thought you said he was shit in bed!'

Carly burst out laughing. 'Yeah, he asked me after we'd done it why I didn't blink. I told him it was because I didn't have time!'

As the two girls cracked up, they restarted *The Notebook* and prepared to ogle Ryan Gosling all over again. The only problem now was they'd run out of chocolate.

With the sun shining and the sea a crystal-clear blue, Brighton looked exactly how he felt, Dermot thought as he strolled along the seafront. The whole operation had gone better than he could have hoped. This was going to be one of the easiest interviews he'd ever done. *Probably because he'd got Storm, interview expert, to do it for him.*

Dermot smirked. It had been a stroke of genius, hiding a tiny recording device in her bag as she left the flat to see Carly. Dermot wasn't much of a follower of fashion but he loved a gadget and always kept ahead of the latest techno developments. He never liked to leave the house without his passport, iPhone and Apple laptop. When he'd spotted this tiny voice-activated recording device a couple of weeks ago he'd known it was another essential he had to have.

Slipping it into the bottom of Storm's bag earlier that morning as she showered, he'd taken a bet with himself

that very soon the device would be filled with Carly's candid comments about Aston. After all, it would be the second topic they talked about after Storm's announcement. All he had to do was sit back and wait for her to come back. Then, when she was getting ready to go out, he'd retrieve the device, type up the girls' conversation, and . . . hey presto! Full interview to Miles.

Pausing to stop for a beer at one of the pubs on the seafront, he ordered a pint of Guinness, slipped off his leather bomber jacket and rang his new editor.

As he waited for Miles to pick up Dermot found it hard to believe how much things had changed in the past twenty-four hours. Yesterday, Miles Elliot barely knew who he was. Today, Dermot had access to his direct line.

'What have you got for me, Dermot?' Miles demanded, straight to the point.

'Just letting you know I'll have the interview with the girl for you later.'

'Nice work. Email me your copy as soon as you can. Looks like you've got your first front page, son.'

As Miles rang off, Dermot gulped his celebration pint and texted Storm. The sooner he could get her home, the sooner he could get his interview over to Miles, and then he was on easy street.

Babe when are you coming back? I miss you and can't wait to play!xxxxxx

While he slurped the froth off his Guinness, Storm texted straight back.

Back in ten. Love you. xxxxx

Finishing his pint, Dermot knew he was home and dry.

This time tomorrow he'd be celebrating his first national scoop. The only thing he had to worry about now was dealing with Storm. If he was honest, her reaction was something he'd been pushing to the back of his mind, but now Dermot knew he was going to have to come up with a plan. After all, this time tomorrow she would know that he'd eavesdropped on her conversation with her friend. Plus she'd more than likely want to kick the shit out of him for betraying her trust and selling Carly down the river.

He thought carefully while he ordered another drink. There was no denying it, things were going to get a bit rocky with Storm once his story broke. When he'd initially gone to Miles and asked for a job he had thought that if Storm kicked off too much he'd dump her then hightail it to London to make his name alone. It wasn't that he didn't love Storm – he did – but he loved his job more.

However, Miles had thrown him a curveball yesterday when he'd said that he had already offered her a job. Now it was in Dermot's best interests to try and win her over; he hated to admit it to himself but he needed her. Usually he knew exactly how to push her buttons to get what he wanted. As he downed his second pint, Dermot could only hope his tried and tested formula of begging for forgiveness would work for him tomorrow.

59

Chapter Four

The banging was so loud Storm's neighbours woke before she did. Peering out of their sash windows they couldn't believe a tiny woman, red faced with fury, was responsible for making such a racket first thing on a Sunday morning.

'Keep it down, love,' one woman shouted. 'You'll wake my baby.'

But Carly didn't care if she woke the living dead. 'Storm, open the door this minute!' she yelled.

Storm, who'd been happily in the Land of Nod dreaming about a night out with Jay-Z and Beyoncé, woke with a start. Realising it was Carly at the door, she slotted her feet into fluffy slippers and padded downstairs, leaving Dermot still sound asleep.

Flinging the door wide, Storm did a double take. Her friend looked to be in a real state. Dressed in trackie bottoms and UGGs, with mascara streaming down her face, Carly was obviously upset. Shit! Had she bumped into Dillon again?

'What's going on, babe?'

'You know exactly what's going on. This!' Carly spat.

Seeing the copy of that morning's *Herald*, Storm ran her eyes over the headline.

Top Totty scores with Aston. Underneath was the selfie Carly had taken and next to it were three little words Storm had definitely not expected to see: *By Dermot Whelan.*

Her blood ran cold. Ignoring her friend, she snatched the paper from Carly's hands and flicked through the story, which ran across four pages. The details they'd got hold of were eye-watering. It was as though they'd sat down with Carly and interviewed her for hours. The piece revealed just what her night with Aston had been like, and even featured Carly's revelation that he was well hung but out of practice.

It didn't end there. Photos of Carly throughout her youth filled the pages, including one of her at school with a bucktoothed smile and hair in bunches. Then another of her at a fancy dress party where she'd donned a flesh-coloured bra and pants to look like Miley Cyrus, complete with foam finger. There was Storm too, in a striped suit, pretending to be Robin Thicke. Shaking, Storm turned back to the front page and looked in bewilderment at Dermot's name in big, bold letters.

Ignoring the stares from her neighbours, who by now had appeared in the hallway to see what all the fuss was about, she sank to the floor. What was Dermot's name doing on the front page of the *Herald*? Had he really betrayed her and Carly? How could he do this to them? She'd trusted him to keep it to himself when she'd told him

about Carly and Aston, and he'd used her and her friend in the sickest way possible. Storm knew how desperate Dermot was to make a name for himself, but would he really go to these lengths? God, was this how he'd scored his new job? By selling out Carly? The revelations came thick and fast.

'Don't act like this is all some big surprise to you, Storm,' Carly spat. 'You tricked me into telling you and Dermot everything just so you could finally get your dream jobs. I hope you're proud of yourselves now.'

'That's not true, I knew nothing about this.'

But Carly wasn't buying it. 'Do you think I'm stupid?' she sneered. 'Don't forget, I know you. And I know how long you've dreamed of working as a showbiz reporter. You'd do anything to succeed.'

Storm was shocked by the look of hatred and disgust etched on Carly's face. Was this what her friend really thought of her? 'You know I'd never do anything to hurt you. You're like a sister to me, Carly.' Storm reached out, but her friend pushed her away.

'So if you didn't do it, how did your bastard of a boyfriend find out?'

Seeing Dermot walk down the stairs then, rubbing his eyes, Carly turned her attention to the man of the moment. Eyes blazing, she was on a roll and nothing would stop her.

'Get everything on some sort of secret tape yesterday, did you?'

'What's going on?' he murmured blearily.

Both girls looked at him, disbelief in their eyes. 'How could you do this?' Storm asked quietly.

'How could you both do it?' Carly screamed. 'This is a disaster, my life's over.'

'No, it isn't, babe,' Storm soothed her as the neighbours shuffled back inside, preferring another cuppa to a morning spent watching a row. 'It might seem like it now, but everyone will have forgotten about it by tomorrow.'

'Easy for you to say,' Carly fired back. 'Your life's not in tatters. So just how did you two plot this? Get me to forget my phone on purpose at Nico's party, did you, by getting me wasted?'

'No, Carly, you did a pretty good job of that all by yourself,' Storm snapped.

Dermot stood in the hallway in his tatty pyjamas unable to believe his eyes. He'd never seen the girls fight like this. Of course he'd witnessed the odd scrap over silly stuff like who got the last chocolate in a box of Thornton's but they'd never gone for each other before. Dermot knew he ought to feel guilty, but he was itching to take the paper from Storm's hands and read his story cover to cover. Seeing his name on the front page, he was bursting with pride – this was his big break, his very first national front page. He'd meant to get up first thing in the morning and savour the moment as he walked into the newsagent's, but he'd been so knackered last night after answering all Miles's queries he'd slept in.

One thing was for sure, Carly was in serious danger of ruining the moment. After all, she was the dumb slapper who'd slept with a married footballer. Girls like her deserved to be outed in the press. But he didn't want her falling out with Storm. They were off to London in a week to start their new life, and he knew he was going to have enough of a hard time winning her around, without Carly making it any more difficult for him. Time for him to fall on his sword.

'Girls, let me just say I'm sorry,' Dermot interrupted. 'Carly, it's true, Storm knew nothing at all about this. She told me about you and Aston after the party and I went to the *Herald* alone. But the press would have found out anyway in time. This way at least people get to know the girl behind the selfie.'

'Are you kidding me with this shit, Dermot?' Carly yelled. 'All my clients are going to think I'm scum for sleeping with someone else's bloke, and as if that isn't enough, Dillon told me he'd ruin me if I went to the press.'

'That's not going to happen,' Storm interrupted.

'Oh, you're going to sort it, are you, Storm?' Carly shot back. 'Just like you sorted this . . . by running to your boyfriend and telling him about my private life, even though I told you to keep it to yourself.'

'I did keep it to myself!' Storm protested.

'You didn't, you stupid cow, you told your lying scumbag of a boyfriend.'

'I didn't think he'd do this,' she said helplessly.

'No?' Carly looked at her in disgust. 'I did. You might not see him for what he really is, but I marked his card long ago. He'd sell his own grandmother if it meant he would get ahead.'

'That's a bit unfair,' Dermot grumbled. 'Both my grandparents died years ago.'

64

'You're not even taking this seriously. How did you get all those details anyway? I only told Storm about this.'

Dermot looked sheepish. 'I bugged her bag when she came over to yours yesterday. Then I listened to your conversation and emailed it to my editor.'

'Un-fucking-believable!' Carly spat. 'I spill my guts to my best friend, and you listen like some sort of perv. Funny how this story doesn't say how guilty I felt and how I couldn't believe I'd been so stupid. Why is that? Frightened it wouldn't make such a juicy read? I've a good mind to sue you, you bastard.'

'For what?' Dermot fired back. 'Correct me if I'm wrong but you did shag a footballer, and he was married?'

Storm had gone white. Looking at her boyfriend and best friend sparring in the hallway, she couldn't help wondering who Dermot really was. She'd thought she knew him, but the past ten minutes had been a wake-up call. To think she'd once thought he was the love of her life! No chance. Looking at him now, his face twisted and contorted with rage as he laid into her friend, Storm realised it was over between Dermot and her, and there was no way she was going to London if it meant being within spitting distance of his lying, cheating face.

'Look, Carly, I never wanted to hurt you . . .' Dermot said, trying to calm things down.

'Don't bother. All I can say is, revenge is a dish best served cold. And as for you, Storm, you and me are through – I never want to see you again.'

With that, Carly stepped out of the front door and

65

slammed it shut behind her. With a withering look at Dermot, Storm pulled open the door and raced after her.

'You can't mean that,' she said, as she caught up with her friend.

'Yes, I do,' Carly said as she coldly pushed Storm aside. 'What you've done is totally out of order and I'll never forgive you.'

'I'm so, so sorry,' Storm pleaded. 'I never thought Dermot would do this. I thought he loved you like I did. I would never do anything to hurt you, Carly, you're my world. Think of all we've been through – we've been friends for a lifetime. Please don't throw that away.'

Carly stared contemptuously at her friend, sweaty and out of breath, standing on the seafront dressed in her pyjamas.

'Up until this morning I would have said that nothing would ever come between you and me, Storm. I would have said we were best friends for life. But the moment I saw that headline I knew it was over. I never want to see you again, you're dead to me.'

For the rest of the week, Storm felt as if she was trapped in a nightmare. After eventually returning to the flat on Sunday, she'd had the mother of all rows with Dermot. Storm had never been so angry and they'd argued for hours over his betrayal.

'How could you do this to me . . . to us . . . to Carly?' demanded Storm.

'Don't be stupid, darling. You know as well as I do how brutal journalism can be.'

'But it doesn't have to be. There is such a thing as loyalty, you know.'

'When will you realise, I did it for us?'

'Please!' Storm snorted with disgust. 'You didn't do it for me or for us. You did it for yourself.'

Dermot stalked towards her, putting his face close to hers. 'That's not true. When I learned Miles had offered you a job, I couldn't stand the idea of being without you so I went to London with what I had.'

'Bullshit! The earliest you would have known about that was if Miles had told you when you were already *in* London, so if you think I'm falling for that you can think again.'

Realising he'd been caught out, Dermot went for her, all guns blazing. 'Well then, you'll know that in this business it's all about who you know, Storm, and you know Carly – who just happens to be a slapper who shagged a footballer. Now, enjoy the benefits of having your boyfriend working alongside you on a national tabloid and wake the fuck up!'

White-hot fury rose in Storm's chest. Before she knew what she was doing, she'd raised her hand and slapped Dermot hard across the face. First he had the nerve to deceive her, then he was having a go at her for being furious with his behaviour. He could fuck right off after the damage he'd caused.

'You bitch,' he said, clutching his right cheek.

'That's nothing compared to what you deserve. And in case you were wondering, I won't be taking that job in London . . . and you're dumped! If I never see you again it'll be too soon.'

Not waiting for a reaction Storm had flounced out of the flat, so angry she didn't even take a coat despite the fact it was snowing outside. Running all the way to Carly's, she hammered over and over on her door. She had to speak to her. Carly was her best friend, there was no way Storm could live in a world where they weren't pals. She was desperate to make things right. 'Open up, please, Carly,' Storm called through the letterbox. 'Let me in. I know you're in there. I just want to talk, I won't budge until we've talked.'

Five hours later, with teeth chattering and fingers so cold she could no longer feel them, Storm had to admit defeat. Shivering and with her eyes blurred with tears she walked slowly home, the bitter wind nipping at her ears. As she rounded the corner to her flat she walked straight past a group of carollers singing *'Tis the season to be jolly*.

Yeah, if you're anyone but me, thought Storm grimly.

The following morning she got into work early, intending to write an email to Miles saying thanks but no thanks for the job offer. She'd tossed and turned all night, agonising over what to do. On the one hand there was no denying that a full-time post working in showbiz journalism was a great opportunity. It was her dream, after all. But she couldn't stomach the thought of being so near to Dermot, and if working on a national tabloid could make you sink so low as betraying a friend, she just wasn't interested. It wasn't right for her. So instead Storm decided to stay put, and by getting in early hoped to prove to Ron just how committed she was to the *Post*, even if Dermot wasn't.

But Ron had other ideas. Storm had barely shrugged off

her coat and fired up her computer when her editor's dulcet tones were heard, bellowing across the office. 'Storm, my office, now.'

Gathering her notepad and pen, she hastened across the floor, aware of everyone's eyes boring into her.

'I've had your daft as arseholes boyfriend in here first thing and now it's your turn to be read the Riot Act,' Ron began as he slammed the door shut.

'But . . .' Storm began.

'I don't want to hear it,' he snapped. 'Now sit down and shut up.'

She perched on an uncomfortable wooden chair by the filing cabinet and braced herself.

'I thought you were better than this, Storm,' he sighed. 'I like to sell papers, but selling out your own best mate's a level even I wouldn't stoop to.'

'But I didn't . . .' Storm began, only for Ron to cut her off.

'You're a good reporter, but after witnessing everything you're capable of I'll be glad to see the back of you. You and Dermot make me sick.'

Wide-eyed with panic, Storm started babbling. 'What are you talking about? Ron, please believe me, I never had anything to do with that story. I want to stay here and keep working at the *Post*.'

'Correct me if I'm wrong, Storm, but Dermot insists you told him something your mate told you in confidence. Don't you remember the first rule of journalism school? Always protect your sources. No, I'm sorry, Storm, if you weren't resigning, I'd have to fire you, I don't want people like you working for me.'

She looked at her editor aghast. How had her life blown apart like this?

'Dermot tells me you're both off to pastures new, so I wish you luck with that,' Ron continued. 'Make sure you clean your desk before you leave.'

'But, Ron, seriously, I can explain all of this . . .'

He opened the door, signalling that the conversation was over. 'I'm sorry Storm. I like you, but I don't like what you've done. There's no job here for you any more.'

Walking back to her desk, head hanging down in shame, she thought quickly. Despite her best intentions she'd have to take the job in London after all. Journalism college hadn't come cheap and she was still paying off her student loans. She needed a job, and fast. She might not have wanted to take the job at the *Herald*, out of loyalty to Carly, but that was the only offer on the table right now. With the job market the way things were, who knew when she might find something else?

But the last thing she wanted was to spend any more time than she had to with Dermot. It was bad enough that they were still living together for the rest of the week. No way was she allowing the situation to continue in London.

'Look, there are two bedrooms in the Clapham flat. We can just be flatmates until we both find something more permanent,' Dermot pointed out when she confronted him about it later.

'Yeah, right. You've already proved you're a liar. For all I know this *Herald* flat could be a studio where we'd have to live in each other's pockets. I'm calling Miles and asking if there's anything else available.'

70

'Don't be ridiculous, Storm. The last thing you want to burden your new editor with is your personal life. It will make you look stupid and both of us unprofessional. The flat has two bedrooms, I promise, and I also promise that I'll leave you alone. I mean it, I'd do anything to get you to forgive me.'

'Yeah?' Storm fired back. 'Hell will freeze over first. We're not moving in together, and we're never getting back together. Got it?'

After that her week went from bad to worse. All her friends shunned her for her apparent betrayal of Carly. As for her colleagues, they continually made snide comments about her being a sell-out. The only one who offered any kind of support was her mother. Sally had been genuinely delighted when Storm told her she'd got a job on a national paper. Now Storm was touched that Sally had realised her daughter was in the middle of a crisis.

'I've read the papers,' she said, ringing Storm at work one morning. 'I sense there could be trouble for you.'

'That's an understatement, Sally.'

'Well, I'm here if you need me. You only have to ask. We all make mistakes, love.'

As for Dermot, he devoted much of the week to trying to win Storm back. Clearly he thought life would be easier if they could share the flat as planned, and Storm was sick of his campaign to make her give in. He showered her desk at work with flowers, cards and love tokens, all of which she dumped in the bin beside her desk.

One evening Storm got home late from work to find him on his knees, naked apart from a rose in his mouth.

'What do you think you're doing?' she shouted.

'I never should have done it. Honestly, Stormy, I just got carried away. I had this idea that selling the story would mean we could finally get the jobs of our dreams. I was thinking of us.'

'What do you mean, selling?' Storm asked.

Dermot shifted uncomfortably on his knees. 'Just an expression, babe. I promise you. I never would have done this if I'd thought Carly would be seriously damaged, or that you and her would fall out so badly. I mean, I figured she'd be a bit pissed off but that you would sort things out eventually – you two are solid.'

Storm had heard enough. 'Yeah? That's what people used to say about Brad Pitt and Jennifer Aniston, and look how that turned out the moment Angelina Jolie got in the way.'

'I'm no Angelina,' Dermot said hastily, getting off his knees.

'No! And you're no bloody Brad Pitt either.'

Walking over to the worn sofa, the only thing they hadn't packed for the move, Storm sank down heavily on to it. She was so tired she could hardly think straight. Cross with Dermot, devastated and sorry for Carly, not to mention keyed up at the prospect of a new job, Storm didn't think she could take any more. 'What do you want from me, Dermot?' she asked wearily.

'Well, I wondered, if you won't take me back, if we could at least keep up the pretence that we're still together when we start work?'

Storm lifted her head from her hands and eyed him

with suspicion. Was he taking the piss?

Sensing he was about to get slapped all over again, Dermot reached for his white towelling dressing gown and held out his hands as a shield. 'Now, Stormy, hear me out. The last thing we want is any more gossip about us. At the moment everyone at the *Herald* thinks we're a couple. If we tell them we've split, people are going to be too busy talking about how and why to pay any attention to the work we do. Surely it's better to break the news a few weeks after our arrival, when people have got to know us and it won't be the first thing they associate with us.'

Storm looked at him in disgust. He really was the most spineless man she'd ever had the misfortune to meet. She didn't care what people thought, and so much the better if they realised she'd dumped the loser. 'No, we bloody well can't pretend,' she hissed. 'And FYI you'll need to find somewhere else to live as I'll be in the Clapham flat alone.'

With that she turned on her heel, leaving him open-mouthed with shock.

Thankfully it at least looked as though Carly was weathering the media storm.

Earlier that week when Storm had turned on her TV before going to work, to find Carly making an appearance on the sofa of *Morning Cuppa*, looking innocent and demure in a high-necked blouse and knee-length skirt.

Sitting opposite the nation's sweetheart and *Morning Cuppa* host Poppy Mason, telling the world how lonely she'd been since she'd been dumped, and how much she wanted to make it up to Aston's wife, Carly had the audience eating out of her hand.

Suddenly the papers were full of Carly's pain as she went from tramp to victim in a matter of days. Storm was pleased Carly's life wasn't going to end in tatters as she'd feared but it seemed she was still no closer to regaining her friend's trust. Logging on to Facebook, she was horrified to see Carly's latest post in her newsfeed was a postcard with a quote about how it can often take years to find out who your friends really are. Scrolling down, she saw hundreds of people had 'liked' her comment and reposted it to their own feeds For God's sake! Storm knew she was in the wrong, but since when did she and Carly communicate through the Internet? It was beyond childish.

By the time Friday morning rolled around Storm didn't want to stay in Brighton a minute longer. She was itching to put this whole mess behind her.

Arriving for work to see out her last day, she found herself largely ignored. 'It's because everyone expected better from you, Storm,' explained Wendy.

There was no arguing with that. As Storm cleared the last of her belongings from her desk and headed out of the newspaper building for the last time, her eyes brimmed with tears. She hated to admit it but Wendy's words had stung. Reaching the flat and packing the last of her stuff into the back of the van she had hired, she had to face facts

she no longer belonged in Brighton. There was a time she'd imagined a huge send off when she left for London, with all her friends gathering at her flat to say goodbye, complete with champagne and maybe even a few moving in gifts, but that was no longer on the cards.

Dermot had already left, saying he would sleep on a

mate's floor in London so only Sally was there to wave Storm off as she began her new life. Kissing her mother swiftly on the cheek, Storm fought back tears. Here she was, leaving her hometown after twenty-five years, and nobody other than the mother who had all but abandoned her as a teenager had bothered to say goodbye. Everything was such a mess. She was just about to get into the van when Sally grabbed her arm and pulled her close for a last hug.

'Storm, I know you won't believe me but Carly will come round and forgive you eventually. And it may not mean much to you but I'm proud of you for pursuing your dreams. You owe it to yourself to make the most of this opportunity.'

'I don't know, Sally,' Storm said quietly. 'I don't feel like I deserve this break.'

Sally released her daughter from her grip, and looked straight into Storm's eyes.

'Listen, my girl,' she said fiercely. 'You may have made a mistake, but you've more than paid your dues in this life already. This is a once-in-a-lifetime chance for you, don't be stupid and screw it up.'

Chapter Five

Checking her reflection in the huge mirror that dominated the ladies' loos, Storm brushed some imaginary dirt from her blouse, smoothed down her hair and took a deep breath to calm herself.

She hadn't felt so anxious for years, but that morning as she'd collected her new pass and made her way into the lift with all the other *Herald* employees it had hit her that this was her new life.

Suddenly the nerves had kicked in, and she'd felt so nauseous she'd been tempted to walk out and never come back. Thank God for her dad's watch. She'd had a feeling she'd need it more than ever this morning so had slipped it into her pocket for good luck. Now as she stroked the face the action grounded her. She remembered that she was a woman in control.

Since her arrival at the new flat Dermot had gone out of his way to help Storm settle in and prove that he wanted her back. He'd turned up offering to clean the

place, to unpack her boxes, even go to the supermarket to stock up on food for her, but Storm had taken great pleasure in slamming the door in his face each time, telling him in no uncertain terms to get the hell out of her life and drop dead!

His behaviour had been nothing short of irritating if she was honest. Storm wasn't about to change her mind and take him back. He was a rat. A rat who had cost her the most precious relationship she'd ever known. No, as far as Storm was concerned, Dermot was ancient history.

Squaring her shoulders, she stopped at the sub-editor's desk and asked where she could find Sabrina Anderson. After she was pointed in the right direction, Storm said thank you and walked towards her new boss. Sabrina was on the phone and Storm hung back rather than interrupt. Something told her the call wasn't going well.

'I don't care if she's dead. Find someone else to talk or I'll get another freelancer who will!' Sabrina shrilled as she slammed the phone down. 'Amateurs,' she muttered, turning to an anxious-looking Storm.

'Who are you and what do you want?'

'I'm Storm, new writer on the showbiz desk.'

Sabrina said nothing but looked her up and down.

'Er, we haven't met before as I've done some Saturday shifts in features,' Storm continued, holding out her hand for Sabrina to shake. 'But I just wanted to thank you for this opportunity.'

Sabrina stared at Storm's outstretched hand as though it was something nasty stuck to the bottom of her shoe.

After leaving Storm hanging for what felt like an eternity, she shrugged and turned back to her desk.

'Your "opportunity" had nothing to do with me. But you can show me how grateful you are by getting me a coffee. Black, no sugar.'

Turning to Dermot who had already settled into his new desk opposite the news editor, Sabrina cocked her head to one side and plastered on her best smile. 'Dermot, how wonderful to see you. Our lovely new starter has offered to go on a coffee run, what would you like?'

'Flat white, please, babe,' he replied, not even looking at Storm. 'So, Sabrina, I've got some great leads I wanted to talk to you about . . .'

Storm flushed bright red with embarrassment before turning away and keeping her head down. She joined the queue in the canteen to get the drinks. The cheek of Dermot, calling her 'babe'! And that bitch Sabrina! What a bloody welcome this was turning out to be — she didn't even know where she was sitting yet.

'Don't worry about Sabrina,' said a voice behind her. 'She's rude to anyone who's not a bloke.'

Turning around, Storm saw a smiling blonde, dressed in a sharp black pencil skirt and grey biker jacket. 'I'm Chelsea, and I'll be working with you on the showbiz desk,' she said.

As Chelsea held out her hand, Storm took it and returned her grin. Thank God she'd met someone normal. 'I thought it was just me she'd taken an instant dislike to.'

'Oh, no, she hates all women so don't even think about trying to be friends with her.' Chelsea smiled. 'We

nicknamed her Supertramp 'cos she's shagged her way to the top.'

Storm couldn't help herself, she burst out laughing. That was just the sort of thing she'd have expected Carly to say. At the thought of her old friend, Storm felt a stab of pain. But today was meant to be a new start – it wasn't the time for letting old hurts get in the way.

Reaching the front of the queue, she gave her coffee order and, with Chelsea's help, successfully managed to deliver the drinks to Sabrina, Dermot and her new colleagues on the showbiz desk without spilling a drop.

'You must be a good influence on me. Normally I'm so clumsy these drinks would have gone everywhere.'

'Then consider me your guardian angel.' Chelsea smiled as she steered Storm to her new desk, and showed her where the tea bags and instant coffee were kept, along with the emergency stash of chocolate biscuits for when Sabrina was being particularly bitchy.

'There are only two left,' Storm noticed.

'Which should give you some idea of just how much of a cow she was last week. We had three packets of these in the drawer last Monday.' As Chelsea winked, Storm breathed out a sigh of relief. She didn't want to jinx things but she had a feeling she and Chelsea might become friends.

She wasn't wrong. All that week Chelsea showed Storm the ropes, telling her who and what to look out for. There was plenty to keep her busy. Although Sabrina was the news editor and officially oversaw the showbiz department, Chelsea was the one who'd been there longest and she ran the desk. She knew where to go, what to see

and what to miss. Best of all, she knew all the celebrity goss on the circuit. Not a thing got past Chelsea and Storm had already been gobsmacked to learn one or two secrets about celebrities she would never have guessed.

'But they look to be so in love,' she protested after Chelsea had revealed the truth about one high-profile married couple.

'That's the point, Storm. They look committed, but they're living completely separate lives – she even lives in her own house next door to his.'

'But why all the pretence?' Storm asked innocently.

'You've still got a lot to learn, kid,' laughed Chelsea. 'They're celebrities, the public are supposed to want their lives. It's not going to look very good for them if the world discovers they're no different from everyone else, is it?'

'Which is where we come in,' Storm confirmed.

'Exactly, babe. That's why I want you at your first showbiz do tonight. It's a handbag launch and Mr and Mrs Golden Couple should be there – they haven't been seen together in months so if they show up tonight this is a big deal. I want you to look for any signs of a split, sit in the corner and just watch what goes on between them. Don't knock back the free champagne, tempting though it is. Getting pissed is not an option. Got it?'

Storm nodded her head. And later during the party at London's swanky Guildhall she did just as she'd been told. Although the promised Golden Couple failed to turn up, the place was wall-to-wall with other celebs and Storm hobnobbed with TV and reality stars, making sure she came up with loads of gossip for the paper's party pages.

As promised she'd sipped sparkling water rather than the free-flowing champagne on offer, but she'd been more than happy just to find herself on the fringes of this glamorous new world. She'd been unable to tear her eyes away from the latest *Big Brother* winner snogging the face off one of the *TOWIE* girls, and an *EastEnders* star emptying an entire gin bottle down her throat while pole dancing in a thong. As if that wasn't enough she'd bumped into another reality star, who announced she'd been offered a walk-on part in a Hollywood movie and was due to sign contracts next week.

'It's such a big opportunity,' she gushed. 'I wasn't supposed to say anything yet, but I feel like I could tell *you* anything! God, don't let me bump into you next time I end up snogging a man I shouldn't!'

The following day Storm wrote up her copy with pride, only to find it wasn't good enough for Sabrina.

'Your piece on that new handbag launch party was shit,' she said, slamming down Storm's copy on her desk.

'Sorry, Sabrina,' Storm mumbled. 'I did my best.'

'Well, your best was shit. It may have been good enough for the little backwater paper you came from, but not here.'

'Sorry again, Sabrina, I'll do better next time.'

'You'd better, otherwise it might be best for you to have a career rethink. I hear Sainsbury's are after shelf-stackers, perhaps that's more your thing.'

Storm just glared at her. Bitch! It was as if Sabrina had a hotline tapped directly into her junior's insecurities.

As Sabrina stalked over to her own desk, Chelsea gave her new friend a smile.

'Just ignore her, we all do.'

'Easier said than done,' Storm whispered back.

'She does this to every new girl who's any good. Sabrina thinks she can get away with it when someone's just arrived – trust me, she'll get bored in the end.'

'I hope you're right.' Storm sighed. 'There's only so much "yes, Sabrina, no, Sabrina, how many coffees would you like today, Sabrina" I can manage before I smack her around the face with a stapler!'

'Don't give her the satisfaction,' Chelsea chuckled. 'She's easily threatened by anyone with a hint of talent – don't let her get in the way of your big chance.'

Storm sighed. She knew Chelsea was right, and Sabrina wasn't the first awkward cow she'd ever encountered and wouldn't be the last. But it was Storm's first week. Couldn't the news editor at least cut her some slack?

'Does this qualify as a chocolate biscuit moment?' queried Storm.

Chelsea threw her head back and laughed. 'Not even close, babe.'

If nothing else at least the challenge of her new role helped to take Storm's mind off Carly. Although she had done her best not to think about her friend, Storm couldn't help it, she really missed her mate. Ever since they were small, they'd talked several times a week at the very least. Not being able to tell Carly all the details of her new life broke Storm's heart. It wasn't so much that she had lots of excitement and drama to fill her in on, but it was the chance to talk about the small things she'd taken for granted all these years – like whether she should be healthy

82

and have grilled chicken for dinner or give into a craving for a greasy burger. Not only that, she would have killed to have confided in her friend about Dermot.

She kept checking her phone every five minutes to see if she had any missed calls, but nothing. Storm hadn't given up, though, and had rung Carly every day since she'd moved but her phone just rang and rang. Yesterday she'd rung and heard a disembodied voice tell her this number was out of service. Storm had stared at her mobile in horror. Had Carly really changed her number to avoid her? Storm couldn't believe it. But there was no getting away from the truth. Carly never wanted to hear from her again.

Storm was worried. Not just about the fact that she may never hear from Carly again, but also about how her former friend was coping. Desperate for information she texted the one person she hoped might still be speaking to her – Jez. Thankfully he texted her straight back, explaining he was working nearby and could meet her for lunch later that day.

Walking into the salad bar he'd suggested around the corner from her office, Storm was delighted and relieved to see a virtually orange man sitting in the corner, waving at her frantically. 'I've ordered us the carb-free lentil bake. It's disgusting but fabulous for the figure.' He smiled, pulling her in for a generous hug.

'Jez, it's wonderful to see you, thank you so much for meeting me.'

'Any time, sweetheart. I think it's madness you and Carly aren't speaking. I've told her there's no way she

should be shutting you out like this but she won't listen. She knows as well as I do how the media blows things out of proportion.'

Storm fiddled with the corner of her napkin and fought back tears. What with splitting from Carly and Dermot in the space of a week, she'd needed to see a friendly face more than she'd realised.

'I honestly didn't betray her, Jez. I made the mistake of telling my boyfriend about her fling, a man I thought I could trust. Big mistake, which is why he's now my ex.'

Jez paused before he said, 'Storm, we've all made mistakes where men are concerned. Me more than most. One day I'll have to tell you all about a little indiscretion I enjoyed with a former boy-band member. He was such a swine in the end, I thought I was going to have to change my name and go into witness protection!'

Storm chuckled. 'That bad?'

'Worse. But what I'm trying to say is that, even though I made a huge mistake, things sorted themselves out in the end, and I know you and Carly will patch up your differences.'

'But she's changed her number, Jez. I don't think she's ever going to forgive me. Besides all that, I'm worried. We both know how badly she took it when Paul cheated on her. I'm concerned all this press attention will send her right back to square one.'

As their food arrived, they took a break from the conversation to tuck in.

'Look, Storm,' Jez said, reaching for the pepper grinder. 'This has done Carly no harm whatsoever. You might as

well know she's never been busier at work and has even been offered a segment on *Morning Cuppa*, to dole out fashion and relationship advice to wronged women.'

Fork midway to her mouth, Storm paused. 'Are you joking? I thought Dillon said he'd ruin her?'

'Far from it. Carly may still be painted as a home-wrecker by some sections of the press but if anything she seems to be climbing the career ladder more quickly as a result, so I'd stop beating yourself up quite so badly if I were you.'

'I want her back in my life, Jez. She's my best friend, and being without her is unbearable.'

'And you'll get her back, you've just got to be patient. If nothing else you've got to get on with your own life, gorgeous. Carly's moved on, you have to as well. Why don't you try giving her some space for a while? Show her what she's missing.'

'You mean like when you've been dumped by a bloke?'

'Exactly like that.' Jez grinned. 'But don't hit the ice cream, my love. Now you're on the London party circuit, not to mention young, free and single, you need to stay in shape.'

After lunch Storm walked back to work feeling more light-hearted than she had in days. She was pleased Carly's career was soaring and that her friend was making the most of the situation she'd found herself in. If only she could find some way of forgiving Storm then life would be perfect for them both.

Flashing her pass at the security guard, she made her way to the bank of lifts. Waiting for one to hit the ground

floor and whisk her back to her desk, she realised Jez was right. She couldn't keep chasing Carly like this. She'd go mad. There was only one thing for it, she realised. She'd just have to get on with her new life.

Thank God for Chelsea, who'd been an endless support since Storm had joined the paper. Not only had she been delighted with the way the new recruit had handled herself at the handbag launch, she now had a new assignment she knew Storm would be perfect for.

'You, Makayla and a hotel suite at five p.m. tonight,' Chelsea announced, handing her the details of an interview that had been set up.

Storm looked startled.

'What . . . THE Makayla ?'

'The one and only,' Chelsea agreed. 'Now she's plugging her new album and has agreed to give just two or three interviews to the press. Try and get something new out of her – I reckon you're good for it.'

At that Storm felt a little pulse of excitement. Makayla was one of the hottest pop stars on the planet. With a bigger following than Katy Perry and Lady Gaga put together, Makayla was seriously A-list. Was Storm really up to the challenge?

'I'm not sure I'm ready,' she said.

'Bollocks,' Chelsea replied cheerfully. 'Besides, I've got a hot date in Paris with a stockbroker tonight and can't be late.'

'Paris, France?'

'I only know one Paris. Come on, you'll be doing me a favour.'

Touched by her new friend's generosity, Storm vowed to do her best. Yet walking into London's swanky Dorchester Hotel later that day, she had to admit her palms and everything else felt more than a little sweaty as she was whizzed up to the penthouse in a private lift. Thankfully, Makayla couldn't have been more welcoming and immediately put Storm at ease.

'Come in, babe,' she said, pushing her PR people out of the way and greeting the reporter from the lift herself. 'Champagne?'

'Not for me, thanks,' Storm replied regretfully. 'On the job and all that.'

'Ooh, a bit like a policeman?'

Storm laughed. Whenever she'd seen Makayla on the telly, she'd always thought she was some super-professional icon who seemed untouchable. Now, she realised the star was a sweet, down-to-earth girl from Dagenham.

'Just like a copper, but without the uniform.'

Unleashing a Barbara Windsor-style belly laugh, Makayla reached for a fresh bottle.

'Well, don't mind me.' She smiled and poured herself a large glass. 'Bottoms up.'

After that Makayla answered everything Storm asked her, even when her publicity team butted in to tell her their client wasn't answering those sorts of questions.

'I can speak for myself, thank you,' the star said bolshily. 'Now then, babes, where were we . . . oh, yes, plastic surgery. Well, of course I've had me knockers done. Who hasn't?'

'I haven't.' Storm giggled. 'And I was sure I'd read you hadn't either.'

'I was embarrassed and ashamed to admit it at the time,' Makayla explained. 'I did it because I thought that was the way to sell more records. Now I realise that's bullshit, and I don't care who knows it.'

'Really?' Storm was puzzled. 'But why do you want to 'fess up now?'

'I don't know.' Makayla laughed. 'It's you! I never meant to tell you about that but you've got a way of getting the truth out of people. I like you!'

Once the interview was over, and Storm and Makayla had air kissed with genuine warmth, Storm walked through the hotel foyer and made her way out into the cool night air. With two days to go until Christmas, the West End pavements were jam-packed with last-minute shoppers, desperate to find gifts for their loved ones. As she negotiated her way around huge shopping bags and pointy elbows, she felt like running down the street cheering. Nothing could put a dampener on her good mood tonight. She'd secured a massive exclusive for the paper, and she'd only been in the job a week!

Nearing Marble Arch station, Storm felt like she was flying. Secretly, she'd been worried that after years of interviewing councillors about planning applications she would be out of her depth when faced with such a huge star. After all, Makayla filled stadiums. But she and the singer had bonded speedily. So much so that Storm had gone way over her allotted ten minutes. It was going to be quiet back at the office but she thought she'd go in to write up her notes.

Thinking of the scoop she'd just landed, she hoped this

was something that would not only give Chelsea a thrill, but finally put a smile on Sabrina's face.

'Nice one, babes,' Chelsea said, when they met in the lobby and Storm told her about the interview. 'I'd help you with your piece but Paris calls and all that.'

'My heart bleeds,' Storm bantered as the lift doors shut.

There was nobody else in the office apart from the night news guys and Storm was determined to make the most of the opportunity she had to get her piece word perfect.

By midnight she was knackered, having slaved over every sentence. She pressed send. With her copy safely delivered to Chelsea and Sabrina, Storm headed out to catch the drunk express. As usual at this time of year the night bus would be rammed with Christmas revellers determined to throw up in their handbags or pass out on her shoulder. What a shame she didn't have the energy to join them, thought Storm, already fantasising about crawling into bed. As she shivered at the bus stop, she thanked her lucky stars tomorrow was Christmas Eve, which meant it was her last day in the office before Christmas Day itself. Although there would still be a paper to produce, only a skeleton staff was on duty, meaning Storm could catch up on some much-needed sleep.

As for Christmas Day itself, she had thought hard about where to spend it. Sally would be in Canada this year with her relatives there, while Bailey and Lexie would both be away, they rarely came home these days – Lexie was fulfilling her dream, travelling the world working on cruise ships, and Bailey had joined the army and was currently stationed in Cyprus. Although they'd all speak on the day, Storm hadn't known what to do for Christmas.

Usually she and Carly saw one another on Christmas Day, but this year Storm had a horrible feeling her special day would mean a meal for one eaten slumped in front of the telly, with only her favourite box sets for company. Still, she'd had worse Christmases.

The following day in the office Storm was determined not to let Sabrina rattle her. She'd worked hard on the Makayla interview, and Chelsea had been thrilled with the story she'd produced, texting her late last night to thank her for a job well done.

It's brilliant babes! What an exclusive! Couldn't have done better myself. xxxx

Balancing a cappuccino and a bacon muffin in one hand and her mobile in the other, Storm was just about to sit down when Miles shouted that he wanted to see her in his office.

Predictably, she spilled coffee everywhere.

'Bollocks!' she hissed, mopping herself frantically with a wad of tissue.

'Stop mucking about, Storm,' Sabrina called. 'Miles is a professional even if you're not. We don't keep him waiting.'

With a heavy heart, Storm walked towards his office. She'd only been on the staff just over a week and had been working her fingers to the bone. What could she possibly have done wrong? Or was this down to Sabrina? It was obvious the woman hated her guts. Perhaps she'd successfully arranged for Storm to be fired. The perfect Christmas present, she thought.

Nearing her editor, she tried to read his expression. He

was smiling, which wasn't usually the look of a man who was about to give someone the sack. But perhaps he was like one of those killer assassins who grinned to put you at ease before shooting you straight in the chest.

'Don't look so worried.' He smiled more widely, ushering Storm inside. 'I want to congratulate you on a job well done.'

'Really?'

'Yes, I've just read your Makayla story – very nice work.' He gestured for her to take a seat. 'It's great you've landed such a big scoop so quickly – you're obviously settling in well.'

'Er, well, you know,' replied Storm, settling herself into the squashy armchair opposite Miles's desk, which was angled to overlook the Thames.

'Any new job takes time to settle into,' he replied reasonably. 'But it's clear you've got a knack for getting people to talk, which is why I've got a special undercover assignment for you. It means working on New Year's Eve but I don't think you'll find it too much of a hardship.'

He slid two first-class British Airways tickets across the desk towards her.

Storm gasped. 'What's this for?'

'Little job. We've got word that a celebrity couple host sex parties and are heading to a New Year's Eve party in Rome to enjoy themselves, with other like-minded individuals. Your job is to befriend them on the plane as they'll be on the same flight, so that they'll feel comfortable at the party revealing their saucy secrets to you.'

Storm wasn't sure she'd heard him correctly. 'You want me to go to a sex party?'

91

'That's right.' Miles chuckled. 'Don't worry, you don't have to have sex at the party and you don't have to stay for the whole thing, just long enough to get the details and some photos of our devoted celeb couple in action.'

This had to be a joke. Staring out of the window at all the other worker bees in offices across the Thames, Storm wondered how many of them were discussing sex with their boss.

'Look, it's just a bit of fun,' he continued. 'Besides, you'll have Dermot with you the whole time. I know you two aren't a couple any more but it won't kill you to spend some time together – and there's nobody else I can send. I can't imagine you'll need to be at the party for more than a couple of hours, meaning you two will have the rest of the night off. Think of it as a mini-break, no expense spared.'

Storm's mind raced. Her life was like some bad sitcom. Any minute now Ashton Kutcher was going to leap out of the filing cabinet and tell her she'd been punked.

Not only was she spending New Year's Eve at a sex party, but she'd be spending it with her ex. Life just got better and better. If only she could tell Carly, she thought. Her friend would die laughing. But no. She had to stop obsessing over her former friend. Jez was right. For now, she had to let Carly go.

Chapter Six

Sweeping into a Mayfair store on Boxing Day morning with the *Herald*'s company credit card burning a hole in her pocket, Storm felt like a million dollars.

'It's vital you look the part,' Miles had told her. 'All the other women at the party will be dressed in designer frocks so you need to be too – don't spare any expense. And don't forget the shoes either.'

But now, after traipsing up and down the shops for hours, Storm realised in despair that this was one of those days when nothing felt or looked right on her. She was staring at some hideous shiny dresses displayed in the window of a very expensive boutique when a man rounded the corner and collided with her.

'Jez! What on earth are you doing here?' she asked, delighted to see her new friend.

'I could say the same to you. I didn't think you were into granny frocks,' he teased, jerking his head towards the shop.

'Eurgh! I'm shopping,' Storm groaned. 'But everything I try on looks like it's come from a dressing-up box.'

'Well, of course it does if you've been looking in places like this. It isn't fit for anyone unless they're ninety-five or blind,' replied Jez, peering in the window and shuddering at the sight of a gold floor-length creation in the window. 'So what do you need a new dress for?'

Quickly Storm filled him in on her latest assignment. 'I thought it would be fun but I've been trudging up and down the shops for hours now and haven't found anything,' she wailed.

'Time for your favourite fairy godmother to step in.' He smiled, hailing a taxi and steering Storm inside. 'Harvey Nichols, please,' he told the taxi driver. 'Honestly, Storm, it's a one-stop designer paradise and you're going to love it.'

Entering the store, she quickly realised Jez was in his element as he flounced around each concession.

'Boring, boring, boring . . . perfect!' He grinned, reaching for a hot pink number and flinging it into her arms. 'I love shopping!'

'Me too,' Storm agreed weakly, by now barely able to see over all the outfits Jez had already piled into her arms for her to try on.

Finally, after Jez had exhausted the store, he herded her over to the changing rooms and insisted she show him every single outfit.

Storm, who was by now starving, was not in the best of moods.

'I'm not a model,' she whined. 'Can't I just show you the one I think will work best?'

Jez looked as if he could slap her. 'No, you can't. If it was down to you I know you'd turn up dressed in a bin bag. I want to see every single outfit – even if *you* think it's minging, *I'll* be the judge.'

Twenty minutes later Storm had found the dress of her dreams, a floor-length, cap-sleeved red gown, that clung to every curve, while still looking classy. 'Divine!' Jez declared as she stepped out of the changing room. 'You'll be the belle of the ball.'

'I hope not!' Storm protested as she gave him a twirl. 'The last thing I want is some dirty old perv picking my car keys out of the bowl.'

'Oh, sex parties aren't like that any more, Storm,' he assured her. 'That's so seventies. These days the venues are often very high-class.'

'How the bloody hell do you know?' she asked, gobsmacked, as they headed to the cash desk.

Jez shrugged. 'I've been around.'

Surrounded by shopping bags, Storm gratefully sipped a Dirty Martini in the bar of the plush W Hotel. She was exhausted after spending hours wandering around after Jez, who had insisted she bought accessories to match the dress. Storm had somehow ended up with a clashing hot pink clutch, diamond earrings, a beautiful ruby necklace, and a pair of red strappy Zanotti sandals that were so high, Storm was sure she'd topple over at any minute.

'They're more expensive than the dress!' Storm had gasped, gazing longingly at the shoes.

'It's on expenses, darling,' Jez wickedly suggested as he

guided her around the store. 'They expect you to spend all this money, so you might as well. Enjoy it while you can, I say. And anyway, with that dress and those shoes, you look like a goddess, darling. No one would dare touch you. Now enjoy it.'

Storm opened her mouth to protest, but realised there was no arguing with that, so she spent with abandon.

As for Jez, he'd refused to leave empty-handed and treated himself to an eye-wateringly expensive Omega watch. 'This is the life.' Jez smiled and clapped his hands together in delight as he rifled through Storm's bags. 'Nothing like a bit of shopping in the Christmas sales.'

'We didn't actually get anything in the sales,' she pointed out.

'No, but it is Christmas. Speaking of which, how was it for you?'

Storm sighed. She knew how much Jez loved this time of year, and it was no secret he liked to get all his nearest and dearest together for the perfect Christmas. This year he'd spent the day with Rufus and their best friends Gemma and Tony, as well as gorgeous glamour model Angel Summer and her über-hot husband Cal Bailey.

The last thing Storm wanted to do was rain on Jez's parade and reveal she couldn't give a toss about Christmas. Still, as Christmas Days went, this one hadn't been too bad. After speaking to Sally, Bailey and Lexie, she'd channel surfed, only to stumble across Nico Alvise presenting a festive cooking show. As she'd stuffed her face with a Christmas ready meal and chocolate Yule log, Storm couldn't tear her eyes away from the screen

– he was as gorgeous as she remembered. Watching him expertly slice a turkey crown, Storm felt butterflies in her tummy. She'd wondered if she'd imagined the strength of her feelings when she'd bumped into him at the party, but watching him on-screen it was clear she hadn't imagined anything.

After that she'd read a book and gone to bed early, but on the whole it hadn't been a bad day. Nobody had got drunk, passed out, vomited or hurled abuse. If it hadn't been for the fact she'd missed Carly every moment of the day and had drunkenly tried to see what she was up to on Facebook every half an hour, Storm would have said the day had been OK. If nothing else she'd at least had the chance to catch up on some sleep.

'It was all right.' She shrugged.

'How much time did you spend on Facebook trying to work out what Carly was up to?'

Storm looked at him in surprise. 'Sorry, did we spend Christmas together after all?'

'No, sweetness, it's just exactly the sort of thing I would do,' Jez said with twinkling eyes.

Storm laughed. Maybe she wasn't as insane as she'd thought she was. 'I've been doing my best to get on with my life, just like I know Carly's doing, yet I keep feeling guilty. I'm not sure I deserve to be happy after what I did to my best friend.'

Jez signalled to the waiter for another couple of Martinis, before turning to face Storm.

'You've got absolutely nothing to feel guilty about! I adore Carly, but she isn't hanging around feeling sorry for

herself. Her work's going well and she's started seeing a new man.'

Storm gulped her drink in shock. Carly was dating again? Wow, that was brilliant news. She really was moving on. Storm knew it was none of her business but curiosity got the better of her.

'Who is he? Have you met him?'

Jez nodded. 'He's totes gorgeous with abs of steel like a Grecian god! His name's Roberto and he's an events manager in Brighton. He organised Nico's Christmas party, and after that awful story came out he called Carly to check she was OK.'

Storm's mind was in a spin. That party had changed both their lives, it seemed. She had a million questions, but there was just one she needed an answer to immediately.

'Is she happy?'

'Blissfully! And it's time you took a leaf out of her book. You can't put your life on hold like this for ever.'

Storm knew Jez was right. But knowing and doing were two entirely different things.

As the limo pulled up to the grand five-storey villa, Storm felt a thrill of excitement. She'd known the venue for the party wouldn't be a seedy dive, but even in her wildest dreams she'd never expected anything this posh.

The villa was gorgeous. It was painted a deep yellow, complete with little wrought-iron balconies and elegant shutters that framed the windows, while a huge stone archway decorated with ornate cherubs welcomed guests inside.

'Care to step this way, milady?' Dermot grinned as he stepped from the back seat of their limo and reached for Storm's hand.

'Don't mind if I do.' She smiled at him.

Dermot had been a perfect gentleman since they'd arrived at Heathrow. He'd treated Storm like a princess, carrying all her baggage, constantly ensuring her glass was topped up with champagne in the first-class lounge, and insisting she took the window seat on the plane.

By the time he had offered her his extra blanket, she'd had enough.

'What's going on?' she demanded. 'You're being too nice and it's weirding me out.'

Dermot looked hurt. 'Storm, I just want to make sure you're OK. We may not be together any more but I still care about you. Not only that but tonight's a big job for us, and I want to make sure you're properly relaxed.'

'Sorry,' she replied softly. 'I guess I just wish you could have been a bit more considerate when we were going out. It's a lot to take on board, that's all.'

'I know I messed up, Storm. You'd be mad ever to give me a second chance and I know I don't deserve one, but at the very least I want you to know I'm not all bad.'

Storm softened then and was about to reach for his hand when she saw Andy Markham, Olympic 1500-metre runner, and his wife Lisa – the reality star turned fashion designer, AKA their celeb swinging couple. They were last to board and sauntering down the aisle as if they had all the time in the world. Andy got Storm's back up straightaway by talking loudly on his mobile phone

as he tried to cram half his lifetime's possessions into the overhead locker.

'Just think outside the box,' he bellowed before turning to the female flight attendant, who had asked him to get into his seat quickly as the plane was ready for take-off. 'I'll get off the phone when I'm good and ready! Don't you know who I am?'

Storm cringed. Cabin crew had enough of a hard time without dealing with wankers like him. Fury rose in her and she had half a mind to stand up and tell Andy to stop being such a dick when she caught Dermot's eye.

Leave it, he seemed to say.

Storm sat fuming in her seat, and when the stewardess came round with glasses of Prosecco for everyone, she took it gratefully. Hopefully it would help her relax and make Andy and Lisa a little more talkative. Dermot swung into reporter mode and leaned across the aisle, pretending to be nothing more than Andy's biggest fan, offering him sincere congratulations on his gold medal.

'Brilliant job, Andy. You made the country proud – you're an absolute legend.'

Storm wasn't sure such an obvious display of arse-kissing would go down well. But Lisa and Andy lapped up Dermot's praise.

'Thanks. 'Course winning the medal cost me. I had to get my legs insured for one hundred million each.'

'He really did,' chimed in Lisa. 'I insisted they were worth so much more, but the insurance company wouldn't go above one hundred mil.'

Storm squirmed in her seat in embarrassment, but she

knew she couldn't let her real feelings about the couple show.

Slapping on her biggest, fakest smile, she nodded encouragingly at Lisa.

'I know what you mean. My Dave's made a mint in stocks and shares so I wanted to get his brain insured.' She giggled inanely.

For this assignment, they'd both had to change their names. Dermot had imaginatively chosen Dave while Storm had gone for something a bit more mysterious with Destiny.

'This is my wife,' Dermot said, wrapping his arm around Storm and pulling her in for a squeeze. 'Destiny's got her own spray tan business.'

That was music to Lisa's ears. She wasted no time in asking Storm for a discount next time she needed her tan topping up. Storm assessed her as she sipped her Prosecco. If it weren't for the stringy hair extensions and badly applied slap, Lisa would have been jaw-droppingly pretty. With her long blonde hair, Barbie figure, piercing blue eyes and perfect skin, there was no denying she had model looks.

Sadly, she hadn't been to the less is more school of make-up. With her badly applied blue eye shadow, clumpy mascara and dodgy roots, she looked a lot older than her twenty-seven years.

By the time the four of them were on their second glass of Prosecco they were all getting on so well, Dermot casually mentioned they were off to a party near the Spanish Steps that night to celebrate the New Year.

'We like to do something special, don't we, love?' he said, turning to Storm, and kissing her lightly on the mouth.

'OMG!' Lisa whooped. 'We're hosting a party there tonight!'

'No way!' Storm exclaimed. 'What a coincidence.'

'Yeah, ours is strictly invite only,' Dermot explained. That much was true. The *Herald* had had to pull a number of strings to get invitations for him and Storm as the parties Andy and Lisa held were notoriously high end.

'Can I ask, is it the Four and Up Party you've been invited to?' Andy said in hushed tones.

'That's right,' Storm replied.

'Shit, babes! That's our party!' Lisa exclaimed. 'I thought there was something about you two that screamed good time! I can't wait to show you how to really party later.'

With that she shimmied the top half of her body in a side-to-side motion causing her boobs to jiggle at an alarming rate.

Andy didn't look impressed. 'Lisa, shut up!'

'Oh, don't be such a misery. If they're coming to our party then I'm not telling them anything they don't already know, or at the very least will find out about later.' She winked before beckoning to the flight attendant for another four glasses of Prosecco.

'To our new friends!'

By now Storm felt uncomfortable. Just how far would she and Dermot have to go to make their story convincing? Determined not to land herself in a sticky situation, she found her voice.

'It's our first time,' Storm babbled. 'But we've just celebrated our wedding anniversary and wanted to mark the occasion by doing something special.'

How easily the lies were flowing. Lisa squeezed Storm's hand, long manicured fingernails digging into her flesh.

'Don't worry, Destiny. It's all good clean fun,' she teased.

Andy nodded in agreement. 'I must say, it'll be nice to enjoy a bit more quality time with you both. Especially you, Destiny.' He leered at her suggestively.

Storm swallowed the bile rising in her throat. Cheeky bastard! Andy was bald, skinny, had pockmarked skin, and was also an arrogant prick. He hadn't stopped going on about how rich he was since winning gold. Apparently he'd been offered so many endorsement deals he was earning more money than he could count, and their house was now so big they needed two cleaners! And as if that wasn't enough, all his fans did his head in by asking for autographs.

'They should understand, I need my space,' he said uncharitably.

Storm wanted to smack him there and then. And had a feeling that if it hadn't been for Dermot she probably would have. As for Lisa, or Loser as Storm had secretly nicknamed her, she had her own set of issues.

'Sometimes the amount of clothes I own makes me feel physically sick, Destiny,' she confided. 'Honestly, since Andy won that medal, I've had designers throwing so many clothes at me we've had to build a new closet just to house all my shoes.'

'That is tough,' Storm sympathised, secretly thinking

how much she'd like to build a third walk-in wardrobe big enough to bury Lisa and her whining in.

By the time the stewardess told them to buckle up in preparation for landing, Storm felt that if they'd offered her the option to jump out now she would have taken it. She wasn't sure how much more she could take.

Later, Storm linked her arm through Dermot's and entered the Roman villa where the party was being held. The scene took her breath away. Everything was so elegant, a million miles away from the lurid sex den full of perverts she'd been expecting. As she took a glass of champagne from a passing waiter, her eyes darted everywhere. She drank in every little detail. Ornate mirrors that were twice the size of Storm herself hung on the stucco walls, while a white marble spiral staircase seemed to climb for miles overhead. In one corner stood a chic white velvet chaise-longue, so pristine Storm doubted anyone had ever sat on it. In the opposite corner she noticed a young man with thick dark hair and almond-shaped eyes, playing the harp as guests continued to flood into the room.

Moving into the grand ballroom, she scanned the crowd for famous faces. She spotted an MP who'd recently resigned over yet another expenses scandal, and over by the huge sash window, nibbling on canapés, stood a couple of minor royals, each married with children! Filthy buggers, she thought.

In the centre stood Marcus, master of ceremonies for the evening, who was in charge of welcoming everyone. Short, with blond hair and a northern accent, he'd been

nice enough, and hadn't seemed to suspect anything when they were introduced. 'Always a pleasure to meet newcomers,' he'd said as he warmly shook Dermot's hand and planted a very slobbery kiss on Storm's cheek. 'Now, if you don't mind handing over your phones – we don't want any pictures getting out when we play later.'

Both Storm and Dermot had known they would have to give up their mobiles, so Dermot had found them both a couple of special camera key rings that doubled up as recording devices. As they slipped their phones into the plastic bag Marcus's assistant was holding out, the host was busily going through the rules for the event. Don't be pushy, don't disturb others, don't be rude, be explicit about your desires but don't exceed other people's limits.

'This sounds more like a boot camp than a sex party,' Storm grumbled under her breath.

At that moment Marcus caught her eye. Licking his lips, he wasted no time in showing her who was boss.

'If you have any specific questions, Destiny, ask me, Andy or Lisa, at any time.' Before turning his attention back to the crowd, Marcus ran his greedy eyes over her body. Despite the warmth of the red-hot fire burning in every room, Storm shivered. The bloke was worse than a drunk eyeing up a doner kebab. Gross!

When Marcus invited them to follow him for a tour of the house, Storm was entranced to see luxurious suites with flashy four-poster beds, chaise-longues and silk bedding. This was another world, and momentarily she forgot why she was in the house. There was nothing she loved more than poking around someone else's home and she had

watched every episode of MTV's *Cribs*, desperate for a glimpse of the celeb lifestyle. Now she was living it – though she never would have imagined it would be quite like this.

Finally, as Marcus finished his tour and invited them all to enjoy a meal in the grand dining room, Storm began to relax.

Picking up her freshly filled wine glass, she took a long sip and tried to focus on the job in hand. She couldn't fail to notice that their hosts, Andy and Lisa, hadn't turned up yet. Storm nervously took another swallow of wine. Miles had specifically engineered it so that she and Dermot would be seated next to the couple, so Storm could work her magic on them and without their presence, the whole story would fall apart. And then, just as the starter arrived, Andy and Lisa – who was wearing a hot pink, skin-tight dress that left little to the imagination – burst through the double doors looking out of breath. Lateness seemed to be their speciality, Storm thought.

'Apologies!' Andy boomed as he marched into the dining room with Lisa tagging behind.

'Yes, Andy bought me a huge pearl necklace worth at least a million, which got us both in the mood for tonight,' cackled Lisa while everyone else tittered.

Andy had to have the last word. 'Certainly did! Looked marvellous against the new double-F boobs I paid for last summer. You blokes would all be lucky to get an eyeful of my wife, let me tell you.'

As the couple sat down, it was obvious that Lisa was blind drunk. Her eyes were unfocused and she virtually collapsed into her chair. Ever the professional, Storm

smiled and got into character as she leaned towards them.

'So nice to see you again. It's a wonderful party.'

'And you, Destiny. We've been thinking a lot about you two this afternoon. We think you're our kind of people, if you know what I mean,' Andy replied, unable to resist ogling Storm in her figure-hugging red dress.

She gulped down more wine. Just the sight of Andy and Lisa was making her skin crawl. Thankfully, Dermot stepped in.

'Kind of you to say so, Andy. We were talking earlier and feel just the same way, don't we, sweetheart?' Dermot replied smoothly as he put his hand on Storm's thigh.

She didn't know which was worse. Being leered at by a creep or groped by her ex.

'Definitely,' she said, swiftly removing Dermot's hand from her knee.

'But enough about us. We want to know more about you – this place is incredible, how did you get started with these parties?'

But Storm's question was interrupted by the arrival of large plates of seared sea bass. Watching everyone around her tuck in, Storm felt increasingly nervous. How on earth were she and Dermot going to pull this off? Nibbling on a tiny piece of fish, she realised she'd lost her appetite, something that didn't go unnoticed by a drunken Lisa.

'You'll want to eat now.' She giggled. 'It's no good just drinking, Storm. We make sure we feed everyone so they've got plenty of energy for later!'

Storm simply smiled and shrugged. 'I'm fine, Lisa – watching my weight!'

Lisa rolled her eyes. 'You're gorgeous. Your weight's the last thing you need to worry about.' Looking down at her own busty figure, she sighed. 'Unlike me. All my weight goes to my bum, and sometimes I'd like to lose a bit. And now with my new boobs, men only ever want me for one thing. You know what I mean, don't you?'

Storm sipped her wine, and looked pityingly at Lisa. She was sure that any minute now the girl was going to burst into tears and start crying about how nobody loved her, a fact that hadn't gone unnoticed by Andy who shot Storm another suggestive glance before he glared at his wife. 'Lisa, leave the poor girl alone for a bit,' he said, then turned to Dermot. 'How would you like to come and enjoy a cigar with me in the library and have a look at my Olympic gold medal?'

Dermot took a sip of his wine and eyed Andy thoughtfully. 'Grand. I'd love to take a look.' Getting up, he bent down to kiss Storm on the cheek and whispered in her ear, 'Perfect timing. Don't worry, I'll get him to tell me all his sordid secrets now.'

As Dermot wandered off, Storm smiled brightly at Lisa and did her best not to panic at being left on her own. What on earth was she going to talk about? A list of dos and don'ts when it came to hair extensions?

But she needn't have worried as Lisa reached for the wine bottle and topped up both their glasses. She couldn't wait to get back to talking about her favourite subject – herself – and chatted with ease about her modelling career and recent attempts at fashion design.

'I've always enjoyed designing. Even when I was

modelling I was always drawing my own creations – you know, things I'd love to wear on the catwalk– but it's only lately it's really taken off,' she slurred. 'I'm hoping to show my first collection at London Fashion Week next year.'

Storm looked at her in surprise. Lisa might have been drunk, but it was the first time since they'd met that she had talked about something real.

'So why these parties?' asked Storm, genuinely curious. 'It seems a world away from Fashion Week!'

Lisa smiled at Storm and drained her glass before answering. 'Andy's always had a bit of an eye for the ladies, shall we say? I quickly worked out it was better to keep him interested with these parties than have a go at him about affair after affair. This way I don't have to worry about what he gets up to or who he's with because I'm there myself and know exactly what goes on.'

To her horror, Storm found herself pitying Lisa. She was doing all this just to keep her man. 'So when did it all start?' she asked, gesturing around the room.

'A few years ago. Then, after Andy won gold last year, we decided to start hosting exclusive parties for rich people just like us.'

'And do you always host parties in Rome?' Storm continued, ignoring Lisa's comment.

'Yes. Italians tend to be a bit more discreet.' Lisa smiled. 'Unlike Brits and the scumbag paps we have to put up with there. They're filth, Destiny. You've no idea what life's like for us. They follow us everywhere.'

Storm saw her chance and took it. 'Well, that's just it. How do you make sure the press don't find out?'

Refreshing their glasses once more, Lisa shrugged. 'We only invite our very best friends to our parties.'

'What do you mean?' Storm asked innocently.

Lisa, who by now had consumed nearly three bottles of wine, rolled her eyes. 'Well, we know the press go through everything . . . Christ, we even caught them going through our bins recently . . . so we only invite people we know we can trust or who have come recommended.'

Storm nodded understandingly and looked around her. 'This house is amazing, Lisa, and all this luxury and gorgeous food. These parties must cost a lot to put on.'

'Oh, they do. You wouldn't believe how expensive they are. But worth every penny.' Lisa winked suggestively, leaning closer to her.

Sensing she was on to something, Storm carried on with the questions. 'So Andy's endorsements pay for all this, do they?'

Lisa looked confused for a moment, and drank some more wine before answering. 'You know, I'm never quite sure where we get the money, to be honest, Destiny. I mean, don't get me wrong, we have loads of the stuff, and it just keeps coming, but Andy always says we should keep that just for us, you know? I think we pay for the parties by using any money that's left over from our charity. You know the one that helps amputee victims? Well, Andy's accountant says there's always so much money left over from the charity that we may as well use it to have fun.'

Gulping a mouthful of wine, Storm couldn't believe what she was hearing. Surely Lisa couldn't be stupid enough to believe that charities would have leftover money.

'So you don't help anyone through the charity?' she asked incredulously.

'Duh! 'Course we do, Destiny!' Lisa slurred. 'It's just, there's so much money, there's enough for us to have these parties too.'

Storm felt sick. The whole country thought Andy was a hero, and yet he and his wife were creaming off charitable donations. Any pity Storm had felt for Lisa quickly disappeared. Their life wasn't just dishonest, it was fraudulent too. They both deserved to be stitched up by the *Herald*. Quickly she glanced at the key ring attached to her bracelet. The light on it glowed a solid red, telling her she'd caught every last word.

As the lights went up, Dermot and Andy joined Storm and Lisa as everyone moved into the lounge area where more drinks were served. Storm was keen to go and finish the job. Dermot, however, pulled her down on to his lap and kissed her full on the lips.

'It's just for show,' he said softly, pulling away. 'We have to act like a couple to pull this off.'

Storm knew he was right. But all this pretence was doing her head in. Not only did she have a fake name but a fake boyfriend too. It wouldn't be so bad if she knew she could go back to her hotel room and chill in her trackie bottoms with a huge mug of builder's tea after all this was over, but she and Dermot were sharing a room – the only saving grace was the fact they'd been given twin beds.

Given the scoop she knew she'd landed, Storm realised it was vital they got out of here fast. Getting up, she pulled him off the chair and over to an alcove, where she quickly

told him what she'd discovered. His eyes were as wide as saucers by the time she'd finished.

'Bloody hell, Storm! That's brilliant. I got nothing out of Andy, except an exhaustive account of his training schedule during the run up to the Olympics.'

Dermot looked at his ex-girlfriend with grudging respect. A year ago he wouldn't have been sure she'd have the courage to go through with something like this, but her new job was giving Storm a confidence he'd never seen in her before and, Dermot had to admit, he was finding it very sexy. She really did have the magic touch when it came to stories. However, he had a horrible feeling she was worth a lot more to the *Herald* than he was. Dermot wasn't stupid. He'd seen the look in Miles's eyes when Storm had pulled off that Makayla story. This was only going to send her stock soaring higher and Dermot realised it would make sense if he tethered himself to Storm, and fast. He hated to admit it, but he needed her.

'So do you think we can get out of here now? These people make me feel sick, and I'm not sure I can take any more,' she said.

Discreetly they found Marcus's assistant in the hallway, retrieved their phones and stepped outside into the cool night air.

An hour later Storm and Dermot had put their night of misery behind them and were enjoying champagne cocktails in a boutique hotel with a bar overlooking the Trevi Fountain. Rome was definitely in the mood to party, with everyone cheering excitedly, hugging and smiling as

they took photos around the fountain and got ready for the countdown to the New Year.

Finally feeling relaxed, Storm checked her watch. Just half an hour to go before she could kiss goodbye to this miserable year and welcome in a new one. As she looked around she saw that the bar seemed to be full of happy couples having a good time. They all appeared to be so in love, with the world at their feet. Storm had never been one of those girls who needed a man to complete her. When she was at school she'd had no time for dating, and as she grew older she always put her mates first and blokes second. Feeling sorry for herself wasn't something Storm did, but at that moment she couldn't ignore the little voice inside her head that wondered: When am I ever going to find love like that?

With Dermot in the gents, she sat alone at the bar and flicked through the photos on her phone. There were so many of her and Dermot together, laughing, and having fun. Storm gazed at one Carly had taken when they'd enjoyed a barbecue on Brighton beach last summer. Dermot had treated them all to champagne and there was a picture of him shaking the bottle all over her as if he was a Formula One driver. Storm hadn't been able to stop laughing. She had to admit they'd had some happy times; it killed her they were over now. Taking a long drink of white wine, Storm felt a pang as her eyes came to rest on a photo of her and Carly, taken just after Dermot had soaked her with booze. With their arms wrapped around each other, it looked as though nothing could ever tear them apart – that all seemed like a million years ago. Since that photo

was taken she'd lost her best friend and her boyfriend. And then there was Dermot. She was still furious with him, and though she hated to admit it, in her darkest hours she missed him.

'Thinking about Carly?' Dermot said as he returned to his seat.

His words surprised her. That was the second time tonight he'd seemed to know exactly what she was thinking. Dermot was many things, but intuitive wasn't usually one of them.

'Yes, something like that.'

'I know you won't believe me, Stormy, but I really never meant to hurt her and I certainly never meant for you two to fall out. Most of all, I never expected us to break up over it.'

'Don't be stupid, Dermot,' Storm snapped. 'You knew exactly what you were doing and you didn't give a shit. You were too busy thinking about your own precious career.'

Casting his eyes down, Dermot fiddled nervously with the stem of his wine glass. 'Thing is, I miss you so much it's killing me. I've been a complete twat, and I know that now. But I love you, Storm, and I want you to forgive me. The truth is I'd do anything to win you back.'

Storm was shocked. Never in all the time they had been together had he expressed his love for her so openly. Of course he'd frequently told her how gorgeous she was, and how wonderful it was to be with someone who completely understood his job, but this was the first time he'd ever spoken with such feeling. Seeing him close to tears moved her. For the first time since this whole mess had begun

Storm wondered if maybe Dermot genuinely was sorry for the upset he had caused.

She opened her mouth to speak, but just as she did the crowd in the bar started loudly counting down in Italian.

As they reached *uno*, Dermot locked eyes with Storm and leaned towards her. Realising he was about to kiss her she turned her head, leaving her ex with a mouthful of her hair.

'Stormy,' Dermot whispered, reaching for her hands.

Backing away from him, she shook her head. 'Dermot, I've told you before, you and me are over. I know you say you're sorry about what happened with Carly but you have to realise . . . we are never getting back together. Since we work together I'm happy for us to try and be friendly, but as a couple we're finished.'

Chapter Seven

'Good time in the land of pizza and pasta?' chuckled Chelsea, finding Storm sipping a latte at her desk.

'You could say that.' Storm smiled as she fired up her computer.

'Well, come on, I want all the details.'

Storm paused. Even though she'd told Chelsea about her history with Dermot over a bottle of wine during her first week at work, she was in no mood to dwell on the fact that he'd tried to kiss her on New Year's Eve. She shuddered at the memory – how funny that the idea of kissing him now was as tempting to her as snogging a fish. Instead she kept it simple and stuck to discussing work.

'The job went brilliantly.'

'So I hear. Miles has been full of your scoop all morning – Sabrina's mad with jealousy. I think she was expecting it to go spectacularly wrong.'

Storm smiled wryly. 'Yeah, I assumed that, seeing as she was so encouraging before I left.'

She reached for that Sunday's edition. After their Italian trip she'd had a few days off, but the thrill of seeing her name splashed across the front page still hadn't lost its novelty. *Swing When You're Scamming* had been the headline to the piece about Andy and Lisa. So far the response to Storm's scoop had been overwhelming. She'd worried that because Andy was considered a national hero and Lisa the nation's sweetheart, everyone would hate her for exposing them. But, in fact, the public were revolted by Andy and Lisa's behaviour and the police had launched an investigation. The comments on the paper's website had been incredible. Some had even thanked Storm for doing a public service in disclosing what a pair of scumbags they really were. Storm wouldn't usually have taken pleasure in seeing someone's career take a nosedive, but if anyone deserved it, Andy and Lisa did. As for Storm herself, Miles had rung her at home the moment she'd filed her story and given her a pay rise – effective immediately.

'Money well spent if you keep this up,' he'd told her.

At that moment Sabrina appeared before Storm's desk. As usual she was dressed to kill in a black power suit, sky-high heels and immaculate make-up. There was no denying Sabrina was gorgeous, but there was nothing warm about her beauty. Cuddling her must be a bit like hugging a cold radiator, Storm thought.

As Sabrina smiled sweetly, Storm waited for the ruthless attack about to come her way.

'Well done on the Italian job,' Sabrina announced while Storm inwardly waited for the sucker punch. 'You exceeded Miles's expectations.'

'Well, that's really good to know,' Storm replied cautiously.

'Yes. Of course, I did say attending a sex party in disguise was something I knew you'd be good at. In fact, I said to him, our Storm will have no trouble pulling off the part of a good-time girl.'

There it was, the inevitable put down, delivered with perfect timing. She might be the boss but Storm thought it was about time she let Sabrina know she wasn't putting up with her cheek for ever.

'Well, thank you for the vote of confidence, Sabrina. And I know you too understand how wonderful it can be when you get the chance to mix business with pleasure,' Storm replied with assumed innocence.

Out of the corner of her eye, she could see Chelsea smirking as she buried her head in her paperwork. Sabrina gritted her teeth and fixed Storm with an icy stare.

'I certainly don't know anything about that. Everything I've achieved has been down to good old-fashioned hard work.'

'Well, there's nothing like getting down on your hands and knees in the name of hard graft,' Storm agreed, still in apparent innocence of her double-entendre. 'Now is there something I can help you with, only I know how busy you are?'

Sabrina looked as if she was itching to give Storm the finger. Instead, she coolly turned her attention to the sheaf of paper in her hands.

'Yes, actually. Miles has asked you to go to a few celebrity parties this week, including the new Daniel Craig premiere

tonight. Wear something nice, but this time don't put it on expenses. I hear Aldi occasionally carry women's wear, if you need to upgrade your wardrobe.'

Storm refused to take the bait. Instead she simply smiled at Sabrina and took the pile of invitations. With Sabrina safely out of earshot, Chelsea let out a snort of laughter, unable to contain her giggles any longer.

'You really told her!' she chuckled.

'Stuck-up cow deserves it. Anyway, aren't you meant to put rabid dogs down? I should call the RSPCA and put her out of her misery.'

Chelsea smirked. 'Forget her, babe, we all know she's a bitch. Anyway, I've got some good news for you. Tonight you won't be all on your own as you attempt to chat up Daniel Craig because I'll be joining you. And I have even got a gorgeous hot pink halterneck number you can borrow. What do you say?'

Storm smiled. What could she say? It sounded like she was in for yet another night of glamour.

Back at her flat Storm was determined to look her best just in case she came face to face with a certain Mr Craig. She slipped on Chelsea's pink halterneck dress and admired her reflection in the full-length mirror. It wasn't bad. She didn't usually do pink but this creation fitted like a glove, with a plunging neckline that made her fairly average-sized boobs look massive. To complete her look she blow dried her hair so that it fell in its usual soft waves around her shoulders. With smoky eyes and a slash of soft pink lipstick, she was done.

'Christ! You'll have someone's eye out with those,' Chelsea laughed as she spotted Storm rushing out of Leicester Square station.

'You don't have to tell me! I've already had my fair share of city boys perving over me on the tube. You could have told me this dress would give me Lisa Markham-style assets.'

Chelsea laughed as she linked arms with her new friend. 'Why else do you think I bought it? Us girls who don't have Lisa's legendary boobs need all the help we can get and I reckon you're going to have celebrities eating out of the palm of your hand tonight . . . or maybe your cleavage!'

'Chelsea,' Storm warned her, 'my name's not Sabrina, and I'm not that kind of reporter.'

'Don't worry, babes. I'm just teasing. To be honest, I think I'm a bit out of sorts because that stockbroker turned out to be more of a cockbroker, if you know what I mean?'

Storm realised with a sudden jolt of guilt that she hadn't asked Chelsea anything about her date in Paris just before Christmas. How self-involved was she? Usually there was nothing Storm loved more than a good gossip, particularly where sex was concerned.

'Was it that bad?'

Chelsea groaned. 'Bad doesn't cover it. Fair enough, he whisked me off to Paris in his private plane and we enjoyed a fabulous meal at the Plaza *Athénée*, but all he did was talk about himself all night long, then shag me before the plane had even left the tarmac on the way home.'

'Was he shit in bed?' Storm asked, getting to the heart of the matter.

'Yes! And the worst thing was his dick wasn't just the size of a party sausage, he had the nerve to tell me afterwards that I should get bum implants and he'd give me the number of a friend of his who was a cosmetic surgeon.'

Storm was astounded. 'He didn't! I hope you told him where to go?'

''Course I did. I said to him, you want to ask your surgeon friend if he's doing a two for one offer. That way you could get your dick and your personality surgically enhanced.'

Storm threw her head back and roared with laughter and was still chuckling as they arrived at the cinema. She'd wanted to watch all the stars walk up the red carpet, but Chelsea had told her not to be so lame.

'Only tourists do that, or mad fans,' she hissed as they marched straight past the crowds and into the foyer.

Storm desperately tried to be discreet and cool just like Chelsea but couldn't help scanning the achingly stylish room with its wall-to-ceiling glass front and hip white stools.

There were lots of wannabes, sipping cocktails and desperately trying to look as though they belonged, but so far no genuine celebs had arrived to watch the film.

'They don't watch the flick,' Chelsea explained. 'They walk the red carpet, get noticed, then head straight to the after party. Most of the stars have seen the film about a thousand times anyway so I'm afraid you're going to have to wait a little longer to meet Mr Craig.'

Storm sighed impatiently. She'd never been to a premiere before and had secretly hoped she'd end up sitting next

to Mr Bond himself. She imagined him yawning as he casually put his arm around her shoulder – it was a move every fifteen-year-old could count as a winner. There was just the small fact that Daniel was married, but as Storm was strictly dealing in fantasy she didn't give herself too much of a hard time about it.

Slipping into her seat in the back row, she looked around her. This was one of the poshest cinemas she'd ever been in. Forget the tatty red velour of the multiplex; these seats were covered in leopard print and embossed with the names of the stars who'd sat in them at various premieres and award ceremonies. It was incredibly glam, and Storm would have loved to have taken some photos on her phone to show her sister Lexie, but they'd been made to hand in all mobiles before being seated. Now, as she scanned the audience, she realised that although there weren't many celebs in attendance, the place was packed with plenty of civilians, dressed up to the nines.

With Chelsea bagging the aisle seat, Storm slyly glanced to her left and found she was sitting next to a bloke in a charcoal grey suit. She couldn't help feeling sorry for him. At well over six foot, he was squeezed so tightly into his seat that his knees were practically around his ears. Storm took pity on him and patted him gingerly on the arm. 'Would you like me to ask my friend to switch seats with you?'

As the man turned, he treated her to a megawatt smile, sending Storm's heart racing. Bloody hell! It was only Nico Alvise. What were the chances? And what if he remembered their last meeting?

122

'I'm fine, I'm more than used to sitting like this.' He smiled, about to turn away from her, then he asked, 'Hey, don't I know you?'

Determined to style it out, Storm kept her face averted and pretended to find her arm rest fascinating. 'Er, no. Don't think so.'

But Nico was insistent. 'Yes, I do! You're that flight attendant who spilled red wine all over me at my Christmas party in Brighton.'

Storm groaned. That bloody party was going to haunt her for the rest of her life.

'Oh, yes! Sorry, didn't recognise you in here, you look so different with . . . er . . .'

'. . . with a white shirt that's not covered in red wine?' Nico bantered.

Storm scowled and wished for the thousandth time she'd never even gone to Nico's party when it seemed she was still dealing with the fallout.

'Look, I'm sorry, I feel terrible about that,' she began.

'I'm teasing, Storm.' As Nico smiled broadly at her, his gorgeous brown eyes twinkled with mischief.

Storm blushed. 'You remembered my name.'

'Hard to forget – like the rest of you.'

Oh, he was smooth, Storm had to give him that, and any awkwardness she felt disappeared as she laughed at the corniness of the line.

'So you're laughing at me now! Storm, I could take this personally. At our last meeting you threw wine at me and now you sit here cruelly snickering at my attempts to make you feel better.'

'If you want to make me feel better, I'd appreciate an invitation to dinner in one of your restaurants a whole lot more.'

Oops – she hadn't meant it to sound as if she was inviting him on a date. That had always been her trouble, Storm thought, she never knew when to quit while she was ahead. As for Nico, if he was taken aback he didn't let on. Instead he treated her to another smile. He was about to open his mouth and reply when the cinema lights dimmed and the opening credits of the film began.

Storm found herself unable to concentrate with Nico sitting next to her. His every move caused her pulse to quicken and the hairs on the back of her neck to stand on end. There was something about him that sent her pulse-rate soaring. When his leg accidentally brushed against hers, she felt the same charge of electricity she'd felt when he'd gripped her wrists at his party. Momentarily shocked, she sneaked a glance at Nico only to lock eyes with him. Had he felt it too? By the time the film had ended Storm felt giddy with lust and couldn't wait to get out of the cinema. Grabbing Chelsea, she murmured a hurried goodbye to Nico and raced from the auditorium. What was it about that man? She wasn't usually shy around blokes, but she felt like a schoolgirl around Nico.

'What's got into you?' Chelsea grumbled as Storm hustled her outside. 'I need the loo and to rid my cleavage of all the popcorn I dropped down it.'

'You can pee when we get to the after party,' Storm said, signalling to a passing taxi and practically shoving Chelsea into the back seat. 'And, babe, newsflash. Your

124

cleavage isn't big enough to hold a lot of popcorn!'

By the time they pulled up to The Chiltern Firehouse, Storm had put Nico out of her mind and instead was buzzing with excitement about the after party.

'Bloody hell! Is that really a giant inflatable Daniel Craig?' she exclaimed to her friend.

Chelsea laughed. 'You ain't seen nothing yet, girl. Trust me, when we get inside there'll be more A-listers guzzling Cristal and pressing more flesh than you saw at your sordid sex party the other night!'

Storm considered Chelsea. 'Just how do you know all this, babe? Exactly how long have you been doing this job?'

'Long enough to know that any celeb worth their salt doesn't really want to be here, they just want to get in, get out, and get into bed before they have to do it all over again tomorrow. What was it Cameron Diaz once said: "The movies I do for free, the publicity I get paid for".'

'You old cynic, anyone would think you hated your job,' laughed Storm.

'Don't get me wrong, I love it. But I can see through the bollocks of the celeb lifestyle. Trust me, I'd rather be me than some A-lister.'

'Even when you date dickhead stockbrokers?' Storm put in.

'Even then,' Chelsea agreed as she flashed her press pass at the bouncer on the door.

Once inside, Storm struggled to get used to the low lighting. As usual Chelsea was right: the place was wall-to-wall with celebrities. This time there were genuine A-listers

too, like Bradley Cooper and Kate Upton. Up close they were just as gorgeous as they were on screen.

'Wow!' sighed Storm, momentarily star-struck.

'For fuck's sake, babe,' chimed Chelsea. 'You look like every other civilian in here, gawping at Bradley like that. You're a professional, so act like it. Plus you've got no chance of pulling if you keep your gob open like that. Keep your fingers crossed for me – I'm off to work the room.'

With Chelsea out of the way Storm headed to a table in the corner to observe the action. Just as she sat down a waiter approached her table with a glass of Cristal. 'From the gentleman at the bar with his compliments,' he said, setting the glass on the table. Storm swivelled around and saw Nico at the bar. Shit! She should have known he'd be at the after party. Catching her eye, he raised his glass as if to toast her and then walked slowly towards her table. She felt a thrill of anticipation as he gestured towards the seat next to hers and sat down, making Storm feel unusually tongue-tied.

'Thought I'd give you the chance to spill another drink over me,' he joked.

'Generous. But I wouldn't waste good champagne on you,' she bantered, not wanting to let Nico know how much his presence was unsettling her.

'So why do I keep finding you at showbiz celebrations? Shouldn't you be up in the skies somewhere, jetting off to glamorous destinations?' he asked.

'Oh, you know, us flight attendants get the occasional day off.' She shrugged, not keen to elaborate on the lie.

She knew she ought to tell Nico the truth, that she was a journalist, but somehow didn't want to break the spell she was caught up in and swiftly changed the subject. 'My friend Chelsea invited me. But what about you? Shouldn't you be cooking up some gastronomic feast in a kitchen somewhere?'

'Us chefs do get the occasional night off, you know,' he mocked. 'No, my manager tells me I have to come to these events to keep my profile high. To be honest, I'd feel more comfortable in the kitchen.'

'Celebrity lifestyle not agreeing with you then?' Storm asked as she sipped her drink.

'I wouldn't say that. I'm grateful for everything that's happened, it's just the TV thing has taken off so quickly, I'm still finding my feet.'

Storm arched her eyebrows as she noted Nico's designer suit and a watch that would have cost thousands of pounds.

'But I'm guessing the pros outweigh the cons.'

He followed the direction of her gaze and shrugged. 'Fair point. Yes, the money helps. But still, all the press attention can be intrusive and I'm sick and tired of women sending me their underwear.'

But Storm couldn't resist teasing him some more. 'Well, that's what happens when you top those sexiest man lists. It's your girlfriend I feel sorry for. How does she cope with women throwing their knickers at you, left, right and centre?'

Nico looked awkward as he replied, 'Francesca and I have known each other many years. She trusts me and thinks it's funny.'

'Well, she's more understanding than I would be!' Storm continued, now in full flow as she finished her champagne. 'If I were your girlfriend, I'd be furious.'

Now it was Nico's turn to look surprised by Storm's outburst. 'Well, if I were your boyfriend, I'd feel like the luckiest man on earth to have such a loyal, beautiful woman by my side.'

His words hung in the air and Storm wanted to brush them aside with a joke, or shoot him down with a feisty reply about keeping his corny comments to himself. But something stopped her. From nowhere an image of Nico kissing her, overwhelming her with his strong, tall body, flooded her mind. For a second she lost herself, wondering what it would be like to lie on top of him and feel his fingers glide over every inch of her skin. Something told Storm she was in dangerous territory. He was attached – flirting was the last thing they ought to be doing. Getting to her feet, she pushed her chair back and smiled at him. 'I think I should go.'

Needing a few minutes to calm down, Storm rushed up the stairs to the ladies and went to open the door. She froze in shock as she realised who was standing directly in front of her – Carly. She looked incredible, dressed in a black chiffon strapless dress and Jimmy Choo pumps. Carly's hair gleamed and her eyes sparkled. In fact, she seemed a world away from the last time Storm had seen her just before Christmas. Now she appeared happy and in control, unlike Storm. Looking down at her borrowed pink dress, she realised she'd spilled champagne down it.

Carly noticed, of course. Wrinkling her nose in disgust,

she gave Storm the once over. 'So it is true what they say.' She looked directly into Storm's eyes. 'Shit really does rise to the surface.'

But Storm barely registered Carly's hurtful words, so great was her astonishment at seeing her. 'Carly! It's amazing to see you. You look so well . . . Jez told me you'd got a new boyfriend too, and of course I've seen you on TV. Looks like everything is going brilliantly for you.'

Storm knew she was babbling but didn't care. There was so much she wanted to say to her old friend, she didn't know where to start. Maybe this was an opportunity for them to talk and repair their relationship. But Carly shut her down in an instant.

'No thanks to you! My whole life could have been in tatters after what you did, and you've got the cheek to stand there telling me how well everything's going for me!'

Even though they were just inches apart on the marble floor, Carly pressed her face close to Storm's and jabbed one perfectly manicured finger into her chest.

Storm tried to remain calm. 'I'm not going to row with you, Carly. How about I let you go? There must be people you need to see.'

But Carly was gunning for her. 'I'm in no rush, but perhaps you are. Desperate to get back to your dick of a boyfriend, are you?'

Bollocks! Storm knew how badly she'd hurt her friend, but those words stung. 'Like I said, Carly, I'll let you get on if we can't at least be civil.'

'You'd like that, wouldn't you?' Carly spat. 'For me to roll over and pretend everything's fine. Well, forget it, you

129

skank. I couldn't give a shit if everyone here found out what you did. 'Cos let's face it, if you hadn't stitched me up you wouldn't be here. In fact, the only way you'd know anything about this premiere would be by reading about it in your precious *Vida!* magazine! So, no, Storm, I won't play nice with you because, unlike me, you don't deserve any of this.'

Carly's words stung, but it seemed she still wasn't satisfied. 'You know what? You remind me of someone in that dress,' she continued as she peered down at Storm's outfit. 'Yes, with all that booze down your front, you resemble your mother.'

Storm felt as if she'd been punched. She knew she'd hurt Carly, but this was a step too far in retaliation.

All she wanted to do now was go home, but as she shook herself free from Carly's hand and turned her back on her former friend Storm was greeted by a fresh horror as she saw Nico standing at the top of the stairs.

Carly paused, brushed some imaginary fluff from her dress as she composed herself and pushed past him to return to the party, leaving Storm flushed with shame.

Nico walked straight over to her. Despite her anguish, Storm felt a flash of desire as his fingers wrapped themselves around hers.

'Silly question, but are you OK?' he asked, brown eyes brimming with concern.

'Fine, fine,' Storm lied, trying unsuccessfully to stop hot tears from spilling down her cheeks.

She could have kicked herself. Storm hated to show weakness at the best of times, let alone in front of a

stranger. Shyly she glanced up at Nico, but he didn't seem to mind. Instead he carefully brushed her tears away with his thumb. The kindness of the gesture only set Storm off again. She couldn't put her finger on it, but there was something about Nico that made her feel as though he'd known her all her life and understood who she was.

'That was my former best friend.' She sniffed. 'We had a disagreement before Christmas because she felt I'd betrayed her, and I'm ashamed to say I did. Tonight was the first time we've seen each other since then and I deserved everything she threw at me.'

'You've tried making up with her?' Nico asked gently.

'Almost every day. But Carly's not interested and I don't know how to reach her.'

At the thought of all she'd lost, Storm felt exhausted and dropped to the floor. Nico joined her and sat beside her, cross-legged.

'I know what that's like,' he confided. 'I used to have several very good friends in Italy but many years ago we had a disagreement and we never spoke again.'

Storm rested her head on Nico's shoulder as though it were something she'd been doing for years. 'What was your row about?' she asked.

Nico buried his face in her hair and paused for a moment. 'To cut a long story short, they didn't stand by me during a very difficult time.'

Storm nodded. It sounded tough. 'Do you miss them?'

'Every day,' he replied simply. 'But there's still a chance you and Carly will make up.'

'I don't think so,' Storm replied. A gaggle of girls

rounded the stairs towards the loos. At the sound of their cackles of laughter the spell was broken and she got to her feet.

'Time for me to leave . . . again.' She smiled at him. 'But thank you for everything.'

Nico squeezed her hand once more, reluctant to let her go. 'Any time, Storm,' he whispered.

Too tired to negotiate the tube home, Storm treated herself to a cab. After the night's events all she wanted was to crawl into bed. The sound of Ed Sheeran's 'Drunk Again' coming from her handbag interrupted her thoughts – Sally. Storm stared at her smartphone. Could she really deal with her mother right now? Whatever she had to say, it wasn't likely to be something that would add to Storm's evening. She checked the time. Just after eleven, a bit late for a routine call, perhaps something was wrong.

'Hi, Sally, what can I do for you?' Storm answered cautiously.

'Nothing, love, just ringing to see how your posh premiere went.'

She sounded remarkably upbeat. Was it possible she'd been boozing?

'Yeah, fine. Sal, are you OK? You sound strange.'

'Fine, love. The real reason I rang is because I've got something to tell you.' There was a brief pause as Sally cleared her throat and took a deep breath. 'Thing is, I've met someone at bingo. I've known him for years, and he's a good, kind bloke. You'd like him, Storm.'

She began to feel sick. Sally hadn't dated anyone since

her husband had died and had always insisted she wasn't interested in finding love again, arguing that Alan had been the only man for her.

'Who is he?' Storm finally asked.

'His name's Jeff. He's a gardener, and like me he lost his partner.'

Is he a drunk like you too? Storm thought uncharitably as pictures of her mother falling down the stairs time and again after drinking too much vodka flooded her mind. Sally sensed what her daughter was thinking.

'I've told him everything, Storm. He knows all about my drinking and how I relied on you to take care of the family, plus he knows how proud I am of you and all you've achieved. He's curious about you and wants to meet you. Why don't you pop down for Sunday lunch sometime? There's no rush.'

Storm stared out of the cab window and watched the lights of the city pass her by.

As they neared Chelsea Bridge her mind wandered. Of course she wanted her mum to be happy, it was just a shock to hear there was someone else in her life after so many years. From nowhere she remembered the Saturday morning ballet lessons her dad always insisted on taking her to, and the strawberry milkshake they'd enjoy together afterwards. Then there were the school holidays when Alan would teach her vital life skills, as he called them. As his trusty assistant Storm had learned what went on under a car's bonnet, how to bleed a radiator, fix a plug, put up a shelf and paint a wall. It was almost as if Alan had a sixth sense his daughter would need those skills around the

house when she became mother, father and handyman after he died.

'Trust me, Storm. You don't want to rely on a fella for everything. You keep your independence for as long as you can, earn your own money, pay your own way, and only be with a man because you love him,' he'd advised.

But Storm at just eleven then had been too embarrassed to heed her father's words. Instead she'd clamped her hands over her ears, willing her dad to go back to talking about anything but boys.

'Dad!' she'd protested. 'Boys are disgusting! I don't ever want a boyfriend.'

At that Alan had smiled knowingly. 'It won't always be that way, Stormy. Believe me, when you're older you'll find a man out there who'll give you everything you need.'

Storm hadn't thought about those conversations with her dad for years. Somehow her mum's shock news had sent her mind spiralling back to the past.

'I'm not replacing your father, Storm,' Sally insisted, bringing Storm back to the present. 'I'm just grabbing a little bit of happiness before it's too late. You know better than anyone what that's like.'

Storm knew she wasn't being fair to her mum. 'I'm really happy for you, Sal, and I'd love to come down some time and meet Jeff. I'm a bit busy at work at the minute, but I'll call soon, I promise.'

Chapter Eight

For the next few weeks Storm buried herself in her work. Sally's bombshell had left her feeling unsettled and she knew she needed a distraction. The paper's annual awards ceremony, celebrating the nation's favourite stars and their charities, was coming up so Storm volunteered her services on top of her regular reporting duties and threw herself into organising interviews with people that each charity had helped. That task, combined with ringing each star's agent and asking about their dietary requirements for the awards do, kept her busy and more often than not she wasn't home before midnight.

Apart from the occasional coffee with Jez and glass of wine with Chelsea, Storm spent a lot of time alone. She didn't mind on the whole, but there were times when she felt lonely. Since she and Dermot had returned from Rome, she'd kept her word and been friendly. She'd asked how things were going sleeping on his mate's floor, enquired after his Christmas back in Dublin and even had lunch

with him. Friends they were not, but she was doing her best to keep things cordial for the sake of their jobs.

Now, after another day spent running around chasing stories, Storm poured herself a huge glass of wine and ran a long hot bath. She had always done some of her best thinking in the bath. Immersed in a tub full of soapy bubbles she considered her mother. Sally had emailed her earlier in the week to say she'd told Lexie and Bailey about Jeff, and they'd both taken it well. A lot better than Storm, by the sound of things. They'd agreed to meet him for lunch when they were next in Brighton, something Storm knew she wasn't yet ready for. Instead she'd fobbed her mum off with excuse after excuse, hoping that if she closed her eyes and wished hard enough all her troubles would go away.

Her mind wandered to Nico. Despite trying to lose herself in her work, Storm hadn't been able to stop thinking about him. His eyes, his touch, the way he made her feel.

Being with him was like being with a lifelong friend, except with all the best stories yet to be revealed. Storm felt he had a hotline straight to her heart, and knew just what to say and do to connect with her. She dreamed of seeing him again, but knew it was a lost cause. She felt like a stupid teenager – it wasn't as if they'd even kissed and of course he lived with his girlfriend Francesca who adored him, if what she'd read in the press was anything to go by.

But no matter how hard she tried to tell herself Nico was out of bounds, Storm had felt a real connection to him on the night of the premiere, and she wished she could see him again. As she began sloshing water over her face, an

image of Alan with his head firmly under a car bonnet as he explained how to check the oil popped into her mind. She could almost hear him now, reminding her that she should never need to be with a man. She should be with him because she wanted to, and because she loved him. It really was that simple.

Just then a knock at the front door interrupted her thoughts. Stepping out of the tub and roughly towelling herself dry, she hurried to open it, only to find a beaming Dermot on the doorstep.

'I was just passing,' he said as he gestured towards the bottle of red wine he was carrying. 'Thought we could split this.'

Storm looked at him in amazement. 'Why would I want to do that, Dermot?'

He shuffled his feet, looking sheepish. 'Well, you know, I just thought . . .' He stopped talking, and looked at her uncertainly.

Storm bit her lip. She wanted to tell him to bugger off, but she'd meant what she'd said about them being friends for the sake of working together so where was the harm? 'Come in then,' she said, 'but I warn you, I'm exhausted and was planning on going to bed quite soon. I just need to put something on.'

'No problem,' he replied, pushing past her and into the kitchen to root around for a couple of glasses.

Coming out of her room a few minutes later, she saw that Dermot had made himself at home and was slumped on the black leather sofa, eating peanuts and watching *Question Time*.

Storm glanced at him. 'Make yourself at home, why don't you?' she said sarcastically.

'Hope you don't mind,' he said. 'Thought I'd get myself settled while I was waiting for you.'

Storm fought the urge to thump him. Instead she sat down and reached for the glass of wine he had poured for her.

'So what were you doing in this area?'

'Sorry, what was that?' murmured Dermot, unable to tear his eyes away from the TV screen.

'I said, what were you . . . oh, never mind,' Storm snapped.

'Sorry, Stormy,' Dermot said, giving her his full attention. 'To be honest, I wasn't passing, I wanted to talk to you about something.'

She was immediately on red alert. 'Oh, yes?'

Swinging his legs off the sofa and turning to face her, Dermot cleared his throat nervously. 'Well, the thing is, Storm, my mate's asked me to move out – he's got a girlfriend and she doesn't like me being there. Truth is I don't have anywhere else to go, and after our lunch the other day, I thought, now you've forgiven me and we're friends again, well . . .'

'. . . you thought you could move in here with me?'

'Not with you,' he said quickly. 'Just as flatmates. You've plenty of room. And you know I can knock you up a mean fried breakfast in the mornings.'

Storm looked at him. Not for the first time he'd left her speechless, and not in a good way. She felt like a prize idiot. Here was she, doing her best to keep things friendly and

professional for the sake of their careers, and here was Dermot, wondering how he could best use that situation to his own advantage. Sod being professional. Enough was enough.

'Sure. Why not?' she said.

'Really?' replied Dermot, unable to wipe the smug grin off his face.

'Yeah. I'll tell you what . . . the place is all yours, in fact.'

Dermot looked confused. 'What do you mean?'

'I mean, you move in here and I'll move out. You seem to think I'll just forget what you did, but I won't. I don't want you in my life, Dermot. You're always looking for a way to get something over on someone, searching for an opportunity to haul yourself up, and I'm sick of it. Other than to say hello, goodbye or anything work related, I want nothing to do with you. I was going to move out soon anyway. You've only got a couple of weeks left here, they want the flat back.'

'Look, Storm, you're tired, you're upset, you don't know what you're saying . . .'

'Jesus, Dermot, what do you take me for? You and me are finished. You're the worst thing that ever happened to me. If you're coming here, I'll move out.'

''Course you can move in with me, babe,' Chelsea exclaimed when Storm told her how Dermot had tried to worm his way back into her good books. 'Spare room's all yours for as long as you need it.'

'Thanks so much, Chelsea. I wouldn't ask if I wasn't desperate,' Storm sighed.

'Are you trying to tell me you're too good to stay at my place?' Chelsea teased. 'I know Stratford's a bit of a come down after Clapham but we're very trendy in East London these days.

'Look,' she continued kindly, 'I think you're great, Storm. Sadly, I've never felt the same way about Dermot. He's always given off an air of what I like to call eau de weasel.'

Storm looked surprised. Usually everyone loved Dermot. 'What do you mean?'

Chelsea sighed. 'Sorry, I didn't mean to speak out of turn, but to be honest with you, Storm, you were way too good for him. I've seen Dermot's type come and go before. He's been hanging on to your coat tails for long enough. You've got more talent in your little finger than he'll ever have. It'll be interesting to see what happens now he no longer has you to fall back on.'

Storm was speechless. She'd half expected Chelsea to tell her she was making a big mistake. If his true character was that obvious, Storm wished she herself had wised up a bit sooner.

'Anyway,' Chelsea continued, swiftly changing the subject, 'I've got something to take your mind off your troubles – I've been invited out to Barcelona for a couple of days to stay with Angel Summer at her mansion and cover her new wedding dress launch. I need you to come with me as it's going to be a really big deal, with lots of celebs.'

Storm looked like a rabbit trapped in headlights. 'Are you serious?'

'Deadly. Why?'

How could she explain? Angel was something of a hero to Storm. The fact that Angel was just a few years older, had gone to the same school, grown up just a few streets away and had enjoyed a meteoric rise to fame, wasn't lost on Storm as a kid. When she'd flicked through her beloved *Vida!* magazine and seen pictures of Angel living her glamorous celeb life, her spirits always lifted. If Angel, a girl from just around the corner, could live out her dreams, who was to say Storm couldn't as well? After all, Angel was living proof that you could change your life; not only had she enjoyed a stratospheric modelling career as one of the world's most stunning women, but she'd bagged the ultimate prince in Cal Bailey, the ex-England footballer who had recently been tipped for the England manager's job.

'When do we go?' Storm breathed.

Chelsea grinned. 'Valentine's Day.'

Angel's wedding dress launch was being held in a luxury mansion just a short drive from Barcelona city centre. In true celeb style she'd arranged for a limo to collect Storm and Chelsea from the airport, and even though she couldn't be there to greet them herself, had ensured there was a bottle of vintage champagne on ice waiting for them in the back to celebrate their arrival.

'I could get used to this.' Storm smiled, taking a delicate sip and enjoying the feeling of the bubbles fizzing all over her tongue.

'Say what you like about Angel,' Chelsea replied, 'but the girl is class all the way.'

'How do you know her?' Storm asked.

'Oh, we go way back,' Chelsea said as she explained she had been fortunate enough to interview Angel several times over the years and they'd always got on well. When Angel had revealed she'd suffered from post-natal depression, Chelsea was the only showbiz reporter who had insisted their paper shouldn't cover the story. 'Women suffering like this should be encouraged to speak out and get help, they're not going to do that if we reduce Angel's condition to nothing but gossip,' she'd told Miles, much to Sabrina's disgust. When Angel had heard of the lengths Chelsea had gone to on her behalf, she'd been more than impressed and had taken the unusual step of inviting her over for dinner – something she had never done with a journalist before, as she usually hated them all on sight. Since then the unlikely pair had become firm friends, with Angel realising Chelsea would always have her back.

When they arrived at the mansion they found a whirlwind of activity in progress. Technicians were setting up lights, carpenters were building the stage, while a team of engineers were rigging up a complicated sound system ready for the models to strut their stuff to. Storm couldn't help noticing Angel's signature colour, pink was splashed everywhere, from the fairy lights and chandeliers to the colour of the stage. Storm thought it all looked incredible and, if she was honest, felt more than a little overawed. Everything was so glamorous and perfect, including the glossy pristine paintwork and giant marble staircase that was so grand it could be considered a work of art in its own right.

But there was no time to dwell on her own feelings as together with Chelsea she moved through the venue. They found Angel giving instructions to a team of florists.

'I thought you were too posh to get your hands dirty these days and had people to do this sort of shit for you?' Chelsea joked as she leaned in for the obligatory air kiss.

'Oi! Don't bite the hand that feeds you.' Angel grinned, kissing her in reply.

'And you must be Storm,' the model exclaimed. 'I've been dying to meet you. Chelsea's told me so much about you, including how you've been telling your cow of a news editor where to go.'

Storm shot Chelsea a WTF face.

Angel sensed Storm's discomfort. 'Don't worry. I've told Sabrina Anderson to fuck off a few times myself.'

Angel had never forgotten how Sabrina had hounded her night and day after she'd briefly split from Cal following his short-lived affair with an Italian WAG. When other reporters had gone home Sabrina had stayed put, determined to land a scoop, and had thought nothing of trying to interview her daughter Honey right in front of Angel.

While Angel finished giving instructions to her team Jez and Rufus sidled into view. Smiling in delight, she waved at them and the two hurried over. The couple kissed Chelsea and Storm hello and Jez wasted no time in getting to the point. 'You've seen the pink palace then?'

'Mmmm, I think you mentioned something about it looking a bit Gypsy Wedding this morning. Cheeky bastard!' Angel smiled as she spoke.

143

'I was merely pointing out that there are other colours in the world besides pink.'

'It's Valentine's Day and a wedding dress launch, Jez! I think for once pink is entirely appropriate.'

He shrugged. 'I suppose I'll let you off just this once. But more importantly have you shown them your new rock yet?'

'They've only just got here,' said Angel, playfully batting her best friend on the shoulder.

Rufus winked at her. 'You know my husband . . . large pretty things excite him.'

'Yes! Enough with the bullshit, show me the bling,' Chelsea exclaimed as she reached for Angel's right hand.

'Crikey, that's bigger than Ayers Rock,' Storm gasped, unable to tear her eyes away from the huge pink diamond nestled on Angel's ring finger.

'It's a Valentine's Day present from Cal.' She sighed contentedly. 'An eternity ring and good luck gift for today. He had it 'specially made.'

Storm was stunned. She'd never seen such a large diamond.

'So what's the plan . . . or are we going to admire your diamond all day long?' Chelsea asked cheekily.

'I've booked you in for some treatments at the spa around the corner, and then we're off to Lasarte for dinner later.'

'Fabulous!' said Jez, clapping his hands in delight. 'I'll need to be relaxed before I get my hands on some of your brides tomorrow. I will not be held responsible for my

actions if I see one bride-to-be wearing a scrunchie or a Croydon facelift.'

As part of the launch, Jez and Rufus had teamed up to offer a wedding bootcamp campaign. Jez was going to be giving hair demonstrations while Rufus would demonstrate wedding day workouts guaranteed to get results.

'As you can see, Jez went to the "customer is always right" school of hairdressing,' Rufus teased.

'Let me stop you right there!' he replied theatrically. 'The customer is never right. Got that? Never! Some of them deserve to be hung, drawn and quartered for crimes against hair.'

'And you see it as your role to tell them that?' Storm couldn't help joining in.

Jez sniffed. 'What can I say, Storm? It is a tough job, but someone really does have to do it.'

There was no other way to describe it, the day had been truly perfect, reflected Storm as she got ready for dinner. After Angel had shown them all to their rooms, which turned out to be luxurious suites, complete with mini-bars stocked with nothing but champagne, Storm had considered the contents of her suitcase. She hadn't known what to pack for a weekend with her heroine so had decided to keep it simple and settled on a short black shirt dress. As she sat down to do her make-up she realised the full body massage, hydrotherapy treatment, facial and mani/pedi she'd just enjoyed, courtesy of Angel, were exactly what she'd needed after everything she'd been through recently.

The therapists had magic hands, and Storm had left the

spa feeling like a new woman. After Carly's outburst at The Chiltern Firehouse, Storm had felt hurt for several weeks, but eventually she realised it had given her the closure she badly needed. It was as though she could shuck off her guilt once and for all as, despite her best attempts, she hadn't been able to mend bridges with Carly. Now Dermot was finally out of her life, she felt as though a giant weight had been lifted from her shoulders and she could move forward. It was just a shame he hadn't got the message yet. Since Storm had moved out of the Clapham flat he'd sent her flowers and texted her every day.

She found this all a bit creepy, especially as she strongly suspected he was now sleeping with Sabrina. God only knows what *she* thought about the situation – or if she even knew.

'Cocktails or champagne?' Jez asked as they were shown to their table in the restaurant.

'Let's start with cocktails. Slippery Nipples all round?' Angel grinned.

'Oh, you can take the girl out of Brighton but you can't take Brighton out of the girl!' Jez mocked, rolling his eyes at his old friend.

Angel protested, 'And what's wrong with a Slippery Nipple? Or Sex on the Beach . . .'

'. . . or a Screaming Orgasm?' joked Storm.

'Ooh, I enjoyed one of those last night.' Jez smirked as he turned to his husband. 'Or should I say, we did?'

Rufus playfully squeezed his hand and calmed him down. 'Nobody likes a show off. Now let's order.'

Two rounds of cocktails later the conversation was flowing. Storm was giving them a blow by blow account of the swingers party, Chelsea was moaning about her love life, and Angel proudly showed the group pictures of Honey along with her new baby boy Ryder, as well as giving them the lowdown on Cal's new football academies.

'He's got four now. As well as the Lewisham and Brighton ones, he's set up one in Chatham and another in Clacton-on-Sea,' she revealed proudly.

'I don't know how he does it,' Jez marvelled. 'Though I like to think I do my fair share for the disadvantaged youth of today.'

'Making interns run around picking up your dry-cleaning, fetching your coffee and searching the Internet for vaguely pornographic pictures of Ryan Gosling, is not the same thing, sweetie,' Angel shot back as the table hooted with laughter.

Storm had to admit, the whole evening was going brilliantly. Although she had got to know Jez and Chelsea quite well by now, she'd been worried she wasn't quite in Angel's league. But she realised she had nothing to worry about. Angel was such a brilliant host, and so wonderfully grounded despite her superstar status.

The following morning Storm woke up starving. After slipping on a pair of grey skinny jeans and a t-shirt, she hurried down to breakfast in the vast, sunny kitchen that overlooked the city. There she found everyone apart from Angel, who had been up for hours, busy devouring a feast.

147

'Those waffles look amazing, Chelsea.' Storm beamed, pulling up a stool next to her friend.

'That's because they are,' she said, mouth full of waffle, chocolate and banana.

'Yes, they're so good that in fact they're Chelsea's third helping,' Jez pointed out.

'Who are you? The food police? Mind your own business,' Chelsea shot back as she reached for more chocolate sauce.

'Just saying, a moment on the lips is worth a lifetime on the hips,' he said, smugly tucking into half a grapefruit.

'Say that again and you'll be wearing that grapefruit instead of eating it!'

'Children, children!' Rufus interrupted, desperate to avoid war until at least lunchtime. 'Storm, can I get you a coffee?'

'God, yes, please!' she said gratefully. Storm didn't feel remotely human until she'd had at least three cups of the black stuff before even attempting food.

'How did you all sleep?' she asked, taking the espresso gratefully.

'Badly,' Jez replied playfully. 'There's nothing like a little European getaway to inject romance into a relationship.'

Rufus looked at his husband warningly. 'Nobody wants to hear about our love life. Again.'

'Definitely not. At least not when we haven't had a bit for ages,' Chelsea moaned.

'No! Are you in the middle of a sex drought?' Jez asked. 'That's terrible. Happened to me once, so I went to visit a white witch who gave me a spell . . .'

148

Storm couldn't resist interrupting. 'Sorry. You went to a white witch and got a *spell*? There's so much wrong with that sentence, I don't even know where to start,'

Jez glared at her. 'FYI it worked. I hadn't had sex for months, but the witch told me to race around Glastonbury Tor after dark, naked, with a white feather in one hand and a white candle in the other, while chanting "My body is yours to worship" three times. Then I had to wait.'

'Oh, yeah! And how long did you have to wait?' Chelsea scoffed.

'Not long actually,' he said conspiratorially. 'On my way back down the hill, I bumped into this gorgeous hippie with huge rippling biceps and dreadlocks down to his navel. I don't normally go for hippies, but on this occasion I made an exception and . . . *voilà* – drought broken.'

Storm gazed at him in surprise. 'Are you serious?'

Jez tipped his head to one side and paused before he burst out laughing. 'Nah! But you should see the look on your face!'

She shook her head. 'You bastard! I believed you then. Still, let me just say this. I may be single, but I don't care how bad it gets . . . no hairy hippy will ever get anywhere near my muff!'

Chapter Nine

After breakfast Storm was determined to make herself useful and threw herself into the launch, admiring all of Angel's hard work. Their host really had thought of everything. Towering plates of chocolate truffles stood proudly at the entrance, along with romantic displays of vibrant red roses and glossy pink peonies, ready to get the guests in the mood for love. Elsewhere, huge photos of Angel and Cal's weddings, the first and second time around, lined the immaculately painted walls, while a string quartet played classic love songs in the garden and caterers set up plates piled high with to-die-for canapés. Outside, the thick grassy lawns had been mown into immaculate stripes, the kidney-shaped swimming pool was a vivid blue, and the marquee (pink, of course) had just been erected. As for the driveway, the beautiful white gravel had been replaced with pink stones. Best of all, there wasn't a cloud in the sky as the sun gently beat down.

The whole place looked as though it had come straight

from the pages of a style magazine and Storm felt a little out of place. She was just some chancer from Brighton – she had no business being here.

'Come on, stop dreaming, there's work to be done.' Angel smiled, cutting into Storm's thoughts. 'Could you be my meet and greet person for a couple of hours, to give me a break from the press? You and Chelsea are one thing, but the rest of them I can't stand and I know they'll be trying to trip me up.'

'Absolutely,' Storm exclaimed. 'What do you want me to do?'

'Stand at the entrance, look pretty and hand them a press pack and goody bag,' Angel said briskly as she guided her to the front of the house.

'Ooh, what's in the goody bag?' Storm asked, curiosity getting the better of her as she peered into one of the pretty pink carriers that stood on a long table by the solid oak front door.

'Just a selection of my perfumes, a slice of pink wedding cake, a voucher for a set of bridal lingerie and some jewellery.'

'Very generous,' said Storm approvingly.

'Well, the one thing I've learned with these bastards, Storm, is that the press can be bought very easily!'

As Storm went upstairs to change out of her jeans, she thanked her lucky stars she'd had the foresight to bring the dusky pink bandage dress she'd bought from ASOS in the sale last summer. She'd almost left it at home, thinking it was far too summery for Barcelona in February, but thank God she'd given in to temptation. The dress was

unbelievably flattering, making her look slim without being skinny, and somehow it made her feel a little less tall. Teaming it with the trusty pair of nude slingbacks, she was good to go.

Two hours later, Storm had seen at first hand exactly the kind of shit Angel had to deal with from the press on a daily basis. Not only had the handful of journalists Storm had met been rude, surly and downright ungrateful, she'd even caught a couple of paps taking pictures of her when she'd bent down to adjust her shoe strap, inadvertently flashing a bit of cleavage! They really do give us a bad name, she thought, giving them another eyeful by flipping them the finger.

'Don't do that, they'll never get over the shock.' Chelsea smirked as she came to relieve Storm from her post. 'Some of those paps see you as the new girl who can't put a foot wrong at the moment. Watching you flip the birdie at them like that will give them palpitations.'

'Well, they shouldn't try and take pictures of my boobs, should they? Pervs,' Storm muttered darkly.

'Looks like I've arrived just in time. Go and get a glass of fizz and enjoy yourself. I'll deal with this shower of shit . . . sorry, colleagues!' Chelsea said, shooing her away.

As Storm joined the throng in the garden she helped herself to a glass of pink champagne from a passing waiter dressed in a fuchsia-coloured tuxedo and watched Angel do her thing. The whole place was teeming with beauty and gossip journalists, actors, actresses, pop stars and sporting heroes. As for the star of the show herself, Angel

was in her element, smiling and welcoming all her guests, ensuring that nobody felt excluded.

'Darling! That dress looks sensational. So lovely to see you in something a little less funereal.' Jez had appeared by her side. Dressed in a pink linen suit that was on the verge of clashing with his slightly orange skin, he looked surprisingly macho.

Storm considered his outfit carefully. 'I think you are the only person I know who could pull that off,' she said finally.

'What can I say? You've either got it or you haven't.' He smiled, doing a little twirl. 'What are we doing anyway? Eyeing up the journalist competition. Rest assured, Storm, Angel will make sure you leave with a little exclusive that should keep Sabrina Anderson off your back for a while.'

At the sound of Sabrina's name, Storm groaned and helped herself to another glass of champagne. That woman had a very sobering effect on her. 'Can we please discuss anyone but her?'

'Anyone but who?' asked Angel as she joined them mid-conversation.

'Sabrina,' she and Jez chorused in unison.

At the mention of the news editor's name, Angel grimaced. 'Yeah, you're right. Can we please discuss anyone but that woman today?'

Storm was about to open her mouth and say something else, when she saw Angel wave at a man in the distance.

'There's someone I'm desperate for you both to meet,' she said.

'I'd brace yourself for a chat about football if I were you,' Jez whispered in Storm's ear. 'I might have a thing

for the players, but if you're anything like me you'll find discussing the sport about as interesting as watching paint dry.'

Storm giggled as she gratefully sipped her glass of champagne.

'Happy Valentine's Day, Storm. Don't tell me, another day off?' a voice bantered behind her.

Storm turned round – Nico. 'What are you doing here?' She was amazed to see the man she couldn't stop thinking about before her once again

'Oh, you two already know each other? I was just about to introduce you. Nico's doing the catering for me today,' explained Angel.

He turned to Angel and Jez, his eyes full of mischief. 'We've met a couple of times, but usually I've found Storm likes to spill her booze rather than drink it.' Nico chuckled softly.

Cheeky bastard! Two could play at that game.

'What can I say, Nico? If you serve quality refreshments like Angel does, then there's less temptation to get them everywhere but down your throat.'

Just being next to him was doing something to her. Even now, dressed in sparkling chef's whites and with his hair slightly dishevelled, he looked gorgeous.

'Actually I was going to invite you into the kitchen to test some of my new dishes. I believe last time we met you mentioned something about dinner . . .'

As Nico's voice trailed off, Storm found herself blushing. Jez and Angel looked at them, surprised expressions on their faces.

'That wasn't how it sounds . . .'

'I'll just bet it wasn't,' sniggered Jez. 'Well, I suggest you hop to it. When a man's offering you a private viewing of his canapés, Storm, it's rude to say no.'

After giving Jez the evil eye, she smiled at Nico. 'If you'll excuse my friends, I'd love the opportunity to see you at work.'

'And I'd love to show you,' he replied softly. 'So will you join me?'

Storm nodded and followed him across the garden towards the house. As they walked inside the mansion she realised that the sound of her high heels was the only thing punctuating the silence.

'Where is everyone?' she asked, spooked by the quiet.

'Most of the team have gone home now the party's underway.'

As the kitchen door loomed ever closer, Storm found herself feeling strangely guilty. She hated telling lies, and knew it was time to tell Nico the truth about what she did for a job. As he opened the door and led her inside she vowed to tell him the truth immediately, but then the sight of the kitchen distracted her momentarily.

'Not bad, Mr Alvise.' She smiled, looking around. The kitchen was small and industrial-looking, with steel worktops and cupboards, but extremely well organised, with pots and pans hanging from the ceiling and knives stuck on a magnetic board on the wall.

'This is where the magic happens.' Nico took her hand and led her towards the fridge. Pulling out a tray of miniature beef tartlets, he held one up to Storm's mouth.

'Taste this.'

Storm didn't need asking twice, and bit into the tart with enthusiasm. 'God, that's so good,' she groaned in appreciation, taking another bite. As the hairs on the back of Nico's hand tickled her top lip, Storm felt consumed with lust. It took every ounce of self-control she possessed for her not to devour that hand as well as the canapé. Instead she focused on the food.

'If nobody's ever said it to you before, let me tell you you're a miracle worker when it comes to food.'

'It's been said before!' Nico laughed, running his eyes over Storm's face. 'Wait a minute, you've got something on your lip.'

As he gazed into her eyes and rubbed his thumb across her mouth, Storm felt it was one of the most erotic and intimate gestures she'd ever experienced. Closing her eyes with longing, she suddenly heard the unmistakable sound of the click of a camera from the kitchen window.

Swinging round at the same time as Nico, she saw a paparazzo flee, camera swinging from his shoulder.

'You scum! Get back here now!' Nico shouted, his face red with anger. 'Who do these people think they are . . . interfering in my life?' He reached for one of the pans hanging from the ceiling and threw it across the room.

Storm jumped back in shock. How had the paps even known they would be in the kitchen, or had they just got lucky? It wasn't as if they'd been doing anything newsworthy. Still, Storm could just imagine the look on her face as she'd eaten from Nico's hand. Innocent it was not.

'I can't believe that just happened,' she said, voice shaking.

At the sound of it, Nico calmed down. 'Forget them. Those paps are nothing, but this is the price of fame. Everything in my life is up for grabs. Even you,' he said sadly.

Storm hesitated. She wanted more than ever to tell Nico what she did for a living but instinct told her that now wasn't the right time. The last thing she wanted to do was make him even angrier. Instead she reached for his hand and squeezed it reassuringly. 'Maybe we should return to the party?' she suggested.

But Nico shook his head. 'No, *bella*, I must go back to my hotel and speak to my manager and Francesca about what's just happened. Maybe I can track down the scum that did this too. I'll see you soon.'

As Storm watched him walk out of the kitchen, she was gripped by a feeling of sadness.

After a night spent worrying about what she was going to find in the next morning's papers, Storm woke after a couple of hours' sleep at about 11 a.m. Desperate for a cup of coffee, she reached for her dressing gown and went downstairs to the kitchen, only to find Angel, Chelsea, Jez and Rufus in full flow.

'Have you lot been to bed?' Storm asked. 'You were all in exactly the same seats when I said goodnight.'

When Nico had left, she had agonised over their encounter for hours with her friends, who'd all done their best to cheer her up, but it was pointless. She couldn't stop

thinking about how if that snap got into the wrong hands it could damage both her career and Nico's. The rumour mill would go into overdrive, accusing her of having an affair with him behind his girlfriend's back – something she would never do, no matter how tempted she was – and Storm wasn't sure she could take any more scandal.

'Grab yourself a mug and stop looking so worried.' Chelsea smiled as she pulled out the chair next to hers so Storm could sit down. 'I've sorted out your little problem with the paparazzi so you can stop fretting about that photo making it into the press any time soon.'

'What have you done?' Storm gasped.

Chelsea shrugged as if it was no big deal. 'Let's just say I made a certain pap see reason, and he realised it was in his best interests not to let that image get out.'

Storm was touched Chelsea had gone out of her way like this to help.

'Honestly I don't know what to say,' she replied, helping herself to coffee and buttering a piece of lukewarm toast.

'All in a day's work.' Chelsea smiled. 'So can you stop worrying now, please?'

'Yes. And I ought to tell Nico, he'll be so relieved.'

Angel held up her hand. 'Already done. I phoned this morning to let him know Chelsea had sorted it.'

'What did he say?' Storm asked, her heart pounding.

'He was obviously delighted, but realises that this won't be the last pap intruding on his personal life. It's the price of fame,' Angel replied, shaking her head sadly, understanding only too well.

Storm chewed her bottom lip absent-mindedly. It

sounded silly, but she'd been hoping to break the news to him herself.

'Did he ask about me?' she said finally, only for Angel to shake her head.

'There was no time. It was only a short call.'

'Just what is going on between you and Nico?' Chelsea said, getting straight to the point. 'It's obviously none of my business, but I think I speak for everyone when I say the sexual chemistry between you two yesterday was as obvious as Jez's fake tan.'

'Do you mind?' he fired back. 'It costs money to maintain this level of bronzing.'

'Really? I thought you just went out and got yourself Tangoed!' Chelsea giggled.

But Storm was hardly taking in a word of the chatter around the table – she was too busy breathing a sigh of relief that a crisis had been averted.

'We're just friends,' she said quietly, finding the idea unsettling. How could she say what they were when she really had no idea herself?

Jez raised an eyebrow. 'Friends with benefits more like.'

'You haven't shagged him?' Chelsea exclaimed.

'No! 'Course not,' Storm protested.

Chelsea wasn't convinced. 'Well, be careful. Mr Alvise might be shacked up with the lovely Francesca, but he's no stranger to the ladies.'

'What do you mean?' Storm demanded.

'I mean that Nico has a girlfriend on the side. Or did up until very recently.'

'Really!' exclaimed Angel. 'I never knew that.

Chelsea shook her head and took another sip of tea. 'No, he's very discreet, doesn't want to upset Francesca.'

'So why hasn't it been in the press?' asked Jez.

'Because Nico's just too nice. He treated his last girlfriend like a goddess, with spa days, first-class hotel stays and so on.'

Chelsea glanced at Storm, who had gone as white as a sheet.

'But he seems so devoted to Francesca,' she protested. 'He as good as told me he was the last time I saw him.'

'Yes, he is devoted to her – but I dunno, they've grown apart or whatever.' Chelsea shrugged. 'Let's face it, the only people who really know what's going on in a relationship are the ones directly involved, so don't judge him too harshly. Nico's a good guy. Just be careful. You could get your heart broken by someone like him.'

'Perhaps the reason he's so into you, Storm, is because he's hoping for a free upgrade next time he goes back to Italy!' Jez chipped in.

'What's he on about?' Angel asked, puzzled.

Storm shot Jez a look of reproof and quickly outlined the facts to her new friends.

'So he's got no idea you're a reporter?' Chelsea asked.

Storm nodded. 'It's so stupid, I had no reason to lie to him, and the story's spiralled out of control. I've a feeling if I tell him now it won't go down very well.'

Angel agreed. 'I think you have to tell him eventually, Storm, but given what happened with the pap yesterday, now may not be the best time.'

*

160

As Storm and Chelsea weren't flying back to London until later that night they had plenty of time to relax. After breakfast Angel, the boys and Chelsea decided to head into Barcelona for a bit of retail therapy, but worried she wouldn't be good company, Storm offered to stay behind and cook lunch for when they got back as a thank you to Angel.

'You cook? Wow, Storm! I'm impressed, I can't even boil water,' Angel laughed. 'What time do you want us?'

'How about two-ish? That should give you plenty of time to shop 'til you drop.'

After air kissing everyone goodbye Storm changed into her blue and white striped bikini and dived into the outdoor pool. Even though it was February, the pool was heated and the water was so refreshing. The more she swam, though, the more she thought about Nico, the same questions going round and round in her mind.

Was he really a cheat? Did he view her as just another potential notch on his bedpost? Was that why he hadn't asked about her when Angel called him? Was he angry with Storm? Had he already worked out she wasn't a flight attendant? Or had she been imagining things all along and any feelings in this situation were purely one-sided. After thirty laps she admitted exhaustion, having never been a strong swimmer. Hauling herself out of the pool, Storm had just started to dry off when she heard the doorbell.

Knowing she was alone in the house, she hastily wrapped a towel around herself, went inside to open the door and came face to face with Nico.

'What are you doing here?' she gasped.

'I just wanted to check you were OK after what happened yesterday.' He shuffled anxiously from foot to foot.

'I'm fine. Chelsea managed to convince the pap not to sell the photo.'

'Yes, I heard,' he replied. 'Are you going to invite me in or should I just stay on the doorstep and watch you drip water everywhere, half-naked?'

At the mention of the word 'naked' Storm flushed bright crimson. In her surprise at seeing Nico again she'd completely forgotten she was wearing just a towel. Worst of all it was freezing – her nipples were doing all the talking. Shit! Of all the times to be caught out. Quickly she hoisted up the towel and opened the door wider to let him in.

'Can you give me five minutes to change?' Without waiting for an answer she sprinted up the stairs, dried off and slipped on a cute navy mini-dress. Running a slick of balm across her lips, she raked her fingers through her hair and hoped Nico was a fan of the just got out of bed look.

'Can you pass me the chicken stock please, Chef?' Storm smiled, pointing to the steaming hot jug just behind Nico. Today she was cooking her famous chicken risotto and, now that she had invited Britain's sexiest chef to join her friends, she knew she had to pull out all the stops. He had of course offered to help, but instead Storm had told him to sit in the corner and look pretty. This was her turn to cook, and Nico was not going to ruin it.

'I'm impressed you're attempting a risotto, Storm,' he mused, handing her the jug. 'Many people would be far

too frightened to cook this classic Italian dish, especially for a classic Italian chef.'

Storm laughed as she ladled the stock into the heavy-bottomed pan. 'You don't frighten me. Trust me, my risotto is the business, and when you've tasted it you'll be begging me for the recipe.'

'Is that right? I think you'll find my risotto has won awards. And of course I'm Italian so, let me assure you, it'll be impossible for you to cook one better than I do! Still, it doesn't look to me as though you're doing a bad job,' Nico bantered, as he watched her dicing the onions. 'Where did you learn to cook?'

'I taught myself mainly. My mother wasn't much for cooking so I did most of it.' She shrugged.

'Why was that?'

Storm snuck a glance at Nico. He wasted no time in getting to the point, she'd noticed. Usually she avoided questions about her childhood but something about Nico's questions made her want to open up. It was just a shame she hated talking about her past. It wasn't that she was ashamed, far from it. Storm had grown up tough and independent, but her memories of her younger years were still painful. Unexpectedly, she felt a pang as she recalled one Christmas where she'd spent hours decorating the house and wrapping the presents, then preparing the dinner, only for Sally to destroy it all while she was drunk. The kids had got up early and found Christmas lights ripped from their sockets, the tree upended and their presents, that Storm had worked so hard to buy, smashed in a drunken rage.

Reaching for a clean wooden spoon, she focused her attention on stirring the creamy rice as she explained how she'd had to cope with Sally's alcoholism and raise her brother and sister for years. The fact that they'd had no immediate family to help didn't make life any easier. Alan's parents had died before Storm was born and Sally's mum and dad had emigrated to Canada years earlier. Once Alan's life insurance ran out Storm became mum, dad, sister and breadwinner, juggling two cleaning jobs around school as Sally was incapable of working. Together with the benefits Sally received they had just about enough to cover the bills and rent on their three-bedroomed council home, but Storm's wages put food on the table, clothes on the kids' backs and bought a few treats at Christmas.

'It wasn't what I would have wished for, but it's made me strong and the person I am today,' she finished.

For what felt like ages Nico said nothing and Storm worried her story had shocked him. After all, some people judged alcoholics very harshly, unable to understand that alcoholism was a disease. But if Storm thought she'd successfully hidden her tears from Nico, she was mistaken. He'd seen the quaking of her shoulders and the tears sliding down the sides of her nose. As a salty tear dripped into her risotto pan he felt a pang of concern. Getting up from his stool, he strode towards her and pulled her into his arms.

'It's getting to be a habit, this,' Storm blurted. 'You mopping up my tears.'

Nico hugged her tighter. 'I don't mind. I get the feeling

your past isn't something you talk about very often.'

'How did you guess?' she replied, burying her head in his shirt.

The smell of fabric conditioner mixed with the tangy scent that was unmistakeably Nico's immediately soothed her. Taking a deep breath, she looked up into warm, chocolate brown eyes that were filled with nothing but kindness.

'It's not good to keep things to yourself. You should talk, get your feelings off your chest,' he said gently.

'I can't,' she said. 'I feel too guilty about it all.'

Dipping her head back against his shirt, Storm tried to suppress her feelings about her childhood. The memories were too painful, and for years now she'd successfully managed to distract herself from thinking about old hurts. But Nico refused to let it go.

'What could you possibly have to feel guilty about, Storm? I'm sure you did the very best you could.'

Nico's perception left her rattled. He was right, she had done the best she could, but it wasn't enough. 'I'm ashamed to admit it, but for all those years, I cared more about raising Bailey and Lexie than I did about being there for Sally. Of course I tried to encourage her to get the help she needed, but she put us through hell. I know I should be able to forgive her now. I feel terrible I'm still so cross with her when it wasn't her fault. She was ill. She was grieving for her husband.'

Burying her face back in his shirt, Storm tried to hide her face from him.

Damn him. She'd never talked over her real feelings for

her mother with anyone, not even Dermot or Carly. What was it about Nico that had her baring her soul?

'We all live with secrets and demons, Storm,' he said, breaking the silence. 'Even me. You probably think I have a perfect life filled with fame and fortune. On the outside it must seem that all I have to do is click my fingers and I get whatever I want, whenever I want, but the truth is I want a simple life. I'd give anything to come home from work, cook a simple meal for my girlfriend, and for us to spend the evening curled up in front of the telly together. But that will never happen.'

'Why? You and Francesca always look so happy together in the press.'

'We are happy. I've known her since I was ten years old and we've been through so many things together. She's supported me from the very beginning of my career, but now the only meals we share together are ones I prepare for her fancy lawyer friends when she's entertaining.'

Storm frowned. So Francesca worked a lot – that didn't give him a licence to cheat on her. Storm was just about to open her mouth and point out as much when Nico started to speak.

'The press isn't always right,' he continued. 'Nobody but me and Francesca knows what really goes on between us. What I will say is that since meeting you, I've been thinking a lot about my mother.'

Storm rolled her eyes. 'Please don't tell me I remind you of your mum?'

Nico nudged her and smiled. 'No, you're nothing like her. But something she said to me before I left for London

166

was that I shouldn't close myself off from marriage.'

'Is it something you're against?' Storm asked.

'It's not something I ever saw in my future, and it's not something that's right for me and Francesca,' he replied carefully.

Storm was confused. Was he saying their relationship wasn't special? That he didn't want to be with Francesca? That he'd met someone else? She paused before asking her next question, aware that directness might offend him.

'Have you met someone you think might be a better fit for you than Francesca?'

Nico looked at the floor, eyes downcast as he nodded. 'But it's hopeless. I can't leave Francesca . . . not now. And this girl, this woman, deserves so much more than a cheap affair.'

'Unlike some of the other one-night stands you've had?'

A look of anger then disappointment flashed in Nico's eyes. 'Who told you that?'

Storm shrugged. 'I hear things, but wasn't sure they were true.'

Letting out a long sigh, Nico sank down on a stool and put his head in his hands.

'It's not true. But this is all such a mess,' he groaned.

'What's a mess?' she asked, sitting down next to him. 'You can talk to me.'

'All this,' he said, raising his face to look at her. 'I always thought *Mamma* was talking rubbish, all those years ago, about "the one".'

'You don't believe in "the one" then?'

'You do?'

Storm thought for a moment. For years she'd thought Dermot was the one for her, but if she was honest their relationship had always been riddled with problems. That and the fact there was something about the two of them together that had always felt a little off key. He hadn't been her one, but that didn't stop her from believing that somewhere out there he existed.

'I do believe there's someone out there who is meant for me. I just hope one day I'll find him.'

'What if you already have?' Nico asked quietly.

'Then I'll grab him with both hands.'

'But what if you can't? What if he lives on the other side of the world or is already involved, for example?'

Storm looked at Nico in shock. The realisation of what he was saying hit home. Nico was involved, but her feelings for him were reciprocated. She felt breathless.

'Then it would be a no go,' she forced herself to say. 'Because if he really was my one it would be easy for me to be with him. There would be no complications to keep us apart,' she whispered.

'Even if you thought you were meant to be together?'

'Even then.' She fell silent.

Nico was the first to speak. 'Then I can't keep doing this, Storm.'

'Doing what?'

'This.' He shrugged helplessly. 'Bumping into you when I know I can't have you. It's killing me. I think about you all the time, but if I know there's no chance of any kind of future for us, I think it's better if we stay away from each other.'

Storm felt as if she'd been punched in the stomach. How could they go from talk of the one to never seeing each other again? Pain seared her heart as she contemplated a life without Nico. It was unbearable, unthinkable, but deep down she knew it was the best solution all round. He was spoken for, end of.

'I think you're right,' she replied, raising her eyes to meet his.

They were so close she could feel the warmth of his breath. Suddenly she felt Nico's lips on hers. It was every bit as good as Storm had imagined it would be. Soft at first, then as their passion for each other built, their kiss gained intensity. It felt so good, so warm, so natural, Storm thought she could lose herself in kissing Nico for the rest of her life. Waves of desire rippled through her as she felt his fingers in her hair. Then all too soon reality kicked in and she pulled away.

'We shouldn't have done that.'

Nico's forehead rested against hers. 'I know,' he breathed. 'But I couldn't help myself. I wanted to say goodbye properly.'

As he got to his feet and walked away Storm's heart sank. It was the sweetest, saddest first kiss she had ever known.

Chapter Ten

Six Months Later – August Bank Holiday

'*Et voilà!* Just scramble the egg into the pan.' Nico beamed out from the TV screen. Watching the programme as she flung clothes from the hotel wardrobe into her suitcase, Storm felt a pang of desire. She hadn't seen him in person since Angel's launch, but that didn't stop her missing him, thinking of him, wanting him. Their kiss had been sensational, everything a first kiss should be, but it had also made it a lot harder to stay away from him. It was as though she'd had a bite of the very best chocolate cake in the world only to have it taken away from her – she knew what she was missing. Of course their pact hadn't stopped her from looking out for him on TV and in the press. She ransacked the gossip magazines for news of what Nico was up to and made a point of watching him on TV. Every word he uttered, every dish he made, every interview he gave, brought him closer to her heart.

Looking at him now, smiling so easily into the camera, no doubt causing hearts to flutter up and down the country, Storm smiled back. She had to hand it to him, he made great telly. He made great everything, she mused longingly. When she'd turned the television on an hour ago she hadn't expected to see Nico – she was in Venice after all.

But it seemed fitting that she should find him here in his home country just as she was returning to the UK. For the last few days Storm had been lucky enough to cover the Venice Film Festival, and had been excited to hobnob with the likes of George Clooney, Matt Damon and Cameron Diaz. A year ago she'd have been too star-struck to do much apart from stutter in the presence of A-listers, but she'd come a long way since her days on Brighton's *Daily Post*. And thanks to Chelsea's guidance, Storm had mastered the art of appearing cool towards a celeb.

Now she was headed back to the UK for a meeting with her editor. Miles had rung late last night and demanded Storm return to the office immediately.

'It's urgent – I want you to come straight from the airport when you land.'

'But, Miles, I'm meant to be here all week,' Storm had protested. She was having a lovely time in Venice. The weather was warm, the parties were stylish, the champagne flowed (not that she could drink much of it), the people were beautiful and the hotel room overlooking St Mark's Square was Storm's idea of paradise, but Miles had been less than understanding.

'I don't give a shit,' he'd blasted her. 'Get your arse on the first plane back.'

As she expertly zipped her suitcase shut, Storm shivered when her eyes caught sight of a huge bouquet standing on the dressing table. It had arrived yesterday, and was so large the poor bellboy who'd been forced to deliver it had struggled under its weight. Taking the blooms from his arms, Storm had set the arrangement down and found the card. As she tore the envelope open her heart was pounding. She found herself hoping the bouquet had come from Nico. If only.

Hope you're having a wonderful time in Venice. Thinking of you today and always. Yours for ever, Dermot xxxx

She'd dropped the card as quickly as if she'd been burned. What was he doing sending her flowers in Venice? The barrage of texts and late-night calls over the past few months had been bad enough. It was always the same message. He was sorry, he wanted to make amends, he wanted her back. But Storm was adamant and repeatedly told him no. When that hadn't worked he'd called and called at any hour, trying to get her to pick up. A few weeks ago she'd been horrified to discover she had endless missed calls from him and immediately changed her number, giving the office strict instructions not to hand it out to anyone without her permission. She'd hoped that finally Dermot had got the message as she hadn't heard a peep out of him since, but the bouquet was further proof that he hadn't.

As the plane hurtled along the runway and soared into the air, Storm looked out of the window. She knew she

172

shouldn't be too upset about going home early. The last six months had been hard work but a lot of fun as she had landed scoop after scoop after scoop. Still, a lot of the stories she'd been assigned to had troubled her, if she was honest. Reporting on people's failed relationships or drinking habits didn't really feel like proper journalism to her. Back when she'd been dreaming of becoming a showbiz reporter she hadn't thought the job would entail so much muck-raking. But Storm was determined to do her best and although she was still living in Chelsea's spare room, had thrown herself into her job following the split from Dermot, working all the hours under the sun. Her diligence hadn't gone unrecognised. Just a month ago Miles had made Chelsea showbiz editor, and she had insisted Storm was promoted to be her deputy, meaning neither of them need have anything to do with Sabrina any more.

Both girls had been delighted with their promotion, especially when Miles treated them to champagne to celebrate. Everyone around the office made a point of congratulating them – everyone that is apart from Sabrina and Dermot.

Inevitably, Sabrina told Storm she'd been sleeping with him for months behind her back. Collaring her in the ladies' loos one day, as Storm was peering into the mirror reapplying her lipstick, Sabrina couldn't wait to share all the gory details.

'Just thought you should know – Dermot and I are together,' she drawled, leaning against a cubicle door. Storm said nothing, merely glanced at her in the mirror.

For a woman who made a big show of having everything, Sabrina looked strangely unhappy. She had huge bags under her eyes, her skin was grey and her mascara smudged. Turning her gaze back to her own reflection, Storm checked on how she felt to hear this news and realised she wasn't remotely bothered. Dermot was a loser and Sabrina was welcome to him.

'I hope you'll be very happy together.'

This calm response was clearly not what Sabrina wanted to hear. Eyes flashing, she walked towards Storm and stood menacingly behind her. 'Oh, we will be. I know how to make sure he's satisfied in every way. In fact, I've been keeping him satisfied for months.'

Storm snorted and shook her head in disgust. Dermot was a lying, cheating wanker, she'd lost nothing and certainly wasn't going to give Sabrina the satisfaction of getting into a catfight with her about him.

Putting her lipstick back in her bag, Storm turned away from the mirror and walked towards the door. She paused there to eye Sabrina coldly. 'You know, I'm curious – if you're not a slut, what are you?'

With that she'd walked out of the bathroom, Aretha Franklin's 'R-E-S-P-E-C-T' her own personal soundtrack as she returned to her desk.

Arriving back at London's City Airport at a little after four, Storm jumped in a cab and twenty minutes later strode into a deserted office. She wasn't surprised, it was a bank holiday after all. Dumping her luggage under her desk, she raked her fingers through her hair and walked towards

174

Miles's office. Her heart sank when she saw Dermot and Sabrina waiting on the sofa outside.

'Storm. So glad you could join us, and so sorry to tear you away from Venice.' Sabrina smiled cattily.

'What can I say, Sabrina? Life's a bitch. Oh, no, wait . . . that's just you.' Storm knocked firmly on Miles's door before entering. She perched on the nearest chair as Dermot and Sabrina filed in behind her.

'So what's all this about?' she asked pleasantly.

Miles leaned back in his office chair, hands clasped behind his head. 'Got a special little job for my star reporter,' he explained. 'It's a delicate one, and needs careful handling.'

'What, more careful than catching out the Markhams?' she teased.

'Dermot here's been working on a story for several months now and we need a bit of help bringing it to life,' Miles continued, ignoring Storm's last comment. 'Are you up for the challenge?'

'Of course Storm's up for it,' Sabrina put in. 'Our rising star is always up for it, if the graffiti in the ladies is anything to go by.'

Storm couldn't even be bothered to reply. The stupid cow was only showing herself up with comments like that, something that didn't go unnoticed by Miles.

'That'll do, Sabrina. Why don't you pop out and get us a round of coffees?' he said to her before turning back to Storm. 'So what do you think?'

She shifted uncomfortably in her chair as Sabrina flounced out of the office. Normally Storm wouldn't dream of turning down a job but she had a horrible feeling

that if Dermot was involved then there was every chance someone was going to get stitched up and she didn't want anything to do with that.

'Well, er, I'd need to know more about it.'

Miles turned to Dermot and gestured for him to take the floor. 'Perhaps you can fill Storm in.'

She watched nervously as he got to his feet holding an A4 file.

'I'll get to the point – a few sources have told me that a very high-profile celebrity has been cheating on his girlfriend. This certain someone routinely has had a long-term relationship with a woman and is no doubt in the market for another, despite having lived with the same woman for years. We've tried to get his previous girlfriend to talk, but she's not having it. We want to expose him for who he really is.'

Storm raised her eyebrows. How ironic that Dermot wanted to expose someone else's duplicity when he was a cheating bastard himself. 'Where do I fit into this?'

'We want you to be the honey trap. Go on a few dates with the guy, see if you can get him to invite you back to his place, that sort of thing.'

Storm was speechless. Her instincts had been right. This job was as dodgy as hell. 'Let me get this right. You want to turn me into a hooker?'

'No! It's not like that, Storm,' said Miles, leaping to Dermot's defence. 'It's just an undercover job, like the Markhams' party. It's all legit, we certainly don't expect you to have sex with the bloke. We just need enough pics and info to prove he's up for it.'

Storm sat in her chair stubbornly looking down at the floor. 'Well, you can get someone else. I'm not doing that.'

Cheeky bunch of bastards. She wasn't the resident sex reporter. But Dermot wasn't put off. Turning his attention to his file, he leafed through a sheaf of papers until he found what he was looking for.

'I think you will do this, Stormy,' he said softly. 'Otherwise I've got something here that could cause you to be in the press for all the wrong reasons.'

As she took the sheet of paper from her ex, her heart almost stopped beating. It was a printout of the pap shot of her taken with Nico at Angel's launch.

'How did you get this?' she gasped.

'Like I said, Stormy – contacts. Now, if you won't do it Miles has suggested we print this instead and then you'll be the focus of the story. I've a few lurid tales of my own I could share, and I'm sure Carly would be good for a comment or two to really spice things up.'

Storm looked at her editor. 'Really?'

He shrugged. 'Papers don't sell themselves. I obviously don't want to print a story about my best reporter, but it's a bloody good picture. I'm disappointed you didn't come to me yourself with this, Storm, but instead tried to cover it up. It shows a certain lack of trust. You should realise nothing gets past me. Although, I'll admit, I didn't realise you and Mr Alvise were quite so intimate, but that's one of the reasons we've picked you for this job.'

'What do you mean?' she asked quietly.

'You've already got a relationship with the man himself

– that's why it'll be easy for you to lure him further. Unless you're already at it?' he added.

Storm's head was spinning as the penny dropped. 'You want me to honey trap Nico Alvise?'

'The one and only,' Dermot said cheerfully. 'You can start tomorrow. He's launching a new charity at Tower Bridge – perfect opportunity to start chatting to him there.'

'But I haven't seen him for months,' she protested. 'He probably doesn't even remember me.'

'Well, tomorrow will be the perfect time for you to find out,' Dermot put in. 'When you see him at his press launch.'

Taking a deep breath, Storm knew she had to think quickly. Deep down she wanted to tell them all to shove their job but she knew that wouldn't help Nico. Even if he was playing away he didn't deserve to get stitched up like this – but there was a chance that if she went along with their plan, agreed to play her part in the honey trap, she could protect him, make sure there was nothing to report. After all Miles, Dermot and Sabrina clearly thought that the fact she knew Nico would be an advantage. Instead she intended to make sure nothing got back to any of them about Nico's private life.

'Fine,' she said.

'Excellent,' replied Dermot as he walked towards her with the file.

Handing her the paperwork, he whispered in her ear, 'How did you like the flowers by the way?'

Storm shot him a look of pure hatred. This, the job, the flowers, the phone calls, had to be his version of payback.

And all because she'd had the nerve to dump him. Refusing to give him the satisfaction of an answer, she stalked out of the office.

Watching his ex march back to her desk, Dermot smiled. The meeting had gone so much better than he'd expected. When a pissed off pap had shown him the photo of Storm and Nico taken in Angel's kitchen months earlier, Dermot had been shocked to see what could only be described as a look of pure desire in Storm's eyes. He couldn't take his eyes off the image, stricken with jealousy. She looked beautiful, and she'd certainly never gazed at him that way. For years now he'd run rings around Storm, and exercised complete control over her. It killed him to admit it, but she'd been good for his career, was a far better reporter than he would ever be. He couldn't help noticing that while her reputation soared at the paper, his was foundering, something that hadn't gone unnoticed by Miles either. Just last week he'd called Dermot into the office and laid down the law.

'I'm wondering what happened to that go-getting reporter I hired at Christmas,' Miles snapped at him. 'The biggest stories you've brought me so far have all been ones you've worked on with Storm. What's the problem, Dermot, got no ideas of your own?'

He had been furious. 'It's not like that, Miles. My stories require investigation and guts, unlike Storm's. She just has to bat her eyelashes and show a hint of cleavage.'

'I think we both know she does a lot more than that,' Miles blasted him. 'There'd better be an improvement in your success rate. I'll be honest, I'm starting to think I

179

made a mistake in hiring you, Storm's clearly the only one with the talent – what that makes you, I'm not too sure.'

The meeting had left Dermot rattled. He knew he needed to up his game, which was why he desperately needed this story about the chef to come off. If he hadn't started dating Sabrina, who he'd been shagging on and off since they'd met, he doubted he'd even have a job at all by now – it was only because she'd put a good word in for him that his six-month contract had been extended on a month-by-month basis. The truth was his life was no good without Storm in it. He needed her back – and fast.

Over the past few months Dermot had tried everything to win her over but Storm had resisted his charms and he was secretly furious with her. Nobody ever said no to Dermot. When he'd discovered Nico had had a girlfriend on the side, he felt like he'd won the Lottery – if he couldn't have Storm, he'd make darned sure her heart's desire couldn't either.

As Storm forced her way on to the Central Line and jostled for a space with her nose pressed into another commuter's armpit, she tried to shake off her feelings of anger and prepare for the day ahead. Since her meeting with Dermot and Miles she'd felt sick to the stomach. Honey trapping wasn't news and Nico sure as hell didn't deserve what Dermot wanted to dish out to him. All she could do was hope against hope that her plan would work and she could save Nico from having his private life splashed across the front page. Last night she'd barely slept and this morning had agonised over what to wear.

In the end she chose an outfit she felt comfortable in, teaming her favourite black boyfriend blazer, white slub t-shirt and navy skinny jeans with a pair of metallic gladiator sandals.

Emerging into the daylight at Tower Hill station and marching towards the venue, Storm shivered despite the early-morning sun and tried to ignore the knot of fear in her stomach. She'd been desperate to speak to Chelsea for advice, but her boss and friend had been sent out to Venice to cover the Film Festival after Storm had been ordered home and she hadn't been able to reach her. More than anything she needed Chelsea to help her keep a level head about all this. Her heart and her mind felt as if they'd been put through a washing machine. Nerves and guilt were eating away at her, but more than anything else, the prospect of seeing Nico again was overwhelming. She dreamed of him most nights. Happy dreams where somehow they would find each other and live happily ever after. When Storm woke, she often felt an overwhelming sense of grief that her dream wasn't the truth. That she and Nico weren't together, and never could be.

All too soon she reached Tower Bridge and saw a huge crowd had already gathered for a glimpse of the man himself. His newest project was incredibly worthwhile, it was no wonder it had drawn such public interest. This time he wasn't opening a fancy restaurant or announcing a new TV show. Instead he was launching a new cookery training scheme for disadvantaged kids – a brilliant cause that had caught the attention of a couple of royals who had offered their support. Today was the launch event,

where Nico had invited members of the press and public to find out about the course.

As she reached the venue and showed her press pass to security, she noticed a large part of the bridge had been sectioned off ready for Nico's arrival. There was a small stage at the front that had been set up with a kitchen, and a bar area with drinks and refreshments for later on. The plan was obviously for Nico to show off some of his cooking skills to the crowd. Behind the makeshift kitchen hung huge posters of the chef dressed in a sharp charcoal suit. Looking at them was like looking at the man himself and she felt a pang of nerves – could she really do this? Storm wasn't sure and half considered running back to the office until she remembered that if it wasn't her it would be someone else sent to ensnare him and then Nico really would be stitched up. She might hate what she was doing, but she'd hate someone else doing it more, and at least this way she could keep him safe from harm.

Ignoring her instinct to run, she pushed her way towards one of the nearby restaurants that was helping to host the event. There she milled about, picked up some press information and even managed to talk to a couple of the students who had already enrolled on the course. One was a former burglar who'd been released from Feltham Young Offenders just last week and the other an ex-drug addict desperate to turn her life around. Hearing their stories was heart-warming, and reminded her of just how worthwhile and necessary this cause was. Once again she felt a flash of fury with Dermot for turning her into the muck-raking reporter she'd never wanted to be. They were meant to

expose scumbags like the Markhams, not decent people like Nico. Still, his launch would make a good enough story in itself. She decided to pass it on to the features team and encourage them to use it this Sunday as one of the paper's more in-depth pieces.

As she walked back out of the restaurant towards the crowd, she arrived at the fringes just in time to hear everyone erupt into a deafening round of applause. Flushed with embarrassment, Nico walked on to the stage flanked by two women. One looked like his press officer, while the other Storm recognised from the press photos she'd studied – Francesca.

Storm did a double take. There was no denying it, Nico's girlfriend was stunningly beautiful. With long glossy black hair, olive skin and deep brown eyes, she radiated success and warmth, and seemed very proud of Nico. With her arm linked through his, she accompanied him on stage then stepped behind to applaud and give him his moment. They really did make the perfect couple.

Wearing a fitted navy suit and pale blue shirt unbuttoned to reveal just a flash of chest hair, Nico glanced at his notes before addressing the crowd.

'*Signori e signore*, thank you so much for coming here today to the launch of my new cookery school. It means a great deal to me that so many of you have come to show your support, or maybe you are more interested in the free food I'll be offering later?'

As the crowd laughed, Storm saw Nico scan them with his eyes. He paused and locked his gaze on her. She froze. For what felt like hours it seemed as though she and Nico

were isolated in their own private world where the crowd didn't exist. Storm watched Nico recover himself, look down briefly at his notes and then address the crowd once more. The rest of the launch passed her by in a blur. So much so she didn't even notice when it was over and Nico was walking through the crowds, appearing suddenly by her side.

'Storm, how lovely to see you.'

She jumped at the sound of his voice and spun around in shock, only to find the chef wasn't alone.

'I'd like you to meet Francesca,' he said, kissing Storm twice with genuine warmth.

Storm returned the kisses to his cheeks, catching the musky scent of his aftershave as she leaned in against his stubble.

'A pleasure.' She beamed, holding out one hand to Francesca, who immediately batted it away and also leaned in to kiss her.

'Nonsense, we greet the Italian way with kisses not handshakes,' she said.

As Francesca kissed Storm warmly on each cheek she locked eyes with Nico once more. Despite their pact, his delight at seeing her again was obvious in his eyes.

'So what are you doing here?' Nico enquired. 'No flights to tend to today?'

'Er, no, I've actually left the airline.'

'Really? What are you doing instead?'

Bugger! Storm quickly looked around for inspiration until her eyes caught sight of the posters about his cooking school.

184

'I've decided to change careers and go into the hospitality trade,' she lied. 'I've just enrolled at the same college where your cookery classes are held and I heard about your launch there so thought I'd pop down.'

Nico regarded her closely before his face broke into a huge smile.

'But that's wonderful news, *bella*. I worried about you up in the air with so many crashes and planes going missing . . .' His voice trailed off.

A smiling Francesca told her, 'As you can see, Nico is a worrier. But a change of career is always a good thing. Life is too short. You must grab your opportunities with both hands . . . something else I am always saying to Nico.'

Storm found herself warming to this woman who was so natural and welcoming. In any other circumstances she was sure they could have been friends. 'Well, it's early days,' she found herself saying. 'Who knows how many drinks I'll spill before I'm thrown out?'

'You're too hard on yourself, Storm,' Nico replied. 'I bet you'll be brilliant.'

'Me too,' Francesca assured her. 'Now if you'll excuse me I really need to find the bathroom.'

With that she turned and half walked, half ran to the nearest bathroom. Funny, thought Storm, she would never have expected a top barrister to be so down to earth and she could see why Nico adored her – Francesca seemed perfect.

'I hope you're not angry I'm here,' Storm began to say to him. 'I just saw the posters at college, and well, it seemed like fate.'

Nico shook his head, his face lit up with his megawatt smile. 'Not at all, *bella*. It's the best thing to have happened to me in a long time. I've missed you.'

Storm couldn't stop smiling back at him. Any feelings of anxiety were long gone as she basked in Nico's obvious delight at seeing her again. With butterflies in her stomach and her heart pounding, she felt like a teenager all over again.

'Come for coffee with me?' he suddenly suggested.

'What?'

'A coffee. You, me, some *biscotti*, a table. We'll talk, get to know each other properly,' he babbled.

Storm felt rattled. Nico was making her job much easier than she'd anticipated. 'But I thought we'd agreed it was best not to see each other again.'

'You're the one who turned up to my launch,' he pointed out.

Storm lowered her eyes and toed the ground with her shoe. She had a feeling she was going to regret this. 'You got me. OK, coffee sometime.'

Nico lit up, his already handsome face suddenly becoming more attractive. 'Perfect. How about after I finish up here?'

Storm laughed at his eagerness. 'No. I have things to do later. But how about next week sometime?'

'Next week would be good. I'll call you.'

'You'd need my phone number for that,' Storm teased.

He fished inside his jacket pocket. 'Here's a card with my personal mobile number. Feel free to call any time and we'll fix a meeting.'

As Storm took the card from him, she trembled with anticipation.

Putting the card carefully into her satchel bag, she pushed her hair out of her eyes and squared her shoulders. 'Well, I'd better be going. Do say goodbye to Francesca for me, it was a pleasure to meet her.'

Nico leaned forward and softly kissed her cheek. 'Until next week, Storm,' he said, his eyes never leaving hers.

As Storm got off the tube at Stratford and walked slowly home, she couldn't stop smiling. Even though pretending to be a college student wasn't the way she would have chosen to see Nico again, it had been worth it. She replayed the scene in her mind. As their eyes had met across the crowd it had felt so romantic, like something out of a film. And now she had his number and a plan to meet for coffee next week. Storm knew this was probably going to end badly, that somehow she was going to get her fingers burned, but at this precise moment she didn't care. Nico had appeared in her life once more and suddenly everything was sunny.

Rounding the corner, she stopped in her tracks. Sitting on a bench near Chelsea's flat was a man who looked suspiciously like Dermot.

It couldn't be. He was at work. And she'd only popped home herself to change into something more business-like before returning to the office. She was going mad, she thought, as she neared the front door.

But edging closer to the bench, she realised there was no mistake. There he was, her ex, larger than life and twice as ugly, sitting there smiling at her.

'What are you doing here?' she growled.

'How was it?' he said, ignoring her question as he got up and walked towards her.

'Yeah, fine,' she replied, barely glancing at him as she took her front door keys out of her bag.

But Dermot wasn't put off. 'Come on – you can give me more than that. I saw the photo, Stormy, I know you've got the Italian Stallion eating out of your hand. Share the wealth.'

'I repeat, nothing went on. I don't think he's even interested in me – perhaps he prefers blondes. And who uses phrases like Italian Stallion any more!'

'Ah, don't give me that, Stormy, I've seen you work your charms when you want to. I'm sure you can get him to do anything you want him to.'

Storm looked her ex squarely in the eyes as she unlocked the door. 'Dermot, you can't make a guy fancy you if he doesn't fancy you.'

'But that picture showed you looking pretty cosy.'

'Not really. He was probably just helping me wipe sauce off my face. Anyway, you haven't answered my question. What are you doing here?'

'Just thought I'd check you were OK.' He grinned. 'Can I come in?'

Storm grimaced and blocked the doorway. 'No, you bloody can't. Now was there anything else? Only I have to get ready for work.'

Sensing he wasn't getting any further, Dermot backed away from the door.

'Well, keep me or Sabrina updated, we'd like to know how our story's progressing.'

Storm looked at him in horror. Keeping Dermot up to date was one thing but there was no way she was talking to that skank. 'What's Sabrina got to do with any of this?'

'In case you hadn't noticed she's still news editor, and she and I have worked very hard to put this together.'

Storm finally lost her temper with him. 'Dermot, there's a café on the corner. Why don't you do us all a favour and pop over there for a nice hot cup of fuck off and die?'

'You told me she was gorgeous but you didn't say just how gorgeous,' Francesca commented once they were safely in the back of their chauffeur-driven Bentley.

'Storm?' Nico asked.

Francesca rolled her eyes. 'No! The waitress doling out the Prosecco. Of course Storm.'

Nico smiled at Francesca. 'You really liked her?'

'I thought she was wonderful. Pretty, genuine, bright . . . I can definitely see why you would like her so much. She's perfect for you, *moroso*.'

Nico trailed his fingers across the back of Francesca's perfectly manicured hand and let his mind wander. He had done his best to forget about Storm over the past six months, but she was always on his mind. He'd stopped going to showbiz events so he could avoid seeing her, but that didn't stop him from hoping he would run into her again. Every time he boarded a flight he looked out for her, and he had even toyed with the idea of getting in touch with Angel and asking her to help him by passing on a message. But he'd stopped himself. He knew it wasn't fair to Storm – he couldn't give her what she deserved.

189

That didn't stop him from thinking about her all the time, hoping fate would intervene. And then suddenly, as he'd looked out into the crowd, there she was – like some sort of miracle. Inviting her out for coffee had been an impulse. Finding her in front of him like that, he couldn't stand the idea of never seeing her again. Of searching strangers' faces in the restaurant, the street and on the tube, hoping one of them would be her. He hadn't really expected her to say yes, but was delighted they would see each other again at least once.

He was suddenly aware of Francesca clicking her fingers in front of his face.

'Earth to Nico.' She smiled. 'Hello. Anyone home?'

'Sorry. I was a million miles away.'

Francesca snorted. 'Yes. With Storm, I imagine.'

Nico shrugged. Was it that obvious?' Francesca wasn't stupid. Even though he hadn't seen Storm for months, he occasionally dropped her name into conversation. Just saying it was a way of keeping the connection alive. It hadn't gone unnoticed by Francesca.

'I've known you for twenty-five years, Nico Alvise, and I've never seen you like this over a woman before.' She sounded astonished.

'It's nothing. I just . . .'

'You just?' Francesca encouraged.

'I just really like her.'

'So why aren't you pursuing her?'

Nico shook his head and smiled. Nothing got past Francesca. 'I don't want to just sleep with Storm,' he said, brushing a piece of imaginary fluff from his trousers. 'And

190

I can't offer her any more than that so I don't know where that leaves us.'

As he stared out of the car window at the London skyline, he felt stumped. He wanted Storm, but she was worth more than some cheap affair. He loved Francesca, she was his best friend and he'd never wanted to end their relationship . . . until now. What he felt for Storm left him both elated and miserable. Never in his life had he been so confused. He was not a dishonest man, yet he'd been living a lie for years.

'Why don't you tell Storm the truth about us?'

Wide-eyed with shock, Nico spun his head to stare at Francesca. Her mouth was set and she had her head cocked slightly to one side. He knew she was serious. But no, it wouldn't be fair on her, on either of them, and could do irreparable damage to their careers.

'I couldn't . . .' he began, shaking his head.

'I want you to be happy, Nico – you have a real chance of that with Storm. Meeting her today has proved to me what I've suspected for months. She likes you as much as you like her. When you see her for coffee, tell her about us then let her make up her mind.

'After all, doesn't everyone deserve a chance at true love? It turns up when you least expect it, and you shouldn't waste this gift. I haven't.'

Nico glanced at Francesca as she admired the delicate platinum eternity ring that sparkled on her hand. He knew she had found the one, and more than anything wanted him to do the same. His best friend had always had the power to amaze him. They had known each other since

191

they were children, becoming friends initially through the church they both attended. They were so close, both families had assumed it was only a matter of time until the couple married, but Nico and Francesca had other ideas. They'd moved to the UK when they were both eighteen. Francesca qualified as a barrister and then helped Nico establish his first restaurant in the city.

He soon made a name for himself with customers loving the theatricality of his cooking. Then there were the customers he was unafraid of standing up to, even going so far as to throw out objectionable diners on occasion. It was no surprise he quickly caught the attention of TV execs, who wasted no time in signing him to front his own show.

Since then his success had grown and grown, along with his popularity with women. Nico had never known anything like it, but he'd not taken advantage of it, sticking to his long-term girlfriend. But despite her, he had never once fallen in love, and suddenly he realised he was terrified of the prospect.

Chapter Eleven

'Those filthy bastards!' Chelsea exclaimed as she downed her second shot of limoncello. 'I can't believe they're making you do this. I'll talk to Miles, this is completely out of order.'

'I don't think it'll do any good, Chelsea,' Storm said, shaking her head. 'He pulled me back from Venice himself to set this up – he thinks it's a brilliant story, and the fact that I already know Nico makes me the perfect bait.'

'Fuckers!' Chelsea growled, pouring them both another generous measure of limoncello. 'I've never heard of anything like this.'

Storm raised her eyebrows. 'But you've heard, seen and done everything.'

'I thought so, babe. But using one of our own in a honey trap's a new one even on me. And the deviousness of Dermot, getting hold of that pap pic, is shocking. I'm going to have a word with my sources.'

'Would that be a word or a slap?' Storm enquired.

'Same difference.' Chelsea shrugged. 'So what's your plan?'

'To protect Nico and give them nothing,' she replied, taking a sip of limoncello and wincing. 'Shit, Chelsea! Why did you buy this? It's gross.'

'It was on offer at the airport.'

'So is meths at the corner shop but we don't buy it,' Storm pointed out.

'Any port in a storm,' Chelsea replied, finishing her drink and topping herself up. She had only arrived back from Venice a couple of hours earlier and had insisted on catching up with Storm immediately.

Dumping her luggage in the middle of the living room, Chelsea had barely even taken off her jacket before she'd pulled two bottles of sticky lemon liqueur from her duty-free carrier bag and insisted Storm tell her everything.

'So you're meeting him for coffee?'

'That's the plan. I've got to ring Nico next week to set something up.'

'And have you told Dermot?'

Storm choked on her drink. 'No way! I'm not telling that weasel anything.'

Chelsea smiled. 'Good! With a bit of luck this story will be his downfall. I'll help you all I can.'

Storm looked at her gratefully. 'Really?'

''Course! You're my mate, and whatever the hell is going on between Francesca and Nico, neither one of them deserves to have Dermot Whelan upending their lives just so he can get his by-line in the paper. Something I've noticed has been a bit lacking lately.'

Storm paused. She had noticed that too. Despite Dermot's hunger for stories, he didn't seem to be reporting on an awful lot these days.

'Between you and me,' Chelsea said conspiratorially, 'Miles is really pissed off with Dermot. All his stories keep falling down, and he hasn't had a good idea in months.'

'Great!' replied Storm uncharitably as she flopped back in her chair. 'About time the bastard got his comeuppance. Anyway, enough about him. Tell me about Venice.'

An enormous grin spread across Chelsea's face. 'All right, I met someone when I was out there. A gorgeous unknown actor called Adam Stark who's played a few minor roles in a couple of action blockbusters. He's just getting his big break after fourteen years of trying and was out there raising his profile.'

'Oh, yeah! Sounds like it wasn't just his profile he was interested in raising.' Storm smirked.

'Come on, a lady doesn't kiss and tell. But as you know I'm no lady, and quite honestly he was hung like a donkey! I told him he was wasted in Hollywood, and he should give soft porn a go.'

'You didn't?' Storm chuckled.

Chelsea slid further down the sofa and let her legs dangle over the edge. 'Nah, I didn't, but he's definitely got what it takes.'

'So I take it you spent most of the festival shagging rather than scribbling?'

'Afraid so, Stormy. It's a hard life, but someone has to do it.' Chelsea grinned.

'And are you going to see him again?'

'I hope so. We've exchanged numbers and he's already Skyped me.'

'Bloody hell, he's keen! You only got back a few hours ago.'

Chelsea looked smug. 'What can I tell you? I've got the X-factor.'

'You certainly do, babe. And of course this means the drought's finally over.'

'Yep! The drought is well and truly over. In fact, it's more like the floodgates have been opened.'

'Oh, gross.' Storm shuddered as the unwelcome image entered her mind.

'How about I fix us a real drink? I can't face any more of this lemon shite,' she said, getting to her feet.

'Thought you'd never ask,' Chelsea replied, handing over her empty glass.

Storm walked to the huge American-style fridge that dwarfed Chelsea's tiny galley kitchen. She pulled out a bottle of ice cold Chablis and poured them both large glasses. Just then there was a knock at the door.

'I'll go,' Chelsea called, as she raced down the stairs to the front door.

Carrying the glasses back into the living room, Storm had just set them on the coffee table when Chelsea shouted up the stairs. 'Storm, get down here.'

Sighing, she made her way down. What was it this time? More Jehovah's Witnesses? She was quite sure Chelsea didn't need help telling anyone to get lost.

'Delivery for you,' explained her friend, jerking her head towards the florist's driver who was busy pulling bouquet

after bouquet after bouquet of white roses from the back of his van.

'What's going on?' Storm hissed.

'Storm Saunders?' asked the delivery driver. He handed her an electronic notepad and pen. 'Sign here.'

'Wait, what is all this?'

'Twenty-five bouquets for you.'

Storm's ears rang with shock. 'What?' she gasped. 'Who from?'

The driver shook his head as he hauled yet more bouquets from the van.

'No idea, love. There'll be a card on one of them, that ought to tell you. Quite the gesture though. Usually people say it with one bouquet, not a van full.'

Chelsea giggled as the flowers piled up on their little patch of front lawn. 'Maybe they're from Nico,' she suggested.

Storm didn't think so. So many blooms suggested something sinister rather than sweet. Snatching up the bouquet that contained the card, she ripped the envelope open.

It eats away at my heart that you won't return my calls. Maybe the flowers in Venice weren't enough. But I hope these bouquets, one for every year of your life, will convince you to take me back. Dermot xxx

Staring at the card in disbelief, Storm felt sick.

'What is it?' Chelsea asked, taking it from her. As she read Dermot's words she put her arm around Storm, who seemed to have gone into shock.

'Jesus, this sounds weird. One for every year of your life? What's he planning? To make sure you don't reach twenty-six? And what does he mean about flowers in Venice?'

'He sent flowers to my hotel room while I was away.'

'What! Why? And what does he mean about the phone calls?'

Storm looked at her friend. She'd been trying to shrug off Dermot's weird behaviour for a while but she had to admit this latest stunt was getting to her. Quickly she outlined what he'd been doing.

'This is seriously creepy.' Chelsea frowned. 'Are you OK, babe?'

Storm nodded. 'Fine. I just wish he'd get the message once and for all that we're over.'

Chelsea called over to the delivery driver, 'Mate. Any chance you can take these back to your shop?'

But the driver shook his head as he piled the last of the bouquets into Storm's arms. 'Not a chance. I'm paid to deliver, not return.'

'But she doesn't want them,' Chelsea pointed out. 'They're from her weird ex-boyfriend who's making her life a misery. Seriously, what normal person sends this many bouquets?'

The delivery driver looked sheepish. 'I'm sorry, love. Wish I could help.'

With that he turned on his heel and clambered back into the van. Looking at the mound of flowers on their tiny patch of lawn, Storm couldn't help noticing that the huge number of white blooms resembled funeral flowers more than any declaration of love.

'Look, we'll both keep an eye on Dermot. As for these flowers, let's stick them in the back of my car and deliver them to the local hospital. They'll be grateful for Dermot's

insanity even if nobody else is,' said Chelsea.

Storm let out a sigh of relief. Typical Chelsea, she had an answer for everything. 'Brilliant idea. Thanks, babe.'

Chelsea pulled her in for a hug. 'Any time. What are mates for if not for sipping disgusting lemon drinks and sorting out deranged exes?'

'What do you think, the blue or the red?' Storm asked nervously.

In the middle of reading some juicy gossip about Blake Lively over a bowl of granola, Chelsea didn't appreciate the interruption. 'What are you on?' she exclaimed. 'These are more like red-carpet dresses. Storm, seriously, this is getting well out of hand. It's coffee, go for jeans – keep it simple!'

'But what if it turns into something besides coffee?' Storm protested.

Chelsea smirked. 'Thought you said you didn't shag men with girlfriends?'

'I'm not worried about that!' she gasped. 'I mean, what if we go on somewhere?'

'Storm, you're meeting at eleven on a Friday morning – it's not exactly cocktail hour.'

'I s'pose not,' she muttered. 'Fine, I'll go with the jeans.'

Frustrated, Storm wandered back to her bedroom, only for Chelsea to knock on her door a few minutes later.

'Can I come in?'

Storm nodded, clearing away clothes, make-up and magazines to create space on her double bed for Chelsea to perch on.

'You're getting this meeting way out of proportion,' she said gently. 'Remember, you're going to make sure nothing ever gets out about Nico so you're doing him a favour. Now just enjoy this for what it is – coffee with a bloke you really fancy.'

In spite of her fears, Storm laughed. If nothing else this was a chance to spend more time with Nico, something she definitely wanted though she didn't like to admit it.

'Jeans it is then,' she said, slipping on her favourite pair.

Nico had suggested Storm meet him in an old Italian café in Soho. Feeling the warmth of the late-summer sun on her back as she turned into the narrow street, Storm was pleased she'd gone for an outfit she felt comfortable in rather than dressing to impress. She had teamed a striped blazer with her favourite pair of wedges and kept her make-up simple, choosing a hint of brown shadow and a slick of her favourite Clinique Chubby Stick on her lips.

Reaching the coffee shop, Storm took a deep breath and opened the glass door, pausing at the entrance as she scanned the room for Nico.

It didn't take her long to find him, fiddling with his smartphone at a table along with what looked like ten cups of coffee. Amused, Storm walked straight over.

'Either you've been here a long time or you really like coffee.' She smiled gesturing to the different varieties on the tiny table. Along with an espresso, there was a cappuccino, Americano, flat white, and God knows what else.

'Storm!' Nico smiled, immediately getting to his feet and kissing her on both cheeks. 'Please sit down. I realised

I didn't know what sort of coffee you like so I got you a choice.'

'Thank God for that.' She grinned as she sat down on a banquette opposite him. 'I thought you had some awful caffeine addiction. But FYI, I usually order a double shot cappuccino without sugar.'

Reaching for a cup and taking a careful sip, she took in Nico's appearance. As always he looked gorgeous. His olive skin gleamed with health. He was wearing a pair of loosely fitted jeans with a classic navy polo shirt. Storm found her heart thumping as he treated her to a broad grin.

'It seems funny to see you somewhere so normal, somewhere that's not an event or launch party,' he said shyly. 'Just you, me . . .'

'. . . and a table full of coffee! People will definitely talk,' Storm laughed as she interrupted him. 'So how come you can squeeze me in for a drink today, Mr Alvise? I thought you celebs never got a minute to yourselves.'

'Shhh!' Nico teased, putting his finger to his lips in mock seriousness. 'I don't want to dispel the rumour. No, actually I have taken a few days off. The restaurants run themselves thanks to my team of brilliant managers and head chefs, and the TV stuff doesn't start again for a few weeks. So I have all the time in the world for you, Storm.'

She sipped her coffee while she thought about how to reply to him. There was so much she wanted to know about this intriguing man. 'So come on then,' she said finally. 'Tell me about yourself. And not the stuff I've read in the press, tell me things I wouldn't know.'

As Nico spoke Storm became intensely aware of his voice, each word sounding as warm and velvety as chocolate. God! She could listen to him talk all day.

He told her all about his childhood, growing up in a small village on the east coast of Italy, with three elder sisters who thought nothing of dressing him up as a fourth sister in their mother's old clothes, and how he and his friends had always played football in the garden until they put the ball through his parents' living-room window and afterwards he hadn't sat down for a week.

Nico was a good storyteller with a passion for detail. Storm realised she hadn't enjoyed herself so much in ages. As he moved on to telling her about how he'd developed a passion for cooking when his mum taught him to make everything from *antipasti* to *dolce*, all thoughts of her job and the honey trap were forgotten.

'I knew then there was nothing else I wanted to do with my life,' Nico finished.

'And now?' Storm pressed him. 'What's next for you? Is cooking still something you love?'

Nico gazed at her thoughtfully and then smiled. 'I'm not sure. Maybe another restaurant, maybe more cookery courses . . . But enough about me. I want to know more about you.'

Storm told him stories about her own childhood. For once, instead of focusing on the unhappy memories, she told him about growing up in Brighton: days spent at the beach with Alan, helping Lexie learn to ride a bike, taking her brother for a McDonald's milkshake when their parents had expressly forbidden it. Then there were the

books and films she liked to read, plus the soft spot she had for Ryan Gosling.

'Honestly, I think Carly and I have watched *The Notebook* at least a hundred times,' Storm laughed. She hadn't felt so light-hearted and unburdened in a long time. Aside from Carly, she couldn't remember anyone before who had been so interested in her life and it felt good.

'I loved living by the sea. That's the one thing about London I can't stand. There's nowhere to go fishing,' Nico commented.

'Leigh-on-Sea?' Storm suggested.

Nico arched an eyebrow. 'I'm very fond of Leigh-on-Sea, Storm, but fishing in an Essex estuary doesn't compare with the blue waters of the Adriatic.'

Storm giggled. 'Point made.'

'Anyway, how are things going for you at college?' he asked.

'Oh, fine. I haven't started properly yet so I've just been doing a bit of pre-course reading. So far, so good.'

Her latest lie was the last thing she wanted to talk about. An image of Pinocchio came into her mind, and as she shifted uncomfortably in her chair Storm found herself rubbing her nose. She wouldn't have been surprised if it had suddenly grown in the last thirty seconds, the lies tumbled from her mouth so quickly.

Sensing she wanted to change the subject, Nico signalled to the waiter for two more cappuccinos and decided to go all out. 'And what else is going on for you, Storm? I cannot believe a girl as beautiful as you is single. Do you have a boyfriend?'

'You don't waste time getting to the point, do you?' she chuckled.

'Sorry. Always a habit of mine. I didn't mean to offend you.'

Storm shrugged and dipped her finger into the froth of her cappuccino. As usual Nico had got her to open up and be who she really was. 'You didn't. For a long time I thought my last boyfriend Dermot was the one,' she admitted. 'I thought we would be together for ever. But the truth is he was a lying, cheating bastard who did his best to destroy my life and I'm better off without him.'

If Nico was surprised by this outburst he didn't show it. Instead he reached across the table for her hand and traced his fingers across its palm. As he touched her Storm felt a pang of desire. She wanted to spend every moment of every day with this man. Locking eyes with Nico, she saw his expression suddenly become grave.

'There's something I want to discuss with you.'

'Sounds serious?'

'It is. And you can tell nobody, especially not your reporter friend Chelsea.'

Storm's heart started to thump wildly. What if he knew about the honey trap plan? What if he'd lured her here to have a go at her, accuse her of fraud, deception, or, worse, tell her he never wanted to see her again? In that moment Storm didn't think she could stand it. Not for the first time she wished she had never gone along with Dermot's stupid plan. Being unemployed was better than duping someone like this.

Nervously, she withdrew her hand from Nico's and

braced herself. 'OK, I'm listening.'

'There's no easy way to say this,' he began. 'I've developed feelings for you, and I don't mean to sound arrogant but I think you care for me too. You're the first person I think about when I wake up and the last person I think about when I go to bed. When I create a new dish it's your opinion I want, and when I'm in bed it's your arms I want to feel around me.'

Storm didn't know what to say. These were the words she'd longed to hear, but it was pointless. Nico was with Francesca and if he couldn't remember that then she had to help him. Suddenly she felt very tired. It would be so easy to let herself be swayed by his words but there was just the little matter of his girlfriend getting in the way. She knew she was falling for Nico but it was time he realised it wasn't ever going to happen.

'Francesca joining us in this little scenario, is she?' Storm leaned forward so that her face was close to his. 'I liked Francesca. I thought she was warm, fun, classy. She deserves better than this.'

Nico winced, and reached for her wrist. 'Francesca very much likes you too. She's part of the reason I'm here. It's with her blessing that I want you to learn the truth about us. I've hardly told anyone what I'm about to tell you, Storm, but the truth is, I'm single. Francesca isn't my girlfriend, we're not getting married – she's gay.'

'What?' Storm gasped. Leaning back in shock, she considered all the photos she had ever seen of Francesca and Nico together. They'd seemed so happy and in love – everyone said so. 'What are you talking about?' she asked finally.

Nico looked at her anxiously.

'It's true,' he said quietly. 'Francesca's gay. Always has been, always will be. She has a girlfriend, Paula, and they have been together for a couple of years and are very much in love.'

'But why lie?' Storm spluttered.

'Even in this day and age people are prejudiced, Storm.'

'But not that badly,' she protested.

'You'd be surprised,' he replied. Taking a deep breath he told her how Francesca had been brought up by her very strict grandparents after her parents were killed in a car crash when she was only a baby. 'From the moment I met Francesca when we were just ten, I sensed she was vulnerable – her grandparents were very strict with her and both devout Catholics. It was a cold existence so I made it my own personal mission to look out for her, make sure she was OK. I sat next to her at school, invited her around to my home to play with me and my sisters, and made sure her grandparents thought I was a good influence on her, so that Francesca would have a little more freedom.'

'Wow, what an amazing friend you were!'

'It wasn't all one-sided,' Nico put in. 'One day she punched a much older boy who had tried to bully me at church. Her bravery and strength impressed me. And you know what, Storm? After twenty-five years she is still doing that today.'

'How do you mean?'

'Well, after that day, Francesca and I became inseparable, sharing each other's secrets as we grew up in and out of each other's houses in our tiny village. But then when we

206

were eighteen both our lives were turned upside down after a group of kids caught Francesca behind the village church, kissing a girl she went to school with.'

'What's wrong with that?'

'This was in the early nineties,' he explained. 'It doesn't seem so long ago but things have changed dramatically since then, especially in small-town Italy. Francesca became the subject of nasty gossip. In a small village like ours, it was hard to get away from the whispers and name calling . . .'

'That's awful,' Storm breathed. 'Poor Francesca.'

'That wasn't the worst part,' Nico replied grimly. 'Her grandparents considered Francesca's behaviour so disgusting they threw her out. It was a terrifying time for her, and she came straight to me. I was furious, couldn't believe her grandparents could behave in that way. I went to see them to try and get them to change their minds.'

'And did you succeed?'

Nico shook his head. 'I didn't come close. They threw me out too. Said I'd encouraged her by not asking her to marry me! It was a joke. They refused to believe Francesca was the kind, loving person she has always been and instead viewed her as some sort of terrible sinner. I hated seeing her treated that way. Because her grandparents were so well-respected in the community, many people – even former friends – shunned us both.'

Storm winced. 'That's horrible.'

'It was, but I didn't need friends like that, and neither did Francesca. But that's why she has never come out. She still worries now about what people will say should

she choose publicly to reveal her sexuality. When all this happened I had a place at a top London cookery school and invited her to join me in the UK, to make a fresh start. She'd been due to study law, and once we got here, she studied hard and managed to win a place at a London university . . .'

'Then what?' Storm asked.

'Francesca began her law degree and I vowed to love and protect her no matter what. She's my best friend and there is nothing I wouldn't do for her, she's been through far too much already.'

'So that's why you let everyone assume you're a couple?'

Nico nodded his head. 'It hasn't done either of us any harm. Francesca has never been back to Italy, and pretending we're a couple makes her feel safer. It's suited us both to keep up the pretence.'

'And your parents have supported you?'

Nico nodded. 'They're the only ones in our village who have. I have always stood by Francesca and always will.'

'And what about the affairs you've had?'

Nico shrugged. 'I'm single, Storm. I haven't had lots of affairs. I had a long-term girlfriend for many years, who understood my situation with Francesca. But then she wanted more, wanted me to encourage Francesca to come out so we could be together once and for all, but if I'm honest I didn't love her anywhere near enough to do that. So I ended it. Now Francesca's away a lot at Paula's, or rather at the house they both own in Dorset, and when she is I do my own thing here.'

'So you're not really cheating then?'

He shook his head. 'I would never cheat, Storm. It's not who I am. Before my restaurant career took off we talked about Francesca finally coming out and living the life she wants with Paula. But she became nervous and insecure, and I couldn't see the point of putting her through it. As I said before, I hadn't met anyone else I wanted to get serious with . . . until I met you.'

'And when you did . . .' Storm's voice trailed off.

'I couldn't stop talking about you, and she . . . how do you say? . . . cottoned on that my feelings for you were strong. When she met you, she saw how I felt and said I owed it to her, you and me to tell you the truth. And maybe, just maybe, there was a way we could be together.'

Nico finished his speech and looked at Storm, waiting for her to say something.

She let out a deep sigh and leaned back against the banquette. She couldn't get her head around any of this. But the one thing she realised was that she had to protect Francesca now as well as Nico. If this ever got out they'd be splashed across the front pages for weeks as skanky reporters and paps delved into their private lives and dug up all kinds of horror stories. She shook her head sadly. Neither of them deserved that. It was up to Francesca when and how she came out. Storm knew she had to carry on with the honey trap plan. She felt unbearably trapped in a situation she just did not know how to handle. She needed to get away from Nico so she could think clearly.

But that wouldn't be fair after he'd just bared his soul to her. She tried to say something, anything, that would relieve

the tension that his words had caused, but nothing came. Instead, she picked up her bag and rushed out the door, leaving Nico staring after her with a dejected expression on his face.

Chapter Twelve

'You ran out of the coffee shop? Have you lost your freaking mind?' Chelsea blasted.

It was gone six and the two girls had gone for post-work drinks at a pub in Covent Garden well away from the prying eyes and ears in the office.

Storm shrugged and sipped her glass of Sauvignon Blanc.

'I didn't mean to. I was just so overwhelmed by Nico's confession.'

'It must have been quite something to rattle you like that, babe,' Chelsea said thoughtfully. 'It's not like you to go off on one.'

Storm took another sip of wine. She hadn't told Chelsea the details of Nico's news. It wasn't her secret to share. It wasn't that Storm didn't trust Chelsea; she hadn't known the other girl for very long but already felt she would trust her with her life. But after everything that had happened with Carly, Storm had learned her lesson. Some things

211

were meant to stay private – and Nico's relationship with Francesca was definitely one of them.

'It was the last thing I was expecting,' was all Storm said.

'I can see that, babe,' Chelsea said quietly. 'What did he do when you legged it?'

'I didn't look back to find out. I just grabbed my stuff and raced out of the café.' Storm sighed and took another sip of her wine. They'd done well to grab a table outside, usually the place was packed with tourists and day-trippers.

'I feel terrible about it. There was Nico, baring his soul, and I just left him there. It was a horrible thing to do. I haven't heard from him since.'

Chelsea folded her empty crisp packet into a triangle and wedged it into the hole in the middle of the table before regarding Storm carefully. 'Do you think that whatever he told you was the truth?'

Storm nodded her head sadly. 'I Googled where Francesca works straight after I saw Nico and called her. She confirmed what he'd told me.'

'I see,' replied Chelsea, nodding. 'Did you tell her you'd deserted him?'

Storm nodded. 'She laughed and said it was the first time a woman had ever ditched Nico.'

She paused then and thought about the conversation she'd had with Francesca. Much as she'd wanted to stay with Nico, the pressure of everything had suddenly become too much for her and she had fled from the coffee shop to a nearby churchyard. Perching on a bench, she had thought long and hard about what to do before deciding to

find Francesca. Punching in the number for the chambers general office, she'd asked to be put through to Francesca. Storm had half expected her to tear strips off her when she heard what had happened, but the other woman had been nothing but warm and sympathetic.

'He's falling for you,' she said. 'We have kept my sexuality a secret for many years, but now I have found love. It would make me very happy if Nico could do the same.'

'But I just left him there,' Storm wailed.

Francesca sounded unconcerned. 'He'll get over it,' she said soothingly. 'Leave Nico to me.'

Swallowing a pang of guilt about the lies she had told him, about working as a flight attendant and then about studying catering, Storm had hung up and returned to the office where she'd done little more than daydream over her computer screen and leave unanswered messages for Nico every half hour. The only glimmer of sunshine in her whole day had been the fact that nobody at work had asked her how she'd got on with him. Sabrina and Dermot had been out on a job all afternoon and Miles had been tied up with meetings so hadn't called her into his office for the lowdown.

Now, almost two glasses of wine down, Storm could see the error of her ways. 'I shouldn't have run off like that. It was a shit thing to do.'

'So tell him, apologise.'

'Not that simple. He won't answer his phone and I don't like to bother Francesca again.'

'Go over there.' Chelsea was surprisingly single-minded sometimes.

'Duh! I don't have his address. And even if I did, I couldn't just turn up.'

'Why not?'

Storm looked at her friend as if she was an alien from another planet. 'Paps, babe! They see me, they'll think I'm there for a booty call.'

'No, they won't. They're all across town at some huge premiere with Jennifer Aniston – they're not hanging about to catch Nico out.'

Storm drained her glass and got to her feet. 'Another?' she asked.

As she waited to be served, Storm considered Chelsea's advice. Maybe she should go over there, explain and tell Nico how sorry she was. She knew she wouldn't sleep a wink if she didn't speak to him this evening.

By the time she'd ordered two more drinks and a couple of bags of salted peanuts, Storm had made up her mind.

'OK, it's a good idea,' she said, placing the drinks carefully on the table and for once not spilling a drop. 'But I don't know where Nico lives.'

'Well, luckily for you, I do,' Chelsea replied, fishing in her bag for a notepad and pen and scribbling down an address in thick black print. Tearing the page from her pad, she handed it to Storm. 'There you go. Now get yourself in a cab and get over there.'

Storm took the piece of paper and stared at the address in front of her. Was there nothing Chelsea couldn't do?

'Thanks, but I can't leave you here in the pub alone.' She pointed to their two full glasses. Chelsea reached across the

table and helped herself to Storm's glass of wine and bag of nuts.

'Problem solved,' she said firmly, noticing a gorgeous dark-haired stranger at a nearby table giving her the eye. 'Besides, I don't think I'll be alone for very long.'

It was one of those beautifully warm nights that made the summer feel like it would last for ever. The sound of laughter and good times provided the soundtrack to Storm's evening as she left the pub and walked towards the nearest taxi rank. It felt to her as though her senses were on fire as she noticed how alive the city seemed, with people spilling out of bars and cafés on to the street, enjoying drinks as they soaked up the late-summer sunshine. She was about to fish out her mobile and check for messages when a movement across the street caught her eye. Glancing up, she was horrified to see Dermot standing across the road, smiling and waving at her.

Shock pulsed through her. What was he doing here? She and Chelsea had only just decided to go for a drink in Covent Garden after they left work. How did he know where to find her?

Determined not to show she was rattled, she ignored him and instead focused on catching the attention of a passing taxi. Right now all she wanted was Nico, not Dermot. Clambering into the back of the next cab, Storm gave the driver Nico's address in Hampstead then turned to look out of the back window.

Dermot was still there, mouthing 'I'll call you'.

Shuddering, Storm did her best to forget him. Tonight

was about Nico, not Dermot. She pulled her compact from her bag to check her appearance. Not too bad, she thought, grateful she didn't have mascara rings around her eyes. Reaching into her bag for the packet of mints she always carried, Storm put two into her mouth to freshen her breath.

Nico's home was every bit as gorgeous as Storm had expected: a large, detached red-brick house, set back from the road behind trees and with a tall hedge at the front to keep out prying eyes. After she'd paid the cabbie, she made her way towards the red front door. As her feet crunched on the gravel drive she did her best to calm down; at least the place was free from paps just as Chelsea had promised.

Raising her hand to rap the brass knocker loudly, Storm couldn't help hoping nobody was home. Apart from a couple of lamps on in what looked like the living room, the place seemed deserted. Just as she was convincing herself it would be for the best if Nico weren't in, the front door swung open and there stood the man himself, dressed in cut-off grey sweatpants and a baggy white t-shirt that showed off just a hint of his tanned, taut stomach muscles, Storm was mesmerised. God, he was sexy! Nico could wear a bin liner and still be the most gorgeous man in the room.

'What are you doing here?' he asked, shocked to see her.

'Er . . .' Storm suddenly felt so nervous, she couldn't get the words out. 'I just wanted to say I'm sorry. I shouldn't have run out on you like that this morning. It was an awful thing to do after you'd told me something so personal.'

The words didn't seem to be enough when she looked at Nico's impassive face. He was giving nothing away and

Storm realised that turning up out of the blue had been a very bad idea. 'I'm sorry, I should never have come.'

As she began to walk away, Nico grabbed her wrist and spun her back round to face him.

'Don't go.'

As his eyes met hers, Storm weakened and her pulse raced. 'I'm sorry, I was overwhelmed . . .' she began. Nico silenced her by gently placing a finger over her lips.

'Shhh,' he whispered, bending down to kiss her. As his beautiful mouth met hers she was sure she heard fireworks going off around her, the passion of it all leaving her breathless. Nico's tongue darted into her mouth and Storm reacted instinctively, moving her lips to the rhythm of his. Butterflies fluttered wildly inside her as ripples of desire pulsed through every part of her body. By the time Nico had gently pulled away she had the strangest feeling it was as if she'd finally come home.

'Do you want to come inside, Storm?' he murmured. 'I'm not ready to let you go when I've only just found you.'

'I think I never want to leave,' she replied softly, taking his hand as he guided her inside.

As Nico led her into the huge open-plan kitchen-diner, Storm couldn't believe the luxury of it all. The room was decked out with glass and steel and by rights should have looked overpowering and masculine, but instead it looked and felt warm and inviting.

But there was no time for a guided tour as he pushed her gently on to the red leather sofa at the end of the kitchen and kissed her again. This time his lips were greedier. 'My God, Storm,' he breathed, breaking away and looking at

her in wonder. 'I've fantasised about this moment for so long, but wasn't sure it would ever happen.'

By way of reply she kissed him back, hungry for more, feeling like a different version of herself, more confident, daring, and alive with a craving she had never experienced before. Her hands moved to his torso. She slid her fingers underneath his t-shirt and savoured the feel of his smooth, warm skin. As she caressed his rock-hard abs, Nico tugged off her dress and knickers. He unclasped her bra, leaving her totally naked, and she realised she would usually have felt self-conscious, a new lover seeing her without any clothes on, but not today.

This time Storm felt powerful in her own skin, excitement coursing through every nerve in her body. At the thought of what lay ahead her nipples stiffened in anticipation – all she could think was how much she wanted this man. Drunk on love and lust, Storm couldn't get enough, wanting to consume every inch of him. Melting into his touch, she slipped her hand into his boxers and moaned with pleasure at the feel of his hard, waiting cock. Storm's touch sent Nico into overdrive. Lustfully, he scooped her into his arms.

'Are you always this masterful?' she giggled as he carried her up to his bedroom.

'Only when I'm really turned on,' he said gruffly, kicking the door closed behind him. Suddenly Storm's laughter gave way to pure passion as they fell on to the bed. Their hands were everywhere, each desperate to touch and please the other. Storm shucked off Nico's sweatpants and gazed at him. He was as perfect as she'd imagined.

Reaching for her, Nico trailed his fingers across her shoulders, then sucked and kissed at her hard nipples, sending waves of desire through her core. As he travelled further down her body, slipping a hand between her legs, Storm bucked and writhed with sheer pleasure. There was no denying it, Nico was an expert lover, his touch sensuous, slow, and at the same time thrilling. He made her feel as though he had all the time in the world just for her. But Storm wanted to prove to Nico just how much she wanted him. Pushing him onto his back, Nico gasped as she slid her mouth lower and lower, eager to taste all of him.

'Let me just put something on . . .' he murmured, pulling her up and reaching into his bedside drawer for a condom.

'Now, Nico, now!' Storm begged, lying back on the bed, unable to wait any longer.

Pausing just for a moment to look at her face, Nico found his way inside her, the sensation so pure and perfect each of them shuddered in delight.

As Nico plunged deeper, all too soon Storm felt her orgasm build, until finally she couldn't hold back any longer. Burying her face in his chest she screamed in ecstasy as wave after wave of pleasure rippled through her body, and then Nico was reaching his own climax. As she felt him thrust into her he called out her name, and Storm thought it was the most beautiful thing she had ever heard.

Storm woke up the next morning to find herself alone in Nico's king-size bed. Sitting bolt upright, she took in the scene – there were clothes everywhere, including her best lacy briefs. Just as she was trying artfully to reach for them

and shove them under her pillow, Nico appeared wearing nothing but a pair of boxers and holding a huge tray laden with coffee, croissants, fresh fruit, and what looked suspiciously like huge bacon sandwiches.

'Wow! Is all that for me?' Storm asked, unsure which was more impressive, the contents of Nico's tray or the contents of his closely fitting boxers.

'I was thinking we might share, but having discovered last night just how greedy you can be, you can eat the whole lot if you want,' he teased, putting down the tray on a bedside table and leaning over to kiss her good morning.

Feeling Nico's lips on hers, Storm too was reminded of last night. It had been amazing, incredible, she didn't think she'd ever had such good sex before in her life. After they'd made love the first time, they'd lain together, limbs entwined, laughing and talking before making love again, and again, and again. Nico had serious prowess, and Storm had lost count of the amount of orgasms he'd brought her to.

Smiling at the memory, Nico brushed a stray tendril of hair from her face. 'What are you smirking about?'

'Nothing.' She laughed, sneaking a bite of buttery fresh croissant. 'Just remembering last night.'

Nico playfully batted her arm before leaning over to gently suck her nipples. 'Last night was just the warm up.' He smiled, inching his boxers down. 'Let me show you just what us Italians can really do.'

'Mmm. I like the sound of that, Mr Alvise. It sounds like it's going to be a long day.'

*

Exhausted, that was the only word for it, Storm thought later as her head hit the pillow. Exhausted, but definitely ecstatic. If she'd thought last night was good, then Nico deserved a medal for the performance he'd just put in. Actually, they both did. Turning her head towards him, she gazed at his closed eyes.

'Stop watching me, Storm,' he whispered, making her jump out of her skin.

'You nearly gave me a heart attack,' she cried, wrapping the duvet tightly around herself.

'Hmmm, don't cover up your beautiful body,' he protested, wriggling closer. 'You're too gorgeous to be covered up. In fact, I think you should be naked all the time.'

'Yeah? I think people in the street might have a problem with that.'

'Well, if they do, they can take it up with me. I know a top barrister who will make their lives a misery!'

Storm felt guilty then. How could she have been so thoughtless as not even to consider Francesca? She'd been so swept up in the heat of the moment she'd totally forgotten about her. OK, so Francesca was a lesbian, and involved with someone else, but Storm reckoned she still might not like to find Nico in flagrante in the house they shared.

'Relax.' He smiled as if reading her thoughts. 'Francesca and Paula are in Dorset for the week. We've got the whole place to ourselves.'

Storm felt a rush of relief. 'Really? So what do you feel like doing?'

221

Nico pulled her towards him and started caressing her neck. 'I think you know exactly what I'd like to be doing.'

By early evening Storm begged for mercy. She'd never had so much sex in all her life.

'Seriously, I'm knackered!'

Nico pretended to look put out. 'Oh, Storm! Come on, let me make love to you once more.'

As he leaned over to kiss her, she playfully pushed him away.

'No! I need to get up, I'm starving. I can't believe I've spent all day with a chef, and only had a croissant.'

'And there was me, thinking I'd filled you up in other ways.'

Already recognising the lustful glint in Nico's eye, Storm put her hands up. 'Stop! I'm getting in the shower and then we are going out to eat.'

Leaving Nico wanting more, she hopped into his huge en suite and turned the rain shower on to full blast.

Over dinner in a gorgeous neighbourhood Thai restaurant Nico counted as one of his favourites, the two of them swapped more stories about their lives. Being a journalist for so long, Storm naturally found it easier to listen to others rather than to reveal details about her own life. With Dermot it had taken her months to open up and share, but with Nico it was different. She felt instantly connected to him. Storm was able to be herself, so when Nico asked how she was coping following her row with Carly, she was honest.

'I haven't seen or heard from her in months,' she

admitted sadly. 'I still miss her every day and wish we could make up – she's been such a huge part of my life for so long – but I know I have to face facts, I doubt it will ever happen.'

'Never say never, Storm.' Nico smiled at her. 'A couple of my old friends from Italy emailed me the other day, apologising for their behaviour. We ended up having a very long conversation. They said they were sorry for not standing by us when we fell foul of Francesca's grandparents. They were just kids who didn't know what to do. It made me realise you never know what's around the corner.'

'Wow, Nico, that's incredible.'

In spite of her own friendship problems, she was delighted for him. He had seemed so sad, almost haunted by the loss of so many friends. It must be a huge weight off his shoulders to know they would be in each other's lives once more.

'Does Francesca know?' she asked shyly.

Nico nodded. 'She's my best friend, Storm. There's nothing I keep from her. And yes, before you ask, she knows you stayed over last night and is incredibly happy for us.'

Storm flushed with delight. The rest of the evening passed in a blur of happy laughter and chat. As she reached into her bag to pay for her half of the meal, Nico waved her gesture away.

'Don't be silly,' he insisted. 'This is on me.'

She was flattered but not easily put off. 'I'm not one of those girls who thinks a man should pay for everything, you know. I insist on paying my share.'

Nico grinned. 'How about a compromise? You pay for breakfast in the morning?' Storm roared with laughter at his forwardness. The cheeky bastard! Just because she'd put out once, he expected her to stay over again.

'You know what they say about assumptions, don't you, Mr Alvise?' She stared at him stern-faced. 'To assume makes an ass out of you and me.'

'Don't talk about your ass, Storm – just the sight of it drives me wild,' he groaned.

She laughed again. The man was shameless!

'Well, I hate to see someone in pain, so as a favour to you, yes, I'll stay.'

Nico smiled broadly. 'Excellent. Now grab your stuff and let's get out of here. You're wearing far too many clothes for my liking.'

Hand in hand, they left the restaurant and walked back to his house. They were just metres from his front door when Storm's mobile rang.

Letting go of Nico's hand, she reached for her phone and peered at the screen – Chelsea.

'I should get this. I haven't managed to speak to her so she's probably wondering where I am.'

'I'll give you some privacy,' Nico offered considerately, unlocking his front door as Storm pressed answer.

'Thank fuck for that! You haven't answered your phone all day, I thought you were dead in a ditch somewhere,' Chelsea said dramatically.

'Don't be daft, I'm with Nico,' she replied, before lowering her voice. 'Actually I'm staying over again tonight.'

Chelsea cackled. 'You dirty bitch! Good on you. So how was he?'

'None of your business.' Storm laughed. 'But I'll be back in the office on Monday.'

'Well, that's what I rang to tell you. I've told the office that you've got a nasty case of tonsillitis and the doctor's signed you off for a week, so nobody's expecting you in for a few days, meaning you and lover boy can spend some time getting to know each other. Don't worry, I've cleared it with HR.'

Not for the first time Storm felt beyond grateful that Chelsea was her friend.

'I don't know what to say. Thanks, babe.'

'I'm not that selfless. I want you out of the way because I've persuaded Adam to come over for a few days and I'd quite like a bout of hot, dirty sex myself without you interrupting, thanks very much.'

Storm giggled. Typical Chelsea. Still, she appreciated the gesture. Heading inside the house to find Nico, she couldn't wait to tell him they had each other all to themselves for the next few days.

Chapter Thirteen

Thanks to Chelsea, Storm and Nico were in a complete and utter state of loved-up bliss. With time to spend together without any pressure from paps, friends, family or work, the couple were able to enjoy the simple luxury of falling in love.

They went everywhere together and couldn't stand being apart, though Storm did insist on returning to Chelsea's flat briefly to pick up some fresh clothes.

It might have taken them a while to get their relationship off the ground but the two of them were more than making up for lost time now. Storm had assured Nico that her college course didn't start for another week, meaning they were free to enjoy days out, including a romantic trip to Bath where Nico arranged for them to have the gorgeous Roman Baths all to themselves. When they weren't out, they would lie in the garden talking and laughing for hours, or Nico would whip up a delicious meal while she perched on a stool at the countertop, chatting and sipping wine.

They never seemed to run out of things to say to each other and Storm felt totally absorbed in his world. When she was with him nothing else seemed to matter. And at night they enjoyed mind-blowing sex.

Over the next few days they felt untouchable, locked in their own private world, and Storm felt happier and more free than she had in years. Her connection with Nico was so intense, it was like nothing she had ever experienced before. She had never really believed in the idea of soulmates, but now she felt sure that's what Nico was. He already seemed to understand her better than she did herself, and they had been eager to learn as much as they could about each other, no detail too small for them to share.

Storm had loved finding out just how he liked his coffee (cappuccino first thing in the morning, followed by espresso throughout the day), that he hated butternut squash, and was secretly fond of *Grey's Anatomy*.

'It's Patrick Dempsey's hair,' he admitted as Storm caught him engrossed in an episode. 'It's so thick and beautiful, it should have its own show.'

As for Nico, he found everything Storm did enchanting. The way she liked to eat satsumas in bed, carried dental floss in her bag, using it after every meal, and had a crush on all the boys in One Direction.

Nico wanted a life with this woman, and already knew he had fallen head over heels in love with her. From the few details he'd learned about Dermot though, and how badly he appeared to have treated Storm, Nico knew he had to tread carefully. He wanted to prove his feelings

for her. Whizzing up a homemade pesto sauce for dinner one night, he looked at Storm who sat in her usual place opposite him.

'So I was thinking, why don't I drive you to Brighton some time and join you for lunch with Sally and Jeff? We could eat in my restaurant, that way it's neutral ground for you both,' he suggested casually.

'Really?' Storm stared at him in amazement, surprised that he was volunteering to get involved in her family life. With Dermot she'd got used to doing things on her own, and on the rare occasions he could tear himself away from work he'd frequently moaned about having a million and one other things to be doing – it had to be said, she appreciated the difference. But old habits were hard to break and she was just about to open her mouth and tell Nico that she was fine and could manage by herself when he leaned across the breakfast bar and silenced her with a kiss.

'I know you were about to tell me thanks but no thanks, but for once stop trying to be so independent and let someone help you. I want to meet your mum, and I want to be there for you.'

'OK then.' She smiled, won over by his thoughtfulness. It had been a long time since she'd felt cared for, and she realised just how close she and Nico had become in a short space of time. Which was why it pained her that she had kept some huge secrets from him, such as the fact she wasn't a hospitality student and had never been an air hostess.

More than anything she wanted to tell him she was really a showbiz reporter who had been asked to entrap him,

but she knew if she did then the spell would be broken. Storm felt terrible about deceiving him. The only thing that stopped her from telling him was knowing that what she was doing was the best way to protect him, since she had no intention of selling him out.

But all too soon Monday morning arrived and their magical week was over. Not only was Storm due back at work, or college as Nico assumed, but he himself had to return to his flagship restaurant. He was recruiting a new sous-chef and always made sure he did the hiring and firing personally.

'Don't look so sad.' He smiled, catching sight of Storm's expression as she layered on her mascara in the bathroom mirror.

'I'm not sad,' she said, doing her best to sound as if she wasn't bothered.

Nico snorted. 'Yeah, right! Never play poker, Storm, your face would give you away every time.'

Doing her best to hide a smile, she eyeballed him in the mirror. 'So you're not bothered our week together is over?'

'Is that all I am to you?' He laughed, slipping his arms around her waist and kissing her neck. 'Some irresistible boy toy you can put down after a week.'

'I hate to break it to you but you're in your mid-thirties so you're less of a boy toy and more of a man plaything.'

'Hah! Well, if that's all I am to you then I'd better make sure I leave you satisfied for the day.'

Pushing her up against the bathroom door, Nico unbuttoned her blouse and started kissing and sucking her breasts.

229

'I'm going to be late,' she protested weakly.

'Who cares? Storm, you drive me wild,' he said, expertly tweaking her nipple in a way he knew she loved. After this she would be smiling for the rest of the day.

'You're a sight for sore eyes.' Chelsea smiled as she saw Storm sashay across the room holding two giant cups of coffee. 'Glad to be back?' she asked, gratefully taking the paper cup Storm offered her.

'What do you think?' she sighed, throwing her bag on the desk and taking a long swig of coffee.

'Yeah, I bet it sucks to get back to reality.'

Storm glanced at her friend, unsure if she was taking the piss. 'Hey, I mean it.' Chelsea insisted. 'Adam's gone back to LA now, meaning it's just me, and my Rampant Rabbit for company on a nightly basis.'

'Oh, babe! TMI!' Storm shuddered. 'How was lover boy then?'

'Brilliant.' Chelsea smiled. 'We got on amazingly well all week and he's even asked me to move in with him.'

Shocked, Storm choked on her coffee.

'What did you say? You've only known him five minutes.'

'Talk about judgey,' Chelsea grumbled. 'Anyway, for your information, I may be loved up but I'm not totally stupid. I told him it's far too early for anything like that.'

'Thank God. What did he expect you to do about your career anyway?'

'Well, exactly,' Chelsea replied. 'I told him it would be a nightmare trying to get a job in the States, but he reckons he knows people and could wangle something.'

'Or he could come over here in a few months' time and you could try living together on a trial basis before you commit to something more serious,' Storm put in sensibly.

'Who died and made you the relationships guru?'

'Nobody. I'm just saying, you've got a life here and he shouldn't expect you to drop everything.'

'It's not like that,' Chelsea protested. 'Look, I know it's early days but everything feels so right with him. I can't put my finger on it, it just feels easy.'

Catching the flicker of emotion that crossed her friend's face, Storm softened.

'I'm sorry. I just worry about you, that's all.'

'Right back at you. How's it all going with Nico anyway? Still shagging for Italy?'

Storm chuckled. 'Something like that. God, Chelsea, I think I've really fallen for him. I hate us being apart. I want to be with him all the time, and I'm pretty sure he feels the same way. He's even offered to come with me to meet Sally and Jeff.'

Chelsea raised an eyebrow as she took another sip of coffee. 'Wow! That is serious. And I take it he's still got no idea who you are or what your job really is?'

Storm frowned. 'None at all. And I hate all this deception. I've already come close to blurting out the truth about my job and what I've been asked to do. The only thing that's stopping me is the worry about what will happen if I don't pretend I'm doing the job. I have to protect him.'

'I know, babe. I haven't said a word, though that slimebag Dermot's been round here sniffing for dirt like a

231

fly around shit. That bastard would sell his own granny if he thought it would help him get ahead.'

Storm considered what Chelsea had said. She hadn't told her friend that he was still bombarding her with text messages urging her to give their relationship another go. Last week he'd sent her a load more, asking how she was, begging forgiveness and telling her Sabrina meant nothing to him. Obviously Storm hadn't answered, but she was worried he'd guessed Chelsea had been lying about her being ill. Knowing him, he'd have turned up at the flat while Chelsea was at work and realised she wasn't there. He was starting to really get to her, his behaviour was seriously unhinged, so she had started to keep a log of all his weird behaviour in case things got out of hand.

Spotting Storm across the office, Dermot wasted no time in coming over to her 'Ah, you look gorgeous as ever, pet. No one would ever guess you'd been ill for the last week. Hope you don't mind my asking, but now you're better when are you planning on seeing Nico? It would be great to get something on him soon.'

Storm eyeballed him. 'I've just got in, Dermot. I'll keep you posted.'

'And I've got a couple of jobs I need covering this week that'll keep Storm pretty busy, but I'm sure she'll fit you in when she can,' Chelsea added sweetly.

Dermot walked around to the back of Storm's chair and whispered in her ear menacingly.

'How was Bath, Storm?'

Storm dropped her pen and turned her head in shock to

232

face him. How would he know she'd been there? Had he followed her to Bath? 'What do you mean?'

'Nothing,' he replied smoothly. 'Now, to business. I know you're already screwing the chef, but I meant what I said. If you don't give us a story soon then I'll print what I've got, and believe me, I think it will be enough. *Capisce*?'

Anger pulsed through her veins. She stood up so she could look him in the eye. 'If anyone should be issuing threats, dickhead, it's me . . . or have you forgotten all those text messages you sent me last week, telling me it was over with Sabrina and you'd never stopped loving me? If you don't leave me alone and let me deal with this in my own way, I'll tell her everything. And while I'm about it, I'll go straight to Human Resources and have you for sexual harassment.'

'You wouldn't dare,' Dermot hissed.

'Try me. And FYI, even Italians don't say *capisce*, you loser. Now fuck off back under your rock.'

'What a dick! I'm glad you told him where to go,' Chelsea said as Dermot stalked moodily back to his desk.

Groaning, Storm sat down. She didn't know how much more of him she could take. How many other people had to put up with seeing their exes on a daily basis? Not many, she bet. Glancing at her phone, ready to text Nico, she saw she already had a missed call from him along with a voicemail.

Dialling her mailbox, she couldn't help smiling as she heard his chocolatey tones flooding into her ear.

'I just called to see how your day's going and to tell you I miss you,' he said. 'Also, I wanted to check you

were still coming over later. Your man plaything is eager to please.'

Laughing, Storm put the phone down.

'I take it all is well in paradise then?' Chelsea asked.

'Never been better,' Storm replied dreamily.

The rest of the week passed in a blur. Storm spent her days interviewing and writing, then at night would rush home to Nico and make love until the small hours. All too soon Friday arrived and Storm was over the moon – for two days it would be just her and Nico. OK, so she'd promised her mum she'd meet her for lunch on Saturday but that wouldn't take long, then Storm would have Nico all to herself again.

But on Saturday morning she woke up in his luxurious bed with a heavy ache in her heart. Not only were they driving down to Brighton for lunch today with Sally and Jeff, but Nico had announced when she got in from work last night that he was heading to Italy for a fortnight on Monday, to do some research on street food for his next TV show. The idea of fourteen days without him in her life seemed like torture to Storm. Determined to shut the world out for a little while longer, she buried her face in her pillow.

'Hey! Cheer up,' Nico whispered, snaking his arm around her waist and pulling her close. 'I won't be away long.'

'I know.' Storm sighed. 'I just don't know what I'll do without you.'

Nico lightly ran his palm over her face, then kissed her gently on the mouth.

'Who said anything about you having to do without me? It's only a fortnight. Besides, there's such a thing as phone sex, you know.'

With that he inched himself under the covers, trailing kisses softly down Storm's back.

'Giving me an idea of what I'll be missing, are you?' she gasped.

'Something like that,' he whispered as he slipped his hand between her legs, bringing her quickly to a shuddering orgasm.

By the time they finally got up, they were running dangerously late to meet Sally and Jeff so skipped breakfast.

'I warn you, I'm moody when I'm hungry,' Storm growled as she settled herself into the passenger seat of Nico's Range Rover.

Sliding his key into the ignition, Nico snorted. 'I thought I left you more than satisfied this morning, Ms Saunders!'

Storm raised an eyebrow. Cheeky bastard. But before she could come out with any quip in return, Nico reached into the back seat and pulled out a picnic hamper.

'Gorgeous Storm, I know you better than you realise, and the one thing I've picked up on is the fact you're no good when you're hungry, so I threw together a simple breakfast picnic for you this morning.'

Staring at the wicker basket Nico had placed on her lap, Storm was lost for words. 'I don't know what to say. Nobody has ever been this thoughtful before.'

'Take a look inside,' he urged, unfastening the leather straps to reveal a fresh fruit salad, hunk of ham, bread, a flask of coffee and even *Panettone*.

'You made all this for me?' Storm was amazed.

'Of course,' Nico whispered, as he stroked her face. 'When will you realise, Storm, I would do anything for you.'

Looking into his eyes, she felt a lump come into her throat. This had to be the most romantic thing anyone had ever done for her. How had she got so lucky, finding the most perfect man in the world?

When they finally arrived in Brighton, and Nico had smoothly parked the Range Rover near Churchill Square, Storm's palms felt sweaty. She hadn't been back since moving to London and she felt strangely nervous.

Sensing Storm's anguish, Nico reached for her hand and together they strolled towards his restaurant. Sally and someone Storm assumed was Jeff were waiting outside.

'Sally,' she said, plastering on a fake smile and kissing her mother lightly on the cheek. 'You should have waited inside.'

Her mum, dressed in a long floral skirt and plain white t-shirt, looked uncomfortable loitering on the pavement, as did Jeff, who was standing just behind her looking incredibly smart in dark trousers, white shirt and navy blazer.

'Oh, you know me, love. It didn't seem right when we hadn't booked a table,' she said, shuffling from foot to foot.

Storm tried to refrain from rolling her eyes. When she'd rung Sally earlier that week to suggest meeting for lunch her mother hadn't been keen on eating at Nico's restaurant, arguing it was a bit fancy for her and Jeff.

But Storm had insisted it was Nico's treat, and Sally had reluctantly agreed.

Now Storm wondered if it had been a good idea to force the issue. Thank God for Nico, who swung into action. He kissed Sally warmly on each cheek, then pumped Jeff's hand furiously. 'Such a pleasure to meet you both. Storm and I have both been looking forward to this very much. Now, please, let's go inside, eat and enjoy ourselves.'

As Nico opened the door for her mother and boyfriend, Storm shook her head in amazement. If he ever fancied a career change, he could enter the diplomatic service, she thought.

Surprisingly, it turned out to be a good lunch. After her initial nerves had settled, Storm took the time to get to know Jeff and was delighted to discover he was a lovely bloke, kind, gentle and warm, with lots of funny stories about his job as a gardener, and the bingo hall where he and Sally had met.

'We'd been friends for years,' he told her. 'And one day, when the girl behind the bar told me they'd run out of chicken and chips, your mother overheard and generously offered to let me have her plate.'

''Course he didn't take them,' Sally chuckled.

'What sort of bloke would I be if I took a woman's chicken and chips, eh?'

'So you two fell in love over . . . what is the dish you say? A bird in a basket?' Nico asked.

The whole table fell about laughing at his mistake. 'It's chicken in a basket,' Sally corrected him.

'A bird in a basket is a very different thing,' Jeff put in. 'But, yes, I think that is how we fell in love.'

'Certainly is.' Sally beamed, giving him a peck on the cheek.

Storm was very surprised by the change in her mother. She seemed so different, relaxed and happy. Storm hadn't seen this side of Sally since before Alan died. Perhaps Jeff was just the tonic her mother needed.

'Am I right in thinking you used to work there, Storm?' Jeff asked, interrupting her thoughts.

'Did you?' Nico looked amused. 'Were you the one who shouted "two fat ladies" and "Kelly's eye"?'

'Not quite, I was just an assistant. I used to stand there with a microphone and when someone called House, I'd run over and read the numbers.' She laughed. 'When I was bored I used to try making up stupid rhymes for the numbers. Don't think many people found it very funny, though.'

Sally tutted. 'Stop putting yourself down. You worked very hard, just as you do now. What you've achieved at work has been incredible . . .'

Before her mother could say anything else, Storm kicked her furiously under the table, reminding her to keep her mouth shut. When Storm had spoken to Sally earlier in the week, she'd explained she had a new boyfriend, and after Sally had got over the shock of her daughter dating a TV chef, Storm had revealed the fact that Nico didn't know what she did for a living.

Listening to herself explain, Storm felt it made their whole relationship sound like a sham, but her mother had

238

agreed not to say anything. Keen to cover her mistake, Sally quickly changed the subject.

'So tell me about your family, Nico. What do they do?' she enquired.

'My parents live in a village on the east coast of Italy. My father is a train driver, my mother runs a small café.'

'And is that where you get your love of cookery from?'

'I think so. My mother and I are very close. She passed her skills on to me from a young age, and it helped that my sisters had no interest in cooking at all. For years it was just me and my *mamma* together, and later I helped her when I could in the café. She helped to fire my passion for cooking. I thank God I was blessed with a loving and happy family.'

As Sally choked on her mineral water, Storm turned bright red while Nico looked horrified as he realised he'd been tactless, considering Sally and Storm's troubled past. He was about to open his mouth and try to smooth things over, when Jeff reached across the table and patted his hand.

'Don't worry, lad. We know you didn't mean anything by that.'

Storm caught Jeff's eye and gratefully mouthed 'thank you'.

Thankfully the rest of the meal passed without incident. After rounding off lunch with a calorific helping of delicious *tiramisù*, they went for a walk along the seafront.

Nico had Sally eating out of the palm of his hand, showing an interest in her and her life that Dermot had never done, giving Storm the opportunity to chat to Jeff. She had been unsure what to expect, but he was easy to

talk to and chatted about his work and his two sons, who had grown up and left home.

They were nearing the Pier when Jeff stopped walking and turned to her. 'Can I be frank with you, Storm?'

'Sure,' she said, hesitantly, worried about what was coming next.

'I just want to say I know that after your dad's death, along with everything you and Sally have been through over the years, it can't have been easy for you to come here today, but both Sally and I appreciate it.'

'Well, thanks . . .' she began, before Jeff cut her off.

'I just want to say I know this is difficult, but I love your mother and we're serious about each other. I realise you and she have had your issues, and I understand why. Heaven only knows how I would have felt if I had been the one who had to cope with bringing up two kids and dealing with a drunk for a mother, but I can see why Sally is so proud of you. It's important to me you realise that while I will never, ever try to replace your father, if ever you need someone to talk to . . . you know, a bloke's opinion sort of thing . . . then I'm here for you.'

Tears sprang into Storm's eyes. Jeff's words had unexpectedly moved her. She hadn't wanted to like him, if she was being honest, and had been looking forward to a good old-fashioned moan in the car with Nico on the way back about what a dick her mother seemed to have found, but incredibly she had taken to Jeff from the moment they'd met. He seemed to get her relationship with Sally, and didn't want to push her or try and get her to accept him as a daddy figure either.

Wiping tears from her eyes, she cocked her head to one side and looked at him. 'You're not what I expected. But you know what? I think I'm going to like you.'

Out of the corner of her eye, she could see Nico and Sally waiting for them to catch up. Struck by an unexpected pang of emotion, Storm linked her arm through Jeff's. 'We'd better hurry up before those two get sick of waiting for us.'

'Well, that went well!' Nico exclaimed as they drove along the A23 towards London.

'It did,' she replied. 'I really liked Jeff.'

'And I thought your mother seemed nice,' Nico put in carefully.

Storm thought for a moment. 'Yeah, she's OK. I'm glad she's met Jeff. It's like the old mother I knew and loved as a kid has come back.'

'How do you mean?'

'Well, normally, Sally's so keen to please and make up for lost time that she totally overdoes the perfect mother act. It was nice to see her relaxed and having a laugh for a change.'

'Maybe Jeff isn't the big bad wolf you thought he was going to be.'

Storm laughed. 'No, I definitely don't think he's the big bad wolf. If anything I think he's bloody Prince Charming, putting up with Sally.'

'He does really seem to love her,' Nico mused. 'And your mum really seems to love you.'

Storm groaned. 'What did she say to you once I was out of earshot?'

241

'That's between me and her,' Nico said, tapping his nose. 'But she loves you, Storm.' His voice softened. 'And all she wants is to make up for the past. She's so proud of you. As am I. I told her she must have done something right because you are perfect. Perfect for me.'

Storm looked over at him, feeling completely dumbstruck. She knew she had fallen for Nico, and she'd hoped he felt the same, but hadn't expected this now. She wanted to fling her arms around him and never let him go.

Nico cleared his throat and looked back at her, his expression serious. 'So, I was thinking, now might be a good time to talk to Francesca about publicly revealing the truth about our relationship.'

Storm gasped in shock. 'What? Why?'

'Because I've fallen in love with you, Storm. I've never felt like this before, and I know I never want to lose you.'

Chapter Fourteen

Watching Nico sling his black leather wash bag into his expertly packed Louis Vuitton suitcase, Storm felt a twinge of sadness. Since the moment they'd got back from Brighton she'd been dreading this parting. She could have kicked herself for it as well. Christ, this wasn't who she was. She didn't need some bloke to complete her. But Storm had a horrible feeling that life without Nico was going to feel very empty indeed.

But if she was honest, his departure wasn't the only thing on her mind. Over the weekend she had been unable to switch off from work. The previous week she'd gone to Claridge's to interview a soap star who had just been killed off and the chat had gone better than anticipated. The star had been a hugely popular character, and now had her sights set firmly on Hollywood. But halfway through the interview Storm got her to admit life wasn't quite as peachy as it seemed.

The actress wasn't sure she was going to like LA. Worse

than that, she was worried about what was going to happen with her boyfriend, a fellow soap star. She didn't trust him as it turned out he'd cheated on her with a lap dancer the year before last. Storm had been nothing but sympathetic, but came away from the interview with a heavy heart. Other people's dirty washing wasn't news, and it wasn't anyone else's business either. She'd written up the interview as sympathetically as possible, but when Miles had praised her for a job well done, and told her it would make the front page on Sunday, she hadn't felt any sense of achievement. In fact she felt as if she'd betrayed a confidence. It wasn't the first time she'd felt it, but this time it was stronger than before, and finally she knew what she needed to do.

The past couple of weeks, spent largely away from the office with a man she knew she loved, had given Storm time to think. She realised that although she loved journalism, the dream of becoming a showbiz reporter was in fact turning into a nightmare. The events the paper asked her to cover weren't glamorous or newsworthy. In fact, she was discovering the job of showbiz reporter was actually quite grubby, pretending to be a swinger one minute and embroiled in a honey trap the next. It wasn't what she'd thought the job would entail.

OK, she was delighted to have been given a promotion, but all this deception and spilling other people's secrets wasn't her. Not only that but it occurred to her that she should never have taken the job after what happened with Carly. If anything should have put her off, that should. Especially as she had to work with Dermot. She felt as if she'd profited from a friend's downfall, and that was out of order. Now she

knew she had to make things right between her and Nico, so they could enjoy a trusting and happy future.

She couldn't believe she was thinking it but she wished more than anything she could go back to covering council meetings and planning hearings, reporting on things that really mattered to people. She just couldn't carry on in showbiz any more and she vowed to talk to Chelsea and Miles about it and ask to be transferred to features. Once she had a new position, she would be able to tell Nico the truth and warn him the press were after him. Perhaps she could encourage him to talk to his lawyer and take out one of those super injunctions.

'I promise I'll call you as soon as I land,' said Nico, interrupting her thoughts.

'OK, but don't stress if you can't,' she said, doing her best to sound casual even though her heart was breaking into a million pieces at the thought of even one night away from him. Looking up into his face, she memorised every detail of it: the slope of his Roman nose, the thickness of his brows, the mole on his left cheek. All ready to store in her own personal memory library, to call up at a moment's notice when her desperation at not seeing him got too much for her.

Pulling Storm close to him, he cupped her face in his hands. 'It's no stress, I want to. When are you going to realise you're never getting rid of me?

'Can I have that in writing?'

'You can have it any way you want it.' He smiled, kissing her with such force, Storm was left in no doubt of how he felt.

'How about I have you now?' she replied, running her hand down his chest and slipping it into his boxers.

'You're a wicked woman, Storm Saunders,' he murmured, already pushing up her pencil skirt.

Storm had toyed with the idea of not going into work and playing hookey all day. The thought of trudging into the office and pretending to feel excited about some pointless celebrity interview before a talk about Nico with Dermot and Miles made her feel sick. She thought she could go shopping instead, have a bath, read a book . . . but finally realised that skiving wasn't the solution. She'd made up her mind about her job and wouldn't rest until she'd spoken to Chelsea and Miles about it.

Walking into the office with two extra-large coffees for her and Chelsea, Storm got straight to the point.

'I need to talk to you,' she said, tracking down her boss by the photocopier.

'Sure. Is here OK?'

Storm shook her head. 'Can we go somewhere more private, please?'

Chelsea nodded and they both walked through the double doors towards the lifts. Once they were outside in the fresh air, Storm couldn't hold back.

'I can't do this any more, Chelsea. This job isn't me.'

'What do you mean, babe?' she asked gently.

Storm hung her head, tears springing to her eyes. 'I don't want to let you down, Chelsea, you're my friend and you've been so good to me, but I don't want to be a showbiz reporter any more. I can't hack it. Swingers, honey traps,

lies. I'm turning into someone I don't recognise, and I don't like what I see.'

Chelsea bit her lip as she pulled her friend in for a hug. 'Don't be daft, babe, I'm the one who should feel guilty. You've been looking downbeat and sad for week. I thought it was because Nico was off for a couple of weeks but I should have realised it was more than that. I may only have known you a few months, but I know you're not the kind of girl who puts her life on hold the minute you get a new bloke.'

Storm pulled away and smiled sheepishly at Chelsea. 'Not my style, hon.'

'I know. And you know what? No job's worth feeling like this for. You've been put through more than your fair share of shit here and that's out of order. I should have done more to help, so let me help you now. What do you need from me?'

'I want to be transferred to features. It's nothing personal, I love working for you, Chelsea, but this isn't what I want . . . which is terrifying because for the last twenty years being a showbiz journo has been my dream.'

Chelsea gave her friend a rueful smile. 'I understand, Storm. Please, babe, don't worry about this any more. Let me see what I can do.'

Storm shook her head. 'You've done more than enough for me, Chelsea, I'll talk to Miles myself. I need him to understand that I'm not cut throat enough for this life. The press has cost me one best friend, I can't afford to let it wreak any more havoc in my personal life.'

But Chelsea was insistent. 'As your boss, I'm asking you

to let me talk to Miles and see what I can sort out. You can speak to him yourself later, but trust me, this will be a lot easier for him to deal with coming from me. I know Miles of old, and I understand exactly how to handle him.'

As Storm let out a sigh of relief, Chelsea brightened. 'Now, do you reckon I can get you to edit some freelance copy for me while you're still here? A five-year-old could have done better, which is surprising because I think this woman actually got her five-year-old daughter to write it.'

Storm laughed in spite of herself. ''Course I can Thanks, Chelsea.'

Hailing a black cab, Nico pulled open the door, told the driver to take him to Heathrow as fast as he could and hauled his luggage on to the seat beside him. He was running seriously late! If he missed this flight he'd be in trouble. He was meeting some of the TV crew in Rome and had a feeling his producer wouldn't be too forgiving if he was made to wait for hours until Nico got on the next plane, even if he did have a good excuse.

At the thought of Storm a smile played around Nico's lips. Their morning together had been amazing, and he knew that if he did miss his flight it would all have been worth it. Storm was incredible, and there was nothing he wouldn't do for her. He couldn't put his finger on what it was about her but he just couldn't get enough of her. She hadn't been the only one with sad eyes that morning. In fact, half the reason he'd initiated sex was because he'd felt himself on the verge of tears and had wanted to lose himself in her.

Still, they would be apart for only two weeks, it would pass in a flash, he told himself. And there was always phone sex, as he'd mentioned to Storm on more than one occasion. He had a feeling she'd thought he was joking, but when he checked into his hotel that evening it might be time to let her know he was deadly serious. He smiled at the thought. Everything about Storm took his breath away, in bed and out, it all felt so right and he was overwhelmingly grateful to Francesca for encouraging him to follow his heart.

Smiling, Nico allowed himself a moment to catch his breath. He looked out of the window as the cab sped through west London before the city gave way to the urban sprawl that led to one of the world's busiest airports. Nico liked flying, and enjoyed the feeling of constantly moving, it kept his overactive mind engaged. Taxi journeys, however, he wasn't too keen on, and found it hard to settle in traffic.

Spotting a discarded paper on the seat next to him, Nico idly reached for it and flicked through the sports section. He made a point of never reading the paper itself but on the brief occasions he did glance at the tabloids, he usually only looked at the sports section to find out how his beloved Lazio were faring.

Ten minutes later he was bored. Bad enough the paper was a day old, but football season had only just begun and there wasn't much to report yet. The rest of the news about cricket, horse racing and darts didn't appeal either. Darts, he mused. Yet another crazy English custom he didn't think he'd ever understand. He threw the paper back on to the seat, but glancing down, something on the front page

gave him a start. Picking up the copy of the *Herald*, Nico's hands started to shake as he stared at it in disbelief.

The front page carried a story about an ex-soap star's betrayal, but that wasn't what bothered him. It was the by-line next to the headline: *By Storm Saunders*. Could this really be by his beloved girlfriend? After all, the name Storm wasn't common. But surely there had to be a mistake? Storm was an airline stewardess. A student. But according to this she was also a reporter. What was going on?

Storm was doing her best, trying to inject some life into a particularly bad piece of freelance copy, when she heard her mobile ring.

Peering at the screen, she couldn't help smiling as she saw Nico's name flash up.

'Hello, gorgeous. Missing me already?'

'How could you?' Rather than the warm, soothing voice she'd expected to hear, Nico's tone was ice cold.

Storm was gripped by fear. 'How could I what?'

'Don't play me for a fool. How could you lie to me like that? I've just seen yesterday's paper with your fucking story on the front. Did you really think I wouldn't find out, Storm?'

Dread coursed through her body as she felt her entire world come crashing down around her. The last thing she'd wanted was for Nico to find out like this. She'd pictured breaking the news to him when they were in bed, maybe after a leisurely breakfast once she'd got her transfer to features. She'd expected him to be a bit hurt that she hadn't told him the truth straightaway, but once

she'd made him understand her reasons for keeping her job from him, he would understand. Stupid as it sounded she hadn't factored in the possibility of Nico seeing one of her stories. He'd told her he didn't read English newspapers, and most people never registered journalists' by-lines, so what were the chances?

'Please, Nico, let me explain . . .'

'Explain? That's the best joke I've heard all year!' snarled Nico, cutting her off. 'Let me guess. You and your journalist friends thought it was funny to dupe me into believing you were an air hostess so you could dig up all the dirt you could on me. Well, you got lucky, didn't you, sweetheart? Bet you never thought you'd get wind of a juicy story like mine.'

'No, Nico, please! It wasn't like that . . .' she began.

'I bet all that stuff with Carly was part of it as well,' he continued. 'I trusted you. I thought we were going to build a life together, to think I was actually stupid enough to fall in love with you. Shit! Scum like you make me sick.'

Hearing Nico use the past tense, tears flooded Storm's eyes. This couldn't be over, she had to make him understand.

'Nico, I know you're upset, but you've got to listen to me.'

But he wasn't interested in hearing anything Storm had to say.

'I thought you understood . . . I hate journalists and paps. They're like parasites, feeding off my life.' By now Nico's voice had taken on a cruel edge that Storm had never heard in it before. Gone were the chocolatey tones that made her feel loved and protected. 'I thought I'd seen

251

it all until I met you, but you've stooped to a new low. I may have misled people about my relationship, but I've never tricked someone into loving me and fucked them under false pretences. You are worse than a whore, Storm Saunders. I never want to speak to you again.'

He hung up the phone and Storm raced from her desk and bolted to the ladies where she threw up the contents of her breakfast. It felt as though her heart was shattering into a million pieces, she had never been in so much pain. Nico had said some terrible things, labelling her worse than a whore. If it had been anyone else she would have hoped for a chance to explain, but she had always known how Nico felt about the press. The fact he had been lied to didn't help, and the worst thing of all was that she had nobody to blame but herself. It was time to face facts. Once again she'd destroyed her chance of happiness with someone she loved.

In the end Nico did miss his flight to Rome, and the one after that too. He'd been so angry after speaking to Storm he couldn't face being cooped up on a plane and had paced up and down the airport, not knowing what to do with himself.

Eventually he'd realised there was only one other person who would understand and called Francesca. She'd been as stunned as Nico to learn the truth, but was upset to learn he hadn't given Storm the chance to defend herself.

'I agree, Nico, that what she has done is terrible, but there must be some mistake here. You should have let her give you her side of the story.'

'What? So she could spin me more lies,' he spat. 'Christ, Francesca, she's already got more than she bargained for from us, and to think I trusted her! I can't believe I was so stupid.'

'You weren't stupid and I don't think you were wrong to trust Storm either. She loves you, Nico, that much I am sure of,' Francesca said carefully.

He laughed angrily. 'You're a bigger fool than I am if you believe Storm ever loved me. The only things that girl loves are herself and her career. We're just two more victims along the way.'

Sinking on to a nearby bench, he sat there for a moment allowing the enormity of his discovery to sink in. It seemed hard to believe that just a couple of hours ago he had been ridiculously happy and in love. For a moment he wished he hadn't ever seen that newspaper and had gone to Rome as planned. But he would only have been living a lie, something he was sick and tired of doing.

'I have to go. I just wanted to warn you there's every chance the press will be sniffing around you and Paula. I want you to know I'm sorry, Francesca. I was wrong to believe there could be any passion in my life other than in the kitchen. From now on that's where I'll focus my energies.'

As Nico hung up, he realised there was nothing Francesca could say or do to change his mind. He'd been betrayed in the worst way possible. As he headed to the flight gate, all he wanted now was the chance to heal.

Once Storm had thrown up she rinsed her mouth out with cold water and splashed her face. Then she returned to the

office where she found Chelsea and told her exactly what had happened. Chelsea was too shocked to come up with any of her usual quips. Instead she listened in disbelief as the words tumbled from Storm's mouth.

'I'm sure he's just upset. Once he's calmed down, he'll give you the chance to explain,' Chelsea told her.

'No, he won't,' replied Storm, shaking her head. 'You didn't hear him, Chelsea, he was so bitter and angry. Nico never wants to see me again, let alone give me the chance to explain.'

Storm looked around her. Pap shots of various celebrities lined the walls, along with a planner and tear-sheets of scoops they were particularly proud of. It all seemed so meaningless now. To think this stupid office was once her idea of a dream come true was crazy. It had brought her nothing but trouble. She felt winded, as if all the stuffing had been knocked out of her. How could she ever have believed in a happy ending?

'I really don't think that's true,' Chelsea continued. 'I think you should just give him time. Why don't you let me try and talk to him in a couple of days? I can put your side of the story across and get him to talk to you.'

Storm shook her head. 'Please don't. I've caused Nico enough trouble for one lifetime, I don't want to upset him any more. I've just got to accept it's over. Just as I have to accept I don't belong at the *Herald* any more.'

Reaching for her bag, Storm stuffed her notepad and pen inside then cleared out her drawer. Aside from a spare pack of tights and some mints, she didn't have many belongings at work, preferring to keep things minimal.

'Where are you going?' Chelsea asked as Storm stood up and pulled on her coat.

'To do something I should have done long ago. I'm quitting.'

'Don't be daft!' Chelsea gasped. 'Let me talk to Miles about that transfer to features, he won't want to lose you.'

Storm walked over to Chelsea and hugged her tight. 'You've been brilliant, a better friend than I could ever have hoped for, and I'm going to miss you. But my mind's made up. I don't belong at this paper or in London.'

'Where are you going to go?' Chelsea wailed.

Storm pulled away and looked her friend in the eye. 'I'll be fine. I just need some space to figure out what I'm going to do next.'

As expected her resignation hadn't gone well. Miles had begged her to reconsider, mentioned a pay rise, and when that didn't work he brought out the big guns.

'This is deeply unprofessional, Storm, I expected better.'

But she was in no mood for Miles's bullying. 'Just as well I don't want to work in journalism any more then, isn't it?'

Life at the *Herald* had left a bitter taste in her mouth. She worried what she'd turn into if she didn't get out while she could.

'I'm sorry, Miles, but my mind's made up. I want to leave immediately.'

He looked defeated. He could see Storm was serious but wouldn't give her the satisfaction of knowing how much her departure would hurt him personally. 'Just as well I want you out now then, isn't it? We don't need people like

255

you cluttering up the place. But let me be quite clear with you, Storm. You will regret this decision and you will come to me begging for your job back.'

'I don't think so,' she said quietly, before racing out of the office and returning to Chelsea's apartment for the final time. There she stuffed a few things into a suitcase and scribbled a note to her flatmate.

Will be back for the rest soon. Thanks for everything! Sxxxxxx

By the front door she looked around the place she'd called home for the last few months, then banged the door shut behind her. She flagged down a passing cab and threw herself inside, desperate to get out of London as soon as possible.

'Where to, love?' the cabbie asked.

'Victoria station, please,' she replied, letting out a sigh of relief as the London streets whizzed past her.

When she'd woken up the day had been sunny and warm. Now the weather had turned and, despite the fact it was only mid September, the afternoon had taken a decidedly wintry turn. Like so many others before her, Storm realised she'd come to London full of hopes of a brighter future, only to have her dreams crushed.

As the rain lashed down on the cab windows, Storm pulled her parka tightly around her and fished out her mobile. She scrolled through her contacts, paused when she saw Nico's number and deleted it. There was no point in keeping that now, they'd never speak again, it didn't seem right to store his number any more. Instead she found the number of the one person she was sure wouldn't turn her away.

Clicking on the message icon she tapped out a text.

I need a bit of time out. Would it be OK if I stayed with you for a couple of days? x

She received a reply almost instantly.

Course you can. I've got the day off today, let me know what time you're getting here and I'll come and pick you up. x

Twenty minutes later the cab pulled up to Victoria station and Storm rushed inside. Anxiously she scanned the departures screen for the train to Brighton and was delighted to see the next service left in ten minutes. Storm walked determinedly towards the train she hoped would take her away from her pain and misery. Maybe she'd had it wrong all these years and had been looking for love in the wrong places. Perhaps unconditional love began with her mother after all.

Chapter Fifteen

'Another drink, love?' Sally asked brightly. Curled up on her mum's sofa, hands wrapped around a stone cold mug of tea, Storm stared blankly at the TV screen as *Morning Cuppa* blasted through the living room.

'Storm! Did you hear me?' Sally asked, standing in front of the telly, waving her hands in front of her daughter's face. 'Do you want another cup of tea?'

She reluctantly lifted her gaze from the TV and looked at her mother. 'No, thanks. I'm fine.'

'Really? Because you've been hanging on to that mug for over an hour now, and haven't moved a muscle,' Sally exclaimed. Walking over to the sofa, she sat down next to her daughter and took the mug from her hands. 'You've been like this for the past week now and I'm worried about you,' she said carefully. 'You barely eat and have hardly left the house.'

Storm tucked her legs underneath herself and returned her gaze to the telly. These last few days had been a major

role reversal for mother and daughter. From the moment Sally had picked Storm up from the station she'd been brilliant: listening for hours as she sobbed over Nico, not to mention cooking, cleaning and trying to coax Storm out of the house with trips to the cinema or local café. She'd even taken time off work to look after her daughter. Storm had been grateful, and a little surprised. Rushing back to Brighton had seemed like the right thing to do, but Sally's determination to look after her had knocked Storm for six. For the first time in years she was able to see the woman her mother was now, rather than the drunk she used to be. But despite Sally's best efforts to help Storm heal, the idea of getting on with her life was too much for her. Right now all she wanted to do was slob out in her pyjamas, watch telly and drink tea.

'I'm OK, I promise. I'm sorry I'm being a pain but it won't be for long. I'll sort myself out soon.'

But Sally wasn't giving up. 'You're not being a pain, love, but this isn't you. I liked Nico very much, he seemed the perfect match for you, and I know you're hurting, but Storm, if you two are meant to get back together then you will find a way. What I do know is you can't sit here on the sofa day after day. You're a bright and determined girl, you need to start getting your life back on track.'

Storm felt her hackles rise. It was all too much. She couldn't cope with anything at the moment and had been silently sobbing herself to sleep every night, grieving for everything she had lost. 'I just told you, I will soon,' she said, struggling to keep her voice even. 'I need a bit more time first. In case you hadn't noticed my whole life's fallen

259

apart, so it's not surprising if all I want to do is sit around the flat, is it?'

'But it's not like you, Storm,' Sally said gently. 'I'm not saying you haven't had a rough ride, but trust me, wallowing in self-pity will not make you feel better. Today I want you showered and dressed, and as I've got to go back to work, I'd appreciate it if you'd nip to the post office and pay a couple of bills for me.'

Storm looked at her, about to protest, but spotting the heady mix of frustration and concern in her mother's eyes, changed her mind. Storm knew if it hadn't been for Sally she'd have gone under – she owed her.

'OK,' she said, giving Sally a kiss on the cheek as she walked towards the bathroom.

Storm hated to admit it but strolling down Western Road in clean clothes, with her hair washed and brushed, she realised Sally was right – she did feel a lot better. After paying her mum's bills it struck Storm she now had a whole day to fill. As she had finally worked up the courage to leave the flat all by herself she didn't feel much like going back so decided to wander down to the seafront.

Zipping her parka tightly around her to keep out the coastal breeze, Storm strolled past the pubs, art galleries and merry-go-round. She tried to make sense of her life. She had always loved it by the sea, and the sound of the waves crashing against the shore helped focus her mind as she started thinking about the very thing she'd been avoiding over the past seven days – where she went from here. Sally had been more than generous, saying she could stay with her for as long as she wanted, but

Storm knew it wasn't exactly ideal. The flat was tiny, and Jeff, lovely as he was, would understandably want Sally to himself as he'd only just moved in. Storm knew she needed to get her own place, and fast. Thankfully she'd managed to save some money while staying with Chelsea, and had enough for a small deposit and a couple of months' rent, but she would need a job – doing what she wasn't sure.

Anything so long as it wasn't journalism.

Then there was Chelsea. She'd rung and rung Storm every day for the past week to find out how she was doing, and Storm knew she owed her a phone call. Truth was she couldn't face speaking to anyone at the moment. She knew it was cowardly, especially after everything Chelsea had done for her, but she'd sent a quick text earlier that morning letting her know she was OK, in Brighton, and that she'd be in touch soon.

Storm realised as she strode across the beach that she needed to take baby steps if she wanted to move forward. It was time to stop crying and pick herself up. OK, she hadn't expected to have to start life all over again but if that was what it took, then that's what she was going to have to do. Shit happened! If anyone knew that she did. It was time to deal with it, and throwing herself a pity party wasn't going to help.

Passing a beachside coffee shop, Storm ducked inside for a break from the chilly air and ordered herself a latte. Perching on a stool, she looked around her as she waited for the barista to make her drink. This place was only small, with a handful of rustic wooden tables and chairs

and a small fridge by the door filled with freshly made sandwiches and healthy smoothies, but it was surprisingly welcoming. On the counter stood an eye-catching display of chocolate cakes that made Storm's mouth water.

Peering across the counter for a better look at the calorie-busting treats, she caught sight of an open copy of *Hot* magazine and saw two pap shots of Nico in Bari shooting his latest TV show. At the sight of him, laughing along with a group of local schoolchildren who were taking part in the show, Storm felt like she'd been kicked in the stomach, the pain and grief of the way they'd split still so fresh and raw. Pulling the magazine closer to her she scanned the picture, drinking in every last detail. Nico looked just the same as he had when she'd last seen him: happy, vibrant and full of energy. She realised the picture must have been taken recently as he still had a nick on his cheek from where he'd cut himself shaving the morning he was flying out to Italy.

As the memory of their last moments together flashed into her mind, Storm lost control and let out an anguished howl, making the barista spill hot milk all over the wooden countertop, soaking the magazine.

'You all right?' he asked as he frantically mopped up.

Miserably, Storm nodded her head. 'Yes. Sorry, I didn't mean to startle you. Here, let me help you clean up.'

As she dived into her bag for the tissues she always carried, the barista waved away her offers of help. 'Forget it. My fault, not concentrating as usual.' He grinned at her and, pouring some fresh milk into her latte, pushed the steaming mug towards her. 'On the house.'

Storm looked at him in surprise as she wiped away her tears. 'You don't have to do that.'

'I don't, but I want to. Besides, anyone who cries in my café deserves a free coffee.'

'Thank you.' As Storm took a sip she considered him gratefully. He looked to be a couple of years older than her, with curly blond hair, big blue eyes and a sloppy grin. She found she felt strangely relaxed in his company.

'What's making you so unhappy?' he asked.

'I wouldn't know where to start.'

'I know the feeling. Come on, try me.'

Storm shrugged. 'OK. In the past week I've lost my job, my house and my boyfriend.'

The barista raised his eyebrows. 'Ouch!'

'Yep. And now I'm living with my mum, which is great . . .'

'. . . but you don't want to stay there for ever.'

Sheepishly Storm nodded.

'What did you do?'

'I was a journalist. Used to work on the *Post* up until last Christmas when I moved to London and worked on the *Herald* as an entertainment journalist.'

'Wow! You hit the big time.' The barista let out a whistle of appreciation. 'So what happened?'

'To cut a long story short, I decided the job was a bit scummy and I'd sooner be homeless, jobless and penniless than spend another minute of another day turning over celebrities.'

'Ah.' The barista paused before asking his next question. 'And the boyfriend?'

'He was a celebrity I'd been asked to screw over. He found out.'

'Bloody hell. You don't do things by halves. I suppose it's pointless me asking who the celeb boyfriend was?'

Storm shot him a murderous stare. He held up his hands and backed away.

'Fair enough. Well, I reckon today is your lucky day. How do you fancy a job here?'

Storm threw back her head and laughed. 'Do you usually go around offering strangers jobs? Besides, if you knew me, you definitely wouldn't hire me. I'm the clumsiest person I know.'

'Well, I'm hardly God's gift myself, am I?' he said, gesturing to the milk-sodden worktop. 'Come on, you'll be doing me a favour, my last waitress ran off to join the circus. Seriously, it's true.' He grinned, clocking her stare. 'And I'm stuck here on my own all day. It's not rocket science. It's coffee, slicing up cake and working the till.'

Storm paused. It wasn't exactly a natural leap from journalism but maybe that was just what she needed. What did she have to lose?

'You're on! But before I start, I think I should know your name.'

'Ed.' He grinned, sticking out his hand.

'Storm,' she replied, returning his grin.

'Well, you've cheered up since I saw you this morning,' said Sally as she bustled through the front door and saw Storm cooking dinner.

'I got a job.' She grinned while she sliced tomatoes.

'That's great, love!' Sally exclaimed as she kicked off her shoes and threw her coat on the back of a kitchen chair. 'And that smells great too. What is it?'

'Just Bolognese sauce. Thought we'd have pasta tonight.'

'Perfect. Now what about this job?'

'It's in a coffee shop on the seafront. The little one tucked under the arches. I just walked in, and after I'd made the owner spill my coffee, he offered me a job.'

Sally laughed. 'You made him spill a drink! That's a new one. Seriously, though, I'm delighted. This is brilliant news, Storm. When do you start?'

'Thanks.' Storm grinned. 'I start tomorrow. Didn't think there was much point in delaying it. I need to get on with my life so might as well start sooner rather than later.'

'That's my girl.' Sally beamed. 'How about we celebrate with a nice cup of tea?'

Flicking the kettle on, she pulled out two mugs and put a teabag in each. 'I'm so proud of you, Storm. I just want you to know that,' she said, handing her daughter a steaming mug.

'Thanks, Sal. But it's just a job in a coffee shop.' Storm shrugged.

'No, it's more than that,' said Sally seriously. 'You never fail to surprise me. You pick yourself up, refuse to let life defeat you, and who knows where this will lead?'

'Thanks,' replied Storm, getting a bit teary-eyed. She knew she was too old to want her mother to heap praise on her but, she had to admit, it felt nice hearing it.

'Anyway,' said Sally, sensing they were both getting a

bit emotional, 'more importantly, what's this guy you're working with like? Is he fit?'

Storm laughed as she thought about Ed. 'He's really sweet. But he's not my type. Think Justin Bieber before he came over all foul-mouthed and got done for drink driving.'

'Oh, that's a shame. I was hoping you were going to tell me he was just like Harry Styles.'

Storm looked at her mother in surprise. 'What do you know about Harry Styles?'

'I know he likes an older lady.' Sally winked.

As the two women erupted into laughter, Storm thought how nice this was. Cooking in the kitchen with her mother, laughing and drinking tea. She never would have thought it was possible a year ago. It was funny how life changed.

Dermot had barely slept following Storm's resignation, he'd been so angry about losing his story and, if he was honest, worried about his future at the *Herald* too. This scoop had been his lifeline, his chance to show Miles he was talented, but now his stupid cow of an ex had ruined it for him. Concerned, he'd tried to talk to Sabrina about other ways of setting up Nico, but she wasn't interested.

'Just move on,' she had said. 'You used to be full of good ideas, don't get hung up on just the one scoop.'

But moving on was the one thing Dermot couldn't do. He knew there was a story on Nico Alvise somewhere, one that could make his career, he just had to prove it.

'I don't understand how the stupid bitch could allow herself to get caught out like that?' Dermot had raged to Sabrina.

'Because she's talentless and was out of her depth,' replied Sabrina, who in truth had no idea what she herself would have done in that situation.

'And in the meantime where does that leave us?' Dermot moaned.

'Look, Dermot, you've got to let this go,' Sabrina insisted. 'This isn't doing you any good at all. Why is this story so important to you? There are plenty of others out there.'

Dermot fell silent. He couldn't explain why exposing Nico was so important. He just knew he wouldn't be satisfied until he'd revealed the truth about the chef one way or another.

About a week after Storm's departure Dermot still couldn't sleep. Sick of spending his nights tossing and turning until the alarm went off, he decided to kill time by pacing up and down Sabrina's kitchen instead.

Flicking the kettle on, he reached for a mug and teabag and waited for the water to boil. Leaning against the worktop, he realised he was as tightly wound as a coiled spring. He knew going over and over Nico's story in his head wasn't doing him any good, that he was on the verge of becoming obsessed. But throughout his entire career he'd never let a story go, and he wasn't about to start now. There had to be some way of proving Nico was a cheat without using Storm.

As the kettle boiled he made his tea then walked over to the chrome breakfast bar, his eyes resting on Sabrina's mobile. Funny, she had exactly the same fluffy pink case as Storm had. Then it hit him: he'd hack Storm's phone and

267

email. Sure, it was technically frowned upon these days after all those celebrities had wept crocodile tears about invasion of privacy and all that bollocks, but this was different. Storm was his ex, and he was pretty sure that she wouldn't have changed the password to her voicemail. She was always so terrible at remembering security information she wrote all of it down in the back of her diary. This wouldn't be phone hacking, this would be more like liberation of information, he told himself.

Besides he'd already placed a GPS tracker on her phone so he knew where she was at every minute of the day. He'd done it when they split, sure it would help him to wreak revenge on her in some way. When she'd changed numbers, all he'd had to do was sweet talk Becki on reception and he'd had Storm's new digits in a flash. He'd hoped his plan to freak her out with flowers, messages and surprise appearances would send her round the bend, but she'd been surprisingly unfazed by it. He'd show her Dermot Whelan was a man you didn't forget, and what better way to do that than by hacking her phone?

Sitting at the chrome breakfast bar, Dermot reached for his phone and punched in Storm's number. Crossing his fingers, he entered her voicemail password and let out a silent whoop of delight when a disembodied voice told him he had no new messages and several saved messages.

Pulling a pad and pen towards him with his free hand, he started listening to all of Storm's voicemails. The first was a boring message from Sally, thanking Storm for lunch, but the next three were from Nico. Each more or less the same as the other: he missed her, he loved her, the

sex between them was incredible and he couldn't wait until he saw her again.

Dermot's cheeks flamed with excitement. This was the proof he needed that Italian sweetheart Nico Alvise was no more than a cheating bastard. Still, he thought as he listened to the messages again, he was surprised Storm had actually gone to the trouble of sleeping with Nico. He didn't think she would do that for a story. Then, like a bolt from the blue, the reality of the situation hit. Storm hadn't slept with Nico for the scoop, she'd done it because she'd fallen in love with the guy. He'd known it since he saw that pap shot of them together but had told himself it couldn't be true. Hearing Nico's voice, warm with love, he knew there was no way Storm would come back to him. He'd give anything to listen to Nico's messages. In fact, he thought, why didn't he listen to Storm's messages to Nico? All he had to do was press whatever key gave him the message details and the number would be there for him to hack.

Minutes later Dermot had successfully managed to get hold of Nico's number. He checked his watch. It was shortly after 5 a.m. Chances were Nico would still be in bed and his phone on silent – worth trying to hack in now. Trembling, Dermot dialled Nico's number and tried accessing his voicemail, already thinking of various number combinations that might form his password. But, incredibly, Nico didn't have any security set up on his phone! Dermot could hardly believe it. Were these celebrities stupid? They deserved to get hacked if they didn't even try to protect their information.

As a second disembodied voice told him he had one new message and one saved message he waited with bated breath. The saved message was from Storm. She was crying into the phone, begging and pleading with Nico to call her. The message rambled on for ages as she wept about how sorry she was, how much she loved him, how he was her one, and how she would do anything if he would only talk to her. Dermot made a note of every word, ready to use in the future. It was all the proof he needed that Nico was a cheat but curiosity got the better of him as he pressed the right key to listen to the new message. This was from the girlfriend, Francesca.

Nico, please listen to me. You have to talk to Storm. I have never seen you so in love, you two are made for each other just as Paula and I are made for each other. Nico, don't be stubborn. You owe her the chance to explain herself. Please, I just want you to be happy.

Putting the phone down, Dermot was both excited and confused. Why was Nico's partner encouraging him to be with Storm and who the hell was Paula? Dermot knew he had some digging to do, but something told him this story was going to be one hell of a lot bigger than he'd originally thought.

Chapter Sixteen

It was a busy few days for Storm as she got used to life working in a coffee shop. Although she was no stranger to hard work, she'd forgotten how physically demanding being on your feet, rushing around after customers and constantly clearing and tidying, could be. She found she was too busy to think much about Nico or her old life in London. After a day at work in the café, Storm would rush home and fall straight to sleep, too exhausted to cry, then wake up, ready to do it all over again the next day.

The job was exactly what she needed. She got to stare at the sea, drink coffee and eat cakes. She had access to as many free newspapers as she liked, though she did her best to avoid them. Not only was she terrified of seeing more pictures of Nico doing God knows what, but she didn't really feel like seeing Dermot's name in the *Herald* either. Thankfully he'd left her alone since she'd resigned. Now she was no longer in the journalism game, she had stopped being of any use to him whatsoever.

Brighton was turning out to be a great fresh start for her. She had hoped that some of her old friends would have been ready to welcome her back, but it seemed they were still siding with Carly, and just like her former best friend nobody else here was ready to forgive and forget. Not for the first time Storm found herself thanking her lucky stars she'd found Ed. Sweet, lovely, funny Ed. He was like the big brother she had never had. Although they didn't have a lot in common, they spent their days chatting, laughing and joking. Ed was a typical surfer dude, who was relaxed, unambitious and had recently left his beloved St Ives for Brighton after falling in love with the place during a stag do with his mates.

'So why coffee?' Storm asked.

'I own a coffee bar in St Ives. Opening one here as well seemed like the next step, until I realised there was no surf but by then it was too late.' He grinned as he cleaned the expensive cappuccino machine before they opened.

Storm whistled in appreciation. 'I never knew there was so much money to be made in coffee?'

'Pah! Have you never heard of Starbucks?' he teased. 'No, it's not a huge money-spinner, but it's chilled and gives me enough money to fund my dream.'

'Which is?' Storm probed.

'To surf my way around Australia for a year. Catch some of those really big waves.'

'Wow! That sounds amazing.'

'Yeah! But I need to sell a lot more coffee to do that.'

'So what do you do when you need a surf fix?' she asked. 'I mean, Brighton's great, but like you say it's not known for its surfing.'

272

'I go back to Cornwall whenever I know the surf's going to be good, which is probably why my last assistant ran away to the circus!'

'But Cornwall's hours away!'

Ed laughed. 'It is. But I like the chance to get in my Beetle with my surfboard strapped to the top, just me, the open road and the dream of catching the perfect wave. Anyway what about you? What are your dreams?'

Storm continued sweeping the floor as she reflected on Ed's question. For years the answer would have been obvious: editor of a major newspaper or magazine. Now she had no desire to do either and was at a bit of a loss. 'You know what, Ed? I've got no idea any more.'

'Well, sometimes that's good. Means you're more open to whatever new opportunities come your way. Speaking of which, I can give you a hand to move your stuff tonight, if you like?'

Storm looked at him gratefully. She was moving into a studio flat above a newsagent's in town later that day and although she didn't have many belongings she didn't fancy shifting them all by herself. Jeff had offered to give her a hand, but Storm wouldn't hear of it. He'd done more than enough finding her the flat in the first place, never mind getting him to shift heavy luggage when she knew he had a bad back.

Jeff had looked so embarrassed when he'd got in from work a couple of days earlier and asked Storm if she was interested in living in a studio. 'I don't want you thinking you're not welcome here,' he said nervously. 'But a mate of mine has got a little flat, and knew you were staying

with us, so he asked if you might be interested. I've been to see it and it's small but very nice. It needed a bit of redecoration, so I've painted it all bright white to make the most of the space. Other than that it's got all mod cons, and it's right in the heart of town with views of the sea . . . if you crane your neck and stand on one leg!'

Storm had been both surprised and touched that Jeff had gone to so much trouble on her behalf, but couldn't resist teasing him. 'Finally got tired of me cramping your style then?'

'Don't be like that,' Sally said, swatting her daughter's arm as her boyfriend went puce. 'You know Jeff's just trying to help.'

'And you know I'm kidding.' Storm grinned at them both. 'Seriously, you two have been great letting me stay here, but I need my own place and this flat sounds perfect. Thank you!'

After that Sally had gone into maternal overdrive, sorting out bed linen and food ready for Storm to take with her.

'I have moved out before, you know, Sal,' she said as she watched her mother fly around piling things together.

'I know, I know, I just want to help,' she insisted.

Now, as Storm opened the café door, ready to welcome in the first customers, she was surprised to see her mother striding purposefully towards her.

Dressed in jeans, trainers and biker jacket, Sally looked like she meant business.

'You're up early. What are you doing here?' Storm asked. 'Can I get you a coffee?'

'No, thanks love, I can't stop,' Sally replied breathlessly. 'I just wanted to ask you if you'd prefer white or navy towels? There's a sale on in town, and I thought I'd treat you to a few new things – fresh start and all that.'

'You don't have to!' Storm exclaimed, touched that Sally was going to so much trouble. 'I'll sort something out later this week.'

'I don't want you too, Stormy,' her mother protested. 'Let me do this for you.'

Storm said nothing. She knew she had to let Sally get on with it. This was her way of making up for those lost years and she was clearly relishing her second chance to play mum again. Storm found she didn't want to spoil it for her.

'Well, classic white would be lovely – thank you. But I insist you come in and have a coffee on me before hitting the shops. Besides you haven't met Ed yet.'

Not taking no for an answer, Storm hauled Sally inside and sat her at a cosy corner table.

'Ed,' she called to her colleague, who was emptying the bins out the back. 'Come and meet Sally.'

Hands full of sacks of rubbish, Ed appeared with a huge smile on his face. 'Mrs Saunders. Lovely to meet you at last. I'd offer to shake your hand, but as you can see . . .' he said, waving the bags around to make his point.

Right on cue rubbish spilled everywhere, leaving Ed red-faced as he bent down to start picking it all up.

'Please, call me Sally,' she said, leaping up from her chair to help him. 'Mrs Saunders makes me feel very old.'

'Oh, Sal, sit down,' Storm chided, shooing her mum away from the rubbish. 'You'll get your nice coat all grubby.

Besides, me and Ed have got a system going. This happens on an almost daily basis.'

'Please don't tell me you're clumsier than Storm?' Sally chuckled, returning to her seat. 'I don't think the world could stand another one of you chucking tea, coffee and heaven knows whatever else everywhere.'

'I'm afraid so, Sally.' Ed grinned as he shovelled the last of the rubbish back into the bag. 'I make Storm look graceful.'

'Wonders will never cease,' she said in mock amazement as he walked past her to the commercial bins outside, leaving Storm to make her mum's drink.

'Cappuccino, Sally?' she called over her shoulder to her mum, who was now engrossed in the latest copy of *Me Time*.

'Yes, please, love.'

As Storm filled the cappuccino maker with water, she heard the sound of the door opening and a pair of heels click-clacking their way across the flagstone floor.

'Can I get a latte to go and one of those skinny blueberry muffins too, please?'

At the sound of the pure Brighton accent Storm froze. It couldn't be? Not again. With a heavy heart she peeked over the coffee machine and saw it was just who she was terrified of bumping into again – Carly. Even though her head was bent over her smartphone and her blonde curls covered her face, Storm would have known her anywhere.

Taking a deep breath, she emerged from behind the machine and wiped her palms on her black apron.

'Carly, hello,' she said cautiously.

At the sound of her old friend's voice, Carly's head jerked up. She looked shocked.

'Storm! What are you doing here?'

'I work here.'

'You work here?' Carly exclaimed. 'Since when?'

'Since a couple of weeks ago. Things didn't work out for me in London,' she said quietly as she reached for a muffin and placed it in a brown paper bag. 'Did you want the latte and muffin to go?'

'You've got to be kidding me!' Carly spat as she stepped closer to the counter. 'I don't want *anything* from you. In fact, if you're working here, I'm never coming in again. I don't know who you think you are but this is my local coffee shop. You know I only live up the road. You've done this deliberately, just to annoy me. You're well out of order. I'm talking to Ed and getting you fired!'

Sally, who had previously been sitting in the corner minding her own business, leaped straight to her feet.

'Now just you wait a minute, my girl,' she butted in.

'Sally!' said Carly, visibly shocked. 'I didn't see you there.'

'Obviously,' Sally fired back at her. 'Now I know you think you've got the right to lay into Storm but you need to hear a few home truths, Carly. It's time you faced up to the fact that Storm has never been anything but a bloody good friend to you. Her stupid ex-boyfriend might have hurt you, but the only thing Storm has ever been guilty of is having terrible taste in men. Something you know all about if the papers are anything to go by. I mean, correct me if I'm wrong, but it was you who slept with a married

277

man, and you who was stupid enough to take a bloody picture on your phone of the two of you.'

Carly flushed bright red, lost for words. 'Er, well, I . . .' she began, but Sally was just beginning to warm to her theme and in no mood for interruptions.

'It's time you took responsibility for your part in all this, lady. Nobody held a gun to your head and made you sleep with that bloke, you did that all by yourself. And Storm here has apologised until she's blue in the face for something she had no control over. It's time you got a bloody grip and stopped being so childish. Life's too short for stupid grudges, if anyone knows that it's me. My daughter's been like a sister to you, Carly, and I know you think I was so drunk when you two were kids I didn't know what was going on, but I did. I know Storm helped you with your homework, stood up for you in class when you were always getting into trouble, and I know that she was there for you when that scumbag you were engaged to cheated on you.

'Can you say that, Carly? Have you always been there for Storm? If you would but see it, she's been through hell and high water this year and could have done with a friend. But you've been too badly wronged, haven't you, to see any of that? Not only that, but correct me if I'm wrong . . . since you were in the papers you seem to have bagged yourself a nice little telly job. I suggest you start looking in a mirror, love – you might not like what you see.'

As Sally finished her verbal attack Carly raced out of the coffee shop in tears, almost knocking Ed over in her haste to get away.

'What happened?' he asked, standing in the doorway, covered in muck and scratching his head.

'Something and nothing,' Sally replied, before turning her attention back to her daughter.

'Now, love, do you mind if I get that coffee to go? I want to make sure I find you those towels before the shops sell out.'

Storm was dumbfounded. She'd had no idea her mum knew what had gone on at school, and couldn't believe she'd stood up for her like that. Looking at Sally, she felt a sudden rush of love. 'Coming right up, Mum,' she said softly.

Arms laden with boxes and bags, Storm and Ed pounded up two flights of stairs. Reaching the front door of her new home, Storm dumped her stuff on the floor, pulled the key from her jeans pocket and fiddled with the lock.

'Ta-dah!' she said, opening the front door.

Ed whistled as he walked in behind her. 'Not bad.'

'It's OK, isn't it?' exclaimed Storm as she walked around her new surroundings, taking them in.

There was no denying the place was tiny but all the furniture had been carefully chosen to make the best use of the space. A double bed had been raised to create a mezzanine, while underneath stood a small sofa, desk and large wardrobe. To the right stood a door to the en suite bathroom complete with shower and loo, while on the opposite side of the room stood the kitchen that looked as if it had been completely refurbished with glossy white cabinets and granite-effect worktop. Freshly painted white

walls and birch-effect laminate flooring finished the flat off to perfection.

'I reckon this place is perfect for you,' said Ed.

'Me too.' Storm beamed. 'And the rent's super cheap.'

'Just as well, given that your boss is tighter than tight.'

'Agreed,' bantered Storm.

Walking over to the large bay window that overlooked Brighton's hustle and bustle, she realised Jeff had been right. If you stood on one leg it was just about possible to make out the sea.

It wasn't where she would have expected to find herself, or if she was honest the flat she would have chosen if she had gone house hunting herself. But as fresh starts went, this one wasn't bad. She had a home, a flat, a family . . . what more did she need to start the healing process?

'How about a takeaway?' Ed asked, interrupting Storm's thoughts. 'I'll nip out and get a curry, if you fancy one?'

Storm clapped her hands in delight. 'Perfect. You have given up your Friday night to help me, so it's only right we salvage some of it! Jeff also gave me a bottle of wine somewhere, I'll dig it out and we can start celebrating.'

'Sounds good to me. I'll be back in five.'

In fact Ed was gone the best part of an hour, but Storm didn't mind. It gave her the chance to sort out her new bed, dig out her pyjamas and give her fresh towels pride of place in the bathroom. By the time he returned with a huge bag of chicken tikka, lamb bhuna, rice and onion bhajis, Storm had only just found the wine and all-important glasses.

'You timed that well,' she said as he set the takeaway down on the breakfast bar. 'Red OK?'

'Lovely,' he replied, already digging into the poppadoms.

As Storm handed him a glass, she got to work dishing out the curry on to two mismatched plates.

'So, I'm curious,' Ed began. 'What was all that business with that woman earlier?'

'What woman?' replied Storm, buying time by playing dumb.

'The one your mum was screaming at earlier.'

Storm sighed. So much for the fresh start.

'She's an old friend. Very old actually as she now hates my guts. Mum was giving her hell for it. Anyway, I thought she was a friend of yours. She told me she'd get you to fire me.'

Ed snorted on his poppadom. 'I hardly *know* her. She's been in for a coffee twice. Though she does look familiar.'

'She's on the telly,' Storm explained. 'She has a style section on *Morning Cuppa.*'

'That's not where I know her from,' he said, shaking his head. 'No . . . wait! Got it. Wasn't she the one that was in the papers a while back for shagging that footballer?'

Storm groaned. Despite her promises to Carly that the story would be forgotten, it seemed sleeping with a footballer was still the one thing she was known for.

'Yeah, that's her.'

'So why does she hate you? You didn't go to the press with her story, did you?

Storm avoided Ed's gaze; he obviously didn't know how close to the mark he'd got. Storm had hoped that when she returned to Brighton she could finally stop talking about all of this, but it seemed her past was always going

to haunt her. Taking a deep breath, she told him about Carly, Dermot, her move to London, job at the *Herald*, and why she'd left.

'Blimey!' Ed exclaimed when she'd finished. 'You've crammed more drama into the past year than most people get in one lifetime.'

'Tell me about it,' Storm sighed.

'And you're still not going to tell me who your celebrity boyfriend is?'

Storm laughed, and threw an onion bhaji at him. 'No way! All I want now is to leave this all behind and move on with my life, I'm saying no to any more drama!'

'I'll drink to that.' Ed smiled and raised his glass. 'Cheers!'

Dermot had to admit it. The last few days had been wildly stressful as he stalked, chased, researched, and sat in his car for hours, following both Nico and Francesca to get to the bottom of what was really going on in their relationship. It had been relentless and he had hardly had a chance to get home, but now as he saw Miles reading over his story with a huge smile on his face he knew it had all been worth it.

After listening to Storm and Nico's voicemails, Dermot had leaped into action and hacked into Storm's email. He hadn't uncovered much, but he did find a brief message from Francesca expressing her sorrow that Storm and Nico had split up. The message itself hadn't been a lot to go on but as Francesca had sent the email from her work account it told Dermot exactly where she worked and he vowed to go straight there. He'd sat outside all day until

she left and then followed her home. He'd expected her to go to the Hampstead house he knew she shared with Nico, but instead she'd taken the tube to Waterloo station where she boarded a train to Bournemouth. Dermot hadn't had time to buy a ticket so had to buy one on the train at a heavily inflated price.

When Francesca got out at Bournemouth he followed her out on to the concourse and watched a petite young woman with auburn hair and blue eyes wave frantically at her. Francesca caught sight of the woman and her face broke into a huge smile. She rushed towards her and kissed her passionately. Together the two walked hand in hand out of the station and got into a nearby Volkswagen. Dermot, thinking on his feet, summoned a cab and told the driver to follow them. Twenty minutes later, they'd arrived at their destination – a little cottage near the sea. Watching the petite woman unlock the front door, Dermot realised the house belonged to her and wondered if this could be the mysterious Paula. After asking the cabbie to take him back to the station, he got the train to London and immediately started researching the house and its owner.

It didn't take long to get results. He soon discovered the house was jointly owned by Francesca and Paula. More digging into Paula's background revealed she was an architect and a proud lesbian, frequently campaigning for gay rights. Dermot's head was spinning as he tried to make sense of it all but more trips to Bournemouth, taking secret shots of Francesca and Paula together, told him what he wanted to know – they were lovers, meaning Francesca's relationship with Nico was a sham.

Realising his scoop had the potential to be one of the biggest of the year, Dermot had confided in Sabrina, sheepishly admitting he'd learned the truth through phone hacking.

'Well, don't tell Miles that, for fuck's sake,' she'd said. 'All you do is say you did an interview with Storm. There's enough in there on the voicemails she left Nico for it to sound as though you've spoken to her directly. Then we can put in the truth about Nico, Francesca and Paula afterwards.'

Dermot kissed Sabrina passionately on the mouth. 'You're a genius!'

Now, as he finished the final line of his article, Dermot felt like punching the air with delight. Finally he'd got his scoop, and it was a much better story than the stupid honey trap he'd tried to make Storm go along with. Popping his head around Miles's door, he checked that his editor was happy.

'Good work, Dermot,' he said thoughtfully, as he finished reading the story. 'This will make a brilliant front page on Sunday, and well done for getting Storm to give you an interview. I don't know how you managed it but you've obviously got better people skills than I gave you credit for.'

Dermot flushed with pride. 'Thanks, boss.'

He walked back to his desk, gathered his coat and headed to the pub to celebrate. Life had never tasted sweeter.

Chapter Seventeen

Storm woke to the sound of seagulls outside her flat. Climbing down from the mezzanine, she walked over to the window and looked out across the city beneath her. It was her first Sunday morning in her new home and although it pained her to admit it she had been dreading it. She had never lived alone before, and over the years had got so used to spending the day with family, Dermot, and later Chelsea, she wasn't sure how to fill so many lonely hours. Before she met Nico, she and Chelsea often headed to Spitalfields on Sunday mornings where they'd grab coffee, bagels and a vintage bargain. Then, they'd gossip over a couple of glasses of champagne at Bedales.

Then there were the few precious Sundays she had spent with Nico. Lying in bed, talking, laughing, watching movies and making love, she had felt such hope for their future. Naively she'd thought they had years and years of Sundays to spend together. At the memory of it all she felt

a stab of fresh pain. Nico was gone for ever, there was no point in thinking of him any more.

Now it was just Storm. With nobody else to please or consider she watched the street beneath her preparing for the day ahead. Tourists had arrived early to soak up the atmosphere, while directly below locals were popping into the newsagent's for papers and pints of milk. She frowned as she saw them walk out of the shop armed with copies of the *Herald*. If there was one thing she didn't miss about her old life, it was working for that newspaper. She knew it had been the right decision for her to leave. She still felt bad about the way things had been left with Miles, though. Checking her watch, she realised it was only 8 a.m., far too early for her to be up on a Sunday morning. Taking her tea, she went back to bed and pulled the duvet high over her head. Time to shut out the world for a couple more hours.

The sound of the phone ringing woke Storm from a bizarre dream where she was making coffee in a racing stables. The job was relentless as she handed steaming hot cups out to everyone, from the jockeys to the grooms. Scrambling for the mobile that was right by her bed, Storm saw that she had three missed calls from Sally and now her mother was calling again. Shit! There had to be something wrong.

'Mum, is everything OK? Are Bailey and Lexie all right?' she asked frantically.

'They're fine, love,' Sally replied urgently. 'They're not why I'm calling. Have you seen the paper?'

'No. What paper?' Storm was confused.

'The *Herald*,' Sally replied.

Storm's blood ran cold. What had happened? Had Dermot somehow managed to turn Nico over after all?

'What is it, Mum?' she begged.

Sally took a deep breath before she answered. 'There's a story about you, Nico and Francesca.'

Storm didn't need to hear any more. Shocked, she dropped the phone and raced downstairs to the newsagent's, still dressed in her pyjamas. Quickly, she scanned the shelves for the paper and soon found a pile of them on one of the bottom shelves.

Snatching a copy, she was horrified to see her own face staring back at her, underneath the headline *Sex, Lies and Lesbians*.

The picture was a pap shot Dermot must have taken of her and Nico holding hands as they walked along Royal Crescent in Bath. Seeing it, Storm felt a wave of fresh hurt. The glance the two of them were sharing was so intimate – it was the look of two people falling in love. Shaking with rage, she glanced at the story below and immediately saw the piece had been written as though she had talked directly to the paper about her feelings for Nico.

She checked the paper again to see who had written it. As if there could be any doubt – *Exclusive by Dermot Whelan*.

The rat! The rat! The fucking, double-crossing, slimy, cheating rat.

Slamming a handful of change down on to the newsagent's counter, she ran back into her flat and read the piece. It spanned seven pages in total and the amount of information Dermot had managed to get hold of was

extraordinary. Every gory detail of her affair with Nico had been laid bare for the world to know about. How they'd met, how they'd fallen in love, and how they'd split up along with Storm's pleas for them to be reunited, how sorry she was that she hadn't revealed she was really a journalist.

The reporter, who was worried her career would impact on her new relationship, told Mr Alvise she was really an airline hostess.

'You mean the world to me, Nico, how can I ever make this up to you? I have never loved anyone in the way I've loved you, I would do anything to make this right,' she was quoted as saying.

She had never told anyone that. How had they got this? She read the rest of her so-called interview, feeling sicker by the second. It was peppered with quotes, things she and Nico had said to one another during and after their relationship, personal things she would never have told anyone. The rest of the piece was all about Francesca being a lesbian and how she had been in a relationship with Paula Manning for some time. Dermot had managed to find out that they had bought a home together near Bournemouth and even got hold of a pap shot of the two of them sharing a kiss.

Further down, he had pointed out that Nico was as guilty as Storm of telling lies. That his pretence of being in a committed relationship was nothing more than a sham, and he'd been making money off the back of his wholesome image when in fact he was nothing more than a playboy who slept his way around town. Which was a blatant lie.

By now Storm had read enough. Throwing the paper in

the bin, she felt fury growing within her. That fucker! How dare he do this to her, Nico, and poor, poor Francesca? Storm's heart went out to them both – this would devastate their lives, and the lives of their families. They didn't deserve this. And neither did she.

Instinctively she reached for her phone to try and call them, before common sense kicked in and she put it down. Storm realised she was the last person they would want to hear from. The whole piece had been written as if she had spoken to the paper first hand – there was no way either of them would forgive her or believe that she'd had no idea this was going to be in the press. She wondered how on earth Dermot had got hold of all those details, never mind the quotes. The things he had unearthed were so personal, things Nico had only ever said to her, and she had only said to Nico . . . well, more specifically, Nico's voicemail as he had never actually taken her calls.

Suddenly the truth dawned on Storm – Dermot had hacked her voicemail. She'd rip that lying little bastard limb from limb! She would have said this was a new low, even for him, but she already knew there was nothing he wouldn't do to further his career. Looking back, she should have reported him to the Press Complaints Commission when he'd confessed to bugging her conversation with Carly all those months ago. And she should have been suspicious that he'd suddenly stopped sending flowers, texts, and calling her after she'd left the paper. She could have kicked herself – she'd been so stupid, making mistake after mistake. Storm assumed he had left her alone after she'd quit the *Herald* because she was no longer of any use

to him; she should have known better. It was clear as day to her now – he'd been plotting the ultimate revenge.

Rage tore through her as she reached for her phone and punched in his number. But it went straight to voicemail and she was in no mood to leave a message. Instead she rang Miles.

'Storm, admiring your front page?' he said, picking up on the first ring.

'Don't be stupid, Miles. I want to know what Dermot told you about this story. It looks as though I spoke to you exclusively about this.'

'Well, you did, didn't you? He told me that he'd spent days talking you into it. I actually thought he had no chance, but he surprised me. Perhaps he picked up some interview tips from you.'

'No, Miles,' Storm sighed. 'He picked up nothing from me. What Dermot has actually done is spent days hacking into my voicemail, and then pretending I spoke to him directly.'

'What?' Miles was incredulous. 'You mean, you didn't give him an interview?'

'Do you honestly think that's something I would do?' she fumed. 'I mean, I know you hate me for the way I left, but I never thought you would stoop as low as him and dress up phone hacking as an interview.'

The editor sounded flustered for once. 'Storm, I'll get to the bottom of this, you have my word, but if what you're telling me is true, I'll fire Dermot.'

'I don't care what you do to him, but I'm suing you for this. You've ruined my life, and the lives of others, and for

what? You should be ashamed of yourself,' Storm blasted him. 'If I ever had any lingering doubts about leaving a career in journalism, you've just convinced me I made the right decision.'

She slammed the phone down and stared glumly at the handset. Shock and disgust were pulsing through her veins. She couldn't believe this was happening. All she wanted to do was curl up in her bed and shut out the world. She glanced at her phone. There were three missed calls from Chelsea and one voicemail. Flinging herself back on to her bed, Storm propped herself up on her pillows and dialled her mailbox. As she heard Chelsea's voice she felt a pang of loneliness. If ever there was a time she needed a friend it was now.

'Babes! I've just seen the paper and want you to know I'm sickened. I've told Miles there was no way you'd ever have given an interview about Nico, certainly not to Dermot, and I've handed in my notice, babe. Since you've left the place has gone from bad to worse, and I told him there was no way I'd work for a paper that would behave like that. The bastard's making me work my three months' notice, but I don't care . . . I'm on my way to LA now to see Adam, but I'll give you a call in a few days. Maybe you could come out here for a break? I know Adam would love to meet you and have you stay. Anyway, babe, chin up and forget those fuckers.'

Storm couldn't believe her friend had quit her job over this. Not for the first time she realised she owed Chelsea big time. And if she was capable of making a grand gesture then so was Storm. Reaching for her diary, she looked through her contact information for Nico's mobile

number. Storm might have deleted his number from her mobile, but she'd still kept a physical note, just in case she ever needed to contact him.

Slowly she punched in the digits and waited for the call to connect. As the phone rang Storm found she was holding her breath, trying to think of the perfect thing to say when Nico answered. But after two rings her call was diverted straight to voicemail. Worried there was a fault on the line she hung up and redialled, but this time there was no mistake. Nico's phone had been permanently switched off, and after realising Dermot had hacked her voicemail she didn't wait to leave a message.

She pressed the end call key, tears welling in her eyes. All she wanted to do was explain to Nico what had happened. But this was no time for a pity party. She wouldn't give Dermot the satisfaction. Instead she rooted around her wardrobe for her trainers and trackie bottoms and decided to deal with her frustrations by going for a run.

She wasn't a good runner, but it was the only thing she could think of that would help blow off some steam. The day was as overcast as Storm felt, wet, cold and windy, and as the rain beat down around her, Storm pounded the pavements harder and faster, each strike making her feel stronger. She would get through this latest nightmare, she told herself. She still had her family, her job and a new flat, this would not ruin her fresh start.

As if to prove the point, as she ran along the promenade and passed the coffee shop she decided to head into work and talk to Ed.

'Fancy seeing you here.' He smiled as she appeared in

292

the doorway, a hot sweaty mess. 'What's the matter . . . can't keep away?'

'Something like that.' She grinned. 'Any chance of a smoothie?'

He grinned back. 'Take a seat and I'll bring it over.'

As Storm took a seat by the window, she ignored the prying stares of other customers and instead turned on her smartphone. She saw there were over fifty missed calls, all from numbers she didn't recognise, as well as a text from her mum.

The house is overrun with paps, love. But they've no idea where you are and I've no intention of telling them. Jeff says he's going to throw a bucket of cold water over them soon if they don't bugger off. In the meantime, stay strong, love. Mum xxx

Reading the message, Storm felt her heart melt. Thank God for her mother. At least she was taking on the paps for Storm. That really would be the last thing she could cope with. Interrupting her thoughts, Ed placed a glass of green gunk in front of her.

'Power smoothie,' he told her proudly. 'It's got kale, spinach and wheatgrass in there – just the thing for the recovering athlete.'

Storm looked suspiciously at the glass. It looked gross, but she wasn't about to say so.

'Thanks.' She smiled, taking a tentative first sip.

'How is it?' Ed asked eagerly, pulling out the chair opposite and sitting down.

Trying desperately to choke it down, Storm smiled at him. 'Very, er, nice. A bit lumpy, but then kale can be hard to break down.'

Ed burst out laughing. 'You should see your face! Sorry, I made you a berry one, I just thought this might take your mind off what's been going on today.'

Storm arched an eyebrow. The cheeky bastard! Still, he was right. Drinking that disgusting concoction had been the first time all day she'd thought about something other than being on the front page of the country's leading weekend tabloid.

'So,' said Ed, as he returned with Storm's favourite berry blast smoothie, 'I wasn't expecting to see you on the front page this morning. Are you all right?'

'Fine.' She shrugged, taking a big gulp of her drink.

'Did you know the paper was running the story?' he asked, getting straight to the point.

Storm shook her head as she drained her glass. 'Not a clue. I'm used to being the one writing about other people, not the one being written about.' She smiled ruefully.

'Well, that must suck.'

Storm eyeballed him, unsure if he was taking the piss. 'Yeah, it does. Still, I'm sure some people would say I deserved it.'

'Bullshit. Everyone should be allowed a private life. I take it that story was written by your ex?'

Storm nodded.

'What a bastard!' Ed exclaimed. 'He would only have done that out of revenge.'

Despite her pain, Storm couldn't help smiling. Ed certainly had the measure of Dermot. What a shame she hadn't seen straight through him herself three years ago.

'Well, on the bright side, at least I don't have to keep

asking you who your celeb boyfriend was.'

'Every cloud . . .'

'So, can I ask, how much of that story was true?' Ed spoke more gently this time.

Storm sighed, pushed her empty glass to the edge of the table and wondered just how much to tell him. She'd wanted to keep her life with Nico a secret; it sounded silly, but she'd felt that the fewer people who knew about him, the more easily she might be able to move on. Little chance of that now.

'Most of it was true,' she admitted.

Quickly she outlined the facts to him. How she'd met Nico, and how she had been asked to honey trap him.

'Nico and I did fall in love, and, yes, Francesca is a lesbian, but they didn't let people assume they were a couple to try and fool the public, as Dermot tried to make out. It's because her grandparents disowned her when they discovered her sexuality when she was a teenager, and in the end the gossip drove her out of her village. The whole experience has left her paranoid it could happen again. And after reading this pack of lies, I can't honestly say I blame her. The worst thing is, I think they were on the verge of coming clean when Nico found out I was a reporter and assumed I was screwing him over.'

'Which you weren't,' Ed put in.

'I wasn't,' Storm agreed. 'I only went along with the honey trap plan to try and protect him from something like this. I was about to ask my editor for a transfer to another department so I could tell Nico the truth, but then he found out and the rest is history.'

'So what are you going to do now?' Ed continued.

'Nothing.' She shrugged. 'What can I do apart from carry on with my life and hope it all blows over?'

'Not tempted to ring Nico and explain?'

Storm shook her head. 'I tried, he wouldn't take my call. I'll keep trying, but I'm not holding my breath. He made it pretty clear when we last spoke that he never wanted to hear from me again. I can't imagine now he and Francesca are front-page news that he's changed his mind.'

Ed's expression softened as he leaned over the coffee table to give Storm's arm a reassuring squeeze. 'Well, I suppose you could always take a leaf out of your friend Carly's book, and get your own style segment on a morning TV show on the back of all this.'

Storm laughed bitterly. 'Yeah, because I'm a real style icon, aren't I? I think battered trainers and faded trackies, combined with eau de stinky sweat, are very this season. Nah, think I'll stick to making coffee if it's all right with you?'

Ed smiled. 'That's more than all right with me.'

Nico walked over to the window and gingerly peered through the Venetian blinds.

'Don't do that,' Francesca warned. 'You'll only encourage them.'

As if by magic, a flurry of flash bulbs went off and what seemed like hundreds of journalists screamed his name. *'Nico, Nico, just give us five minutes.' 'Aren't you going to say anything, Nico?' 'How do you feel about deceiving the British public, Nico?'*

Scowling, he snapped the blind shut and sat down at the

kitchen table next to Francesca, who was trying to get on with some paperwork.

'Fucking scum,' he hissed. 'Haven't they got anything better to do than harass innocent people? I feel like going out there and tearing them apart.'

'You've been saying that all morning,' Francesca pointed out, head bent over some files. 'Can't you just ignore them? They'll get bored and move on to someone else soon enough.'

'They shouldn't be bothering us at all,' he shouted, leaping to his feet and pacing up and down the room. Usually, if Nico had a problem or stress to work out, he'd go for a run, but with paps on his doorstep there was no chance of that. Instead he'd had to resort to pacing up and down inside the house and felt like a prisoner in his own home.

Ever since his agent had rung late last night to tell him about the story that was due to break, he had been livid. Seeing the front page in the morning had done nothing to lighten his mood. He'd read it and re-read it over and over, unable to believe that Storm would betray him like that. And with Dermot, her ex, of all people. That is, of course, if she really was his ex. Maybe they'd never split up in the first place. Sighing, Nico ran his hands through his dark hair. He didn't know what to think any more. What he did know was that he should have realised Storm was just stringing him along. And to think he'd actually fallen in love with her!

Being in Italy for a couple of weeks had given him chance to think. Perhaps he had been too hasty. Perhaps

there had been a perfectly good explanation. He hated to admit it but he missed her . . . where was the harm in talking to her? Francesca had been right, he'd mused. He owed her that much at least.

But waking up to this mayhem had shown him how much of a sucker the girl obviously thought he was. And he'd thought he'd found the one! What a joke. No, as far as Nico was concerned, Storm had taught him a very valuable lesson. All women were trouble and he was steering clear from now on.

As for Francesca, his heart went out to her. To her credit she had taken it remarkably well, Nico thought. When he got the call last night, he'd rung her immediately at Paula's and warned her about the breaking story. He'd expected her to stay put in Dorset or even to go away somewhere with Paula, but she'd driven straight back to London to support him. She'd also called her friends and bosses at work and told them the truth about who she really was.

'Are you sure you're OK about all of this?' he asked, flopping on to the huge leather sofa.

Francesca looked up from her work, and pulled her glasses off her face. 'You know what? I'm surprisingly calm about it. I've been dreading this day for a long time, but now it's happened I realise that I can't keep hiding my true self from the world. It's time to be me.'

Nico looked at Francesca with admiration. She really was incredible. It was just a shame her grandparents never came round to seeing that. They had died years ago without ever forgiving her. But it was their loss, Nico had always felt.

'Are you sure?' he asked.

Francesca smiled and nodded at him. 'Very sure. And, Nico, I feel like I need to apologise to you. If anything, I've held you back all these years. Your *mamma* was right, you should never have given up on love and marriage just to protect me. I can cope on my own. It's time for you to go out and live your real life now.'

Smiling, he pulled her into his arms and held her tight, He would always be grateful that this incredible woman had entered his life, he was proud to call her his best friend.

'How did it go with your boss?' he asked, releasing her from his arms.

Francesca sighed. 'They've really surprised me. When I told him he said he was proud of me and that I should have come to him sooner. He laughed and said I had some very old-fashioned ideas if I thought that being gay might impact my career. It's all going to be fine.'

'How has Paula taken it?'

'Well, she's delighted I'm ready to face the world as myself but worried about the effect this horrible story will have on all of us.'

'She's not the only one,' he growled. 'I've made an appointment with my lawyer in the morning, to see if we have any kind of case against the *Herald*. I still don't know how Storm could do this to us.'

'I'm not so sure she did,' replied Francesca thoughtfully. Pushing her paperwork aside, she got to her feet and joined him on the couch. 'It all seems very out of character.'

'Pah! Don't make the same mistake I did, Francesca.

She played you and me for fools, and I never want to hear that woman's name mentioned again.'

'I take it I can't persuade you to hear her out then?' Francesca said, swinging her legs up and resting them on top of Nico's.

'Hell will freeze over first.'

'But she's called you several times today. She wouldn't do that if she was as guilty as you suspect.'

Nico frowned. There was nothing Storm could say to make any of this better, and she was the last person he wanted to hear from. As if by magic, his phone rang again – Storm.

'Just talk to the girl,' Francesca insisted, spotting his caller ID. 'It's not fair to blame her for all of this without at least finding out her side of things.'

Nico thought for a minute and picked up his phone. 'Storm, if you ring me again I'll have you prosecuted for harassment. Now leave me and my friend alone.'

'I thought you were going to talk to her!' Francesca wailed.

'I listened to everything she had to say.'

'But you didn't let her say a word.'

'Exactly. That girl tells nothing but lies, I wasn't going to give her the opportunity to tell a few more.'

Nico turned his phone off and threw it on the coffee table. Storm might have played him once, but he was damned if he was giving her the chance to do it again.

Storm stared at her phone in despair. When Nico had finally answered her heart had leaped. Finally she was

going to get the chance to talk to him. But he had sounded so menacing, she'd felt almost frightened. She didn't think it was possible for him to have been any angrier with her than when he'd last spoken to her, but somehow he'd outdone himself. She felt like screaming. They'd both been stitched up and yet she was going through this alone.

Wandering over to the fridge, she pulled open the door and examined the contents. Aside from some leftover curry and half a pint of milk, it was bare. She sank to the floor and buried her face in her hands. She wasn't sure how much more of this she could take. Seeing Ed at the coffee shop earlier had left her feeling positive and she'd jogged back to her flat in the rain in a surprisingly upbeat mood.

But turning on her phone again and seeing over one hundred missed calls, all from journalists begging her to reveal more of her story, she felt trapped. How much longer was she going to have to keep paying for one stupid mistake? Ever since she'd told Dermot about Carly she'd been plagued by bad luck. Usually she prided herself on her ability to bounce back after any setback, but now Storm's resilience was wearing thin.

Too exhausted to stand, she crawled over to her bed and pulled the covers over her head. She didn't care that she was still dressed in her sweaty running gear, and even had her trainers on. What did any of it matter any more? Her eyes wandered towards her bedside table where her dad's gold watch was lying next to her alarm clock. She reached for it and gently rubbed the face as she so often did when she needed reassurance. But it was no good, even her usual

301

comforts were failing her now. As the rain lashed down against the window, she drifted off into a dream-filled sleep where queues of people snaked outside her front door, all screaming and shouting at her that she was a terrible person.

As the rain turned to thunder, Storm found the shouting only got louder and louder.

'Open up. I want to talk to you!' one insistent voice was yelling over and over again.

Coming to, Storm sat bolt upright in shock only to discover the claps of thunder that she thought she had dreamed were actually the sound of someone banging at her door.

'Storm, will you open this door?'

Scrambling out of bed, Storm unlocked her front door only to come face to face with the last person she'd expected to see – Carly.

Chapter Eighteen

'What are you doing here?'

'Thought it was time you and me had a talk,' Carly replied.

Storm ran a hand through her hair, sweaty and tangled from her run, as she drank in Carly's appearance. Although she was wet from the rain, she looked as gorgeous as ever. Her long blonde hair looked as if it had been recently highlighted and her natural make-up made her eyes sparkle. Dressed in a fitted black wool jacket, jeans and knee-high boots, her appearance screamed style and Storm could fully understand why she had become such a hit on *Morning Cuppa*. It was wonderful to see her doing so well, but Storm was too tired to deal with any more today.

'Carly, I know you want to tear strips off me, but not now, all right?' she said, about to shut the door in her former friend's face.

'Actually that's not why I'm here. Can I come in?' she said quietly.

Surprised, Storm opened the door and ushered Carly inside.

'This is sweet,' she said, standing in the middle of Storm's flat and looking around her.

Looking at her flat through Carly's eyes, Storm almost felt like laughing at her ex-friend's politeness. With cardboard boxes and dirty washing all over the floor sweet was the very last thing the place could be described as

'No, it's not. But thanks for saying it. Can I get you a drink?'

'Tea would be nice,' Carly said, perching on a large cardboard box and setting her bag on the floor. 'So how are you?'

'Fine, you know,' Storm replied as she flicked on the kettle and quickly rinsed two mugs under the kitchen tap.

'Good, good. And the job at the coffee shop?'

'Well, I haven't been fired yet, if that's what you mean? Look, I don't mean to be rude, but what do you want? I've had a hell of a day and if it's all right with you I'd love to postpone our next fight.'

Carly took a deep breath. 'I've seen the papers this morning. Storm, you must feel awful.'

'I do,' she replied, pouring boiling water into the mugs and adding milk to the tea. 'Is that why you're here then? To gloat over my downfall?'

'Actually, I've come to say I'm sorry for the way I've treated you.'

Shocked, Storm dropped the mugs she was holding,

304

causing scalding hot tea to spill everywhere.

'Bollocks!' she shouted, brown milky liquid running down her legs. Grabbing a roll of kitchen towel, she frantically started mopping up. Carly joined her.

'I see you haven't changed,' she said wryly. 'Still as clumsy as ever.'

'Yeah, well, why change the habit of a lifetime?' said Storm, standing up. 'So . . . tea?'

Carly shook her head. 'I've a better idea. How about we go to the pub? I reckon you could do with it after the day you've had.'

Storm stared at her in surprise. Of all the endings to this day she could have imagined, she would never have predicted this.

'Sure. Give me ten minutes to get showered and changed.'

The pub at the end of Storm's road was a quiet traditional place. With large fireplaces, wooden beams and red velour banquettes, it was a world away from any bright, trendy London watering hole, but Storm had always found the place homely. Sitting in a quiet corner, she poured two large glasses from the bottle of red Carly had bought and eyed her cautiously.

'So . . . you mentioned something about an apology?'

'Christ!' Carly groaned. 'You're not going to make this easy for me, are you?'

'I'm just curious,' Storm explained. 'You've got to admit that our last few meetings haven't exactly gone well. I'm wondering what's changed.'

Carly paused and took a sip of wine before she spoke. 'I've been so cross with you for such a long time now, Storm. I hated you for telling Dermot about what had happened between me and Aston.'

Storm hung her head in shame. If she could turn the clock back she would. 'I know, I wish I could change it. In fact, I wish I could change a lot of things, including ever getting involved with Dermot Whelan.'

'Well, that's the thing. All this time I've been cross with the wrong person. It wasn't your fault, Storm, it was mine,' Carly said. 'Sally gave me a wake-up call the other day when she yelled at me. I was so upset after she said all that stuff, but you know what? She was right. I was the one who slept with a married man and I was the one who took a stupid picture on my phone. I blamed everyone but myself.'

Storm shook her head. 'No, Carly, you made a mistake, that's all. You didn't deserve to have your face splashed all over the papers. Dermot's the one who's to blame. He lied to us both, but I was stupid for not seeing any other way out other than to move to London.'

'We've both made mistakes,' Carly agreed. 'But the biggest one has to have been letting this affect our friendship. Sally was right again about that. You have always been there for me, and I was stupid ever to forget that.'

Storm smiled. 'Mum's been right about a lot of things lately.'

'Wow, you've started calling Sally Mum! When did that happen?'

'When she started behaving like one.' Storm shrugged. 'A lot's happened, and I felt we should forgive, forget and move on.'

'Any chance we can do the same?' Carly asked quietly. 'I can't tell you how much I've missed you, Storm.'

She nodded. 'I know how you feel. It seems so weird that I don't know what's going on in your life. Although I know you've got a job on the telly now.'

Carly rolled her eyes. 'It seems sleeping with Aston Booth wasn't such a bad career move, but I'm still not proud of what I did. However, yes, the telly job is going well, but the public haven't let me forget my mistake. I still get hate mail sent to the TV studios calling me a home-wrecker, or journalists raking up my past when I'm mentioned in the press.'

'I'm still very proud of you, Carly. You've done so well after everything that happened,' Storm assured her.

Pouring them both another glass of wine, Carly shrugged. 'If there's one thing I've learned it's that you've got to make the most of any opportunity that comes your way.'

'And what about this boyfriend of yours? Jez told me you were seeing some events organiser?'

'Oh, him. Nah, that was over months ago,' she replied, shaking her head. 'But I have started dating this hot TV producer at work.'

Storm smiled at her. 'What's he like?'

'Young and fit.' Carly smirked. 'It's not serious. But what about you? I read the paper but I'm so confused. When did you start dating Nico Alvise? And why the hell did you

give Dermot an interview? Finally why are you back in Brighton, working in a seafront coffee shop? What's going on with you, Storm?'

Shaking her head, she topped up their glasses. 'This story definitely requires more booze.'

Slowly, she filled Carly in on everything that had been happening in her life since she'd moved to London. Careful not to leave out any detail, she told her everything in a way that only two women who have been friends for a lifetime can communicate.

When she'd finished Carly was speechless. 'I don't know what to say, babe. Shit. I'm so, so sorry.'

Storm shrugged. Nothing anyone could do would change anything. She would just have to get through it all as best she could.

'So what are you going to do now? I mean, you're not giving up journalism, are you?'

'I think so, yes. It doesn't feel right to me any more.'

'But it was all you ever wanted to do,' Carly pointed out.

Storm fiddled with one of the paper coasters on the table, shredding it into tiny bits.

'Dreams change,' she replied. 'I'll find something else that excites me the way journalism used to. Who knows? Maybe I'll become the UK's go to barista.'

'Not the way you spill drinks!' Carly teased. 'But what about Nico? You still love him, I guess?'

At the mention of his name, Storm felt a rush of emotion. She'd been so strong all day but now the combination of shock, exhaustion and alcohol sent her over the edge.

'Yes, I love him.' She sighed hopelessly. 'But I have to start getting over him. He never wants to see me again, Carly, and I have to accept that.'

Dragging her chair over to Storm's side, Carly wrapped one arm around her old friend.

'Storm, let me tell you something you told me all those years ago, when that cheating bastard devastated my life. You will get through this, and you won't always hurt this much. I promise.'

As Storm rested her head on Carly's shoulder, she wiped her tears away with the back of her hands.

'When did you get so wise?'

'When I started hanging out with the smartest girl in the class,' Carly whispered. 'My biggest mistake was letting her go. What do you say, Storm? Do you think we can be friends again?'

Storm drew back from Carly's embrace and looked her up and down. For so long now she'd thought they were over; that she would never make things up with Carly no matter how hard she tried. She'd grieved for their broken friendship, the loss hitting her as hard as if someone had died. But now the unthinkable had happened. Carly was here, begging for forgiveness and offering Storm the chance to make things up. Was it really possible they could wipe away everything that had happened and go back to being friends once more? Or had too much happened and this was all too little too late?

Storm sighed as she opened her mouth to speak. 'Carly, I've always been your friend and always will be,' she

replied, pulling her in for a hug. 'I love you like a sister, and you'll never, ever get rid of me.'

As Dermot sat down outside Miles's office, waiting to be called in, he tapped his feet up and down nervously. This morning, wearing his best navy suit and arriving at work with Sabrina by his side, he'd expected to be greeted like a conquering hero. Usually when a reporter landed a scoop this big there'd be high fives, pats on the back and talks of long pub lunches with plenty of booze. But since sitting down at his desk he'd felt like he was being given the cold shoulder by everyone. When Karen, Miles's secretary, told him the editor wanted to see him immediately, Dermot felt a rush of fear. Usually Miles came straight out to the huge open-plan office and announced hearty congratulations on a job well done. Being called in for a private meeting didn't signal anything good.

Finally Miles was ready for him, and as Dermot walked into the glass-walled office, he knew he was in trouble when he saw not just the editor but Polly from Human Resources.

'Take a seat, Dermot,' Miles said, gesturing to the hard office chair opposite his desk. 'Before we begin I want to ask you a question. How was Storm when you interviewed her?'

Miles's bluntness left Dermot on the back foot. 'Sorry. What do you mean?'

'Storm. You remember, your ex-girlfriend, a highly gifted journalist and former colleague. How was she when you interviewed her?'

310

'Fine. You know, getting on with her life,' he replied quickly.

Miles regarded him thoughtfully. 'I notice the article didn't say anything about where Storm's living now, or what she's doing. We've referred to her in the article as an ex-*Herald* journalist, but usually we mention people's current jobs and the town they're living in. Why are those details missing from your piece?'

Dermot flushed. Shit! Why hadn't he thought about that? He knew she was back in Brighton, the GPS tracker told him that much, but he had no idea what she was doing there. He should have asked Chelsea. She and Storm had been as thick as thieves. But then Chelsea also hated his guts, Dermot reasoned. The chances of her telling him anything would have been zero. Quickly he thought on his feet.

'Just an oversight, Miles,' he replied smoothly. 'But it doesn't affect the story. We've had so many hits on our website along with emails from people saying how much they enjoyed the piece.'

What Dermot didn't add was that most of the emails he'd received congratulating him on a job well done had been from his mum and his aunt. And actually the public had been surprisingly hostile to the story, saying things like they felt sorry for all three people involved and why couldn't they be left to live their lives in peace? If that was the sort of story the *Herald* wanted to cover the readers would be buying another paper in future.

But Miles had heard enough. Getting to his feet, he walked menacingly towards Dermot. 'It wasn't an

311

oversight, you didn't know. And the reason for that is because you didn't bloody interview her! Now tell me the truth about how you got that story.'

'That is how I got the story. I called Storm, and asked for her side of things and she agreed, out of loyalty to me, to give me an interview,' he said, panicking.

'Bullshit!' Miles roared. 'I know the truth. You hacked her phone and then you hacked Nico Alvise's. I've had them both threatening legal action, thanks to you. When will you learn that nothing gets past me? Now, for once in your life, tell me the truth. Did you get Storm's story by hacking her phone?'

For a minute Dermot said nothing. Then, realising the game was up, he nodded. He knew there was no getting out of this one.

Miles returned to his seat beside Polly, and pursed his lips. 'You don't need me to tell you how serious this is, Dermot. Phone hacking is illegal, and we don't use stories like that here. You've left me with no choice. You're fired. Clear your desk and get out immediately.'

'What! You can't be serious,' he protested. 'I made one tiny mistake but the story was all true. Storm did have a relationship with Nico and his alleged girlfriend is a lesbian.'

Miles said nothing. Instead he turned to Polly.

'Dermot, phone hacking is grounds for instant dismissal,' she said. 'Security will be here shortly to escort you from the premises.' She opened the office door, gesturing for him to leave.

'Miles, please don't do this to me,' Dermot pleaded,

turning to his editor. 'Look, I'll do anything . . . please give me another chance. I'll find you even greater stories, the right way, I promise.'

Miles laughed. 'I don't think so, Dermot. You're so bent, you can't even lie straight at night.'

But Dermot wasn't going anywhere without a fight. Leaving his dignity at the door, he got down on his knees and clasped his hands together. 'Miles, I'm begging you, please don't fire me. I'm nothing without this job.'

'You're nothing anyway, Dermot,' Miles sighed. 'The biggest mistake I ever made was hiring you in the first place. Now get out of my office and don't come back.'

Realising his career was over, Dermot let out a massive howl as two security guards walked into the office. They hauled him to his feet and pushed him towards the door, but he had one last thing to say.

'You'll be sorry you did this to me!' he screamed. 'I'll make you pay for this. You haven't heard the last of Dermot Whelan!'

After being front-page news Storm had worried her world would be turned upside down, but in fact life settled down fairly quickly for her. Of course, she still had several requests from journalists asking her to tell her story, and Carly also offered her the chance to go on *Morning Cuppa* and explain how she'd been a victim of phone hacking, but Storm refused. As for the paps, once they realised Sally and Jeff weren't going to give them Storm's location they too gave up, meaning Storm could get back to living her life in peace.

Over the next few weeks she hired a no win, no fee lawyer to help her sue the *Herald* for hacking her phone. Her lawyers had been more than happy to help and told her she had a watertight case. Worryingly, Chelsea had called a few days earlier, telling her that Dermot had rung asking where Storm lived. He'd worked out thanks to some old friends of theirs who had seen her in Brighton that she was working in the beachfront coffee shop. Chelsea wanted to warn Storm that he might come looking for her. 'Give him a kick in the nuts from me if you see him,' she fumed.

Meanwhile Storm threw herself into her job at the coffee shop, constantly thinking of ways Ed could improve the business. It was the only thing she could do to take her mind off Nico. Since he'd told her he never wanted to speak to her again, Storm had thought long and hard about trying to reach him. She toyed with the idea of going to his house, calling Francesca or even writing to him, but something always stopped her. He had made his feelings perfectly clear and she ought to respect that after all the damage she had caused him. And she couldn't really blame him for wanting her out of his life. They might have had a connection, but she'd lied to him, and caused his private life to be splashed across the front pages. No, Nico would see her as nothing but trouble now, and as the old saying went, if you loved someone you had to let them go.

That didn't mean she stopped missing him or thinking about him though. Every morning when she woke he was the first thing she thought about, and if she happened to

catch his TV show, she'd look at the screen and pretend he was talking just to her.

Bustling into work one cold and drizzly November morning, Storm couldn't wait to show Ed her latest Christmas ideas. She'd been up half the night devising festive plans and, with Christmas around the corner, had come up with a file full of recipes and new ideas to tap into the hungry shopper market.

'Why don't we do a late-night opening on Thursdays to coincide with late-night shopping?' she suggested before they opened. 'We could encourage all those shoppers to unwind with a glass of mulled wine, or a Christmas coffee with a mince pie.'

'That's not a bad idea,' Ed replied. 'Though it would mean overtime for us both.'

Storm shrugged. 'So what? It would be great for business and we could add other events over the month.'

'Have you been watching Dragon's Den?' he teased her. 'It's brilliant. Have I told you, hiring you was the best decision I ever made?'

'Not since yesterday,' Storm bantered. 'But I've no problem with you telling me again.'

It was funny, she thought as she started clearing coffee cups and wiping tables. She had never seen herself working in a coffee shop, but she had to admit she was really enjoying it. Ed was a dream to work for, and it was brilliant not having to worry about deadlines or sit at a desk for hours on end. She might have been earning a pittance and was back to doing her clothes shopping in Tesco, but Storm realised she was a lot happier these days than she

315

ever had been working at the *Herald* doing her supposed dream job. But then a lot of that might have something to do with Carly.

Since the two girls had made up, they'd quickly fallen into old habits and saw each other most days. Carly always stopped off for a coffee on the way to the station in the morning, and after work the two of them would either enjoy a gossip and a bottle of wine at each other's flats or go to catch a movie. It had been like old times.

'That reminds me, Carly had a good idea as well,' Storm said to Ed as she finished wiping the tables ready for the day.

'Oh, yeah?' he said cautiously. 'It's nothing to do with reinventing my style, is it?'

Storm frowned. 'No, why?'

'Ever since you two made up she keeps telling me I need to change my image. She says I'm never going to attract a woman if I wear camo shorts all year round and flip-flops. Plus she keeps fiddling with my hair.'

Storm tipped her head to one side and took in Ed's appearance. 'She does have a point. Don't you get cold dressed like that? I mean, it's almost the end of November – don't you think you ought to at least put long trousers on?'

Ed shook his head. 'I don't feel the cold. Besides, too many clothes make me feel trapped.'

'You're a funny boy.' Storm smiled fondly, shaking her head at him. 'Anyway, Carly suggested holding a Christmas party outfit session at the coffee shop. You know how everyone always struggles with what to wear at the

Christmas party? Well, she thought it might encourage more customers.'

'I like it,' Ed replied. 'As long as she doesn't start trying to style me. I'm happy as I am.'

'Even with the beard?'

'What's wrong with it?' he exclaimed, touching his chin self-consciously.

'Nothing, nothing.' She smiled. 'You just look a bit like Tom Hanks in that movie where he's stranded on a desert island for a year with only a football for company.'

'You cheeky cow. I'll have you know women love a beard.'

'If you say so.' Storm chucked her wet cloth into the sink and walked over to the door to open up for the day.

'I say so! And, Storm, you missed one of those tables.' He waited for her to turn round then threw the wet dishcloth straight at her, hitting her full in the face.

Storm had spent the day rushed off her feet. They'd been overrun with shoppers and day trippers, and by the time Carly came to collect her for a drink and a gossip in the nearby pizzeria, Storm was done in.

'Don't even think about cancelling on me,' Carly warned her. 'The thought of you, me, a glass of wine and a lot of carbs has been the only thing that's kept me going all day.'

'All right, all right,' replied Storm, taking off her apron and checking her appearance in the café window. Not bad after a day spent wiping, clearing and serving, she thought. Storm ran her hands through her hair and reached into

her jeans pocket for her lip butter. That would have to do, she mused. Turning to Carly, she reached for her bag and coat.

'Come on then. Tell me all about your hectic day as the face of British television, and I'll reward you with tales of how I had to unblock the sink.'

'You do lead a very glamorous life,' Carly teased.

'Tell me about it. One minute washing dishes, the next slopping coffee over my favourite customers.'

'Still not tempted to go back to journalism then?' Carly asked.

Storm shook her head. 'I don't think so. Don't get me wrong, I miss writing. You know, actually talking to people, finding out about their lives and who they really are, but I don't miss all the bullshit that goes with it.'

'How do you mean?'

'Well, all the pressure, the deadlines, the boring council stories.'

'Come on, it wasn't that bad at the *Post*,' Carly reasoned.

Storm paused. No, it hadn't been all bad. There were times when she'd got a genuine thrill out of covering stories. Especially the crime ones. She loved the high drama of a criminal trial. And she'd liked her work when she'd reached out sympathetically to any family who had been a victim of crime or loss, and offered them the chance to talk freely.

'No. It wasn't all bad,' she said finally. 'I think my trouble was I got so fixated on the idea of being a showbiz journalist, I didn't think about any other area of journalism.'

'So what about going back into another field then? You're very talented, it would be a shame to waste that.'

Storm smiled. 'Yeah, my old editor Ron came in this morning and said much the same thing.'

Carly dropped a fork full of pizza. 'Why didn't you say? Bloody hell! How was it seeing him again?'

'Fine. He was really nice actually. Told me he was proud of me for resigning from the *Herald*.'

'Really? What did you tell him?'

'I said that I'd finally realised what was important in life.'

In truth, the meeting with Ron had rattled her. He'd had no idea she worked there and had popped in for a coffee on his way back from a meeting with one of the local councillors. Seeing Storm making lattes had given him a start.

'Storm! How lovely to see you, but what are you doing here?' he'd asked.

'Working,' she replied. 'But it's good to see you too. How's everything at the *Post*?'

'Fine.' Ron grinned. 'But we miss you. Things haven't been the same since you left. Me and Miles Elliot were at journalism college together. He rang to tell me you'd quit your job in London and, I have to say, I'm proud of you, Storm.'

She blushed as she made Ron his flat white. 'Thanks. But you shouldn't be. My life has lurched from bad to worse since I left the *Post*. And didn't you always tell me that a good journalist should write the news, not be the news? I messed up that golden rule, didn't I?'

Ron took his drink and slapped a fiver on the counter. 'You're too hard on yourself. You've handled a difficult situation very well and I'm proud of you. If you ever want your job back, just say the word. I was too harsh on you once, Storm, but there will always be a place for you at the *Post*.'

Giving Ron his change, she'd looked at him in surprise. Given the way they had left things, she'd been sure he would never want to see her again. Still, her mind was made up. No good could come from a career in journalism and she was better off doing anything else. 'Thanks, Ron, I appreciate that, but I don't think journalism is for me.'

'So now you've ruled out journalism, what's next?' Carly asked her.

'You sound like my mum!' Storm groaned. 'I don't know. I guess I'll find the right thing eventually. I'm really enjoying working for Ed at the moment.'

At the mention of her boss's name, Carly flushed, something Storm noticed straight away.

'Oh my God!' She grinned. 'Have you got a crush on Ed?'

'No way!' Carly exclaimed. 'He's nice, but he's really not my type. He's got no sense of style, lives in shorts, and his big ambition is to go surfing around Australia. No, thanks.'

'He's also got a heart of gold, a sweet, kind nature, and runs his own business,' Storm pointed out loyally. 'Also, he's given your style night idea the go ahead.'

'Really?' Carly beamed. 'Wow, that's great! When does he want to do it?'

'He suggested next week. First week of December, when Christmas really gets into full swing.'

'Great. I've got a stack of ideas.'

'Does one of them include snogging Ed under the mistletoe?' Storm teased.

'No, it does not!' Carly flushed, before cheekily adding, 'Maybe. You have to admit, he's cute.'

'He's very cute.' Storm smiled. 'I think he'd make someone a lovely husband one day.'

Chapter Nineteen

As Storm draped tinsel around the pictures in the coffee shop she did her best to ignore the sounds of Mariah Carey belting out her classic hit 'All I Want for Christmas' on the radio.

'Stupid song,' she snarled. 'Should be banned at this time of year, when people are feeling lonely.'

'What's got into you?' asked Ed in surprise. Storm had been grumpy all day – scowling at customers, moaning when she had to take out the bins – and despite his constantly asking her what was wrong, she'd refused to confide in him.

'For the final time, nothing,' Storm growled, just as Carly walked through the door with her arms full of clothes for that night's style event.

'Hi, guys.' She beamed as she looked around her at the twinkling Christmas tree lights and decorations. 'How's everything going?'

'Wonderful, thanks, Carly.' Ed beamed at her. 'You're

a breath of fresh air. Storm's been in a mood all day and refuses to tell me what's wrong. I can only think it's because she's secretly Scrooge.'

Carly glanced at her friend, currently wrestling with a piece of mistletoe. 'Yeah, it's not her favourite time of year. But I think she's probably more upset about the fact that Nico was in the papers this morning, looking loved up with a mystery blonde.'

'Carly!' Storm snapped as she slammed the mistletoe down in frustration. 'It has nothing to do with Nico. I'm just a bit tired, that's all.'

'Yeah, right,' Carly said. 'Storm, it's OK to be upset that Nico's seeing someone else. God, I'd be devastated.'

'Me too,' put in Ed, only for both girls to give him a glare, warning him to shut up. 'How about I pour us a glass of wine before the punters arrive?'

'Best idea you've had all day,' Storm replied, sinking into a nearby chair and throwing the remaining mistletoe across the room.

'So,' Carly began gently, 'how are you feeling?'

'Really pissed off!'

'Nico's a good-looking guy. He wasn't going to stay single for ever. Not only that but he's been badly hurt. I'm sure this is just a rebound thing, it doesn't mean anything.'

'Well, they look pretty close to me,' said Storm, snatching a tabloid from a nearby table and opening it to the page where Nico and his mystery woman had been papped.

Carly stared at the image. 'You're right. They do look close. But you know better than anyone how wrong the press can get things.'

'I know.' Storm sighed. 'It just hurts so much to see him with someone else like that. They look as though they're in love.'

Peering at the picture of Nico with his arm wrapped around the blonde sent a stab of pain through Storm and she burst into tears.

Putting an arm around her, Carly did her best to calm her friend down. 'I know this sucks, babe, and I know how much it must hurt to see him with someone else, whether it's real or not. But to be honest even if Nico is seeing someone, although it hurts it doesn't matter any more. You and he are done now; it's time for you to move on. New Year's around the corner, what better chance for a fresh start?'

'Yeah, except I just have to get through Christmas first.'

'It won't be that bad surely. Are you going to Sally's?'

Storm shook her head. 'No. Mum's going back to Canada and taking Jeff to meet her family there. Lexie and Bailey will be away with work again. They like Christmas as much as I do.'

Carly bit her lip. 'I'm sorry I won't be here either, Storm. Mum and Dad booked this ski-ing trip months ago to Val d'Isère. I can see if there's room for you, though, everyone would love to have you along.'

Storm was touched Carly would try to include her in her family's plans. 'No, don't worry. It's really sweet of you but I can't afford it. That's why I'm not going to LA to see Chelsea or to Canada with Sally either. I just haven't got the money.'

'Which is why I don't understand why you won't let

me loan you some?' put in Ed, appearing with three large glasses of red wine.

'Because I'm not a charity case!' she protested. Seeing Ed's hurt expression, she felt a pang of guilt. He had been nothing but nice to her, and certainly didn't deserve to be shouted at.

'Sorry. I just feel bad. You've done so much for me already. It wouldn't feel right to take your money as well.'

'What are you doing, Ed?' Carly said, changing the subject.

'Going back to St Ives for Christmas. It's the same every year. The whole family get together, sing carols, eat turkey and go to midnight mass at Truro Cathedral.'

'Wow, you sound very close.' Carly smiled at him.

'We are. Well, apart from my brother and sister, who refuse to go to mass and instead drink Dad's whisky and watch Clint Eastwood films.'

'Ah. Thought it sounded too perfect.' Carly nodded knowingly.

'See, Carly, there's no such thing as a perfect family,' put in Storm. 'Which is why I will be fine on my own, eating a ready meal and watching telly. Let's face it, it won't be any worse than last Christmas.'

Carly smiled sympathetically at her. 'Well, let's look forward to New Year then. You and me can go out on the pull together and look for Mr Right.'

'What happened to that hot TV producer you were seeing?'

'I binned him. He was more interested in how I could rework his wardrobe than a relationship with me.'

'So does that mean you're single then?' Ed asked bluntly.

'Single and very ready to mingle.' Carly smiled straight at him.

Storm looked at the two of them beaming into each other's eyes and smiled to herself. They weren't a likely couple but she reckoned there was a chance they could really suit each other. Perhaps she could give them a shove in the right direction.

Letting out a huge yawn, she stretched and got to her feet. 'I'm really sorry, you two, but would you mind if I went home instead of giving you a hand tonight? All this Nico stuff has really knocked me sideways and I don't think I'll be that much use to you.'

Concerned, Carly pulled Storm in for another hug. ''Course not, babe. You go home, have a nice hot shower and chill.'

'Thanks so much,' Storm said gratefully. 'Why don't you tell me all about it when you stop by for coffee in the morning?'

Carly stepped back and turned her attention to the huge bundle of clothes she was organising. 'I'm not going in tomorrow. I've got a day off.'

Storm was confused. 'Really? Since when?'

'Since I asked for one because I knew I'd be knackered the day after organising this event.'

'But it's the run up to Christmas. Surely the TV show needs you now more than ever?' Storm quizzed.

'No,' Carly said. 'They were fine with it. Now get off home before I change my mind and make you stay.'

Frowning, Storm was about to ask her friend for more

details but something told her that pushing Carly wouldn't do any good. She would come clean when she was good and ready, and Storm would be waiting. In the meantime she was off home, well aware of the expression two's company, three's a crowd.

Nico drummed his fingers on the Formica-topped table and wondered again why on earth he'd agreed to this meeting. When his agent had suggested it, his instinct had been to say no immediately but Natasha, who had worked with him for years, was very insistent, making it clear no wasn't really an option.

Realising there was no getting out of it, Nico tried to look on the bright side and thought that at least this would be a chance to lay some demons to rest. What he hadn't counted on was this particular demon being over twenty minutes late. Getting to his feet, he left a handful of pound coins on the table and reached for his coat just as the door swung open.

Spotting a short blonde woman standing at the doorway, frantically scanning the crowded café, he raised his hand to attract her attention.

'Carly,' he said quietly. 'Over here.'

Seeing Nico had waited, Carly rushed over to him, looking apologetic. 'I'm so sorry I'm so late. The train from Brighton was delayed. I tried to reach Natasha to get a message to you but she was stuck in meetings.'

'It seems our agent has been very busy lately,' Nico mused, sitting back down and gesturing to the waiter for another round of coffees.

Carly pulled a face. 'Yes. I know it was a bit naughty to get her to insist you meet me, but when I realised you and I shared an agent I saw it was the only string I could pull.'

Nico smiled. There was something very charming about Carly. She seemed so calm and poised on television, but in person she was unashamedly honest and warm. He could see why Storm had been so devastated to have lost her friendship. At the thought of his ex, his face darkened.

'So why did you want to see me so desperately?' he said. 'I have a funny feeling it has something to do with our mutual enemy.'

Carly flinched at his use of the word. 'Actually Storm and I have made up.'

'Pah! What lies did she tell to get you to come round? I thought you'd seen the light, Carly. I admired you for seeing straight through that girl's bullshit and getting out before she did any more damage.'

Carly shook her head. 'Storm's not like that. She's been hurt as badly as you have. You've got to understand.'

Nico shrugged. 'I don't have to do anything. So, it's Storm you've come to talk to me about, is it? I take it she sent you?'

'No. She has no idea I'm here. But, Nico, she's so unhappy without you. I know I never saw you two together, but what I do know is I've never seen Storm this besotted with a man. You clearly got under her skin.'

Nico frowned at Carly. Why had she come all this way to plead Storm's case? She was wasting her time; he should put her out of her misery right now.

'You should know that I'm suing both Storm and the

Herald for damages. My phone was hacked and my lawyer tells me I have an excellent case.'

Carly looked at him coldly. 'Well then, your lawyer should have informed you that Storm's phone was also hacked and she's also suing, which is how that dickhead of an ex of hers got hold of the story about you two in the first place.'

'You mean, she never gave an interview?' Nico asked, incredulous.

'No! That's the last thing she would ever do. She doesn't even work at the *Herald* any longer. She quit the day you dumped her, saying she'd realised how much of a shit job being a showbiz reporter was. She was going to tell you the truth about her job once she'd asked for a transfer to another department, but you beat her to it by dumping her.'

'And what about this honey trap business?' he scoffed. 'Oh, yes, I know Storm was asked to take part by her ex, Dermot, that's if he even was her ex. My lawyers have found out Storm was only going out with me in the first place to try and uncover the truth about my life, so she could run an *exposé*. I'm sorry, Carly, but that doesn't sound very innocent to me.'

'She was just doing that to protect you,' Carly replied, sounding exasperated. 'I know it's a lot to take in, but it's absolutely true. She never wanted anything to appear about your private life, and felt that if she pretended to go along with Dermot's plans then she could keep you out of the limelight. The last thing she ever wanted to do was hurt you.'

329

'I don't believe you,' Nico jeered.

'It's true. She's back in Brighton, with a broken heart, living in a tiny studio, earning a pittance making coffee in a seafront café. She says she never wants to work as a reporter again, which to be honest is stupid because she's a brilliant journalist.'

Nico sank back in his chair and swept his hands through his hair as he tried to take in everything she was saying. Storm was as much of a victim as he was. Storm was going to tell him the truth. Storm didn't want to honey trap him Storm loved him. He shook his head. It was all too little, too late. Storm was gone, and no matter what he may or may not still feel for her, she'd done nothing but wreak havoc in his life.

'I'm sorry, Carly. My mind's made up. I never want anything to do with her again. And even if she had organised a transfer for herself to a different department it still wouldn't have made a difference. I hate journalists, they're the scum of the earth – she knew that.'

'What? You'd let someone's job stop you from loving them?' Carly exclaimed. "Scuse my French but how fucking stupid!'

'It's not stupid at all. In fact, I'm surprised you've sorted things out with her after what she did to you.'

'How do you know what Storm did to me?' Carly asked, surprised.

'She told me a version of the truth, and my lawyers did some digging and found out the rest.'

'Well then, you should realise that my life without Storm was pretty miserable. On the outside I pretended to hate

her because I was so hurt. But I realised her only crime really was telling someone she thought she could trust a secret.'

'Well, that's the other thing, isn't it?' hissed Nico, jabbing his finger on the table. 'Even if I did talk to Storm again, I would never, ever trust her. There's no getting away from the fact she lied to me. I'm sorry, you can't have a relationship without trust.'

Convinced he'd made his point, Nico looked at Carly triumphantly.

'It's true, trust can be hard to regain. But if the love is there then it doesn't have to be gone for ever,' she said thoughtfully. 'Sally told me some home truths a little while ago, which made me realise it was wrong to blame Storm for everything that happened. Ultimately I was the one who slept with a married man and you were the one who lived a lie. I mean, if we're getting down to it, wasn't that the real reason you hated reporters? Because you were worried they'd uncover the truth?'

Nico's face flushed with anger as Carly hit a nerve with her question. 'That is the biggest load of bollocks I've ever heard. My relationship was my business, and even if I let people believe we were together, I was doing it for the best of reasons.'

'So was Storm.'

Neither of them spoke for what seemed like an eternity, each staring at the other in frustration, until finally Nico got to his feet.

'Carly, I'm sorry but you've had a wasted trip. I hate Storm and never want to see her again.'

'Well then, it's nice to see you've moved on so quickly ... if those pap shots of you in the papers with that blonde are anything to go by.'

'That's none of your business,' replied Nico smoothly as he pulled on his coat. 'Please leave me alone now. Storm and I are over.'

Carly grabbed his wrist as he made to leave. 'Wait just a minute,' she begged, pulling a pen from her bag. Reaching for a napkin from the chrome canister on the table, she scribbled something on it and pressed it into his hand. 'This is Storm's address. Just in case you change your mind.'

Nico released his hand from Carly's. 'I won't!' he called as he reached the door.

The Christmas atmosphere all around town and at work was beginning to do Storm's head in. Everywhere she went people seemed to be whistling carols, wishing each other a Merry Christmas and discussing their holiday plans. Usually this time of year didn't bother her; after all, she'd long ago got used to Christmases that were less than happy and instead looked forward to the new beginnings January always brought. This year was different, though, and Storm couldn't put her finger on why. She had a lot of reasons to be cheerful, including the new relationship she'd forged with her mother.

For the first time since she could remember Sally felt like a proper mum, and now Storm looked forward to their time together. They met every week for a gossip and a cup of tea, and Storm had even accompanied her and Jeff to their beloved bingo!

No, Storm knew she had more reasons than most to feel thankful, but this year she was finding it impossible to get into the Christmas spirit. Deep down she knew the reason – Nico. During their time together they'd actually made Christmas plans. Nico had offered to take her away to his holiday home in the Italian Lakes where he said they'd light fires, relax by the water and eat a huge Christmas dinner before spending the day making love. Storm had been doing her best to remain strong since returning to Brighton, but this endless Christmas cheer was bringing back memories of him and all she had lost. She knew there was no point getting upset, that what was done was done, but being without him still hurt and there were times she struggled to get through the day without crying.

Storm felt as though she was walking around under a great big cloud of unhappiness. More than anything she wished it would lift. As she opened her front door ready to leave for work, she ran through her mental checklist, phone, purse, keys . . . then realised they were the one thing she didn't have. Scrambling around her flat, desperately searching for her keys, she let out a torrent of swear words. She wasn't usually this disorganised and could only put it down to the curse of Christmas. Frantically she checked her watch and groaned. She should have left ten minutes ago if she had any hope of being on time and she'd promised Ed she'd open up this morning.

He and Carly had gone on their first date last night after they'd shared a kiss at Carly's style event. Knowing it was such a special occasion, Storm had offered him the chance of a lie in, just in case he got lucky! Not that Carly

333

was that kind of girl, she'd assured him as he flushed bright red with embarrassment. She hoped it worked out for them; they both deserved someone special, although Storm had noticed Carly had been really weird for the past week. Always dropping in on her at home and at work to check she was OK, bringing her clothes from the set of *Morning Cuppa* which apparently she didn't have to return, and being generally over-attentive and positive about a brand new start in January. Storm didn't know what had got into her and had tried asking her what was wrong, but Carly had said everything was fine with such a bright sunny smile on her face that Storm had given up asking.

She could only put it down to the fact her friend was worried about how Storm would feel about Ed and her best mate going on a date, but she had nothing to worry about there. Storm was delighted for them both. It was nice to see Cupid fire his bow at this time of the year and she couldn't wait to find out how their date had gone.

Finally spotting her keys on top of the fridge, Storm heaved a sigh of relief as she grabbed them and raced out of her front door. Half jogging and half walking towards the café, she didn't notice the man on the opposite side of the road, who had been watching her flat waiting for her to leave.

'Storm!' a voice called. At the sound of her name, she whipped around and got the shock of her life when she saw Dermot.

Astonished, she stood rooted to the spot as he crossed the road and hurried towards her.

'Storm,' he said again, more warmly this time. 'It's so good to see you.'

As he leaned in to give her a kiss on the cheek she backed away, speechless. What the hell was he doing here? And how did he know where she lived?

'Why are you here?' she croaked, finally finding her voice.

'I had to see you,' he said, putting his hands in his pockets to ward off the chill of the December air. 'One of our old colleagues at the *Post* told me you were living here.'

As Dermot spoke, Storm took in his appearance. With greasy matted hair, an unshaven face and dark shadows under his eyes, he didn't look a well man. Still, Storm had no inclination to feel sorry for him as shock gave way to anger.

'Well, I don't want to see you, Dermot. Now fuck off and leave me alone.

'Please, Storm,' he begged. 'Just listen to me . . . there's something I need to tell you.'

'What?'

'I need to tell you how sorry I am. I should never have hacked your phone and I should never have got you to honey trap Nico. I was jealous, and wanted revenge. You were doing so much better than me at work, and you'd fallen in love with another man. I didn't know what else to do, but I'm so, so sorry.'

'Wow, Dermot, thanks, I feel so much better about it all now,' she said sarcastically.

'Really?' He smiled, a flicker of relief passing across his face.

'No, not really!' she snarled, as she angrily jabbed her finger into his chest. 'You ruined my life, you piece of shit. Now, for once in your life, think of someone else and leave me alone.'

Pushing past, she picked up her pace and walked quickly away from him, but Dermot wasn't giving up. He chased her down the road.

'Just give me a chance to talk to you, Storm.'

'You've talked. I listened. Now go,' she said, continuing to walk faster down the street.

'Don't be like that. Please! I came here to ask you for another chance. I know I've asked before, but I got it wrong sending you all those flowers and text messages. I see that now. But what *you* need to understand is that ever since you and I split up our lives have fallen to bits. Look at us. You're here in Brighton again, doing a shit job and living in a shit apartment, and I'm kipping on a mate's sofa without any hope of getting a job in journalism again. We belong together, Storm. I need you and you need a grand gesture.'

To her horror, Dermot ran in front of her then blocked her path by getting down on bended knee. Reaching into his coat pocket and pulling out a tiny black box, he opened it to reveal a ring. 'Storm, you're my world. Please will you marry me?'

Looking at Dermot, down on one knee, holding a ring in the air, his expression brimming over with seriousness, Storm couldn't help herself. She broke into peals of laughter. 'Have you lost your mind?' she said, when she'd finally calmed down.

'No,' he said earnestly. 'This feels so right. We should be together, we belong together.'

'Really?' said Storm, arms folded against her chest. 'And what does Sabrina make of all this?'

'That's over,' he said, waving one hand. 'Has been for a while now. She blamed me after she was fired.'

Storm frowned. Sabrina was Miles's rising star – what on earth did she do to get fired? Still, it proved there was some justice in the world. The woman was the biggest bitch on the planet.

Seeing Storm's confusion, Dermot put her in the picture. 'She knew I'd hacked your phone. Miles fired us both.'

Instantly, Storm backed away from him. This was all too much, him being here in her life, with all his lies and deceit, after she'd worked so hard at a fresh start.

'Just go away, Dermot,' she said, losing her patience. 'How many times do I have to tell you before you get the hint?'

But he wasn't listening. 'Storm, I'm serious. All this has made me realise what's important in life, and I know for me that's you. I can't live without you. Since you left me everything's gone wrong, I need you back.'

Storm had not been expecting any of this and suddenly felt exhausted. 'You just don't get it, do you, Dermot? I know what love is now; I know what it feels like. Even if I never love anyone else again, I've experienced how good it can be when you're with the right person, and what you and I had was not love. At best it was good sex, but it wasn't love. Why on earth would I ever go back to life with a selfish twat of a man like you, who has tried to ruin me over and over again?'

337

'Don't be stupid, Storm,' snapped Dermot, getting to his feet. 'Nico will never have you back. You're wasting your time if you're waiting around for him.'

'Thanks, but I'm not waiting for Nico,' Storm replied. 'I know it's over, but I'd rather have nothing and be alone for the rest of my life than be with someone like you.'

'But it's Christmas,' he protested. 'Surely you don't want to be alone at Christmas?'

'It never bothered you when we were dating, and quite honestly I'd rather spend a lifetime of Christmas Days eating meals for one than spend another minute in your company!'

'And what am I supposed to do with this ring?'

'I couldn't care less what you do with it. Give it to Sabrina, give it to charity, throw it in the sea, but just leave me alone, Dermot,' she said. 'And if I ever see you near my flat again, I'll take out a restraining order.'

'Don't worry, I'm going,' he hissed. 'You know your trouble, Storm? You always look a gift horse in the mouth.'

She couldn't resist one final putdown.

'And you know your trouble, Dermot?' she called, walking away from him. 'You're like school in August – no class.'

Nico strolled purposefully along the seafront, feeling more hopeful than he had in months. When he'd woken early that morning this was the last place he'd expected to find himself, but he'd had the strangest dream. He and Storm had been lying in bed, eating croissants. Storm had been flicking crumbs at him, and he had pinned her to the bed

and made delicious love to her. When he woke, sleepy and blurry-eyed, he reached across the bed expecting to find her by his side and felt a stab of shock when he realised she wasn't there. Propping himself upright against his pillows, he realised how much he missed her. How everything in his life had seemed brighter, shinier and simply better with her in it. He missed the way she smiled at him in the mornings, the way she scrubbed her teeth rather than gently brushed them, he even missed the way she sang really bad show tunes in the shower each morning. Had he made a mistake? Were Carly and Francesca right? Should he at least give Storm the opportunity to tell him her side of things?

His gaze fell on his bedside table where he saw the napkin on which Carly had scribbled Storm's address. It had been lying there in a crumpled heap along with a pocketful of change, receipts and a spare button. He'd wanted to throw it out the minute Carly had given it to him, but for some reason had kept hold of it. Now he knew why.

For a tantalising moment Nico considered the possibility that he could end this misery just by talking to Storm. That they could spend Christmas together after all. He fantasised about the two of them waking up on Christmas morning together. They'd open presents, eat dinner and spend all day locked in each other's arms. Life could be perfect, Nico realised, if he'd just swallow his pride. Too keen to get going to bother with a shower, he slipped on jeans and a jumper and grabbed his car keys. With a bit of luck he should catch Storm before she left for work.

On the drive down, Nico practised what he was going

to say. How he had been wrong not to listen; how although he was still angry with her for lying, he was now ready to work things out. He would blame his crazy Italian temperament, and ask her if she thought there was some way back to being the happy, loving couple they'd been before. By the time Nico reached Brighton he was fired up and ready to see Storm. As there was no parking outside her home, he left his car near the seafront and walked along the promenade, the brisk air helping to calm his nerves. Turning into Storm's road, he took a deep breath and walked towards her flat, only to see her in the street talking to someone.

Getting closer, he realised the man could only be Dermot Whelan. Nico recognised him from the dossier his lawyers had compiled, and unless he was very much mistaken, it looked as though their conversation was getting intimate. Nico's mind went into overdrive as he tried to work out why on earth Storm could be talking to her ex. After all, he had set her up and betrayed her just as badly as he had Nico. Suddenly his heart was in his mouth as he saw Dermot get down on one knee, reach into his pocket for a tiny box and hold it aloft. Storm looked shocked, he noticed, before she broke into what he could only assume were peals of delighted laughter.

A mixture of shock, anger and nausea washed over Nico as all the pieces of the jigsaw slotted into place. More deception. Storm hadn't had her phone hacked, she'd obviously been in on the whole thing with that scumbag of an ex. Except it was now very clear to Nico, that Dermot was not her ex. Dermot was very clearly her future. How

could he have been so stupid as not to see this coming?

He turned on his heel and stomped back towards his car in the freezing cold. He'd seen all he needed to see and wasn't going to hang around. When would he realise Storm had never been interested in him, that she had been playing him for a fool all along? Carly, the stupid bitch, had probably been in on it too. Getting their agent to set up a meeting to tell even more lies . . . It was sick. But what had been the point of it? To set him up for an even bigger story? To make more money out of him? Well, forget it. Storm wouldn't make a fool out of him twice.

God, she was a piece of work, he had to give her that. Cunning and clever. He thought back to just a couple of hours ago when he'd dreamed of the two of them spending Christmas together. What a joke! No, he was better off alone, sitting in his beloved kitchen, dreaming up new recipes for his restaurant.

Shaking his head in sorrow, Nico hurried back to his car and clambered inside. Letting out a howl of despair, he thumped the steering wheel over and over again, repeatedly cursing his own stupidity. He swore there was no way he would ever allow Storm back into his life again.

Chapter Twenty

Christmas Eve

'Oh my god, babe! This is gorgeous,' exclaimed Storm, unwrapping a beautiful black, sequin-encrusted designer dress.

Storm and Carly had decided to get into the Christmas spirit by treating themselves to lunch in the pub near Storm's home. It had become quite the local for the girls since they'd made up, and they had spent many a happy night there swapping stories about their days over a bottle of wine.

'I feel so bad now. I only got you that rucksack,' Storm sighed.

'Are you kidding me?' beamed Carly, who knew Storm was struggling to make ends meet. 'That rucksack's just what I need for my adventures next month.'

'I still can't believe you're going.'

'Neither can I.' Carly grinned at her. 'I wanted to go with

Ed for the whole year, but *Morning Cuppa* refused to hold my job open for me, and much as I love him, experience has taught me not to give everything up for a man.'

'So you're only going to Australia for a month then?' Storm confirmed.

'Yeah. I think a few weeks of living out of a backpack will make me more than ready to come home.' She shuddered at the thought. 'But I'll be with Ed, and that's all that matters.'

'So what will you do after that?' asked Storm, nibbling on a plate of chips. 'Ed's going to be gone for six months, do you think you'll cope?'

'We've both compromised,' explained Carly. 'He wanted to go for a year, but doesn't want to be without me, and I've said I'll come out for a fortnight in April when I can take more time off. It won't be that long.'

Storm looked at her admiringly. Since Carly and Ed had started dating, she'd really blossomed. She'd gone back to being the confident, sassy, gorgeous girl Storm had known and loved. The romance was going well and Storm couldn't have been more pleased for her friend.

'Still, you're in for a hectic few weeks travelling across the globe.' Storm smiled. 'Flying out to Val d'Isère this afternoon, then off to Melbourne the day after you get back from ski-ing. When will I see you?'

'It is going to be hectic,' agreed Carly. 'But, hey, life's short. So screw it, why not? As for you and me, no doubt I'll be Skyping you constantly about the tortures of slumming it in a youth hostel with no access to any of my designer toiletries.'

343

'You'd better,' Storm urged, mopping up a mound of tomato ketchup with her last chip.

'Anyway, more importantly, have you decided what you're going to do now?'

Storm sighed. 'I think so. I did offer to run the café for Ed while he was away, but he seemed adamant about selling it.'

'It hasn't been doing very well,' Carly admitted. 'Despite your best efforts to turn things around. So he's just going to keep the one in St Ives open, which is a little gold mine apparently.'

'I know. It's a shame. He never told me how bad things were and I'm really sad today's my last day,' sighed Storm. 'Then tomorrow I'll be home alone, watching box sets and eating mince pies.'

Carly reached across the table and squeezed her friend's arm. She had never told Storm she had gone to visit Nico, convinced that hearing how much he hated her would only halt her friend's healing process. 'Are you sure you're OK with spending Christmas on your own? Because, honestly, if you want, I'll fork out for you to come ski-ing?'

'Don't be daft, babe. A last-minute ticket would cost a fortune. Honestly, I'm fine. You know Christmas doesn't bother me.' She shrugged.

Carly eyed Storm thoughtfully as she took a sip of her wine and changed the subject. 'So what are you going to do next? Any more news on your case against the *Herald*?'

'Yes. My solicitor is working on an out-of-court settlement with Miles. I'm not sure what Nico and Francesca are doing, I think they're planning on taking their case all the way to

court as they want to make a point. Unlike me. I've had enough of being in the spotlight and my solicitor reckons Miles will make sure the settlement is quite generous so that should mean that in the New Year I'll be able to put a deposit down on a flat.'

'That's brilliant news, babe. It seems like it's all happening for you! Let's hope next year's better than this one.'

'For both of us,' Storm agreed.

'And what about work? Are you going to accept Chelsea's offer?'

'No. I thought about it, but it doesn't feel right.'

'And is she OK with that?' Carly asked.

Storm nodded. Chelsea had rung her the week before and told her that she was moving to LA permanently and Adam had offered her enough cash to start up her own luxury travel magazine. As a result Chelsea had offered Storm a job travelling around the world, writing about gorgeous hotels.

'Babe, just think how glamorous life will be as you jet from country to country, staying in the best hotels in the world!'

Storm had paused before answering. 'I know you're going to think this is mad, Chelsea, but actually I think I'd rather stay in Brighton. Now I've made up with Carly and established a new relationship with Mum, I want to focus on what I've got at home rather than travel halfway around the world looking for glamour. I've realised that all the time I was chasing a glam, party lifestyle, all I really wanted was my family – I've got that now.'

'Oh, Storm,' Chelsea replied tearfully. 'I don't think that's mad, I think that's beautiful. I completely understand. But any time you fancy a holiday, I insist you come to stay with me. Let me give you a glam life for at least a couple of weeks.'

Storm grinned. 'I can't think of anything I'd like more.'

'So does that mean you'll be taking Ron up on his offer then?' Carly asked.

Storm nodded. 'Yes. As of next month I'll be the *Post*'s chief crime reporter, and you know what? I can't wait. I've actually really missed journalism, something I never thought I'd say, and this job will be brilliant as I'll be based mainly in court and will be able to talk to many of the victims of crime as well.'

'No more boring council meetings for you then?'

'No! And no more showbiz stories either. Ron has promised me there won't be a celebrity in sight.'

Carly raised a glass to her friend. 'Well, I'm really proud of you. You were wasting your talents making coffee. You're a brilliant journalist, Storm, and you should never have turned your back on it.'

She grinned as she clinked her glass against Carly's. 'Maybe that's why Ed's business wasn't doing well. I probably spilled more coffee than I served!'

Glancing at the clock above the bar, Storm groaned as she realised she'd taken well over her allotted hour and was a little bit tipsy to boot.

'I'd better be getting back,' she said. 'Ed wants to get on the road back to Cornwall, and I promised him I'd lock up.'

'Poor old Ed,' Carly said, draining her glass and getting to her feet. 'I know he's going to be devastated to say goodbye to the business here.'

'That's why I offered to lock up for him one last time,' Storm replied. 'Goodbyes are tough, and he's got enough on his plate organising this trip to Australia.'

'You're too generous.'

'I know.' Storm shrugged. 'Perhaps I'll put this lovely new dress on for my last afternoon at the café. Say goodbye in style.'

'You'd better not, Storm Saunders,' Carly warned. 'That dress is designer and meant for pulling only!'

'Fine,' she groaned, as they left the pub and braced themselves against the cold sea air. 'But I hope you realise that means this beautiful dress will more than likely remain in the back of my wardrobe for ever. The first of my New Year's resolutions is to avoid men and falling in love.'

Nico slammed his foot down angrily on the brakes as the car in front stopped suddenly. It was always this way at Christmas, he fumed. The roads were full of Sunday drivers and he needed this like a hole in the head.

Earlier that morning the chef at his Brighton restaurant had called to tell him he had to leave work immediately. There'd been some kind of family emergency and the chef couldn't work Christmas Day as planned. Was there any way Nico could find someone else to cover his shift? Nico had felt like screaming. Of course there wasn't anyone else who could work Christmas at short notice – Nico would have to do it himself.

Ungraciously, he'd told his chef not to worry. After paying through the nose for the last remaining room at the Hotel du Vin, he got in his car. It was just as well he didn't have any plans of his own other than sitting alone eating turkey sandwiches. Francesca had been sweet when she'd learned he would be alone for Christmas and had invited him to go away with her and Paula, but he'd refused.

'Why don't you go to your own family's then?' she had suggested. 'I hate to think of you here all by yourself at this time of year.'

'Please,' Nico had scoffed. 'You know how *Mamma* has been since the newspaper article. She can't wait to sit me down, find out all the details, and talk to me about settling down with a nice Italian girl. Much as I love her, her fussing is the last thing I need right now. I'd rather be here, trust me.'

'If you're sure?' Francesca had said.

Nico was sure. In truth, he couldn't wait to spend some time alone and get his head around everything that had happened over the past year. It had been a horrible few months, and much as he hated to admit it to himself his heart was still broken. He'd done everything he could to get over the woman who'd betrayed him, including dating another woman, but it had been a disaster. Despite his best efforts to forget Storm, his new girlfriend had seen straight through him and recognised he was on the rebound, breaking up with him immediately. Nico wasn't bothered, but he was determined to get his life back on track. He intended to spend Christmas coming up with new ideas for the restaurants and for making his career bigger and better

than ever. Thankfully, the public had been sympathetic after the story about him and Francesca was published and business had boomed, but he was still keenly ambitious.

Funnily enough, though, driving to Brighton on Christmas Eve and working in his restaurant there hadn't been part of his master plan. Once again he cursed his bad luck, along with the traffic, for another hour as he finally crawled past Preston Park and into Brighton itself. Spotting a space near the Pier he slung his car into the spot, not caring if he was parking on private property or if he would get towed. He'd made it, that was all that mattered.

He wandered along the seafront towards his restaurant. Brighton really was pretty at this time of year, he thought. Although the sea was grey and the sky cloudy, the promenade was illuminated with beautiful twinkling lights, while everyone around him seemed happy and excited about the fact that Christmas Day was less than twenty-four hours away. Kids clung excitedly to parents' hands, groups of lads were dressed as Santa, in the mood to party, while loved up couples snogged in shop doorways, ready to celebrate the romance of the season.

Nico looked around him and found the atmosphere was rubbing off on him. Passing a seafront coffee shop, he decided to get into the Christmas spirit by treating himself to a mince pie and an espresso.

Pushing the door open, he saw a young woman balancing on a stool while reaching for a box at the back of the store. 'Be with you in a minute,' she called.

'No rush,' he said, looking around him. There were boxes everywhere, he noticed, and all the tables and chairs

looked as though they were being stacked ready to store. On the counter he noticed a large sign pointing to cakes and a small array of sandwiches. *Closing down. Everything must go!* it said. Nico felt sad. Too many small businesses were being forced to shut these days. It was a worrying sign of the times. He watched the woman get down from the stool.

'What can I get you?' she said, turning round to face him.

'Storm!' he spluttered, coming face to face with his ex. 'What are you doing here?'

Her pulse raced as she drank in the sight of Nico. She'd thought she'd never see him again, and yet here he was in the flesh, still as handsome as ever. His brown hair was ruffled, but his skin glowed and his eyes sparkled. With a start, she realised the single life must be suiting him.

'I work here,' she said quietly.

'Pah! Is this another career you're pretending to have, like being an air stewardess or a hospitality student?'

Storm sighed and rested her hands on the counter. She knew Nico's anger was justified, but it seemed especially cruel to have to deal with it now on Christmas Eve.

'Yes, I was a showbiz reporter but I handed in my notice the day you left for Italy. I'd intended to transfer out of showbiz and into another department, but when you ditched me I realised I didn't want to work there at all.'

'So you came back to Brighton?'

'That's right. I had no job, no home, nothing, but I knew I couldn't be in London any more. It seemed too hard to stay in the place where you and I had been so happy. I

made up with Sally, got a job here, moved into a studio flat and sorted things out with Carly.'

'Sounds like everything's worked out for you,' he said quietly.

Storm looked him in the eye. He seemed consumed with pain and anger, and she felt terrible, knowing she was the one who had caused him so much sorrow.

'I know I hurt you, Nico,' she said softly. 'And I cannot apologise enough for all the lies, but I had good reason. It was stupid of me to go along with the air stewardess joke that Jez came up with but I couldn't seem to find the right time to tell you the truth about what I really did. Then you and I agreed we'd never see each other again, and it seemed pointless to confess.'

'Until you decided to set me up for a story in your paper,' Nico pointed out, leaning closer to her, his face twisted with rage.

'I didn't set you up, Nico. You have to believe me, I had no choice. Dermot had got hold of that pap shot of us. He threatened to publish it unless I agreed to take part in a honey trap. I told him I'd do it, but really I was protecting you. I knew if I didn't go through with it, then they'd just get another reporter. When I left, he wanted revenge and hacked my phone, which is how he got the story about us. The last thing I have ever wanted to do, Nico, is hurt you. You have to believe me.'

'Why would I believe anything you say? Even now you're telling me a pack of lies. Dermot never set you up, you were in it together. Or why would you be marrying him?'

'What? I'm not marrying Dermot.'

351

Nico ran a hand through his hair and sighed. 'Storm, you have to stop lying. There's no point any more. I saw you, OK? And I saw Dermot the other week, down on one knee in the street, and you giggling excitedly as you saw the ring.'

Storm couldn't help herself. Great waves of laughter rose within her as she realised how badly wrong Nico had got things.

'Why are you laughing again, Storm?' he snarled. 'This isn't funny.'

'But it is!' she giggled. 'You obviously didn't hang around otherwise you would have seen me send Dermot packing, with the threat of a restraining order if he ever bothered me again. He and I have been over for a year. I never loved him, Nico, not like I love you. You're all I've ever wanted.'

Storm felt she had nothing to lose by speaking so bluntly; after all, she'd probably never see Nico again after this. At least by telling the truth there was a possibility she could set the record straight. Looking at him now, his mouth set in a grim line, his eyes filled with hatred, Storm felt a sharp stab of pain in her heart. She would never get him to forgive her. She had to accept that. The two of them stood in silence in the empty coffee shop for what felt like hours until he spoke.

'Did you know Carly came to see me?'

'No,' replied Storm, stunned. 'When?'

'About three weeks ago. She told me you were working here and living in a studio flat. She told me everything, in fact. Why you entrapped me, how you gave up your job,

how Dermot had betrayed you. She even gave me your address, urging me to come and see you.'

Storm was astonished. 'I had nothing to do with that, honestly, she never told me anything about it. I wouldn't have encouraged her.'

'She gave me a few things to think about actually,' Nico confessed. 'Asked me if the real reason I disliked journalists so much was because I had something to hide. She had a point. It was something I'd never considered before, but she was right, that *was* why I hated journalists, so I decided to come and see you. Talk to you, see if there was some way we could work things out.'

Storm looked him in the eye. 'And?' she whispered.

'And I saw that bastard propose to you, Storm. It felt like my whole world had come crashing down around my ears again. To see you getting engaged to another man . . . it felt like someone had taken out my heart and shredded it into tiny pieces.'

Storm's eyes filled with tears as she saw the strength of his emotion. 'But, Nico, I didn't say yes to Dermot. I was as surprised to see him as you must have been and I certainly didn't want him around. The guy ruined my life, he ruined my relationship with you,' she cried. 'That's something I have to live with for the rest of my life, knowing how close I was to finding true happiness.'

To her surprise, Nico walked around the counter towards her. 'Please,' she continued. 'I never meant for any of this to happen. At the very least, please don't walk away from here hating me. I was set up and I made some bad choices for the right reasons, but Carly was telling the truth.'

'I know that now, Storm. I can see that everything she told me is true,' Nico said, reaching for her hands.

She shuddered with delight as that tell-tale charge of electricity and desire shot down her spine at his touch.

'I'm the one who should be apologising. I leaped to so many conclusions. I never gave you the chance to explain when I should have done. If I had, maybe we could have avoided all this pain. All these months of misery, being without each other.'

As Nico locked eyes with Storm, he bent down to kiss her and she felt her body melt into his. No kiss had ever tasted so sweet or felt so right. It was time to forget the past and look to the future. It had only just begun.

'Wow, you look gorgeous!' Nico breathed as Storm sashayed into his restaurant.

'Thanks.' She smiled, silencing his compliments by kissing him full on the mouth.

When Nico had invited her that evening to a private dinner for two after the restaurant closed, she had known exactly what to wear. As she'd hoped, Carly's present fitted her like a glove, and Storm couldn't resist texting her friend a selfie.

Who are you wearing that for? Carly had texted back immediately.

Nico, Storm had replied.

Unsurprisingly, Carly had rung from Gatwick airport straightaway, desperate for the details.

'What's going on?' she squealed.

Storm had quickly filled her in, telling her how Nico

had found her at the coffee shop and it was there they had kissed and made up.

'So does that mean you're back together then?' Carly asked.

'Yes,' Storm replied happily.

But Storm didn't tell her everything. For example, she didn't tell her that after Nico had kissed her and kissed her, she had walked over to the door, turned the open sign to closed then turned the key in the lock. Behind the counter they'd made love, each so desperate to hold, touch and feel the other that they couldn't wait to make up for lost time. She also didn't bother to explain to Carly how, after they'd made love, they'd talked and talked, about the past and the future. Storm had told him how much she wanted to be a part of his life, and how much she'd missed him, but that she was planning on returning to journalism. She told Nico she'd understand if that would be too much for him to cope with, but after everything that had happened she knew she had to be honest.

Incredibly, he had been more than understanding. He knew what it was like to feel driven in a career, and to feel real passion for work.

'No more honey traps or kiss and tells, though,' he said warningly. 'Deal?'

'Deal,' agreed Storm happily.

Now, she couldn't help noticing how beautiful the place looked. Every table was lined with crackers, table decorations and gorgeous little gifts for all the customers Nico would be cooking Christmas lunch for the following day.

'I've got a confession to make,' he said as he led her by the hand through the restaurant.

'Oh, yes?'

'I'm afraid I haven't got you a present. This all happened so suddenly . . .' He broke off.

'What!' Storm teased. 'You cheapskate.'

'I was going to suggest you come back with me to my hotel tonight,' he whispered, nuzzling her neck. 'And I was going to suggest waking up together on Christmas morning and enjoying breakfast in bed.'

'Sounds good,' Storm purred. 'How about I lie in bed naked all day, so I'm ready and waiting for you when you finish work.'

'Now that would be the perfect Christmas present,' he agreed. 'In the meantime, though, I can offer you this.'

As he led her to a table that was laden with roast turkey, potatoes, and all the trimmings, she wondered when on earth Nico would have had time to pull off something so elaborate, not realising he had made one phone call to his sous-chef and asked him to organise something before he left for the day. One thing Storm couldn't help noticing was the fact that the table Nico had chosen for them was behind a large pillar towards the back of the restaurant.

'Why are we here? I thought you might like us to sit near the kitchen or by the window.'

'Because . . .' He smiled, reaching for her hand and bringing it to his lips. 'It was at this very spot you spilled wine all over me and our story began.'

'I can't believe you remembered.'

'I remember everything about that night. I remember

356

you looked gorgeous in your navy dress, how you spent most of the night consoling your friend Carly, and how your smile lit up the room. I looked at you, Storm, and I knew then what I know now: that I want to spend the rest of my life with you.'

She looked at him in shock. 'Are you asking me to marry you?'

Nodding, Nico stared into her eyes. 'I don't have a ring, Storm, but I do have a heart filled with love all for you, if you'll have me?'

'Yes.' She smiled and wrapped her arms around him. 'Yes, I'll marry you.'

Storm wiped the tears from her eyes as Nico reached for the champagne bottle.

'You didn't ask me to marry you to get out of buying me a present, did you?' she asked cheekily. 'Because FYI, a marriage proposal is *not* a Christmas present.'

Laughing, Nico popped the cork and filled their glasses.

'You mean, I have to get you an engagement ring *and* a gift?'

'Afraid so!' Storm teased.

Nico groaned. 'I knew getting married was expensive but this is taking the piss!'

Handing her a glass, he kissed her lightly on the mouth and proposed a toast.

'To us.'

'To us,' Storm whispered. 'And to years of very Merry Christmases together.'

He's the One

Katie Price

Can you ever forget your first love?

Liberty Evans hasn't. She has a beautiful daughter, a successful career as an actress, and she's married to one of Hollywood's most powerful directors.

But behind the glamour, things are not what they seem. Her daughter Brooke is turning into a spoiled teenager, her husband controls everything she does, and Liberty longs for Cory, the man she loved before she became famous.

Unable to live a lie any longer, Liberty returns to England with a reluctant Brooke to start a new life. While her daughter has to cope with a massive lifestyle change, Liberty finds that she cannot get Cory out of her head.

'Glam, glitz, gorgeous people... so Jordan!' *Woman*

'A real insight into the celebrity world' *OK!*

'Brilliantly bitchy' *New!*

arrow books

Santa Baby

Katie Price

'I thought Tiffany should know that she has a half sister. She's Angel Summer – the famous model.'

With these words from the mother who gave her away, Tiffany Taylor's life is turned upside down.

To Tiff's surprise, Angel welcomes her with open arms and suddenly Tiffany has gone from being a waitress to working as a stylist on Angel's TV show.

If only Angel's seriously sexy bodyguard Sean could be as welcoming. But with the threat of kidnap hanging over Angel and her daughter Honey, he has to stay vigilant.

Then, as everyone gathers at Angel and Cal's mansion for a big Christmas celebration, Sean's defences finally drop. But as he relaxes, the danger moves closer, and Tiffany finds herself in serious trouble

'Glam, glitz, gorgeous people... so Jordan!' *Woman*

'A real insight into the celebrity world' *OK!*

'Brilliantly bitchy' *New!*

arrow books

ALSO AVAILABLE FROM ARROW

The Comeback Girl

Katie Price

Once upon a time, Eden had it all; she was one of the most successful young singers in the UK, and the darling of the pop industry. Life couldn't have been better. But just two years after a sell-out tour, Eden is regarded as a has-been, better known for her drinking and the kiss-and-tell stories that a string of men have sold to the papers.

Desperate to get back in the big time, Eden begins recording a new album with songwriter Jack Steele, a man who drives her crazy for all the wrong reasons. But when she's asked to be a judge on the TV talent show *Band Ambition*, it's just the break she needs, and she's determined not to mess it up. So falling in love with Stevie, a contestant on the show, is probably not a very good idea. But Eden has always followed her heart, and she is sure that Stevie is 'the one'.

But is Eden setting herself up for another fall?

'Glam, glitz, gorgeous people . . . so Jordan!' *Woman*

'A real insight into the celebrity world' *OK!*

'Brilliantly bitchy' *New!*

arrow books

Also available by Katie Price

Fiction
Angel
Angel Uncovered
Paradise
Crystal
Sapphire
The Comeback Girl
In the Name of Love
Santa Baby
He's the One

Non-Fiction
Being Jordan
Jordan: A Whole New World
Jordan: Pushed to the Limit
Standing Out
You Only Live Once
Love, Lipstick and Lies

Make My Wish Come True

THE STRUCTURE
OF BRAZILIAN
DEVELOPMENT

THE STRUCTURE
OF BRAZILIAN
DEVELOPMENT

Edited by
Neuma Aguiar

Transaction Books
New Brunswick, New Jersey

Library of Congress Catalog Number: 78-55936
ISBN: 0-87855-138-7 (cloth)
Printed in the United States of America

Library of Congress Cataloging in Publication Data

Main entry under title:

The Structure of Brazilian Development.

Includes bibliographies and index.
1. Brazil—Rural conditions—Addresses, essays, lectures.
2. Peasantry—Brazil—Addresses, essays, lectures.
3. Brazil—Politics and government—Addresses, essays, lectures.
4. Brazil—Social conditions—Addresses, essays, lectures. I. Aguiar, Neuma.
HN283.S77   301.44'43   78-55936
ISBN 0-87855-138-7

to Irving

Contents

Chapter

List of Tables

Acknowledgements

Editing this book about Brazil written by Brazilians is an endeavor mostly due to the stimulus I received from Professor Irving Louis Horowitz, who always used every possible chance to listen to other people's voices, especially from what has come to be called the Third World of development. I am also indebted to Professor Richard Morse, who during his recent stay in Brazil lent great support to the idea of assembling the work of young Brazilian authors and giving an international audience to the effort. Professor Candido Mendes de Almeida provided support and obtained UNESCO resources for the development of a small survey to gather data on current work and trends in the Brazilian social sciences. I am grateful to Dr. Almir de Castro for the same reason, but above anything else, for the personal encouragement and credit he has given my work. In the data gathering, whose product is mostly included in the bibliography and partially in the introduction, I have been helped by a dedicated, efficient, and intelligent person—Laura Dantas P. Guimaraes, whom I warmly thank.

Most resources to put this book together, however, come from a Ford Foundation grant for which I am most thankful. I thank them not only for the financial resources provided but also for the information they made available on research and publications they have sponsored.

I would like to thank CAPES (Coordenaçao do Aperfeiçoamento de Pessoal de Nível Superior), a department of the Brazilian Ministry of Education, which has sponsored graduate schooling in Brazil and made available evaluation surveys they carried out on the academic production of the institutions they sponsored. For the same help I thank the Conselho Nacional de Ciência e Tecnologia (CNPq) and the Financiadora de Estudos e Projetos (FINEP), both departments of the Brazilian Ministry of Planning. The Brazilian Council of Science and Technology (CNPq) sponsored the data gathering for my own essay, which was also presented at the Employment-Unemployment study group of the Latin American Council for the Social Sciences (CLACSO).

All translations but two were done by Lupi Mirón, a very conscientious professional who goes out of her way to find the proper word to a phrase. The other two works (the first and last chapters) were presented in English by their authors. Anthony Seeger and Renato Raul Boschi helped revise, respectively, the translation of the articles by Moacir Palmeira and Antônio Otávio Cintra.

Most of the manuscript was patiently typed and retyped by Lúcia Inêz Teixeira da Cunha and also by Graça Maria Nunes and Carolina Rosa Borges de Holanda. I would like to thank all the Brazilian graduate schools in the social sciences, which provided information on their current work.

All articles but one were specially prepared for this book. The only exception is part of Antônio Otávio Cintra's chapter, which appeared in Portuguese in a book edited by Jorge Balán, *Centro e periferia no desenvolvimento brasileiro* (Sao Paulo: DIFEL, 1974). I wish to acknowledge their granting the English-language rights throughout the world to appear in this edition.

I want to thank all the contributors to the book—fellow friends and companions in the hardship but also pleasure of professing the social sciences in Brazil.

THE STRUCTURE OF BRAZILIAN DEVELOPMENT

Introduction: Current Trends
in Brazilian Social Sciences

The main purpose of this book is to introduce the international public to recent analyses of the social structure and development of Brazilian society performed by a group of young social scientists. The contributors to this collection are younger than those Brazilian authors whose works have until now enjoyed broader coverage outside the country.[1] Their portrayal of Brazil involves not only their writings but also the intellectual picture of a generation which had to face and solve, or attempt to solve, the difficulties brought about by the rise to power of an authoritarian regime with an initial attitude of undisguised intolerance toward the social sciences.[2]

After completing their training abroad, these authors returned to Brazil and began their research work as an inquiry on the crisis affecting the country. They sought to analyze the nature of the authoritarian state, the social structure within which such a regime could emerge, the modifications and continuities observed at the outbreak of the crisis, the continuities and differences found in comparing the current administration with previous authoritarian regimes in Brazil, and the Brazilian case as compared with equivalent situations experienced by other countries, whether under liberal or authoritarian rule.

To embark on this intellectual journey, they had to modify liberal training, acquired in the United States and Europe, and find new ways of practicing the social sciences in Brazil. In response to the crisis then affecting the country's social science teaching and research centers, some of which had seen many of their staff members purged, attention was focused on strengthening other institutions. The most critical effect of this move was the emergence of graduate schools with credit systems patterned after the American model, in contrast with Brazil's traditional center of graduate training in the social sciences, that of the University of Sao Paulo, which followed the European model, based on the tutorial

1

system and, until recently, the country's chief source of academic production. The emerging schools soon proved to be an important source of new knowledge and led to a diversification of social science production centers which this book seeks to reflect.

Compared with pre-1964 practices, this period became one of data storage for social scientists as they paused to reappraise their methods of production of knowledge. The effects of this are only now beginning to surface in the form of a substantial intellectual production centered around the graduate programs.[3] The liberal outlook acquired abroad by many of today's social scientists has undergone some change in the Brazilian national context, since the parameters involved in the production and dissemination of knowledge are completely different.[4] The assumptions of freedom of research have had to be constantly checked within a two-fold inquiry framework whereby the social scientist conducts his research projects and at the same time analyzes the conditions available for the production of such knowledge. The result is always a search for greater rationality and more dispassionate language. Discourse becomes less polemic and more precise.[5]

The passionate side of social science production is often linked to the application of the ethnographic method. This method provides a higher degree of identification with society through direct contact and allows for questioning abstract proposals, promoting discovery, and adding value to the qualitative aspects of research (Palmeira, Aguiar, Berlinck and Hogan, Alcântara de Camargo).

Fear has not precluded academic production but led, at first, to a high degree of isolationism in the scientific community which is only now beginning to break. It is common for Brazilian social scientists to meet only abroad, when invited to international conferences in which both the topics and the organizational scheme, though productive, are not tailored to the controversies resulting from the day-to-day research practice within the national borders.[6]

International sponsorship has promoted the growth of Brazilian social science. In both the development of graduate programs and the creation of national archives, international institutions as diverse as UNESCO and the Ford Foundation have been and continue to be extremely important. Several other foundations and international agencies such as the Canadian Agency for International Development, the Misereor Foundation, the Rockefeller Foundation, the Social Science Research Council, the French Technical Cooperation Agency, to mention a few, have also played a relevant role in sponsoring academic activities and are gradually being joined by the Brazilian government, which is becoming one of the major financiers of social science research. Government agencies are still conducting their sponsorship activities in disorganized fashion. They sometimes support research projects high in academic substance and sometimes adopt extremely restrictive practical definitions, thus confining the social sciences to a degree of instrumentality which stifles scientific creativity as a result of the low level of abstraction permitted. As regards international sponsorship, limitations arise when social scientists are forced to mold their scientific inquiries to topics derived from the international definition provided by the foundations' bureaucracy and not from local research practice.

Several of the research projects on which some chapters in this collection are based were originally funded by international sponsors, succeeded later by the Brazilian government which is gradually becoming the main sponsor of academic activities. The role played by foundations in the United States, anticipating the American government in areas where it dared not tread, may have had the same effect at the international level, anticipating the Brazilian government by providing substantial grants for social science research. The results of this double sponsorship have been to associate the plurality of perspectives, which has traditionally been a part of international funding for research, to an academic continuity in the work which can only be guaranteed by government financing. International cooperation also appears in cases of migration or extended visiting professorships from the United States and European and Latin American countries. One example of this cooperation is offered in this book by Daniel J. Hogan.

From the classic standpoint, whether by training or by tradition, the authors refer back to Marx, Weber, and Durkheim. But the trend is away from orthodoxy and towards a merging of perspectives. Prior to 1964, Brazil's development had been rigidly analyzed in terms of the feudalism versus capitalism controversy, explicitly detailed in this volume by Cintra and Alcântara de Camargo and extensively criticized by another contributor in an earlier article (Palmeira 1973).

Some of the authors herein included (Velho, Palmeira, Aguiar) have taken the concept of mode of production as a basis for understanding Brazil's agrarian and agroindustrial structure, identifying some modes of production not found in the classic typologies which have become depleted as sources of thought-provoking ideas.[7] Feudalism has been replaced as a key concept by the plantation, the frontier peasantry, the handicrafts, and the household industry. In the frontier areas a peasant population coexists with the capitalist system or has been generated by it. Velho explains that the state plays a mediating role among different modes of production in Brazil's expanding frontier areas. The coexistence of various modes of production in the Northeast is also described in another one of these chapters (Aguiar).

The relationship between the social structure's political and economic levels is a key issue in two chapters, which offer different explanations for this phenomenon. Velho is concerned with showing that authoritarianism is common to both the plantation and the national state. The plantation's traditional role in repressing the peasant population has been taken over by the state, which is now defining the limits of political participation. Palmeira points out that these limitations to peasant participation, whether imposed by the plantation or by the national state, tend to politicize economic disputes arising either in the context of specific jobs or from within the unions.

The combination of Marxist and Durkheimian approaches leads to an analysis of collective representation linked to the social division of labor. This outlook is found in two chapters (Aguiar and Palmeira) and is a departure from the traditional Marxist approach which countered any analyses based on the notion of a hierarchical continuum with a dichotomous view of social classes (Stavenhagen 1966). In the analytical framework presented by these authors the representational system is derived from the division of labor and allows for consolidating hierarchies into classes (Aguiar 1974).

The comparative approach is also applied in the use of Durkheimian and Marxist analytical models. Two chapters refer to the comparative method (Velho and Alcântara de Camargo), used by one of the authors as a strategy for moving from conjuncture to structure (Velho). The United States and the Soviet Union are the main reference points for comparison in the chapters dealing with the frontier peasantry and with the development of populism, which allows us to infer that a Third World perspective is strong in Brazil and that the countries used as reference points are industrialized nations which, like Brazil, have large territories.

Also represented in this collection is the perspective which discusses the relationship between economics and politics within the context of a combined Marxist and Weberian tradition, or of a more exclusively Weberian outlook.[8] This relationship between economic and political power is also analyzed in four other chapters (Alcântara de Camargo, Cintra, dos Santos, and Brasil de Lima Júnior), within a different framework than the ones introduced above (Velho and Palmeira), utilizing the Weberian perspective, widely used in Brazil, in an analysis of "colonelism" (the rule of local bosses of "colonels") in terms of political decentralization and the growth of the patrimonialist state with its strong centralizing tendencies. Two chapters focus on this problem and, in the process, discuss the sociopolitical literature produced on the subject. Both contributions will be discussed further on.

The political science tradition is also represented in this book (Cintra, dos Santos, and Brasil de Lima Júnior), providing still another approach to the relationship between political and economic power, as derived from public policy analyses. Wanderley Guilherme dos Santos and Olavo Brasil de Lima Júnior challenge the legal distinction between the concepts of public and private and discuss the difficulties posed by such definitions for public policy analyses. The authors prefer an analytical model whereby the institutions so far studied from a legal standpoint as private, but whose policies involve external implications for the public, can be used in accounting for the external effects of such policies. The point here is the importance of creating an analytical model that will account for the public consequences of a private decision.

Antônio Otávio Cintra develops the thesis that the central government delegates public powers as a result of its inability to maintain public order within a country as vast as Brazil. Through different means, Velho finds an analogy among the labor related policies in what he calls "authoritarian capitalism" and the "authoritarian state."

It would be erroneous to conclude that these contributions are derived from the classic traditions listed above. The latter should be viewed as a vehicle rather than an influence on the authors' approach to society. A dialogue takes place not only in relation to classic authors but also to contemporary ones. In this regard, we can mention theories of modernization, frontier development, and public policy analysis introduced by American sociologists and criticized and reappraised here (Aguiar, Velho, dos Santos, Brasil de Lima Júnior).

There is a strong tendency in these contributions to reflect on Brazil's classic sociological tradition through such authors as Azevedo Amaral, Victor Nunes Leal, Oliveira Vianna, and Capistrano de Abreu. In keeping with this tradition, social scientists analyze the authoritarian state, colonelism and the political mechanisms through which it relates to the state, the family's importance within Brazilian social structure, and the role of the frontier in Brazil's socioeconomic development.

An analysis of colonelism in terms of political decentralization and its interrelationships with the authoritarian state is used by two contributors (Cintra and Alcântara de Camargo) as a theoretical starting point for their studies. I will try to present some of these chapters in greater detail, since they offer an important frame of reference within which to consider the crisis that struck Brazil's agrarian society as well as the outbreak of the 1964 military movement leading to the authoritarian state, effective in Brazil to this day.

Antônio Otávio Cintra supports the theory that political centralization goes hand in hand with a high degree of administrative decentralization when order-keeping powers in the interior are delegated to local oligarchies. He describes the pact established as far back as the imperial era in Brazil between the centralizing interests of a bureaucratic state and a slavocratic class whose interests ran parallel to those of the empire, to the extent that this class continually extended its landholdings in accordance with the central government's expansionistic designs. Throughout Brazilian history this pact has been modified and reinstated. The central government has used it to keep the municipalities weak, as a way of guaranteeing local submission. The municipality is thus left with very limited institutional resources or none at all. However, a strong colonel who commands a large contingent of votes can use his influence to obtain favors for the municipality, in terms of the resources allocated by the federal government.[9]

The lack of power resources leads to frequent local disputes, while the strength of the central government and the municipalities' weakness result in political factionalism. Local disputes are always kept within a competitive rather than a conflictive framework and always involve factions of peers, that is, class barriers are never crossed. Manipulation by the central power is therefore obvious from the submission it fosters in the interior. Cintra concludes that municipal weakness is not incompatible with a strong local power.

Aspásia Alcântara de Camargo believes that where political and economic power do not correlate, the state often distributes its resources in such a way as to grant political power to regions or groups lacking in economic power. Specifically, in the case of the Northeast, the government from time to time applies differential criteria to provide support and representation for groups affected by economic crises or economic decadence. In granting differential representation to areas which are economically less representative the government operates as a redistributive force. Such is the case of the sugar-supplying regions where, as the author reminds us, one area whose sugar production sells at less competitive prices guarantees production quotas maintained through the intervention of the Institute for Sugar and Alcohol (IAA).

Nevertheless, as Antônio Otávio Cintra points out, an analysis of these regional mechanisms should not lead us to conclude that if an economically strong system does not have sufficient political representation its interests will not be taken into account by the state. Not only does Cintra provide examples of the forms of pressure available to the economically stronger states when they lack direct representation, but in addition he points out that, as such states discover that there are other states with compatible interests, new alliances are bound to emerge. This author also points to the economic measures which favored the state of Sao Paulo despite its lack of representativeness on given occasions. He also mentions that at the present time the state has more freedom to implement redistributive measures, although in the long run these measures are not sufficient for successful redistribution. In fact, economic incentive policies often increase some regional disparities.

The economic domination system is discussed by Moacir Palmeira in the specific context of the sugarcane-producing area. Aspásia Alcântara de Camargo proposes the existence of a conflict between sugarcane growers and industrial processors, to the extent that the sugar factory owners *(usineiros)* replaced the traditional sugar mill owners in the exploitation of sugarcane and became the product's chief industrial processors in that region by using modern techniques which were far more efficient than those of the old sugar mills. The sugar mill owners are no longer sugar producers as of old but have become suppliers of sugarcane for the modern factories or *usinas*.

Another chapter in this collection (Aguiar) describes a type of industrialization which is similar and complementary to the existing modes of agricultural exploitation but has prevented any change from taking place in the area's traditional labor relations.

The sugar mills which often rented land to the peasants became the center of conflicts leading to the emergence of peasant leagues. The background and development of these conflicts are described by Camargo and Palmeira. Among other things, the peasants demanded a stop to the practice of imposing upon them compulsory services in addition to the rent paid for the land.

Moacir Palmeira deals with the sugar mills and the sugar factory as different components of the same social organization. He points to conflicts of interest which arose between the factory owner and the suppliers by referring to a statement from the president of the Pernambuco Suppliers' Union who complained that a much smaller amount of resources was allocated to the supplier than to the *usineiro*.

Palmeira discusses the general crisis which affected sugarcane agriculture in the state of Pernambuco, the area chosen for his study and the setting in which the peasant leagues emerged, by referring to the competition between sugar-producing interests in the Northeast and their southern counterpart in the state of Sao Paulo. Because of its richer soils, better technology, more capital, and less effective labor unions for this particular type of production, added to a higher level of mechanization, Sao Paulo is better equipped than its northeastern competitor to produce low-priced sugar and has the potential to supply the entire country. State intervention through the creation of the Institute for Sugar and Alcohol precluded this possibility, ensuring the Northeast's production quotas, though at less competitive prices.

Palmeira also mentions other difficulties such as the product's periodic price fluctuations and the state's confiscation of profits through mediation in placing the product on the export market. There are also references to a third type of situation affecting sugarcane production in the Northeast. It involves competition from within the same region. Sugarcane production in the state of Alagoas has greater potential for mechanization and the peasants there are less belligerent, all of which has encouraged many of Pernambuco's *usineiros* to move to the neighboring state.

The process of peasant mobilization is described by Aspásia Alcântara de Camargo. We can now evaluate this movement in light of the political pact between the state and colonelism, a point which is mentioned by Camargo and analyzed in detail by Antônio Otávio Cintra.[10] Camargo makes a distinction between a mobilizing tendency that is the populist movement, and a populist policy. Populism would be the union of a populist movement with a populist policy, in an attempt to redefine alliances and arrive at a new balance among the centers of power.

Camargo shows that state interference through the Institute for Sugar and Alcohol affected both the state of Sao Paulo and the Northeast when the central government took it upon itself to define export relationships, impose export tariffs, purchase agricultural surpluses, and so on. According to Camargo, industrialization did not lead to changes in the political pact between the oligarchy and the central power. Under these circumstances, the lack of local resources encourages dependency on the government, which in turn guarantees the monopoly of power by one local political faction. Thus the Pernambuco oligarchies surrendered almost willingly to state control and operate as interest groups within the Institute for Sugar and Alcohol in order to guarantee their businesses either as sugarcane suppliers or as industrial processors of sugar. Through state mediation, both the colonels of the interior and the northeastern states manage to maintain ample representation.

As Palmeira points out, the crisis leads to an extortionist attitude on the part of factory owners and sugarcane suppliers, considered here as members of the same dominant class, although their positions within the productive system are different. The system of agricultural property includes the factory and the sugar mill, as well as their respective owners, the *usineiro* and the *senhor de engenho,* the latter having become in recent times a sugarcane supplier for the factory, as opposed to processing the product himself. Aspásia Alcântara de Camargo points out that the factory is technologically more complex than its predecessor, the sugar mill. Their interests, although conflicting in some cases, are coordinated by the Institute for Sugar and Alcohol. Camargo also refers to the colonels, who enjoy greater political representation and who, as a category, seem to overlap with the sugar mill owners or sugarcane suppliers. In using these concepts, with a distinction between the more modern and more decadent sectors of the sugarcane region in the Northeast, Alcântara de Camargo holds that economic decadence does not imply political decadence.

Moacir Palmeira points to the high degree of politicization which ensues when the sugarcane-producing region, trapped between crises, feels threatened by any change in the rules of the game. Efforts to extract the laborers' surplus value can lead to extremes which practically duplicate conditions preceding the 1964 political movement, although the political conjuncture is, of course, different. Moacir Palmeira focuses on the aftermath of the peasant mobilization, expounding on the exploitation suffered by the tenant worker, the renter, and the outside worker, upon facing the plantation hierarchy, or the sugar mill and factory owners' direct aides, the subcontractor, the supervisor, and the overseer or supervisor's assistant. In describing the various forms of labor exploitation prevailing in the area, Palmeira discusses the political context in which the unions must operate, closely controlled in their activities but nevertheless playing an important political role in relation to complaints constantly raised by the workers. Palmeira describes not a process of mobilization, but the situation in which such mobilization was once possible, and underscores the fact that the mobilization stage is still an important reference point for the peasants.

The oligarchies favored the urban populist policy as long as the mobilization mechanisms used with urban industrial workers did not reach the countryside. The populist pact was broken when that policy penetrated the rural milieu. Through a new openness in the political system, the state attempted to channel the peasant movement by capitalizing on the basic conflict of interests then developing between peasants and landowners. This was achieved by denouncing the oligarchies which the state had until then supported. The rise of this new alliance at a time of crisis frightened the oligarchies. According to Camargo, it is also important to note that peasant organization comprised a broad ideological spectrum which ranged from moderate reformists to radical extremists. Peasants whose participation had not been solicited up to then were being consulted in connection with different community programs. The new political openness implied that the peasants found themselves in a position which they had never before experienced. It also implied that alliances had shifted and that the oligarchies were under pressure to change. Social mobilization became a populist movement through the political direction it received from the state.

It is here that Alcântara de Camargo makes a distinction between a populist state and a popular movement. The former amounts to a political alliance of mutual cooperation, while the latter refers to a political merger where the social movement elects its representatives instead of being coopted by the state. Upon merging with the popular movement, the popular front created impasses which were even more radical than those caused by the populist state, and thereby triggered the institutional alternative of the authoritarian state. The advent of the authoritarian state reestablished the previous alliance, thus proving that the role of the oligarchies as social peace-keeping agents continues to be important within the political system.

The decline of the plantation and the peasants' move to the frontier areas are also a starting point for Velho's analysis. The plantation's periodic crises are not a recent phenomenon in Brazilian society. Berlinck and Hogan call attention to a theory proposed by Celso Furtado to the effect that the plantation's crises are cyclical, responding to price fluctuations in the international market. At times when business is bad, the area assigned to subsistence planting increases, while when prices are more favorable such an area decreases. Additional problems are caused by the seasonal nature of production. These cyclical problems, in addition to the government's current developmentalist interests with respect to the export market, the specific attention being devoted to food production, and the westward move by some northeastern factory owners toward the state of Maranhao, in search of areas with more regular rainfalls, lead us to question the diagnosis of decadence applied to the agrarian elites of the Northeast. Under the circumstances, the term *crisis* might be more accurate than *decadence*.

There are differences between peasant populism in the Northeast and southern urban populism in Sao Paulo (Alcântara de Camargo, Berlinck and Hogan), representing different types of political participation.

A comparison of prospects for union participation developed by Berlinck and Hogan, on the one hand, and by Palmeira, on the other, shows a lack of correlation.[11] This might be due to differences in methodology. If we take ethnographic accounts of voluntary associations between popular sectors in the state of Rio de Janeiro, we may conclude that, at least during particular times of the year, there is substantial participation in such associations as samba schools and *terreiros* (religious gathering grounds) (Sávio 1975; I. Velho 1975). The fact that Palmeira's analysis was based on the unions may account for the impression of intense participation projected in his chapter. On the other hand, the survey followed by intensive interviews provides a general framework, but does not allow for an assessment of the same wealth of details as provided by the ethnographic method. Exclusive use of the latter is not satisfactory in terms of the possibilities for generalization. Berlinck and Hogan attempt to use the ethnographic method as a complementary resource with which to interpret the results of the survey. Their approach, however, is not based on an analysis of labor relations. At any rate, once the populist policy had been depleted, popular mobilization was also exhausted in Sao Paulo, whereas in the case of the Northeast, specifically for the type of worker studies by Palmeira in the Pernambuco Woodland Zone, the potential for mobilization is still there. Alcântara de Camargo does not refer, as does Ianni (1968), to the collapse of populism, but proposes alternatives which are built into the structure, authoritarianism and populism, foreseeing a resurgence of the latter.

The chapters in this collection also allow us to question another perspective regarding populism. The analyses by Weffort (1965) and Cardoso (1970) lead us to conclude that there was an alliance bewteen sectors of the bourgeoisie and the working class against the agrarian export sector, which was the key to populist mobilization. Considering the problem in the Northeast, rather than the center-south, Alcântara de Camargo suggests, as an alternative, that agrarian and urban working class interests could converge. After all, the agrarian sector was not threatened by urban populism. It was only when the latter reached the countryside that the rules of the political game changed.

The peasants' alternatives for migration are also discussed (Velho, Berlinck and Hogan). The main choices are either to migrate to the frontier areas, under government incentive plans, or to head for Sao Paulo or neighboring areas.[12]

Assessments of regional policy have repeatedly appeared in the national and international academic literature (Furtado 1959; Hirschmann 1963; Robock 1962; Goodman 1972; Albuquerque and Cavalcanti 1976). Within the authoritarian context, Cintra outlines some shortcomings of the distributivist policy. The chapter by dos Santos and Brasil de Lima Júnior proposes an analytical model for public policies geared in that direction.[13]

The social consequences of the structure of production in rural areas affect the national industrial cost of labor (Aguiar, Velho, and Camargo), which constitutes attractive conditions for multinational industries (Camargo).[14]

The results of many of the changes mentioned in this introduction affect various sectors of society in ways which are now becoming apparent. Space limitations allow us only to mention some of them.[15] Movements toward the frontier are triggering conflicts with the Indian population, which have long been a matter of concern to Brazilian anthropologists, but to which society is only now beginning to respond.[16] The slavocratic origins of the plantation have generated a racial stratification system which even today affects the upward social mobility of Black Brazilians.[17] Women find that the social position they held in agrarian society, where the family was the mainstay of the production system, is reproduced in the urban-industrial context where the university's increasing accessibility interacts with social stereotypes which restrict women's increased participation in the productive system (Barroso and Namo de Mello 1975; Aguiar 1976).[18]

Neuma Aguiar
Rio de Janeiro, Brazil

NOTES

1. For example, the work of Fernando Henrique Cardoso was recently reviewed in a book by Joseph A. Kahl (1976). He is a representative of a widely known group, the Centro Brasileiro de Análise e Planejamento (CEBRAP). Other examples are the work of Gláucio Ary Dillon Soares, Hélio Jaguaribe, Florestan Fernandes, Maria Isaura Pereira de Queiroz, and Gilberto Freyre (see the general bibliography for references).
2. For a sociological concept of generation akin to the one employed here see Nanci Brigagão (1976).
3. While in 1965 there was one school in the country which offered the course at the master's and doctoral levels, in 1974 there were twenty-nine master's programs and four doctoral programs in the social sciences. Data collected by the Brazilian Council on Science and Technology and kindly made available to us show that, from a sample of six graduate programs in the social sciences which were declared centers of excellence by that council, 64 percent of a total of sixty-one graduate professors had done their graduate studies in the United States and Europe (out of a total of thirty-nine professors, thirty-five had studied in the United States, two in France, and two in England). The remaining 36 percent had completed their graduate work in Brazil.
4. See Wanderley Guilherme dos Santos's (1975) important paper on the Brazilian social imagination entitled "Paradigma e história," in which he develops the concept of institutional matrix to differentiate between the institutional practice of the social sciences and the independent practice which prevailed before 1930. The author believes that this should not lead us to consider independent work as either nonscientific or prescientific. This concept, as well as another one used by the author (the bourgeois order), were used as reference points in an earlier study I conducted (Aguiar 1975) on current trends in the Brazilian social sciences. Other studies could be mentioned in relation to the analysis of the Brazilian sociological imagination, such as dos Santos (1967); Alcântara (1967); Diniz Cerqueira and Soares de Lima (1971); and Barros (1975). The article by dos Santos (1975) mentioned above covers most of the local reflection on the topic.
5. Elaborate metaphors are sometimes used to characterize social situations. The result, although aiming at rationality, is obtained at the expense of clarity.
6. It was this realization concerning the isolation and lack of controversy that led Carlos Estevam Martins once to deplore (in a verbal communication) the current state of affairs in the social sciences: the lack of controversy and the

fact that authors sought more readily to accumulate data than to discuss the paradoxes generated by their research.

7. The concept of mode of production has been the subject of intensive debates in both the national (Tragtenberg 1974; Giannoti 1976; Palmeira 1971; Velho 1976) and international literature (Long 1975; Hindess and Hirst 1975; Aya 1976).

8. For an analysis of the Weberian tradition in Brazil see Fernando C. Dias (1973). For one of its major exponents see Raimundo Faoro (1975).

9. Voting studies have become a matter of wide academic interest since the pioneer survey study of Soares (1961). See Lamounier and Cardoso (1976). See also Campello de Souza (1976) and *Revista Brasileira de Estudos Políticos 43* (July 1976).

10. For the most recent analysis of colonelism under the Weberian tradition see Fernando Uricoechea (1977). His dissertation provides a wide coverage of literature in the area. For an American work arguing with the Brazilian traditional literature on this topic see Eul Soo Pang (1974).

11. For a review of books on labor unions in Sao Paulo see Aguiar (1975). For a recent work focusing on labor unions in the southern urban-industrialized part of the country see Vianna (1976).

12. An analysis of the informal labor market in metropolitan areas is made by Luiz Antonio Machado da Silva (1971).

13. See also the important analysis by James Malloy on the Brazilian social security system.

14. For an analysis of national entrepreneurs and their attitudes toward the state a study is being made by Luciano Martins, Mario B. Machado, and Sergio Abranches (forthcoming). See the work of Eli Diniz Cerqueira and Renato Boschi (1977) for attitudes in relation to multinationals. See also Cesar Guimaraes (1977).

15. An example of a pioneer publication on the social organization of the military is the work of Edmundo Campos Coelho (1976).

16. See the work of Roberto Cardoso de Oliveira (1964), quoted in more detail in the general bibliography. See also Matta (1976) and Ramos and Taylor (1968), among others.

17. This has been a tradition largely due to the work of Florestan Fernandes (1965, 1972) and the school he formed. He reviews the work done in the area for the last twenty-five years in a recent publication (Fernandes 1976). See also Carlos Hasenbalg (1977). For a contrast see the ethnography on the hedonistic lifestyle of the White, upwardly mobile middle class in Rio de Janeiro made by Gilberto Velho (1975).

18. For detailed references on women's situation see the bibliography compiled by Rosemberg and Namo de Mello (1975).

REFERENCES

Aguiar, Neuma. 1974. *Hierarquias em classes*. Rio De Janeiro: Zahar Eds.

_____. 1975. "Tendências atuais nas ciências sociais no Brasil." Rio de Janeiro: IUPERJ, mimeographed.

———. 1975. "Industrialization, Organization, and Unionization in Sao Paulo." *Studies in Comparative International Development* 10:100-106.

———. 1976. "The Impact of Industrialization on Women's Work Roles in the Northeast of Brazil." In June Nash and Helen Safa (eds.), *Sex and Class in Latin America*. New York: Praeger.

Albuquerque, Roberto Cavalcanti; and Cavalcanti, Clóvis Vasconcelos. 1976. *Desenvolvimento regional do Brasil*. Brasília: Instituto de Planejamento Econômico e Social.

Alcântara, Aspásia. 1967. "A teoria política de Azevedo Amaral." *Dados* 2-3:194-224.

Aya, Rod. 1976. Book review of Barry Hindess and Paul Q. Hirst's *Pre-Capitalist Modes of Production. Theory and Society* 3 (Winter 1976).

Barros, Alexandre S. C. 1975. "Gulliver em Lilliput ou a imagem que os cientistas sociais tem de si mesmos: introduçao à ediçao brasileira." In Oscar Cornblit et al., *Organizaçao e política da pesquisa social*. Rio de Janeiro: Fundaçao Getúlio Vargas.

Brigagâo, Nanci V. C. 1976. "Geraçoes que fazem história." Rio de Janeiro, mimeographed.

Barroso, Carmem Lúcia de Melo; and Namo de Mello, Guiomar. 1975. "O acesso da mulher ao ensino superior brasileiro." *Cadernos de Pesquisa: Revista de Estudos e Pesquisas em Educaçao* 15 (December): 47-77.

Campello de Souza, Maria do Carmo. 1976. *Estado e partidos políticos no Brasil, 1930 a 1964*. Sao Paulo: Alfa e Omega.

Cardoso de Oliveira, Roberto. 1964. *O indio e o mundo dos brancos. Sao Paulo: DIFEL*.

Coelho, Edmundo Campos. 1976. *Em busca de identidade: o exército e a política na sociedade brasileira*. Rio de Janeiro: Forense-Universitária.

Dias, Fernando C. 1973. "Presença de Max Weber na sociologia brasileira contemporânea." Universidade de Brasília, mimeographed.

Diniz Cerqueira, Eli; and Boschi, Renato Raul. 1977. "Magnitude das empresas e diferenciaçao da estrutura industrial: caracterizaçao da Industria paulista na década de 30." *Dados* 14.

Diniz Cerqueira, Eli; and Soares de Lima, Maria Regina. 1971. "O modelo político de Oliveira Vianna," *Revista Brasileira de Estudos Políticos* 30.

Dos Santos, Wanderley Guilherme. 1967. "A imaginaçao político-social brasileira." *Dados* 2-3:182-193.

———. 1975. "Paradigma e história." Rio de Janeiro: IUPERJ, mimeographed.

Faria, Luiz Castro. 1974. "Populaçoes meridionais do Brasil: ponto de partida para uma leitura de Oliveira Vianna." Museu Nacional da Universidade Federal do Rio de Janeiro, mimeographed.

Faoro, Raimundo. 1975. *Os donos do poder*. Porto Alegre and Sao Paulo: Editora Globo/Editora da Universidade de Sâo Paulo, 2nd ed.

Fernandes, Florestan. 1965. *A integraçao do negro na sociedade de classes*. São Paulo: Editora Dominus and Editora da Universidade de Sao Paulo.

_____. 1972. *O negro no mundo dos brancos.* Sao Paulo: Difusao Européia do Livro.

_____. 1976. *Circuito fechado.* Sao Paulo: Hucitec.

Freyre, Gilberto. 1963. *Mansions and Shanties: The Making of Modern Brazil.* New York: Alfred Knopf.

_____. 1969. *Masters and Slaves.* New York: Alfred Knopf.

Furtado, Celso. 1959. *Operaçao nordeste.* Rio de Janeiro: Instituto Superior de Estudos Brasileiros.

Gianotti, José Arthur. 1976. "Nota sobre a categoria 'modo de produçao' para uso e abuso dos sociólogos." *Estudos CEBRAP* 17:161-68.

Goodman, David. 1972. "Industrial Development in the Brazilian Northeast." In Riordan Roett (ed.), *Brazil in the Sixties.* Nashville: Vanderbilt University Press.

Guimaraes, César. 1977. "Empresariado, tipos de capitalismo e ordem política." *Dados* 14:34-47.

Hasenbalg, Carlos A. 1977. "Desigualdades raciais no Brasil." *Dados* 14:7-33.

Hindess, Barry; and Hirst, Paul Q. 1975. *Pre-Capitalist Modes of Production.* London and Boston: Routledge and Kegan Paul.

Hirschman, Albert O. 1963. *Journeys Toward Progress.* New York: Twentieth Century Fund.

Ianni, Octávio. 1968. *O colapso do populismo no Brasil.* Rio de Janeiro: Editora Civilizaçao Brasileira.

Jaguaribe, Hélio. 1968. *Economic and Political Development.* Cambridge, Mass.: Harvard University Press.

Kahl, Joseph A. 1976. *Modernization, Exploitation, and Dependency in Latin America: Germani, González Casanova, and Cardoso.* New Brunswick, New Jersey: Transaction Books.

Lamounier, Bolivar; and Cardoso, Fernando Henrique (eds.), 1976. *Os partidos e as eleiçoes no Brasil, 1974.* Rio de Janeiro: Paz e Terra.

Long, Norman. 1975. "Structural Dependency, Modes of Production, and Economic Brokerage in Rural Peru." In Ivar Oxaal et al. (eds.), *Beyond the Sociology of Development.* London and Boston: Routledge and Kegan Paul.

Machado da Silva, Luiz Antonio. 1971. "Mercados metropolitanos de trabalho manual e marginalizaçao." Museu Nacional da Universidade Federal do Rio de Janeiro, M.A. dissertation.

Martins, Luciano; Machado, Mario Brockman; and Abranches, Sérgio, Forthcoming. "Recursos humanos e problemas operacionais do estado." Research Report. Rio de Janeiro: IUPERJ and FINEP.

Matta, Roberto da. 1976. "Quanto custa ser indio no Brasil? Consideraçoes sobre o problema da identidade étnica." *Dados* 13:33-54.

Palmeira, Moacir. 1971. "Latifundium et capitalisme: lecture critique d'un débat." Faculté de Lettres et Sciences Humaines de l'Université de Paris, doctoral dissertation.

Pereira de Queiroz, Maria Isaura. 1968. *Réforme et révolution dans les sociétés traditionelles.* Paris: Anthropos.

Ramos, Alcida; and Taylor, Kenneth I. 1968. "Sugestoes para a criaçao de um parque indígena no território dos indios no norte do Brasil." Universidade de Brasília, mimeographed.

Robock, Stefan H. 1962. "Northeast Brazil: A Developing Economy." Washington, D.C.: Brookings Institution, Foreign Policy Studies Division, mimeographed.

Rosemberg, Fulvia; and Namo de Mello, Guiomar. 1975. "Levantamento bibliográfico preliminar sobre a situaçao da mulher brasileira." Fundaçao Carlos Chagas, Departmento de Pesquisas Educacionais, mimeographed.

Sávio, José. 1975. "Escola de samba, ritual e sociedade." Museu Nacional da Universidade Federal do Rio de Janeiro, M.A. dissertation.

Schwartzman, Simon. 1974. "Back to Weber: Corporatism and Patrimonialism in the Seventies." University of Pittsburgh, mimeographed.

_____. 1975. São Paulo e o estado nacional. São Paulo: DIFEL.

Soares, Gláucio Ary Dillon. 1961. "Classes sociais, stratas sociais e as eleições presidenciais de 1960." Sociologia 23 (September):217-38.

_____. 1963. "Brasil: la política del desarrollo desigual." Ciências Políticas y Sociales 32 (april-june):159-95.

_____. 1964. "The Political Sociology of Uneven Development in Brazil." In Irving Louis Horowitz (ed.), Revolution in Brazil. New York: Dutton.

_____. 1967. "The Politics of Uneven Development: The Case of Brazil." In Seymour Martin Lipset and Stein Rokkan (eds.), Party Systems and Voters' Alignments. New York: Free Press.

Stavenhagen, Rodolfo. 1966. "Estratificaçao social e estrutura de classes." In A. R. Bertelli, M. Palmeira, and O. Velho (eds.), Estrutura de classes e estratificaçao social. Rio de Janeiro: Zahar Editores.

Tragtenberg, Maurício. 1974. "O modo de produçao asiático." In Burocracia e ideologia. Sao Paulo: Editora Ática.

Uricoechea, Fernando. 1976. "The Patrimonial Foundations of the Brazilian Bureaucratic State: Landlords, Prince, and Militias in the XIXth Century." University of California at Berkeley, Ph. D. dissertation.

Velho, Gilberto. 1975. "Nobres e anjos." Universidade de Sao Paulo, doctoral dissertation.

Velho, Ivonne. 1975. Guerra de orixás. Rio de Janeiro: Zahar.

Velho, Otávio G. 1976. Capitalismo autoritário e campesinato. Sao Paulo: DIFEL.

Vianna, Luiz Werneck. 1976. Liberalismo e sindicato no Brasil. Sao Paulo: Paz e Terra.

Weffort, Francisco C. 1965. "Raízes sociais do populismo na Cidade de Sâo Paulo." Rivista Civilização Brasileira 1 (May):39-60.

The State and the Frontier

Otávio Guilherme Velho

Brazilian and United States Frontier Developments

It has been a long-standing tradition for Brazilian scholars to compare Brazilian and U.S. development. This is natural, owing to the great similarities and contrasts between the two countries. It is not a purely scholarly attitude, but reflects a spontaneous interest within Brazilian society. Many conclusions scholars have come to are in a way systematizations of general beliefs (Freyre 1963: 67-92; Moog 1969).

These comparisons usually start from a historical point of view. Thus the question of the occupation and colonization of the two territories is raised from the start. Such comparisons have until now usually led to serious deadlocks. Absolute analogies (colonial background, large territories, etc.) and absolute contrasts (mainly U.S. development and Brazilian backwardness) are hard to fit and one is usually forced into cultural, religious, and racial explanations which are not of the same nature as the facts (mainly economic) with which one started.

This is due to two main methodological errors that have their origin in ideological preconceptions of a historicist nature. One of them is that these studies tend to project unilinearly the present into the past. Thus if one is confronted with U.S. development and Brazilian backwardness, these must be sought and found *as such* in the past. The different social formations that came into being in the two territories are not considered in terms of their meaning in their contemporary setting (Moog 1969).

The other error is that to the extent that this comparison is based on very immediate historical references, one not only implicitly excludes from consideration comparisons which may be theoretically relevant and whose points of reference would be structural rather than historical, but one may also lose sight of important structural references in the initial

17

comparison itself. One of the consequences of this position is that the spontaneous or legal categories which describe these different phenomena are usually not questioned and their content is not carefully analyzed.

The first error mentioned can be seen, for instance, in the development of a system mainly based on free labor and family economy in the territory later to become part of the United States, versus a system based on labor repression and export production in Brazil.[1] This is viewed as "development" and "backwardness" in their original forms. These two systems would be better understood in terms of what these different territories represented at the time. Brazil would then be seen as a typical colony having a clear role in the process of primitive accumulation of capital. New England, on the other hand, would in this sense not be at all typical due to a very specific feature of British development: the fact that Britain, through the enclosures, had created a "surplus population" of a sort that did not occur in any other European country before the nineteenth century, least of all Portugal. New England served to siphon off this "surplus" and other territories would serve for primitive accumulation. It seemed much more important for England in the eighteenth century to maintain its hold in the West Indies and even Canada than in New England. Consequently, U.S. present development is not positively correlated to a former predominant role as a colony. On the contrary, the fact that it did not have such a predominant role permitted a classic internal accumulation of capital. Reaction to the metropolis came only when such a situation was threatened. This seems a better basis for explaining this initial difference which, in spite of all qualifications, has been important for further development.

A symptom of the second error can be felt, for instance, in the fact that in spite of the interest in comparing Brazilian and U.S. territorial expansion, the work of Frederick Jackson Turner is practically unknown in Brazil.[2] Although Turner was mainly interested in the American frontier, it should be mentioned—as Gerhard (1958-59) has pointed out—that he "also referred to the frontier as a phase in a general process of evolution, the significance of which in the formation of other societies ought to be investigated." This is probably the main reason why Turner was not tackled by Brazilian scholars. If he was referring exclusively to the American frontier his observations could be contrasted with Brazilian developments and cultural explanations could still hold to account for the obvious differences. But his "thesis" is transcultural. It is the frontier as such and as an element of a wider structure that is important, irrespective of cultural factors and initial motives.[3] Turner's thesis is basically structural and any definite discussion of it would also have to be structural, a point of view incompatible with the historicism that characterizes a good part of Brazilian literature on the subject of territorial expansion.

Authoritarian Politics and Labor Repression

In true Turnerian fashion my interest here is much more on a sociology *from* than *of* the frontier. Let us start by going back to the question of free versus repressed labor. It has been suggested that the latter in Brazil, basically through the plantation system, had to do with primitive capitalist accumulation. This does not answer the basic question as to how such a system was able to structure itself and why repression of labor was necessary for the extraction of a surplus. Turner would say that a frontier forges a spirit of independence which would be more consistent with a system of small independent producers. He was not alone in that position. Karl Marx (1906.843), in a very different context, implied something similar. In the chapter on the theory of modern colonization in *Capital* he ridiculed the attempt to transplant the capitalist mode of production to Australia in a situation of open resources.

> The regular reproduction of the wage-labourer as wage-labourer comes into collision with impediments the most impertinent and in part invincible.... The wage-worker of to-day is tomorrow an independent peasant, or artisan, working for himself. He vanishes from the labour-market, but not into the workhouse. This constant transformation of the wage-labourers into independent producers, who work for themselves instead of for capital, and enrich themselves instead of the capitalist gentry, reacts in its turn very perversely on the conditions of the labour-market. Not only does the degree of exploitation of the wage-labourer remain indecently low. The wage-labourer loses into the bargain, along with the relation of dependence, also the sentiment of dependence on the abstemious capitalist.

Is this not the hidden side of the coin that Turner presented to us and which explains it? So it seems. But what about the plantation? After all, in Brazil and elsewhere it established itself in a situation where free land was available. Evsey Domar (1970) in a recent article has put together some ideas already present in less systematic form in earlier writers (Marx included), that may be of help to us. Domar has suggested that "free land, free peasants, and non-working landowners — any two elements but never all three can exist simultaneously." This is very close to Marx's argument just presented. But Domar (1970) goes on to add that "the combination to be found in reality will depend on the behaviour of political factors," and that "a change in the land/labour ratio can set in motion economic and political forces acting in opposite directions.'' That is, given an area of free land, instead of witnessing the dispersion of labor a ruling class may impose an immobilization of the working force. This is a very interesting suggestion which adds an important alternative to Turner's reasoning. According to him, if one has free land one would expect the development of small-scale family farms. Marx himself would generalize: if one has free land one has independent producers and, at the limit, the impossibility of a centralization of capital and production based on a combination of labor. But Domar's argument suggests — putting it in more theoretical terms — that this view would only hold when the economic instance is dominant. In fact, the opposite may result if through political means, in a broad sense, one immobilizes the working force through the establishment of slavery or serfdom, thus avoiding the transformation of a physical frontier into a sociological one. In both cases the physical frontier would not be favorable to the formation of a free labor market, but in each case this would lead to different and even opposite systems of social and economic organization.

Domar's argument is important for our discussion not only because the issue of the frontier and that of repressed labor are put together, but also because he gives us some clues for clarifying what authoritarianism is about. Where most authors would simply see the unspecified action of noneconomic or even artificial forces, he broadly sets for us the possibility of considering different kinds of articulations between economic and political instances and ultimately the different roles of the state.

Brazilian and United States Frontier Myth Makers

These different modes of articulation between politics and economics, although rarely presented in theoretical terms, often emerge clearly from an analysis of ideological texts. Such is the case, for instance, when one compares the work of two myth makers who used the frontier as raw material for their myths: Frederick Jackson Turner and Cassiano Ricardo. The existence of large tracts of almost unoccupied land in Brazil (until recently practically half the country), which seems to have been the necessary consequence of a system based on labor repression, has been for years an important element of a rhetoric that came to be synthesized in the phrase: ''Brazil, land of the future.'' This rhetoric, which initially served as a compensation for actual backwardness, became more important after 1930 and particularly with the establishment of the New State in 1937.[4] In 1938 the government announced a Westward March.

A leading intellectual figure who like Turner, confirms the excellence of the frontier in providing raw material for myth making, was Cassiano Ricardo. His main book — *Marcha para oeste* (Westward March) — appeared in 1940 and was very well received by the regime. In 1970, at the time the building of the Transamazonic road was announced, it went through its fourth Brazilian edition. Ricardo's main ideas shed light on the ideological relation between authoritarianism and the frontier, while constituting a significant contrast with Turner's ideas on the frontier. Like Turner, Ricardo was aware of the importance of the frontier as a myth and seemed to consciously assume the role of mythmaker. As he said in the preface to the second edition of his book, which Richard Morse (1967:204-5) included in his readings on *The Bandeirantes:*

> The bandeira transcends the domain of history and mingles with the mythological. To explain its heroes, does not a learned man like Saint-Hilaire find himself obliged to classify them as a "race of giants"? To his way of thinking only giants... could have conquered a continent on foot... today's "mechanical" world, unsentimental and anti-human, heightens in us the tendency to place the bandeira in the mythological world. It thus acquires a new force in our collective dynamism. What is "ephemeral" in historical fact becomes eternal in legend, perhaps because the myth is an "image" which in history acquires the power of a symbol.... And even today, the chief of the Nation himself [President Getulio Vargas], when he speaks of a new Westward march, is careful to say that "it has nothing to do with an image." More than a mere image, "it is an urgent and necessary reality to cross over the plateau and pick up again the train of the pioneers who planted the territorial boundary markers in the heart of the Continent, in a vigorous and epic thrust."

Similarly to Turner, Ricardo (1970:8) believed the East coast maintained close ties with Europe (especially Portugal), while the West (the *sertao*) was conquered by those who were willing to loosen these ties. Thus at the beginning of colonization, "the positions were thus defined: the ships attracted the Portuguese linked to their cultural matrix; and the *sertao* attracted those (*mamelucos,* i.e., mixed bloods of European and Indian descent) who gave their backs to the sea." And "when the first *bandeira* goes into the woods, the history of Portugal ends, and the history of Brazil begins" (Ricardo 1970:229).[5]

The agrarian plantation society that established itself on the coast became "feudal," while the *bandeira* society which had its main base in inland Sao Paulo looked for new solutions. While the Negro was the main influence on the European of the plantation, the Indian was the main influence on the *bandeirante,* which explains the mobility of the *bandeira* (Ricardo 1970:27). "The *bandeira,* is an ethnic sense, is born with the first generation of *mamelucos*. Democratization through race mixture is thus its birthplace" (Ricardo 1970:42).

"Biological mobility" shortened racial and social distances (Ricardo 1970:109). This in turn made for "social democratization" (Ricardo 1970:120). The *bandeira* was thus born in a "democratic" milieu; in the *bandeira* there was a "division of labor according to skin color" (Ricardo 1970:322) and a "hierarchization of skin colors in the civil and military organization of the group" (Ricardo 1970:323).

> In the formation of this rude democracy, the Indian contributes with social mobility, the Negro with abundance of sentiment and human warmth, the White man with his spirit of adventure and command....It is not possible to think of *bandeirante* democracy without the hierarchical organization of the group, which permits the use of all human values by the living capacity of each one and not by abstract, irrational, or standardized equality. The Indian as a rower, hunter, and police is as clearly explainable as the Negro as an agriculturalist and miner. There would neither have to be any violence for the White man to be in command. In the division of labor, as in that of political posts, each human element has his role, determined more by the tendency of each group than by violence or the imposition of racial prejudice (Ricardo 1970:324).

This "functional hierarchization" was presided by a "spirit of cooperation" that permitted everyone's development (Ricardo 1970:324-27). In this it was supposed to be very different from the "feudal" organization of the plantations. The plantations did not like pathways, for they were a menace to their prestige. The plantation represented conservative power, while the *bandeira* represented the revolution from which would burst forth democracy and independence (1970:452-53). The *bandeira* channeled the runaways from the plantations and avoided their violent reflux against the plantations (1970:454).

On the coast, Brazil could not develop on the basis of small properties, since that would be an obstacle to its territorial expansion. But the *bandeirante* — since he was not really primarily interested in land but in mobility — when he settled, he did so on small property (Ricardo 1970:70-71). Being inland, the *bandeirantes* were far away from crown authorities. Since they had to defend themselves from Indians and all sorts of dangers, they had to become organized. They gave origin to the only real Brazilian experience in self-government (1970:187).

The *bandeira* chief concentrated all powers in his hands: executive, legislative, and judicial. The *bandeira* would not be able to subsist without an authority. The *bandeira* had to be conducted by its chief in a military, Roman fashion. It was, according to Ricardo (1970:479), a state in miniature: "The *bandeira* chief thus represents, in our social and political genesis, the creator of strong government, courageously American." This had to be so because the "natural" tendency in a tropical milieu, which the Indian embodied, was for "savage communism" to prevail. Only authoritarian, antiliberal *bandeirismo* could bring order and impose rationality on this tendency, establishing a "hierarchical democracy." According to Ricardo (1970:482-83) this is the origin of Brazil's attachment to strong government and to a leader who — contrary to "feudal" practice — full of community spirit and personal valor arises from the masses which have felt the need to be governed.

After independence, the coastal cities structured democracy politically (Ricardo 1970:526). They were prey to "exotic liberalism," which has little to do with real democracy, since each people should organize liberty according to its own ways.

> These facts mean...that one thing is our social-democratic formation and another one is our liberal and urban "de-formation." The *bandeirante* has already proved that "liberal" has nothing to do with "democratic." Imperialist (internally) and anti-liberal, he had built his rude but true democracy in opposition to the sugar aristocracy and to Indian communism....The *bandeirante* is not domineering as many think. He is the protector, the creator of strong and autocratic government   (Morse 1967:198).

The *bandeira,* like the state is a sort of extension of the family. And the bandeira chief is a sort of father for all.

From Decentralized to Centralized Authoritarianism

Ricardo's work would enchant any myth specialist. It seems to have most of the elements of a myth and many myth substructures can be distinguished (Esterci 1972). And of course, it all has to do with justifying and legitimizing state authoritarianism. It is a sort of myth of the origin of authoritarianism.

A comparison with Frederick Jackson Turner's work and his myth of the origin of American democracy is interesting. They have several important points of contact, such as the East/West (coast/*sertao*) opposition and the belief in the "conservative" character of the East. The "natural" tendency perceived as resulting from the frontier seems to go in the same direction in both authors, although Turner positively labels it "democracy" and Ricardo considers that it would not be self-regulating, thus going further in terms of the nonexistence of law, and approximating "anarchy" and "savage communism."

Here we have the decisive twist: the *bandeirante* has to become primitive like the Indian, but — almost as if parodying the idea of the domination of politics — Ricardo says that *because* of this natural tendency the *bandeira* has to develop an authoritarian structure as a reaction. Thus from a similar starting point he arrives at the opposite of Turner's view. It is not the frontier as such which gives the Brazilian frontiersman his fundamental characteristics, but a frontier coupled with his reaction to its anarchic influences. While for Turner the frontier is the locus where American democracy develops, for Ricardo the frontier experience leads to the development of Brazilian authoritarianism. In both cases the frontier is used as raw material for the creation of myths of origin. However, each one of the myths turns out to be the opposite of the other. This is extremely revealing in terms of the contrast between authoritarianism and classic bourgeois development.

The analogy between the *bandeira* and the New State is clear. They are both genuinely Brazilian or American and not imported (although significantly, Ricardo does approximate them several times to "Roman" experiences). Through "hierarchical democracy" they both have to face and defeat "feudalism" (colonelism for the New State) and communism ("savage" communism for the *bandeira* and "Russian" communism for the New State). And they both have a territory to conquer or occupy.

Ideologically the Westward March of the New State was of the utmost significance as a bridge with the Bandeirante movement and a reenactment of it through the cultivation of a Bandeirante spirit. Now the territory had to be definitely occupied. It was no longer only a question of a Westward March, but also of a march to the west. And Ricardo's stress on small property as being characteristic of the settled *bandeirante* (a feature which, to say the least, is historically unimportant), in contrast with large "feudal" property, also determines the kind of occupation he had in mind and its balancing functions.

The Bandeirante movement did not establish any independent or dominant structure in the long run. The territory it covered was either incorporated into the dominant system or not really occupied, simply politically guaranteed. The main interest Ricardo's writings present is ideological. But ideology is not a synonym for falsehood. Although in a distorted way, ideology may express genuine social processes. For our purposes the main point that comes out of Ricardo's writings, together with the general connection between state and frontier, is the idea of authoritarianism as a reaction against spontaneous or "natural" trends which would be dissolving. If one substitutes *economics* for *natural* — and this underlying identification is also "natural" in our present societies — one has the idea of political dominance clearly presented.

Once the broader notion of political dominance is established, one can try to rethink the state as one possible locus for political dominance among others. The notion of political dominance helps to establish a relationship between systems based on labor repression and state authoritarianism. Labor repression may or not be established directly through state action, but it will always reveal political dominance.[6] One could then establish the notion of decentralized authoritarianism in contrast with centralized authoritarianism. However different, they represent different varieties of loci of political dominance. Contrarily to other authors that maintained an absolute contrast between private and public power, Ricardo expressed this relation between the two in his mythological language when he considered the *bandeira* as a miniature state.

The shift from decentralized to centralized authoritarianism as a quest for survival under pressure from the international system in an era of combined and unequal development, in spite of all contradictions that may appear, would today be consistent with the development of authoritarian capitalism. This would be the case even where internal and external circumstances force this development into a radical posture that may eventually and for a time make it seem anticapitalist or part of a socializing or Third World phenomenon.

In Brazil this transition from decentralized to centralized authoritarianism never had to become particularly radical in this sense. Now that through the establishment of a new authoritarian regime it has successfully completed the shift from its initial and necessary nationalist phase (most clearly represented by the former authoritarian regime of the New State) into a more mature cosmopolitan one, this possibility seems ever more remote.

Political Unity and Authoritarian Integration

One of the ways one can view authoritarian capitalism is as a special mode of capitalist development which comes about in backward or underdeveloped countries as a consequence of the preexistence of an international capitalist system. It is based on political dominance in contrast with bourgeois capitalism once its primitive accumulation is completed. It is characterized by a sort of nonorganic development by leaps and bounds and not by retracing all the steps taken by prior capitalist development in other countries. This creates a great strain, particularly on the need for capital accumulation. To make an analogy with classic capitalist development, it is as if these strains and needs never permitted authoritarian capitalism to leave behind its "savage" primitive accumulation. One of the consequences of this is continuous reliance on political dominance. Another important consequence is continuous reliance on exploitation of labor. In Brazil the latter has appeared disguised in debates such as that of so-called concentration of income, but usually seen as a mere consequence of a particular and reversible economic policy. In regard to its basic features (in contrast with certain obvious situational exacerbations) it is a much deeper problem.

A case analogous to exploitation of labor is the exploitation of geographic regions (such as the Brazilian Northeast) or of whole sectors of the economy to the detriment of others. An example could be those sectors of the agriculture linked to the production of foodstuffs for the internal market. The relatively low prices of foodstuffs do not permit these sectors to accompany the average rate of profit in the economy, and by keeping the cost of the urban labor force low, favor industry. This may be one of the reasons why peasant production, whose very nature is based on imposed self-exploitation, is usually not superseded by capitalist production in agriculture in these circumstances. It seems impossible to conceive authoritarian capitalist development without these phenomena of structural heterogeneity and overexploitation. As we shall see further on, this is where the frontier areas in Brazil come into the picture.

Successors of the Plantation Labor-Repressive System

During most of Brazilian history part of its territory was taken over by the plantation system or its subordinate subsystems, while another large part simply had its political conquest guaranteed, but without any large-scale definite occupation. This is the broad picture. There were some episodic activities connected to mineral and vegetal extraction, but these were consistently labor-repressive. Here and there appeared what Oberg (1965) has termed a "marginal peasantry," but the term itself punctuates their limited structural importance, except as a reverse side of the coin of repressed labor — the exception that confirms the rule.[7]

The development of state centralization and authoritarian capitalism as the "legitimate" successor of the labor-repressive system of the plantation and as the main locus of political dominance[8] has gradually changed the meaning of the frontier in Brazil. In a sociological sense only these developments have given origin to a real frontier. The effective and definitive occupation of Central Brazil and the Amazon River region is largely a phenomenon of our time, contemporary to the centralization of authoritarianism. It has owed much to state action ignoring criteria of immediate economic viability. Although already present as a trend (and on an ideological level), this became particularly evident with the building of the Belém-Brasília road during the Kubitschek administration (1956-60), and was itself an instrument in strengthening the state through broadening the social arena beyond the physical limits where established local and regional interests prevailed. Does this mean that labor-repression is no longer an issue? The problem is much more complex, and that is one of the reasons why it has been difficult for the state in Brazil to create a consistent and systematic policy regarding agriculture in general and the frontier in particular. As we have seen through Ricardo's writings, the perception of the ideological importance of the frontier was not new. Getulio Vargas (n.d.:284-85) himself, in 1940 said:

> After the reform of November 10, 1937 [the coup d'état that inaugurated the New State], we included this crusade in the program of the New State, saying that the true direction of Brazil is that of the West. To clarify the idea I must say to you that Brazil, politically, is a unit. We all speak the same language, have the same historical tradition, and would be capable of self-sacrifice in order to defend our territory. Considering it an indivisible unity, no Brazilian would admit the hypothesis of giving up one inch of this land, which constitutes his flesh and blood. But if politically Brazil is a unit, it is not so economically. Regarding this aspect it resembles an archipelago made up of islands interlaced with empty spaces. The islands have already achieved a high degree of economic and industrial development and their political frontiers coincide with the economic frontiers. The vast empty spaces, however, continue, and have not achieved the necessary renovated climate due to the lack of a whole series of elementary measures whose execution figures in the government's program and in the aims of the administration — foremost among them sanitation, education, and transport. The day they are furnished with all these elements, the empty spaces will be filled. We shall have demographic density and industrial development. In this way the program of the Westward March represents the resumption of the campaign carried on by the builders of nationality, the *bandeirantes* and *sertanistas,* with the integration of the modern cultural processes. We must promote this takeoff, in all aspects and with all methods, in order to delete the demographic vacuums from our territory and make the economic frontiers coincide with the political frontiers. This is our imperialism. We do not ambition one inch of territory which is not ours, but we have an expansionism which is that of growing within our own frontiers.

This is all full of powerful ideological images, and the idea that the political frontiers are ahead of the economic frontiers and that the latter must catch up seems to represent the noncorrespondence between politics and economics in a backward country. The stress on the frontier movement, as a way of filling up the empty spaces between the "economic islands" that made up Brazil, also looks like a reinforcement of the classic authoritarian theme of national unity and integration and of a national outlook as opposed to particularistic regional ones.

There were also other more pragmatic functions that the frontier was supposed to perform, besides the mainly ideological ones that prevailed in practice at first. The concrete "functions" of the unoccupied areas perceived by the state were connected to the general need on the part of authoritarian capitalism to chart the course of its development in such a manner as to steer away both from the old structures which it wanted to transform and from the whirlpool of uncontrolled change which could result if the old structures, instead of being transformed, were destroyed. One of Getulio Vargas's most mythicized personal qualities was, significantly, his "political realism," which appears to be an inevitable manifestation of authoritarian capitalist development at the time.

Social scientists such as Gláucio A. D. Soares (1964) called attention to the fact that industrialization and populist mobilization in the cities coexisted with an agrarian structure left practically untouched. This constituted an outflanking of the old structures and a way, through the appearance of new social actors, of creating the conditions for a new balance of forces inside the system and consequently also the conditions for its ultimate overall transformation. The two poles of this dualism maintained a complex relationship, which was not reducible either to a complete incompatibility between them or to a total mutual functionality. But what has not received so much attention is that the Westward March movement, analogously to industrialization, was, in a way, conceived as a possibility of outflanking the system from the other side.

Vargas spoke frequently of the evils of latifundia such as its low productivity, and of the advantages of small property for the creation of abundance and wealth (in Neiva 1943:237). But instead of trying to substitute one for the other through direct confrontation, he saw the unoccupied frontier areas as loci for the development of this small property. This would mean channeling tensions away from the established agrarian structure and giving it a chance of transforming itself without being destroyed. This kind of policy, according to the point of view of the observer, could be negatively labeled "demagogic" or "reactionary," and it suffered the opposition of both extremes of the political spectrum.

Peasant Development and Capitalist Growth

Except for a few isolated attempts (Esterci 1972) all this was not put into practice during the New State, either because it had not yet become urgent and there were other possibilities still to be explored or due to the still limited resources of the state at the time. A systematic, concrete policy would only start taking shape in the late 1950's with Celso Furtado's SUDENE scheme for the colonization of the humid lands of the state of Maranhao. Furtado also called attention to the possibility of trying to fill the gaps in the food supply of the big cities left by the established agrarian structure through the use of small peasant agriculture on unoccupied frontier land in state-directed colonization projects (Grupo de Trabalho para o Desenvolvimento do Nordeste 1959).

Viewed from the mid 1970's there are important points of general reasoning that persist, while others seem to change. One of the problems is that government policy is not formulated and put into practice in an absolutely passive milieu. Two particularly important factors must be taken into account: first is the so-called spontaneous movement of small peasants into frontier areas which is often prior to government action and usually difficult to fit into government schemes; and second, the growing capitalist interest in those areas once government has opened them up and created by its own action formerly inexistent economic viability for many kinds of enterprises, particularly cattle raising for beef export and mineral extraction.

These two movements toward the frontier are often in opposition to each other and these last few years have witnessed many serious clashes. The position of the state regarding this issue will certainly be basic concerning the future of the frontier areas in Brazil and of state action itself. The confrontation between the two movements is mainly the result on the one hand of the disintegration of the old plantation system and its subordinate subsystems; and on the other hand of the development of capitalist forces.

From a classic point of view this is a confrontation between archaic precapitalist forces and developing capitalism and the inevitable result will be the triumph of the latter. There are even critics on the Left who suggest that the sooner this happens the better, since the strengthening of the bourgeoisie will lead to the superseding of authoritarianism by bourgeois democracy, permitting the eventual development of the confrontation between bourgeoisie and proletariat (in this case, a rural proletariat). This view is connected to a more general rather Menshevist view of the development of Brazilian society which is gradually taking shape. To the extent that it becomes a reality the formerly perceived functions of the frontier linked to small peasant agriculture will lose meaning. The main question is whether there is a real possibility of this bourgeois hegemony ever coming about.

State, Bourgeois Entrepreneurs, and Peasants

The three main actors in the frontier areas are the state, the bourgeois entrepreneurs, and the developing frontier peasantry. Something should be said briefly about the latter and its relations with the other two, since it is the least acknowledged and understood of the three. This peasantry is composed mostly of northeasterners. Directly or indirectly this mass movement has to do with the breakdown of the plantation system. Its origins can be traced to the migration of northeasterners into unoccupied areas of the state of Maranhao in the 1920s (Velho 1972). Other less numerous groups migrated to parts of the Amazon region, but in terms of a mass movement linked to peasant production the migration trend to the state of Maranhao was the most significant. It went on little noticed by public opinion, and when the Belém-Brasília road (which links the capital of the state of Pará) was built in the late 1950s the peasants were already crossing over into the state of Pará. The building of the Transamazonic road in the early 1970s would find them well established in the Tocantins River Basin area of Southern Pará and spreading in several directions, one of which would be the Xingu River in the general direction the road was to follow. Simultaneously other currents were developing. One of the most important spread in Acre and Rondônia at the other extreme of the Amazonas region and was made up not only of northeasterners, but also of small farmers from southern Brazil. When the building of the Transamazonic highway and official colonization projects along its route were announced in 1970, intensive migration into the region had already been in progress for several years. Since then this trend has proceeded and developed.

The "archaic" quest for land and for setting up independent production units is indeed a strong motivation, and even the establishment in government-sponsored projects is sometimes strongly resisted (Velho 1973). The transformation of proletarians into peasants that Marx alluded to is constantly taking place in the region, with a rapid turnover of individuals who are hired as workers in big capitalist projects (mainly as cowhands) and as soon as possible try to establish themselves as independent producers (Almeida 1974).[9]

This is where the issue of labor repression creeps into the picture once more. It is curious how in a situation of open resources labor repression is again present inspite of a supposedly modern capitalist dominance. Many devices — traditional and new — are used to try to secure a stable supply of labor, and accusations of "slave labor" are not infrequent even in the press (Almeida 1974). The main issue for the future is the access to land and property rights. The position of the state is of course basic in this matter, in a situation where the built-in social (and not "natural") rights to property are much more evident and undisguised than in long established areas.

State Balance between Peasants and Entrepreneurs

There are two general attitudes on the part of dominant interests regarding peasant movement into Amazonas. One of them (which we have already alluded to and could be considered the "bourgeois" position) would change its character, thus avoiding any competition for natural resources (particularly land) and turning the peasants into wage earners. The other would try to limit and control this movement by means of government-directed colonization projects. Let us examine the viability and consequences of each position.

One of the main difficulties for carrying out such a "bourgeois" program has to do with the structural heterogeneity that characterizes Brazilian society. In the particular case of agriculture if the rate of profit in the production of basic foodstuffs for the internal market (such as certain varieties of rice, beans, manioc, etc.) does not accompany the general rate, in the long run why should capitalist entrepeneurs go on producing them when soya beans, beef, and other products are so much more interesting? And if they do stop producing, Who else can fill the gap but the peasant who uses these products for his own consumption and whose unit of production does not work on a capitalist profit basis?[10] There does not seem to be any easy alternative. It is accepted knowledge that Brazilian industrialization is based and dependent on the cheap price of the labor force, and the exploitation of urban workers has practically achieved its physical limits. Thus the price of basic foodstuffs simply cannot be allowed to float on a free market, even when policymakers would like it to.

One of the characteristics authoritarian capitalism shares with the so-called phase of primitive accumulation is that much that is necessary for the system does not come about automatically. This means that in spite of its "spontaneous" origin the development of the neopeasantry may in this phase partly depend on state action.[11] This is not the case only on the frontier, but it is there that this development could occur, at least on a large scale, without unduly upsetting the foundations of the system. The alternative would not only be unthinkable in the long run from the point of view of basic supply, but would also force state intervention in a most repressive form to guarantee land exclusively for large enterprises. Results would be doubtful, and if ultimately successful would depopulate the region and create problems of labor supply for the large enterprises themselves. As things stand the lack of an adequate supply of labor due to migration is already a limitation to the generalization of capitalist agriculture in Brazil and one more factor favoring peasant agriculture not basically dependent on extrafamily labor. The creation of a balance between these two types of production seems unavoidable.

The colonization projects have not so far shown themselves to be a practical way out. In fact it is their apparent failure that has been hailed lately as an evident sign of the need for the occupation of the frontier to be left to large enterprises. It is possible, however, that this failure is not inevitable, but is due to the yet unaccepted development of a free peasantry, that although subordinate to dominant authoritarian capitalism, has to have a large degree of social and physical space in order to be successful (Velho 1972, 1973). This makes the difference between a free peasantry and a complex division of labor inside large enterprises, and the peasants, in contrast with the promoters of the colonization projects, are very aware of it.

Overcoming this limitation may be forced by events themselves and by the development of the regime's "social face" and of a "mature" authoritarian ideology. This will not mean the end of large enterprises in the Amazonas region. They are also absolutely necessary for the system. In spite of all contradictions it is a question of coexistence (and at least in the middle run also of combination). There is certainly enough physical space for this at the moment and the government's presence has to serve as a guarantee for a Solomonic division of areas.

Peasant Democracy and Authoritarian Capitalism

Is it possible that the regime's doubts about a freer rein for the development of a frontier peasantry are totally ungrounded? This development would certainly be part of a larger strategy of gradual transformation of social structures without upsetting the foundations of the system in the way a revolution from below would. The predicament is not new, even in the use of unoccupied land as an additional trump in this delicate game. This is how Donald Treadgold (1957:189), analyzing a situation which presents some curious analogies, sums up Prime Minister Stolypin's intentions and misgivings regarding the colonization of Siberia at the beginning of the century:

> He hoped to bring social stability to the mass of the people, the peasantry, by way of land settlement and migration together. Unlimited movement, unaccompanied by measures intended to secure solid settlement, would entail risks. If the safety-valve of migration operated smoothly, economic pressures in the homeland might be gently and gradually relieved, and the monarchy would be easier to preserve. If migration should entirely escape the confines of governmental assistance and direction, the result might be the

"rude democracy" about which Stolypin mused. Some kind of upheaval from below might upset the regime, even though a doctrinaire revolution of the intellectuals were successfully averted. Stolypin and the officials of the Resettlement Administration supported migration steadily and firmly, but they thought it neither economically warranted nor politically prudent to stake everything on it.

This sounds like a certain practical vindication of Turner's ideas, although with different and revolutionary consequences due to the authoritarian milieu.[12] It also shows the predicament of authoritarian capitalism. This is part of a broader contradiction linked to the fact that its development leads it to favor the emergence and growth of social forces which may subsequently turn against it. In the case of the peasantry, it seems connected to the growth of a sort of grass roots democratic capitalism that Lenin identified with the American variety of capitalism in contrast with a Junker line of development. Stolypin's great dilemma came from the fact that he saw the development of this peasantry (particularly on the frontier and in contrast with a decadent and archaic peasantry) as being both necessary and threatening to the system. Differently from what one man hoped and the other feared, however, history has already gone too far to permit the dominance of a new democratic capitalism. But the forces it represented were nevertheless basic in the complex conjunction that led to the overthrow of capitalism itself.

In the case of Brazil this threat alone would certainly be much smaller due to the relatively lesser social weight of the peasantry. It can be visualized, however, and also some of the peasantry's contradictions with the dominant system. These appear, for instance, in the struggle for land, in the whole process of commercialization of their products, and in the limitations to their expansion (Velho 1973). As part of a more general process of development of new social forces all this might have its importance. It will be interesting to observe in the next few years, through all its wavering and policy changes, how the state will eventually face this dilemma.

NOTES

1. The expression "labor repression" is taken from Barrington Moore, Jr. (1969). It is not used by the authors I am refering to, such as Moog (1969).
2. Brazilian historians seem to know a little more about him than sociologists. Still the few references I have found are not very illuminating. There are also a few scattered references to Turner throughout some of Gilberto Freyre's works (1965: 73, 94, 103).
3. This is an important point Lipset (1968) seems to ignore when he accepts

Moog's (1969) explanations for the varying nature of the Brazilian and U.S. frontiers in the context of a discussion on Turner.
4. Name given to the period during which Vargas governed under authoritarian rule.
5. *Bandeiras* were organized expeditions into the interior of Brazil, and which resulted in frontier expansion.
6. This comes out very clearly from Jerome Blum's (1968) discussion of the establishment of a "second serfdom" in Eastern Europe from the sixteenth century onwards.
7. There are large gaps in our historical knowledge regarding intermediary groups and it is possible that their presence has been underestimated in the past. But this does not seem to have occurred to the point of invalidating the general notion of the dominance of a system based on labor repression.
8. For an analysis of the plantation system and the different and even quite recent forms of labor repression see Palmeira et al. (1972).
9. For a discussion of the ideological representation of this preference for independent labor see Velho (1973).
10. For a discussion of the particular nature of peasant production see, among others Chayanov (1966), Galeski (1972), and Shanin (1972).
11. The traditional plantation system did not permit the emergence of more than a marginal peasantry. The rise of a real mass peasantry seems linked to the breakdown of this system and the development of capitalism.
12. For a further discussion on a possible transformation and incorporation of Turner's ideas see Velho (1973).

REFERENCES

Almeida, Alfredo Wagner B. de. 1974. "Movimentos migratórios nos vales do Tapajós e do Xingu." Rio de Janeiro: Museu Nacional, mimeographed.

Blum, Jerome. 1968. *Lord and Peasant in Russia: From the Ninth to the Nineteenth Century.* New York: Atheneum.

Chayanov, A. V. 1966. *The Theory of Peasant Economy.* Homewood, Ill.: Richard D. Irwin.

Domar, Evsey. 1970. "The Causes of Slavery and Serfdom: A Hypothesis." *Journal of Economic History* 30 (March).

Esterci, Neide. 1972. *O mito da democracia no país das bandeiras.* Museu Nacional da Universidade Federal do Rio de Janeiro, M.A. dissertation.

Freyre, Gilberto. 1963. *New World in the Tropics.* New York: Vintage Books.

Galeski, Boguslaw. 1972. *Basic Concepts of Rural Sociology.* Manchester: University Press.

Gerhard, Dietrich. 1958-59. "The Frontier in Comparative View." *Comparative Studies in Society and History 1.*

Grupo de Trabalho para o Desenvolvimento do Nordeste. 1959. Uma política de desenvolvimento econômico para o nordeste. Rio de Janeiro: Imprensa Nacional.

Lipset, Seymour Martin. 1968. "The Turner Thesis in Comparative Perspective: An Introduction." In Richard Hofstader and S. M. Lipset (eds.), *Turner and the Sociology of the Frontier.* New York and London: Basic Books.

Marx, Karl. 1906. *Capital: A Critique of Political Economy.* New York: Modern Library.

Moog, Viana. 1969. *Bandeirantes e pioneiros.* Rio de Janeiro: Editora Civilizaçâo Brasileira, 9th ed.

Moore, Barrington, Jr. 1969. *Social Origins of Dictatorship and Democracy.* Middlesex, England: Penguin Books.

Morse, Richard M. (ed.). 1967. *The Bandeirantes: The Historical Role of the Brazilian Pathfinders.* New York: Alfred A. Knopf.

Neiva, Arthur Hehl. 1943. "A imigraçao e a colonizaçao no governo Vargas." Supplement from *Cultura Política* (no. 21) in *O pensamento político do presidente.* Rio de Janeiro.

Oberg, Kalervo. 1965. "The Marginal Peasant in Rural Brazil." *American Anthropologist,* p. 1 (December).

Palmeira, Moacir, et al. 1972. "Emprego e mudança sócio-econômica no mordeste." Rio de Janeiro: Museu Nacional da Universidade Federal do Rio de Janeiro, mimeographed.

Ricardo, Cassiano. 1970. *Marcha para oeste,* 2 vols. Rio de Janeiro: José Olympio, 4th ed.

Shanin, Teodor. 1972. *The Awkward Class.* New York: Oxford University Press.

Soares, Gláucio Ary Dillon. 1964. "The Political Sociology of Uneven Development." In Irving L. Horowitz, *Revolution in Brazil.* New York: E. P. Dutton.

Treadgold, Donald W. 1957. *The Great Siberian Migration: Government and Peasant in Resettlement from Emancipation to the First World War.* Princeton, N. J.: Princeton University Press.

Turner, Frederick Jackson. 1921. "Social Forces in American History." In id., *The Frontier in American History,* vol. 12. New York: Henry Holt.

_____. 1932. *The Significance of Sections in American History.* New York.

_____. 1967. "The Significance of the Frontier in American History." In George Rogers Taylor (ed.), *The Turner Thesis Concerning the Role of the Frontier in American History.* Boston: D. C. Heath, rev. ed.

_____. 1967. "Contributions of the West to American Democracy." In George R. Taylor (ed.), *The Turner Thesis Concerning the Role of the Frontier in American History.* Boston: D. C. Heath, rev. ed.

Vargas, Getúlio. n.d. *As diretrizes da nova política do Brasil,* Rio de Janeiro: José Olympio.

Velho, Otávio G. 1972. *Frentes de expansao e estrutura agrária.* Rio de Janeiro: Zahar Editores.

_____. 1973. "Modes of Capitalist Development, Peasantry, and the Moving Frontier." University of Manchester, Ph.D. dissertation.

_____. 1976. *Capitalismo autoritário e campesinato.* Sao Paulo: DIFEL.

Division of Labor, Technology and Social Stratification

Neuma Aguiar

The purpose of this chapter is to analyze several forms of social organization of production and the status value of the occupations they comprise through the study of the social hierarchies determined by different ways of classifying people in society, according to the division of labor. The effects of technical innovations on social classification, as well as on the status value of the occupational categories involved, have been the subject of a series of studies which I have reviewed elsewhere (Aguiar 1974). It should suffice here to present a quick overview of the various theoretical positions in order to establish the approach to be used here.

Some studies of occupational stratification propose that the evaluation of occupations becomes generalized as societies become more industrialized. A relatively stable hierarchy of occupational prestige is associated with the industrial system (Inkeles and Rossi 1956; Hutchinson 1960), and this representation extends beyond the evaluation of occupations to a broad range of concepts, when the factory is viewed as a major influence in the formation of modern values (Inkeles 1960, 1974; Kahl 1968). The proposition that industrial societies are convergent is usually coupled with a functional integration which renders them relatively unvaried or undifferentiated (Davis and Moore 1945). These assumptions have been seriously questioned since neither industrialized nor traditional societies have proved to be convergent (Nash n.d.). I will take a different standpoint, assuming that both traditional and industrial societies present internal variations which involve not only their value systems but also the use of technology and the social division of labor.

The literature points to a difference between the forms of industrialization, occupational structure, and social stratification found in Latin American societies which followed the classic pattern of an industrial revolution (Cardoso and Reyna 1967; Soares 1967). The emerging industries may be linked to various forms of social organization and even interwoven with rural production systems such as the plantation (Perruci 1974; Aguiar 1976). This form of industrialization in rural areas and the interaction between handicraft forms of production and the type of industrialization associated with the plantation have seldom been explored in the sociological literature. Marx studied a type of industry which developed after a transition through the stages of handicrafts and manufacture. In his analysis of change, he studied the forms of social organization of labor and the emergence social hierarchies, and proceeded to outline a theory on the use of technology and distribution of manpower. Marx claims that in the handicraft economy every worker carries out all stages of the production process. The worker directs and controls his own work tools, and the force and organization of labor driving the production system are set in motion by the craftsmen. One way to increase labor productivity consists of combining a group of workers to perform a given task. Several workers may gather under the same production organizer either performing the same task in one place, or each engaging in a different task. Simple cooperation may be a matter of team work in cases where the number of workers is small, or when one worker alone can carry out the task, or it may become a community undertaking when a large number of persons is involved and the work is temporary (Marx 1906, 1966).

Combining several workers in a social system of labor frees the employer from manual tasks which for this reason become indirectly linked to production. The gathering of workers under a cooperative system demands a body of supervisors to ensure a smooth functioning of the human machinery, the collective worker. In addition to fostering cooperative labor, the capitalist system leads to the specialization of workers who then become responsible for an independent and separate stage of the work. Individual tasks demand different degrees of technical training. Whereas some assignments can only be performed with a high degree of skill, others require no technical training whatsoever.

According to Marx (1906), a hierarchy of labor then develops determined by the workers' innate or acquired skills and linked in turn to a hierarchy of wages. The main division occurs between specialized and nonspecialized workers. Parallel to this stratification which applies to the working classes, another one holds within the propertied class which uses control and supervision systems to ensure the production efficiency of a factory. This one has bureaucratic ties with the dominant class and completes the concept of hierarchies within the social classes (Aguiar 1974).

The hierarchies are linked to the material part of production and inter-related in a particular manner. At the same time as the division of labor favors the creation of hierarchies, the dominant class offers material or symbolic rewards that strengthen them. This does not imply that the values assigned by the dominant class or by the dominant stratum within it are the only valid classification, since each stratum has a self-image derived from its position in the social stratification system (Lockwood 1966; Sigaud 1971). The images may, however, be interrelated, prevail-ing through several strata. While adopting the hypothesis that hierarchies are linked to the division of labor, the chapter will depart from the evolu-tionary outlook of the previous theories by focusing on the complexity of the handicrafts system.[1]

It was previously proposed that both traditional and industrial societies are varied in terms of value systems, use of technology, and social division of labor. When industrialization first appears, societies do not suddenly abandon their former way of life. Although industrial capitalism may become the dominant form of production, a relationship is established between old and new forms of production. A considerable part of the old pattern is duplicated in the new one and modes of rela-tionships or ways of coexisting are developed between them. The interac-tion which takes place is not consistent with theories on the formation of enclaves. Instead of the succession of two integrated systems, the emergence of a more complex system occurs. To illustrate this model, I will now describe the case of a region in southern Ceará, a state in the Brazilian Northeast.

Coexisting with manufactures and handicrafts, and socially connected to the plantations, there are industries organized under a capitalist model and set up with the help of fiscal incentives from governmental and paragovernmental agencies. In subsisting industries, the highest ratings are given to activities involving control and supervision. However, in many sectors human strength and physical involvement in production, with its resulting bodily risks, are the most highly valued activites. With these and some additional facts regarding the relation of industry to the land and family organization, we can examine a cross-section of forms of production that coexist in the area. This relationship concerns not only the morphology but also the representation of productive activities within a system of social values.

The Research Study

The research study was performed in Cariri, an area of Ceará where a rural structure prevails consisting mostly of *minifundios* (small landholdings) and a few coexisting latifundia. This zone has undergone two processes of industrialization: an initial one involving sugar mills and cotton gins and a recent one, with a structure of corporations where the most modern machinery was introduced for the production of roof tiles, bricks, flour, shoes, sweets. The area also includes a growing urban nucleus which is the region's commercial center and has a diversified handicrafts system. Some of the industries, new as well as old, produce items similar to the handicrafted products and coexist with them. In this study I tried to take advantage of that coexistence by focusing on the process of internal differentiation of handicrafts, domestic enterprises, and small and medium-sized industries which transform those same products, made of clay, corn, and manioc.

The research involved a six-month period of participant observation during which I studied two ceramics industries and two cornstarch industries. In addition, I used interviews and documents to collect data regarding a fifth factory of manioc starch which had closed down. In the first four, 192 questionnaires were administered. Another 58 were obtained in eleven "flour houses" (domestic flour-producing concerns) and six brickyards; one flour house and one brickyard were also closely studied. Additional data on these last two activities were later gathered with the help of two research assistants. On the basis of the questionnaires, I developed lists of occupations for each manufacturing activity and obtained ratings for them by using a technique designed by Robert Hamblin (1971). Here I will present data on three types of activities: a brickyard, a small ceramics factory, and a large ceramics factory. All three manufactured the same product—tiles and bricks. In the course of its operations, however, the large ceramics factory diversified its production and eventually specialized in earthenware tiles. While it manufactured only roof tiles and bricks, the ceramics factory was in serious danger of closing down. By changing the line of production, it ensured its eventual success. The small ceramics factory and the brickyard were part of the same complex and will be described jointly in the following section.

Case Studies

The Factory Farm

The factory farm involved an entire complex of activities: it is presented as a case here because a ceramics factory and a brickyard operated on its premises. Also included in the complex were a sawmill, a sugar mill, and cane, rice, and sunflower plantations. The owner had five pieces of property, three of them classified as productive latifundia by IBRA (Brazilian Institute for Agrarian Reform), while other two were small landholdings. The owner referred to one of his cattle farms as a bank since, according to his own statement, the cattle was a resource which increased, and a purchase could be financed or a debt paid by simply selling a head. However, he resorted to bank loans and had made use of USAID resources to finance the purchase of machinery and set of a drying area for the ceramics products. He claimed to have a variety of interests and placed the highest value on agriculture: "First of all, my biggest worries are over the ailing son: the ceramics factory. Because the ceramics factory still has debts. It's sickly and I must look after it. But my chief interest is in agriculture, because I have a number of regular plots. They bring in enough to manage on easily; I don't really need the ceramics factory" [interview data].

In the factory farm where the ceramic factory and the brickyards were located everything was intregrated. The clay, removed from the clay pits left holes in the ground which were filled in with sawdust from the sawmill. The timber for the sawmill was in turn supplied by the owner's plots. The holes were also filled in with rice chaff from the rice plantation, bagasse from the sugarcane mill, and cattle manure. The fertilized land was then sown with rice, sugarcane, and sunflower. The planting, as will be explained later, was carried out by the factory workers as a part-time activity.

The Brickyard at the Factory Farm

Before describing the ceramics factory, we will study the case of the brickyard which operated alongside it. The roof tiles for the kiln used at the ceramics factory had been made at the brickyard. Both activities coexisted in harmony, each with its own style of production, work schedules, type of relationship with the landowner, and forms of pay.

The labor employed at the brickyard for the production of roof tiles and bricks was contracted by the landowner's partner, Mr. Joao. Within the partnership, the owner, Mr. Antonio, provided the land from which the clay was dug, a donkey-drawn cart used to transfer the raw materials from the clay pit to the brickyard, a shed to dry the tiles in, and a campaign-type kiln, as well as the firewood which was brought from another one of his properties. The small production tools were furnished by his partner, Mr. Joao. The latter was responsible for supervising the manufacture of tiles, hiring labor for the task, and exploiting the part-nership resources with the landowner. As the need arose, he would re-quest new resources, the replacement of old tools, working capital to purchase materials such as firewood, and payment for the hired hands. Mr. Joao explained how the partnership operated in terms of the tools of production:

I got four workers to build the shed and things. The hemp grew wild here; it belonged to the landowner. We pulled it out, tied it, covered the holes, and leveled the ground. We also built the kiln; the kiln belongs to Mr. Antonio. The shed also belongs to him, but I paid to have it built. The labor for the shed cost Cr$100.00.[2] If I'd bought the thatching and lumber it would've been Cr$300.00. The fronds from the *babaçu* palm tree which were used for thatching were brought from Mr. Antonio's land, tied together with hemp from the property. The thatch has to be changed every year and the wood planks every other year. Repairing the shed is my duty. I do that in November. The board [used to hand-press the tiles] comes from the sawmill; it can be *brauna, aroeira,* any kind of wood will do as long as it's hard and heavy. The ashpit — I made it — sometimes breaks down, but on the whole it doesn't wear out much. The "turtle" and "grid" molds are mine. I bought the turtle mold for Cr$3.00 and the grid for Cr$1.00. Every other week I have to buy a new grid, but the turtle lasts a long time — two years. The grid mold was made by one of the boss's cabinet makers — Mr. Cícero over there. The turtle mold was made by one of the boys from the machines [at the ceramics factory]. I have three turtles and three grids. During the peak season I set up three boards and three teams, but at this time I only have two teams [a team consists of two men working together — one hand-presses the tiles, the other one catches them] [interview data].

The division in terms of partnership which provides for subcontracting labor, was explained by the contractor: "Mr. Antonio doesn't like me to say I'm his partner. He wants me to say I'm the owner, because if anyone from the INPS [National Institute of Social Security] shows up, he tells them he has nothing to do with this; that these are my employees. But I am his partner and that's what I say" [interview data].

The national system demands the establishment of a formal employment bond between worker and employer;[3] the risks of circumventing the law are shared through the partnership system. The contractor, who is employed by the landowner, is a beneficiary of the social security system as an autonomous worker. However, he would give anything to have his work card signed by the owner. His relationship with the latter is plagued with ambiguities. While, on the one hand, he hires workers, they tend to view him as the owner and he has to clarify his position as the owner's partner. While, as a contractor, he pays dues to the INPS (National Institute of Social Security) as an autonomous worker, he would prefer to pay the fees as a registered employee and claims that it would look better for the owner to have him as an employee rather than a partner.

Although as a contractor he hires workers, he performs work as well. His participation varies with the fluctuation of available labor. However, on another scale, the risks imposed by nature are channeled toward the laborers. They are hired to work on a piecework basis, which means that their pay depends on their output. If the weather is against them, they produce less and consequently earn less. If the weather is favorable, they can achieve greater yields, in a production system which varies on an individual basis and determines their daily earnings. Sometimes a day-labor wage is paid instead of piecework wages, depending on the fluctuation of the work itself. However, this is the exception rather than the rule. As the contractor remarked:

> The kiln charger earns either Cr$3.00 for every 1,000 units fired, or a day-labor wage of Cr$2.00; but for the day-labor wage he does very little work. I seldom hire on a day-labor basis — only when I need help with work I cannot manage alone — and they show up. I pay the laborers on a piecework basis, they work on their own. They get the clay and make the tiles at Cr$15.00 per 1,000; they get the clay from the pit, bring it, press it, and deliver the tiles to me. The Cr$15.00 are divided between two of them; the 1,000 units are delivered before firing. Each team makes 700 units a day at this time of year. In the winter they make 900 to 1,000, depending on their mood. The man who does the firing is also hired on a piecework basis. He works only for me for Cr$6.00 per kiln charge — it takes him one day to fire a charge and he fires 3,000 units at a time. The firing is done once a week in the winter and twice a week in the summer. At this time [in the winter], the sun won't dry them.[4] The kiln charger also makes bricks in the clay pit, for my needs, and carries them there and places them in the kiln with my help. [interview data].

One of the workers, Mr. Raimundo, described the stages of work and their corresponding wages which depend on the tasks performed under the piecework wage system.

> I only do steady work here. I earn Cr$3.00 to Cr$3.50 a week. When it rains, it's 2,000 or 1,000 units. I get Cr$7.50 to do 1,000 alone. I like it here better than out in the country because I can go home whenever I want. In the country there's no freedom. If at one point you don't get to work somebody starts yelling. Here if you stop, no one says anything. The man who mixes and presses gets two shares or Cr$10.00, the man who only presses gets five. If it's two men mixing and pressing, each one gets half or Cr$7.50 for 1,000 units [the presser and the catcher form a team]. The selling

price for 1,000 is Cr$60.00. From that, Mr. Joao takes out the costs, gets the balance, and pays for his own work [interview data].

Mr. Raimundo had pressed 400 tiles and was going to get Cr$4.00 because he had done the pressing, and Mr. Joao was going to earn Cr$2.00 for having completed the team with him, but doing only the catching. The task of carrying the clay back from the clay pit is described as follows: "I mix the clay, load it onto the cart, and bring it here, driving the cart which is drawn by a donkey. The cart belongs to Mr. Antonio, but the one in charge is Mr. Joao" [interview data].

This is a particularly heavy task because it involves going barefoot into a clay pit and naked from the waist up to dig out the clay and shovel it out of the hole. Another strenuous task is that of the kiln charger who has to feed the fire day and night until the bricks and tiles are ready to be removed. The work involves some skill since it requires keeping the kiln at the right temperature, neither too cold nor too hot, and keeping it lit for exactly the time needed for firing. The charger who is also a brick presser describes his job as follows:

I earn Cr$15.00, Cr$18.00, Cr$16.00 per week, it depends on the output. In the summer it's Cr$15.00 or more. It's more in the summer than in the winter. I work on a piecework system. Whatever I can get done determines what I earn. I start whenever I choose, quit whenever I choose. At 11 P.M. everybody [from the ceramics factory] has left and we [at the brickyard] are still working. Today, I'll be working till midnight; at times I even see the sun rise. Right now the kiln is firing; when it's ready, the fire comes out up there. Contracted labor on piecework doesn't have to pay the institute [of social security]. After I fire the kiln, I'll go home and come back tomorrow [interview data].

All these tasks were divided in order to allow for piecework contracting. The work of preparing the kiln for firing was done by the entire group, although the contractor did the arranging. This task involved stacking bricks and tiles properly to ensure their even firing. Mr. Joao did this himself with the help of other laborers. He carefully arranged the bricks and tiles in courses, for a total of approximately 2,000 tiles and 3,000 bricks until the roofing was finished and the slots were sealed with clay, at which point the kiln was ready for firing.

We can compare this hiring of labor on a piecework basis with a different form of payment in kind used at a brickyard in the municipality of Juazeiro. There, capital resources were so low that the owner had installed it in a plot of land for which he paid rent. The laborers made bricks and gave one-third of their production to the contractor. The bricks were sold in the city, but were often used in making housing for the brickworkers themselves or for their families. In this sense, the system was part of a subsistence economy inasmuch as it provided shelter from exposure to the elements.

We now understand the various stages in the production process of tiles and bricks: mixing the clay, carting it, hand-pressing the tiles, catching them, stacking them, placing them in the kiln, putting firewood in it, and firing the material. These tasks were subcontracted as three separate activities; two of them were the work of a team, another one was the firing. The contractor acted as a liaison between the workers, coordinating the various stages of production.

The workers were rewarded in cash for what they produced and shared losses with the contractor. The risk of having the product destroyed by the rain was theirs until the dry tiles were delivered to the shed.[5] If the clay was too wet due to winter weather, the work was slower, because the clay had to have a specific degree of moisture to allow for molding. Excess humidity is detrimental to tile manufacturing, unless there is an initial drying process which, in this case, was impossible to obtain given the lack of technical resources for artificial drying. From there on, the contractor bore the risks. Notice that, in the absence of money, the risks for the contractor increased; however, they could not compare with the risks incurred by the workers. The owner received half the sales returns. When the output was light, the owner earned less, when it was high, he earned more. But he would always profit as long as something was produced, inasmuch as half the production returns went to him. The owner guaranteed the product a place in the market through political influence. All construction works undertaken by the town hall were covered with tiles from that brickyard. Mr. Joao bragged about the schools he had roofed, as well as the bricks and tiles he had provided for the construction of the local stadium. The risk of lacking a market was counteracted in this fashion. The risks of being fined by the INPS (National Institute of Social Security) was borne by the contractor and not by the owner.

There are yet other risks to account for. These activities were under way in the winter that never came in 1970. The brick workers had a decision to make: either to plant a plot of rented land or work in the brickyard. The owner, in addition to running the brickyard, also rented out land. However, he would only do this for some workers. Mr. Joao had another source of income, a garment business he ran with his wife and son, which decreased his risks. However, the previous year he had planted rice in Mr. Antonio's land. Here is how he described his experience.

Last year I planted rice in Mr. Antonio's land. I spent Cr$500.00

> and made Cr$50.00. This year I refused to. Mr. Antonio called me and I said no. It's as if I'd guessed that there'd be no winter. Mr. Antonio called me all sorts of names when I said I wouldn't work there. Last year I planted one *tarefa* of rice. There was a caterpillar plague and just the stumps were left. I wanted to quit, but Mr. Antonio swore at me, called me every name in the book, and I stayed to see the rice grow again. I spent Cr$500.00 and got fifteen *quartas* of rice.[6] As a sharecropper I had to give the owner half. The rest got me about Cr$100.00. I sold for Cr$30.00 and drank it all away in frustration. The rest was left there to rot because I didn't care any more [interview data].

In short, the partnership relation implies a series of risks which are divided and subdivided, and those who have more to lose are also those who own less, since the losses cut directly into their livelihood. The partnership relationship holds here as it does in agriculture in the sense that the weather affects production. However, the direction is reversed since these activities are favored by the dry season rather than the winter.

The Small Ceramics Factory at the Factory Farm

This ceramics factory was set up in 1966-67. The machinery included a complex of three engines used for clay extrusion and brick pressing. There was a grinder, a compressor, and a machine that molded the clay and allowed for cutting the extruded tiles, bricks, and pipes. This set of equipment had fifty-five horsepower. Both the site and the machinery belonged to the same Mr. Antonio, who also owned a limited variety of brick molds. Some of them had been made locally, copied from an original acquired in Sao Paulo along with the machinery. Next to the machines were five sheds, three with thatching and two with tile roofing. This covered area was used for drying bricks in the shade. Although the sheds provided protection against rain and sun, there were considerable moisture problems. The workers were worried about this and explained:

> The pace is slowing down now. Six months ago. Mr. Antonio got a contract for 3,000 bricks for the new ceramics factory. Then he got another contract for 3,500. After that, who knows how it'll work out. Nobody buys these six-hole bricks. A large amount is in stock, but only a few go out every month [interview data].

Another man said:

> Antonio has that other contract for six-hole bricks of the smaller kind, but I don't see how he'll be able to meet it. The winter came and he wasn't prepared for it. He should've had much more clay

sent up here. Now the rain has destroyed the clay pits and flooded everything. There was no organization. Now I don't see what he's going to do. It should be like in the large ceramics factory where the clay is dried with a fan [the worker was idealizing the situation, because the drying process was nonexistent in the area]. Now, in the winter, the clay doesn't dry properly. Look at those bricks, in a sunny day they'd be yellow. That dark color shows that the bricks in the middle of those rows are still as wet as when they left the machine [interview data].

Another laborer said:

The old man is going to lose out on that kiln. It rained and the rain seeped into the kiln. We were mad because of the rain when we covered it and we didn't do a good job. We took out the firewood and the rain got in. Wet bricks go all soft [interview data].

The three campaign-type kilns had a capacity of 8,000 to 10,000 bricks each, and their condition was rather precarious. They had been repaired a number of times and one of them finally collapsed toward the end of the period when I was observing the factory. It was quite difficult to obtain information on the cost of the tools here (whereas it was not so in the brickyard) because these figures belonged to the owner who kept his accounts under lock and key. He kept most of the books at home in the hands of an accountant who worked part-time. Accounts for the labor, which were done on the factory premises, were more easily obtained.

At the brickyard there was no set schedule. The workers used those hours when the heat was milder to carry out their activities. In contrast, the ceramics factory had a seven to eleven and one to five shift, separated by a lunch break. The daily output was 6,000 to 9,000 bricks. The production process could be divided into the following stages: preparation of the clay which includes digging up the clay at the clay pit and loading it onto carts. This task was parallel to that performed at the brickyard, but the carts used by the ceramics factory were bigger and drawn by horses. This was followed by the transferring of clay from the pit to the curing sheds where it was mixed and watered by a laborer (called a waterer). The wet clay was then loaded onto the rolling dies, a task which required strenuous physical labor since the conveyor belts had worn out and this part of the machinery had been replaced by manpower. In the words of one worker:

The big belt wore out. Now it's a lot of work to load the clay onto those planks up there. Where there was one man before, there are now five working. I think paying them is still cheaper. A conveyor belt is only good for a year and apparently it costs Cr$2,500.00 [interview data].

The next task was the extrusion which called for one machinist in charge of the equipment, one retriever, and a variable number of carriers. This was followed by the drying process which involved placing the bricks in the sun for approximately six hours and in the shade for two days, before they were ready to be fired. The task of preparing the kiln was called grating and required skilled labor. The system of firing required that all the firewood be checked first, since each kiln needed a certain amount to bake the bricks. Finally, the firing took place, a process lasting thirty-six hours and involving a kiln charger and an assistant. The ceramics factory grouped the workers not by activity but by types of activity. There had previously been two types: ceramics (working around the machines) and drying. Since a major part of these activities involved carrying the bricks, and since both were paid for on a day-labor wage system, they were later regrouped. The cart drivers who brought the clay to the factory constituted a separate category. The number of cart drivers varied up to a maximum of four who were all paid piecework wages. Each worker was required to unload sixty cartloads into the curing sheds every day. This task earned them Cr$10.00 and every additional cartload was worth Cr$0.20. Brick firing was contracted on a piecework basis at Cr$25.00 per kiln charge, and the assistant was paid Cr$6.00 plus board. The charger earned another Cr$2.00 for every cartload of firewood he checked. The firewood, bought by the meter, had to be piled and cut into meter-length logs next to the kilns. Payment for the firewood was also made on a piecework basis. The task of preparing the kilns had only recently been changed from piecework to day-labor wages. The owner seemed pleased with the day-labor system. Finally, those in charge of supervising the factory — the foreman, the recordkeeper, and the watchman — were paid on a weekly basis. The first two earned Cr$20.00 and the third Cr$15.00; the foreman was a tenant of Mr. Antonio.[7]

The wage categories for agricultural work hold true in the ceramics factory as well. It is important to analyze the labor system in greater detail, especially in relation to day-labor wages, since here we have a system which employs technology as well as a complex network of cooperation. How does the owner retain skilled manpower in the factory? The occupational categories used in the area point to the existence of fixed employment and unattached labor. Workers at the ceramics factory made the following distinctions as to the types of bonds which link a worker to the factory: subcontracted labor; odd jobs or doing a day's run, a system in which the worker is unattached, receiving day-labor wages; fixed or permanent employment involving a commitment with the firm; steady or continuous work which is carried out in the same place; being idle or unemployed.

Day-labor wages were actually paid in half-day work units. The day wage was set at Cr$1.40 to Cr$3.00, depending on age and occupation. When it rained, a major part of the workers were left idle; the owner would only take those he wanted to retain and who would work in the fields rather than in the factory. As the foreman explained: "During the winter, I use the men from the clay pit. Yesterday the clay was too soft because the boy who waters it overdid the watering. Since the clay was already wet, it wasn't necessary to water it as much" [interview data].

One rainy afternoon, many workers failed to show up and the foreman dismissed some others, keeping only a few to repair damages caused by the rain, and sending the boys who worked on the machinery out to the sunflower fields. The boys were fourteen to eighteen years old and were retained because the work around the machinery was important to production. Two of them were brothers of the machinist; they lived in a house which Mr. Antonio had given them just outside his property, on the street, so that an inspector making his rounds would not take them for tenants on his property. Their father came from a family of tenants who had worked for the owner's father and grandfather. The workers worried about the insecurity of their jobs and said that only young men without family responsibilities worked there. Those that had families were permanently employed. Those who did not would not show up when the business needed them and would therefore be dismissed. This statement however, concealed the status of the youngest employees who worked around the machines and had their jobs guaranteed. The work accounted for in half days was registered by the record keeper. Previously, the system had been supervised exclusively by the *factor* who acted as a foreman. However, he was hardly literate, and had to commit the records to memory, remembering every worker by his nickname; eventually, this duty was assigned to another employee. The foreman, as a wage earner, and having relatives among the workers, had a rather close relationship with the latter who took advantage of this fact to constantly request loans. The arrival of a record keeper decreased the number of requested cash loans which then began to be registered. Records were also begun of the workers' attendance for every half day of work, the factory's daily output, the incoming and outgoing money, and the total amount owed to each worker, as well as a general summary of work-related expenses for the week. The foreman and the record keeper fell in the same category as the brickyard's contractor, although their relationship to the owner was that of salaried employees. The record keeper wanted to have his work card signed in order to qualify for social security benefits. The fireman had a tenancy relationship with his employer, which meant that the owner felt more responsible for him, yet the ambiguity of the factory farm obscured employment categories, preventing it to be either factory or farm, and having either salaried workers or tenants. As the owner put it: "I don't have tenants, I don't want to take care of anybody. The INPS [National Institute of Social Security] can take care of them if it wants to" [interview data].

In this case, the owner denied having tenants for fear of IBRA (Brazilian Institute of Agrarian Reform) inspectors, and denied that his workers did not have signed work cards for fear of the INPS inspectors. One laborer reported that all the work cards were in the hands of the boss. Another stated: "I think he wants to keep the work cards there. If an inspector comes around he signs them and then cancels them that same day. Those work cards are there since June. The owner did that with a friend of ours. He cancels them on the day he signs them" [interview data].

The workers' awareness of their employment situation was heightened by contact with laborers from the new ceramics factory which had commissioned the factory farm to make bricks for its construction. When a truck from the new ceramics factory arrived, one of the factory farm's workers said: "Those aren't from around here; they all have their work cards signed" [interview data]. The visiting laborers spoke with them and told them about their life at the new ceramics factory. One worker asked whether they punched a time clock. The answer was yes. Another remarked: "it's like at the oil factory." The latter's whistle could be heard by the ceramics workers who used it as a signal for beginning and ending work, since their own factory had no clock.

Some chose this type of work instead of agriculture in the hopes that the firm would establish a more definite employment relationship with them by instituting the minimum salary, a time-clock schedule, and a signed work card. As one youth remarked:

> I had hoped things would get better here because the old man asked for our work cards in May of last year. Thinking I'd get the salary, I didn't go out to the country to plant. Working in the country gets you a little bit extra over what you get in this job. It'd be good not to have to work here in the winter. Planting here in the boss's land doesn't work out. I wanted to plant but there wasn't any land. Besides, sharecropping doesn't work. Last year I spent Cr$50.00 planting; the sun was too hot, the summer stretched out, and the rice never sprouted. I was scared and didn't plant again [interview data].

Another stated:

> I've planted beans and corn on the owner's land, but this year I

didn't plant anything. I planted just a small area last year, at the end of the winter [interview data].

And another still:

I find this job [the current one] better than agriculture ... [here] a man suffers but gets that little bit of money .... The owner here gives out harrowed land, seeds, and the water which he pumps with an engine; he waters if it doesn't rain — as much water as it takes. He rents everything on a sharecrop basis; in other places you pay by the output. A man here pays a set amount, for example three *quartas* of rice. If the land yields eighty-five, he gets eighty-two; if it yields three, he gets nothing [interview data].

Yet another worker said:

This year I spent Cr$400.00 planting seven *tarefas* of rice. The irrigation ditch was not ready on time, the old man doesn't water, only waters once in a blue moon; the rice is going to spoil [interview data].

The statements quoted above and the previous description of the brickyard help us understand the effects of introducing machinery into a labor system vulnerable to natural phenomena. The day-labor wage system which is also used in agriculture worked better than the piecework system. Day-labor wages allow for greater flexibility in assigning tasks, because the work unit is not an amount of a given task that needs to be performed, but the number of hours that must be worked. In the piecework system, the tasks are specific, the hours are not. The brickyard laborers begin to work at dawn and continue into the night to avoid the sun. The kiln charges at the brickyard and the ceramics factory work through the night because they have to. The day-wage earners sell the number of hours worked rather than the output produced (700 tiles). In practice, the other system is maintained as a check. The order for six-hole bricks placed by the new ceramics factory at the factory farm required that the bricks be fired for a longer period. The kiln charger at the ceramics factory complained of not having received the right overtime pay for the additional hours he put in, in order to deliver every fired charge of bricks to the new ceramics factory. The record keeper, on the other hand, had to demand that a certain number of bricks be produced for a half day's pay. The data on daily output of bricks show that this requirement was not upheld in practice.

On the day-labor system, industrial workers could be transferred to agricultural activities in order to compensate for natural hazards. This system favored discrimination against workers whose only marketable asset was physical strength and who could therefore be dismissed when not needed. It also left room, on a different level, for retaining those who performed special tasks, combining this with a day-labor wage system. The owner used a peculiar system of agriculture to retain these workers. He combined their labor activities with tenancy. One house afforded several workers from the members of one family. The houses provided as dwellings were built with materials from the ceramics factory. The land rented to the industrial laborers for agricultural work was only assigned to those whose families had a long-standing work relationship with the owner's family.

Both the piecework and the day-labor wage systems allow for the dismissal of labor during the bad weather season. The dissociation of labor through the day-labor system requires other ways of controlling the work which are different from those involved in operating a farm, where the foreman prevails as production supervisor. The foreman in this case was a wage earner but, as a man who had the owner's trust, he was also a tenant. The accounting of day-labor wages and production could not be performed by the foreman due to his lack of schooling. The records were kept by another wage earner who, nevertheless, lived outside the property and did not have the same loyalty relationship with the owner.

The Large Ceramics Factory

One last case, the large ceramics factory, will further illustrate the effects of introducing technology into the computation of and payment for time worked. This factory was part of the national industrialization system, since it received financial aid from regional and state planning bodies. In addition, it had been part of a larger development project for the area and had originally been planned to function as a corporation. Much can be learned about the relationship between handicrafts and industrial production from the problems and solutions encountered by this factory. According to the original plans, the industry was to manufacture tiles, bricks, and earthenware pipes. The first two products were also produced in the area by brickyards and ceramics factories of the type previously described. The factory was planned in such a way as to allow for the survival of the area's handicrafts production. The first error involved here was planning a factory to manufacture goods already produced in the area at lower cost, since the competition paid its workers according to the system described earlier. In addition, the large ceramics factory had to face other hurdles such as a mistake in their choice of technology. The kiln which had been designed for the firing of its ceramics products (as the Ph.D. thesis of a UCLA engineer) proved inoperative. The tiles and bricks in it would break under thermic shock.

The firm was forced to build other kilns to fire its products, and once these were built the factory had become an expanded version of what was described earlier for the factory farm. There was a process of extrusion, a drying area, and kilns. Two of the kilns resembled those of the factory farm. Others were subsequently built using a higher degree of technology: downdraft and bottle-shaped kilns. This part of the factory eventually became known as the "old factory." A new area was built with a continuous kiln bought in Sao Paulo which operated on oil burners; this expanding sector became the "new factory."

The failure of the first continuous kiln plus a type of production geared to the local market almost led to the factory's closing. One of the workers said the plant's electric power had actually been cut off during the crisis. Another reported that at some point vouchers for Cr$10.00 were being circulated instead of money, and that the workers sold them to one another for Cr$5.00. The factory overcame its initial failure thanks to a young engineer, its current industrial director, who managed to solve some of the firm's most pressing problems. As a result of a rule established by SUDENE (Superintendence for the Development of the Northeast), the company could not acquire second-hand machinery. But the directors decided to sidestep the supervising officials and bought the first presses from a Sao Paulo industry which had closed down. They changed the line of production to earthenware tile, an upper middle class product that was easily sold in the large coastal cities. The raw material was an excelent type of argil which eventually led a ceramics firm from the state of Sao Paulo to install another large-scale plant in the area. The large ceramics factory was soon in a position to develop a new project and enter a different stage of production. The old section of the factory remained only as an accessory to the new one.

The factory operated on a three-shift system, although some sections worked on a single shift. It had, at the time, 418 employees scattered throughout four departments: production, engineering, programming, and maintenance. The first department included the extrusion, tile production, and glazing sections. This department, linked to the civil construction section in charge of building the new factory, included the bulk of the plant's workers. The extrusion section operating in the same fashion as the small ceramics factory earlier, except for the fact that here humidity readings were taken daily. The temperature of the kilns where the extruded material was fired also followed a carefully traced temperature curve, despite the fact that the kilns used firewood for fuel. Next to the extrusion section, there were mills to grind the raw material which was later passed through a sieve. One part was set aside for extrusion, the other for the presses. The powder which passed through the sieves had to be rigorously dry. In this sense, humidity was also a problem at the large ceramics factory. The kilns took much longer to fire in the winter, according to one kiln stoker. The factory strove to provide technical solutions for every problem encountered and sought means of controlling humidity at every stage of production. The introduction of the continuous firing kiln demanded a constant rate of work, since its unending activity set the entire factory moving in order to feed its enormous appetite. Solutions were not always easy to come by. Sometimes the problems were not within immediate reach of the firm. The electricity was occasionally cut off causing major damages to the ceramics factory which eventually purchased a powerful generator in order to offset the deficiencies of power supply.

In the process of extrusion the clay had to be wet in order to allow for molding. The tiles are made by dry-pressing the clay and humidity can lead to breakdowns in the equipment. If the talc obtained from the clay was damp, it would cause cloggings in the system which carried the raw material from the grinding section to the presses. The problem of dampness was exacerbated in the winter when the clay flowed more slowly and the productivity of the presses was consequently lower. Even the presses had a decline in productivity during the winter, although the overall annual trend is toward increased productivity (Aguiar 1973). This trend reflected the factory's efforts. The humidity problem decreased after the plant decided to apply an initial drying process to the raw materials. A rustic wood-burning oven was set up in which the *taguá* or raw material was stirred until it lost the greenish tint of moisture. This process would soon be replaced by an oil-burning oven which was put to use a few times before I left the factory. The new oven had continuous rotating tracks which took the raw material from moisture to dryness.

The factory realized that it could increase the productivity of the presses by introducing incentives. Thus it shifted from a fixed-salary work system, that is, one where there was a formal or informal bond between the workers and the industry, to a combined system of salaries and production premiums. This soon also showed effects on productivity. The premiums were introduced in two stages; a third one is being contemplated by the factory. The first stage was the establishment of increases on the minimum salary for output exceeding the factory's average of 8.5 m² of tiles produced in one hour's work. The premium system never involved decreases, that is, if the presses remained stationary and productivity was less than average, the minimum salary was still maintained. The premiums were set for four presses whose mechanical potential was equal. The increases could go as high as half the minimum salary.

The next stage was to establish premiums for supervision, which involved not only the number of tiles produced, but also their quality. The system for supervisors was not successful, however, because there was considerable dissatisfaction among them, since they did not understand their system of incentives. According to one of the supervisors:

> I was the first one here to complain about the salaries. The workers at the new kiln have it easy; they don't go through the hardships we have here. We're the ones who support that section, who give it production. And we work hard. They come in with clean clothes and leave as clean as they came. We do the real dirty work here. We're filthy by the time we leave. The output I used to yield was 450 boxes; now the director isn't even happy with 550 boxes. The kilns has an insatiable appetite. And we're the ones who keep that going. There used to be a car going in every hour, now they say it's every forty-five minutes, and it's still not enough [interview data].

And according to another:

> Last week, with this business of a [salary] raise over there, I actually stopped production. I only put out 250 boxes. It wasn't exactly that I stopped. The guy at the sieves was mad too and not putting out enough powder. I didn't rush him either. He was there and I was here and it went on like that. Thursday I went to talk to the director and told him this just can't go on, I have payments to make, I have to pay the installments on my stove. The raise has been about to go through for three months now and there's no way. Now they say they're going to do away with the premium. The stupid little premium of Cr$20.00 a week we were getting. And the people here are clever, they pay for quality, not quantity. If it was quantity, well it's right there — just fine! It seems the system hadn't worked out too well and now the experts are going to come up with another premium. We'll see how it goes and how much the raise amounts to [interview data].

The factory was planning still a third stage of incentives to production by setting salary premiums in kind for the women who retrieved the pressed tiles from the machine. One of the supervisors had noticed that a good relationship between presser and retriever led to a considerable increase in production. A pairing of this nature raised the productivity of one of the "slow" presses to the level of those who had qualified for premiums.

Production control was highly developed in this industry. In the first place, there was a hierarchy of supervision whose members had undergone special training for the post. There was an aspiring or second line of supervision which in practice did not operate and a line of supervisors above it. The factory had recently hired a production manager;

and the industrial director was at the apex of the control pyramid. In addition to direct supervision of work, there were indirect production controls through a statistical department which collected data on the entire factory's production and calculated the premiums, the proportion of flaws, the fuel spent, and productivity of each section, and plotted a considerable number of productivity graphs. Another form of indirect control was effected in the laboratory where samples were gathered daily by shift, and were measured, weighed, analyzed for humidity and granulometric composition, and so on. The laboratory also performed experiments with pigments and glazes, as well as analyses and measurements of earthenware tiles from various factories across the country for quality comparison purposes. The way in which the presses were utilized elicited the admiration of a specialist who had just arrived from a ceramics factory in the south. The shift system provided for this intensive use of the machinery. The rest of the labor was not on a shift system, but worked on an overtime basis. The classification section worked Sundays because the continuous firing kiln never stopped ejecting those fired tiles.

The factory had a policy of hiring relatives, because female labor was cheap and because the industry made it a point to avoid disturbing the rural family order. The family groups employed there earned a relatively high joint income and reinvested their earnings in agriculture. The employment status of workers at the factory was not standard; it varied according to section, profession, seniority, sex, and education. The possibility of increased earnings offered by the factory and the constant need for manpower brought about by industrial expansion partly compensated for the fact that most workers lacked official registration.

Regional industrial planning bodies try to ensure that industries will create jobs for the region. This was one of the justifications for the plan to industrialize the Northeast introduced by SUDENE (Superintendence for the Development of the Northeast). The Bank of the Northeast adopted this same policy. These bodies, however, try to maintain a realistic overview of the possibilities of modern industrialization and one aspect of their inspections involves noting the proportion of fixed and variable manpower. Included in the ceramic factory's variable labor force was the civil construction section. These were laborers in charge of the factory's expansion works, hired by a contractor at Cr$18.00 per week for the bricklayer's assistant and Cr$5.00 per day for the bricklayer.

The civil construction section set itself apart from the factory and differentiated in its statements between "those at the factory and ourselves." They also resented the lack of registration. The workers described one incident in which the roofing collapsed, due to a flaw in one of the beams, and several men were wounded including a carpenter who broke both legs. The workers continued to be paid for some time, but complained because the compensation ended soon and those workers had to leave. Fear of unemployment was considerable: "A worker without registration is like a sheep lost in the middle of a storm. When there's an accident like the roofing you can end up jobless, out on the street to starve" [interview data]. Other statements make reference to the meeting place of the municipality's unemployed: the church courtyard, where there are sometimes up to 200 men, sitting around with nothing to do.

The factory administrators spoke in elaborate circles when referring to the lack of registration for workers, and maintained two sets of accounts. This ambiguous system was functional in dealing with inspectors from the INPS (National Institute of Social Security), because no one was ever certain of the total number of workers or the sections to which they belonged. A meeting with the supervisors would have been enough to set the workers' files up to date. In comparison with the rest of the region, however conditions of employment here were considerably better. The factory used this as an important fact in renegotiating its debts with the social security system. The INPS in its periodic inspections knew some of the businesses where it was likely to get funds. However, places such as the factory farm were never inspected. The large ceramics factory was much more conspicuous and from a total of 397 to 418 workers, 57 to 65 percent were not registered. The salaries of the nonregistrees were lower than those of the registered workers. In spite of this, the factory offered some of the best opportunities in terms of employment and a considerable number of young high-school girls were employed there in the tile classification, glazing, and pressing sections. Data concerning forms of payment are important here, since this is one of the indicators of social stratification I make use of.

Comparison of Activities

I will now compare the occupations involved in the preparation of tiles and bricks within the three types of social organization of production I chose for analysis. Table 2.1 lists the various occupations involved in the manufacture of tiles and bricks at the brickyard of the factory farm. Several of the occupations listed were carried out by one same person. For example, the workers who pressed tiles were usually the same ones who made the clay dough or who delivered the product to the charger who would place it in the kiln. At times, the kiln charger also pressed tiles. However, he never prepared the clay, which was the heaviest and dirtiest task. The work of arranging the kiln was done by the contractor, who occasionally substituted for one of the members of a team, in case of absence. The workers who carried out all these tasks were asked to rate the occupations in terms of degree of skill required by each one. The standard for rating was given as the task of "making bricks at the clay pit" with a score of 10. The occupations were presented in random order so as to minimize error. The technique used for measuring the ratings was described earlier (Hamblin and Smith 1966; Hamblin 1971; Stevens 1951, 1957). The medians were obtained using the same technique.

TABLE 2.1

Median Ratings and Wages Paid for Occupations in the Brickyard at the Factory Farm

Occupations	Median Ratings	Monthly Wages
1. Making clay in the clay pit	3.00	66.50
2. Carting the clay	1.25	66.50
3. Hand-pressing the tiles	3.50	66.50
4. Catching the tiles	3.50	66.50
5. Stacking tiles in the sun	3.50	66.50
6. Delivering to the kiln charger	3.00	66.50
7. Firing	7.00	51.00
8. Placing bricks in the kiln	8.50	90.00

* Standard used for the ratings: Making bricks in the clay pit, with score 10. The estimated monthly wage for this occupation is Cr$51.00.

The same table shows the wage paid for each activity. The earnings for each occupation were first calculated on the basis of a kiln charge, although this is not always the unit on which the productive activities are paid. The computation unit for labor productivity at the brickyard is 1,000 bricks or tiles. The kiln has a limited capacity (3,000) for tiles and bricks. The unit of payment for firing is the kiln charge, just as the computation of the production share which goes to the contractor is also the kiln charge. This facilitates the standardization of wage estimates on the basis of a kiln charge. We converted the data on wages into monthly earnings. However, it should be made clear that this information is subject to considerable variability and it was only obtained in order to compare it with the small and the large ceramics factories.

The multiplicity of tasks that each laborer performs allows us to explain the low correlation between income and status value for the occupations. The correlation was practically nil. The variance accounted for was 11 percent. Every worker carried out several tasks in his job, some involving heavy work, some involving craft.

The occupational ratings were in all cases lower than the standard. The scores seem to be linked to the order in which tasks are performed. As stated previously, due to the rain, brickyards face a high risk in the manufacture of tiles and bricks. We have already referred to the fact that this activity is markedly seasonal and performed mainly during the dry months. The winter or rainy season hinders the drying of material. The number of kiln charges decreases with the rain. Activities generally stop during the winter, except in drought years such as the period when this research was carried out. In this case, however, the rain had not stopped completely; it was simply less abundant and less frequent. Occupations related to the final stage of processing were consistently rated higher than the earlier ones, with only two exceptions. Making clay at the clay pit precedes the activity of carting the clay. However, it is a much more strenuous activity which also demands skill in determining the right amount of moisture for manufacturing the product. The work of delivering tiles to the kiln charger was rated lower than that of stacking the tiles in the sun. This last activity is crucial for the workers, because if it rains at this point the loss falls on them. When this task is completed, any losses fall on the contractor, who in this case adds his main activity to that of a kiln charger in the production process. Having overcome this risk, the workers get their earning regardless of the final outcome for the tiles. From here on it is the contractor who must continue the production process up to the final stage of firing the product.

Work at the small ceramics factory shows a higher degree of association between status value and income. The variance explained is 52 percent. The wages in this case were paid on a day-labor system, with the exception of some tasks carried out on a piecework basis. This was the case of carting the clay to the curing sheds and firing the kilns. Until shortly before the beginning of the research study the task of placing bricks in the kiln was also contracted on a piecework basis. Later on, the pay was transferred to a day-labor wage system which prevailed in most of the other occupations in this business. The activity chosen as a standard for rating the occupations was that of "stacking bricks in the sun to dry."

Notice that, as shown in Table 2.2, and contrary to the brickyard's situation, all the ratings were systematically higher than the standard. Also note that both for the ratings and for the wages of each occupation there are no extreme scores. Occupations which involved physical strength and skill have the highest ratings, which is not always the case with the pay scale.

TABLE 2.2

Median Ratings and Wages Paid for Occupations in the Small Ceramics Factory at the Factory Farm

Occupations	Median Ratings	Monthly Wages
1. Carrying clay to the machine	32.50	48.00
2. Carrying bricks to the sheds	20.00	48.00
3. Removing bricks from the kiln	20.00	48.00
4. Arranging the product for drying	15.00	48.00
5. Carrying bricks to the kiln	20.00	48.00
6. Firing the kilns	32.50	64.80
7. Placing bricks in the tile-covered shed	15.00	43.20
8. Preparing the clay pit	27.50	48.00
9. Loading clay onto the rolling die	25.00	48.00
10. Retrieving bricks from the machine	15.00	33.60
11. Delivering bricks to the kiln charger	20.00	43.20
12. Placing bricks in the kiln	20.00	54.00
13. Supervising and repairing the machinery	30.00	52.80
14. Cutting bricks	12.00	36.00
15. Watering the clay	13.50	43.20
16. Carting clay to the curing sheds	26.25	52.80

* Standard used for the ratings: Stacking bricks in the sun, with score 10. The estimated monthly wage for this occupation is Cr$43.20.

Occupations at the large ceramics factory had the highest correlation between income and status value. The variance explained is 88 percent. Notice that only one section of the factory is being considered here whereas in the previous cases all occupations at the firm were included. One of the questions put to the raters involved not only the occupations of their section or those closest to them, but a sample of occupations from the entire factory. This question, however, will not be analyzed here. Table 2.3 shows consistently higher ratings for occupations related to supervision and direction of the production process.

TABLE 2.3

Median Ratings and Wages Paid for Occupations in the Extrusion Section of the Large Ceramics Factory

Occupations	Median Ratings	Monthly Wages
1. Classifier of small tiles	7.50	64.00
2. Tractor driver	12.50	185.00
3. Warehouse manager	8.00	200.00
4. Clay presser	10.00	84.00
5. Retriever	9.50	84.00
6. Loader of clay onto the rolling die	10.00	72.00
7. Arranger of material for drying	10.00	72.00
8. Cleaner of residues	9.00	64.00
9. Box presser	10.00	64.00
10. Industrial director	30.00	4,000.00
11. Box presser's assistant	7.50	64.00
12. Supervisor in the production department	14.50	1,000.00
13. Carrier	8.00	84.00
14. Section supervisor	15.00	360.00
15. Box repairman	5.00	72.00
16. Box selector	9.00	72.00

* Standard used for the ratings: Mechanic's assistant, with score 10. The estimated monthly wage for this occupation is Cr$98.40.

The obtained correlation coefficients show that the higher the degree of complexity in the organization, the higher the degree of association between income and evaluation of occupations. The ratings reported here involved different numbers of judges, since only those workers familiar with the activities were asked to give their evaluation. The activities presented for rating also varied in number: eight in the case of the brickyard, sixteen for the small ceramics factory, and sixteen for the extrusion section of the large ceramics factory.

At this point a comparison can be established for the systems of occupational stratification prevailing in the three types of activities, by focusing on some of the tasks common to all. Since in the large ceramics factory the firing does not take place in the extrusion section but in the firing section, data concerning this activity were attached to the table. We can compare the activities presented in Tables 2.4 and 2.5 by using

TABLE 2.4
Median Ratings for Occupations Common to the
Three Types of Production

Occupations common to all types of production:	Brickyard	Small Ceramics Factory	Large Ceramics Factory
1. Clay preparer	3.00	27.50	10.00
2. Clay carrier	1.25	26.25	12.50
3. Arranger of material for drying	7.00	15.00	10.00
4. Retriever of molded material	3.50	9.50	15.00
5. Kiln Stoker	7.00	32.50	12.00
6. Kiln Charger	8.50	20.00	20.00
7. Carrier of material for firing	3.00	20.00	12.00
8. Loader of clay onto the rolling die	–	25.00	10.00
9. Supervisor	–	30.00	15.00

Occupations 8 and 9 exist only in the ceramics factories. Evaluations for occupations 5, 6 and 7 of the Large Ceramics Factory were provided by workers from the downdraft kiln section.

TABLE 2.5

**Median Wages Earned in Occupations Common to the
Three Types of Production**

Occupations common to all types of production:	Brickyard	Small Ceramics Factory	Large Ceramics Factory
1. Clay preparer	66.50	48.00	84.00
2. Clay carrier	66.50	52.80	185.00
3. Arranger of material for drying	66.50	48.00	72.00
4. Retriever of molded material	66.50	33.60	84.00
5. Kiln Stoker	51.00	64.80	84.00
6. Kiln Charger	90.00	54.00	84.00
7. Carrier of material for firing	66.50	43.20	84.00
8. Loader of clay onto the rolling die	-	48.00	72.00
9. Supervisor	-	52.80	360.00

Occupations 8 and 9 exist only in the ceramics factories. In the case of the Large Ceramics Factory, the occupations of kiln-stoker, kiln-charger and carrier of material for firing belong to the downdraft kiln section.

the ratio between two ratings or wages. The numerical scale used to rate the activities allows for computing the ratio between two of them. These ratios can therefore be compared in order to have a clear picture of the distance between two occupations. The data for the tables were obtained through the use of an occupational standard that varied from one type of production to another, although the value assigned was always 10.

There are many possibilities for comparison; I will analyze only some of them on the basis of the theoretical background developed in the introduction to this chapter. Keeping the data on the clay preparer's position as the common denominator, we can see through Table 2.6 just what happens when we change the occupations in the numerator according to degree of skill required. The clay-mixing occupation requires strength and is dirty. It demands some skill, nevertheless, to determine the proportions for the mixture. Should the dosage be inadequate, the tiles and bricks may crack. The dosage, however, depends mainly on the supervisor and the clay carrier.

TABLE 2.6

Occupations Whose Required Skill Varies from One Type of Production to Another

Occupations*	Ratio of the ratings			Ratio of Wages		
	Brickyard	Small Ceramics Factory	Large Ceramics Factory	Brickyard	Small Ceramics Factory	Large Ceramics Factory
$\frac{2}{1}$	0.41	0.95	1.25	1.00	1.10	2.20
$\frac{4}{1}$	1.16	0.34	1.50	1.00	0.70	1.00
$\frac{8}{1}$	-	0.90	1.00	-	1.00	0.85
$\frac{9}{1}$	-	1.09	1.50	-	1.10	4.28

* Clay mixer (1); Clay carrier (2); Retriever of molded material (4); Loader of clay onto the rolling die (8); Supervisor (9).

Let us now take occupations requiring different degrees of skill as the numerator. The ratio between the status of occupations requiring different degrees of technology increases in proportion to size of the organizations. In the first case in which the numerator is the occupation of the clay carrier, the production instrument used varies from donkey-drawn cart to tractor. In the case where the numerator is the occupation of retriever of the molded material, the worker receives the material from another one who has initiated the molding process which can be an entirely manual task, or go as far as involving extrusion machinery with compressors, where the ability demanded of the worker is almost nil. In the case of the small ceramics factory, where an extrusion machine is also used, the relative position of this occupation decreases. I attribute this to the use of minors as manpower for this task. The task of loading the clay onto the rolling die also involves the use of machinery. There is no corresponding task in the brickyard's work. It is also a task which requires the use of physical strength as in the small ceramics factory, given the lack of conveyor belts which wore out and were not replaced. The gradual loading of clay onto the machines demands care in order to avoid clogging and the consequent breakdown of technical tools. The use of conveyor belts in the large ceramics factory results in less physical exertion on the part of the worker. The task of gradually loading the clay also becomes simpler by the use of this technical instrument. This explains the drop in this occupation's relative position at the technologically more sophisticated firm. The relative position of the supervisor rises with the manufacturer's degree of complexity. This comparison between supervision work and various specialized tasks may be further studied by means of Table 2.7

TABLE 2.7
Ratio of Occupational Ratings for Supervision Work and for Tasks Requiring Varying Degrees of Specialization

Occupations*	Ratio of the ratings		Ratio of Wages	
	Small Ceramics Factory	Large Ceramics Factory	Small Ceramics Factory	Large Ceramics Factory
$\frac{9}{8}$	1.20	1.50	1.10	5.00
$\frac{9}{7}$	1.50	1.25	1.22	4.28
$\frac{8}{7}$	1.25	0.83	1.20	0.85

* (7) Carrier of material for firing; (8) Loader of clay onto the rolling die; (9) Supervisor.

Once again, when the small and large ceramics factories are compared, the relative position of the clay loader drops. In this case, the denominator is the occupation of carrying material for firing, a manual task requiring strength but no skill and which can be performed by minors in the case of the small factory. The occupation of supervisor has a relatively higher ranking, especially when the wage variable is considered. However, I had the opportunity elsewhere (Aguiar 1975) to show that the supervision of occupations may receive lower ratings in terms of status value than occupations involving physical risk or considerable exertion for the worker. Within this system of values, supervision work is considered easy or light. The occupation of supervisor in the present case shows much higher ratings than the others, and not only for reason of seniority. The extrusion section is the oldest in the factory and the supervisor is also one of the oldest employees of the firm, making a salary double what most of the factory supervisors received (Aguiar 1975). The responsibility attributed to the occupation is my major concern here.

Now let us look at Table 2.8 and see what happens to the kiln charger's job in relation to the other occupations, according to the technical complexity of the firm. The table shows a relative loss of status for this occupation in relation to the others. The situation is more clear-cut when we look at the wage variable. This task requires specialization, since a poorly arranged kiln can bring enormous damages through cracks or collapses during the firing process. The major responsibility, however, can be transferred to the process of supervision, as is the case in the large ceramics factory. In this case the occupation comes closer to that of arranging material for drying. Notice that the small ceramics factory introduced some changes in this occupation when it stopped paying on a piecework basis for the task of arranging the kiln and moved to a day-labor wage system, once the factory began to gain more control over this activity.

TABLE 2.8
Relative Position of One Occupation in Relation to Others

Occupations*	Ratio of the ratings			Ratio of Wages		
	Brickyard	Small Ceramics Factory	Large Ceramics Factory	Brickyard	Small Ceramics Factory	Large Ceramics Factory
$\frac{6}{1}$	2.83	0.72	2.00	1.35	1.12	1.00
$\frac{6}{2}$	6.80	0.76	1.60	1.35	1.02	0.45
$\frac{6}{3}$	1.21	1.33	2.00	1.35	1.12	1.16
$\frac{6}{4}$	2.42	2.10	1.33	1.35	1.60	1.00
$\frac{6}{5}$	1.21	0.61	1.66	1.76	0.83	1.00
$\frac{6}{7}$	2.83	1.00	1.66	1.35	1.25	1.00

* (1) Clay mixer; (2) Clay carrier; (3) Arranger of material for drying; (4) Retriever of molded material; (5) Kiln stoker; (6) Kiln charger; (7) Carrier of material for firing.

Conclusion

I have analyzed data from observations made in an area of northeastern Brazil where different coexisting forms of social organization are involved in the manufacture of the same types of products. Taking advantage of this situation, I investigated the type of division of labor that occurs in each form of social organization. I verified the relationship between income and status variables which sociological literature claims is high (Duncan 1961), and discovered that the degree of association varies with the degree of complexity of the organization. The lack of correlation between status and income found in the brickyard, as well as the organization of production which combines a contracting system with partnership, cooperation in the form of teams, and payment on a piecework basis, reveals the complexity of the handicraft system in terms of these dimensions. The brickyard, although not highly differentiated as the wages paid, becomes diversified by the value assigned to its occupations. The ratings of activities closer to the final stage of manufacturing the product are higher than those of initial tasks in the production process.

Another observation concerns the status acquired by occupations according to the organizations' degree of technological complexity. The factories differ in terms of social organization of production. One factory farm resembles the model through the tenancy system it maintains with the laborers, associated with the contracting of labor on a piecework basis with day-labor wages as the form of payment for most workers. In both the small and large ceramics factories there is a tendency to differentiate laborers in terms of income and status. To the extent that the occupations use a complex technology, they rank higher in relation to manual activities requiring strength. The higher ranking holds when the introduction of technology demands a greater degree of technical knowledge for the occupation. Should the introduction of machinery result in a simplification of the task, allowing it to be performed even by minors, the occupation's rank drops. Finally, the data indicates that the need for skill or specialization in certain activities is being replaced by supervisory functions, with a resulting loss in status for the former and a concurrent gain for the latter. The style of research combining ethnographic and survey techniques shows new possibilities for analyzing the structure of production in countries as complex as Brazil, which have a variety of coexisting modes of production. Such style of work can improve our knowledge beyond gross typological simplifications which are still in use in the sociology of development.

NOTES

1. This will be exhibited through the social relations of production, the articulation between the system of representation of occupations and the occupational system, and through the specificity of technical relations of production.

2. US$1.00 = Cr$4.39. Weighted average based on official currency exchange rates for the research period.
3. Under this system, the worker must be officially registered and his worker's identification card signed by the employer. A different system applies for autonomous workers who are not permanently employed by any particular firm. In either case, the law provides for payment of social security fees which ensure the worker sick pay, retirement pension, and other eventual benefits. Handicrafts and manufactures generally make no use of the social security system for their workers.
4. *Winter* is the local name for the rainy season.
5. The idea of sharing risks has been suggested by Roger Walker in his unpublished study of sharecropping in cotton plantations.
6. The original measures can be replaced by approximate equivalents for the sake of readability. The contractor actually planted 1 *tarefa* (= 0.896 acres) and harvested 15 *quartas* (= 25.56 bushels) of rice (1 *quarta* = 1.68 bushels). One could read one acre instead of one *tarefa* and twenty-five bushels instead of fifteen *quartas*.
7. He addressed his foreman by an old term for farm supervisors used in plantations, calling him his *factor*.

REFERENCES

Aguiar, Neuma. 1973. "Tempo de transformaçao no nordeste." Rio de Janeiro: IUPERJ, mimeographed.

_____. 1974. "Hierarquias em classes: uma introduçao no estudo da estratificaçao social." In Neuma Aguiar (ed.), *Hierarquias em classes.* Rio de Janeiro: Zahar.

_____. 1975 "Impact of Industrialization on Women's Work Roles in Northeast Brazil." *Studies in Comparative International Development* 10 (Summer): 78-94.

_____. 1976 "Indústria em área rural."*Dados* 12: 46-57.

Cardoso, Fernando Henrique; and Reyna, José Luis. 1967. "Industrializaçao, estrutura ocupacional e estratificaçao social na América Latina." *Dados* 2-3: 4-31.

Davis, Kingsley; and Moore, Wilbert. 1945. "Some Principles of Stratification." *American Sociological Review* (April): 242-49.

Duncan, Otis Dudley. 1961. "A Socioeconomic Index of All Occupations." In Albert J. Reiss, Jr. (ed.), *Occupations and Social Status.* New York: Free Press of Glencoe.

Hamblin, Robert; and Smith, Carole. 1966. "Values, Status, and Professors." *Sociometry* 23 (September): 183-96.

_____. 1971. "Mathematical Experimentation and Sociological Theory: A Critical Analysis." *Sociometry* 34 (no. 4): 423-52.

Hutchinson, Bertram, et al. 1960. *Mobilidade e trabalho.* Rio de Janeiro: INEP.

Kahl, Joseph. 1970. *The Measurement of Modernism: A Study of Values in Brazil and Mexico.* Austin and London: University of Texas Press.

Inkeles, Alex; and Rossi, Peter. 1956. "National Comparisons of Occupational Prestige." *American Journal of Sociology* 61: 329-39.

_____. 1960. "Industrial Man." *American Journal of Sociology* 66: 1-31.

_____. 1974 *"Becoming Modern: Individual Change in Six Developing Countries."* 8th World Congress of Sociology, Toronto.

Lockwood, David. 1966. "Sources of Variation in Working-class Images of Society." *Sociological Review* 14.

Marx, Karl, 1906 *Capital.* New York: Modern Library.

_____. 1966. *Pre-Capitalist Economic Formations.* New York: International Publishers, 2nd printing, 1st U.S. edition.

Nash, Manning. n.d. "Southeast Asian Society: Dual or Multiple?" *Journal of Asian Studies* 23 (no. 3): 420-22. As quoted in Bert F. Hoselitz, "Interaction between Industrial and Pre-Industrial Stratification Systems." In N. Smelser and S.M. Lipset (eds.), *Social Structure and Mobility in Economic Development.* Chicago: Aldine, 1964: 183.

Perruci, Gadiel. 1974. *"Estrutura e conjuntura da economia açucareira do nordeste."* Conference on the Brazilian Northeast, Racine, Wis.

Sigaud, Lygia. 1971. "A naçâo dos homens." Museu Nacional da Universidade Federal do Rio de Janeiro, M.A. dissertation.

Soares, Glaucio Ari Dillon. 1967. "A nova industrialização e o sistema político brasileiro." *Dados* 2-3: 32-50.

Stevens, S.S. 1951. "Mathematics, Measurement, and Psychophysics." In S.S. Stevens (ed.), *Handbook of Experimental Psychology.* New York: Wiley.

_____. 1957. "Ratio Scales and Category Scales for a Dozen Perceptual Continua." *Journal of Experimental Psychology* 54 (December): 377-411.

The Aftermath of Peasant Mobilization: Rural Conflicts in the Brazilian Northeast since 1964

Moacir Palmeira

Peasant movements frequently end in defeat and suffer violent police repression. If we are to believe those who have studied this kind of social movement, that seems to be their usual fate. It has become commonplace in the literature to say that peasant movements either end as quickly as they begin or represent cyclical explosions that interrupt the immemorial conservatism of the peasant.[1] The analysis of the "morning after" one of these movements — one that has had a profound effect on public opinion in the West during the past two decades — may help us assess the periods of supposed conservatism and perhaps to discard some of the stronger stereotypes of peasant political participation.

The authors who have described the emergence of peasant movements in the Northeast of Brazil refer to the incident of the Engenho Galiléia as the starting point (Juliao 1962; Callado 1960, 1964; Forman 1968; Camargo 1973). The *foreiros* of that *engenho* organized the first peasant league, which advanced among *foreiros* in similar situations, whose autonomy was threatened by the return of the big landowners to the sugar plantations attracted by the rising prices of sugar on the world market.[2] During this initial phase, the leagues also recruited *moradores* in danger of being reduced to the status of mere wage earners. Led by Francisco Juliao, the leagues spread, gaining the so-called Agreste (a region of renters and small landholders), and later flowing back into the sugarcane zone. They then faced competition from rural unions, organized mostly by the Catholic church and its denominational and semidenominational associations. While in the early 1960s leagues and unions vied for the support of salaried and semisalaried sugar workers,

71

beginning in 1962, there was a trend toward specialization: renters and small landholders rallied to the leagues, the wage earners joined the unions. Juliao (1962) himself recommended that the political current taking shape within the leagues should also gain strength in the unions. The rural unions, originally inspired by the Catholic church and later divided into several political-ideological trends, developed at an amazing rate. Their strength increased when Miguel Arraes became state governor in 1963. By July of that year, they had already become far more numerically important than the leagues. While the latter had 40,000 affiliates, union members totaled 200,000 in Pernambuco (Wilkie 1964). The Rural Labor Statute, an innocuous legal instrument in other areas of the country, became a powerful weapon for the rural workers' struggle in the Pernambuco coastal sugarcane zone. By remaining politically active almost on a daily basis, the rural masses forced the landowners to abide by the rulings of the statute and to observe the *tabela de campo*[3] issued by the Arraes administration.

The labor rights which in the city took decades to become imperfectly enforced, in the Pernambuco countryside became effective almost concurrently with their proclamation as law (Furtado 1964: 155). This was no chance occurence, but one connected with a specific political conjuncture: the rise of so-called popular forces at the national level and the election of a state government with clear-cut reformist aims. The existence of this conjuncture can hardly eliminate the undeniable importance of the peasant masses' active involvement in the enforcement of the law, nor the repercussions of that law on the area's social structure, particularly concerning power relations between landowner and worker. In contrast to the region's major historical events in that period, the history of peasant participation in the process, in which their own political redefinition was at stake, has yet to be written. However, the depth of those changes can be grasped in the area today, through a study of the rural workers' own "cognitive map" (Sigaud 1971). To rural workers and peasants, not only in the Pernambuco sugarcane zone but in the entire state, Arraes, the union, and the "laws" mark the turning point between two eras, defining a period in which traditionally established relations were completely overturned, and acting as necessary reference points for the thinking and practices of present-day workers (Sigaud 1972).[4]

The Pernambuco sugarcane zone *(zona da mata)*, with its 11,583 km² and 1,076,263 inhabitants (11 percent of the state's surface area holds 20 percent of the population), is one of the country's oldest settlement areas. Always geared toward sugarcane production, it flourished in the late sixteenth and early seventeenth centuries. From then on, as a result of international competition (from Dutch, French, and English capital invested in the West Indies), it very seldom approached the prosperity of its early settlement years. After regaining a strong position in the international market, following the Haitian revolution at the turn of the eighteenth century, the area experienced a series of ups and downs throughout the 1800s. Early in the twentieth century, while undergoing a process of technological modernization which would have assured it of better competitive conditions in the international market, it was affected by the general crisis which was then assailing the whole of Brazil's export agriculture (Prado Júnior 1962: 231-61). In the case of sugar, the crisis was specifically linked to a lack of foreign markets. Thanks to the development of a coffee culture, the area's economy managed to survive, turning increasingly toward the domestic market. Following World War I, its foreign sales had practically stopped, while in Sao Paulo sugar production was expanding to compete for the domestic market. By the early 1930s, the struggle between Sao Paulo's sugar production and its northeastern counterpart was becoming clear: higher-level technology and a richer soil, plus greater availability of capital afforded the state of Sao Paulo a much lower production cost. These differences increased over the years and the crisis was only averted thanks to state intervention which created the IAA (Institute for Sugar and Alcohol) to guarantee the price of the northeastern product. According to experts, Sao Paulo is currently in a position to supply the entire country, including the North east, with sugar cheaper than Pernambuco's.

Over the past few years the state of Pernambuco has been facing competition from within its own region: production in the state of Alagoas has increased thanks to at technological breakthrough of the 1950s, generalized during the 1960s, which made it possible to grow sugarcane on the tablelands, whereas only the *várzeas* (or lowlands) had been used for this before. Alagoas has a much larger expanse of tablelands than Pernambuco, as well as better conditions for mechanization which allow it to draw a considerable amount of investment funds, since the use of machinery is a priority goal for the regional programs aimed at rationalizing the agroindustry. In addition, its labor costs are lower because the unionist movement is practically nonexistent there and landowners are not forced to bear the weight of labor legislation. One of the results of this has been the transfer of capital, and often of the sugar mill owners themselves, from the sugar agroindustry of Pernambuco to the neighboring state.

The present condition of Pernambuco's sugarcane economy is dramatic, according to the area's rural owners. Lacking the means for self-survival whether in the domestic or international market, thanks to state protection it has profited from favorable conditions arising in both. Sugarcane plantations have expanded and the population which depends on the sugarcane agroindustry has grown as well. As a result, problems have also increased in scale. But the situation is dramatic for another reason still. Despite all the inconveniences, sugar continues to be the region's most economically viable product (Du Genestoux 1967: 131-37). Various technical projects designed for localized agrarian reform have failed to overcome the problem. The liberation of lands from the large estates for the development of a subsistence agriculture, to match the government's massive support toward modernizing the *usinas,* a "solution" which delighted the experts, has proved unprofitable.[5] The cause lies less in the investments needed for soil improvement, irrigation, etc., than in the fact that a peasant economy existing on the fringes of the large estates has reasonably met the region's food demands, while offering a degree of flexibility which a "rational" agriculture could not possibly provide (Palmeira 1971; Garcia and Heredia 1972). Even cattle breeding, a "solution" welcomed by the major landowners, specially between 1961 and 1968, is apparently not profitable enough to become an alternative to sugarcane (Du Genestoux 1967: 134-37). Although SUDENE continues to finance the planting of pastures, and despite the fact that pasture grounds have actually expanded in some parts of Pernambuco's sugarcane zone, the *usineiros* and sugarcane suppliers claim to be disappointed with the "solution."[6]

The Pernambuco coastal region is a priority area for agrarian reform. Innumerable attempts have been made to assure the Pernambuco sugarcane agroindustry a competitive position in the domestic market. Sao Paulo's sugarcane agroindustry, although far from being an international model, managed through the introduction of machinery and in the absence of a strong rural unionism to decrease production costs, reducing its labor expenditures to a minimum. In contrast, the Pernambuco agroindustry has an agricultural cost profile in which labor accounts for nearly 70 percent of total expenditures (Du Genestoux 1967: 123-27). Above all, it operates with a relatively more expensive labor force than its Sao Paulo counterpart, while Pernambuco's rural unions ensure at least partial fulfillment of the industry's legal obligations to its workers. Faced with this, Pernambuco's *usineiros* and sugarcane suppliers can only attempt to reduce costs in any possible way, since the government's credit policy and the rising price of sugar in the domestic market are not enough for the owners.[7] In addition to the constant struggle for new increases in the price of sugar, sugar mill and plantation owners seek to minimize labor costs by dismissing groups of workers they consider superfluous, increasing exploitation of the workers employed, and attempting to circumvent rural labor laws and agrarian legislation by any available means.[8] Finally, they struggle at a strictly political level for legislative reform, or for measures which will neutralize existing laws.[9] As their bargaining power in government circles decreases (their political importance is on the wane at both the national and local level, with the arrival of new actors on the political scene), the overexploitation of rural workers and peasants is bound to increase.[10]

For several years, the critical situation affecting the sugarcane agroindustry had been leading the large landowners, in an attempt to decrease labor costs, to evict their *moradores* (Correa de Andrade 1964; Furtado 1964), or at least to break the rules of the game by redefining the status of these workers.[11] The establishment of wage relations proper had been spreading in the area for some time and landowners had been attempting to shed their "social obligations" to the workers. This tendency was intensified by the issuing and implementation in the area of the Rural Labor Statute. The military movement of 1964 gave the go-ahead to landowners eager to evict their workers and frightened by the labor movement's gains during the preceding period. In the words of a rural laborer, evictions began "after they removed Miguel Arraes.[12] They were angry at the workers." The Land Statute, the "law of two hectares," and the extension of retirement with pay to the countryside produced the same effect.[13]

As a result, one of the main sources of conflict in the area is still the landowners' tendency to disown their obligations to the workers. Landowners in the woodland zone are no longer accepting new *moradores* on their lands, and prefer to subcontract the labor through *empreiteiros* (labor contractors). Those who continue to accept *moradores,* or who must bear the weight of their older *moradores,* do not provide them with land for the development of subsistence agriculture in their spare time, as was customary up to a certain period. When they do, the plot is usually located on poor soil or so far from the laborer's house that the latter is unable to exploit the land assigned to him. In addition to the traditional ban on growing fruit trees, more often than not, the plots are mobile. The landowner gives the worker a lot covered with brushwood. The laborer clears the brushwood, often has to "destump" the plot as well (a task considered one of the hardest in the region), and then plants his field. After the produce of this field is gathered, the landowner claims he needs the land to plant sugarcane and sends the worker to another part of the estate.

These procedures are not mutually exclusive. The same landowner uses them all. And the same worker is subject to various forms of manipulation. A large *usina* operating in the area was facing financial difficulties in 1970 and, unable to afford keeping all its permanent workers busy the entire week, was giving them only three days' work. This factory decided, amid much publicity, to grant its workers land in accordance with the "law of two hectares." This was actually done. The catch was simply that the plots given were located at an average six kilometers away from the laborers' homes, and land was either depleted or covered with scrub, permanent plants were forbidden, and the plots were mobile. Few workers were interested in receiving plots under these conditions and the *usina* interpreted this as proof of their lack of interest in land and their unwillingness to work.[14] This is only one aspect of a wider process. Whenever possible, the landowner simply evicts his *moradores*, giving them ludicrous compensation (in terms of what they are entitled to by law) or none at all.

This eviction is not always as simple, nor is it always effected in the same manner. The landowner often begins by "trimming the plot," that is asking the *morador* to return part of the land he had been given in order to "cover it with sugarcane."[15] This is an attempt to force the *morador* into seeking another *engenho*, by depriving him of the means to develop his modest agriculture. At other times, the landowner will request the entire plot, leaving the worker bound to him only through wages. In extreme cases (which are not common in this region) the owner will demand rent for the house or simply tell the *morador* to look for other housing in some nearby hamlet, although the work contract or employment bond is maintained. Another possibility is to provide no upkeep for the worker's house and just let it fall apart. All these practices are often part of the same eviction process. But this is not necessarily the case; the same landowner may use only one of these devices or, conversely, use several devices on different kinds of workers.

The house and plot are not the only pretexts used to dispose of workers. In some areas of the sugarcane zone (specifically the south, where ownership is more concentrated and sugarcane has a more exclusive quality) (Correa de Andrade 1964: 98-126), some of these devices had become irrelevant since the plots no longer existed or were not particularly significant when, in the last few years, the eviction process was intensified. Here the mechanism used is "dismissal due to absences." The landowner will offer the worker only two or three days a week or, more often, assign him tasks which require more than a day to be completed. Since payment if effected on a piecework basis, with an equivalence between output "X" and the minimum salary established for one day's work, the laborer "goes down on record" as having worked three days instead of the six he actually spent. In addition to earning less, he is "lawfully" fired after a certain time for having missed more than thirty days of work. Or instead, by paying more for work done through the contractor, the landowner prompts the *morador* to move out of the *engenho*. Other devices are the constant complaints about tasks which the *morador* is supposedly doing poorly, and the "change in jobs." The latter, perhaps the most frequently used mechanism nowadays, involves the landowner's demand that his *morador* perform a different task each day, including jobs for which he lacks even the vaguest qualifications or which are hazardous to his health; the basis for this is the supposedly un-skilled nature of agricultural work. The moment the laborer refuses a given task, he is dismissed on the grounds that he is refusing to work.

The fact, reported by both landowners and workers, that the eviction rate has risen over the last ten years, does not imply that the process is taking place without a struggle. The unions have tried, by playing with existing legislation, to discover means of fixing the worker to the land or increasing his resistance through cooperative programs, by creating forms of accruement which will make him tougher prey for the large land owners. The *moradores,* for their part, react to eviction throughout all its stages. The most common reaction on the part of a *morador* to the landowner's warning that he leave the plot or the house is to ignore it and wait for the landowner and his vigilantes to destroy his field or remove the roofing from his house, before going to the union or the courts. Others, in response to a mere threat will immediately seek out the union which instructs them on how to behave and to prepare, in many cases, to catch the landowner "redhanded," which is an important ele-ment for the subsequent court process. However, some simply leave, upon being threatened, and then claim compensation for the im-provements they left behind.[16] Paradoxically, the courts and the unions are present in these cases from the very beginning.

Not only the *moradores,* but also the *foreiros* are subject to eviction. The latter cultivate plots larger than those given to tenants, in the lands of the *engenho* or the farm where they live. In exchange for this they pay a yearly rate and have other obligations to the landowner already men-tioned above, and which were contested from the beginning of the pea-sant mass mobilization, having practically vanished after 1963. As the rural workers put it: "After Miguel Arraes, nobody pays *condiçao,* nobody pays *foro,* nobody pays *cambao* .... When the unions started, we gradually got rid of the *cambao,* got those conditions off our backs" [interview data]. Many of these *foreiros* grew permanent plants. In the north of the sugarcane zone, they lived mainly in the *chas,* a type of tableland considered useless for growing sugarcane, where they produced fruits, vegetables, and manioc flour for the region's urban centers. The value of these lands has increased not only due to the eventual use of *chas* for sugarcane, but also as a result of the *granjismo* which led city dwellers to set up "weekend resorts" where fruit growing and poultry breeding were carried out. This rise in land value prompted landowners to seek the *foreiros'* eviction. In the early stages, the most common pro-cedure seems to have been raising the *foro.* Unable to pay the higher rate, the *foreiro* would be forced to seek land elsewhere. The rise of the leagues and unions, however, made things somewhat more difficult for the landowners. More subtle devices were sought, such as *recusa do foro,* whereby in an attempt to eliminate the *foreiro,* the owner refuses to accept his payment. Some time later, accompanied by a few witnesses, he goes to court and requests eviction of the "invader," or of whomever broke the contract by failing to pay the stipulated amount. However, the *foreiros* found an answer to this. If the landowner refuses to accept the *foro,* they go to the union, individually or as a group, and through the union, deposit their payment with the court.

It is common among union leaders in the area to complain about the "individualism" of *foreiros* and small landholders. The bosses would manipulate this individualism, when conflicts arose, by dealing with the *foreiros* separately and proposing solutions which, if accepted, weaken the latter's own bargaining position, since the possibility of union intervention decreases under these circumstances. This image undoubtedly transcends the union leaders' interpretations. It corresponds to an image of the peasant which not only prevails within Brazilian society, but is also accepted in international academic circles, where it has led to unending discussions. For this reason, it may be useful to put it in perspective in terms of the particular case under analysis. Francisco Juliao (1962: 50-68) pointed out that, because the *foreiros* and small landholders are neither so dependent upon the large landowners nor so poor as the mere wage earners, they are better equipped to resist pressure from large landowners. A comparison between conflicts involving *foreiros* and large landowners, on the one hand, and those involving large landowners and what we could call, with due reservation, wage earners, on the other, shows that the former type of conflict lasts much longer, stretching out over several years during which the *foreiro* is not forced to accept the landowner's claims. On the other hand, it is difficult to find a *foreiro* or a small landholder who has not at some point worked as a wage earner in the *engenhos* and *usinas* during the sugarcane harvest time.[17] The prolonged conflicts in which the *foreiros* must fight the owners' constant attempts to divide them may lead to defections. However, they also seem to create social control mechanisms which decrease the number of defectors, and an associative spirit often as strong as or stronger than that of salaried workers.[18] This explains the union leaders' apparently contradictory statement to the effect that, once convinced to join the union, the *foreiro* and the small landholder become the most conscientious members on whom the union can count.

The eviction of *moradores* drives a large contingent of laborers to the neighboring cities, who will compete for jobs with the *moradores* who have remained in the plantations and create for them a state of semiemployment, forcing them to accept whatever working conditions are imposed by the boss. These conditions involve, as we will see further on, everything from accepting lower wages to receiving them off the record, which deprives them of all legal guarantees. Subcontracting of labor, a widespread practice in other areas of the country such as Sao Paulo and Paraná, was not unknown in the sugarcane zone prior to the proclamation of laborers' "rights." Until 1963 and 1964 it was not a generalized procedure, and landowners used it only during the harvest season. Contractors were not even needed as mediators between the harvest workers (at the time, particularly in the Agreste) and the landowners. Since additional labor was always needed to help during the harvest period, landowners "worked" both through contractors and with laborers reporting directly to the plantations or recruited by their employees, who were members of the sugar mill hierarchies. Following the proclamation of "labor rights," "working through a contractor" practically became the rule and was no longer limited to harvest time. Even the tasks of planting and weeding were assigned to contractors. The outside worker who went directly to the owners was referred back to the contractor. In the last few years, as subcontracting became general practice, workers who continue to live at the plantations are suffering the effects of eviction through a mechanism other than the presence of a "reserve army": many landowners have made the continued residence of these laborers conditional on their working for a contractor. This attitude is even more common in relation to the *moradores'* offspring. As soon as they come of age, the children are forced to choose between leaving the estate without any right to compensation or remaining in their parents' house, but working for a contractor.

The contractor can be a free-lancer or a former rural worker commissioned by the owner or by a member of the *usina* hierarchy to find clandestine workers who can assure the owner lesser expenditures by freeing him of legal obligations. The *clandestino* is a nonregistered laborer, without a worker's identification card (or whose card is out of use), with no employment ties whatsoever to the owner (either legal or personal), who is hired by the contractor. The clandestine worker is not recognized by the *usina* or *engenho*. The *usina* pays the contractor who has a worker's identification card signed by the employer and has a portion of his wage withheld according to legal stipulations.[19] After subtracting his share, the contractor pays the workers in accordance with the tasks they have performed at a wage agreed to previously. This wage, which is always less than the legal minimum wage, gives some workers the opportunity to earn more than they would "legally" receive, since no deductions are made from their pay and the contractor does not limit the amount of work they can perform (as is common practice at the *engenhos,* where the owner never lets the *morador* make more than the minimum wage). Although he is hated by many of the workers, especially the *fichados* (registered workers) for whom he represents a double threat in terms of competition and of the likelihood of losing their labor benefits in the near future, the contractor's "liberal attitude" in relation to work limits and wages assures him of a relative amount of prestige with certain groups of workers.

The implications of subcontracting were not limited to economic aspects. Spreading at a time when the unions were disjointed due to the repression which followed the crisis of 1964, and when unemployment in the area was considerably high since several *usinas* had closed down or gone bankrupt, it helped draw workers away from the union. Whereas in 1962-63 having one's worker's identification card in order was almost a prerequisite to getting a job, the converse was true in 1964-65. Only those who had no links with the union and were willing to forfeit their legal prerogatives were in a position to find work. Thus, not only was the landowner suspicious of a worker connected with the union, but considerable pressure was being put on workers to abdicate their rights.

Once regrouped, the unions began to fight against subcontracting, using as a weapon the Rural Labor Statute which forbids rural landowners to employ clandestine workers. The struggle was particularly intense and somewhat successful in 1970, the year when rural workers gained access to the INPS (social security) system. The state, which was also sidestepped through subcontracting (since the workers failed to pay dues in its favor), responded to the unions' campaign. The Ministry of Labor concentrated on this area for some time, making a few *usinas* pay rather stiff fines.[20] The campaign's relative success served to enhance the unions' prestige. However, landowners found ways to overcome that hurdle. When subcontracting was made difficult in some areas, they began to use short-term formal contracts. Following the example set by businessmen in the cities, they would "fire" the worker and "rehire" him for an additional six months, and so on. In this fashion, the landowner was released from having to provide a thirteenth salary each year (the *décimo*), paid holidays, severance pay if a worker was fired, etc. However, subcontracting did not end and was even revitalized when the INPS system was replaced by FUNRURAL, the government's solution to reconciling its fiscal interests with landowner resistance, while allowing certain advantages to remain for the rural masses (Chiarelli 1972: 44-47).

Eviction of *moradores* is not the only source of conflict. Other conflicts involve new forms of labor exploitation applied within the sugar economy's specific working conditions. The same mechanisms used to force the worker to leave the sugar mill are often also used to reduce his wage and make him lose his rights, that is, lose the right to labor benefits to which he is entitled by law. The "three days' work" system mentioned before is used quite frequently to prevent the laborer from receiving his "paid rest," once he has accumulated a certain number of "absences."[21]

The confrontation between landowners and workers takes place above all within the productive process itself. There the landowners see the possibility of continuing to be owners, given the very conditions of the area which we have already mentioned. To them, it is not just a matter of wringing a surplus value out of their workers. It is a matter of their survival as such, and it is increasingly a matter of reducing the share allotted to "necessary labor" from the returns produced by the laborers in order to ensure for themselves a surplus value. Without this overexploitation of the labor force which is expressed in a constant effort to circumvent the laws concerning rural work, the *usineiro* and sugarcane suppliers would not be able to remain within the economic scene, since government protection is becoming relatively lower each day.

This overexploitation involved in extracting that surplus value within the region's specific conditions is what determines the terms of the conflict between workers and owners. Sugarcane workers define their daily struggle as a battle against "the bosses' theft," a formula which has its counterpart among the owners in what they call the "worker's theft" and the "government's theft," to refer to devices used by workers to avoid performing the tasks assigned to them, and the government's "confiscation" of part of the surplus value extracted from the labor, through the differential price of sugar in the domestic and international market. It is very common for a worker to say that the labor laws are good, but are not enforced. Except that the enforcement of these laws seems to be incompatible with the operational patterns of the sugar industry in Pernambuco.

Of the three stages in the sugarcane's agricultural cycle (planting, weeding, and cutting), the last two are decisive for the laborer. Weeding the sugarcane fields keeps him busy for most of the year. And cutting the cane, a task which is paid on a piecework basis, gives him a chance to prepare his "nest egg." The piecework system first came into general use in the 1940s. Originally, weeding was paid on the basis of *tarefas* (a square area measuring 0.896 acres per side, where one man would work from two to four days) and cutting on the basis of *cento* (lots of 120-130 stalks of sugarcane each, cut and tied together by a worker).[22] Subsequently, weeding began to be paid by the *conta* (an area measuring 22 by 22 meters, covered by one man in a day or less) and cutting in terms of the number of tons of sugarcane cut by one person. These measures created various problems since, given certain soil conditions, types of brushwood, quality of sugarcane, etc., the worker had to exert more or less effort in order to complete the assigned tasks. The wage and labor equivalence tables issues in 1963, during the Arraes administration, and in 1964, after the military coup, reflect the problem of reconciling the interests of landowners and workers, particularly after the minimum wage became effective in the countryside. These tables, which establish the relation between tasks assigned in terms of the measures described above (*contas* and tons) and the regional minimum salary, never acquired the status of collective work contracts, although they were signed by legal representatives of workers and landowners. Instead, they remained as a mere point of reference in the arbitration of local conflicts. The 1964 table attempts to provide a maximum of detail concerning conditions under which a given measure is valid. However, these specifications, rather than preventing controversies, provide one more cause for their occurrence. This was probably inevitable, since they open an entire span of possibilities for different ways of manipulating the wording of the agreement.[23]

A permanent source of conflict in the area is the *tarefa exagerada,* an expression coined by the workers who, in this case, use the term *tarefa,* which describes an area much larger than the *conta,* to refer to the *contas* assigned by the owners, exceeding the measures established by usage or by the table. Disagreements over the size of a *conta* arise every day, since the *contas* are assigned on a daily basis. When the laborer reports to work in the morning and finds his *conta* already measured out by the *cabo* (man in charge of measuring the responsible for groups of workers, who represents the next step above the mere laborer in the plantation hierarchy), he can refuse to accept it. The *conta* must be measured in front of him. Still, this is only the first step; the next step concerns the size of the *conta* itself. The owners (or their representatives) have a habit of asking the *cabos* that the *contas* they give the workers in broken land, or in plots covered with brushwood, be measured out in terms of flat or cleared land. In addition, the corporal generally uses a *vara de medir* (a rod which should measure 2.20 meters) whose length does not match the legal and/or customary size. In these cases, the workers, who often carry their own rods, refuse to work and threaten to return home or complain to the union. Whatever arrangement is reached, however, does not put an end to the conflict. If the work is not done to the boss's liking, the laborer is subject to a *corte da conta*. This means that if the cane field was not weeded to perfection (and the criteria for "perfection" are, of course, variable), as a whole or in part, the *cabo* does not record in his work control pad the task performed by that laborer, whose day will not be counted when the payroll is drawn up and who will therefore not be able to buy on credit at the plantation store as is customary. Finally, the owner is constantly concerned about speeding up the work. If on a given day, the most physically fit worker or the one who was given a *conta* in better or clearer land, finishes his work much earlier than the rest, the following day's *contas* will be set according to the working capacity of that particular laborer, the "superman," as the workers themselves call him. Since cuts in the *conta* often result in physical violence or in having to leave the estate, the workers, who can no longer resort to a strike as in earlier days, can only fight this speeding by stalling the work in such a way as to have everyone finish more or less simultaneously and thereby eliminate the pretext used by the boss.

The main deception device applied to the cutting of sugarcane is known as the "scales theft" (*roubo da balança*). The sugarcane cut by the worker is tied up in sheaves of twenty to thirty stalks each, depending on the *usina,* which must be weighed by the *cabo.* Since he cannot weigh every sheaf, he chooses ten, weighs them, takes an average, and estimates the worker's total individual output by multiplying the average weight of the sample by the number of sheaves which were cut. The *cabo* tends to choose sheaves with smaller or slimmer stalks for his estimate. The worker always protests and, to forestall a very heavy "theft," he tries to place stalks of different weights in the same sheaf. This defensive move, however, involves extra effort on the part of the laborers. In addition, according to the workers and to the *cabos* themselves, the *cabo* always uses biased scales. They are generally small scales in which the dial is cut in half, which makes any weight above a given number equal to the scales' maximum weight. A few workers protect themselves by using their own scales.

In some areas, the sugarcane cut by the laborers is still accounted for on the traditional *centos* system. The worker's pay is then estimated, not by weight, but by the number of lots of one hundred sheaves of twenty stalks each, tied together by the cutters. According to the owners, this system makes the "worker's theft" easier: he supposedly cuts the stalks in more than the required two pieces and therefore actually puts fewer stalks in each sheaf, or he places the larger and thicker stalks on the outside of the sheaf, while hiding the slimmer stalks (which are easier to cut) on the inside. However, the practice of tying whole stalks, adopted in the last few years, did away with whatever advantages the system might have offered the worker, and also managed to avoid protests over the change to a system of cutting by the ton.[24]

The "scales theft," added to other devices such as assigning areas of "overgrown cane" (sugarcane with much straw and/or brushwood) to workers who tend to produce more than the *usina's* desired limit, is skillfully used by the *usineiros.* In order to commit their sugarcane suppliers, foremen, and *cabos* to this form of exploitation, they maintain that the sugarcane at the *tomba* (the place where it is cut) must have the same weight at the *ponto* (the place to which it is transferred by donkeys to be picked up by the *usina's* trucks or engines) and at the sugar mill scales (where the sugarcane is weighed before being processed). This is impossible: as soon as the sugarcane is cut, it begins to lose its saccharose content and consequently its weight. In addition, the sugarcane generally spends hours and even days awaiting transportation, and there are inevitable losses associated with that transportation as well. In order to make the impossible possible, the *usineiros* and *fornecedores* pass the responsibility for "losses" on to the foreman and his assistants (*cabos*), paying them on a piecework basis (in terms of the product's weight at the *usina* scales), and threatening the former with dismissal should they retain lenient *cabos* who allow the payroll to suffer large wage outlays.[25]

The wage and labor equivalence tables and the Rural Labor Statute left both owners and workers to choose the most convenient system of payment in each specific case. As we saw earlier, piecework wages tend to prevail, while day-labor wages are restricted, in the case under analysis, only to work which is not linked directly to the sugarcane, such as transportation, road building and maintenance, and trench digging and maintenance. The owners, however, seek to combine both forms of payment. They want the worker to perform on a piecework basis, while serving a minimum of eight hours a day. The laborer then finds himself caught in a work pace which he had been spared through the piecework system, in addition to having to endure, as in the "era of captivity," the presence of the *cabo* constantly at his heels ("you just set down the hoe and it's enough to get a scolding"). This interpretation of the law, invoked by the owners whenever they face a business boom, creates additional conflicts; however, thanks to union intervention, it has not managed to prevail.

The daily struggle between workers and owners at the production level does not stop there. To have done the work to the boss's satisfaction is no guarantee that the worker will receive his wages at the end of the week. Lack of payment and late payment are quite frequent, particularly in between harvests, since many owners do not have access to what is known as "interharvest financing" or use this to pay other debts, especially during crisis periods which are not unusual in the sugar economy. Failure to pay wages is sometimes used by the *usina* as an excuse to invite intervention by the Institute for Sugar and Alcohol which will step in, pay the *usina's* debts, and resupply it. This was the case in 1968 with two *usinas* in a municipality of southern Pernambuco which, for no less than a year, had failed to pay wages, while those laborers who did not quit their jobs managed to subsist thanks to the local union's distribution of food and to the credit facilities available from businesses in the nearby cities which had no other alternative.

Failure to pay wages, however, is not as frequent as failure to provide paid rest, paid vacation, and "thirteenth salary." Delays in paying the latter are a standard occurrence. Instead of receiving it in December, as required by law, the worker gets his *décimo* (thirteenth salary) in May or June of the following year. Sometimes the *usinas* will even try to break it down into installments. Perhaps because, with the establishment of the *décimo*, the owners did away with the custom of presenting their *moradores* with gifts for the holidays (Christmas, New Year's, Epiphany), the workers identify the *décimo* with those holidays and are absolutely adamant on the question of its payment, which will allow them to purchase new shoes and clothes. It seems that failure to receive the *décimo* reaches the heart of the worker's sense of honor. This is one of the areas of conflict where they are less likely to yield. This can be illustrated in terms of the refusal, on the part of one *usina's* rural workers, to receive the overdue *décimo* in installments, in spite of the difficulties they were facing and although payment under these conditions was being proposed directly by the *usineiro* who was ready to pay the first installment on the spot.

Although their wage is paid on a weekly basis, the workers as a rule buy their provisions daily. The plantations' relative isolation forces them to shop almost exclusively at the *barracao*, the plantation store. Every day, at that store, the worker acquires the amount of goods he needs, particularly to meet his family's food requirements, according to his amount of work for that day and his accumulated debt. In extreme cases, this type of bond with the *barracao* leaves the worker in a permanent state of debt as a result of which he often does not receive his wages, since the debt is automatically deducted and the storekeeper (in charge of the plantation store) is, as a rule, responsible for effecting payment as well as drawing up the plantation's payroll. Although nowadays the plantation store system appears to be declining (Palmeira 1971), it is still strong enough to ensure the *usinas* and *engenhos* of a means to manipulate their workers' consumption. Once again it is during periods of crisis that traditional devices such as these are implemented in full force and without the alleviating circumstances or compensations which would offer the worker an occasional advantage, as in the past. In this fashion, another *usina* faced with a crisis preferred, instead of inviting IAA intervention, to solve its problems of working capital, after 1964, by reinstating the store special tokens known in the area as *gabao*. In the past, the tokens functioned as a sort of currency, limited to the premises of the *usina* or *engenho*, which, in a type of bondage by debt, guaranteed the workers' continued stay at the site. In extreme cases, the usinas or *engenhos* would pay only in tokens, while the company store monopolized the workers' means of supply. Yet these tokens always had liquidity, that is coverage in terms of merchandise. In contrast, today's *gabao* is without its true value on the *usina*. It represents the rural worker's in ability to purchase supplies from a source other than the plantation store, in addition to which the prices are higher and its tokens are only accepted through a reduction of close to 30 percent of the nominal value. Nor can the worker be always certain of finding the goods he needs there; at this particular factory, the crisis had depleted the store's supplies. The worker's only alternative is often to sell his token for half the price or less to a dealer associated with the *usineiros* who can provide some cash, and then head for the shops or the outdoor market of a nearby settlement. The situation became even more complicated between 1970 and 1972. Before 1970 the usina was still paying part of its wages in cash. During 1970-72 when the army unofficially intervened following appeals from the area's rural unions and the sugar industry workers' union, the salaries came to be paid entirely in tokens.[26]

The distinction drawn between conflicts linked to the movement of expropriation of *moradores* and conflicts linked to new forms of labor exploitation, in the specific conditions of an economy whose status is marginal in relation to the national economy, are only meaningful in the context of an analytical point of view. From the standpoint of the social agents involved, these theoretical subtleties are irrelevant, particularly so since there is no empirical difference between the mechanism of expropriation and that of extracting surplus value. As we saw earlier, it matters little for the worker whether he is being evicted or overexploited when he realized that the owner is gaining ground over something which is socially recognized as his.

Yet while the theoretical differentiation has no practical consequences, the practical lack of differentiation has crucial implications for understanding the forms and contents which the class struggle acquires in the case under study. This lack of differentiation is responsible for unity in a struggle which could be different in each case since proletarianization, that is, the worker's full involvement in the new economic relations, is not the only way out for those affected by expropriation. It is also responsible for the limits within which these struggles unfold, which are none other than those set by the national legislation.

The laws are often a double-edged sword. On the one hand, the legislation was and continues to be an incentive and a tool for the owners to dispose of their *moradores* and/or exploit their workers by means of devices which can offset any losses they may suffer as a result of legislation. On the other hand, it is just as true that this legislation, for parallel and opposite reasons, is a weapon of utmost importance to the laborers. The area's rural unions, while having been strongly repressed with the 1964 coup and continuing to operate on rough ground, were not annihilated.[27] New leaders and even rightist leaders before 1964 were called upon to play the role which had previously fallen to leaders with a more clearly defined political program.[28] This did not imply the waning of a class struggle which existed without them and could eventually exist against them, given the objective conditions. Within this framework, the mere struggle to enforce legislation often acquires unsuspected radical features, and can even disrupt the continuity of social relations in the agroindustry.

These struggles to enforce legislation are not inconsistent with the struggles preceding the military movement (which were also largely for the enforcement of legislation), despite the change in the political conjuncture. The situation did not change for the area's rural workers and peasants in the same fashion as it did for other national political forces. The irreversible conflict between landowners and workers persisted on the same terms. The cycle of changes which could alter the content of these conflicts had not been completed and the means for the formulation of group interests, that is, the unions and their links to the state machine, were preserved. Since the economic structure and the terms of the class struggle remained the same, as soon as the unionist movement recognized the real channels of the new national political conjuncture, new definitions arise for those groups, akin to those of the preceding period, that is, conjunctures within which the contradictions dividing rural workers and owners could recur.[29] The greatest difficulty in analyzing these conflicts is that they do not follow the "normal" categories into which conflicts are generally classified. They are not exactly union conflicts, nor are they purely local conflicts. They are not political conflicts, nor are they simply economic.

With the emergence of unions, the legitimacy of traditional power based on personal relations was subverted, but dismissing any possibility of simple "local" conflicts, that is, conflicts limited by a single geographic or social unit which could be solved on the level of that unit. Simply questioning the authority and/or power of the owner within his domain necessarily implies another source of legitimacy alien to traditional domination, that is, broader, existing within the national political framework. This is true even for situations in which the union's presence was not needed to resolve a specific conflict. The union's presence is not confined to a physical mode. If as Rosa Luxemburg (1968) said, socialism is present in the least politicized unionism, we could say that the union, in the case under study, is there even in the most spontaneous struggles of the rural masses. It is no accident that the union became a temporal frame of reference crucial to the worldview of rural workers and peasants (Sigaud 1971). Nor is it accidental that an entire union mystique should have developed in the peasants' consciousness. The union is generally credited with an uncommon force — a power which goes beyond what the workers and peasants themselves acknowledge in the actual unions they know through their day-to-day existence. Paradoxically, this mystique seems to have a stronger hold on those further removed from the union, for example, the worker who refuses to join because he feels it is cowardly to face the boss through the union. This is also the case of the unionized worker who opposes his union's present leadership and recalls how the union building was constructed directly, stone upon stone, by the workers who are now being betrayed by something which "is not a union." Actually, he and his fellow workers know that this was not really the case and that the union building was erected by a construction foreman and his crew. Another worker, interviewed in 1972, was critical of the mobilization preceding 1964, which he saw as an excessive show of force through which the union would have eliminated all authority, along with the boss's. He then proposed, as a way to solve their problems, that the laborers all stop working simultaneously — "no need for strikes or agitation." In contrast to other historical situations, the conflicts in this case are not purely, or even primarily, union conflicts.

The authoritarian regime imposes the rules of the game and the unions must abide by them more or less rigorously, depending on the particular set of circumstances.[30] These rules prevent them from acting as agents of conflict unless demands are made from below. They may not appropriate a conflict as their own, or redirect it in such a way as to meet their policy interests at a given moment, nor can they extend the dynamics of one conflict to other related ones. In this sense, a legalistic adaptation tends to develop within the unions, internalized by both leadership and masses, and expressed not only in more explicit statements such as "the laws are good; it's their enforcement that's missing," but also in the way union leaders edit the facts. When a union leader is questioned as to existing conflicts in his area, he will only mention those whose causes can be framed within the labor and agrarian legislation. In the same fashion, the workers usually seek out the union to "discover their rights," before taking up an issue with the owner (see note 16).

It is difficult to draw the line between economic and political struggles in the modern states, given the extent of the influence of the federal government (Jelin 1973). It is even harder to attempt to draw that line in the case of Latin America, where the state tends to replace private enterprise to a considerable degree in the economic sphere and to fill the gap left by civil society in the political sphere (Jelin 1973; Velho 1974; Cardoso 1973). The task becomes practically impossible when we deal with a social sector which is part of a society ruled by an authoritarian regime, characterized by an extremely fragile economy based on devices for exploiting the labor force, and whose survival depends on the state's protection. Under these conditions any conflict is, almost by definition, a political issue which threatens the survival of the region's dominant class as such. It can therefore be treated as are political issues in authoritarian regimes, that is, as a matter for the police. Since this treatment defines the nature of its subject, the latter becomes "politicized" a second time and any vestige of the nonpolitical aspects of its socially acknowledged nature disappears once and for all. This approach has been applied to the major conflicts erupting in the northeastern rural zone, as well as to some others. Within these specific historical circumstances there is room for a certain mystique regarding not the state but its embodiment, the president, as a sort of supreme arbitrator, the only one capable of intervening and solving such conflicts. On the other hand, the government machine is subject to continuous deterioration, as its agencies become increasingly identified with the dominant regional interests with which they are intimately linked, even under circumstances where their objectives are opposed. This identification becomes stronger as further state intervention in the area turns government entities into mere representatives of the economic and paraeconomic agencies of the local dominant classes. INCRA, for example, becomes an enterprise which, like any other in the area works through a contractor, hires clandestine workers, and uses all those devices designed, as we have seen, to extract surplus value from labor.[31] This same firm becomes involved in conflicts with nationwide repercussions, such as the Barreiros case, involving the expulsion of workers from plantations acquired originally for "agrarian reform."[32]

However, a great distance separates these conflicts from purely political ones, the regime's restriction of political activity and the relative isolation of the struggle between workers and owners in the Pernambuco sugarcane zone, gives these conflicts a purely defensive character. This is even true when they go beyond the mere demand for law enforcement, and the workers adopt a more aggressive stand in terms of economic claims. To illustrate: after 1971, the policy outlined by the government in relation to sugarcane was aimed at rescuing the dominant class by using a favorable period in the international market.[33] Beginning in early 1974, the policy provoked a union reaction of collective bargaining because the rise in the true average salary and the relative dearth of labor caused by the sugar rush in some areas has exhausted the struggle for mere enforcement of the minimum salary. Although the reaction was unprecedented in terms of rural unionism, and although it may have been an adequate response to the stimulus, it still remains a defensive attitude.

The term *spontaneous struggles* involves a contradiction. It would hardly be appropriate to speak of spontaneous struggles in referring to those clearly traceable to the extremely complex political mobilization process of 1955-64. It would be more appropriate, following a classic exponent of historical materialism, to speak of an internalization of the (political) class struggle which has lost its more explicitly political features to come to the very core of the productive process. Here the daily output of *engenhos* and *usinas* has become subjected to the outcome of the day's confrontations between workers and bosses.

The loss of "spontaneity" in the struggles of the rural masses is not countered with intensive activity from more or less disguised political bodies seeking to direct the struggles in progress, at close range or from afar. Nor is it offset by the regime's acolytes who are nevertheless present, trying to manipulate the will of the rural masses, as in other Brazilian historical examples. Instead, the union leaders' activities are becoming more spontaneous, as these leaders transcend the strict limits of their role and replace some of the roles of the eroded political parties, without becoming identified with them.[34] In this fashion, the unions directly defend the interests of the class or class sectors they represent in dealing with the agencies in power, as opposed to the traditional ones. The role of union leaders as representatives of the interests of classes or parts thereof is at once juridical and, paradoxically, political.

NOTES

1. This chapter is not the result of a systematic research on conflict. Rather, it represents an effort to reflect on some realities which called the attention of the author during his field work in the Northeast of Brazil in 1969, 1970, and 1972, sponsored by the Comparative Study of Regional Development. This project was directed by Roberto Cardoso de Oliveira and David Maybury-Lewis as part of the *Programa de Pós-Graduaçao em Antropologia Social do Museu Nacional* (Rio de Janeiro).

2. *Foreiros* are small farmers who have a house and land on the *engenho*'s premises, where they plant for their own needs. They must pay a yearly rate, in addition to having some definite obligations to the owner, such as working for the plantation a few days per year *(cambao)*. *Moradores* are rural workers who live on the *engenho*'s premises and are linked to the sugarcane production work. They often have a plot of land *(sítio)* where they plant for themselves. The term *engenho* referred in the past to the plantation–sugar mill complex and, more specifically to the sugar mill itself where the processing was carried out in order to produce sugar. Today, the term is used in Pernambuco, where the last actual *engenhos* stopped grinding in the 1950s, to refer to any large property which plants sugarcane to supply a modern *usina*. The *senhor de engenho,* the property owner of an *engenho,* is also referred to as a *fornecedor de cana* or sugarcane supplier. *Usina* in a sugar mill which besides receiving sugarcane from the *senhores de engenho* has also its own plantations. Usineiro is the owner of an *usina.*

3. Since most of the tasks associated with sugarcane production are performed

on a piecework basis, when the Rural Labor Statute was issued in 1963, it became necessary, according to it, to establish a relation between the work actually performed in the countryside and the regional minimum salary. This was carried out on the basis of a discussion between the state government, on the one hand, and representatives of the sugar mill owners, sugarcane suppliers, and rural workers and peasants (peasant leagues and unions), on the other (Callado 1964:88, I-V).

4. To rural owners, these are also crucial reference points for their perception of Brazilian history, and a necessary topic in any conversation. We interviewed a large number of landowners, at different times. Despite the fact that the subject of the interviews had nothing to do with those political events, they made it a point to gear the conversation to reminisce over the incidents. Next to the expected condemnation, they always attempted to add very personal considerations (such as "it was the time when I was making money," or "I'm not against the unions, but they were heading in the wrong direction," or even, "Arraes meant well, but he got involved with the communists"), which, strangely enough, are shared by all.

5. This attempt to reconcile the interests of *usineiros* and *fornecedores,* on the one hand, and landless or near landless workers, on the other, is written into the statements of SUDENE and its leaders before and after 1954 (Furtado 1959:62; Gomes da Silva 1971:155). It can also be recognized in the goals of GERAN (Executive Group for the Rationalization of the Northeastern Agroindustry), created during the Castello Branco administration and closed in 1971, and of PROTERRA (Program for Land Redistribution and Incentives to the Northeastern Agroindustry), created in 1971.

6. This had led to official statements from the Federation of Agricultural Workers of Pernambuco, issued through the newspapers and through memoranda to governmental authorities. One of the federations's last presidents complained that although SUDENE had been trying to solve the problems of the Northeast for the last ten years, it was accomplishing nothing, since all he saw them doing was finance the plantation of *pangola* grass and replacing people with cattle.

7. Recently the president of the Association of Pernambuco Sugarcane Suppliers (representative body for the plantation owners) complained to the press that the price of sugarcane continued to be lower than its actual value, adding that sugarcane suppliers were losing Cr$28.00 per ton supplied. He further stated that Pernambuco's planters felt alienated because the IAA (Institute for Sugar and Alcohol) has assigned Cr$3.5 billion from the export fund to the industrialists (the sugar mill owners) and resources amounting to approximately Cr$450 million had been channeled to suppliers. He evaluated this as "a case of pure and simple confiscation of our benefits." He considered the biggest problem to be that the price fixed for sugarcane was lower than the production costs: "90 percent of our problems lie in the price of a ton of sugarcane" (*Jornal do Brasil,* October 28, 1974, section 1, p. 14). The presentation of the article containing these statements is in itself significant. The newspaper *Jornal do Brasil* mentioned that the agroindustry continued to complain about financial difficulties in spite of the spectacular rise in the

price of sugar in the international market. A survey taken by *Jornal do Brasil* in the major producing states is also referred in the article as showing that the cause for complaint lied in the excessive control maintained by the IAA on sugarcane agriculture and sales, in addition to the institute's monopoly on exports. The president of the Pernambuco Alcohol and Sugar Industry Association (the sugar mill owner's representative body), General Silvio Cahu, accused the IAA in the same article of absorbing 90 percent of the profits gained from exports, while granting the agroindustry only 10 percent.

8. The Rural Labor Statute was recently incorporated into the CLT (Consolidated Labor Laws), which until then ruled labor relations in urban zones only, now extended to the countryside.

9. These are, for example, the recurrent attempts of the CNA (Brazilian Confederation of Landowners) to change the union framework by making small landholders join the owners' associations. Among the more recent is an amendment submitted by two senators of the government party and drafted by that organization in 1973 (cf. *Jornal do Brasil*, May 21, 1973).

10. Camargo (1973:143-53) points to the rise of the *coronel* from the backlands beginning with the New State, and to the concurrent mobilization of the urban poor, following the populist model. See her study in chapter 4 of the present volume.

11. The eviction of *moradores* taking place in the area is radically different from the expulsion of labor in the northeastern plantation in earlier periods. This is a mass-scale eviction in which the expelled workers are deprived of the possibility of being absorbed by other productive units. The elimination of plots and the large contingent of available labor which settles in the cities around the *engenhos* change the very nature of relations which define the *morador*. The term then comes to refer to hardly more than a wage earner who lives in a plantation.

12. This refers to a decree issued by President Castello Branco in 1965 which reincorporates a ruling from the 1943 Statute of Sugarcane Agriculture, to the effect of granting the worker, free of charge, "an area of land big enough to allow for the necessary cultivation and breeding for the farm laborer's subsistence and that of his family." The decree, which immediately mobilized rural labor unions in the area, was outlined in detail in 1968, giving the firms a ninety-day period in which to submit a plan for granting land. This was never carried out and the decree became obsolete (Crespo 1972). However, from 1965 to the present, landowners have taken precautions against the implementation of that legal measure, disposing of their *moradores,* since the decree would apply, according to Gomes da Silva (1971:210), "to workers with more than one year's continuous service" to whom the sugar planters would have to grant "up to two hectares of land, close to their houses, for the production of subsistence goods."

13. The extension of retirement with pay to rural workers elicited an immediate reaction from landowners, judging from the successive complaints registered by unions and federations. The mere announcement of the law, according to the president of the Pernambuco Rural Workers' Federation, has already led

to threats of eviction (cf. "Sindicato sugere ajuda a aposentado," *Jornal do Brasil,* June 22, 1972.)

14. One worker in that *usina* who had been offered a plot voiced a completely different view, referring to the fact that the plantation foreman offered plots, but in poor soil in which even broad bean, the toughest plant there is, did not grow. He also mentioned that the land given was as hard as a wall, or "land fit only for sugarcane which is a plant with many roots." All complained that at the plantation they give out land for the worker to clear so that the sugar mill owners can then come and plant. Besides that, the plot would have been far away. This is why he did not want the land. And he added: "The *usina* hands out plots so that when the government comes by, they'll see that there are plots for the workers." This same worker felt that the owners "hand out poor land in order to force the laborer to work on whatever type of *conta* he is given." He also felt that "if the worker had good land and a good field he could refuse to accept a *conta* in which he is being exploited." But if the land is bad, "the worker has nothing to fall back on."

15. This image of the physical encroachment of sugarcane plantations on the *moradores'* backyards is probably the most common method used to plan the process of expropriating those tenants.

16. Vera Echenique, a graduate student of the National Museum's Graduate Program in Social Anthropology, has done a systematic research on conflict solving in the sugarcane region. This work is part of the Comparative Study of Regional Development.

17. One of the founders of this seasonal work is the complementary relation between the agricultural calendar of sugarcane and that of the subsistence cultures of peasants in the *Agreste* and in the coastal zone itself. The most intensive periods in sugarcane planting match with the slacker periods in the peasant economy and vice versa (Correa de Andrade 1964:154-71).

18. More so because the *moradores* are not safe from maneuvers to divide them. Because they are immersed in patronage relations with the owner, they find the collective nature of their work compensated for by the particularizing nature of the relationship. This, however, is not peculiar to the area (Wolf 1964). One attitude on the part of the *morador* which makes his joining the union difficult or which hinders his using the union against the boss once he becomes a member, is that he finds it cowardly to pit many people against just one. In the context of this logic, he often chooses to face the boss as an individual, that is under circumstances allowing for the possibility of physical violence.

19. Currently, only union dues are withheld from both contractor and workers. However, throughout 1970, INPS (National Institute of Social Security) fees were also deducted from their salaries.

20. Around that time, one *usineiro* complained that although all *usinas* worked through a contractor, "it so happened that the federal police decided to knock here, precisely the one time we were using a contractor." The union president who had filed the complaint said that he "had orders from the Labor District to discuss nothing with the owner and refer everything to the

Ministry of Labor.'' He added that when a landowner is caught using a contractor,'' he is forced to pay a fine to the INPS and to register all clandestine workers.''

21. *Remunerado* is the term used by workers in the area to refer to the *repouso semanal* (paid weekly rest) to which they are entitled according to Brazilian law.

22. One *braça* is equivalent to 2.20 meters.

23. A publication issued by the Union of Sugar Industrialists of Pernambuco and the Federation of Rural Workers of Pernambuco can give an idea of the possibilities of work manipulation. Article 23 of the publication gives an equivalent in terms of one regional minimum wage or *conta* to the weeding of sugarcane. It establishes that weeding sugarcane in harrowed land with rough brushwood on hard soil is worth 0.60 *conta*. In nonharrowed land with soft brushwood on soft soil: 0.80 *conta*. In nonharrowed land, on loose clay or sand: 1 *conta*. Weeding by stemping in thick brushwood is worth 0.80 *conta*, while in sparse brushwood it is 1 *conta*. Weeding by using a hoe: 2 *contas* (Sindicato da Indústria do Açúcar no Estado de Pernambuco and Federaçao dos Trabalhadores Rurais de Pernambuco 1964:4-5).

24. A *morador* from the south of the coastal zone, where sugarcane is cut by the ton, said that the Brazilian poor got a bit to eat, ''when they cut sugarcane by the hundreds, which didn't leave room for theft.'' A *morador* from the north of the coastal zone, where sugarcane is cut predominantly by the ton, stated that in *Engenho Novo* the man out there took one stretch of good sugarcane and got the contractor to cut by the hundreds, and that the workers would end up cutting by the ton. He added that their cutter ''would cut, cut, cut.'' He further stated that when ''he reached the bad area, he'd take those outside people away from there and make the farm people cut by the ton.'' He further added that many people from his work area thought this was really wrong.

25. Recognizing this mechanism leads the workers to show a certain amount of understanding for the *cabo*'s theft. One worker mentioned that ''the *cabo* thieves in measuring.... And the foreman doesn't give the worker one *braça*.'' He further stated that ''the foreman doesn't end out in the street.'' He observed the vigilance of the foreman on the man in charge of measuring: ''The poor *cabo* is already afraid to lose his cut, so he thieves in measuring.'' He noticed the *cabo*'s fear of the workers and of the administrator, adding that the cabo received his part for every ton measured, pointing that as long as the quota is met, at the end of the week the *cabo* gets his share of five in a ton. He also referred to the fact that ''if he doesn't do that, he can't get it. So to get those extra five, he moves in on the work of the laborer, of his colleague.''

26. Many of the struggles we describe developed naturally within the union sphere itself. However, an analysis of the unions and their work is beyond the scope of this chapter.

27. The ''Relatório Geral da FETAPE no Triênio 1966/69'' is eloquent in referring to the critical situation the unions were facing at that time (1966). The report diagnoses the weakness of the rural union structure as well as the

movement resulting from state intervention in the unions. It reports the drop in union membership and the difficulty in the financial situation of the union federation "which could not help but handicap considerably the implementation of programs planned by the new directors" (FETAPE 1969:1).

28. Shepard Forman (1968) already noticed these facts in 1967.

29. A true transition process had indeed begun in the area with the disruption of social relations which supported the old plantation and ensured its continuation. This process was never completed, in spite of the political changes which affected the country and the region from the rise of the peasant leagues to the present.

30. We could say, using the term and the points proposed by Otávio Guilherme Velho (1973), that such rules, more than being imposed by the authoritarian regime, had been a consequence of authoritarian capitalism itself, since they coexisted relatively unperturbed with the cosmopolitan stage of Brazilian capitalism. See chapter 1 in the present volume.

31. *Empresa* (enterprise) is one of the terms used by the workers to refer to the *usinas*.

32. In the last few months, events connected with PROTERRA's implementation in Pernambuco have been given wide press coverage in Brazil's major capitals. In the municipality of Barreiros and in neighboring municipalities, INCRA acquired some of the plantations of one of the state's largest *usinas* in order to sell them to small farmers, according to the law through which PROTERRA was created. The plan called for giving purchasing priority to the plantations' own rural workers. However, only two laborers profited from this land redistribution which favored mostly businessmen, *rendeiros* (cane suppliers who rent *usina* lands or lands owned by other suppliers), etc. As to rural workers who were previously linked to the sugar mills, a document addressed to the Ministry of Agriculture by the Pernambuco Rural Workers' Federation and the Barreiros Rural Workers' Union reports the dismissal of 219 rural workers from its list of employees of usina Central Barreiros when the transfer of land ownership was completed, complaining that their successors — INCRA or the plot holders, i.e., those who acquired the land — had not taken "the role of employers in relation to the workers in question." They further added that the workers "have now been jobless and wageless for sixty days, the victims of hunger and desperation" (cf. Confederaçao Nacional dos Trabalhadores na Agricultura, oficio nº AJ/1323/74).

33. Although the Export Fund, consisting of the difference between the price of sugar in the domestic and in the international markets, was established in 1965, it was only in 1971, with the plan for the merging of sugar mills, that part of this fund was channeled to refurbishing the agroindustry.

34. Jelin (1973) illustrates how this took place in Argentina, on a different scale and with different implications, during the period in which Peronism was banned from the country.

REFERENCES

Bello, Julio. 1938 *Memórias de um senhor de engenho*. Rio de Janeiro: José Olympio.

Callado, Antônio. 1960. Os industriais do seca e os galileus da Pernambuco. Rio de Janeiro: Civilizaçao Brasileira.

_____. 1964. *Tempo de Arraes: padres e comunistas na revoluçao sem violência.* Rio de Janeiro: José Álvaro, 2nd ed.

Camargo, Aspásia Alcântara. 1973. "Brésil nord-est: mouvements paysans et crise populiste." Université de Paris, doctoral dissertation.

Cardoso, Fernando Henrique. 1972. "O modelo político brasileiro." *Estudos CEBRAP* (no. 2).

_____. 1973. "Estado e sociedade no Brasil: notas preliminares." *Notas sobre estado e dependência.* Sao Paulo: Cadernos CEBRAP.

Chiarelli, Carlos Alberto. 1972. *Teoria e prática do prorural.* Sao Paulo: Ediçoes LTR.

Correa de Andrade, Manoel. 1964. *A terra e o homem no nordeste.* Sao Paulo: Editora Brasiliense, 2nd ed.

Crespo, Paulo. 1972. "Necessidade da aplicaçao do Decreto No. 57.020/65: decreto dos 2 hectares." *Reforma Agrária* (Boletim da Associaçao Brasileira de Reforma Agrária—ABRA), year 2 (no. 1):5-7.

Du Genestoux, Patrick Calemard. 1967. *Le Nordest du sucre.* Université de Paris, doctoral dissertation.

Echenique, Vera. 1974. *Resoluçao de conflitos na plantaçao Açucareira de Pernambuco.* Universidade Federal do Rio de Janeiro, Museu Nacional, M.A. dissertation.

Federaçao dos Trabalhadores na Agricultura do Estado de Pernambuco. 1969. *Relatório Geral da FETAPE no Triênio 1966/1969 (synthesis).* Recife, mimeographed.

Furtado, Celso. 1959. *Operaçao nordeste.* Rio de Janeiro: ISEB.

_____. 1964. *Dialética do desenvolvimento.* Rio de Janeiro: Fundo de Cultura, 2nd ed.

Gomes da Silva, José. 1971. A reforma agrária no Brasil. Rio de Janeiro: Zahar Editores.

Gramsci, Antonio. 1966. *Concepçao dialética da história.* Rio de Janeiro: Civilizaçao Brasileira.

Heredia, Beatriz; and Afrânio R. Garcia Júnior. 1971. "Trabalho familiar e campesinato." *América Latina,* year 14 (no. 1-2):10-20.

Jelin, Elisabeth. 1973. "Espontaneidad y organización en el movimiento obrero." Mimeographed.

Juliao, Francisco. 1962. *O que sao as ligas campesinas?* Rio de Janeiro: Civilizaçâo Brasileira.

Leite Lopes, José Sérgio. 1974. *Os operários do açúcar.* Universidade Federal do Rio de Janeiro, Museu Nacional, M.A. dissertation.

Luxemburg, Rosa. 1968. *Gréve de masses, parti et syndicats.* Paris: Maspero.

Palmeira, Moacir. 1966. "Nordeste: mudanças políticas no século XX." *Cadernos Brasileiros* (September-October):67-86.

_____. 1971. "Feira e mudança econômica." Rio de Janeiro: Museu Nacional, Centro Latino-Americano de Pesquisas em Ciências Sociais, mimeographed.

Prado Júnior, Caio. 1962. *História econômica do Brasil.* Sao Paulo: Brasiliense, 7th ed.

Sigaud, Lygia Maria. 1971. *A nacâo dos homens: uma análise regional de ideologia.* Universidade Federal do Rio de Janeiro, M.A. dissertation.

Sindicato da Indústria do Açúcar no Estado de Pernambuco, Federaçâo dos Trabalhadores Rurais de Pernambuco. 1964. *Contrato coletivo de trabalho na lavoura canavieira de Pernambuco.* Recife: Centro Arquidiocesano de Publicidade.

Wilkie, Mary. 1964. "A Report on Rural Syndicates in Pernambuco." Rio de Janeiro: Centro Latino-Americano de Pesquisas em Ciências Sociais, mimeographed.

Wolf, Eric R. 1964. "Aspectos específicos del sistema de plantaciones en el Nuevo Mundo: comunidad, subculturas y clases sociales." In *Sistemas de plantaciones en el Nuevo Mundo.* Washington, D.C.: Unión Panamericana.

Authoritarianism and Populism: Bipolarity in the Brazilian Political System

Aspásia Alcântara de Camargo

Waves of authoritarianism and populism have successively assailed the Brazilian political system over the years. The bipolar strategy adopted by the political elites seems to impel them to consolidate the power of decadent classes or otherwise freeze emerging social forces — thereby reinforcing the authoritarian state — or else, paradoxically, to become a driving force for popular mobilization, thus triggering populist outbursts.

A unique alliance develops, from the Second Empire on, between the central power and the decadent agrarian elites, blocking social differentiation and the sharing of power with rural strata. As of 1930, the near-symbiotic relation between the emerging unionism and the centralizing state rules out the viability of an autonomous workers' movement, developing along classic lines, through the open conflict among classes.

Quite to the contrary, it was often the state itself (or a section of the ruling political class) which took the initiative in reopening the political system to the popular ranks and their specific claims. Such was the case with the social measures defended by the lieutenants' uprising *(tenentismo),* shortly after the Revolution of 1930, with the *queremismo* movement, toward the end of the New State, and with the intensification of the workers' movement, during Vargas's second term in office. The same phenomenon can be found, in an even more explicit and eloquent from, during the administration of Joao Goulart who, in seeking to resolve the crisis he faced, attempted to extend his sphere of influence to the rural population.

We intend to analyze the bases of the agrarian pact, sealed between the central power and the oligarchies and prevailing historically under different guises. The breach of this tacit agreement, through the alliance between the state and the peasant movement, is one of the foundations of the populist policy which led to the military takeover of 1964 (Alcântara Camargo 1973).

We will endeavor to use the term *populism* with a precise meaning. We believe it to be the result of a symbiotic relation between a process of political mobilization and a state policy which supports it, yet also becomes dependent on it. Populism would thus be the junction of a social movement and a state strategy seeking to redefine political alliances and to achieve a new balance among the centers of power (Touraine 1973). We intend therefore to differentiate, within what we term "populism," between a mobilizing trend — the populist *movement* — and a self-regulating trend — populist *policy* — which interact with one another.

It may be possible to establish differences between the historical examples of Russian and American populism, on the one hand, which belong within the framework of pure populist *movements,* and the innumerable examples of Latin American populism, on the other, which in contrast with their predecessors are characterized by their complicity with the state (Venturi 1972). This duplicity on the part of the state, both an accomplice of decadent elites and a fortuituous ally of popular movements, discloses its supremacy over civil society. The price paid for that supremacy is a permanent imbalance in the political system which throws itself open to participation, in order to resolve the tensions brewing behind closed doors, only to clamp down on it drastically later, in an attempt to break the deadlocks brought on by that very participation.

The State and Oligarchies

The state plays a crucial role in the development of peripheral countries, that is, those whose colonial past conditioned them to joining the international market in a subordinate position, as exporters of raw materials and importers of technology and manufactured goods. State intervention proves decisive even during the period prior to the accelerated development introduced by import substitution. It operates through the manipulation of trade tariffs, which control the price of imported goods, through credit grants, monetary issues, the purchase of agricultural surplus, all with a view to balancing an economy rendered vulnerable by its asymmetric relationship with the world's capitalist centers (Furtado 1959).

Development through import substitution will also be supported and controlled by government intervention, which restrains the command centers of capital accruement and rules on the distribution of newly gained resources. At the class relations level, the state's role will be just as decisive, since its mediating action becomes intensified in the absence of dominant economic elites. This action averts emerging social conflicts to the extent that it operates concomitantly on both businessmen and working class, within the developing capitalist market.

If we attempt to understand the relations between landowners — the oligarchy — and the central power in the course of these changes, our difficulties are bound to increase, partly due to the fact that these are long-standing relations, consolidated before the rise of industrialization. In considering the Brazilian case, we can hardly speak of a single oligarchy. We are dealing with several oligarchies whose interaction with the central power differs according to the role played by their respective regions in the country's economic and political life.

Two academic controversies attest to these difficulties: the first concerns the nature of the production relations predominating within the agrarian sector, that is feudal as opposed to capitalist; the second involves the degree of centralization of the Brazilian political system, viewed by some as an expression of the interests of large scattered estates, and by others as the by-product of a powerful state bureaucracy, a direct heir to the Portuguese patrimonial tradition. The two controversies overlap as a function of the strategic position accorded to the large landowners in each particular argument. To supporters of the feudal thesis, the economic and social importance of the large estate becomes particularly relevant and explains the decentralization of power (Pereira de Queiroz 1957). Those who favor the capitalist thesis see the market mechanism, linked both to the urban world and to the centers of power, as having a more active voice. In this respect, they come closer to the political centralization theorists who contend that the oligarchy was replaced by a section of the commercial bourgeoisie intent on reinforcing the state machine (Prado Júnior 1964).

We will set aside the capitalism/feudalism debate, flawed at the roots by its political-ideological implications, since the manifold indicators and classification criteria used have rendered it insoluble (Palmeira 1971). In practice, the contention inevitably ends in varying degrees of compromise (depending on the relative importance accorded to the various indicators), whereby one school rates the system as more feudal and another as more capitalist, both tacitly acknowledging that, to some extent, a hybrid or dual structure indeed exists.

The controversy concerning political centralization encounters similar difficulties, given its basic theoretical assumption that a centralizing state and a politically dominant oligarchy are incompatible (Faoro 1958).[1] As in the previous contention, both schools succumb to identical contradictions in their analyses of specific historical instances. Both are forced to admit that there are periods of greater or lesser centralization (such as the Second Empire as opposed to the Old Republic), controlled *more* or *less* by the oligarchies or the state.

It is no accident that such discussions appear repeatedly in studies of Brazilian society. Significant historical circumstances have helped shape it, on the one hand favoring the coexistence of autonomous and widespread power nuclei throughout a land of continental dimensions, and on the other anticipating the consolidation of a relatively autonomous state machine controlled, before and after independence, by a political class linked to the colonial bureaucracy. As such, it views the country as a coherent political unit, despite its geographic isolation and economic inconsistencies which intensify regional differences.

Within this framework, we will attempt to outline the political role of the agrarian oligarchies in the process of modernization and development which will be monitored by the state. On analyzing the oligarchy's position during Brazil's transitional period toward an industrialized society, innumerable authors have suggested, either implicitly or explicitly, that the entrance of new actors on the political scene led to a restructuring of the system of alliances, with the resulting displacement or loss or power for the traditional groups which controlled the state. We do not wish to underestimate the importance of the changes taking place during that period, as the result of a shift in the political axis which, as of 1930, supports the developmentalist policy. Nevertheless, as concerns the oligarchy, historical analyses have been either incomplete or oversimplified. An alliance with the more traditional agrarian sectors has been a constant feature in the country's political life. Operating under different guises, to fit the demands of each historical period, this alliance has played an important role within the political system, favoring the process of modernization and state control.

Throughout the Second Empire, the central power strengthens its hold over the provinces by imposing upon them a single political command; it promotes urban expansion by increasing public services and triggering industrial boom periods — when the international situation becomes unfavorable to exports. It also supports and legalizes slavery, already condemned on the continent, and extends it for almost another half century, to benefit the traditional sectors of the Northeast and the Paraíba Valley. In keeping with this same trend, the outset of agricultural modernization in the Sao Paulo coffee industry (still during the days of the empire) coincides with a reduction in the provinces' political power, in favor of decadent groups from the state of Rio and the Northeast which are faithful allies of the central power (Lima Júnior and Gomes Klein 1970). When the pact with slavery is broken, the political class undermines its traditional bases of support and the empire falls.

The Old Republic, erroneously viewed as a composite of oligarchic feuds comprising autonomous regional nuclei, is no more than a refined form of political connivance between the economically dominant region of Sao Paulo and the politically dominant region of Minas Gerais. Sao Paulo favors laissez faire and political decentralization (insofar as each would benefit the expanding regional market) and Minas Gerais, backed by Rio Grande do Sul, maintains a more effective control over the command posts within the state machine (Love 1971; Schwartzman 1975). In this fashion the axis of power converges on the center-south pole, reinforcing its strategic position within the ongoing development process.

The underprivileged regions, comprising the various states of the North and particularly the Northeast and East, are left to play a subordinate role within the political system. The more prominent among those states (Pernambuco, Bahia, and Rio de Janeiro) hold the second rung in the central power ladder: the vice-presidency, a few ministries, the higher posts in the civil bureaucracy, etc. In compensation, the monopolistic power of the oligarchies is further strengthened in the interior of those states. In these regions, lack of local resources as a result of economic decline or lethargy, encourages a dependency on their source of aid: the central power. This dependency is expressed in the political pact operating through the "governors' policy."[2] Under this pact, the central power assures one of the regional factions a monopoly on power in exchange for political loyalty to the center, expressed in a constituency vote which provides an unconditional source of support to the president of the republic through the mediating action of local bosses.

In the most deprived regions, the power of the oligarchies and that of the "colonels" *(coronéis)* is exacerbated even further. Such a state of affairs, far from implying insubordination against the centers of power, is for the most part the product of an overdependence which intensifies political competition for the control and distribution of resources granted by the central bodies. The state, through the president of the republic and his intermediaries in the region, skillfully manipulates the tensions between rival factions, firing them when that suits its purposes or if necessary replacing the dominant group with its adversaries by means of armed intervention. The basic principle which defines the rules of the political game — loyalty to the president of the republic — will never be questioned by the regional bosses, except in those rare cases where political indecision in the centers of power (brought on by dissidence among the dominant states) fosters intrastate disputes which indirectly favor the opposition. The monopoly on regional power, maintained through the colonelist system *(coronelismo)* and the constituency policy, assures the central power of an enormous share of votes in those regions which have been effectively alienated from political decisions (Nunes Leal 1948). In return, they are given an amount of resources which, although limited, will be redistributed among fellow partisans, thus strengthening the dominant position of the local elites.

Following the Revolution of 1930, relations between the central power and regional oligarchies undergo significant changes, as the latter find themselves confined to a direct dependency on the government machine. This is true for both the dominant sectors of the coffee industry and for the more backward regions of the sugar economy in the Northeast. From now on, the state will intervene as a centralized bureaucracy, creating agencies to control production, distribution, and exportation of those goods. This lack of autonomy carries some definite advantages: guaranteed distribution, stable prices in spite of the crisis, assurance of minimum quotas for the producer, etc.

Taking the state of Pernambuco, the most important sugar-producing center in the Northeast, as an example, these mechanisms speak for themselves. To ensure the continuity of a ruling system threatened by the crisis and by changes in market trends, the sugar oligarchy yields almost willingly to state protection, which then imposes upon local elites a set of general criteria to control the sector from the top down. Under the effects of this policy, the two opposing sections of the local ruling class — the sugar suppliers and the factory owners — become "interest groups" which coexist more or less peacefully under government control. The policy adopted by the Institute for Sugar and Alcohol (IAA) assuages the open conflict between sugarcane suppliers and factory owners, ensuring, as of 1941, the survival of the sugar economy's traditional sector (the suppliers) which had been threatened by the factories' expansion. At the national level, the effects of this state policy are even more patent, since the IAA guarantees favorable production quotas for the Northeast, to the detriment of Sao Paulo's flourishing production which is closer to the consumer market and lower in cost (Lima Sobrinho 1962). State interference is no less significant on the political plane. The federal government appoints its own trusted commissioners *(interventores)* to replace the state governors, thereby redefining the regional system of alliances.

In Pernambuco, an area we studied more closely, the political game is restructured by displacing the sugar elites which up to 1930 had controlled the state machine, to the benefit of the colonels from the backlands (Sertao) who were linked to the marginal sector of the Pernambuco economy (Alcântara Camargo 1973). At the same time, Commissioner Agamenon Magalhaes defines new alliances with underprivileged urban groups, encouraging laborers and public servants to unionize and taking favorable steps on their behalf. The axis of political support becomes diversified and brings together both the decadent oligarchies from the backlands and the popular ranks of Recife, the state capital.

The sugar elites are assured, with support from the central power, of a ruling system which had been jeopardized by the crisis affecting the regional economy. On the other hand, however, they witness the loss of the political supremacy they had enjoyed till then, as a result of the state's arbitration which incorporates new actors into the political scene while strengthening the power of the region's peripheral oligarchies.

With the country's return to democracy, following the fall of the New State, the general outlines of this policy become consolidated. Factory owners and sugarcane suppliers will have fewer representatives in the National Congress and the State Assembly than the colonels from the westland (Agreste) and the backlands (Sertao). The former will constitute the opposition part to Vargas — the UDN — and the latter will be organized under the government party — the PSD. The sugar elite is not to be excluded from the power system: factory owners and sugarcane suppliers, from Pernambuco for the most part, take turns serving in the Ministry of Agriculture and infiltrate the IAA, keeping a sharp eye on government policy. Victims of the economic malaise and passive in facing it, the dominant groups exercise their rule by vetoing any attempts to change the power relations prevailing in rural society. In this fashion they ensure their own control as well as the survival of their business concerns whose agricultural and industrial returns are low.

As the political system reopens, as of 1946, the more backward states, and with them their respective elites, will benefit from the electoral law. These states will gain a proportionately higher representation in Congress than the prosperous states of the Center-South (Soares 1962). This does not prevent their subordinate position from becoming even more acute as the development process continues, since the state, through its exchange policy, protects the emerging industries in the Center-South, indirectly increasing the dependency of the traditional exporting centers. Our study of the agrarian elites, particularly those of the Northeast, has led us to the following conclusions.

The rigidity and inequality of class relations have been reinforced by the way in which regional elites interact with the central power. The latter assures them of the monopoly on political power and consolidates the tools of control which allow them to transfer the setbacks caused by regional marginality to the rural lower strata. The deepening of class differences, with the state's tacit consent, offsets the weakness of the ruling class which is no longer dynamic enough to overcome the regional crisis. In the absence of alternatives, any innovative measure must come from the state itself — through the state governments,[3] and, above all, the federal administration.[4]

The state's mediating function ensures the stability of social relations and the continued existence of the elites. Elites with a greater or lesser modernizing tendency find a *modus vivendi* which sets a slow rate of change and rules out abrupt transformations in the social order.

The political game itself is extremely flexible. Regional dependency appears to favor floating coalitions which can adjust to unexpected situations, defined from the outside by national and international conditions. Such coalitions are also highly eclectic and can incorporate popular urban sectors, loyal to the state, into political disputes.

Under special sets of circumstances — such as those which ensued from the 1950s on — the make-up of these coalitions brought oligarchic opposition groups closer to populist electoral ranks.[5] Their political success paved the way for the election, in 1962, of Miguel Arraes, who rose to power backed by the people of Recife, without the support of oligarchic factions.

Feasibility of the Model

The alliance with marginal oligarchies holding a subordinate position in an economic subsystem grants them, both in their spheres of action and, indirectly, in the central bodies, a disproportionate amount of political influence in relation to their actual class position, defined in terms of their role within the national production process. During the Old Republic, the regional clans became autonomous. Beginning with the New State, the colonels from the interior of Pernambuco rise anew and put an end to the political supremacy of the sugar elite.

The state's power of arbitration is reinforced since, by creating "optimal" conditions for the survival of the weakened local elites, it broadens its power to intervene, embracing them all in a strategy imposed by the center upon the system's periphery. The state has displayed particular skill in manipulating the instrumental potential of decadent groups, since the latter are primarily concerned with securing what few resources they can in exchange for electoral support, regardless of the nature of the central power's policies.

The alliance between Vargas and the colonels of the interior of Pernambuco is consistent with his developmentalist policy insofar as it secures the complicity (or neutrality) of the colonels — cut off from economic competition — more easily than that of the factory owners, industrialists, and sugarcane suppliers. As local businessmen, the latter are more seriously affected by the protectionist policy which fosters deflection of resources from the Northeast to the Center-South. The labor guarantees granted by Vargas and the political limits imposed upon factory owners and big businessmen in the sugar zone, consolidate his prestige with the popular sectors. Fortunately, these groups will remain detached from the overall implications of his policies for the country and even the region.

As the political game becomes more intense, whether due to clashes between factions in the struggle to control limited resources or to the predominance of either traditional or modern groups, the state circumscribes political activity to a regional level, as President Campos Salles had done earlier with the "governors' policy." In this fashion, it averts ideological popularization around possible alternatives and, through its bureaucratic bodies, ensures the outlining of basic directives for the national development process.

By protecting decadent or marginal sectors — such as the colonels and the sugarcane suppliers from Pernambuco — the state allows for the consolidation of an instrumental and defensive dominant class. The latter profits from command positions in securing prestige and privileges, since the social structure remains impermeable and actually prevents the rise of a leading class capable of proposing projects and designing models of action which would ensure its political supremacy.

By promoting the controlled institutionalization of urban movements, sharing part of the fruits of economic development with some sectors and guaranteeing their symbolic incorporation into the national community, the state musters its own constituency, increasing its bargaining power with the solidly entrenched traditional groups and with an as yet incipient bourgeoisie. The price of development seems to have been paid by the rural populations which are either politically immobilized (or feudalized) in rural areas or continuously swelling the marginal ranks of the cities.

The State and Political Mobilization

In mustering constituencies, the state often behaves as if it were itself a social force. Thus alienated from its own nature, since its main function is to neutralize and harmonize conflicting groups, it strays away from its "natural vocation," that of promoting social cohesion, and becomes a driving force for participation. Often the growing paralysis of the political system — evident in the increasing difficulty of implementing policies with the existing set of forces — triggers a split in the political class within the state machine or on its periphery, as well as the rise of new political elites.[6] The innovative (or progressive) segment embarks on a search for new allies, and is prepared to negotiate the until then "non-negotiable" interests of the system in order to expand and strengthen the weakened decision-making centers for its own benefit (and that of its allies). Thus it legitimizes emerging social forces, strengthens them, and turns once marginal actors into political actors, redirecting class alliances toward new political coalitions which will allow it to rule.[7] The state is one step ahead of this new partner, as it swells its political resources. It politicizes demanding movements by offering short-term rewards and incorporating them into the scene of current events. It mobilizes these groups against immediate adversaries and even future contenders within its own sphere. In other words, it allows the social forces a more significant political performance than they could achieve through autonomous channels, attempting to make them compatible with its own interests.

The phenomenon we have just described is not a recent one in Brazil. We can trace it back to Florianismo (a movement which followed the proclamation of the republic) or even to the oligarchic ousters associated with the rise of Hermes da Fonseca to the presidency in 1911. During the crisis of 1922 in Pernambuco, the ruling oligarchic segment sides with the workers' movement against the federal government.[8] The masses' intermittent participation in the struggles within the state itself is manifest in all these instances. The most expressive example of this trend is the lieutenants' movement *(tenentismo)* which gains the backing of "public opinion," that is of the urban middle classes. (Santa Rosa 1963).

The trend toward a closer relationship between the state and the masses is reinforced with the Revolution of 1930. During 1930-32, the lieutenants in power attempt to set up an alliance with the workers' movement and thus pave the way for approval of the labor laws. They also attempt to mobilize and organize antioligarchic groups which identify with the middle class. A radical wing presses the social issue and is even prepared to stretch the fabric of new alliances to embrace the rural workers (Santa Rosa 1963).

The lieutenants' removal and the incorporation of the most faithful oligarchic segments severs the direct links between the state and the masses (Santa Rosa 1963).[9] Following a short-lived attempt at autonomy on the part of the social movements (with the creation of a popular front, the ANL), the state takes it upon itself to promote the coexistence of heterogeneous, if not actually conflicting, social interests. It demobilizes emerging social movements by triggering a confrontation between ANL and AIB militants.[10] Through increasing army intervention, it gains control over the powerful oligarchies from Rio Grande do Sul and Sao Paulo. It rationalizes the political system's performance and strengthens its bureaucratic machine. It also protects the exporting groups by giving them the tools to weather the crisis. It coopts the incipient bourgeoisie by incorporating it into the state machine and guaranteeing industrial expansion. Finally, it consolidates its prestige with the working class by enforcing the labor laws. Thus it increases its bargaining power, eliminating political participation in the periphery while promoting it in the center of the system, that is within the state machine. Faced with a disjointed civil society, it incorporates both traditional sectors and emerging groups through various means, uniting them around a single national project. Such an assorted configuration demanded a marked degree of authoritarianism. From the moment the latter is challenged, with the drive toward democracy associated with the end of World War II, the state is confronted with a new deadlock which leads it again to a reshuffling of alliances. The *queremismo* movement then arises, as a reactivation of the unionist movement and the Communist party (severely repressed throughout the New State), with the participation of public servants in the mass movements, demanding the continuation of the Vargas regime as represented by his labor minister.[11]

Under military protection, the forces of cohesion regain power and participation is suppressed once more, only to be restored anew during Vargas's second term as president, with Joao Goulart as his labor minister (Erikson 1970). It is not by mere coincidence that Vargas commits suicide shortly after Goulart's ouster from the Ministry of Labor which is, at that point, again encouraging union autonomy, promoting wage increases, attempting to extend the labor laws to the rural areas, at the same time as Vargas summons the masses to participate in a nationalist and popular government. This new cycle comes to a close when Vargas commits suicide, yet its legacy of ideological support for the labor and nationalist movements remains. These two elements will be the backbone of the social movement inspired by Getúlio Vargas, which revitalizes its ties with the state with the rise to office, in the early 1960s, of Joao Goulart — a loyal disciple and follower of Getulismo.

At this crucial moment the economic crisis begins — with the deterioration of the import-substitution model and the breakdown of the alliances which supported the centers of power. Partisan coalitions are quickly formed and dissolved. Union leaders mobilize, organizing under a single command and putting pressure on the government. New political leaderships arise, encouraging mass demands which lead to a populist movement in the urban centers. At the heart of the crisis lies the agrarian issue: pressures for an agrarian reform increase and an expansion of the domestic market, with the incorporation of the landless and disenfranchised rural masses, appears to be the only viable and lasting solution to the crisis. This new outlook, shared by various members of the administration, is backed by the peasant movements which spread throughout the Northeast as of the mid-1950s and seconded by the urban political, student, and union leaders who are the supporting beams of the populist movement. Nuclei of peasant mobilization proliferate throughout the country.

In political practice, the old (and steadfast) alliance between the state and the traditional agrarian sectors begins a drastic decline, to the extent that it switches directions, inverting existing political relations to the detriment of the oligarchy and the benefit of the rural workers. Considering the latter's numerical significance (more than half the total population), the extent of their economic and political alienation, and their age-old passivity — due to the effective mechanisms of the agrarian pact — the peasant mobilization which ensues grows to unforeseeable proportions: the alliance between the state and the peasant movement heralds far-reaching structural changes which irreversibly affect the nature of social relations prevailing until then, and consequently the basic direction of the political system as well.

The Peasant Movement and the Populist Crisis

The year 1955, a symbolic date which witnesses the reactivation of the Peasant Leagues, opens a new era in the history of Brazil's peasant movement, dissociated up to that point from the urban world.[12] Inextricably tied to the original and controversial figure of Francisco Juliao, the Peasant Leagues become well known as of 1959, through their impact on both national and international public opinion as well as on the centers of power. This impact will foster significant changes in agrarian policy, particularly in the Northeast. It will also trigger significant changes in the very structure of the movement — affected by a populist policy which for the first time reaches the rural population.

As of 1961, the peasant movement gains new impetus with the proliferation of Rural Unions, promoted by priests and communists supported by students, to curb the leagues' expansion and organize their own constituencies among the rural workers. As of 1962, the two streams within the peasant movement — the leagues and the unions — merge, combining the struggle for land with the workers' demands. The peasant movement's leadership incorporates elements from a broad ideological spectrum — moderate reformists from a segment of the Catholic hierarchy, leftist Catholic youths, the reformist opposition of the Communist party, undisciplined radicals from extreme Left minority parties. Bound to the populist movement, as the latter's link with the state, this leadership will play a prominent role in the crisis that ensues.

It is not by accident that the dynamic nucleus of the peasant movement is located in Pernambuco, the geographic and political heart of the Northeast. This fact becomes more meaningful when viewed in the context of the regional economy's ruinous condition, in contrast with the development boom enjoyed at the time in the country's Center-South. In this enormous region covering an area of one million square kilometers with a population of over twenty million, most of the inhabitants live in the countryside, where land ownership is concentrated in the hands of a few. Afflicted with endemic diseases and barely surviving under chronic malnutrition, this population is the national stigma which the period's high development indexes do not manage to conceal. Those who leave the rugged countryside and seek shelter in the cities only manage to increase the ranks of the unemployed which include 31 percent of the potentially productive population. Eighty percent of the rural population in the Northeast is illiterate. Sixty percent of the children die before the age of one and for 80 percent of the population, life expectancy is thirty-five years.

The Peasant Leagues, despite their precarious organization and limited militant contingent, are the first to sound the alert, eliciting a rapid response from the authorities and public powers. In 1956, the Encounter of Bishops of the Northeast, held in Campina Grande, warns the government of the need for planned intervention to level the region's social inequalities. Still in the days of the Kubitschek administration, a technical committee undertakes an evaluation of the economic situation in the Northeast. The outcome of this evaluation is the well-known "Furtado report" which leads, shortly after, to the enactment of a bill creating SUDENE (Furtado 1959; Page 1972). At the time, its pessimistic diagnosis awakens public opinion, intellectuals, and politicians:

> The Brazilian Northeast is unique in the Western Hemisphere as the vastest and most populated area where income per capita is under US$100. Before the war, the Northeast's contribution to the gross national product... was 30 percent; today, it amounts to only 11 percent.... At the present rate, if the Northeast continues to diverge as drastically from the country's South, we will indeed be on the verge of a separatist revolution (Furtado 1959a:14; 1959b:7).

To the traditional elites in political control of the region, the situation does not seem so dramatic, nor does it appear to demand urgent intervention. With the Constitution of 1946, which broadens congressional prerogatives, their representatives gain a higher degree of political influence than they held during the Old Republic — when Congress had limited decision-making powers and no autonomy to speak of — or during the New State — when they were monitored by the central power. By denying illiterates the right to vote, the Electoral Law allows the states in the Northeast a lower electoral coefficient (determined not by the number of voters, but in terms of the population), which means that these states would need a lower number of votes to elect a senator or congressman than the prosperous and populous states in the Center-South, where voters enjoy greater political autonomy.[13]

The elites of the Northeast also controlled some important ministries and agencies: the Ministry of Agriculture and the Ministry of Transport. The National Department of Works Against Droughts (DNOCS) originally designed to fight the droughts which periodically devastate the region, channels federal resources so as to benefit those who control highway and dam construction, increasing their economic and political influence through land speculation.

SUDENE's installation follows a public debate aimed at reinforcing it, to the detriment of the all-powerful DNOCS. Curiously enough, accusations leveled against the "drought industrialists" by the press, in an attempt to strengthen SUDENE, also reinforce and legitimize the region's emerging protest movements. Antonio Callado's articles — the first to give national coverage to Juliao's Peasant Leagues, in 1959 — are significantly entitled "The Drought Industrialists and the Galileans of Pernambuco," and point to a suggestive relationship between executioner and victim, master and subjects, the idle landholder and the exploited peasant, in other words, between who should be excluded and who should be incorporated within a new structure of power alliances (Callado 1960). In presenting a choice between two opposing alternatives — popular violence as foreshadowed by Francisco Juliao's Galileans or a corrective program from the state as embodied in SUDENE — these articles propose the reformist approach as the effective means to avoid a peasant uprising.

In the United States, as well, public opinion and the political stratum, overwhelmed by the experience of the Cuban Revolution, are concerned over the pressing problem posed by the Northeast. The *New York Times* gives front page coverage to the Peasant Leagues.[14] The ABC television network airs a dramatic documentary — "The Troubled Land" — in which a "colonel" appears on screen wielding a weapon intended to kill all peasants who might attempt to organize on his property. President-elect Kennedy states that "no other region deserves greater or more urgent attention than the vast Brazilian Northeast." Shortly after, a USAID delegation settles in Recife.[15]

International personalities visit the Northeast: Sargent Shriver, Edward Kennedy, Arthur Schlesinger, Jr., George McGovern, Henry Kissinger, Adlai Stevenson, Jean-Paul Sartre, John dos Passos, Yuri Gagarin, and Ralph Nader. As the focal point of American cooperation policy, the required stopover for eminent public figures and the source of inspiration for the most innovative regional planning initiative around the continent, the Northeast blends into one with the controversial image of Juliao and the Peasant Leagues. The Galileia league soon becomes a tourist attraction which kindles the interest of public opinion, the press, and politicians.

As an alternative to Juliao's leagues, in the struggle for leadership within the rural milieu, the unions organize under the proper institutional coverage. With unprecedented momentum the peasant movement spreads throughout the states of the Northeast and reaches the country's central and southern states. In the structurally unequal open confrontation between peasants and landowners, the relative position of the former gains strength to the detriment of the latter, to the extent that the state's loyalties are transferred from its former allies, the agrarian elites, to the rural workers. The reshuffling of political alliances is both a product and a cause of the growing radicalization and mobilization of the peasant movement.

Established in December 1959, SUDENE intends to revitalize the region's economy by industrializing it and rationalizing its property structure. The agency proposes the modernization of production techniques in the large estates and the effective use of plots freed by the small landholders involved in precariously supplying the urban centers. Shortly after, Jânio Quadros submits to Congress a preliminary project for agrarian reform. With Joao Goulart, agrarian reform is a key issue in the program of basic reforms which the government announces a few days after its troubled inauguration in office.

In late 1962 the Superintendency for Agrarian Reform is established. In March 1963, Congress approves the Rural Worker's Statute which sets forth regulations for rural labor. With Almino Afonso as labor minister, the existing rural unions are officially recognized. The National Committee for Rural Unionization is created with the purpose of encouraging the organization and recognition of new unions. Their proliferation under official support is staggering: their active membership in the Northeast rises from 123 in July 1962 to 208 in September 1963, and up to 324 by December of that same year. In less than two years it practically triples. Countless state federations are officially recognized and, in late 1963, the National Confederation of Agricultural Workers (CONTAG) is created.

The peasant claims grow. Approval of the statute triggers a struggle for enforcement of labor laws in the countryside, while new demands — for rights to retirement pay and health services, for example — are voiced through class associations. Literacy centers, organized by students, attempt to grant the peasant an effective citizenship. Through consciousness building they intended to integrate him into society. Through literacy, they incorporate him into the political community which, as an illiterate, had barred him from voting. Receptive to all the attention and to a broad range of political pressure, the peasant movement strives, under the impact of various leaderships, to attain institutionalization. The first step toward that goal is the Pernambuco Popular Front.

While hardly powerful in terms of voting strength, considering that it was mostly the votes from Recife's popular neighborhoods which elected Miguel Arraes as state governor, the peasants are undoubtedly the main beneficiaries of his short-lived administration. In Pernambuco's sugar zone, the labor laws will be strictly enforced thanks to official tables relating the time needed to complete different tasks to their respective pay. Labor-management disputes arising from the enforcement of these labor laws will be mediated by a government advisory office — free of interference from local police forces. Government credit grants will be made available to the needy peasants of the wasteland region, and successive wage raises — wrested through negotiations conducted by the government with management groups and federal agencies — will raise the sugar worker to the unprecedented status of a consumer. The Paulo Freire method brings literacy to adult peasants in a matter of forty hours. Itinerant medical teams tour the countryside. Enjoying new goods and services, the peasant is ideologically and practically exposed to participation and thereby driven to modify his own living conditions through community action. Before building a house or a school the people are asked at the unions, neighborhood associations, or sports clubs to discuss their immediate problems and propose ways to solve them.

A unique experiment in housing policy, based on participation, begins in Cajueiro Seco:

> This experiment is simple and easy when the people themselves are in command. What we attempted to do was to make it possible for a man — in an area urbanized by the government — to build his shack or house in whatever way he pleases, in his own fashion and to his own liking, according to his means.... Neither charity nor imposition are involved here. Man discovers and liberates himself through work and community life with other men....This change of attitude with respect to problems is basic to the people's integration into the government process. And this reference to integration is not meant as demagoguery. It is a policy (Cajueiro Seco Housing Program).[16]

Community participation, from this standpoint, becomes the key to a government policy which is to face successive stalemates at the leadership level. It therefore seeks to consolidate its political bases and muster the support needed to meet growing internal opposition and the isolation imposed upon it by the federal government. Within this open system the peasant movement plays a renovating economic role inasmuch as it forces the sugar plantation to modernize in view of the impossibility of indefinitely exploiting the labor force.

> The organized and democratic movement of the sugar workers must be credited with disclosing the artificial climate in which the

sugarcane plantation had been living. It took pressure from below, applied by an enormous contingent of rural workers, to discover that sugarcane involves a production cost. And the discovery is due to the fact that a considerable segment of those included in that production cost — which until then had been kept invisible — made their existence known in a clear and determined manner (Arraes 1965:78).[17]

The organized peasants also ensured the enforcement of social legislation which without their pressure would have remained inoperant.

The movement's consolidation and expansion are not an exclusive achievement of the rank and file or of the peasant leaders. They depend directly on the state's political direction, which uses every available means including its own mobilizing capacity, to encourage all layers of the population interested in the nation's development (Arracs 1965:102). The peasant movement and the state are organically bound in pursuit of a common purpose: agrarian reform, which is also the populist movement's priority goal, as well as that of the president of the republic in his basic reforms program.

The agrarian reform asserts itself at the national level, not just as an ideological banner announcing humanitarian and egalitarian measures, but also as a functional tool to disencumber a development process threatened with stagnation. "It facilitates an improved distribution to the urban population, creates and expands the market for industrial products" (Arraes 1965:102). Or, as Celso Furtado (1962) pointed out in his Three-Year Plan, an agriculture based on an extremely disparate land distribution cannot adequately meet the rising needs of economic development. On a different occasion, Furtado (1962) concludes, voicing the consensus of the times: "Because the agrarian structure is obsolete, development often leads to a relative increase in the returns of the land which favors parasitic groups."[18] To Miguel Arraes (1965:56), the long-awaited agrarian reform was already under way: "Begun by the peasant masses of the Northeast, particularly Pernambuco." "Here," he says in a speech before 100,000 workers, "the people have tired of waiting."[19] He was not the only one to think in such terms. On his side was a significant segment of public opinion — the populist movement — which also believed that the "Brazilian Revolution" had already begun in Pernambuco.

The Dynamics of Political Bipolarity

Nevertheless, the Popular Front faces severe and successive crises and Goulart's populism lives out its last days. In Pernambuco, peasant groups linked to militants from the leagues encourage the occupation of lands, creating serious difficulties for the state government, thus forced to take a stand between peasant demands (to which it claims to be ideologically committed) and the institutional order which it legitimately represents and must guarantee to the very end. In addition, frequent labor-management clashes in the sugar zone point to the precariousness of the sugar industry and to the scope of the changes needed for the peasant movement's effective institutionalization: minimum salary, wage raises, "thirteenth salary," social security, family allowance, severance pay — in other words, what the workers call "the rights," already won by urban wage earners. All these benefits impose high costs on the obsolete sugar industry whose operations depend on large contingents of ill-paid labor, ensured, as was pointed out earlier, by a "pact" which politically guaranteed its survival. Other more strictly political demands are becoming equally important: voting rights for the illiterate, guarantees for union representatives, agrarian reform, constitutional reform. These measures were not under the jurisdiction of the state government, but nevertheless found a receptive audience in that region, giving local conflicts a more comprehensive scope.

The crisis intensifies in late February 1964, demanding a show of political skill on the part of Arraes in order to avoid the worst: federal intervention or the fall of his government. In Vitória do Santo Antao, the peasants illegally occupy the Serra sugar mill, refusing to comply with court orders instructing them to vacate the premises. At the same time, Goulart's decision to dismiss the head of IAPI meets with opposition from the workers who organize a general strike and use it also to demand payment of the thirteenth salary. Groups of students also decide to demonstrate, in an attempt to prevent SUDENE from granting fiscal incentives to foreign investors intending to operate in the Northeast. For its part, management decrees the lockout which was to lead the state to economic paralysis and resulting federal intervention.

The state governor reacts swiftly and forcefully. He warns the peasants of the seriousness of the situation and persuades them to comply with court orders. He negotiates a return to work in the sugar sector and at the same sends an ultimatum to management. The situation quiets down; yet the underlying turmoil continues. The government had exhausted all legal resources in the workers' favor, and more sweeping constitutional changes would have to come from the centers of power. The dominant class was openly hostile to the government and found backing among American officials stationed in Recife (Page 1972:128-44).[22] Extreme Left groups created deadlocks and alienated the middle class, which was less receptive to a policy favoring the peasants. Relations with the federal government deteriorate and there is actual talk of military intervention in Pernambuco.

Goulart's populism is also coming to an end. Having failed in his many attempts to form a stable Center-Left coalition — a "positive Left," according to an expression at the time — he seeks to strengthen his populist backing (unions, students, labor party members). With the referendum of January 1964 he recovers the presidential powers he had lost under the terms of his inauguration, and promises to implement some basic reforms. Foremost among them is an agrarian reform, involving land expropriation without cash compensation, and constitutional reform. The Constitution demanded just compensation in cash and denied illiterates the right to vote, which would have incorporated more than ten million voters, most of them from the rural areas, into the political game.

The agrarian issue becomes the dividing factor which alienates Goulart from representative traditional sectors who fear that the agrarian and constitutional reforms might trigger a radical reformulation of the political and institutional orders, and strengthen Goulart's personal power. Within populist ranks, the make-up of power is no less unstable. The diversity of populist leadership divides the movement into a Jangoist (Joao "Jango" Goulart) faction, a Brizolist faction, and a third wing based on Arraes's legalism. The Communist party's growing involvement pervades the various spheres of influence. The Reform Rally held on March 13, 1964, will be the last attempt at mobilizing the rank and file and unifying the movement's leadership. During the rally, Goulart signs a decree for the expropriation of land bordering on railways and highways, takes over private refineries, and announces rent controls.

Relations between the government and the army deteriorate. Following two attempts to decree a state of siege, whose immediate aims were armed intervention in the states of Guanabara and Pernambuco, a series of incidents exacerbate the restiveness of military leaders: the sergeants' revolt in Brasília, in September 1963; the sailors' uprising in March 1964; and Goulart's speech delivered on March 30 at the Automobile Club, requesting the sergeants' participation in the military conflict. This is the spark which triggers the end of the crisis, with the army's intervention and Goulart's ouster.

The Pernambuco Popular Front and Goulart's populism point in different ways to the precariousness of a system which exhausts its capacity to distribute the resources ensuring its support from the popular movement. Arraes had used up, in the course of his short term as governor, the last legal resources available to meet the demands of the masses, and lacked sufficient financial support to continue his regional reform program at the same pace. Goulart faced a serious economic crisis, with galloping inflation and a stagnant production, reflected in regressive development indexes, which would have rendered contentious any initiative toward redistribution.

The growing mobilization of popular sectors underscores the ambiguous nature of the symbiotic relation between the social movement and the state. The social movement defines and asserts itself through its pressure for demands, through its capacity to generate conflict and improve the position of its actors within the social order. The state plays, above all, a regulating role, aimed at reabsorbing conflicts or rechanneling them so as to form or maintain viable coalitions which will allow it to rule. Within the populist context, the social movement behaves as if it were autonomous. Or rather, it believes in its own capacity to overrule the state by using its mobilizing potential, as if the state were one and the same with the sector of the political class precariously controlling it.

The impasse occurring between the social movement and the state can best be explained by focusing on the leadership mediating relations between them. Divided between the demand-geared social movement from which it draws support, and its command posts, the leadership encourages participation, while at the same time seeking to control it. Faced with difficulties in implementing programs and outlining government policies, they protect the movement at the centers of power, while their own power fades in the face of a unification of political forces on their Right and the disjunction of those forces on their Left. The lack of consensus as to the basic guidelines of social order is exacerbated by the accumulation of contentious measures which shape the final crisis. The reestablishment of political balance will be achieved through the repression of populist leaderships and by smothering participation.

During those last years, the populist crisis was diagnosed as the result of a structural change in dependency relations, arising from the growing involvement of multinational companies in the Brazilian domestic market. The crisis was also viewed as a sign of the failure of a national development model based on the alliance between the workers and a national bourgeoisie whose own existence was questionable and which proved in fact to be more closely linked to its overseas partners than to its ''domestic allies.'' A decisive role has also been attributed to the growing interventionism of the army which, since Vargas's suicide in 1954, seemed ready to take the country's leadership onto itself.

Although with certain reservations, we must underscore another factor which is indispensable for a balanced understanding of the facts: the urban mobilization which gains momentum as of 1959, combined with the peasants' awakening. The driving force behind this movement will include young students and intellectuals, a segment of the political stratum, and the union leaders. At its peak, the agrarian issue becomes the pivotal point of the populist crisis, culminating with the program of Basic Reforms, of which agrarian reform is to be the most important.

The opposition between the coast and the backlands, civilization and barbarism, city and countryside, the central theme of Euclides da Cunha's (1966) reflections at the beginning of the century, rises anew with the populism of the late 1950s intending to narrow the contrasts between the developed urban world and the backward rural masses. This trend is embodied in the "rush to the countryside" between 1961 and 1964, which reminds us of "those who returned to the people" in Tzarist Russia during the 1870s. Like them, the Brazilian populists will fight for a development model closely linked to the interests of the peasant class. Like them, they will be steeped in an ideal: "identification with the people." However, while in the case of Russian populism, the intelligentsia seeks to preserve the peasant community's traditional values, a way of life which belongs to the past and is now nearing its end, Brazilian populism, on the contrary, is essentially aimed at integrating the peasant masses into the development process and sharing its returns with them. In contrast to Russian populism which breaks with a repressive state and fights relentlessly against it, Brazilian mobilization results from an opening of the political system and is backed by the state which actually supports it.

Brazilian populism comprises three elements: (1) The peasant movement and, within its framework, the conflict between peasants and landowners. (2) Urban populism, geared toward the people — underprivileged segments of the cities and countryside — against a parasitic oligarchy (the large estate) and an outside enemy (imperialism), and seeking to integrate them into the nation that they may also benefit from the development process, so that the people, the nation, and the development process may all become part of a harmonious and unified whole. (3) The populist state or populist policy, which seeks to reorganize its support through new political and class alliances.

The peasant movement unveils the rigidity of class relations in the rural world and the obsolescence of a ruling system which is impregnable to progress and development. The (urban) populist movement denounces the oligarchies and intends to incorporate the masses, which depend on them, into the development process. And the populist state sees in these masses an enormous political potential which is liable to help it solve the crisis by supporting new projects outlined within the higher ranks of the state bureaucracy.

A distinction must yet be made between the populist state and its more radical offshoot the Popular Front. While in the former case, relations between the social movement and the state remain at the level of an alliance or of mutual cooperation, in the latter both are intertwined. In the Popular Front, the social movement elects the government which speaks and rules on its behalf. In the populist state, alliances are formed after the rise to power, achieved either by constitutional means or by encroachment, through some type of merger with more traditional groups.

For this very reason, the Popular Front, an extreme model of institutional mobilization, faces even more dramatic deadlocks than the populist state. While for the latter an "authoritarian solution" is always possible or even desirable, no such possibility exists for the Popular Front: it is always and fatally doomed to die with the demobilization of the social movement which gave it birth and with which it has merged. The reason for this is that the state represents it effectively and takes an active part in the class conflicts which develop within the system. As a result, there are even greater contradictions between its role as a "representative" of the social movement challenging the basic norms which rule the workings of society, and society itself which compels it to maintain the position of its dominant class in order to keep it working. The Popular Front will thus be checked by successive impasses as class conflicts deepen and spread.

The element which gave Brazilian populism its radical character was the peasant movement. Its dynamism stemmed from the fact that it questioned class relations which had sustained traditional society, yet coexisted with the modern structures of a developing society. Struggling against the landed gentry and spurred on, from the beginning, by the intelligentsia, the peasant movement reinforces the populist movement — legitimizes it — in its fight against the decadent estate. By placing the peasant as its central issue, the populist project endows him with a universal dimension which transcends the regional context of the conflict, since it demands on his behalf fair wages, the fruits of the land, the right to vote — such measures as will allow him to redefine his place in society and, through participation, ensure his right to the production and consumption of wealth.

As a result of contingencies within the national context, the movement developed on the periphery of the system, far from the developing nucleus, highlighting two contradictions: the exclusion of the masses, particularly the rural population, and the increasing regional disparities in a country where one of the state's major functions was always to maintain political harmony among the various regions. These contradictions weighed heavily on the peasants in the Northeast, burdened by their regional marginality, the drawbacks of which were minimized for the local elites.

At the national level, the system of alliances will be inverted with the advent of populism. The state, committed until then to an agrarian aristocracy which ensured its control over the various regions, seems prepared now to renounce its ally and directly incorporate the peasant to the nation's political life. The undertaking in question appeared feasible, since the importance of these elites had presumably declined with the country's industrialization. However, their role was underestimated, since their past and current political function is of the utmost importance for the central power. Even today, given the limited scope of the political game and the fact that government officials are chosen by the army — which is not dependent on the votes of rural constituencies — the oligarchies continue to maintain order in the countryside, keeping the vast contingent of destitute peasants under close control, so as to ensure that the political system will remain dependent on its good services.

The agrarian society under crisis is a source of cheap labor which, contrary to earlier belief, is not incompatible with the resumption of development. Low wages lure foreign investors into the country and the development process continues, in coexistence with marginality. In the meantime, the agrarian elites gradually adjust to the dynamics of national capitalism. It might be valid to ask whether in a society such as Brazil's — where the state either overrules or anticipates civil society — pure social movements, from within the heart of the economic, political, and institutional system, could ever be launched. Would such a society be capable of launching genuine social movements, or would they lead the fictitious life of a "ghost partner" unable to meet with adverse pressure from the state?

While hardly presuming to answer such questions, which are too complex to be considered merely on the basis of the populist experience analyzed here, we are nevertheless inclined to believe that autonomous movements will not arise in that society as long as it remains subservient to an international context. That context, which fluctuates by definition, defines the parameters of its economic life by altering the configuration of its dominant class, introducing technology which throws the labor market off balance, broadening the gap between skilled and unskilled workers, between the city and the countryside, among different regions, causing a disproportionate increase in the number of unemployed and marginal members, in short — disrupting social relations.

The diversity of norms which rule economic and political relations leads to extreme situations in which the state moves away from the dominant class — divided within itself — in order to correct the system's imbalance. This explains the split between civil society and the political system and the state. The role played by the state serves to structurally reinforce its autonomy: it occasionally fills gaps through intermittent waves of participation, filtered from the top down, which are sometimes indispensable in order to redirect or expand its sphere of action, and sometimes become disturbing or dysfunctional phenomena — whenever the pressure from below surpasses the state's capacity for absorption. Participation and authoritarianism predominate in alternate cycles. While the contest is admittedly unequal, given the slightest leeway, the social movement rises again with renewed vigor.

NOTES

1. For a broader and more diversified discussion see Eisenstadt (1963).
2. A policy implemented by the second civil government of the republic under the presidency of Campos Salles, which reincorporates the regional oligarchies to the central power (Campos Sales 1908). For an analysis of the political significance of these alliances see Alcântara de Camargo (1973). For a more factual analysis see Guanabara (1902).
3. It is attributed to the state government the initiative to stimulate the creation of central sugar mills *(engenhos centrais)* at the end of the past century, and the establishment of *usinas* at the beginning of the present one. The *usinas* become units of both rural and industrial operation which substitute the old sugar mills *(engenhos bangüês)* in the sugar zone. CF. Lima Sobrinho (1971).
4. The Institute of Sugar and Alcohol (IAA) was created by the Vargas provisional government of 1933 and introduced important policy modifications in the sugar economy.
5. We refer to the campaign which elected Cid Sampaio, a *usineiro* (*usina* owner), as governor of Pernambuco, with the support of the left-wing movement which emerged in Recife.
6. We are using Wanderley Guilherme dos Santos's concept of institutional paralysis from his unpublished work "Impasse and Crisis in Brazilian Politics."
7. The expression belongs to Jaguaribe (1974). It corresponds to what Touraine (1973) denominates *historicity*. This means a level of analysis conducted by a system of domination which commands the process of accumulation.
8. This refers to an alliance between Manuel Borba, state governor, and Joaquim Pimenta, professor of law and working-class leader, who support, at the national level, the lieutenant movement which emerges in July 1922, aiming at avoiding that the elected president in March of the same year, Arthur Bernardes, be invested in power.
9. Before the coup d'état of 1937, the central power succeeds in controlling the Sao Paulo oligarchy which had an uprising, the 1932 revolution, and the Rio Grande do Sul oligarchy which, during this period, defied Vargas and the army's authority, preparing themselves for resistance with the help of private armed groups.
10. Vargas seems to endorse the *integralista* faction (a movement of fascist orientation) against the Aliança Nacional Libertadora (a liberal movement), but soon after he also demobilizes the *integralista* movement.
11. A public opinion movement which asserts itself in 1945, demanding Vargas's permanence in power. It includes public officers, communists, and sindicalists who remained faithful to Vargas.

12. In 1955 was created the Sociedade Agricola e Pecuária de Plantadores de Pernambuco (Agricultural and Pecuary Society of Pernambuco Planters) at the Engenho Galiléia in Vitória de Santo Antao with the periodic consultancy of Congressman Francisco Juliao. The society soon afterwards became known as the old Peasant League which worked in the region, the first years before the war, influenced by the Communist party, then legally operating in the country. Since 1948 the Communist party was outlawed and the leagues disappeared.

13. In the Center-South there was one congressman for each 190,000 inhabitants and one senator for each 1,200,000 inhabitants. In the Northeast the proportion dropped to 159,000 and 670,000 inhabitants respectively.

14. Article by correspondent Tad Szulc, *New York Times,* October 31, 1960. A second article then appeared saying that "the Marxists are organizing the peasants in Brazil."

15. USAID installs itself in August 1961, soon after Miguel Arraes's victory as governor of the state of Pernambuco.

16. The pilot experiment of Cajueiro Seco defines the governmental housing policy. Helped by a staff of architects in search for practical, cheap collective solutions, it tries to adapt the necessities to the resources of the region's poor.

17. Cf. speech pronounced during the government's first anniversary.

18. The price of agricultural products rises faster than the industrial products and provokes the transference of income from one sector to the other. This happens without the displaced capital being used to increase agricultural productivity. We observe, on the one hand, that the majority of establishments are too small to raise production in an efficient manner, and on the other, that a very reduced number of properties are too big to succeed in using rationally the available land. Effectively 75 percent of the total surface of establishments (properties with less than fifty hectares); while 16 percent of the establishments occupied 51 percent of the total (properties of less than one thousand hectares).

19. Conference delivered in Sao Paulo on January 25, 1962.

20. For other details see chapters "Enter the Americans" and "The Americans and the Nationalists."

REFERENCES

Alcântara de Camargo, Aspásia. 1973. *Mouvements paysans et crise populiste.* École Pratique des Hautes Etudes, doctoral dissertation.

Arraes, Miguel. 1965. "Discurso diante de 100.000 trabalhadores." *Palavras de Arraes.* Rio de Janeiro: Civilizaçao Brasileira.

_____. 1965. "Discurso pronunciado por ocasiao do 1⁹ aniversário do governo, 31 de janeiro de 1964." *Palavras de Arraes.* Rio de Janeiro: Civilizaçao Brasileira.

_____. 1965. "Introduçao à mensagem de prestaçao de contas..." *Palavras de Arraes.* Rio de Janeiro: Civilizaçao Brasileira.

Callado, Antonio. 1960. *Os industriais da seca e os galileus de Pernambuco.* Rio de Janeiro: Civilizaçao Brasileira.

Cunha, Euclides da. 1966. *Os sertoes*. Rio de Janeiro: José Aguilar.

Campos Sales, Manuel Ferraz. 1908. *Da propaganda à presidência*. Sao Paulo: A Editora.

Carone, Edgard. 1969. *A Primeira República*. Sao Paulo: Difusao Européia do Livro.

Eisenstadt, S. N. 1963. *The Political Systems of Empires*. New York: Free Press of Glencoe.

Erickson, Kenneth Paul. 1970 "Labor in the Political Process in Brazil: Corporatism in a Modernizing Nation." Columbia University, Ph.D. dissertation.

Faoro, Raymundo. 1958. *Os donos do poder*. Porto Alegre: Editora Globo.

Frank, Andrew Gunder. 1967. *Capitalism and Underdevelopment in Latin America*. New York: Modern Reader Paperbacks.

Furtado, Celso. 1959a. *Formaçao econômica do Brasil*. Rio de Janeiro: Fundo de Cultura.

_____. 1959b. *Uma política de desenvolvimento econômico para o nordeste*. Rio de Janeiro: Departamento de Imprensa Nacional.

_____. 1962. "Reflexiones sobre la prerevolución brasileña." *Trimestre Económico* 29 (July-September).

Guanabara, Alcino. 1902. *A presidência Campos Salles*. Rio de Janeiro: Laemmert.

Jaguaribe, Hélio. 1974. *Brasil: crise e alternativas*. Rio de Janeiro: Zahar.

Lima Júnior, Olavo Brasil de; and Gomes Klein, Lucia. 1970. "Atores políticos do império." *Dados* (no. 7).

Lima Sobrinho, Barbosa. 1962. "A experiência de uma reforma agrária setorial." *Jurídica* (IAA) 27 (July-September).

_____. 1971. "Dos engenhos centrais às usinas de açucar de Pernambuco." - *Jurídica* (IAA).

Nunes Leal, Victor. 1948. *Coronelismo, enxada e voto: o município or regime representativo no Brasil*. Rio de Janeiro: Revista Forense.

Love, Joseph. 1971. *Rio Grande do Sul and Brazilian Regionalism, 1822–1930*. Stanford: Stanford University Press.

McCann, Frank D., Jr. 1973. *The Brazilian-American Alliance, 1937–1945*. Princeton: Princeton University Press.

Page, Joseph. 1972. *The Revolution That Never Was*. New York: Grossman.

Palmeira, Moacir. 1971. "Latifundium et capitalisme: lecture critique d'un débat." Faculté de Lettres et Sciences Humaines de l'Université de Paris, doctoral dissertation.

Prado Júnior, Caio. 1964. *A Revoluçao Brasileira*. Rio de Janeiro: Civilizaçao Brasileira.

Pereira de Queiroz, Maria Isaura. 1957. "O mandonismo local na vida política Brasileira." *Estudos de Sociologia e História*. Sao Paulo: Anhembi.

Presidência da República. 1962. *Plano Trienal do Desenvolvimento Econômico e Social*. Brasília. D.F.

Roett, Riordan. 1972. *The Politics of Foreign Aid in the Brazilian Northeast*. Nashville: Vanderbilt University Press.

Santa Rosa, Virginio. 1963. *O que foi o tenentismo?* Rio de Janeiro: Civilizaçao Brasileira.

Soares, Gláucio A. D. 1962. "El sistema electoral y la reforma agraria en el Brasil." *Ciencias Políticas y Sociales* (no. 29).

Schwartzman, Simon. 1975. Sao Paulo e o estado nacional. Sao Paulo: Difusao Européia do Livro.

Touraine, Alain. 1973. *Production de la societé*. Paris: Seuil.

Venturi, Franco. 1972. *Les Intellectuels, le peuple et la revolution*. Paris: Gallimard.

Traditional Brazilian Politics: An Interpretation of Relations between Center and Periphery

Antônio Otávio Cintra

Traditional Political Arrangements

A major share of Brazil's production in the field of political science, as well as a considerable number of studies on Brazilian politics written by foreign authors, have focused on the problems in the relations between center and periphery throughout the country's political development. Some studies, such as those of Oliveira Vianna, Nestor Duarte, Raymundo Faoro, Maria Isaura Pereira de Queiroz, to name but a few, take this problem as their main focus of analysis.[1] In others it appears often implicitly as reference, as a requirement of the topics themselves in their dealing with political and power phenomena, messianic movements, and outbursts of violence (banditry, vendettas) in traditional Brazilian society. In addition, a substantial contribution has been made by legally trained or oriented authors who deal with the center/periphery problem from a different angle and translate it into an intellectual discourse which, to the eyes of sociologically or historically oriented writers, appears formalistic, poorly presented, or limited in scope. Topics recurring throughout this discourse include federalism and its changes, relations among government levels, and the benefits or damages involved in the differential distribution of resources among these levels. Social class, elites, and pressure groups are replaced by different, seemingly more influential actors in the political scene, such as the union, state, and municipalities.

This chapter will study problems in the relations between the political center and periphery through a review of the existing literature and a selection of themes and hypotheses most relevant to an understanding of the various phenomena. We will attempt to include the contributions and concerns of legally oriented writers in terms of a broader set of problems and a more comprehensive approach. The guiding theme is a discussion of "colonelism," a phenomenon which has puzzled some of the sharpest analysts of the various schools.

The term *colonelism (coronelismo)* is derived from *colonel,* a title given to the highest echelons of the Old National Guard. The wealthiest farmers, the highest-ranking and most powerful local bosses could be colonels of the guard. The title remained after the guard was disbanded and is used even today to refer to local chieftains. Colonelism amounts to the ruling presence of local bosses in the interior and their political role as mediators between local and state and federal spheres.

In an earlier study, we approached this phenomenon somewhat restrictedly (Cintra 1971). There attention was given to its local political manifestations, while bypassing the mechanisms and effects which gain relevance in the political system's broader scale, although only as one of the links in a larger chain. This chapter will attempt to make up for that limitation. The study of colonelism highlights the role of mediator played by the village chieftain — usually a landowner, but sometimes also a tradesman, doctor, or pharmacist — between the state or, more generally, the central political institutions, and the population of the interior. The concept of mediation between central political institutions and local populations places the problem within a broader context in which arrangements are made, throughout the history of a society, in an attempt "to achieve the political organization of relatively large areas with the resources offered by an undeveloped civilization" (Hintze 1968:26). Such arrangements are extremely varied, and a strong feudalizing tendency operates in proportion to the distance between the unifying political project — led by an ambitious prince, a dynasty, or a group or class — and the objective conditions which can make that project feasible. Feudalization in this sense refers to what Hintze (1968:6) calls "a peculiar kind of decentralization in which officials who are given land and adopt a personal relation of loyalty, generally become independent local powers in the course of a few generations.

Aside from the question of whether or not feudalism had a place in Brazilian history, an irresistable trend toward the private holding of power was undeniably at work in the encounter between the Portuguese patrimonial state and the vast new area to be ruled, as well as in the broad prerogatives granted to settlers.[2] The political center did not flounder; nor did the king become merely a feudal lord among his peers — the patrimonial and bureaucratized state continued to exist. There was no feudal order with multiple jurisdictions or in which the political center was forced to accept the representation of feudal estates through a constitutional pact.[3] The political order of Brazil's Old Republic came closest to this, but even so, only from a very formal point of view. It seems more appropriate to look at the situation as a traditional bureaucratic empire confronted with centrifugal tendencies, and unable — in technical, economic, military, and political terms — to assert its presence in all points of a territory increasingly adding to its domains through private actions in keeping with imperial expansion projects.

The country's independence from Portugal led to the creation of a Brazilian empire which combined the centralizing interests of the bureaucratic estate located in Rio de Janeiro with the needs for political cohesion of the ruling slavocratic class. The political pact which took shape then lost strength when new strata, no longer using slave labor nor hindered by slavery and the political institutions which supported it, emerged in nineteenth-century Brazilian society. As it gradually settled, the imperial political arrangement developed a peculiar set or relationships between center and periphery. The landed class, in its more aware and politically cohesive segments, realized that, as Victor Nunes Leal (1948:50) puts it, following the theory of Hermes Lima (1948): "In a country as geographically and economically diverse as ours, if the provinces were given broad powers, free labor might well put an end to slavery in some of them."[4] And: "Since it would be impossible for these antagonistic work systems to coexist in the same country, the slavocrats who dominated the national political scene would have to resort to centralization in order to ensure the continuation of slavery throughout the empire. According to historians, centralization saved national unity. It also saved the unity of slave work."

The centralizing effort of the imperial period did not lead to an omnipresent state which pervaded all sectors of society and extended its power throughout the territory. Given the conditions at the time, it was natural for private power to command extensive areas of social relations and fill the gaps of public authority in the country's immense territorial expanse. As in other societies in a similar stage of development, law and order in the interior could seldom be enforced through the state's actual or potential presence, and then only to a minimal degree. The elites in control of the political center renounced the more obvious alternative of reinforcing it through an increase of military contingents serving the state. Autonomous action by the military corporation was feared. The National Guard was created instead, through a law issued on August 18, 1831, which abolished the old ordinances, militias, and municipal guards. As Faoro (1955:164) puts it: "The government was providing for itself a strong apolitical body, accustomed to war and capable of facing the political army if necessary."

By investing landowners and village chieftains with the ranks of colonel, major, or captain, according to their prestige and power, entrusting them with peace-keeping in the interior and with helping the regular army troops in outside conflicts, the National Guard legitimized their effective power and endowed them with a public mission. The situation was not far removed from what Fred Riggs (1959-60:412) described in relation to traditional rural societies:

> Here subsistent rural populations have both little to ask for and not much to fear from the central government. Similarly the center, although demanding that localities maintain peace and pay taxes, makes few demands for positive conformity of behavior. Hence local clienteles have few incentives to cling to the center and the center is generally content so long as there is no trouble in the localities. Thus the substantial real decentralization, even in the most centralized bureaucratic system, is based on mutual indifference as much as on technical obstacles to effective centralization of power.

It seems paradoxical, in terms of territorial distribution of power, that the country's local units, whether provinces or municipalities, have not had greater legal and administrative autonomy. However, this makes sense given the rural landowners' interests, the defense of which allowed for a coalition with the state's bureaucratic groups established in the "primate" city. The imperial bureaucracy was interested in reinforcing the center and, insofar as necessary, also in subjugating the periphery. No matter how progressive one or two prominent members of the political elite, in the final aggregate of political decisions and "nondecisions" the mainstay of slavocratic society could not be brought down. Even liberal political forces, in their struggle for decentralization, went only as far as the provinces in an attempt to strengthen them before the general government. Greater autonomy for the municipalities would threaten that goal and could turn them into "centers of more intensive political activity which could awaken the interests and aspiration of the population's lower strata" (Leal 1948:47). If there were any doubt as to those possibilities, the Regency period made them quite tangible with the threatening surge not only of regional discontent, on the part of the landowning strata, but also of popular claims. It was necessary for the municipalities and provinces to be well harnessed to the center, where agrarian interests were represented and combined with those of the imperial bureaucracy, to be defended in relation to basics but subjected in terms of incidentals. These incidentals were the whims of autonomy and reinforcement of local power, through the electoral process, taxes, police force, and self-administration.[5]

During the Republican period, important changes took place. Since imperial centralization had resulted from an implicit pact between the slavocrats and state bureaucracy, and since the slavocratic order was thus relatively rigid, the way was blocked to emerging interests. The latter included those of the expanding coffee agriculture in Sao Paulo, relatively marginal to governmental power and, little by little, alienated from the monarchy.[6] These interests could count on the army's republicanism. This institution had gained strength after the war with Paraguay, during which it developed a real corporative spirit and came to resent its secondary role in the Empire.[7] With the joining of both forces which, despite their topical identity of purpose, differed with respect to basic aspects, it was not difficult to put an end to the monarchy. The army being the weaker partner of the two, after a brief interregnum in control of government, it yielded to the civilians and returned reluctantly to a secondary place in the political makeup of the Old Republic.

Republican federalism answered the demands of the new coffee-growing class. Having been tied down by the imperial institutions, this group saw new channels for defending its interests with the added autonomy gained by the state.[8] The states could now negotiate foreign loans, maintain their own military forces, and make use of export taxes — a considerably important resource to such exporting states as Sao Paulo. Following the abolition of slavery, and once national unity became consolidated, even the states not linked to coffee production did not see, through their dominant groups, the need for a strong national center. The new set of arrangements was even convenient since it gave them a free hand in maintaining the local status quo on the political, economic, and social planes.

Political cohesion factors were at work even in the new situation brought on by the Republic. Control of state politics was an alluring trophy for the various groups, as a source of employment, fiscal benefits, help from state brigades and the police in confrontations with contenders, channeling of public works to their zone of influence, which raised the value of personal property, and other such rewards. Likewise, since the interests of a given coalition of forces at the state level often depended on decisions at the federal level as well, the fulcrum of influence for these decisions was generally control of the state administration itself. Voting was more important in the Republic than it had been in the Empire, as a result of legislation which substituted a literacy requirement for the electoral qualifications previously demanded, and thereby considerably expanded the electorate (Carone 1971:293-94).[9]

It was not enough for the most ambitious, influential landowner within a given region, who aspired to a higher position of leadership to negotiate with the dominant bosses in his restricted geographic area. The state's "establishment" arose from a composite of bosses from various districts. Among those, some would gradually become preeminent until a coalition, powerful enough to guarantee electoral victory and control of the state machine, eventually emerged. Personal ambition and regional leadership were not the only factors which counted, whether taken jointly or separately, in the formation of a successful coalition. Other assets included the family's traditional prestige and power — sometimes dating back to the Imperial period — long-standing republican status, and similar forms of access to power which operated within the traditional political order. On taking command of the state, the successful coalition sought to perpetuate its reign, using the legal and paralegal tools of the government machine, and gradually forming what throughout the states of the Old Republic became known as "oligarchies."[10] At the state level, the political system was defined not only by the formation of oligarchies — more or less broad coalitions comprising either a large group of kin or a more heterogeneous group — but also by the actual institutionalization of colonelism, that is the pact between the public powers and and leaders of the interior who controlled and supplied votes from their local domains.

The work of cohesive forces was not confined to the state level. Early in the Republican experience, it became obvious that federalism would be damaging to the most dynamic regional sectors, such as those of Sao Paulo, which, in order to promote their interests, would need the federal government's mediation. The country's financial and exchange policies, as well as its fulfillment of foreign commitments, were crucial to these interests (Carone 1970:101).[11] It would be completely impossible to implement a consistent policy were all the states and their representatives in Congress to act autonomously. In the absence of imperial institutions and given the national army's weakness at the time, as compared to the state brigades under oligarchic control, the "governors' policy" *(política dos governadores)* was devised as a centralizing mechanism.

This arrangement acknowledged the national hegemony of some states, particularly Sao Paulo and Minas Gerais, and guaranteed their control of the federal government machine.[12] Power was concentrated to allow for policies which would have proved difficult, if not impossible, within a full-fledged federalist system. These policies involved the fiscal and monetary areas, financial commitments abroad, and assistance to the coffee agriculture. National interests — which for the most part were those of the country's economically dynamic region — were created above local and regional interests, and so were the political mechanisms needed to fulfill them. The central policy expressed the interests of the hegemonic states.

The governors' policy also favored members fo the periphery, the states "establishments" or oligarchies, whose rule remained uncontested by local adversaries and by the population's limited political activity. Favoring the oligarchies did not imply a broader favoring of the regions under their rule. As often happens when the center and periphery are defined in the political power arrangements affecting a given territory, the Old Republic's political pact kept vast regions from developing, while allowing or promoting the progress of others. In the backward or decadent regions, traditional domination continued, supported by the center, in return for local peace-keeping and electoral backing.

This political arrangement was far from flawless. Private violence at the base was beyond the state's — and particularly the national army's — control. State oligarchies lashed out rampantly at any source of opposition and became internally divided in the struggle for the spoils of state and local politics or in the game of alliances played at the federal level. All this led to instances of federal intervention in which the army was used as a sometimes docile, but often reluctant instrument. Ever since it was relegated to a secondary place, after the military governments of Deodoro and Floriano, early in the Republican phase, the army had become increasingly intolerant of the First Republic's political practices, looked upon as the cause of society's problems and deficiencies at the time. The military establishment lacked the strength to oppose the civilian elite, shielded by its own state military forces. The army's attempts to return to government power appeared to have succeeded when Marshal Hermes da Fonseca's candidacy was launched in 1910. However, Fonseca's presidential period was a frustrating experience for the military groups and, in its failure, helped trigger rebel outbursts in subsequent governments, culminating in the lieutenants' movement *(tenentismo)* which was decisive in bringing down the Old Republic. Central control itself was the subject of regional disputes between dominant and aspiring groups (such as the Republican party of Rio Grande do Sul, from 1910 on). The peripheral states took advantage of internal divisions among the major ones to increase their share of the benefits.[13] The whole institutional framework held little in the way of representation or satisfaction for emerging urban groups.

Undermined by all these factors, the Old Republic fell during the crisis of 1929. From then on, the central state, its civil and particularly its military bureaucracies were reinforced. Member states were deprived of a major share of their previous bargaining power through the suppression of elections and the subjection of state brigades and police corps to the national army. Private violence, which was commonplace in the interior, became a target for the state's intolerance (Facó 1963:194-97). The cities grew and gradually undermined the overpowering weight of rural votes. While in the interregnum of the New State rural voting lost its significance, from 1945 on it rose again and was still a decisive factor in elections at all government levels. Colonelism managed to remain, somewhat residually in some regions, where it was forced to adapt to new conditions in terms of urban development, migration, and industrialization, and in others definitely losing ground to the populist vote. In a large section of the national territory where archaic forms of land exploitation and social domination persist, colonelism is alive up to the present, as newscasts will occasionally confirm, particularly during election periods. As to relations between the union and the states, analysts report that, after 1945, a federalist system subsisted in which the union was led by the predominant states, followed in turn by a periphery of backward, politically submissive states, controlled by oligarchic groups settled in the interior and manipulated by the transactions of colonelism.

Representative Democracy in a Patrimonial Order: The Colonels' Mediation

In the preceding section we attempted to focus briefly on the traditional political interrelationships found in Brazilian society. One of the most important links in this chain is the colonelist arrangement. The phenomenon as such was not unknown during the Empire; its basic features were outlined then. However, it only grew to its full political stature during the Republican period with the relative expansion of suffrage and the added strength of the states (which could now elect their own governors, instead of having a president appointed by the center, as was the case during the Imperial state). Temporarily disrupted during the New State, colonelism rose again after 1945 and prevails up to the present in many part of the country. The following description of colonelism's structure and forms of action applies particularly to the Old Republic and the period between 1945 and 1964. From 1964 to the present its importance has been substantially redefined by institutional changes — the same was true during the New State — especially since elections became a secondary factor in the choice of government officials. We will return to some aspects of the problem in the final section of this paper.

If it is only through analytical simplification that voting can be made to fit into an "open market" model, the fit is even more difficult in a society where political factors are still attached to units in which the individual's ascribed status prevails entirely or partly. The literature dealing with traditional politics points to the fact that, until recently, the power of life and death over the population of vast areas of the interior was in the hands of landowners. Unequally distributed, land was the main source of power and most of the population depended on it for subsistence. Security and justice were not provided by public authorities, but by the landowners whose authority "was based, in the final analysis, on the capacity to enforce their decisions, by force if necessary; in other words, it was based on the number of armed men which they were capable of mobilizing" (Souza 1968). A second crucial source of power was controlled by the landowners: the private militias. It is true that with the central government's gradual reinforcement, as of 1930, the rural potentates were, little by little, deprived of this source of power. Nevertheless, considering how slowly the state managed to reach the remotest regions of the interior, the process was far from standard or general.[14] We will now take a closer look at the situation created by the arrival of representative institutions.

The bonds which initially linked the rural population to the national political process could be accurately described as a mediation system. In the literature, the phenomenon has been labeled "colonelism" and defined as a system of mutual tolerance involving the declining private power, which was nevertheless still strong, the power of national and state governments, slowly being consolidated, and the power of the political parties.[15] What elements does the literature provide to allow us to describe the mediation process? As Silverman points out, not all types of intermediary activity fit in with what we here call "mediation"; the process we refer to is critical and performed exclusively by the mediator.[16]

Mediation as Critical

From the clients' viewpoint, particularly among the lower rural classes, with the electoral laws issued in the Republican period, the act of voting and the very right to vote created new opportunities to express and reinforce feudal loyalty. The duty to help the boss during elections was added, quite naturally, to the old system of obligations. If the boss did not need votes, the people would not vote since this, like any other contact with the bureaucratic machine was a bit frightening, as far as the preliminaries were concerned. The act of voting called for traveling out to the registration centers, speaking to an official, taking literacy tests. Election day would bring further problems, to cope with which the boss's help would be indispensable, even if he were not running for office himself.

The landowner's active participation in mobilizing the population is of the utmost importance to outside politicians. If the colonels do not personally enter the contest and consequently do not need votes, the only (or perhaps the most economical) way to have the people rally to the polls is to enlist the services of local bosses. Politicians — both from the administration and from the opposition at the federal and local levels — are thus fully aware that before being given to them, the votes must be collected by the local chieftain. In the typical situation during the Old Republic, as well as in more recent periods, the government party held considerable advantage over the opposition in that it controlled strategic resources for the local boss, not only on the financial plane, through aid and subsidies, but also in the form of nepotism — the nominations for federal or state posts in the community.

To gain a better view of this complicated picture, we must look at the two major government circles outside the municipality — the federal and state levels — and at the four possible positions of political groups seeking votes in the municipality: (1) when the incumbent state elite belongs to the same party as the incumbent federal faction; (2) when the incumbent state elite belongs to the same party as the federal opposition; (3) when the state opposition is on the same side as the incumbent federal party; and (4) when the state opposition group is on the side of the federal opposition party.[17]

		Federal government level	
		Incumbents	Opposition
State government level	Incumbents	A	B
	Opposition	C	D

Given its greater proximity to the municipalities, the state political machine is more important to local authorities than the federal one. This being the case, we could classify groups from outside the area in the following order of diminishing importance, in terms of their potential for intervention in the municipality: *A, B, C, and D.* Particularly during the Old Republic, situation *B* could be extremely vulnerable, given the incentives which the federal government offered to uprisings from the state opposition, leading to the fall of oligarchies. In this fashion, colonels from the interior, at odds with state "incumbents," could come together — more often than not under federal government inspiration and frequently relying on federal military support — and threaten to overthrow the dominant oligarchy. The state "opposition" could sometimes use this fact skillfully by joining the federal government on the one hand, while on the other increasing and organizing the coalition of rebel colonels against the state power (situation *C*).[18]

As disclosed by most studies, the state government tended to associate with the mediator in terms of the abstract role, regardless of the person or family playing it, as long as there was effective control to guarantee votes. The relation was instrumental and universalistic.[19] In contrast, from the clients' point of view, not only was the mediator's role critical, but so was he as a person, since the traditionally institutionalized relation was based on bonds of personal loyalty and actual or ritual family relationships.

The ideal type is thus characterized by a hierarchical system of dependency relations. It differs in some respects from traditional patron-client relations which formerly prevailed, namely: (1) The national and state political machines are much stronger and gradually depriving local bosses of many of the powers they had enjoyed till then. (2) Rural bosses still control a crucial source of power, the land, on which most of the population still depends for a livelihood. The role of rural landowners is vital in mobilizing those populations for elections. (3) Consequently, they have an electoral function in addition to their other sources of power. Mainly as a result of this function, the ranchers and bosses eventually control other important relationships between local and outside (national and state) spheres.[20] Since decisions at the national and state levels become increasingly important to the area, particularly in relation to jobs, credit, public works, and welfare services, the mediation of local political bosses becomes even more important for the population, including the middle strata which find few opportunities in the stagnant economies of most of Brazil's minor cities and towns.

Mediation as Exclusive

We have analyzed the mediators' critical functions. How do they manage to remain exclusive? A loss of exclusivity can take three different courses. In the first course, a given middleman no longer monopolizes the mediation process. This may be caused by competing mediators of like social status and in a position to take over his clientele, or through unlike competitors whose mediation is based not on land ownership but on an occupation which allows them contact with many different persons or gives them frequent opportunities to dispense favors (physicians, pharmacists, notary publics, tradesmen, etc.) The second course involves more than just one individual's loss of his monopoly to competitors. The structure of the situation changes and different mediation channels appear, such as new political parties with a populist ideology, or unions, the government's bureaucratic bodies, and similar groups. A third course is partly favored by the preceding situation and partly the cause of it, as horizontal solidarities arise from within the clientele, promoting its transformation into a social class.

Within the more traditional context, as yet not affected by change, the local boss's command is more likely to be contested by a person of like social standing. Interfamily vying, often ending in bloody confrontations, has been common throughout Brazilian history, although vendettas became unusual after the strengthening of public authority.[21] The new mediation mechanisms described earlier may lead to conflicts between political factions, although not necessarily bloody ones. These factions develop around powerful families, creating a vertical split in society between two antagonistic camps. Since the outside groups, particularly what we refer to as government, are interested in effective mediators, they generally wait for the conflict to end, before supporting the victor, that is the boss or family who proves stronger or shows a broader electoral following.[22] Since the financial resources and jobs the state can offer are limited, the process allows for using a smaller but nevertheless decisive group of voters who will trade their ballots for a relatively lower amount of resources than would be needed if both local factions were united and consequently both sets of demands had to be met. This being the case, once the government secures the necessary minimum to ensure victory, it cares little whether or not the whole world is on its side. But the local boss's strategy must be to seek government support. If he should court the opposition, he runs the risk (repeatedly confirmed) of having the government reach an understanding with his competitors, which would mean the loss of his mediation monopoly. In the ideal situation, government support means not only positive rewards, but also protection from hostility on the part of opponents.[23]

This situation is not just typical of the distant past. We find indirect evidence of it in an article by Julio Barbosa concerning elections in Minas Gerais. His analysis points to changes in the makeup of the state legislature which stemmed from the election, in 1960, of a UDN governor over the PSD candidate (the UDN and the PSD being the state's two major parties) According to Barbosa (1963), "elections for the Legislative Assembly of Minas Gerais are the most vulnerable to direct and indirect influence from the state's executive branch. All parties, except the PTB, are conditioned by their stand in relation to the executive." He goes on to say this phenomenon is clearly and intensely expressed in the elections held during the governor's mandate, free from the effects of a joint election for state governor and president of the republic. The UDN (the governor's party) managed to increase the number of seats it held in the Assembly from eleven, won in the 1958 election, to twenty-two in 1962. The same was true in the municipal elections: in 1958, when the state executive power was in the hands of the PSD (Social Democratic party), this party managed to seat 42 percent of all mayors, and an additional 13 percent by alliances with other parties; while the UDN (National Democratic Union), its main opponent, had less then 10 percent of its candidates elected directly (plus 19 percent in alliance with other parties). In the 1962 elections, the UDN managed to take sixty-one municipalities from the PSD and increase its number of mayors from less than 10 percent to 22 percent of the total; while for the PSD, the opposition at the time, participation dropped from 42 to 35 percent (Barbosa 1963, passim). Although the evidence is indirect, it can be easily inferred that these returns were largely a product of the mechanisms described earlier.

Due to the importance, in terms of individual power, of being a local political mediator, and to the relative arbitration of state and federal leaders in choosing the most efficient individual as a mediator, local elections inevitably tend to promote factionalism. As many case studies show, the most serious conflicts have taken place after the closing of electoral agreements, not before, and the responsibility of outside groups in causing such conflicts is far from negligible.

The landowner's power is not challenged by his peers only. His constituency must of course be safeguarded from the opponents' propaganda; this is done by means of a thorough organization for election day. Nevertheless, other mediation structures stand as potential threats as well, and it is just as important to prevent them from developing on the basis of class interests. This calls for strategies geared less to particular instances and more to long-term results. Some studies describe how the rural landowners watch over their workers' contact with strangers. In some cases, "the workers must request permission before they can seek medical or religious aid — to baptize a child, for example — or go out on trips, visits, and so on, even during weekends or holidays."[24]

Although these cases are extreme, they show that the mediators are well aware of their strengths and weaknesses and act according to the circumstances. Patron-client relationships may survive even in small industrial communities. Well-known case studies show that the organization of workers' unions or other horizontal solidarity institutions was actively opposed by the bosses who sought to maintain vertical dependencies and loyalties intact. It should be recalled that a structural factor favored them in this respect, namely, the shortage of jobs which made the worker view his employment as a special favor on the part of the boss.[25]

The detailed view of the colonels' mediation as it operates in the political system's lower levels should not obscure its effects and relevance within that system's overall functioning. Well attuned to the governors' policy during the Old Republic, yet still comfortably linked to the federalism prevailing after the fall of the New State in 1945, colonelism represented the meeting of a rural social order operating in the interior with the central political order through which the socially and economically dynamic sectors and regions expressed their needs and interests. Let us now review some of the consequences of the interior's integration into national politics by way of colonelism.

Political Participation

In the typical situation under analysis, voting means little in terms of political participation as a public demonstration. It is simply a matter of trading another "good" in the context of a patron-client relationship. This good undoubtedly has its own dynamics which can eventually help break down the mediator's monopoly. As long as this monopoly subsists, however, voting must be viewed as a rather prepolitical form of participation. It is also valid to assume that all efforts will be made to keep it down to a minimum. Why? Because the person who mobilizes the mechanism pays a certain price for it and will therefore be highly concerned about the "marginal cost" involved. This is the conclusion reached from reading, among others, Blondel's (1957) study on political life in the state of Paraiba. The main problem lies in whether or not the election is guaranteed, to which another question may be added: How much bargaining power does mobilizing a marginal vote give the mediator in his negotiations with outside politicians?[26] It is difficult to formulate specific hypotheses concerning political participation, given the need to consider such variables as the degree of competition involved in elections, the type of elections (for the executive, the legislature, etc.), or the electorate (local, state, or national). However, by simplifying the problem in light of the previous considerations, we can propose the following hypotheses: (1) Isolation, unequal land distribution, shortage of jobs in the interior, are all factors which render the population dependent on the landowners and on persons of high standing in general. (2) The population's peripheral position makes voting difficult for most, as well as probably meaningless as a political act. It leads to high abstention rates. (3) An active mobilization of the electorate by local leaders is therefore needed to increase attendance at the polls. (4) Mobilizing the voters requires a certain amount of resources to cover expenses. In the extreme case of a highly dependent population, the total resources needed are determined mainly by the cost of physically transferring the constituents to the voting centers. The less dependent the population, the higher the resources needed, since the electorate will then demand more in exchange for its votes. The presence of other candidates also implies a higher investment of resources to ensure the voters' loyalty. (5) The mediator's active role in mobilizing votes will depend on the following factors: the level of competition with other political leaders participating in the election; the population's degree of dependency; the amount of bargaining power for negotiations with outside leaders to be gained by the mediator through the mobilization of marginal votes. If these factors fail to encourage the mediator to act, attendance at the polls will be meager.

Attendance will increase to the extent that his assessment of those factors leads him to believe that he will not be wasting resources, but may even increase his current ones. These hypotheses are not only applicable to elections for offices outside the community. In many instances, even local elections — that of a mayor, for example — can become important to the higher-level political elites.

From the center's viewpoint, particularly the states', it is not crucial to achieve sweeping political participation, but only the minimum needed to guarantee a winning coalition, eligible to the rewards of power. Excessive popular mobilization through the electoral process may not be favorably looked upon. It can be assumed that the landowning group is expected to retain control of the political struggle at the lower levels — an assumption which could come into question were there greater involvement on the part of the rural population. Influences aimed at reducing political participation also spring from the "central" viewpoint. The following section will corroborate this assumption.

Control of Violence

In contrast to the idyllic conservative image, violence pervades all levels of traditional society. We have already mentioned intraclass conflicts in family feuds which are amazingly frequent in stories about community life in the interior. The potential for interclass conflict was no lower throughout the period of slavery when it led to slave uprisings, escapes, and the creation of slave refugee communities. That potential was not eradicated with the abolition of slave work; on the contrary, it was to reappear time and again in the form of banditry and in the messianic movements.

Material scarcity and insecurity prevail in the remotest regions, characterizing local fights, be they over honor, debts, division of lands, or inheritance, or in the search for political domination or prestige, as a zero-sum game. Traditional powers are not eager to add the horizontal violence of the lower strata, alongside the class rifts. Violence is only acceptable among peers. Only coopted can it cross class barriers.

In the communities of the interior, the rural bosses surround themselves with true private militias, the tools used to impose their will on subjects and keep their peers at bay. The most skillful individuals among the rural workers, in terms of physical violence, are thereby offered a means of vertical mobility within the rigid class structure.[27] At the boss's command they may inflict violence on his enemies, even when the latter are members of the landed class.

The colonelist arrangement is also a parapolitical arrangement for imposing law and order and controlling violence. It involves a parallel system of power, to quote Hobsbawm's (1965:30-56) terms in a study of Sicily's Mafia society, which the central power sees sometimes with indifference, sometimes with active opposition, and is sometimes forced to meet halfway. The weakest, no matter where they are, must seek shelter from the strongest, thereby reinforcing the system of dependency which links the peasant population to the landowners, and the smaller and weaker landowners to the more powerful. Thus the entire population congregates around strong nuclei in pyramidal power systems, among which, but not within which, the struggles ensue. Outside actors can sometimes be called in to intervene in a deadlock or when the outcome of a contest is not being observed. Police partiality in the general protection of the "establishment" are well within the rules of the game. It is important to ensure that violence among the lower strata, coopted by the colonelist arrangement, does not get out of control, becoming autonomous and taking the overtones of a class struggle. When such an event becomes imminent, the reaction does not come only from one colonel or another, but involves the mobilization of greater resources from the political system. The repression of the messianic movements of Canudos and Contestado points to the fear, the actual panic of the political elites when faced with the threat contained in such outbreaks.[28]

It was also important in the conflicts among the colonels that the scope of the struggle should not extend too far — which was always a possibility when the population was armed.[29] A thought-provoking illustration of this phenomenon took place in Cariri Valley, State of Ceará, in 1911. The constant battles among the colonels of that region — struggles which mobilized hundreds of armed men — led to a unique agreement among them, led by Father Cícero Romao and backed by Governor Nogueira Acioli. In addition to consolidating the political forces supporting the governor, the "colonels' pact," as it eventually became known, sought to end the unstable pattern of command in which the local bosses were continually overthrowing each other. In a region where the concentration of peasant populations was growing, drawn by Father Cícero's reputation, it was unwise to mobilize these populations around conflicts which could become uncontrollable. It should be borne in mind that we are dealing with a region where instances of peasant violence, not coopted but spontaneous, were quite frequent, particularly during such periods as the great drought of 1877-79.[30]

Control of the Rural Population through Labor[31]

One important by-product of colonelism in many regions, not always stressed in studies dealing with this phenomenon, is the retention of abundant and cheap labor in rural domains. This fact is brought to light in a recent study of migratory data which shows lower migration rates than expected in some areas of the country: the large estates keep the population scattered, rarely involved in migratory waves and not easily recruited (Graham and Buarque de Hollanda 1971; Facó 1963; Della Cava 1970). Coercive retention of workers is likely to operate in this respect as well. There is evidence pointing to such coercion in the mate-producing (a Brazilian type of tea) region of Contestado, but it is possible that in other areas bandits *(jagunços)* may have helped to prevent defection of laborers, when needed.[32] Father Cícero acted as a major labor supplier in Cariri Valley, and a major share of his political strength rested on this. Farmers and even contractors called on him when there were few hands available for agricultural tasks or public works. Father Cícero could easily recruit them from among the throngs of pilgrims who flowed into Juazeiro (Facó 1963; Della Cava 1970).

Not surprisingly, the oligarchies often struggled within the political arrangements at the federal level, as did the colonels in the municipalities, against the migration of labor beyond state borders. The loss implied by such an exodus was not only economic but political as well, since the migrants would decrease the potential number of voters. For a state in lack of workers, it was often easier to resort to foreign labor than to attempt to recruit them from another state in the country.

Municipal Weakness and Excessive Centralization

Another consequence of colonelism is stressed by the "municipalists," who point to the municipality's weakness within the power division scheme applied to the federation, states, and municipalities. The three levels of power are usually referred to as true political actors, while their source of interest and logic of action are not generally analyzed or clarified. The diagnosis is followed by claims for greater municipal autonomy — in financial, administrative, and political terms — in honor of a loyalty to grass roots democracy whose characteristics are also left unexplained.

It was Victor Nunes Leal (1948) who took up the problem anew with a comprehensive and analytically incisive approach.[33] The municipality's institutional weakness — and, from a different angle within the country's federalism, that of member states as well — is not the mere result of individual whims, or of failures in constitutional prescriptions per se.

The weak municipality is a product of colonelism, but at the same time contributes to perpetuate the latter through a feedback process. The central authorities, the politicians who need votes from the interior, make use of the colonels' mediation whose domain is the municipality. The latter is not viewed as a political administrative unit which renders services. Its legal responsibilities in the financial sphere, for example, are hardly broad, and in practice they suffer further curtailment through action and omission. Concessions for the municipalities are only obtained with the good graces of the central machine (state or federal), but in order to obtain them, the colonel must support the administration. A weak municipality needs a colonel and the colonel needs the government, and for as long as the need persists, he will continue to support the ruling party. It is undesirable then, within the logic of the ruling powers, to have strong autonomous local areas. As far as the opposition is concerned, once it rises to office it does not differ from its predecessors and soon forgets the municipalism which it had earlier praised in the bitterness of opposition.

Municipal weakness is not incompatible with a strong local power. Because the colonels are strong, they must be made to depend on the government, keeping the municipalities weak. But are the colonels' interests not represented in the state power? Even when this is the case, the government coalition must ensure the colonels' electoral submission if it is to continue as a winning coalition. From the individual colonel's point of view, the government has thus become a Hobbesian creation to which they must submit in order not to perish.

The political center has interests which do not quite coincide with those of the colonels and may actually clash with them. These may be, for instance, city interests in conflict with rural interests as regards trade relations between them; the intersts of the capital and urban centers, where the political elite is settled, as well as other groups seeking a parasitic existence at the expense of the interior. These interests may benefit from centralization and institutional weakening of municipalities, on the assumption that further autonomy and resources granted to the latter would only be poorly administered by the colonels and their clienteles.

Center and Periphery in Political Life and the Brazilian Situation

One of the basic dimensions of political power in a total society, particularly when it operates over a vast territory, is its spatial frame of reference. Naturally, the concept "vast" is relative to the technical conditions surrounding the exercise of power (especially the communications technology). To the extent that the society grows more complex, as it differentiates and specializes its institutions, develops a stratification pattern, and gains added mastery over nature through technological progress, not only does the population spread out unevenly over the area, but resources and values are also differentially distributed throughout the territory. Political power, previously dispersed, tends to concentrate, not only within the social structure, but also geographically in certain points where wealth, higher forms of culture, and the leadership of organized religion tend to converge. In other words, a center (or centers) and a periphery are outlined in that society (Eisenstadt 1968:81-88).

In politically organized societies, center-periphery relations provide the substance for a major part of political life. One of the crucial political problems, which must be solved at the institutional level, results from the concentration of power at a specific point in the area — the capital city — from which it extends to all other points. The concentration of power takes place because, in addition to the objective factors acting in that direction — the society's structural differentiation itself — there are social groups pressing for centralization, considered important and necessary to promote their interests. These interests can no longer be contained within awkward local or regional limits, but are viewed in terms of a broader scale, covering increasingly larger portions of the area, even transcending it at times (Eisenstadt 1963; Deutsch 1966; Bendix 1964).

Seldom does the promotion of interests by the central powers coincide with promoting the interests of all groups. Just as a look at the social stratification may lead to suspicion as to the exercise of power by the dominant class, the interests of the center and the groups which identify with it may be contrary to the interests of the periphery and indeed be perceived as such. This is the root of regional secessionist movements and, in a broader sense, of regionalism as well. There are also empirical situations in which the political center does not overlie the economic one. Such a situation may happen during periods of change when the political centers respond to stagnant or declining interests, more than to the call of new dynamic economic nuclei. The fact that the new economic center is not directly represented in the political one should not lead to the conclusion that the former is somehow marginalized, since its interests could nevertheless be prominent in the considerations of the political center's decision makers.

Federalist institutions may be viewed as attempts to establish a balance among regional interests and between these and the central interests.[34] But could it be that all the interests brought together by the political center can be reduced, in the final analysis, to those of the economically dominant region? Even when the economic and political centers overlap completely, it should be borne in mind that the greater a society's economic integration, the stronger the repercussions of the central region's interests on the rest of society. This in turn corroborates the need for the central public power to identify with these interests, as general, not merely regional ones. The periphery is able to assert itself to the extent that its support is needed in promoting "general interests." In exchange for this backing, it tries to extract concessions. Attention to the interests of the periphery does not always result in benefits for its entire population. The concept of exploitation must be resorted to in dealing with the center-periphery relation, no matter from what particular angle of the social sciences the problem is approached. The relationship between center and periphery can be just as easily be one of mutual promotion as one of reciprocal exploitation.

Exploitation by the center is seldom carried out without the dominant groups of the peripheral regions or settlements. Nor is it always the case, when, through the spokesmen for its dominant classes, the periphery cries out against exploitation by the center, that such exploitation is actually taking place in terms of a majority of the population. Within the periphery's internal stratification, the landed and politically dominan classes can exploit the rest of the population and use the central elites support to ensure their local rule. These elites may sometimes seek to weaken the local domination, promoting the rise of other groups and even favoring strata which until then have been exploited.[35]

In this respect, Fred Riggs's (1959-60) proposals are extremely useful and we have drawn on them, perhaps all too freely, for our subsequent treatment of the problem. The interest groups, both local and central, which he calls "clienteles," can be classified as either "supporters" or "dependents." Dependents are those who, in terms of their economic behavior, consume more from a given area than they produce there; supporters, those who produce more than they consume. The idea need not be approached only from an economic standpoint, but could also be viewed within a social framework. However, the difficulties involved in providing operational definitions for these concepts would be great. From a theoretical point of view, the idea makes sense (Moore 1967:470-83).

In the relationships between the center and periphery, various alliances may develop from the meeting of local and outside interests, in which the groups involved are defined as either exploiters (dependents) or supporters. The following possible alliances may be outlined:

		Local or Internal Clienteles	
		Supporters	Exploiters
External Clienteles	**Supporters**	A	B
(Central)	**Exploiters**	C	D

A type *A* alliance is the typical case of mutual promotion of interests between the local developmentalists and those of the center. In the *B* type, supporters based outside the area or region, perhaps politically dominant in the center — through their control of the more strategic levers of central power — form alliances, either for tactical reasons or due to political contingencies, with traditional local leaderships of the exploiting type. Having agreed to limit their developmentalist energies to some parts of the territory, they give regional groups a free hand, providing the latter do not cause any major problems and, if necessary, supply them with political support. The *C* case is perhaps more difficult to define empirically. We can think of a state, region, or district, whose development is being promoted by a dynamic ruling elite which, due to political reasons, enters into a mutual tolerance pact with national elites of the exploiting type. This case seems to be the most unstable of the four. Finally, type *D* alliances are very common in underdeveloped societies. Taking a simplified set-up, we have local parasitic elites, established perhaps in the capital city and living on the surplus of rural zones where, to a greater or lesser extent, the population is exploited by local landowners. The latter, in connivance with external elites, have a free hand in local domination, and may even rely on central resources, should these be needed. In return, they supply the central elites with political support and a variable share of surplus extracted from the dominated population. The local elite, as a rule, is the weaker partner in the pact and loses in the transactions, both economically (for example, through the deterioration of prices for agricultural produce as compared with those of urban-made goods) and politically. From an institutional viewpoint, the type *D* alliance can leave the locality with very few effective instruments of power. In the center, the curtailment of local autonomy is justified by the alleged incompetence of the local elites and the assumption that were they to have greater resources and power, they would become even more unruly.

The problems of secessionism, regional or municipal demands, complaints against the workings of federalism, and so on, take on a new form when seen within the framework of center-periphery relationships. This is not merely a typology of interrelationships between central and peripheral elites. Specific hypotheses can be formulated about relations among the various possible arrangements and such resulting phenomena as an excessive centralization in some aspects — in taxation powers or in administration, for example — coupled with abusive decentralization in others, as with the practice of private violence. The power structure at a given moment may result from various constellations of these alliances. The central elites may consist of spokesmen for dependent and supporting interests, with varying degrees of influence, who, for political reasons, are backed by various regional interests, likewise definable as dependent or supporting.

How would we describe the center and its interests from a peripheral point of view, in the case of Brazil? When we speak of traditional Brazilian politics we think primarily of the representation of rural landowners at the center. There is a symbiotic relationship which provides a good illustration of the pact between dependents (block *D)*. A mutual exploitation of sorts takes place which is unbalanced in favor of the center. The central elite is not differentiated from the periphery as a class, but becomes a segment gradually gaining preeminence, by its very central position, over the remainder. In contrast to it, the peripheral elites are scattered and lack the resources to act as a cohesive block in the everyday political life, except through their delegations in the center. The central elite watches over the preservation of the traditional rural structure (the intolerance of such peasant movements as broke out in Canudos or in Contestado clearly attests to the interests and ideologies of that group.[36] In like fashion, it keeps every individual colonel in the interior and, on a collective scale, every oligarchy tightly bound to the "official wagon," through mechanisms which weaken the municipalities and states, and renders them dependent on the center and on its fiscal, financial, occupational, and police-related favors. The colonels maintain a symbiotic system of support with the central elites. The latter are they themselves and their representatives, but as political elites they develop interests in self-preservation and continued performance of the role which in turn leads them, with inexorable logic, to the need to dominate and weaken the colonelship inasmuch as it represents a base capable of resisting the summit (reference is made to our earlier considerations in the section on municipal weakness and excessive centralization).

The political center, particularly as it developed in the Old Republic through the workings of the governors' policy, is to a great extent responsive to the dynamic and expanding agricultural sector, the Sao Paulo coffee growers, very well organized at the state level, from where they extend their influence to federal circles. As tends to occur with the dynamic sector in a national economy, coffee interests are not viewed simply as the interests of one group, but actually as national interests which thus become legitimate.

A description of the central elites does not exclude the possibility of conflict within the political center itself.[37] Both during the Old Republic and even later, throughout considerable periods, there were tacit agreements, division of profits, and spheres of influence. Brazilian federalism translated these agreements into a transaction by which the richer states — particularly Sao Paulo — would benefit from the operation of important mechanisms involving taxes, credit, foreign exchange, and trade. Elites from other states would rise against these favors because the tacit bargaining ensured them of life-long rule. They managed to demobilize the local population through the very stagnation and decadence of the region under their control. In like fashion, they drew power from the regional poverty during times of economic crisis, when federal assistance to the region was channelled through them by way of compensation.

Simon Schwartzman (1970) recently called attention to a possible contradiction between the interests of Sao Paulo and those of the Brazilian political center. The center would rather voice the interests of other states, led by Minas Gerais. As we see it, the Old Republic's machine was not all that removed from the Sao Paulo oligarchy, but was to a great extent a product of its action. The Old Republic's federalism gave this oligarchy a free hand in defending its interests and, when needed, the backing and protection of the federal government, although this was sometimes given rather reluctantly.[38] Any such reluctance, however, was not particularly due to more federal receptivity to the demands of Minas Gerais. The coffee valorization policy which was crucial to the Old Republic, often found these two state oligarchies working side by side to pressure the same federal administration to give them its approval. Federal unwillingness to yield was often linked to the interests of the central state itself which would have to be responsible to foreign creditors, as an underwriter, or else resort to a policy of currency issues. During the 1920s for example, Sao Paulo governor Washington Luiz managed to obtain from President Epitácio Pessoa the issuance of paper money and intervention in the market to guarantee the price of coffee, plus, some time later, a loan of nine million pounds for the product's third valorization. The president's reluctance to implement these measures elicited reactions from both the Sao Paulo and the Minas Gerais elites. The federalist solution did not just bring benefits to Sao Paulo, but was undoubtedly better for the state than seccession. There were other partners with claims to be met, but they were satisfied with relatively little — the division among them of formal command posts and offices — in exchange for the Sao Paulo oligarchy's freedom of action within its own state and for the possibility of using federal power when it became necessary to socialize losses, as in the third valorization of coffee described.[39] In contrast with Sao Paulo, the most outstanding situations were those of the Northeast and, closer to the center, Minas Gerais. While Sao Paulo developed using the federalist mechanisms, these other regional elites were content to secure "consummatory" political power (Minas Gerais) or regional oligarchic control and mediation in federal distributive policies (Northeast).[40]

At the state level, the interests of regional political organization and

coordination result in the colonels' gradual submission to their own creations, the oligarchies. This, insofar as institutions and political practices
are concerned, leads to political, financial, and administrative atrophy
for the municipalities, as well as to a strong governmentalism. On the
federal level, the interests of the dynamic state, through control of the
central machine, lead to pacts with the oligarchies from the more backward states. The use of those discriminating mechanisms does not elicit
protests, as long as the bases of oligarchic domination are not threatened
but actually strengthened.

Could we speak of central interests that are not those of the dominant
groups which controlled the center or made use of it? Our analysis leads
to a negative answer, not in the trivial sense that the state merely ex-
presses the strongest private interests, but because the national center
arises as an endeavor of groups acting on an increasingly national scale.
Their interests, at a given point, become national, collective in scope, or
representative of the common good, however we choose to see it. From
this viewpoint, private interests become public, being raised to the level
of state goals. The interests promoted by the political center can be those
of the dominant region — whether or not they are counterbalanced by
concessions to regional interests which are secondary in the constellation
of political forces.

An analysis of the Old Republic shows that, in addition to the interests
of the dominant groups and regions, more autonomous state interests
seemed to arise which at times even conflicted with private ones. This
was the case with the exchange policy, in which both coffee and industrial interests fought for lower rates, while the state sought high ones as a
result of its continuous need to cover foreign public debts and remit-
tances of foreign capital earnings. The state's viewpoint was often
defended by leaders who had risen to the presidency as defenders of
dominant regional interests but who, once sworn in, assimilated some of
the views of the federal state. The financial policies of Campos Sales
were far from being unanimously accepted by the Sao Paulo elite. The
coffee valorization policies did not find in Rodrigues Alves the support
expected from a representative of the Sao Paulo elite. In the military corporation, more than in the civilian bureaucracy, the germ of state level
collective projects could be glimpsed in the ideas behind such movements
as *tenentismo*. After 1930, the state's prospects became more easily
discernible.

Center-Periphery After 1964

In describing traditional Brazilian politics, we referred mostly to its
golden age within the overall political system, which was the Old

Republic. We nevertheless pointed out that many of its elements persisted through time, some of them lasting up to the present, not only at the local, but also at the national level. Arrangements analogous to those previously described are still found in the ties between center and periphery. Many mechanisms which preserve or promote regional inequality between center and periphery have survived, and in some localities and regions there are still elites with their coteries, which benefit from local stagnation.

The old arrangements are relatively secondary elements today. With the new centralization of Brazilian politics after 1964, with the weakening of legislative power in relation to the executive and the suppression of elections, except for posts at the municipal level or in the legislature, colonelism and traditional politics have witnessed the drying of much of the sap that had previously nourished them. Elites from such states as Minas Gerais, whose sizable electorate accounted for the power they wielded in the center, have fallen into ostracism. Political transformations in the wake fo the political-military movement of 1964 broke off developments in the macroinstitutional plane — the populist alliances, for example — largely attributable to such changes as urbanization, population growth, the country's physical integration, expansion of the domestic market, industrialization — all of which had also affected the smaller urban centers of the interior and reached the very core of colonelism and local power. Changes such as these, extensively mentioned in the literature, are still taking place at a relatively fast pace, varying in accordance with the region involved, but present even in the remotest corners of the land.[41] However, we do not believe that they alone can eradicate colonelism, unless backed by institutional changes.

From an institutional point of view, the forces of change sometimes operate in opposite directions. The rise, in the more dynamic sections of the interior, of new parties and leadership experimenting with the populist theme was met with obstacles of all sorts. Given the need to legitimize the regime by proving its backing by solid electoral majorities, the institution of "subtickets" makes the present government party almost invincible. No matter how persistent the rivalries may be, the families and groups involved in municipal politics are motivated to join and seek shelter with the official party which can ensure them a good relationship with the state executive without forcing them to forsake their old political ties, concealed by the "subtickets." Thus, although it may be growing, the electorate which until 1965 would have voted for a party like the old PTB (Brazilian Labor party), seldom manages to overcome the forces of the old UDN (National Democratic Union) or the old PSD (Social Democratic party), whose local political rivalries persist. The votes of the "subtickets" which hide the old parties are added together in the same total — the government party's. This "gimmick" permits the landslide victory of the government party in both state and federal elections, but keeps dissent and polarization very much alive in the municipality itself. Within the framework of classic colonelism, the scepter of officialdom was awarded to that faction which could muster a local majority. The interests of the landed classes would be served by whatever faction held the local government. In the period following 1945, the rise of new parties and populist alliances in the major cities and their gradual penetration into the interior threatened the uncontested rule of such conservative parties as the UDN, the PSD, and the PR. This was recognized both at the national level — with many leaders proposing the creation of a truly conservative party through a union of party forces scattered until them — and at the local level.[42] After 1965, the institution of Arena (National Renovating Alliance) and the acceptance of "subtickets" gave the party both state and federal hegemony, while maintaining factional conflicts in the municipality without any major risks.

Certain institutional changes — particularly in relation to taxes — may well be causing gradual modifications in the style of local politics.[43] Many analyses of traditional political life emphasize the vicious circle of municipal poverty wherein colonelism finds fertile ground to flourish and which its own activities help to perpetuate. In the words on one of its creators, former minister Roberto de Oliveira Campos, the new tax legislation set forth in the Eighteenth Amendment to the Constitution of 1946, and subsequent measures, sought among other things to facilitate the rise, at the local level, of executive political vocation. It was hoped that in the long run the political stratum would be revamped from below. In the previous tax structure, the municipalities were left with a deficit of resources, since the legal provisions for their sharing in the taxes collected by both the state and the union were implemented either poorly or so slowly that the money's value would decrease as a result of inflation. One important source of revenue for municipal authorities, for instance, was a quota of the income tax, which the union assigned to each Brazilian municipality. However, in the battle among the states for the acquisition of resources from the federal system, new municipalities were created as a means to secure more money within state boundaries, a process which actually reduced the quota to be received by each municipality.

In the new system, two important transfers are channelled much more reliably to municipalities: a 20 percent share of the single stage sales tax (state) collected in the municipality, and such shares of the income tax and the excise tax (federal) as gathered in the Municipal Participation Fund. The first tax benefits the municipalities whose dynamic economy offers a greater number of taxable operations. The fund share is assigned on the basis of population size and therefore more beneficial to poorer municipalities, as long as they have a large number of inhabitants. In both cases the big difference is the practically automatic channelling of resources to municipalities, whereas previously, demonstrations of loyalty and political serfdom as well as the application of colonelistic abilities were required even to receive funds constitutionally stipulated for the municipalities. Considering that even in the larger and more urbanized districts there is a tendency to avoid making the building and urban property taxes a major source of revenue, given their unpopularity, the impact of those two transfers on the municipal budget is easy to assess. Even the poorest of mayors can rely on a definite income.

The question which naturally arises is: Are these changes facilitating the rise of new executives, the forerunners of new political elites born out of the municipal grass roots? In certain localities it seems to be so, while in others, at least for the time being, the new resources have led to instances of corruption and abuse. However, one thing is certain: the complaint over lack of resources has lost substance as an argument to justify lack of action. Can the municipalities subsist without state favors, and thus break one of the mainstays of colonelism? For the smaller towns, political favors still weigh heavily, even when the mediation process has been transferred to other groups, for instance from congressmen to technicians and bureaucrats of the state and federal administration. For the larger municipalities, the answer to this question can only be "yes" for the basic level of local needs. The more ambitious programs still depend on state and particularly federal financial investments, relatively free from political pressure, guided by technical criteria or national interest and security factors, as seen by the military or higher-level bureaucrats.

The realities of the new tax system have resulted in greater municipal autonomy in relation to routine services, in this sense decreasing the dependency of local elites. The higher government levels, particularly the federal administration, still retain important instruments to subjugate the local units as they grow and their needs increase. This, combined with the political and legal mechanisms which guarantee a broad majority, can ensure that the local lifestyle will retain the governmentalist emphasis so frequently mentioned by scholars concerned with municipal problems. And while the system may allow for the renewal of many local elites, this merely changes the trappings of the mechanisms which subject local political life to the political center.

The same applies on the larger scale of federal operations. The changes, if not the development itself, of state economies create greater needs for federal aid, which the union certainly knows how to use, in conjunction with other political and administrative instruments peculiar to the new political regime, in order to keep them well harnessed to the central government. The question could be raised whether reinforcing the center does not have its advantages. One could argue that the center has the means to act relatively free or regional pressures and pacts with the local dependent elites, and that, given the present concentration of political and financial resources at its disposal, it could embark on ambitious redistribution programs, especially at the territorial level.

A change seems to be taking shape, whereby the initial polarization of Brazilian development in the Southeast would lead, both through spontaneous mechanisms and intervention from the central government, to a filtering of benefits toward the periphery. A look at government intervention shows a number of policies which would confirm this impression: tax reform, creating state and municipal participation funds from shares of federal taxes (income tax and excise tax) and assigning them on the basis of redistributive criteria; the fiscal incentive policies designed to channel private investment to the Northeast (Articles 34/18); the housing, sanitation, and urban development financing policy whose differential interest rates are designed to favor the lower-income states and municipalities; and finally, the policy of direct federal investment in public works (highway and railway networks, for example).

The redistributive effectiveness of these mechanisms has been questioned. A recent study of federal transfers to the municipalities and states shows that:

> Following the tax reform, the lower-income states' dependency on transferred federal resources has increased to the point that in some states of the North and Northeast, this income amounts to more than 50 percent of the 1970 total. Since the bulk of income from federal transfers was considered to be earmarked for capital expenses and functions, there is a reduction, beginning in 1967, of state autonomy in terms of allocation of resources....The redistributive nature of these transfers from the State Participation Fund and the Special Fund is actually diluted in the sum total of transfers (Barbosa de Araujo, et al. 1973:116-18).

It is even more serious to find that the new single stage sales tax (ICM) inspired by the French *sur la valeur ajoutée* (on added value) has been regressively biased in its application to the Brazilian states. Since it is collected on each value-adding operation it naturally benefits those states (and municipalities) having the greatest number of taxable operations (or, in other words, where the added value is higher), as a result of an integrated productive structure. Thus consumer states lose to the producers in interstate transactions. All this seems to confirm the truth of Navarro de Brito's (1970:59) statement to the effect that the "new system of taxes...consolidated the union's financial hegemony and favors industrialized states."[44] The policy of fiscal incentives has also been accused of favoring the capital-intensive industrialization model, contributing relatively little to the growth of the internal regional market and promoting undertakings which benefit outside capital (from the more dynamic centers of the Southeast) and whose production is geared to markets other than those of the region.

The financing policy, particularly through the National Housing Bank funds, which at first sight appeared to benefit the poorer states and municipalities has in turn been questioned because despite its low interest rates for these states and municipalities, it still provides expensive money as compared to cheaper financial alternatives (international, for instance) or self-financing which is available to more prosperous areas. Aside from this, it has been claimed that the union dumps great responsibilities on the lesser units when, instead of embarking on works and services paid with its own funds, it forces those units to resort to financing, contending that such projects are actually of state or local scope.

Let us then review the recent transformations in center-periphery relations. Changes affecting central political institutions after 1964 impounded the residual political trump available to the municipal bosses and state elites for bargaining with the center, that is the votes needed for a majority in the legislature or, to a lesser extent, in presidential elections (or elections for state executives, if we are to limit the scope of this analysis to the states).[45] The legislature and political parties became accessories to the government machine, operating mainly as its legitimizers. The functions of colonels and state elites were concurrently vacated. As long as elections are an important method of choosing government officials, and while the legislature retains some decision-making power, traditional politics will continue to live, though somewhat modified to meet the demographic, economic, and social changes of the past thirty years. Up to 1964, the politics of colonelism, although declining, still had some weight in the power balance. Today this is only residually true.

The new regime attempted to encourage a renewal at the very core of traditional politics, as a by-product of the federation's new differential tax scheme. This renewal is naturally slow, confronted by opposing forces — such as the "subticket" mechanism — and, like the current diminished prestige of the conventional political career, may be limited to the local level. The municipal need for state and federal aid and the state need for federal resources, although redefined, are still considerable and growing. Tax reform benefits are not being homogeneously distributed among states and municipalities; instead, the distribution is uneven, following stratifying mechanisms. Therefore the periphery continues to depend on the center and, to a certain extent, is paradoxically weaker than before in the political bargaining, since it has little to offer in return.

The situation can be criticized from a liberal point of view in which greater autonomy for intermediate groups — including territorial units such as states and municipalities — is part of the basic ideology. But it could be positively interpreted if the center's domination over the periphery — once the latter was relatively and increasingly free from the colonels' mediation — implied a direct flow of benefits to localities without concessions to local elites granted at the expense of the population. Without this leakage, the center could conceivably act more generously in promoting development policies for peripheral areas, backed by their emerging elites.

This is not what happens. The inversion of concentration flows in the dynamic regions is seldom spontaneous, and when it is, the radial span of the trickle-down effects seems to be short, condensing the flow over the immediate vicinity of the center itself. Peripheral regions may benefit from the presence of some of their representatives in the decision-making bodies, who manage to extract a few benefits for their state, municipality, or even region as a whole. Still, it seems that more substantial interregional redistribution policies would demand closer ties among the supporting elites at the national level, further discussion and questioning of the union's policies in relation to the various regions, and a greater capacity to wrest concessions and support equalization policies through majority coalitions. The representative institutions' loss of power makes the range of influence of the supporting peripheral elites far too short and the possibility of establishing such coalitions infinitesimal. Instead of an interregional redistribution policy, consistently formulated and obtained through an open political process, there are isolated measures which operate in the same direction as what political scientists call a "distributive policy." In contrast to a redistributive policy, it is the sum total of many individualized topical decisions which fall into the "pork barrel" type, none of which is actually an expression of consistent government action. It is usually achieved through ad hoc negotiations between specific bureaucracies and localized constituencies.[46] While the distributive policy[47] has a minimum of compensating effects, the mechanisms of accumulation, concentration, and polarized development, are bound to act vigorously. We thus witness a renewal of an old tendency, this time as a result of a new type of political arrangement. If the latter helps to weaken and may even lead to the annihilation of the old parasitic elites, it has not been equally successful in stimulating the growth of new leaderships, potentially capable of promoting peripheral development.

NOTES

1. I am grateful to Fabio Wanderley Reis and Jorge Balán for their reading of a first version of this chapter which brought many valuable criticisms and suggestions I have tried to incorporate into the present version, hopefully with some success.
2. This problem pervades major interpretational works on Brazilian development. Two major trends can be identified. The first falls within the Marxist framework and its exponents are divided between those who claim that Brazilian history had no feudal past and no remnants in today's society (Prado Júnior 1967; Gunder Frank 1969), and those who argue for both the existence of a feudalist past and its remnants such as Passos Guimaraes (1964), among many others. The other school stresses the political problems of centralization as against decentralization. Faoro (1958) and Duarte (1966) are exponents of this position in the opposite camp.
3. The concept of feudalism implied here is taken from Hintze (1968).
4. See Lima (1945), as quoted in Leal (1948). See also Mercadante (1965).
5. For a discussion of this problem, see Leal (1948: passim). For an analysis of imperial policy, see Jaguaribe (1968).
6. See Schwartzman's (1970:29-33) important discussion of this problem. Also, Gomes Klein and Lima Júnior (1970). Available data show that the economic and social center and the government's political base in the country moved in opposite directions, with two states, Sao Paulo and Rio Grande do Sul that were to become the main supporters of the Republic, being clearly underrepresented in the Second Reign (Schwartzman 1970:31). Regarding the characteristics and causes of Sao Paulo's republicanism, see Pereira de Queiroz (1956-57).
7. The army's secondary role can be traced as far back as the First Regency, when the political elite chose to decentralize the military forces and created the National Guard as an auxiliary body to the army. It served to offset the army's influence, considered excessive in the events of the end of the First Reign.
8. As described by Carone (1971:13,16,18) the Republic finds the Sao Paulo elite well organized.
9. Although the 1891 Constitution enlarged suffrage, it excluded women, beggars, illiterates, paid soldiers (except students in the military schools of higher learning), and members of religious orders who were subject to obedience (Leal 1948:285).
10. Regarding the oligarchies, see Carone (1970:267-84). See also Carone (1972) and Mello Franco (1955). For a study of politics in Minas Gerais during the Old Republic and of the mechanisms involved in recruiting the political elite, see Fleischer (1971). Also, Rebelo Horta (1956). Concerning the situation in Ceará, see Della Cava (1970).
11. See also Carone (1971:175) and, along the same lines, Love (1971:96). See also Carone (1971:13, 16, 18).
12. The "governors' policy" was created by President Campos Sales, a representative of the Sao Paulo political establishment. Carone (1971:175-77)

describes the plea for national union made by Campos Sales and the mechanism used to implement the unifying policy. It consisted in controlling the "confirmation of power" through Congress. As a result of a change in its procedures, the chamber's president, who appointed the credentials committee, is no longer the senior congressman, but the presiding officer of the last legislative session, should he continue in office. His close relation with the president ensured the chamber of a minimum number of opposition members. As a complement to this change, the confirmation of winners in the state election was made to depend on the majority in the municipal chambers which, in keeping with the colonelist and oligarchy policy, were subject to the state establishment. Rebel congressmen were therefore barred.

13. Prospects were not quite compatible with the interests the dominant group could develop in the center itself, as a result of the state's attempt to assert its own interests through groups identified with it, such as the military. Furthermore, the pact between Sao Paulo's dynamic sectors and the oligarchies of less developed states led by the political establishment of Minas Gerais was somewhat precarious. In this connection, see Schwartzman's (1970) interpretation.

14. Regarding societies in the interior, in a very isolated region, see Lins (1952), among others.

15. The key study on this topic is Leal (1948). The term *colonelism* is derived from *colonel,* the title by which rural bosses, ranchers, and influential figures became generally known, as a carryover from the days of the National Guard.

16. Anthropologists have used the concept in studies of local societies being integrated into emerging national societies. An important paper along these lines is Silverman (1965). A thought-provoking essay is presented by Scott (1972). See also Duncan-Powell (1970) and Wolf (1956).

17. Harmonious relations between the federal and state governments were the rule throughout the Old Republic since the governors' policy made it difficult for opposition governments to survive the federal administration's hostility. Interventions were resorted to without much scruple, in order to bring down recalcitrant groups. See Leal (1948), Morazé (1954), Pereira de Queiroz (1956-57), Carone (1970), and Mello Franco (1955).

18. There were many such situations. Perhaps the most outstanding example is the Franco Rabelo uprising in Ceará State, led by Father Cíccro and Floro Bartolomeu. See Della Cava (1970) and Facó (1963).

19. Among others, see Leal (1948: passim), Carvalho (1946: passim), and Calvalcanti de Albuquerque e Villaça (1965), in addition to local-power studies published in several issues of *Revista Brasileira de Estudos Políticos,* the most important of which are included in this bibliography.

20. A similar phenomenon is described by Silverman (1965) in Central Italy. Pizzorno (1967) describes others in Sardinia.

21. The classic study of vendettas in Brazil is Costa Pinto (1949). See also Souza (1968).

22. See Leal (1948: passim). The available literature on local power in Brazil is plentiful. In a recent review of the material, Murilo Carvalho (1968) points

out its methological and theoretical flaws. Lamounier (1965) offers another critical review, with an emphasis on the more positive contributions. The author of this chapter has made extensive use of Lamounier's analysis. Some of the more representative studies are included in the bibliography.

23. It is extremely important for the local boss to control appointments of local police authorities, rural tax collectors, and public prosecutors. Considering that it is unlikely for these officials to be entirely neutral to local rivalry and that considerable leeway is involved in law enforcement, property assessment, etc., it is safer for the boss to have such persons on his side. Police authorities are often openly partial and persecute the "opposition." As a result, the opposition leader seeks justification to side with the government. For the ethics involved in this see Leal (1948:25) as quoted in Lamounier (1967).

24. The same source, Oracy Nogueira, quoted in Brandao Lopes (1967:29), tells us of a landowner who provided liquor for his employees at night to keep them from going to the nearby city. In Stein (1957:267) we found remarks concerning practices which were common after the abolition of slavery, to keep preabolition patterns preventing workers from contact with outside plantation services, opening their own stores to sell food, clothing, and assorted goods to plantation workers. Concerning practices to prevent contact between the voters and rival candidates on election day, see Carvalho (1958), Blondel (1957), and Sampaio (1960).

25. We refer to the fascinating research study conducted by Brandao Lopes (1967) in two cities of Minas Gerais during the late 1950s. Instead of interpreting dependency relations as a cultural-psychological phenomenon, it seems to us more appropriate to look first for structural variables which could account for them. Hutchinson (1966) takes a different approach.

26. See Rokkan (1966:249-50) for some interpretations and hypotheses based on the Norwegian data. The turnout in peripheral areas is low not only because it takes more effort from the average resident to cast his vote, but also because local political leaders, being less directly tied in with provincial and national party organizations, will only rarely assign a high marginal value to the last mobilized vote. Blondel (1957:90-95) studies electoral abstention in the state of Paraiba and offers interesting elements to illustrate the role of rural bosses in mobilizing and demobilizing the population.

27. See Facó (1963) and Souza (1968), from whom we draw much of the inspiration for this section. See also Lamounier (1968).

28. This interpretation finds ample support in the literature, beginning with Euclides da Cunha's (1969) classic Os sertoes. See Vinhas de Queiroz (1966), Facó (1963), and Pereira de Queiroz (1956-57).

29. The background elements of the Contestado movement include the state of war to which the population had become accustomed through border disputes between Santa Catarina and Paraná, the region where the movement erupted. Many of the future "fanatics" became familiar with the use of weapons at that time (Vinhas de Queiroz 1966).

30. Concerning the incidents which took place in Cariri Valley, which are quite

enlightening in relation to the workings of the First Republic in the peripheral regions, see Facó (1953) and Della Cava (1970).

31. I am grateful to Jorge Balán for having called my attention to this function of colonelist domination.

32. Singer (1971) proposes hypotheses in this area.

33. Other important works which elaborate on different aspects of this problem are by Carvalho (1946), Donald (1959), Sherwood (1967), and Lordello (1970).

34. See Deutsch (1966) and Deutsch et al. (1957). Also the following: Davis (1956), Livingston (1952), Riker (1964), Birch (1966), Wildavsky (1967), and Navarro de Brito (1964).

35. The problems involved in the center's exploitation of the periphery are acknowledged in studies of regional development differences, in studies on urban hierarchies, especially in relation to the "primacy" phenomenon, and in studies of political and administrative centralization problems, when approached not merely from the local but also from the sociological and political viewpoints. See the following: Friedman and Alonso (1969), Linsky (1969), Mehta (1969), Berry (1971), Browning (1970), and Riggs (1959-60).

36. See references in note 28.

37. The political center does not respond only to the will of national groups and classes, but is also linked in some important sectors to the interests of foreign capital which in the Old Republic operated through private, particularly British groups. In principle, there are no basic disagreements between these interests and those of the elites who control the political machine. In the political centralization produced by the governors' policy, the national elites respond to basic survival imperatives which include guaranteeing a political climate favorable to foreign loans. Foreign interests, in turn, seek the guarantee of a reliable political center in order to proceed with their operations. See Carone (1970:127-41) and Love (1971:128-29).

38. Within the scheme adopted in this chapter, we are proposing a two-fold view of Sao Paulo's situation: this is a peripheral region, controlled by "supporting" groups which, as a result of political contingencies, are forced to side with the dependent central elites. The latter are aligned with the backward states or may even represent them. At the same time, the region is clearly part of that center and responsible for a substantial share of its action.

39. See Carone (1970: 27-51) for a discussion of the coffee policy during the First Republic.

40. This situation is typical of those arising in ideological discourse, and Sao Paulo had a counterclaim to complaints from other states that they were being exploited by federal mechanisms. Dynamic regions and cities are usually viewed by stagnant regions and rural areas as parasitical, exploiters of their resources, etc. The dynamic regions pay back in kind. In Brazil, the Sao Paulo arguments to the effect that there was one locomotive towing twenty empty box cars illustrates this point. The ideological discourse is not built in a vacuum, and it is true that there were exploitation processes at work, although in a two-way fashion. In the final balance, considering the resulting economic development, the flow seems to be more favorable to the dynamic

regions and the center's political mediation in attaining this result is far from negligible. One of the best analyses of the Northeast's situation in the context of federalist policy, although not specifically centered on this problem, is Hirschman's (1965). See also Navarro de Brito's (1964) excellent study.

41. Political changes which took place in the Brazilian interior within the sequence of structural transformations, have been reviewed by this author (Cintra 1971: 18-23). We discuss the colonels' loss of exclusivity in mediation, as well as the dispensability of mediation itself. In the first case, the importance of the colonels' electoral role declined as a result of population concentration in the cities, improvement of means of transportation, and direct access to the voters by the candidates. This has been shown in studies by Silva (1960), Nogueira (1962), and Blondel (1957), among others. These studies also mention the rise of leaders whose power was not primarily based on land ownership. As a result, ranchers lost their exclusivity in channeling state and federal benefits to the area. There were also demands implied by the "scale" (Wilson and Wilson 1945) in relation to the number of voters which one political leader could control within a clientelistic system characterized by the exchange of favors. This encouraged the rise of competitors. Orlando de Carvalho (1958) and Nelson Sampaio (1960) have found evidence of a relation between the size of the electorate and the existence of one-, two-, or multiparty systems in the locality. According to their observations, should the city have more than 9,000 voters, the existence of many parties as well as competing leaders is almost certain. See also Soares and Noronha (1960). It should not be assumed that the changes are necessarily monotonic or nonregressive. Industries in smaller areas with few other job options can maintain workers under conditions which are not unlike those of rural domains (Brandao Lopes 1967). Traditional political elites can adapt to growth-related changes in the cities under their rule, particularly if they have any influence over appointments to the local bureaucracy. An important case study in this connection was done by Murilo Carvalho (1966). Concerning the dispensability of mediation, we placed special emphasis on changes in tax legislation and in the political regime, which are discussed further on in the chapter.

42. The growth of the PTB was noticed by José Abílio, a famous PSD colonel of Pernambuco State who admonished party leader Agamenon Magalhaes in a letter in this connection. See Cavalcanti de Albuquerque e Villaça (1965: 84).

43. See Cintra (1971) for a discussion of various hypotheses concerning the impact of taxes on local power.

44. See Barbosa de Araújo et al. (1973: 116-18).

45. See Navarro de Brito (1970: 59, 1964), whose work is indispensable to a discussion of Brazilian federalism.

46. The characteristics of the Brazilian electoral system made presidential elections — which encompass the entire country — relatively more sensitive to urban centers. In congressional elections, where the area encompassed is the state, the poorer and more rural states were given a greater weight in the electoral coefficient.

47. See Lowi (1964) for the concept of distributive policy used here.

REFERENCES

Azevedo, Luiz Octávio Viotti. 1959. "Evoluçao dos partidos políticos no município de Sao Joao Evangelista." *Revista Brasileira de Estudos Políticos* (July): 129-30.

Barbosa de Araújo, Aloisio; Taques Horta, Maria Helena; and Monteiro Considera, Cláudio. 1973. *Transferência de impostos aos estados e municípios.* Rio de Janeiro: IPEA, no. 3.

Barbosa, Júlio. 1963. "Análise sociológica das eleiçoes de 1962 em Minas Gerais." *Revista Brasileira de Ciências Sociais* 3 (no. 3).

Bendix, Reinhard. 1964. *Nation-Building and Citizenship.* New York: John Wiley.

Berry, Brian J.L. 1971. "City Size and Economic Development: Conceptual Synthesis and Policy Problems, with Special Reference to South and Southeast Asia." In Jakobson and Prakash (eds.), *Urbanization and National Development.* Beverly Hills: Sage.

Birch, Anthony H. 1966. "Approaches to the Study of Federalism." *Political Studies* 14 (no. 1).

Blondel, Jean. 1957. *As condiçoes da vida política no Estado da Paraíba.* Rio de Janeiro: Fundaçao Getúlio Vargas.

Brandao Lopes, Juarez R. 1966. "Some Basic Developments in Brazilian Politics and Society." In Elik N. Baklanoff (ed.), *New perspectives of Brazil.* Nashville: Vanderbilt University Press.

_____. 1967. *A crise do Brasil arcaico.* Sao Paulo: Difusora Europeia do Livro.

Breese, Gerald (ed.). 1969. *The City in Newly Developing Countries.* Englewood Cliffs, N.J.: Prentice-Hall.

Browning, Harley L. 1970. "Primacy Variation in Latin America during the Twentieth Century." Mimeographed.

Carone, Edgar. 1969. *A Primeira República.* Sao Paulo: Difusao Européia do Livro.

_____. 1970. *A República Velha: instituiçoes e classes sociais.* Sao Paulo: Difusao Européia do Livro.

_____. 1971. *A República Velha: Evoluçao política.* Sao Paulo: Difusao Européia do Livro.

_____. 1972. "Oligarquias: definiçao e bibliografia." *Revista de Administraçao de Empresas* 12 (January-March).

Carvalho, José Murilo. 1966. "Barbacena: a família, a política e uma hipótese." *Revista Brasileira de Estudos Políticos* (January): 153-93.

_____. 1968. "Estudos de poder local no Brasil." *Revista Brasileira de Estudos Políticos* (no. 25).

Carvalho, Orlando. 1958. *Ensaios de sociologia eleitoral.* Belo Horizonte: Revista Brasileira de Estudos Políticos.

Cava, Ralph Della. 1970. *Miracle at Joaseiro.* New York: Columbia University Press.

Cavalcanti de Albuquerque, Roberto; and Vilaça, Marcos Vinicius. 1965. *Coronel, Coronéis.* Rio de Janeiro: Tempo Brasileiro.

Cintra, Antonio Octávio. 1971. "A integraçao do processo político do Brasil: algumas hipóteses inspiradas na literatura." *Revista de Administraçao Pública* 5 (July-December).

Costa Pinto, L.A. 1949. *Lutas de família no Brasil.* Sao Paulo: Cia. Editora Nacional.

Cruz, Levi. 1959. "Funçoes do comportamento político numa comunidade do Sao Francisco." *Revista Brasileira de Estudos Políticos* (January): 129-30.

Cunha, Euclides da. 1969. *Os sertoes.* Rio de Janeiro: Ediçoes de Ouro.

Davis, Rufus. 1956. "The Federal Principle Reconsidered." *Australian Journal of Politics and History* 1 (May).

Deutsch, Karl. 1957. *Political Community and the North Atlantic Area.* Princeton: Princeton University Press.

_____. 1966. *Nationalism and Social Communication.* Cambridge, Mass.: MIT Press.

Donald, Carr L. 1959. "The Politics of Local Government Finance in Brazil." *Inter-American Economic Affairs* 13 (no. 1).

Duarte, Nestor. 1966. *A ordem privada e a organizaçao política nacional.* Sao Paulo: Cia. Editora Nacional.

Duncan-Powell, John. "Peasant Society and Clientelist Politics." *American Political Science Review* 64 (June).

Eisenstadt, S.N. 1963. *The Political Systems of Empires.* New York: Free Press.

_____. 1968. "Estado, sociedade, formaçao de centros: alguns problemas relacionados com o desenvolvimento da sociologia política." *Dados* (no. 4).

Facó, Ruy. 1963. *Cangaceiros e fanáticos.* Rio de Janeiro: Civilizaçao Brasileira.

Faoro, Raimundo. 1958. *Os donos do poder.* Porto Alegre: Editora Globo.

Fleischer, David V. 1971. *O recrutamento político em Minas 1890-1918.* Belo Horizonte: Revista Brasileira de Estudos Políticos.

Friedmann, John; and Alonso, William. 1969. *Regional Development and Planning.* Cambridge, Mass.: MIT Press.

Gomes, Klein; and Lima Júnior, Olavo Brasil de. 1970. "Atores políticos do Império." *Dados* (no. 7).

Graham, Douglas H.; and Buarque de Hollanda Filho, Sergio. 1971. "Migration, Regional and Urban Growth and Development in Brazil: A Selective Analysis of the Historical Record, 1872-1970." Sao Paulo: IPE, USP, mimeographed.

Guimaraes, Carlos Eloy de Carvalho. 1956. "A vida política e administrativa de Dores do Indaiá." *Revista Brasileira de Estudos Políticos* (December): 170-79.

Gunder Frank, André. 1969. *Latin America: Underdevelopment or Revolution?* New York: Monthly Review Press.

Harris, Marvin. 1956. *Town and Country in Brazil.* New York: Columbia University Press.

Hintze, Otto. 1968. *Historia de las formas políticas.* Madrid: revista de Occidente.

Hirschman, Albert O. 1965. *Política economica na América Latina.* Rio de Janeiro: Editôra Fundo de Cultura.

Hobsbawm, Eric. 1965. *Primitive Rebels.* New York: W.W. Norton.

Hutchinson, Bertram. 1966. "The Patron-Dependent Relationship in Brazil: A Preliminary Examination." *Sociologia Ruralis* 6 (no. 1).

Jaguaribe, Hélio. 1968. *Economic and Political Development.* Cambridge, Mass.: Harvard University Press.

Jakobson, Leo; and Ved Prakash. 1971. *Urbanization and National Development.* Beverly Hills: Sage.

Lamare, Judith. 1968. "Political Mobilization: A Study of Minas Gerais, Brazil." University of California at Los Angeles, mimeographed.

Lamounier, Bolivar. 1965. "Violence and Economic Development: Toward a Theory of Political Change in Brazilian Communities." University of California at Los Angeles, mimeographed.

_____. 1968. "Local Politics and Structure in Brazil." University of California at Los Angeles, mimeographed.

La Palombara, J.; and Weiner, Myron. 1966. *Political Parties and Political Development.* Princeton: Princeton University Press.

Leal, Victor Nunes. 1948. *Coronelismo, enxada e voto.* Rio de Janeiro: Livraria Forense.

Lima, Hermes. 1945. *Notas à vida brasileira.* Sao Paulo.

Lins, Wilson. 1962. *O médio Sao Francisco.* Salvador: Livraria Progresso.

Linsky, Arnold S. 1969. "Some Generalizations Concerning Primate Cities." In Gerald Breese (ed.), *The City in Newly Developing Countries.* Englewood Cliffs, N.J.: Prentice Hall.

Livingston, William S. 1952. "A Note on the Nature of Federalism." *Political Science Quarterly* 67 (March).

Lordello de Mello, Diogo, 1971. *O município na organizaçao nacional.* Rio de Janeiro: IBAM.

Love, Joseph L. 1971. *Rio Grande do Sul and Brazilian Regionalism, 1882-1930.* Stanford, Calif.: Stanford University Press.

Lowi, Theodore J. 1974. "American Business, Public Policy, Case Studies, and Political Theory." *World Politics* 16 (July).

Mehta, Surinder K. 1969. "Some Demographic and Economic Correlates of Primate Cities: A Case for Revaluation." In Gerald Breese (ed.), *The City in Newly Developing Countries.* Englewood Cliffs, N.J.: Prentice-Hall.

Mello Franco, Afonso Arinos de. 1955. *Um estadista da República,* 3 vols. Rio de Janeiro: J. Olympio.

Mercandante, Paulo, 1965. *A consciência conservadora no Brasil.* Rio de Janeiro: Saga.

Morazé, Charles. 1954. *Les Trois Ages du Brésil.* Paris: Armand Colin.

Montenegro, Abelardo F. 1965. *História dos partidos políticos cearenses.* Fortaleza, Ceará.

Moore, Barrington. 1967. *Social Origins of Dictatorship and Democracy.* Boston: Beacon Press.

Navarro de Brito, Luiz. 1964. "Um estudo sobre a federaçao brasileira." *Revista de Direito Público e Ciência Política* 7 (September-December).

_____. 1970. "O federalismo na Constituiçao de 1967." *Revista Brasileira de Estudos Políticos* (no. 28, January).

Nogueira, Oracy. 1962. *Família e comunidade.* Rio de Janeiro: Centro Brasileiro de Pesquisas Educacionais.

Oliveira Vianna, F.J. 1955. *Instituiçoes políticas brasileiras,* 2 vols. Rio de Janeiro: José Olympio.

Palmeira, Moacir. 1966. "Nordeste: mudanças políticas no século XX." *Cadernos Brasileiros,* year 8 (September-October).

Passos Guimaraes, Alberto. 1964. *Quatro séculos de latifúndio.* Sao Paulo: Editora Fulgor.

Pereira de Queiroz, Maria Isaura. 1956-57. "O mandonismo local na vida política brasileira." *Anhembi* 24-26.

Pizzorno, Alessandro. 1967. "Rapporto sulla situazione política e sociale." Milan, mimeographed.

Prado Júnior, Caio. 1967. *A Revoluçao Brasileira.* Sao Paulo: Ed. Brasiliense.

Rebelo Horta, Cid. 1956. "Famílias governamentais em Minas Gerais." In *Segundo Seminário de Estudos Mineiros.* Belo Horizonte: Universidade Federal de Minas Gerais.

Riggs, Fred. 1958-60. "Circular Causation in Development." *Economic Development and Cultural Change* 8.

Ricker, William. 1964. *Federalism: Origin, Operation, Significance.* Boston: Little, Brown.

Rokkan, Stein. 1966. "Electoral Moblization, Party Competition, and National Integration." In La Palombara and Weiner (eds.), *Political Parties and Political Development.* Princeton: Princeton University Press.

Sampaio, Nelson. 1960. *O diálogo democrático na Bahia.* Belo Horizonte: Revista Brasileira de Estudos Políticos.

Santos, Edilson Portella. 1961. "Evoluçao da vida política no Município de Picos, Piauí." *Revista Brasileira de Estudos Políticos.*

Schwartzman, Simon. 1970. "Representaçao e cooptaçao política no Brasil." *Dados* (no. 7): 9-41.

Scott, James C. 1972. "Patron-Client Politics and Political Change in Southeast Asia." *American Political Science Review* 66 (March).

Sherwood, Frank P. 1967. *Institutionalizing the Grass Roots in Brazil.* San Francisco: Chandler.

Silva, Luís. 1957. "Cachoeira do Campo: vila das rivalidades." *Revista Brasileira de Estudos Políticos:* 132-47.

———. 1960. "Implicaçoes políticas do desenvolvimento industrial em Barroso." *Revista Brasileira de Estudos Políticos:* 234-51.

Silverman, Sydel F. 1965. "Patronage and Community-Nation Relationship in Central Italy." *Ethnology* 4.

Singer, Paul. 1971. "Urbanizaçao e desenvolvimento: o caso de Sao Paulo." Mimeographed.

Soares, Gláucio A. D.; and A. Noronha. 1960. "Urbanizaçao e dispersao eleitoral." *Revista de Direito Público e Ciência Política* 3 (no. 2).

Souza, Amaury. 1968. "The 'Cangaço' and the Politics of Violence in Northeast Brazil." MIT, mimeographed.

Stein, Stanley. 1957. *Vassouras: A Brazilian Coffee County, 1850-1900.* Cambridge, Mass.: Harvard University Press.

Vinhas de Queiroz, Mauricio. 1960. *Messianismo e conflito social: a guerra sertaneja do contestado, 1912-1916.* Rio de Janeiro: Civilização Brasileira.

Wildavsky, Aaron. 1967. *American Federalism in Perspective.* Boston: Little, Brown.

Wilson, Monica; and Wilson, Godfrey. 1945. *The Analysis of Social Change.* Cambridge, Mass.: Cambridge University Press.

Wolf, Eric R. 1956. "Aspects of Group Relations in a Complex Society: Mexico." *American Anthropologist* 58 (no. 6).

Social Marginality or Class Relations in the City of Sao Paulo?

Manoel Tosta Berlinck
Daniel J. Hogan

One aspect which has been practically ignored by proponents of the concept of social marginality concerns the institutional arrangements guaranteeing the existence of that social system.[1] To propose the existence of a marginal segment of the population is either to suggest a circumstantial and therefore passing phenomenon with no structural significance, or to assume its persistence and therefore its structural nature. In the latter case, it is necessary to identify both the social mechanisms which guarantee its survival and the institutional arrangements which block or hinder its transformation and consequently the alteration of the social structure which includes it.

Only a few studies dealing with these questions are available (Machado da Silva 1969). However, from the outset, they pose a theoretical paradox which leads us to suspect even the approach to the subject. The concept of marginality implies a structural dualism, the notion that a given structure holds both an integrated and a marginal segment, whereas the concept of structure presupposes the idea of wholeness (Berlinck 1974). In pointing out this paradox, one runs the risk of "throwing the baby out with the bath water." It could be that the marginality phenomenon constitutes a unique structural arrangement and therefore requires an analysis suited to its specific nature (Kowarick 1974). If this were to have some empirical basis, it would be necessary to show that there is an institutionalized mechanism, also unique, which guarantees this segment's adaptation within a broader social structure. As we see it, the adaptation problem refers to the development of a relatively repetitive and standardized interaction network which allows

167

the population to obtain the means required to satisfy its needs and desires from the system in which it lives.

From the viewpoint of social marginality, the problem of adaptation refers to those peculiar mechanisms which that segment develops to satisfy its needs and desires. Those who propose the existence of marginality also propose the existence of adaptive mechanisms which are qualitatively different from those adopted by the nonmarginal or integrated population. Whether this is true, or whether the adaptive mechanisms used by the marginal sector hardly differ from those used by the population's upper strata, remains to be seen.

Adaptation to the Urban Milieu

From the adaptation viewpoint, the urban milieu is a system which offers an availability of resources, obtainable as long as a network of organized interaction allows access to them. The availability of resources within a given system is limited. Both the social inequalities and the interaction network itself (because it is organized) guarantee an unequal distribution of such resources. In spite of these difficulties, resources do exist and any given population will always seek to satisfy its needs and desires. A close look at the lower-income strata in the city of Sao Paulo shows that they consist almost entirely of recently arrived rural migrants (Berlinck 1974). This poses an added difficulty to the problem of adaptation, insofar as one admits these migrants to be, by definition, a contingent which leaves one system (rural) and heads for another (urban) (Pastore 1971).

A better understanding of this added difficulty requires the realization that two systems are different to the extent that their structures differ (Berlinck 1968). As concerns social systems, different structures imply different cultures (Williams 1961). In order to adapt, the migrant must resocialize or acquire a new symbolic stock which will allow him an adequate behavior within the new structure. Distinctive social systems are not entirely different. In this case, the national migrants' original and target systems are quite similar. Thus theoretically, an adult from Rio de Janeiro or Belo Horizonte who migrates to Sao Paulo should have fewer adaptation problems than a migrant from Quixadá or Xique-Xique, since in terms of complexity the former are closer to the target system than the latter.[2]

The resocialization process demanded by migration may be ruled by mechanisms considerably different from those involved in socialization, insofar as in the former case the individual has already acquired a life experience which, depending on the circumstances, may facilitate or hinder his learning of a new culture. Therefore, as a rule, the more complex the individual's previous life experience, the more easily he learns to live in new situations. Another important factor which facilitates this process involves an interaction network based on cooperation and mutual assistance, including the transmission of information concerning the new system's resources. The problem posed in this chapter is to discover the mechanisms developed and used by migrant and native populations to become acquainted with the resources available in a city like Sao Paulo.

The Research Study

The data are the result of a research study conducted between 1969 and 1972 and can be broken down into three major stages.[3] The first stage involved an inspection of secondary data and bibliography concerning Sao Paulo, the purpose of which was to familiarize the authors with the city's history and chief socioeconomic characteristics. In the second stage, a sampling survey was taken of 1,015 Brazilian-born families living in the municipality of Sao Paulo during the second semester of 1970. In the third stage, during the second semester of 1971, thirty anthropological interviews were conducted with lower-class men and women living in Sao Paulo.

The sampling survey was performed by means of interviews structured according to a questionnaire developed by the authors and pretested twice in the city. The interviews were conducted by university students especially trained for the task. The sample was drawn up as follows: fourteen areas (described in Table 6.1) were chosen from the municipality of Sao Paulo which, given their ecological characteristics, would be representative of the city's stratification system. The limits of these areas followed specifications from the General Scale Plan of the Sao Paulo Municipal Hall (Planta Genérica de Valores da Prefeitura do Município de Sao Paulo), a map which is detailed to the city block level. Then, a 10 percent random sample of blocks in each area was taken, excluding apartments in the Santa Cecília, tenements, and slums (see Table 6.1), and a quota of three to five interviews was filled in each city block. As regards the Santa Cecília apartments, each building was treated as one residence and therefore a single interview was taken per building. Selection of tenements and slums was made on the basis of certain characteristics (described in Table 6.1), and the interviews were performed according to a quota system. The interviews, which took an average of one and a half to two hours each, were conducted with the man of the house who had to be a native Brazilian, living with a native Brazilian woman and having at least one child living in the same house.

The sample is not representative in the statistical sense. Nevertheless, it will be possible to appraise its representativeness indirectly when the 1970

TABLE 6.1

Areas of the Municipality of Sao Paulo Selected for the Survey, Their Characteristics, and Number of Interviews Performed

Areas	Characteristics	Interviews N	%
Jardim Europa and Jardim América	Elite	(82)	8.1
Brooklin	"New middle class" comprising professionals whose occupations were born of the industrialization which followed World War II	(97)	9.6
Vila Mariana	"Old middle class" comprising professionals whose occupations (e.g. shop keepers, bureaucrats, etc.) existed prior to World War II	(100)	9.9
Santa Cecília	Middle class living in apartments near the city center	(93)	9.2
Vila Nova Cachoeirinha	Lower class, far from an industrial area and on the borderline between the urban and rural zones	(68)	6.7
Braz R. Catumbi	Lower class close to a rather old industrial area	(102)	10.0
Santo Amaro	Lower class, close to a recently developed industrial area	(77)	7.6
Vila Anglo-Brasileira	Lower class; a tenement of sorts adjacent to middle-class areas	(70)	6.9
Santa Cecília, Bela Vista and Consolação	Tenements	(92)	9.1
Favela de Vila Prudente	A large organized slum housing about 8,000 persons	(70)	6.9
Vila Prudente	Small slum close to an industrial area	(12)	1.2
Tatuapé	Small slum close to an industrial area	(78)	7.7
Brooklin Novo	Small slum, far from an industrial area and close to a middle-class housing area	(23)	2.8
Vila Olimpia	Small slum far from an industrial area and close to a lower-class housing area	(46)	4.5

census results are published. For the time being, a check has been provided by a comparison with data from the National Household Sampling Research (PNAD), a quarterly study which covers seven socioeconomic regions in the country. The following two tables contain PNAD data for the first quarter of 1970 and refer to the urban section of Region 2, which is the state of Sao Paulo.

Up to the age of forty-four, the percentage of literate males is lower for the survey sample than for the PNAD. For ages forty-five and over, the survey findings are quite similar to those of the PNAD. The only major discrepancy found in Table 6.3 concerns the lack of representation in

TABLE 6.2

Percentage of Literate Male Population by Age According to PNAD (National Household Sampling Research) and to the Survey

Idade	Percentage of literate males	
	PNAD	Survey
20 - 24	98.2	66.7
24 - 34	95.8	77.6
35 - 44	92.4	84.5
45 - 54	85.0	87.1
55 - 64	84.9	80.9
65 and over	74.4	77.8

Source: Anuário Estatístico do Brasil (Brazilian Statistical

Yearbook), 1970 and Berlinck/Hogan Sampling Survey

the twenty to twenty-four age group. This was due to the demands of our sample, since the young couples, in general, had no children as yet.

The anthropological interviews were made in an attempt to collect information regarding the life of members of the lower class (both men and women) in order to familiarize the authors with a lifestyle which is not their own, provide illustrations for arguments, and serve as inspiration for theoretical developments. These interviews were conducted by two specialists and were not subject to any sampling criterion.[4] The authors believe, nevertheless, that the interviews contain empirical material of high sociological relevance and they will therefore be used here as illustrations for theoretical arguments.

Needs and Adaptation in Sao Paulo

Prior to a study of adaptive mechanisms, it is necessary to describe the needs considered most pressing by the city's poorer population. The anthropological interviews revealed that residence, "legalization," employment, and food are four needs considered pressing by members of Sao Paulo's lower-income strata. Their order of priority may be different from the above. Still, those needs were always mentioned in both the anthropological interviews and those of the sampling survey which included 1,015 families (Berlinck 1974).

TABLE 6.3
Age Distribution of Male Population According to PNAD and to the Survey

Idade	PNAD		Survey	
	%	(N)	%	(N)
Under 20			0.2	(2)
20 - 24	17.0	(1000)	5.0	(51)
25 - 29	12.6	(551)	11.5	(117)
30 - 34	12.7	(406)	13.1	(133)
35 - 39	11.2	(412)	18.1	(184)
40 - 44	11.3	(361)	15.5	(157)
45 - 49	9.7	(364)	11.5	(117)
50 - 54	7.2	(314)	10.7	(108)
55 - 59	6.0	(233)	6.5	(66)
60 - 64	5.1	(193)	4.3	(44)
65 and over	7.4	(164)	3.6	(36)
Total	100.0	(3236)	100.0	(1015)

Source: Anuário Estatístico do Brasil (Brazilian Statistical

Yearbook), 1970 and Berlinck/Hogan Sampling Survey

Residence refers to the place where an individual finds shelter. In addition, a person's residence has a more complex social meaning: it refers to the place where that person can be found if someone wants to see him. In this sense, to have a fixed and definite residence is one of the system's demands; an individual without a residential address runs a high risk of being jailed, and/or not finding employment, in addition to not getting credit.

The need for legalization refers to documents which attribute to the individual a civil responsibility. Large numbers of lower-class individuals migrate to Sao Paulo without any documents (not even a birth certificate). This situation makes their survival extremely difficult in a city where most social relations are ruled by contractual norms. Without documents, the migrant encounters enormous difficulties in renting or even buying a place to live, in finding a job, buying on credit, and even moving freely around the city, since the police will pick up anyone who cannot produce an identification document, particularly a work card, to prove that he is actually employed. For the population's lower strata, having a work card stamped by the firm where the person is employed is more important than having an identification card, since the former prevents arrest for vagrancy and makes it easier to obtain a new job.

Sebastiao Leandro, for example, was born in Ibanopeba, near Boa Vista, State of Pernambuco. In 1970, he came to Sao Paulo with his wife and three children. When they arrived, they went to live to his father-in-law's house. But Sebastiao Leandro could not get a job because he had no documents: since he had not registered for military service, he did not have a reservist's card and could not get work papers. He only had a marriage license and it took him four months to obtain the documents needed to survive in the city. Throughout this time, he simply picked up what odd jobs he could. Once he had documents, it was easy to arrange employment. Benedito Laurindo spent one year without a job after he arrived in Sao Paulo because he did not have documents. During that year, he too picked up odd jobs and lived with his father-in-law in Mauá.

The need for employment is linked to the person's survival within the system; but it is also related to civil guarantees: an unemployed individual may be taken for a bum. Aside form all else, the lack of a job hampers the establishment of a series of contracts which call for references.

The need for food refers to the individual's physical survival itself and is intimately linked to employment. Notice, however, that the need for food involves some social dimensions: where to buy inexpensive food; where to obtain credit to buy food; where to eat when one has neither money nor credit. Solutions to these problems can only be drawn from the interaction network to which the individual belongs.

These needs and desires disclose structural differences between the original and target system. The interaction standards which apply in the rural milieu, ruled by particularizing and difuse norms, dispense with certain resources that the more universal and specific norms prevailing in the urban setting cannot ignore. In addition, social controls differ from one system to the other and, as a result, require different elements. Such differences are historically determined and may vary in time and space. Consequently, as capitalist expansion modernizes the Brazilian rural milieu, interaction standards prevailing there will gradually be guided by norms similar to those which predominate in the urban system.

In any case, the satisfaction of all these pressing needs, which exist owing to structural differences and a surface as a result of migration, depends on three basic factors: (1) the material resources available to the individuals; (2) the latter's information stock on resources existing in the city and the ways to tap them; and (3) their access to different communication channels through which information can be acquired as to both the available resources and the means of obtaining them.

The greater the volume of material resources available, the easier it is to satisfy needs and desires. In other words, the higher the stratum to which a person belongs, the greater the possibility of satisfying his needs and desires, regardless of all other factors, except for his information stock in relation to the resources existing in the city. One should not forget, however, that within certain limits, information can be acquired.

In the case of members of the lower strata, the income available is quite small, although this varies substantially, as we will see further on. For this reason, the other factors become considerably important and therefore warrant analysis. Marginal status is not merely characterized by a lack of material resources. One of the nonmaterial factors which seems to affect access to resources in the city is the individual's location within the urban area. Leeds (1969), for instance, suggests that different types of slums (defined in terms of location, size, and history), are not only likely to house populations with different characteristics, but also to affect the process of urban adaptation. Finally, a third set of factors which is bound to affect urban adaptation is the individual's information stock. In his analysis of the culture of poverty, Oscar Lewis (1965, 1966) suggests that one of its characteristics is its cultural poverty. Members of the culture of poverty have an exceedingly restricted symbolic stock which is used in the communication process both among members of this culture and between them and the surrounding world.

In terms of adaptation, the poverty of this culture creates a problem, in the first place, to the extent that it implies a relatively simplistic life experience and this affects resocialization negatively. It also leads to an isolation which hinders adaptation in that it prevents the transmission of information. Scholars have contended for some time, both in theoretical and empirical terms, that participation in various groups and contact with different channels facilitate the individual's adaptation to new situations, insofar as they allow for cooperation and increase the person's symbolic stock, providing a broader range of alternative actions for a given situation (Durkheim 1964). Hawley (1966) suggests that two or more individuals who join forces through a certain type of cooperative behavior can achieve more in the same period than if they work separately. As individuals cooperate with one another, an organization begins to develop. At the same time, an increasingly broader sphere comes within reach of the organization which thereby maximizes its members' access to available resources. A study conducted by Suttles (1968) in Chicago confirms Hawley's theoretical observations. Suttles studied the situation of Italians and Blacks who, in addition to showing similar levels of poverty, also lived in adjacent areas of the city. His observations disclosed that Italians obtained such things as education, medical assistance, employment, housing, and so on, more easily than Blacks. Suttles attributed this differential facility to a difference in the degree to which each of these two segments of Chicago's population participated in voluntary associations. While the Italians included in the study often took part in get-togethers with relatives (even rather distant ones), religious clubs, and had an intense pattern of primary interaction with different neighborhood shopkeepers, the Blacks were highly isolated, their participation confined to joining street gangs, and even this only in some cases. This is why, Suttles concludes, although both groups are subject to discrimination in American society, Italians manage to satisfy their needs and desires more easily (also discrimination against them is less intense).

Income

For the lower-class population of the city of Sao Paulo, income derives from work. It is subject to a significant degree of variability. According to our sampling survey, in 1970 the average monthly income from the chief occupation of unskilled manual laborers was Cr$275.13 (with a standard deviation of Cr$206.56), while the average earnings of skilled manual workers were Cr$629.82 (with a standard deviation of Cr$702.02) for the same period. Nevertheless, everything indicates that the income-generating unit is not the individual but the family. The wife and children generally bring in additional revenue. Aside from this, individuals occasionally have "side deals" (*bicos*) which also produce more revenue. Thus the average monthly income for the entire family was Cr$430.73 (with a standard deviation of Cr$405.35) for unskilled manual laborers and Cr$878.87 (with a standard deviation of Cr$897.19) for skilled manual workers.

The additional revenue produced by "side deals" and by the other members of the family raises the total income of unskilled manual workers by around 56 percent, while for skilled workers the increase is only of around 40 percent. Thus additional sources of revenue are more important for those who hold jobs which call for lower qualifications, since those sources generate a higher proportion of the total income. These marginal differences in revenue are influenced not so much by different job opportunities for the relatives, but more by the image the lower class holds of the status role of each of its members. The household heads interviewed did not want their wives or children to work. "A wife was made to look after the house," and "children were made to play and study" are the predominant concepts, and the work of either wife or children is tolerated only in view of the family's needs. As soon as there is an increase in the head of the family's income, the wife and children stop working. Both the average monthly wage for the chief occupation and the family unit's total income vary considerably, depending on the ecological niche in which the individuals are located within the city. The data presented in Table 6.4 support this proposition.

TABLE 6.4
Average Monthly Income in Cruzeiros (Cr$) by Ecological Niche*

Location	Income from chief occupation	Standard deviation	Family unit's total income	Standard deviation
Tenements	479.58	482.01	627.80	547.35
Vila Anglo-Brasileira	475.46	302.71	701.52	417.29
Vila Prudente Slum	277.12	146.33	371.35	215.06
Small Slums Far from Industries	264.73	454.70	381.86	1,032.20
Small Slums Close to Industries	197.02	60.76	255.70	95.27

* US$ 1.00 = Cr$4.39 at the time of research study

Notice that both the lowest and the more homogeneous average incomes are generated by those who live in small slums located close to industrial areas. Those who live in small slums far from industrial areas and close to upper-class residential neighborhoods not only generate considerably higher incomes than those of the previous group, but also show a higher increment in the family unit's total income. However, their standard deviation is quite large, as a result of the type of activity which produces the added income. Both the internal variations and differences between these niches are most likely due to the different types of relationships which their members maintain with the outside world. The latter, in turn, vary as a function of the location of each niche. Thus the residents of slums which are far from industrial areas and close to upper-class residential neighborhoods must establish relations with members of that class which provide them with resources unavailable to those who live in small slums close to industries. Slum dwellers located close to upper-class residental neighborhoods manage, in exchange for intermittent services which guarantee a lifestyle for the upper classes, to obtain a higher monetary income than slum dwellers living close to industrial areas. Notice also that the standard deviations reflect a considerable variability of average incomes in the small slums far from industrial areas, while the average incomes of those living close to industrial areas are quite homogeneous. These differences in standard deviations both between small slums close to and far from industrial areas, and between the average income from the chief occupation and the family unit's total income, indicate that the heterogeneity of material resources among members of the lower strata depends on the type of relations which they maintain with other social classes. Because of their intermittent nature, services rendered by slum dwellers who live near upper-class neighborhoods lead to large marginal variations in that segment's revenue.

The notion of social marginality presupposes both homogeneity within the marginal sector and the absence of relations between the marginal and integrated sectors. These premises are not supported by the data presented so far. On the contrary, the data show that variability of material resources within the lower classes is quite substantial and depends on the relations maintained by different members of these strata with the integrated social classes. These observations have complex theoretical implications inasmuch as they reveal an absence of homogeneous class relationships. The unequal income production of the lower-class earning units suggests different forms of relationships between members of different social strata and a heterogeneity within the lower classes which sociological theory has been unable to account for up to now.

On a broader level, relations between classes are based on labor exploitation. However, the social structure's complexity makes these relations complex as well, and leads to a heterogeneity within the so-called lower classes which probably hinders their consolidation as a class in the traditional sense of the word. While classic sociological theory manages to explain relations between classes on a broader level, it does not manage to grasp the specific aspects of these relations which generate complex situations hindering their consolidation as a political category.

Cultural Poverty and the Culture of Poverty: Membership in Voluntary Associations

The sampling survey disclosed (Table 6.5) that most of the municipality's population does not participate in voluntary associations.

The highest rate of participation is found in sports associations where the information exchanged is generally irrelevant to the population's adaptation to the city, except of course as a form of leisure. A comparison of membership in voluntary associations based on a breakdown by social class clearly shows the selectivity of participation. Table 6.6 provides that breakdown.

TABLE 6.5
Membership in Voluntary Associations

Association	Belong (%)	Do not belong (%)	Total (N)
Religious association	2.8	97.2	(1015)
Neighborhood association	3.3	96.7	(1015)
Club at place of work	5.8	94.2	(1015)
Professional group	11.2	88.8	(1015)
Union	15.0	85.0	(1015)
Sports association	23.1	76.9	(1015)

In the six kinds of voluntary associations studied, except for the neighborhood type, participation is always higher for upper-class than for lower-middle or lower-class groups. There are certain types of voluntary associations where membership tends to be limited by social class. Participation in neighborhood associations tends to be confined to the lower classes; membership in clubs established at the place of work tends to be characteristic of the middle class; and membership in professional groups is limited to the upper class. The most interesting result contained in this table concerns union membership, which is more frequent for the upper than for the lower classes.

This fact confirms an observation made in a previous study, namely that those who most need the union are those who participate in it the least, and are thereby vulnerable to manipulation by their employers (Berlinck 1974). Skilled manual laborers and those who hold supervisory positions (members of our lower middle class), as well as white-collar workers, see the unions as relief associations since they have no need for

TABLE 6.6
Social Class Membership in Voluntary Associations*

	Religious		Neighborhood		Club at place of work		Professional group		Union		Sports association	
	Belong	Do not belong	Belong	Do not belong	Belong	Do not belong	Belong	Do not belong	Belong	Do not belong	Belong	Do not belong
Upper	3.1 (4)	96.9 (127)	2.3 (3)	97.7 (129)	6.9 (9)	93.1 (121)	52.3 (69)	47.7 (63)	22.1 (29)	77.9 (102)	63.9 (85)	36.1 (48)
Middle	3.7 (13)	96.3 (334)	2.3 (8)	97.7 (335)	8.5 (29)	91.5 (313)	11.0 (38)	89.0 (307)	20.5 (71)	79.5 (275)	35.1 (121)	64.9 (224)
Lower-Middle	2.5 (6)	97.5 (236)	5.0 (12)	95.0 (228)	4.7 (11)	95.3 (225)	1.7 (4)	98.3 (234)	17.5 (42)	82.5 (198)	8.8 (21)	91.2 (218)
Lower	1.8 (5)	98.2 (273)	3.6 (10)	96.4 (268)	2.5 (7)	97.5 (268)	0 (0)	100.0 (274)	2.5 (7)	97.5 (268)	1.1 (3)	98.9 (272)
No Ans.		(17)		(22)		(32)		(26)		(23)		(23)

* Absolute frequencies are given in parentheses. Relative frequencies were computed separately for each association.

these organizations as instruments for their claims. This may also explain the type of activity performed by unions in Brazil, as well as predict both their future line of action and the structure which will prevail in this kind of organization. Table 6.7 presents the total number of voluntary associations to which these subjects have belonged throughout their lives, in terms of social class.

TABLE 6.7

Social Class and Total Number of Voluntary Associations to Which Subjects Have Belonged Throughout Their Lives*

Social Class	Total number of associations				
	None	1 or 2	3	more than 3	Total
Upper	41.4 (55)	38.3 (51)	12.0 (16)	8.4 (11)	(133)
Middle	56.9 (198)	36.8 (128)	3.2 (11)	2.9 (10)	(348)
Lower-Middle	79.1 (197)	20.5 (51)	0.4 (1)	0 (0)	(249)
Lower	93.2 (262)	6.1 (17)	0.4 (1)	0.4 (1)	(281)

* Data for 4 cases were unavailable.

A comparison between Table 6.7 and the previous one shows that current participation rates are generally lower than in the past, for all social strata except the upper class. Such a comparison suggests that what little participation in voluntary associations there is tends to be lower at present than in the past, particularly for the population's lower classes. Since most members of that group are migrants, it would be reasonable to assume that recent migrants participate less than do older migrants. Table 6.8 confirms this assumption.

Participation in voluntary associations is not common social practice for the population living in the city of Sao Paulo. A comparison of membership by social class shows that the higher the social stratum, the greater the participation in different types of associations. When natives and migrants are compared, the former participate more than the latter, and the more recent migrants tend to show the least participation. These trends do not point to the existence of participant and isolated sub-cultures. They do indicate that there are differences in terms of degree (more so than in terms of quality) which may be related to differential opportunities for access to those associations and/or to their actual roles in relation to members.

TABLE 6.8

Average number of Voluntary Associations to Which Natives and Migrants Have Belonged Throughout Their Lives*

	1900/29	30/34	35/39	40/44	45/49	50/54	55/59	60/64	65/70
Natives	0.31 (283)								
Migrants	0.62 (45)	0.63 (38)	0.50 (50)	0.42 (60)	0.53 (76)	0.33 (64)	0.33 (78)	0.32 (126)	0.25 (164)

* Data for 2 cases were unavailable.

These observations confirm the conclusions reached by Leôncio Martins Rodrigues (1970: 21) in his study of a group of workers belonging to one of the country's major automobile companies, located in Greater Sao Paulo: "Life for most of these workers, both geographically and socially, is confined to the neighborhoods; their participation in the recreational or mass cultural activities offered to other social groups is very meager." This phenomenon is not peculiar to the lower classes, but common to Sao Paulo's entire population.

Cultural Poverty and the Culture of Poverty: Access to Mass Media

Access to mass media may become another mechanism for adapting to the city insofar as such channels can provide relevant information for satisfying the population's needs and desires. Table 6.9 shows the lack of some means of mass communication in terms of social class.

The isolation pattern disclosed in connection with membership in voluntary associations repeats itself here: radio is still the only easily accessible channel for the population's lower strata. When Isaura, one of the interviewees, was asked whether she used the telephone, she said: "To tell the truth m'am, I just don't know how you talk [laughs loudly]. I don't even know how to pick it up. I see all the others pick it up, put it

TABLE 6.9

Lack of Mass Communication Channels, by Social Class

Social Class	Do not own			
	Radio	TV	Record player	Car
Upper	0.0 (0)	0.0 (0)	9.0 (12)	6.8 (9)
Middle	4.3 (15)	6.6 (23)	27.4 (95)	50.6 (176)
Lower-Middle	10.8 (27)	32.5 (81)	66.7 (166)	84.3 (210)
Lower	43.9 (123)	73.2 (205)	91.1 (256)	97.5 (274)
No Ans.	(6)	(5)	(5)	(4)

up to their ear and talk, but I still haven't dared to pick it up and talk, no m'am" [interview data].

A relatively high proportion (26.8 percent) of lower-class families own television sets. Yet a study of the programs most often heard on the radio or watched on TV shows that the population does not view these media as sources of information, but rather as entertainment or relaxation. Isaura's father offers quite an articulate concept of TV which differs somewhat from observations: "Television is an 'educationally' real fine entertainment. It shows good as good and evil as evil. We older people know how to organize ideas; the young in their pride are eager to learn, the young learn to shoot, learn blows, even a performer can come out of that" [interview data]. Even in this case, the message transmitted by TV is perceived as something redundant and manichaean, "it shows good as good and evil and evil," although the young may be able to learn from it. When the young were asked, they also answered that TV was a form of entertainment. Table 6.10 shows other indicators of social isolation in terms of class.

From this we can conclude that the lower the social class, the greater its relative isolation. This phenomenon is only relative since the lower strata have access to certain channels (TV and talking to the neighbors) which express their connection with the city's broader institutional net-

TABLE 6.10
Isolation, by Social Class

Social Class	Do not watch TV	Do not talk to neighbors	Do not listen to radio	Do not have friends	Do not know a museum	Do not read a newspaper	Do not know a library	Do not read books regularly	Do not go to movies
Upper	1.5 (2)	28.6 (38)	3.8 (5)	13.0 (24)	10.5 (14)	2.3 (3)	10.7 (14)	28.6 (38)	46.6 (62)
Middle	2.1 (7)	14.4 (50)	6.9 (24)	13.4 (64)	10.6 (37)	8.3 (29)	18.7 (64)	56.9 (198)	58.3 (203)
Lower-Middle	5.8 (13)	9.6 (24)	11.8 (29)	20.6 (51)	25.3 (63)	32.4 (80)	53.5 (129)	74.5 (184)	79.8 (198)
Lower	11.0 (18)	5.0 (14)	28.2 (78)	27.8 (78)	41.9 (116)	73.9 (207)	79.7 (216)	88.7 (244)	90.7 (254)
No Ans.	(151)	(4)	(13)	(5)	(10)	(7)	(30)	(12)	(6)
Total	4.6 (40)	12.5 (126)	13.5 (136)	21.5 (217)	22.9 (230)	31.6 (319)	42.9 (423)	66.2 (664)	71.7 (717)

work. These observations are still consistent wih those of Martins Rodrigues (1970) who clearly notes the relative isolation of the industrial workers he studied.

Cultural Poverty and the Culture of Poverty:
Informal Contacts Network

Another important adaptive mechanism takes the form of informal primary relations maintained with relatives and friends. A study performed by Rosen and Berlinck (1968) in the state of Sao Paulo showed that the urbanization and industrialization processes did not break down the extended kinship structure and that, for residents of the city of Sao Paulo, that structure was as extended as for the region's more rural communities, or even more so. A subsequent study of Brazilian families in the city of Sao Paulo suggested one possible cause for the preservation of an extended kinship unit within that urban set-up: the exchange of information provided by these groups in an environment in which "secrecy is the heart of business" and where no other efficient means of information exist (Berlinck 1969). Martins Rodrigues (1970: 20-21) points out that among the industrial workers studied:

> The married ones' weekend centers around the family. They usually spend the entire day at home, visit relatives, take the children on outings or go to mass. Only a small percentage take advantage of Sundays to engage in sports, attend a soccer match, or perform any other type of recreational activity outside the family. We are tempted to say that there is a reduction in the areas of personal relations whereby primary contacts increase as compared to secondary ones.

One must search in the extranuclear kinship structure — the extended family — for the major social relationships maintained by members of the lowest classes in the urban milieu.

In our sampling survey the existence or absence of an extended family was measured in terms of three criteria: (1) whether or not there were relatives or other persons living in the same house as the interviewee and his nuclear family; (2) the relatives' geographic proximity; and (3) the frequency of interaction with relatives. Table 6.11 summarizes the data gathered in relation to criterion (1), in terms of social class.

The upper classes tend to have an extended kinship structure more often than the lower classes. However, the structures differ since, while the upper classes tend to have other persons (and no relatives) living in the same house, the lower classes tend to have relatives with them and no other persons. In the case of the upper classes, these other persons are generally domestic servants and therefore this extended kinship structure

TABLE 6.11

Kinship Structure by Social Class: Relatives and Other Persons Living in the Interviewer's House*

Social Class	No one	Only relatives	Only others	Relatives and others	Total
Upper	40.2 (53)	9.8 (13)	47.7 (63)	2.3 (3)	(132)
Middle	63.1 (219)	13.3 (46)	19.9 (69)	3.7 (12)	(347)
Lower-Middle	71.5 (178)	20.5 (51)	6.6 (17)	1.2 (3)	(249)
Lower	79.0 (222)	16.4 (46)	3.2 (9)	1.4 (4)	(281)

* Data for 6 cases were unavailable.

may be classified as "service-related" (Berlinck 1969). Servants perform both typical kinship functions such as socialization and tension management and an important adaptive function as well, to the extent that they provide members of the upper class with spare time which can be used in other tasks such as obtaining relevant information to maintain the status quo (Berlinck 1969). As concerns the lower classes, these same functions are sometimes performed by relatives although, as the table shows, the phenomenon is much less frequent there than in the upper classes. Table 6.12 displays the relatives' geographic proximity, in terms of social class.

Table 6.12 shows that members of the lower classes have relatives living close to them (in the same block or within a similar area) more often than do members of the upper classes. However, members of the upper classes are more likely to have relatives living in the same neighborhood or in the city of Sao Paulo than are members of all classes often have relatives living close to them, or in the city, who can help in times of need. The higher the social class, the greater the probability of having relatives living in the city of Sao Paulo. Table 6.13 shows the frequency of interaction with relatives, in terms of social class.

Results show that members of all classes interact frequently with their relatives. The higher the social class, the greater the probability of interaction. All these indicators suggest that the extended kinship structure

TABLE 6.12

Kinship Structure by Social Class: Relatives' Geographic Proximity

Social Class	Have relatives living		
	In the same block	In the same neighborhood	In the city
Upper	20.3 (27)	55.6 (74)	94.0 (125)
Middle	19.0 (66)	52.9 (184)	93.4 (324)
Lower-Middle	30.5 (76)	48.6 (121)	90.4 (225)
Lower	33.2 (93)	34.6 (97)	71.8 (201)
No Ans.	(6)	(5)	(6)

TABLE 6.13

Kinship Structure by Social Class: Frequency of Interaction with Relatives

Social Class	Spoke with relatives on the day before the interview	Spoke with relatives on the week before the interview
Upper	51.9 (69)	69.7 (92)
Middle	44.8 (156)	66.7 (232)
Lower-Middle	43.8 (109)	55.8 (139)
Lower	33.5 (94)	47.3 (133)
No Ans.	(4)	(5)

is commonly found in Sao Paulo, regardless of social class. They also suggest that the higher the social class, the more frequently an extended family occurs, although its structure is different from the one which prevails among the lower classes. The very existence of this mechanism suggests that kinship relations may be very important adaptive factors in the urban milieu. Isaura, for example, grasps the role of kinship relations quite clearly:

> I'm sure not to starve to death. Sao Paulo is big, isn't it? My family is big, too. I scatter a few kids all around [she laughs]. One gets a bit here, another bit there. We save, little by little and, before you know it, with a bit of patience, we've made it. Now, that madness of going, getting all those kids together, taking them all to Paraná. God only knows where I'd end. Falling smack in the middle of real bush country, in a rough place like that? [interview data].

Further on, referring to her husband's job, the same interviewee said:

> It took him four months of roughing it out there to find a job. My brother helped a bit, my uncle there, my father out there, and slowly we managed to get things under control, one adding to the other's bit of help; one gave this, one gave another thing, another gave something else, until ... well, now we're all there. My uncle gave that room. Those two beds we got from the neighbor lady [interview data].

Kinship relations are not the only adaptive mechanisms relevant in the city of Sao Paulo. Anthropological interviews show that friendship relations are extremely important to the lower classes' adaptation within the urban milieu. Members of these classes generally present a complex but well-defined hierarchy in their friendship relations. Distinctions are made between friends, acquaintances, and "people from back home," all of whom are used as sources of information and assistance at different points in the life of a member of these classes. The concept "back home" has a broad territorial basis, which varies from the same area (city or farm) to the same state or region of origin, and is widely used by the migrants. These mechanisms may be illustrated by some statements taken from the anthropological interviews.

José Jeronimo had the address of one of his brothers, Alberto, who lived in the city of Sao Paulo. He left his wife and children in Campos Sales, State of Ceará, and "came to try things out." It was a fourteen-day ride in the back of a truck. He arrived at his brother's house but stayed only for a few days. He then arranged lodging at a boarding house in Mooca. Two days after his arrival in Sao Paulo, he got a job through his brother. After working there for one month, he left because the work was too heavy. He then found another job through "a buddy from his native Ceará" and held it for six months before going back to fetch the family he had left in his home state.

José Francisco, from Angelin, State of Pernambuco, had several relatives and acquaintances living in the city of Sao Paulo. When he arrived, he went to live in Sapopemba, State of Sao Paulo with one of his brothers. Six days later, he found a job: "Walking down the street in front of some company, I went to ask the man whether he had work for a guy from Pernambuco. The man asked: 'Are you from Caruaru or from Garanhuns? From Garanhuns? Then you have the job' " [interview data]. He quit and found another job with Acesita, quite by chance: he had gone to General Electric and later to Pirelli but "I didn't find anything so I went to Ipiranga. I knew that a cousin of mine worked close by and I explained to him that I was looking for work. My cousin went to talk to the old German and came back saying that I could register and start" [interview data].

Romildo, a native of Cajazeira, in the municipality of Encruzilhada, State of Bahia, came to Cosmorama, State of Sao Paulo, where he worked in the fields for one year, but lost his crop for lack of rain. He then decided to come to Sao Paulo. "When I was up in Cosmorama, I used to watch the soccer games and knew a certain 'Zé Goleiro' by sight, who was a good soccer player, except I wasn't really friends with him there" [interview data]. Zé Goleiro had left for Sao Paulo a year earlier. When Romildo decided to come to Sao Paulo, a friend who knew Zé Goleiro quite well came with him. He arrived at the house of Zé Goleiro with his friend and they asked if he could help. Romildo's friend had come with him only for the trip and later returned to the interior. Zé Goleiro agreed to help Romildo who went back to the interior to fetch his things and then moved into the house. The house had two rooms and was located at Potomaque Street, Jardim das Maravilhas in Sao Paulo. Zé Goleiro has three young children. He had Romildo sleep in the children's bed and the children slept in the parents' bed. Romildo was embarrassed to sleep in the same room with a family he hardly knew. Zé Goleiro sent him to the Swift factory in Santo Andre and Romildo began to work as a helper, since he had no training. He worked in the bull slaughtering section. Two months later, Zé Goleiro built a boarding room in his own back yard and Romildo would then sleep in that shed. His lunch, dinner, and the food he took to work all came from Zé's house. He had no money when he arrived, but Zé said there was no problem, he could pay later.

Problem Solving

The importance of these informal mechanisms can be clearly grasped by studying the way in which the population solves certain problems. Table 6.14 shows how the interviewees solved the residence problem, in terms of social class.

TABLE 6.14

Solution to the Residence Problem, by Social Class

Social Class	How did you find the house you now live in?*						
	Built it	Relatives	Neighbors	Friends	Newspaper	Broker	Street sign
Upper	14.4 (19)	24.2 (32)	2.3 (3)	15.2 (20)	12.9 (17)	22.0 (29)	9.1 (12)
Middle	8.7 (30)	21.4 (74)	3.8 (13)	22.0 (76)	17.4 (60)	14.2 (49)	12.5 (43)
Lower-Middle	13.3 (32)	25.7 (62)	3.3 (8)	35.7 (86)	5.0 (12)	2.9 (7)	14.1 (34)
Lower	39.3 (108)	22.9 (63)	3.3 (9)	25.8 (71)	0.4 (1)	1.1 (3)	7.3 (20)

* Data for 22 cases were unavailable.

Relatives and friends are relevant sources of information in solving the residence problem for all social classes. While the upper classes make use of other resources (such as newspapers, brokers, and street signs), the lower classes tend to confine themselves to those informal sources only, or to solve the problem on an individual basis. Table 6.15 shows how the population found its current job, in terms of social class.

Results shown in this table generally confirm the remarks made in relation to previous ones — that relatives and friends are relevant adaptive mechanisms for all social classes. However, the upper classes have other resources unavailable or inaccessible to the lower ones. The relative isolation of the lower classes is considerably greater than that of the upper classes. This isolation in turn restricts the lower classes' awareness of resources available in the city, as Table 6.16 shows.

This unawareness in relation to resources existing in the environment obviously limits the alternative actions of lower-class members and hinders their adaptation. However, there are no indications that a culture of poverty exists in Sao Paulo, in the sense of a set of norms, values, beliefs, and so on, which are characteristic and common among the municipality's lower classes. The most that can be said in this respect is that members of the upper strata are relatively more central, that is, have access to a greater number of different communication channels (Berlinck 1968). It would therefore not be valid to assume that the poor are marginalized. On the contrary, they have access to informal communica-

TABLE 6.15
Finding of Current Job, by Social Class

Social Class	How did you find your current job?*						
	Relatives	Neighbors	Friends	Newspaper	Radio or TV	Street sign; on your own	Other
Upper	39.4 (52)	—	33.3 (44)	3.0 (4)	—	2.3 (3)	22.0 (29)
Middle	24.2 (83)	—	49.3 (169)	7.9 (27)	0.9 (3)	2.0 (7)	15.7 (54)
Lower-Middle	14.2 (35)	2.0 (5)	53.3 (131)	11.0 (27)	—	8.1 (20)	11.4 (28)
Lower	16.7 (46)	3.3 (9)	53.6 (148)	1.1 (3)	—	10.9 (30)	14.5 (40)

* Data for 18 cases were unavailable.

TABLE 6.16

Urban Resources Unkown, by Social Class

Social Class	Medical Hospital	Health Center	"Peg-Pag" Supermarket	"Mappin"	Zoo	Ibirapuera	D. Pedro II Park	São João Avenue	Where to register to vote	Where to get identification documents
Upper	2.3 (3)	4.5 (6)	—	—	2.3 (3)	0.8 (1)	1.5 (2)	—	1.5 (2)	—
Middle	2.6 (9)	6.6 (23)	2.0 (7)	2.6 (9)	9.5 (33)	2.9 (10)	2.0 (7)	0.6 (2)	5.7 (20)	2.3 (8)
Lower-Middle	6.4 (16)	8.8 (22)	7.2 (18)	11.4 (28)	18.3 (47)	9.7 (24)	4.8 (12)	2.8 (7)	16.1 (40)	8.0 (20)
Lower	19.6 (55)	19.6 (55)	27.0 (76)	36.7 (103)	37.7 (106)	20.6 (58)	12.5 (35)	10.3 (29)	56.2 (158)	29.2 (82)
No Ans.	(4)	(4)	(4)	(4)	(4)	(6)	(4)	(4)	(4)	(4)

tion channels — relatives, neighbors, friends, and "people from back home " — which guarantee them information concerning such problems as residence and employment, and help them to adapt.

Theoretical Interpretation

Our analysis of social adaptation mechanisms used by the population of the city of Sao Paulo points to the absence of what is known as social marginality. We found that the lower-class population manages to generate a limited amount of income which varies as a function of how members of that class relate to those of other classes living in the city. Variations in family income depend on the revenue derived from the work of the head of the family. They also depend on the work of other members of the family who, for their part, vary in terms of their dependence on the head's income and his conception of female and child labor. Finally, income variations depend on the family's location within the urban area, since this partly determines the nature of the group's relations with members of other social classes. Since labor involves an asymmetric social relation, one cannot assume absolute isolation on the part of the lower classes in relation to the upper strata. Furthermore, for this population, unstable work relationships operate mainly as a mechanism which generates marginal income, rather than as a marginal form of insertion in the labor market.

Although satisfaction of the lower-class population's needs and desires depends basically on the income distribution structure, it also depends on that population's access to and use of communication channels which can provide information concerning resources available in the city and access to them. Although the data presented in this chapter point to a relative isolation of the lower classes, evident in the absence of voluntary associations and considerable dissociation from mass media, they also reveal that interaction patterns prevailing in the various social classes show no qualitative variations. Although the upper classes use a greater number of different mechanisms to fulfill their needs and desires, both they and the lower classes make foremost use of relations with relatives, friends, and "people from back home" in solving their problems, and spend much of the spare time cultivating informal relationships. These patterns are quite the opposite of those found in advanced capitalist societies such as the United States and England, where voluntary associations and mass media are considerably varied and widely used by the population. Is Brazilian society, then, a case of national culture of poverty?

The concept of a culture of poverty as formulated by Lewis (1965, 1966) proposes a considerable isolation of the lower class caused by its break from a preexisting structure (generally agrarian) which in turn occurs as a result of the rural-urban migration process. According to Lewis, the culture of poverty is characterized by a cultural poverty in which traditions are absent and the symbolic stock used is substantially restricted. This phenomenon is not present in Brazilian society, or rather, things do not operate as Oscar Lewis conceived them.

In order to understand why informal patterns of interaction predominate in the city of Sao Paulo, one must first understand the nature of interaction patterns prevailing in the preexisting structure — those of Brazilian patriarchal society. Several classic studies of Brazil's patriarchal society (Freyre 1973; Oliveira Vianna 1949; Leal n.d.; Freyre 1951; Duarte 1966) show that it dispensed with voluntary associations and that the interaction patterns which predominated within it were informal, based on bonds of kinship and friendship. However, these studies encounter some difficulties in explaining this state of affairs. Except for Oliveira Vianna's pioneer study, the authors attribute the phenomenon to the colonists' world view (Genovese 1972). In our opinion, interaction patterns prevailing in Brazilian patriarchal society were a result of the colonization project's very nature, that is, the way in which the expansion of European mercantilism materialized in Brazil.

The Portuguese colonial system implanted in Brazil was based on land exploitation and characterized by the creation of *sesmarias* (large rural properties granted by the Crown and very sparsely populated). Parallel to this set-up, a limited number of port cities were established, from which the products of the land were shipped and colonial administration was carried out. Once it was fully installed, the colonial system may be schematically described as comprising: (1) Latifundia labeled according to the products they yielded and the region where they were located: sugar mills (*engenhos*) and cattle corrals (*currais*) in the Northeast; coffee and cattle farms (*fazendas*) in Rio, Minas Gerais, and São Paulo, or cattle ranches (*estâncias*) in the South. (2) Smaller landholdings, generally attached to and dependent on the larger ones, where subsistence agriculture was developed. And (3) an export trade sector, closely linked to the large landholdings and located in the port cities. The large estates had an internal division of labor whereby part of the property was used for subsistence crops and part for export production. As Furtado (1959) points out, the subsistence sector bound the population to the property, guaranteeing its survival and varying in terms of extension and labor employed, according to the size of the area used for export-bound production. During times when prices for agricultural goods were unfavorable in foreign markets, the size of the area used to produce them decreased and workers were left free to perform subsistence cultivation in the lands released. During times when prices for agricultural products rose in the foreign markets, the size of the area used to grow them increased, the area used for subsistence agriculture was reduced, and the workers freed by the subsistence sector were employed in cultivating the exported product. The process varied in time and space and went through a number of alterations. However, the agroexporting framework maintained its balance up to the mid-nineteenth century when the Brazilian economy's dynamic axis changed radically as coffee production expanded toward western Sao Paulo.

The colonial system's balance depended on the social structure it created, based on what Oliveira Vianna (1949) calls "the kinship complex" which, according to this author, comprised the "feudal clan" and the "manorial family complex." We are not concerned here with the appropriateness of Oliveira Vianna's terms but with an understanding of their meaning. The feudal clan was structured within the context of the large estate.[5] Its operations were guaranteed by a normative structure based on: (1) personal property rights (slavery); (2) police immunity according to which no metropolitan authority could intervene inside the large estate without the owner's permission; and (3) the principle of *ut et des* (take there, give here) through which the owner offered his subjects protection and assistance in exchange for their loyalty and obedience. This structure was in turn legitimized by the metropolitan authorities and by the Catholic church (Berlinck 1972).

The manorial family complex was structured at the interproprietary level, that is, among the owners of adjacent estates.[6] The normative structure of the manorial family complex was based on: (1) the collective responsibility of the private talion which guaranteed the property's indivisibility, that is the central column itself of the economic system based on the agroexporting large estate; and (2) the duties of mutual protection and assistance to kin. The export trade sector, up to the mid-nineteenth century, was an appendage of this system regulated by the same normative structure, that is controlled in general by the same families which controlled the large landholdings.

The kinship complex prevented or hindered mobility for free laborers. In order for a laborer to leave the area of influence of a particular kinship complex he had to be accepted by another complex — otherwise he would have no chance of surviving even in the cities. The complex tended to bind both free laborers and members of the manorial family within a definite and indivisible territorial expanse, thereby guaranteeing the labor needed for production and the large estate's survival. The system not only dispensed with associations outside the family, but actually saw them as a threat. This was the case with associations to protect fugitive slaves and later with millenarian movements which were always severely repressed, since they offered alternatives for the subordinate population and threatened the kinship complex. Only three types of voluntary associations seem to have legitimately existed at that time: the holy houses of mercy, the trade associations, and the religious brotherhoods (Conniff 1974). All three were located in the urban centers and, except for the religious brotherhoods, performed functions which reinforced the normative structure centered around the kinship complex (Russell-Wood 1968; Ridings 1970). Religious brotherhoods seem to have performed modernizing mutual assistance functions which ran counter to the kinship complex. A few brotherhoods flourished in Vila Rica, for example, which are known to have defended the interests of freedmen and to have brought the freedom of slaves.

During the second half of the nineteenth century, important economic changes took place in the development of capitalism in Brazil. The prolonged abolition process and the republican movement — social and political answers, respectively, to economic changes   led to the rise of a series of lower-class associations. Not only did the religious brotherhoods of former slaves become important (Viotti da Costa 1966), but secular associations such as Antonio Bento's Caifazes emerged and developed in Rio and Sao Paulo, bringing craftsmen and minor industrialists together and defending their interests (Cardoso 1969; Conniff 1974). Some examples are the *Jornal do Comercio*'s Typesetters Benevolent Association (1869), the Goldsmiths' Corporation Supporting Society (1838), and the Brazilian Central Railway's General Association for Mutual Assistance (1884). Voluntary associations varied in number and nature as capitalist development promoted the rise of new groups in the increasingly complex productive process. Table 6.17 illustrates this point.

Throughout the period of great social and political instability elapsed between Abolition (1889) and the proclamation of the Republic (1891), the number of associations founded is the lowest in the entire period studied. This is due to the considerable degree of repression prevailing during those years. However, one should not discount the fact that the fall of the monarchy was promoted by the Military Club (1887), a voluntary association. The number of state civil servants and workers' associations increased as of 1900, reflecting changes in both the economic and political planes. The expansion of coffee production toward western Sao Paulo and the Abolitionist movement also triggered a major wave of European immigration, encouraged by the Society to Promote Colonization — a voluntary association founded by ranchers and subsidized by the provincial government (Hall 1972).

This wave of European immigration promoted the rise of a series of lower-class voluntary associations in which the immigrants, many of whom would become urban workers, were brought together (Simao

TABLE 6.17
Voluntary Associations Founded in Rio de Janeiro

Type	Time of founding				
	Up to 1879	1880-1889	1890-1899	1900-1909	1910-1919
Religious Brotherhoods	35	7	2	11	5
Mutual Assistance Societies	35	46	16	16	10
Civil Servants	4	9	9	28	28
Workers	12	10	·8	29	29
Professionals	11	3	1	3	4
Employers	5	2	1	2	7

Source: Conniff, 1974, p. 4

1966; Carone 1970). During this period, until approximately 1930, workers' organizations took various forms, from those designed for mutual aid to those which were formed to defend the class from its enemies. However, all were mere transplants of their European counterparts (Simao 1966; Carone 1970). According to Cardoso (1969:205):

> Among the immigrants of European urban origin there were many, particularly Italians and Spaniards, who transplanted to the American Continent the experience, feelings, and goals of European workers' groups which were politicized and discontented with the social spoliation imposed on them by industrial capitalism. Anarchists, anarcho-unionists, unionists, *carbonari,* and other variants of the European workers' movement of the late nineteenth and early twentieth centuries, many of them expelled from Europe, attempted to organize Brazil's incipient workers' groups and make it react as a social stratum with its own characteristics.

The abolitionist and republican associations ended when their goals were reached. But those which brought European urban workers together were permanently and increasingly repressed by the law and the police throughout the entire First Republic, although they subsisted until 1930, when the urban working class began to feel the impact of internal migration, and the government undertook regulation and control of these associations through its labor legislation. However, the repression proved beneficial, because in addition to being an efficient form of social control, it was backed by the working class itself, which could only rely on a politically active minority incapable of unifying the various class sectors. Most workers during this period aspired to social advancement and often attained it because the industrial system was still a handicraft system which was only then beginning to diversify and allow for the installation of a few relatively larger workshops with some technical division of labor (Cardoso 1969). As a result of these structural conditions, the means to fulfill the aspirations of social advancement lay in commanding a more elaborate work technique: a skillful and diligent craftsman could get to be the owner of a small workshop and with a bit of daring and luck, "conquer America" and become an industrialist (Cardoso 1969). In addition, there was still the mass of workers who had come from the coffee plantations and from agricultural work in general. On moving to the city, these workers were either already disappointed by the failure of their first venture (with the radical change in lifestyle it implied), encouraged by the optimistic expectation of better days which the migration never brought, or lacked the minimal sociocultural resources needed to behave as members of a self-aware class (Cardoso 1969).

The period between 1890 and 1930 involved a major transition for Brazilian capitalism, which moved from an agroexporting stage to one of substitution industrialization. In this transitional period, marked by economic and political crises and by the breakdown of patriarchal society, lower-class voluntary associations outside the family flourished in Brazilian society.

The 1930s witnessed the consolidation of substitution industrialization which survived several economic crises and gradually annihilated the preexisting social system's unstable balance. Faced with industrialization, the large estates could no longer maintain their subsistence sectors intact, as a result of the growing demand for agricultural products which arose, this time, from the domestic market. In order to meet this demand, those estates underwent some important modifications: the areas used for subsistence were reduced, thereby freeing a number of workers who would seek jobs in the urban centers and thus fill the growing demand for cheap labor triggered by substitution industrialization. These mechanisms led to a rural-urban migration wave, supported, after the thirties, by a persisting modernization of agricultural production processes. The period also witnessed a vertical drop in the number of foreign immigrants and drastic changes in the class structure of Brazilian society. In addition to the existing agricultural sector and to the industrial sector with its businessmen and workers, the service sector expanded and the growth of public bureaucracy, commerce, and other services created new classes or class segments. The urban-industrial working classes no longer consisted mostly of recent European immigrants. Instead, the majority of their members were now recent national rural migrants who brought with them patriarchalist traditions and no associative experience whatsoever outside the family circle.

Substitution industrialization and the new, much more heterogeneous class make-up allowed for the emergence and consolidation, on the political plane, of a populist state which adopted a paternalistic and corporative style in vertical social relations. This in turn found legitimate support in the lower classes' cultural traditions (Martins and Almeida 1974). The paternalistic quality of populism during the Vargas era was clearly expressed in the New State's propaganda. Thus, the literacy primer published and widely distributed in 1938 by the National Department of Propaganda states that "the head of the government is head of the state, that is, the head of the big national family. The head of the big happy family."

Corporativism vertically harnessed the unions to the state in such a way as to never allow them the initiative of horizontal association which would make the class more powerful. By means of these mechanisms Vargas's populism managed to become a kind of mass political mentality, as Weffort (1965:41) notes when he points out that "populism as a social and political fact takes shape in such a way as to mystify class and ideological differences...because it is always expressed as a mass phenomenon, as a personal relationship between a leader and a conglomerate of the individuals."

Populism came to replace preexisting sociopolitical relations based on colonelist patriarchalism and which were then undergoing a crisis.[7] It brought no dramatic changes to the style of vertical relations, which continued to be paternalistic and were legitimately supported by the lower class's history. The two systems of domination were clearly different in some respects. Whereas in the previous period relations between the owner of the large estate and his subordinates were not subject to mediation of an associative nature, during the populist period such relations were mediated by various associations — beginning with the state itself — and, within these, by various mediators, the best known of which were the *pelegos* (middlemen) and the "electoral corporals" (Lopes 1966). The populist period managed to combine the paternalistic and personal style of preexisting vertical social relations with an authoritarian centralism based on the corporative principle, so that any attempt at parallel association — outside the parameters legitimized by the state — was considered subversive and strongly repressed by the authorities in charge of "maintaining order." The style of populist relations was legitimized by the popular traditions themselves and by the ability of substitution industrialization to satisfy many of the working class's needs and desires.

The collapse of populism which began in the early 1960s as a result of the crisis affecting substitution industrialization (Ianni 1968: Tavares 1972) seems to have brought the working classes, up to 1969, a relative autonomy from the state, expressed in the emergence of a series of voluntary associations, whether illegal or not. Many of these associations were repressed after 1967 when the Brazilian economy recovered from the crisis of substitution industrialization. The new style, by now predominantly monopolistic, which characterized the development of capitalism in Brazil, was now able to dispense with any major associative mediation process in the vertical social relations it established. On the economic plane, monopolistic industrialization did away with all associative mediation inasmuch as the system continued to generate a relatively large supply of labor thanks to the concurrent rural-urban migration. The growing employment capacity and the relatively high salaries offered by monopolistic industrialization contributed to demobilizing the preexisting unionist structure whose main function was to make demands, during a period of high inflation rates. The Brazilian state reorganized in technical bureaucratic fashion, and gradually the legitimacy principle found support in a type of charismatic-institutional domination which eliminated bargaining with the lower classes, as it operated during the populist period (Klein 1973). By incorporating the armed forces into the government and forming strong alliances with the monopolistic sector — eventually performing the functions of a monopolistic businessman — the state discarded relations with the working classes through the types of voluntary associations which had prevailed during the populist period. For this reason, both these and parallel associations were disbanded and repressed by the authorities.

Conclusion

In the absence of an autonomous tradition and facing strong organized opposition to any attempt at organizing and living within an expanding economy, the urban-industrial workers seek the assistance they need in the context of their own traditions, that is in kinship relations, friendships, and ties with "people from back home," in short, in informal and personal relationships. It is no accident that this period is witnessing a substantial expansion of popular religions organized in the churches and sects in which relationships are intimate and mutual assistance is tangible (Souza 1969; Berlinck 1972).

The relative isolation found among members of Sao Paulo's lower classes is a product of the very style of development which characterizes the capitalist system of which they are a part. The predominant forms of association are a result of domination patterns and of a long and rich lower-class cultural tradition whose complex personal and informal interaction patterns were always legitimized by the system, given their lack of broader political characteristics. Macrostructural mechanisms (for example, internal migrations), domination mechanisms developed and used by the bourgeoisie (such as the populist state), and the lower class's cultural traditions, while proving the absence of a culture of poverty, disclose the structural difficulties encountered by the lower class in its organization and in the development of a political self-image.

NOTES

1. This chapter is part of a broader project entitled "Population Characteristics and Social Organization and Adaptation in the City of Sao Paulo," sponsored by the Research Protection Foundation of the State of Sao Paulo (FAPESP), the Sao Paulo Business Administration School of the Getúlio Vargas Foundation, the Brazilian Center for Analysis and Planning (CEBRAP), and the Population Council. We would like to thank these organizations and to make it clear that the ideas expressed in this chapter are entirely under our responsibility.

2. Belo Horizonte is the state capital of Minas Gerais. Rio de Janeiro and Sao Paulo are the capitals of the states bearing the same names. Quixada and Xique-Xique are cities in the interior of the states of Ceará and Bahia respectively, both in the Brazilian Northeast.

3. These stages were not effected separately; there was an overlap of activities. They are described here as if they had been chronologically developed because this makes them easier to understand.

4. One of the interviewers is a worker-priest who for the past ten years has been working in the highly industrialized region of Santo André, Sao Bernardo, and Sao Caetano, and in addition has sociological training. The other is a social scientist from the University of Sao Paulo.

5. The feudal clan includes the owner of a large estate and his nuclear family (wife and children). It also includes: the administration; the technical staff, who are generally freedmen; the foreman; and the chaplain of the estate. All maintain some reciprocal relationships with the owner. It also includes nonreciprocal relations such as: dependents by personal property rights or slaves; dependents by hierarchical power such as farm workers; protégés; "nonproductive" squatters (for electoral purposes); small landholders; neighboring tradesmen and hoodlums.

6. The manorial family complex includes the patriarchical nuclear family with their dependents which are: blood relations (children and grandchildren); col-

lateral relations (brothers, uncles, and nephews); in-laws (sons-in-law, brothers-in-law); ritual kin (godparents and godchildren); and adopted relations (wards).
7. From colonelism — political mediation by local rural bosses (colonels).

REFERENCES

Derlinck, Manoel T. 1968. "População, centralidade relativa e morfogênese sistêmica em areas urbanas do Estado de Sao Paulo." *Revista de Administraçao de Empresas* 8 (December):61-79.

———. 1969. "The Structure of the Brazilian Family in the City of Sao Paulo, Brazil." Cornell University Latin American Studies Program Dissertation Series.

———. 1972. "Algumas consideraçoes sociológicas sobre as religioes no Brasil." *Revista do Instituto de Estudos Brasileiros* (no. 12):139-61.

———. 1974. *A vida como ela é: marginalidade social ou desenvolvimento capitalista periférico na Cidade de Sao Paulo.* Campinas, mimeographed.

Cardoso, Fernando Henrique. 1969. "Proletariado no Brasil: situaçao e comportamento social." *Mudanças sociais na América Latina.* Sao Paulo: Difusao Européia do Livro

Carone, Edgar. 1970. *A República Velha: instituiçoes e classes sociais.* Sao Paulo: Difusao Européia do Livro.

Conniff, Michael L. 1974. "Voluntary Associations in Rio, 1870-1945: A New Approach to Urban Social Dynamics." Mimeographed.

Costa, Emília Viotti da. 1966. *Da senzala à colonia.* Sao Paulo: Difusao Européia do Livro.

DNP. 1933. *O Brasil é bom.* Rio de Janeiro.

Duarte, Nestor. 1966. *A ordem privada e a organizaçao política nacional.* Sao Paulo: Cia. Editora Nacional.

Durkheim, Emile. 1964. *The Division of Labor in Society.* New York: Free Press.

Freyre, Gilberto. 1973. *Casa grande e senzala,* 16th ed. Rio de Janeiro: Livraria José Olympio.

———. 1951. *Sobrados e mocambos,* 3 vols., 2nd ed. Rio de Janeiro: Livraria José Olympio.

Furtado, Celso. 1959. *Formaçao economica do Brasil.* Rio de Janeiro: Fundo de Cultura.

Genovese, Eugene D. 1972. "Materialism and Idealism in the History of Negro Slavery in the Americas." In *Red and Black: Marxian Explorations in Southern and Afro-American History.* New York: Random House.

Hall, Michael. 1972. *Origins of Mass Immigration in Brazil.*

Ianni, Otávio. 1968. *O colapso do populismo no Brasil.* Rio de Janeiro: Civilizaçao Brasileira.

Klein, Lucia Maria Gomes. 1973. "A nova ordem legal e suas repercussoes sobre a esfera política." *Dados* (no. 10):154-65.

Kowarick, Lucio. 1974. *Capitalismo, dependência e marginalidade urbana na América Latina: uma contribuiçao teórica.* Sao Paulo, mimeographed.

Leal, Victor Nunes. 1948. *Coronelismo, enxada e voto.* Rio de Janeiro: Livraria Forense.

Leeds, Anthony. 1969. "The Significant Variables Determining the Character of Squatter Settlements." *América Latina* 13 (July-September):44-87.

Lewis, Oscar. 1965. *La Vida: A Puerto Rican Family in the Culture of Poverty.* New York: Random House.

_____. 1966.; "The culture of poverty." *Scientific American* 215 (October):19-25.

Lopes, Juarez R. Brandao. 1966. "Some Basic Developments in Brazilian Politics and Society." In Eric N. Baklanoff (ed.), *New Perspectives of Brazil.* Nashville: Vanderbilt University Press.

Machado da Silva, Luiz Antonio. 1969. "O significado do Botequim." *América Latina,* year 12 (July-September):160-82.

Martins, Carlos Estevam; and Almieda, Maria Hermínia Tavares de. 1974. "Modus in rebus: partidos e classes na queda do Estado Novo." Sao Paulo, mimeographed.

Mello e Souza, Antonio Candido. 1964. *Os parceiros do Rio Bonito.* Rio de Janeiro: Livraria José Olympio.

Oliveira Vianna, J. F. 1949. *Instituçoes políticas brasileiras,* 2 vols. Rio de Janeiro: Livraria José Olympio.

Pastore, José. 1971. "Migraçao, mobilidade social e desenvolvimento." In Manoel Augusto da Costa (ed.), *Migraçoes internas no Brasil.* Rio de Janeiro: IPEA/INPES.

Ridings, Eugene Ware, Jr. 1970. "The Bahian Commercial Association, 1844-1889: A Pressure Group in an Underdevelopment Area." University of Florida, Ph.D. dissertation.

Rodrigues, Leôncio Martins. 1970. *Industrializaçao e atitudes operárias: estudo de um grupo de trabalhadores.* Sao Paulo: Editora Brasiliense.

Rosen, Bernard C.; and Berlinck, Manoel T. 1968. "Modernization and Family Structure in the Region of Sao Paulo, Brazil." *América Latina* 2 (July-September):75-96.

Russell-Wood, A.J.R. 1968. *Fidalgos and Philanthropists: The Santa Casa de Misericórdia of Bahia, 1550-1755.* Berkeley: University of California Press.

Simao, Azis. 1966. *Sindicato e Estado: suas relaçoes na formaçao do proletariado de Sao Paulo.* Sao Paulo: Dominus.

Tavares, Maria da Conceiçao. 1973. *Da substituiçao de importaçocs ao capitalismo financeiro: ensaios sobre economia brasileira.* Rio de Janeiro: Zahar

Souza, Beatriz Muniz de. 1969. *A experiencia da salvaçao: pentecostais em Sao Paulo.* Sao Paulo: Livraria Duas Cidades.

Santos, José Maria dos. 1942. *Os republicanos paulistas e a aboliçao.* Sao Paulo: Livraria Martins.

Suttles, Gerald D. 1968. *The Social Order of the Slum.* Chicago: University of Chicago Press.

Weffort, Francisco C. 1965. "Raízes sociais do populismo na cidade de Sao Paulo." *Revista Civilizaçao Brasileira* 1 (May):39-60.

Williams, Robin M., Jr., 1961. *American Society: A Sociological Interpretation.* New York: Alfred A. Knopf.

Public Policy Analysis in Brazil

Wanderley Guilherme dos Santos
Olavo Brasil de Lima Júnior

Concepts, Problems, and the State of the Art

The analysis of public policies in Brazil is as old as political and social analysis in general. This is perhaps due to one of the outstanding features of Brazilian intellectual production in the social sciences which from the beginning has been deeply involved in political and social engineering. Starting with independence (1822), and continuing with the debates throughout the Second Empire until today, after more than eighty years of republican life, which included various authoritarian interludes, the activity of political and social analysis has always been predominantly directed toward the performance of different electoral and party systems and regimes, the division or concentration of powers, and their impact, more imputed than effectively measured, on society as a whole.

If one considers the questions that filled Brazilian political life from 1850 onward, one can see the incidence of a rudimentary analysis of public policies concerning the slave system, which was then in force, the fiscal and tributary systems, and the policies favorable or unfavorable to the industrial expansion of the country. Jumping a century we find the same desire to analyze the performance of the political system and its differentiated effects on the social structure, starting in the 1950s and continuing until today, with discussions on income distribution, the social costs of the process of accelerated economic modernization, the relationship between the national economic system and transnational enterprises, a certain assumed association between the form that economic growth has taken in Brazil and the exacerbation of social injustices, regional disparities, which would or would not be accentuated as a result of government policies, and many other themes that presently make up the set of issues of Brazilian political dynamics.

When we speak of the analysis of public policies as a special way of visualizing the activity of the political system, or more specifically governmental activity, what we have in mind is something less vague than the simple presentation of relatively impressionistic opinions on the supposed effects of particular polices. What one is looking for consists of the verification or nonverification of assumed associations between certain types of political structures, and the types or contents of the decisions taken, that is, the policies. Second, it is a matter of clarifying the relationships between the decisions taken and their effective implementation, clarifying the intermediate steps or links, which may slow the process, between decision and action. Finally, it is an attempt to illuminate, if not measure, the real effects brought about by the complete implementation of the decision taken, aiming at establishing possible gaps between the intention of the decision and the actual consequences of the chosen policy.

Another crucial difference between the analysis of public policies as we understand it today and the diagnoses of the past — which incidentally continue to be done on a large scale — lies in the systematic way in which the analysis is carried out. The sophistication and systematization of the analysis depends on the stage of development of available analytical and statistical techniques, which have been greatly developed in the last thirty or forty years. It would be unrealistic to expect the analysts of the past century to be able to go beyond, in their diagnoses, the limits laid down by the instruments available to them. In this respect it is interesting to observe how the first complete economic census carried out in Brazil, in 1907, under the sponsorship of the Brazilian Industrial Center, the main aim of which was to obtain a diagnosis of the different sectors of the economy for the purposes of input and policy recommendations, was content with the simple enumeration and description of the number of establishments, spatial distribution, physical production, and other similar variables, making no attempt to carry out any analysis in a more systematic way (Censo Industrial do Brasil 1907). Today, with the development of techniques for measuring and analyzing data, above all on a statistical basis, it has become possible to submit public policies to more accurate and careful tests.

It was not only the development of statistical techniques that has made it possible to set up a new mode of political analysis. Developments at the level of theoretical elaboration on the relationship between government policy, decision-making structure, and effective performance have also contributed to the increase in the range of pertinent questions and to the raising of problems where previously uncertainty prevailed. The analysis of public policies requires the critical discussion of the presuppositions concerning the relationship, for example, between the representative nature of the state and the type of policies that, as a result of the state being representative, would originate from it. It has become necessary to be sharply aware that decision making does not automatically and necessarily imply either the adequate implementation of the decision or the clear fulfillment of its aims. Before this happened, various reasons contributed to the neglect with which analysts dealt with the performance of the political system.

A major factor keeping researchers from the analysis of effective government action in the past was, obviously, the lack of resources. It is only natural that producers in a relatively free market — that is, the community of social scientists — should be alert to signs indicating the availability of scarce resources and be ready to change the production line to accompany, if not the consumer's, at least the sponsor's changing preferences. Research councils and private foundations, even without intending to, channeled efforts, time, and talent into areas they considered worth studying, to the detriment of the output side of political systems which remains something of a mystery. The hypothesis of an explicit policy aimed at coopting social scientists out of potentially embarrassing areas is attractive but superfluous. The overwhelming majority of social researchers and decision makers in sponsoring institutions shared two unstated, tacit premises which are enough to explain the neglect of output studies, without having to resort to suspicions of intellectual corruption by either party.

Pervading most modern political analysis, at least until recent times, is the voluntaristic assumption that, once policy goals are set by decision makers, practically nothing worth researching remains in the field. Things will develop as charted by the prior analysis that fixed both the goals and the means to achieve them. The interesting part of the political game is limited at one extreme by the social processes that may be held responsible for the generation of specific types of demands; and at the other extreme by the not so visible processes fixing the goals to be pursued and the best means to achieve them. In between, are the questions pertaining to the mechanisms preventing demands from being articulated, the connections between the decision makers and that section of the public allowed to voice its discontent, the processing of occasionally incompatible information, the searching for alternative solutions to meet the problems, and possibly the discovery of patterns of choice. Electoral studies, the analysis of the political functions of private and small organizations, models of party behavior, arguments about the perception of the elite as determined by constituencies or vice versa, predictions of elite behavior based on detailed background knowledge are all familiar investigations translating the questions previously mentioned into explanations of how a problem is born, voiced, perceived, and finally solved at the decision-making level. If we make the voluntaristic assumption that decision makers will in fact do whatever they have planned to do, with no constraints or deviations, plus the assumption that what they planned to do will actually lead to the desired goals, then output analysis will become unnecessary, unimportant, and uninteresting. Political output, in the larger sense, is easily predicted from political input and the political processes involved. (Notice the similarity with vulgar Marxism, whose practitioners dispense with any careful analysis of effective government performance the moment they identify the groups controlling power.)

The naiveté of such a premise is perhaps only too obvious, and perhaps no political scientist has really postulated it in the way described above. However, the voluntaristic premise is associated with traditional democratic theory, and also with radical criticisms of capitalist democratic societies. If a society is democratic, either government output will be congruent with social input — according to democratic theorists — or it will correspond to the interests of the dominant social class — following radical critiques of bourgeois societies. In both cases, the overall performance of any system can be predicted from the knowledge of previous steps in the political process. Yet there is a contemporary model for the analysis of public policies — the so-called ecological model — the findings of which strongly contradict the voluntaristic assumption.

The second premise pertains to the liberal bias of most political analysis. Theoretically in a liberal society the most relevant output for the society as a whole stems not from governmental action but from private agreements and contracts taking place among private, autonomous partners. The system only provides the more general framework within which society will move. And it does that according to the voluntaristic assumption discussed earlier. The government does or should do a minimum. Again, this version of the liberal society is too old-fashioned to be held by sophisticated analysts. However, even accepting that today's liberalism or capitalism is a far cry from eighteenth-century versions of it, relatively few people are aware of what liberalism or capitalism look like today. This is the case independent of the particular competence of political scientists. Not even economists have a clear idea about the limits to be respected by a liberal state, once the concept of a welfare state is accepted as legitimate. Old concepts do not adapt particularly well to new phenomena and therefore just because no one today holds nineteenth-century notions about the functions of the state, it does not necessarily follow that one does hold notions adjusted to current history. Let us be controversial: we know of no political scientist whose ideas about the modern state are sufficiently convincing to solve traditional problems concerning legitimacy and justice, or at least to the point where they receive widespread support from the scientific community. Or, to be even more controversial: contemporary political scientists are almost lost in the face of contemporary political challenges. It is not surprising that long-buried notions keep intruding into one's daily evaluations and behavior, particularly when those old ideas have not been substituted by clearly defined new ones. An old liberal bias accounts for part of the neglect shown for so many decades by political scientists in relation to output analysis.

All this is not enough to provide an accurate picture of the analysis of public policies. Instead of suggesting a definition of this activity which would necessarily be open to a fruitless debate, I will develop a short discussion based on the following questions: What are public policies and who are the participants? What is the purpose of analyzing public policies? What kinds of evidence are appropriate to the analysis of public policies, besides the conventional evidence used in all social analysis?

What Are Public Policies and Who Are the Participants?

The conventional criterion used on large scale to identify both public policies and their participants or matrices is based on the institutional-juridical conception of the public as opposed to the private. Public policies are developed by public bodies, and public bodies are juridically defined as such. The advantage of the juridical-institutional criterion is that it permits clear distinction, in the total set of policies implemented in a society, between those that are public and those that are not. Because the juridical distinction between public and nonpublic is reasonably clear, the use of the juridical-institutional criterion enables the investigator to solve the difficulty of empirically outlining his field of study with a minimum of vagueness. The problem of conceptual vagueness is concerned with the denotative limits of any concept, that is to say, what in the empirical world can or cannot be subsumed under the concept. The vaguer the concept, the harder it is to distinguish the limits which it denotes and what should be denoted by some other concept. Conversely, the less vague the concept, the less difficult is is to decide in each case whether or not the empirical piece under examination belongs to the set of phenomena denoted by the concept.

The juridical definition of who are public policymakers automatically solves the problem of deciding what a public policy is with a minimum margin for vagueness: public policies are those policies implemented by public policymakers, and public policymakers are those defined as such by juridical criteria. Thus there will be no great number of dubious cases, in which the analyst would be in some trouble to decide whether or not the policymaker (the institution) is public. This appealing feature of the juridical criterion explains why public policy analysts focus their attention on governmental structures and policies. Even more, it perhaps explains why there is no single analytical piece discussing this basic question: What is a public policy? Everyone simply assumes that everyone else knows what he/she is talking about, and agrees with it. Yet there is a problem here.

The biggest drawback to the juridical criterion is that it limits analysis to governmental structures and institutions. It is as if policies chosen and implemented by private institutions, according to juridical criteria, had only private consequences and therefore fall outside the legitimate scope of public care and control. An obvious fact in the contemporary world, and above all in the advanced industrial world, is that private decisions taken by giant corporations have tremendous public impact and consequences, even beyond national frontiers. The status of being a privately owned organization does not mean that its decisions should be of nobody else's concern. In the same way, it does not follow that just because the public should have a say in the affairs of any giant private organization that the latter should necessarily become publicly owned. Ownership is one thing, and one should be able to discuss, in each case, the most appropriate status for the organization according to one's perception of the problem. Accountability is another thing, and private property cannot mean that it is not publicly accountable. To define policymakers in a juridical way implies giving a free hand to private corporations, whose decisions are far from having only private costs or consequences. What is needed is a concept of public policies and policymakers that while preserving private rights of ownership would allow the public at large to evaluate the social and public impact of policies decided in private and carried out by large organizations.

A possible way of providing a different definition of what public policies are is to follow the economic tradition in dealing with the definition of public goods and establish that public policies are those policies with externalities. We know it is not easy to put forward a definition of public goods sufficiently persuasive to obtain the agreement of all the specialists. In particular the emphasis on external effects, both positive and negative, as an essential characteristic of public goods, is open to objections and criticisms.[1] We are not going to provide any new definition of public goods. Rather, we would like to draw attention to the fact that compared with the juridical-institutional definition, the definition in terms of externalities has the disadvantage of a wider margin of vagueness. It is much easier to decide what public policies are and who generates or produces them according to the institutional criterion than according to the criterion of externalities. Taken to extremes, the criterion of externalities would end up including in the category of public policies all policies generated in a given society insofar as it is inconceivable that any policy should be bereft of externalities.

Thus, defining public policies as those that produce external effects — for example a petrochemical organization whose production policy leads to pollution of the environment — is less advantageous than the the institutional definition, due to its vagueness. Its positive aspect lies in that it enables us to include on the list of questions of public interest a whole series of decisions which, although juridically private, have undeniable public consequences. Private power need not be, nor should it be, publicly irresponsible, and what the proposed alternative definition does is provide a means of establishing the accountability of the private sector. In this respect, the definition in terms of externalities is undoubtedly superior to the juridical criterion.

Analytically speaking, the problem of the definition — in terms of external effects — lies in its excessive margin of vagueness. We do not believe that there is a logical solution to this problem, which does not mean there is no solution at all. The definition of what is or is not a public policy — the definition of when the magnitude of externalities reaches such proportions that public concern is legitimate — should be politically established. In an effectively democratic system, the public should have the right to decide when the consequences of the private decisions of a complex organization are violating the limits of what is tolerable and consequently the simple fact of ownership ceases to be sufficient grounds for them to exercise sovereign rights in making decisions. The premise underlying this position is that the public in general is fair and will not invade private sovereignty except when its public consequences effectively demand it to be limited. One can accept, as a counterargument, the hypothesis that the public may not be fair. There is, however, no empirical evidence to support this view and consequently the definition of public policies in terms of externalities is superior, until proved otherwise, to the juridical-institutional definition because, besides its comparative advantage — including in the public field questions that would otherwise remain out of its control — it is possible to solve politically its analytical disadvantage.

What Is the Purpose of Analyzing Public Policies?

The objectives that guide the analyses of current public policies are more latent than manifest and need to be inferred. However, there are at least two texts dealing explicitly with the question and they can be taken as representative of two of the most widespread attitudes toward it. Consider first the piece by Richard Hofferbert (1973). This article develops the scientistic position. Statistical association does not mean causality and this cautionary note is found every now and then in academic papers. Nevertheless, it is no less infrequent to construct statistical association as if it represented a sufficient causal connection. Although we know that association does not mean causality, we at least have to admit that, given the statistical association between X and Y, and especially if it is strong, even though the existence of Y may not necessarily depend upon the presence of X — which would be too big an assumption — the presence of X is enough to provoke the presence of Y. If we assume this to be true, we will be in a position to give advice to policymakers in the following way: If you want Y, you should do X.[2]

A daring policy analyst, willing to go even further and to construct the association as representing a necessary connection between X and Y, might advise not only that if one wants Y, one should do X, but also that if one does *not* want Y, one should avoid X. This presumes that Y would not come about, or at least that the chances of it coming about are very slim in the absence of X. When a policy analyst takes the position that his aim is to be able to give advice of the above kind, he is taking a scientistic position, insofar as he does not ask why things are the way they appear to be. Why does X seem to vary together with Y? Is there only one type of inference one can draw from the association found, or can one interpret it in several different ways? These are types of questions a scientistic policy analyst would not ask, believing that the associations he finds and their interpretation are more or less natural and "objective."

A second approach to public policy analysis — the contextualist approach — asks precisely this type of question. Take an article by Martin Krieger (1972).[3] He proposes that public policy analysts should not only look for the motivations and perceptions that have led policymakers to do what they have done, but try to understand why the world behaves the way it does. How does the social context explain the association between X and Y, which might be different were the context different? In addition, what a policy analyst should do, according to this line of thinking, is show how social problems can be seen in a different light, as soon as one changes the context in which the question is framed as a problem.[4] The objective of public policy analysis according to the contextualist approach, implies an effort toward persuading the public and the policymakers that to deal with the problem in question requires a change in the broader context.

A third way of analyzing public policy, which we favor, would be to state clearly and at the outset the values according to which policies will be analyzed. There is no point in analyzing public policies if it is not to propose alternative ways of doing things or to suggest that certain things should be done. This implies that the advice offered will be congruent with the values subscribed to by the analyst, which should be clear from the start. If public policy analysis is not normative, we fail to see what is new about it.

Evidence

Finally, there is the empirical basis upon which policy analysis is pursued. In addition to the traditional evidence handled by social scientists — industrialization and urbanization rates, income indices, votes, parliamentary seats, and so on — policy analysts manipulate monetary flows, mainly in budgetary form, and legal output, that is, decrees, regulations, instructions, and all output not translatable into monetary terms, originating from the government or the social system as a whole, depending on the concept of public policy one adopts. Both types of evidence carry particular problems of codification, classification, aggregation, and interpretation which will not be discussed here.[5] What is perhaps useful to stress is the absorption by the policy analysts of those kinds of empirical materials so far monopolized by economists and jurists.

Evolution of the Public Sector

Let us consider what public policy analysts in general, or Brazilian policy analysts in particular have been doing with regard to the following: the concept, latent or manifest, of public policy that they hold — that is, the analytical unity of analysis; the aims they pursue in their analysis — scientistic, contextualist, or normative; the type of evidence they work with; and the model they use in the analysis. Most of the analyses to be reviewed are derived from a juridical-institutional definition of public policy, and therefore a good starting point would be a discussion of the evolution of the public sector.

The study of the functions of government has attracted the attention of scholars, although these analyses are still highly descriptive. Resende da Silva (1971), for example, concentrates on examining the growth of the Brazilian public sector both from a historical point of view (growth over time), looking at the performance of the economy as a whole (evolution as a percentage of the gross national product), and through some international comparisons. His analysis of the theoretical hypothesis for the growth of public expenditure — generated within an econometric tradition — and the analysis of the diversification of the functions of government, notably in an entrepreneurial capacity and in nontraditional activities sets a landmark for his subsequent work and that of other economists.

More recently, Baer et al. (1973) have undertaken an analysis of the functions of the state carried out on various levels: the periodization of modern Brazilian economic history taking into consideration the growing levels of intervention in economic life and including an assessment of the present control of the economy by the state which uses various institutional channels (official banks, autarchies, publicly owned companies, instruments of price control, etc.). The authors' basic idea is that the growth of the public sector, side by side with a greater degree of economic intervention, has not been the result of planning guided by ideological criteria, but of objective economic conditions coupled with the desire to rapidly industrialize the country. If there is a high degree of continuity in the evolution of state participation in economic life, independent of continuity in the value judgements of the different administrations, it does not logically follow that the instruments of intervention have been the same, satisfying the same preferences for public policies or producing similar effects, intentional or otherwise. Such considerations, of great significance for the analyst of public policies, are not the concern of these authors, which in no way invalidates their basic arguments.

Once the evolution of the functions of government has been defined, the next logical step would be to analyze public policies, which are here understood as the sum total of authoritative decisions for the society as a whole or for significant sectors thereof, decisions therefore made by public officials. The Brazilian output in the field of public policy may, for the purposes of discussion and despite the inherent disadvantages of this definition, be separated into two lines of analysis which do not exclude each other but are mutually complementary. Some analyses tend to view government output as a process of value allocation, which would reflect preferences and/or changes in the distribution of political power. Other analyses of a more economic nature tend to view government output as the allocation of scarce resource within a normative framework whose basic assumptions correspond to the principles of the Paretian optimum.

The analysis of legal production, which is highly comparativist — seeking to explore the relationships between the different powers, particularly between the executive and legislative and simultaneously analyzing aspects of party behavior — was the starting point in Brazil for a whole series of studies on the performance of the public sector with regard to legal output. Along this line are the works of Brigagao (1971) and dos Santos (1973), analyzing legislative output in the period 1959-66 and leading us to believe in a situation of "decisional paralysis," characterized simultaneously by a decrease in the output of decisions and an increase in bills presented in the federal legislature.

Dos Santos (1972) in another analysis extends the period under study of legal output to compare two governments after 1964 in terms of "authoritarian output," defined as "the effective use of the capacity of the executive." It is no longer a question of analyzing power relationships between two political bodies through the legislative output, but to compare two administrations in their use of legislative power which was taken over by the executive, in Brazil, after the 1964 intervention.

The substantive classification of governmental acts — executive decree-laws — identifies these basic categories: economic acts (production and distribution of goods and services), social acts (distribution of status symbols), institutional investment (expansion of government structures), and administrative routines (residual category). Brigagao and dos Santos take as their unit of analysis bills passing through the legislative and laws and decrees of the executive, thereby adopting a legal-institutional perspective of public policy.

An analysis clearly directed toward a macroanalytical perspective is undertaken by Lafer (1970) on the Target Plan of the Kubitschek administration (1956-61). The discussion moves from the planning state to implementation and its results. This study shows that all government planning was defined and carried out on the basis of an awareness of a certain configuration of social forces within a populist system with broad political participation. The Target Plan in all its phases directly reflected the tendencies and pressures of politically active social groups and was, at the same time, an instrument used by the executive to strengthen its political bases.[6]

Skidmore's (1973) analysis of economic policymaking in Brazil is an interesting summary of what has been accomplished.[7] His article is a descriptive account of the nature and content of policymaking processes, he advances some propositions relating policy content to the political regime itself, and attempts to establish a continuity. First he argues that the military-technocratic alliance created a political environment that allowed most policies to be adopted, as all open political mechanisms were either abolished or tightly and effectively controlled. The conclusion being that the success of the policies adopted can be attributed to the established regime, and that economic success, given its nature, prevented opposition from the middle and upper classes. The second aspect is developed in such a way that the period 1945-64 would be seen as an interlude in authoritarian politics and 1964 would not be the breakdown of an imperfect democratic regime, but rather a continuation of the previous system given the similarities in terms of goals and actions between the New State (1937-45) and the post-1964 governments.

Other analyses take, as empirical evidence to test their hypotheses, government expenditures — whose advantages and disadvantages as policy indicators are already well established by the literature. The analysis of nonreducible expenditures has attracted the attention of Garbayo et al. (1974) who, defining them as those expenditures related to personnel in the different bodies of the federal administration (1965-69), conclude that the executive is the branch that shows the greatest spread of variation limits of fixed expenditures in relation to nonfixed expenditures. Within the executive, the ministries that have the greatest flexibility in the reallocation of budgetary funds are mines and energy, transport, and communications. The ultimate objective of the analysis is to establish the limits of the incremental model and the conditions under which its predictive value is altered, utilizing an interval categorization of expenditures for each public branch and organs within the executive, a categorization that would reflect the fact that a certain type of expenditure may be more easily reallocated.

Although the writers are aware that the variation in proportion between fixed and nonfixed expenditures is affected by various general factors (economic stagnation, for example), the historical series being considered is insufficient to adequately assess long-term trends, which does not, however, invalidate the fact that the data clearly point to the existence of political preferences in the reallocation of resources, showing that the most flexible sectors are those to which highest priority is given by the administration, although some additional problems might be added: they are new organs in the administrative set-up of governmental activity. The interesting point of the analysis is, that the nature of the expenditure itself affects the incremental nature (more, or less) of the decision-making process itself. Capital expenditures (investments) as opposed to current expenditures (personnel expenditures) would be the best indicator of political preferences for resource allocation, understood here as budgetary expenditures.

An interesting way of identifying political preferences in the allocation of values would be the establishment of an index reflecting the relationship "personnel expenditures/investment expenditures" for each policy area. The behavior of the index over a period of time would allow us to identify not only preferences but also possible phases in the implementation of a policy, that is, an initial phase in which personnel expenditures predominate (in relative terms), a phase in which investment expenditures predominate, followed again by a phase with personnel expenses. The specific form of the relationship would perhaps correspond to an S-shaped curve or even a U-curve. This procedure would enable us to establish more accurately the conditions under which the incremental model would be valid, overcoming the problem of only analyzing policies being carried out, or in their final stages. The inclusion of the initial planning phase in the analysis, even perhaps at the point when the policy has not yet been translated into significant budgetary terms, would avoid the problem that, in empirical tests of incrementalism, the arbitrary choice as to the length of the historical series affects inferences concerning the incremental nature of the decision-making process. In this way we would also avoid the frequent problem of bias in analysis, insofar as it is possible that the historical series to be studied corresponds only to that intermediate moment in the life of a policy, or rather, to the final stages in which the relationship investment expenditures/personnel expenses reaches a maximum stability in time.

The above conditions are fulfilled in the second part of the work where the writers show first that certain organs, that tend to be incremental over time at some point show signs of nonincrementalism. How can we interpret those results? The results corroborate previous findings obtained for the federal administration in Brazil (Souza 1974). Is it possible that these nonincremental results are due to the nature of the public good produced which, by definition, would imply a personnel/investment relationship? Or are these nonincremental variations a reflection of specific political preferences? Or both? This problem is crucial to the explanation of the process of value allocation through budgets and, if the results presented by the writers still cannot be taken as a definitive test, they certainly point to an important line of reflection and analysis.

The empirical results presented by Souza (1974) and Garbayo et al. (1974) show that the incremental or nonincremental nature of the process depends on how the data are utilized, that is, on their level of aggregation. When one works with total expenditures for each agency, the tendency is toward the positive test of the model. When the analysis is carried out on a more disaggregated level, nonincremental behavior tends to be stressed, which perhaps represents a weakness of incrementalism in which the variation limits accepted by the model are very loosely defined. The model has a very strong tendency to refer to empirical generalizations — the fact that budgetary expenditures at the highest level of aggregation are of the incremental type — at the expense of offering explanations for nonincremental variations at the level of political preferences, which may be one of the model's advantages in the sense that its simplicity allows further refinement. Hence the need to carry out not only tests of the model in different political contexts, but to seek out conditions under which the model has greater or lesser validity in terms of its predictive power (Lima Júnior 1974).

Still within this comparativist and analytical approach to the structure of public expenditures is the work of pioneer Rezende da Silva (1974), who attempts simultaneously to establish the role of the public sector in the economy, analyze the functional structure of the federal and state governments' expenditures and, to a lesser extent, assess the performance of the public sector, stressing the entrepreneurial dimension. In this last objective the work approaches analytical studies of a more political nature previously discussed. The common objective is to establish the limits of the participation of the public sector in the economy and to assess the performance of governmental activities.

The data presented refer to the period 1965-69, a series that is unfortunately rather short for an adequate discussion of the profile of governmental preferences for the allocation of scarce resources and values. The analysis of the performance of the public sector, as the writer recognizes, is still in its initial stages, mainly due to the fact that there is no adequate methodology for the quantification of the objectives and targets established by the government for each sector. The coefficients of performance suggested by the writer connecting expenditures with the needs of the sector constitute an important contribution to subsequent works that would allow an evaluation of distortions introduced into sectoral allocation of resources.

An important distinction is necessary regarding these coefficients. It is essential to establish the determinants of public expenditures and, separately, to establish coefficients of performance. As to the first aspect, the writer restricts himself to dealing with theoretical contributions to the study of the determinants of public expenditure, studies which are economic in nature and in which income is seen as the principal determinant. But the study of determinants must consider the level of aggregation of expenditure, the nature of the sector itself, the administrative level of analysis, and the level of data aggregation, as the structure of determinants may vary according to all these dimensions. If the level of aggregation is high, such as "total expenses in sector X," if the problem of the nonreducibility of the expenditure is eliminated, the variable income will most likely be the only significant determinant.

The problem becomes even more complex if the data are analyzed in a more disaggregated way (economic subcategories or even subprograms) or if one introduces as an intervening variable the level of government. The consideration of the level of government is fundamental, for as the writer suggests, it introduces additional questions of fiscal federalism, where problems of regional imbalance, intergovernmental transfers, and problems of redistribution assume great importance. Analyses of government performance, and mainly the establishment of the determinants of public expenditures, depend fundamentally on how the dependent variable — public expenditures — is operationalized.

A second line of analysis refers to the structure of determination of public expenditures and the trade-offs involved among different policy areas when one takes the whole budget for analysis. These studies are carried out within an interdisciplinary framework, incorporating into the analysis basic economic, political, and social variables. A large number of the studies in this field follow a tradition already established in the United States, taking the states as the unit of analysis.[8] Recently this framework has been extended to other countries, and in Brazil, not only subnational units but also the central government is taken as a basis for analysis. Some international studies are longitudinal and others are cross-sectional.[9]

In the Brazilian case, the definition of a pattern of determinants for public policies and the analysis of trade-offs (interbudget) originate in the work of Margaret Hayes (1973). In her first article, on general patterns of expenditures, the author concludes that some allocations are more volatile than others, both when the allocation is seen in functional terms and when the expenditures are taken as percentages of total expenditures; and that if this functional classification is altered in the sense of obtaining more aggregate categories (expenditures for social development, economic infrastructure, and bureaucratic expenditures), bureaucratic expenditures and infrastructure expenditures are mirror images.

The study, mainly because of its pioneering nature, is of great interest. However, the writer infers on the basis of the mentioned categorization that certain administrations opted for a certain scheme for allocating resources through the budget, while other administrations opted for a different pattern. These inferences, given the nature of the data, are somewhat dubious. First in Brazil one cannot speak of preferences of the different administrations without incorporating into the analysis information relative to the decentralized sector of the administration; and second, neither can one speak of these preferences without assessing the real margin of choice of the different administrations, even in terms of budgetary allocations. The distinction between fixed and nonfixed budgetary expenditures cannot be dismissed.

The second article (Hayes 1973) assesses the impact of ecological factors as determinants of federal allocations in Brazil. The analysis is carried out on several levels. First, a regression is run to determine the individual relationships between a series of indicators and each budgetary allocation for each area of public policy. Two conclusions, irrespective of the nature of the independent variables involved, are the following: different ecological factors (external dependence, indicators of the performance of the economy, and domestic conflict are the three groups of independent variables included in the analysis) affect in a different way each type of expenditure (a step-wise regression is used). There are trade-offs among all three types of expenditures (economic infrastructure, bureaucracy, and social development) verified in the second model of regression in which each type of expenditure is regressed against all the others. The general conclusion is that there is no prevailing bivariate relationship: the pattern of determination of public expenditures varies according to the nature of the expenditure, and both socioeconomic and political variables participate in the pattern of determination.

Finally, it is worth mentioning some specific policy studies, not only because they are concerned with clearly defined substantive policies, but also because they tend to avoid a political-juridical definition and keep much closer to policies identified as public in view of their external effects. The educational sector has been the object of economic analyses concerned with the determination of the costs associated with its performance. The principal studies in the area of educational economics are those by Castro (1971), dealing with the relationships between the cost of education and the quantity produced.

Castro's (1971) first piece, in which he takes a sample of first-year university students in the state of Guanabara, presents us with the following conclusions, among others: Economic variables are particularly relevant to explain the quality of secondary schools. The most important variables involved in the productive function of education are: salary level of teachers, school equipment, and the quality of students. In the final years of senior high school, teachers' salaries and tuition are the variables that best reflect the quality of the school. The students who pass university entrance examinations come from a small number of secondary schools. The schools in Guanabara are highly elitist, confirming for the student the social and educational status of his family.

In a second study, a natural follow-up of the above survey, the writer analyzes the costs and performance of technical education, seeking to determine the social costs of technical education in Guanabara and Sao Paulo (Castro 1972). The book is an excellent manual for the analysis of costs in this education subsector, providing methodological bases for future studies and substantive results for the programs designed to create medium-level technicians.

In his work on the industrial labor force in Brazil, Castro (1974) complements the previous studies analyzing, according to social level, the distribution of personnel characteristics demanded by technical training and the restrictions and biases associated with this particular type of training. The composition of the labor force is seen according to social origin and to the vertical mobility within companies. Besides, and it is here that the study is of direct importance for the analysis of public policies, it also investigates the problem of equating the demand for labor with the structure of the educational system. Finally, the survey looks at the organization of training and the distribution of its costs among the students and firms sponsoring training-on-the-job programs.

Current Research Problems

There are still some gaps that empirical studies should try to fill. We will indicate some research problems that would significantly add to available studies. Generally the budgetary categories with which one works stem from legislative decisions which in turn are based on budgetary proposals of the executive. Thus there must be established the relationship between the budgetary forecasts of government agencies, the confirmation of these forecasts in terms of budgetary proposals of the executive, changes introduced by the legislative, and the level of expenditures disbursed by the state, which constitute the real output of governmental decision making. Whether the analysis deals with the ecological determinants of public expenditure, the decision-making process, or the impact of government policies, it is essential for the understanding of intergovernmental relationships to work within a comparative framework, introducing variations of a state or regional nature, which should be seen here as a "proxy" variable.

Comparative studies of public policies, either from a longitudinal or spatial point of view (diversity of analytical political units), should stress the degree and type of association existing among different substantive policies with a view to detecting possible tradeoffs in allocations. Here the essence of the analysis would be to identify preferences in the allocation of resources among the different areas, considering available resources. Either the resources increase substantially and there exists an uncommitted surplus, or the resources are reallocated with a view to reducing previous levels of allocations in certain areas and increasing them in others. The final goal is to detect preferential allocations resulting from specific policies — be they already in existence or innovative policies. Finally, there is a need for case studies of the decision-making process which should stress substantive policy areas while aiming at the theoretical significance within a comparative perspective.

NOTES

1. An excellent account of several ways of conceptualizing public goods and their problems can be found in Steiner (1970).
2. This is the position taken by Max Weber on the issue related to the connection between science and action.
3. This paper touches upon many other points we will not be concerned with here.
4. Cf.: "Also, I will argue that the effect of most understanding is to change the manner in which we see our problematic situations" (Krieger 1972: 4-6).
5. For a lengthy discussion of these problems, see Santos (1974).
6. See also Lafer (1973) and Daland (1967) for a specific analysis of the historical experiences on federal planning in Brazil.
7. For further references on economic policymaking in Brazil see Baer (1965), Left (1968), and Ellis (1969). Of related interest see Schmitter (1971), particularly chapter 10.

8. For further references on the ecological literature see Dawson and Robinson (1963), Dye (1969), Hofferbert (1966, 1968), Cameron (1972),and Sharkansky (1967, 1969).
9. Some examples of analysis on Latin America are the papers of Barry and Goff (1973) and of Keneth and Wannat (1973), both presented to the 1973 American Political Science Association Meetings.

REFERENCES

Baer, Werner. 1965. *Industrialization and Economic Growth in Brazil.* Homewood, Ill.: Richard D. Irwin.

Baer, Werner, et al. 1973. "As modificaçoes do papel do estado na economia brasileira." *Pesquisa e Planejamento Econômico* 3-4. Rio de Janeiro: IPEA/INPES.

Edward, Ames; and Goff, Barry. 1973. "A Longitudinal Approach to Latin American Public Expenditures." Paper presented at the American Political Science Association Meetings, New Orleans, September 4-8, mimeographed.

Brigagao, Clóvis. 1971. "Poder e legislativo no Brasil: análise política da produçao legal de 1959 a 1966." Instituto Universitário de Pesquisas do Rio de Janeiro, M.A. dissertation.

Cameron, David, et al. 1972. "Urbanization, Social Structure, and Mass Politics: A Comparison within Five Nations." *Comparative Political Studies* 4 (October).

Castro, Claudio Moura. 1971. "Eficiência e custos das escolas do nível médio: um estudo piloto na Guanabara." Rio de Janeiro: IPEA/INPES, report no. 3.

Castro, Claudio Moura, et al. 1972. "Ensino Técnico, desempenho e custos." Rio de Janeiro: IPEA/INPES, report no. 10.

Castro, Claudio Moura; and Souza, Alberto de Mello. 1974. "Mao de obra industrial no Brasil." Rio de Janeiro: IPEA/INPES, report no. 25.

Censo Industrial do Brasil. 1907. *O Brasil: suas riquezas naturais, suas industrias,* 3 vols. Rio de Janeiro.

Daland, Robert. 1967. *Brazilian Planning-Development, Politics, and Administration.* Chapel Hill, N.C.: University of North Carolina Press.

Dawson, A.E.; and Robinson, J. 1963. "Inter-Party Competition, Economic Variables, and Welfare Politics in the American States." *Journal of Politics* 25 (May).

Dye, Thomas. 1969. "Income Inequality and American States' Politics." *American Political Science Review* 62 (March).

_____. 1969. "Executive Power and Public Policy in the States." *Western Political Quarterly* 22 (December).

_____. 1972. *Understanding Public Policy.* New York: Prentice-Hall.

Ellis, Howard. 1969. *The Economy of Brazil.* Berkeley: University of California Press.

Garbayo, Cléa, et al. 1974. "Alocaçao de recursos públicos: um estudo sobre o processo orçamentário no Brasil, 1965-70." Rio de Janeiro: Instituto Universitário de Pesquisas do Rio de Janeiro, mimeographed.

Hayes, Margaret D. 1973. "Patterns of Federal Spending in Brazil, 1950-1967: An Allocational Policy Analysis." Paper presented at the Ninth World Congress of the International Political Science Association, Montreal August 20-25, mimeographed.

_____. 1973. "Ecological Constraints and Policy Outputs in Brazil: An Examination of Federal Spending Patterns." Paper presented at the American Political Science Association Meetings, New Orleans, September 4 8, mimeographed.

Hofferbert, Richard I. 1966. "Ecological Development and Policy Change in the American States." *Midwest Journal of Political Science* (November).

_____. 1968. "Socioeconomic Dimensions of the American States, 1890 1960." *Midwest Journal of Political Science* 12 (August).

_____. 1973. "How the Scholarly Analysis of Policy Outcomes Can Be of Practical Benefit to Policy Makers." Paper presented at the Conference on Perspectives on Canadian Public Policy, Carleton University, Ottawa, February 17, mimeographed.

Keneth, Coleman; and Wanatt, John. 1973. "Models of Political Influence on Budgetary Allocations to the Mexican States." Paper presented at the American Political Science Association Meetings, New Orleans, September 4-8, mimeographed.

Krieger, Martins H. 1972. "Is It Worthwhile to Do Public Policy Research?" No. 167, Institute of Urban and Regional Development, University of California at Berkeley, January, mimeographed.

Lafer, Betty M. 1973. *Planejamento no Brasil*. Sao Paulo: Ed. Perspectiva.

Lafer, Celso. 1970. "The Planning Process and the Political System in Brazil: A Study of Kubistschek's Target Plan, 1956-61." Cornell University, Latin American Studies Program, Ph.D. dissertation, Dissertation Series 16, mimeographed.

Left, Nathaniel. 1968. *Economic Policy-Making in Brazil, 1947-1964*. New York: John Wiley.

Lima, Júnior, Olavo Brasil. Forthcoming. "Incrementalismo e política orçamentária." *Caderno*. Belo Horizonte (Brazil): Departmento de Ciência Política, Universidade Federal de Minas Gerais.

Rezende da Silva, Fernando A. 1971. "A evoluçao das funçoes de governo e a expansao do setor público brazileiro." *Pesquisa e Planejamento* 1-2. Rio de Janeiro: IPEA.

_____. 1974. "Avaliaçao do setor público na economia brasileira." Rio de Janeiro: IPEA/INPES.

Santos, Wanderley Guilherme dos. 1972. "Governing by Decree: An Empirical Introduction to a Theory of Authoritarian Spending." Paper presented at the Conference on National Development Indicators, Instituto Universitário de Pesquisas do Rio de Janeiro.

_____. 1973. "Paralisia da decisao e comportamento legislativo: A experiência brasileira, 1959-1966." *Revista de Administraçao de Empresas* (April-June). São Paulo: Fundaçao Getúlio Vargas.

_____. 1974. "Comparative Public Policy Analysis: Non-Exhaustive Inventory of Queries." Paper presented at the Conference on Public Policy Analysis, Instituto Torcuato Di Tella, Buenos Aires, August 11-15, mimeographed.

Schmitter, P.C. 1971. *Interest Conflict and Political Change in Brazil.* Stanford: Stanford University Press.

Sharkansky, Ira. 1967. *Spending in American States.* New York: Rand McMally.

_____. 1969. *Politics of Taxing and Spending.* New York: Bobbs Merrill.

Skidmore, Thomas E. 1973. "Politics and Economic Policy-Making in Authoritarian Brazil, 1937-71." In Alfred Stepan (ed.), *Authoritarian Brazil.* New Haven: Yale University Press.

Souza, Isabel R.O. Gómez. 1974. "O incrementalismo e a política orçamentária brasileira." Instituto Universitário de Pesquisas do Rio de Janeiro, M.A. dissertation.

Steiner, Peter. 1970. "The Public Sector and the Public Interest." In Robert H. Haveman and Julins Margolis (eds.), *Public Expenditure and Policy Analysis.* New York: Markham.

General Bibliography: A Selection of Brazilian Production in the Social Sciences, 1960-1977

Abranches, Sérgio Henrique Hudson de; and Soares, Gláucio Ary Dillon. 1972. "As funçoes do legislativo." Universidade de Brasília, mimeographed.

Abranches, Sérgio Henrique Hudson de. 1973. "O legislativo no processo político do Brasil." Universidade de Brasília, M.A. dissertation.

Aguiar, Neuma. 1962. "O sindicato dos trabalhadores nas indústrias do Estado da Guanabara." *"Revista de Direito Público e Ciência Política* (January-April): 62-80.

———. 1964. "The Organization and Ideology of Brazilian Labor." In Irving Louis Horowitz (ed.), *Revolution in Brazil.* New York: E.P. Dutton.

———. 1967. "Movilización de la clase obrera en el Brasil." *Revista Latinoamericana de Sociología* 3 (November): 359-87.

———. 1968. "Corporativismo y clase trabajadora." *Desarrollo Económico* 30-31 (July-December): 313-48.

———. 1969. "The Mobilization and Bureaucratization of the Working Class in Brazil, 1930-1964." Washington University, Ph.D. dissertation.

———. 1969. "Condicionamentos sócio-culturais da industrializaçao do Ceará. *Revista de Ciências Sociais* 1: 96-109.

———. 1969. "O modelo de mudança por detrás das teorias da anomia e mobilização." *América Latina* 3: 90-116.

———. 1972. "Ideologias competitivas e um projeto de industrializaçao do Nordeste." *Dados* 9: 21-71.

———. 1973. "Totem e tabu no Nordeste." Instituto Universitário de Pesquisas do Rio de Janeiro, mimeographed.

———. 1973. "Tempo de transformaçao no Nordeste." Rio de Janeiro: IUPERJ, mimeographed.

———. 1974. "Urbanizaçao, industrializaçao e mobilizaçao social no Brasil." *Dados* 11: 146-72.

———. 1974. "Brazil: Residents of the Road" (with Hugo Denisart). *Society* 11 (September-October): 81-83.

_____. 1974. "Hierarquias em classes: uma introduçao ao estudo da estratificaçao social." In id. (ed.), *Hierarquias em Classes*. Rio de Janeiro: Zahar.

_____. 1975. "Industrialization, Organization, and Unionization in Sao Paulo." *Studies in Comparative International Development* 10 (Spring): 100-106.

_____. 1975. "Impact of Industrialization on Women's Work Roles in Northeast Brazil." *Studies in Comparative International Development* 10 (Summer): 78-94.

Albuquerque, Roberto Cavalcanti de; and Vilaça, Vinicius Marcos. 1965. *Coronel, Coronéis*. Rio de Janeiro: Tempo Brasileiro.

Albuquerque, Roberto Cavalcanti; and Cavalcanti, Clóvis Vasconcelos. 1976. *Desenvolvimento regional do Brasil*. Brasília: Instituto de Planejamento Econômico e Social.

Alcântara, Aspásia. 1967. "A teoria política de Azevedo Amaral." *Dados* 2-3: 194-224.

_____. 1972. "Brésil nord-est: mouvements paysans et crise populiste." Ecole Pratique des Hautes Etudes (Paris), doctoral dissertation.

Aléssio, Nancy. 1970. "Urbanizaçao, industrializaçao e estrutura ocupacional." *Dados:* 103-107.

Almeida, Ana Lucia Malan. 1970. "Abertura empresarial, percepçao de papel e participaçao política do empresário brasileiro." Instituto Universitário de Pesquisas do Rio de Janeiro, M.A. dissertation.

Almeida, Maria Hermínia Tavares de; and Marcondes, Cassiano. 1968. "As greves políticas de 1962 e 1963." Sao Paulo, mimeographed.

Almeida, Maria Hermínia Tavares de. 1975. "O sindicato no Brasil: Novos problemas, velhas estruturas." *Debate e Crítica* (July).

Alvim, Maria Rosilene Barbosa. 1971. "Misticismo e artesanato." *Revista de Ciências Sociais* 2: 67-82.

_____. 1972. "A arte de ouro: um estudo sobre os ourives de Juazeiro do Norte." Museu Nacional da Universidade Federal do Rio de Janeiro, M.A. dissertation.

Amorim, Maria Stella Faria de. 1975. "Homens burocráticos: sociologia das organizaçoes públicas do nordeste Brasileiro." Universidade Federal Fluminense, *Livre Docência* dissertation.

Amorin, Sonia David. 1973. "Urbanizaçao e expansao agrícola: o caso de Mato Grosso." Universidade de Brasília, M.A. dissertation.

Andrade, Rachel Maria de Araujo. 1973. "Migraçao e industrializaçao." Universidade Federal da Bahia, M.A. dissertation.

Avelar, Sônia Maria. 1971. "Desenvolvimento e tensoes sócio-políticas." Universidade Federal de Minas Gerais, M.A. dissertation.

Azevedo, Sergio. 1975. "A política habitacional para as classes de baixa renda." Instituto Universitário de Pesquisas do Rio de Janeiro, M.A. dissertation.

Azevedo, Thales. 1966. *Cultura e situaçao racial no Brasil*. Rio de Janeiro: Civilizaçao Brasileira.

Azzoni, Carlos Roberto. 1975. "Fatores locacionais, incentivos municipais e a localizaçao de indústrias no Estado de Sao Paulo, 1958-1967." Faculdade de Economia e Administraçao da Universidade de Sao Paulo, mimeographed.

Bacha, Claire Savit. 1971. "A dependência nas relaçoes internacionais: uma introduçao à experiência brasileira." Instituto Universitário de Pesquisas do Rio de Janeiro, M.A. dissertation.

———. 1972. "Elites Empresariais no Brasil." Instituto Universitário de Pesquisas do Rio de Janeiro, mimeographed.

Baer, Werner; and Villela, Anibal. 1972. "Crescimento industrial e industrializaçao: revisoes nos estágios do desenvolvimento econômico do Brasil." *Dados* 9: 114-34.

Barriaveli, José Claudio. 1972. "O teatro, a política, a ideologia." Universidade de Sao Paulo, mimeographed.

Barros, Alexandre S.C. 1975. "Gulliver em Lilliput ou a imagem que os cientistas sociais tem de si mesmos: introduçao à ediçao brasileira." In Oscar Cornblit et al., *Organizaçao e política da pesquisa social*. Rio de Janeiro: Fundaçao Getúlio Vargas.

Barreto, Vicente. 1973. "A ideologia liberal no processo da independência do Brasil, 1789-1824." Brasilia: Câmara dos Deputados.

Barroso, Carmem Lúcia de Melo; and Namo de Mello, Guiomar. 1975. "O acesso da mulher ao ensino superior brasileiro." *Cadernos de Pesquisa: Revista de Estudos e Pesquisas em Educaçao* 15 (December): 47-77.

Bastos, Rafael José de M. 1975. "Um sistema de classificaçao kamayura." Universidade de Brasília, M.A. dissertation.

Bazzanella, Waldemiro. 1963. "Industrializaçao e urbanizaçao no Brazil." *América Latina* 6.

Beiguelman, Paula. 1965. "O processo político no Império de 1840 a 1869." *Revista Brasileira de Estudos Políticos* 12 (January).

Beisiegel, Celso. 1972. "A educaçao de adultos no Estado de Sao Paulo." Universidade de Sao Paulo, mimeographed.

Benevides, Maria Victoria de Mesquisa. 1976. *O governo Kubitschek: desenvolvimento econômico e estabilidade política*. Rio de Janeiro: Paz e Terra.

Berlinck, Manoel T. 1968. "Populaçao, centralidade relativa e morfogênese sistêmica em áreas urbanas do Estado de Sao Paulo." *Revista de Administraçao de Empresas* 8 (December): 61-79.

———. 1968. "The structure of the Brazilian family in the City of Sao Paulo, Brazil. Cornell University Latin American Studies Program Dissertation Series, Ph.D. dissertation.

———. 1972. "Algumas consideraçoes sociológicas sobre as religioes no Brasil." *Revista do Instituto de Estudos Brasileiros* (no. 12): 139-61.

———. 1974. "A vida como ela é: marginalidade social ou desenvolvimento capitalista periférico na Cidade de Sao Paulo." Universidade de Campinas, mimeographed.

Berquó, Elza Salvatori. 1971. "Estudos da seqüêcia dos sexos em famílias do Distrito de Sao Paulo." *Cadernos CEBRAP* 4.

Berquó, E.S.; and Camargo, C.P.F. (eds.). 1971. "diferenciais de fertilidade." Sao Paulo: CEBRAP, mimeographed.

Berquó, Elza S.; Camargo, Candido P.F. de; Singer, P. Lamounier Bolivar; Gonçalves, M.; and Lopes, Juarez R.B., n.d. "O crescimento da populaçao brasileira." Sao Paulo: CEBRAP, mimeographed.

Berquó, Elsa Salvatori; Milanesi, Maria Lucila; and Prandi, J. Reginaldo. 1971. "Estudo da influência da idade dos pais, do uso de meios anticoncepcionais e do número de gestaçoes anteriores no resultado de uma gestaçao." *Cadernos CEBRAP.* 4.

Berquó, Elza Salvatori; Milanesi, Maria Lucia; and Silva, Eunice Pinto de Castro. 1971. "Análise prospectiva de fertilidade no Distrito de Sao Paulo." *Cadernos CEBRAP* 1.

Berquó, Elsa Salvatori; and Oya, Diana R.T. 1971. "Estudo da esterilizaçao em Sao Paulo." *Cadernos CEBRAP.* 1.

Blay, Eva Alterman. 1967. "A participaçao da mulher na indústria paulistana." *América Latina* 10: 81-95.

———. 1969. "Mulher, escola: profissao-estudo sociológico do Ginásio Industrial Feminino na Cidade de Sao Paulo." Universidade de Sao Paulo, mimeographed.

———. 1972. "A mulher o trabalho qualificado na indústria paulista." Doctoral dissertation, Universidade de Sao Paulo.

———. 1972. "Trabalho, família e classes sociais em Sao Paulo." *Revista do Instituto de Estudos Brasileiros* 13: 87-99.

———. 1973. "O trabalho feminino." *Cadernos do CERU,* 8: 129-45.

Bolaffi, Gabriel. 1972. "Aspectos sócio-econômicos do plano nacional da habitaçao." Universidade de Sao Paulo, doctoral dissertation.

Bolan, Valmor. 1970. "Religiao e secularizaçao: introduçao a secularizaçao no Brasil." Universidade de Sao Paulo, mimeographed.

Boschi, Renato Raul. 1970. "Marginalidade urbana, educaçao e aspiraçao: uma contribuiçao à teoria do comportamento político do favelado." Instituto Universitário de Pesquisas do Rio de Janeiro, M.A. dissertation.

Braga, Célia. 1970. "Relaçoes de trabalho no meio rural." Universidade Federal da Bahia, M.A. dissertation.

Brandâo, Carlos Rodrigues. 1974. "Relações de trabalho e identidade étnica em Goiás." Universidade de Brasília, M.A. dissertation.

Brasileiro, Ana Maria. 1976. "The Politics of Municipal Finance: A Comparative Study of Local Government in the State of Rio de Janeiro." University of Essex, Ph.D. dissertation.

Bressan, Matheus. 1973. "Determinantes da estrutura ocupacional brasileira." Universidade de Brasília, M.A. dissertation.

Brigagao, Clovis. 1971. "Poder e legislativo no Brasil: análise política da produçao legal de 1959 a 1965." Instituto Universitário de Pesquisas do Rio de Janeiro M.A. dissertation.

Brigagao, Nanci V.C. 1976. "Geraçoes que fazem história." Rio de Janeiro, mimeographed.

Britto, Sulamita (ed.). 1968. *A sociologia da juventude.* Rio de Janeiro: Zahar.

Brumer, Anita. 1971. "Sindicalismo rural e participaçao dos agricultores em sindicatos: Candelária." Universidade Federal do Rio Grande do Sul, M.A. dissertation.

Calazans, Julieta. 1969. "Le Syndicat paysan comme instrument de participation: le cas du nord-est du Brésil." Ecole Pratique des Hantes Etudes, doctoral dissertation.

Camargo, Aspásia Alcântara de. 1973. "Brésil nord-est: mouvements paysans et crise populiste." Ecole Pratique des Hautes Etudes, doctoral dissertation.

Camargo, C.P., et al. 1974. "Composiçao da populaçao brasileira." *Cadernos CEBRAP* 15.

Camargo, C.P.F., et al. 1970. "Marriage Patterns and Fertility in Sao Paulo." *Social Biology* 17: 260-68.

Camargo, C.P.F.; and Levy, M.S.F. 1970. "Catolicismo e abortamento." *Universitas:* 343-57.

Campello de Souza, Maria do Carmo. 1976. *Estado e partidos políticos no Brasil (1930 a 1964).* Sao Paulo: Alfa e Omega.

Cardoso, Fernando Henrique. 1962. "Proletariado no Brasil: situaçao e comportamento." *Revista Brasiliense* 41 (May-June).

_____. 1964. *O empresário industrial e o desenvolvimento econômico.* Sao Paulo: Difusao Européia do Livro.

_____. 1967. "Hégémonie Bourgeoise et dépendance economique." *Temps Modernes* (October).

_____. 1967. "Dependencia y desarrollo." Santiago de Chile: FLACSO, mimeographed.

_____. 1969. "Proletariado no Brasil: situaçao e comportamento social." *Mudanças sociais na América Latina.* Sao Paulo: Difusao Européia do Livro.

_____. 1971. "Teoria da dependência ou análise concreta de situaçoes de dependência?" *Estudos* 1: 25-46. Sao Paulo: CEBRAP.

_____. 1971. "Alternativas políticas na América Latina." Sâo Paulo: CEBRAP, mimeographed.

_____. 1971. *Política e desenvolvimento em sociedades dependentes.* Rio de Janeiro: Zahar.

_____. 1972. "A cidade e a política." *Cadernos CEBRAP* 7.

_____. 1972. "O modelo brasileiro de desenvolvimento: dados e perspectiva." Sao Paulo: CEBRAP, mimeographed.

_____. 1973. "Notas sobre estado e dependência." *Cadernos CEBRAP.* 11.

_____. 1973. "As contradiçoes do desenvolvimento associado. Sao Paulo: CEBRAP, Mimeographed.

_____. 1973. "As classes sociais e a crise política da América Latina." Sao Paulo: CEBRAP, mimeographed.

_____. 1975. *Autoritarismo e democratizaçao.* Rio de Janeiro: Paz e Terra.

_____1976. "Estatizaçao e autoritarismo esclarecido: tendéncias e limites." *Estudos CEBRAP* 15 (February-March).

_____. 1976. "Bibliography of Works." In Joseph A. Kahl, *Modernization, Exploitation, and Dependency in Latin America: Germani, González Casanova, and Cardoso.* New Brunswick, N.J.: Transaction Books.

Cardoso, Miriam. 1972. "A ideologia do desenvolvimento do Brasil JK-JQ." Universidade de Sao Paulo, doctoral dissertation.

Cardoso, Ruth Corrêa Leite. 1972. "A integraçao do imigrante japonês em Sao Paulo." Universidade de Sao Paulo, doctoral dissertation.

Carone, Edgard. 1969. *A Primeira República.* Sao Paulo: Difusao Européia do Livro.

_____. 1970. *A república velha: institutuiçoes e classes sociais.* Sao Paulo: Difusao Européia do Livro.

_____. 1971. *A república velha: Evoluçao política.* Sao Paulo: Difusao Européia do Livro.

_____. 1973. *A Segunda República.* Sao Paulo: Difusao Européia do Livro.

Carvalho, Inaiá Maria Moreira de. 1971. "Operários e sociedade industrial na Bahia." Universidade Federal da Bahia, M.A. dissertation.

Carvalho, José Murilo de. 1968. "Estudos de poder local no Brasil." *Revista Brasileira de Estudos Políticos* 25-20 (June): 231-48.

_____. 1974. "Elite and State Building in Imperial Brazil." Stanford University, Ph.D. dissertation.

_____. 1975. "As forças armadas na Primeira República." *Cadernos DCP* 1: 113-88.

Casas, Roberto Las. 1969. "Formation et comportement du prolétariat au Brésil." *Sociologie du Travail* 2.

Castro, Josué de. 1965. *Une Zone explosive: le nordest du Brésil.* Paris: Seuil.

Cesar, Waldo A. 1970. "Urbanizaçao e religiosidade popular." Centro de Estudos, Pesquisa e Planejamento do Rio de Janeiro, mimeographed.

_____. 1970. "Attitudes e manifestaçoes religiosas dos membros da Igreja Presbiteriana de Ipanema." Centro de Estudos, Pesquisa e Planejamento do Rio de Janeiro, mimeographed.

_____. 1973. *Para uma sociologia do protestante brasileiro.* Petrópolis: Vozes.

Chacon, Vamireh. 1969. *História das idéias socialistas no Brasil.* Rio de Janeiro: Civilizaçao Brasileira.

Chaloult, Norma B.R. 1971. "Migraçao Rural." Universidade Federal do Rio Grande do Sul, M.A. dissertation.

_____. 1971. "Educaçao integral em uma comunidade rural: Candelária." Universidade Federal do Rio Grande do Sul, M.A. dissertation.

Chaves, Luiz Gonzaga Mendes. 1971. "Um aspecto relevante da contribuiçao de Silvio Romero às ciências sociais no Brasil." *Revista de Ciências Sociais* 2: 87-113.

_____. 1973. "Trabalho e subsistência: abrangendo aspectos da technologia e das relaçoes de produçao." Museu Nacional da Universidade Federal do Rio de Janeiro, M.A. dissertation.

Cintra, Antônio Octávio; and Reis, Fabio Wanderley. 1966. "Política e desenvolvimento: O caso brasileiro." *América Latina* 9 (no. 3): 52-74.

Cintra, Antônio Octávio. 1968. "Partidos políticos em Belo Horizonte: um estudo do eleitorado." *Dados* 5: 82-112.

_____. 1971. "A integraçao do processo político no Brasil: algumas hipóteses inspiradas na literatura." *Revista de Administraçao Pública* 5 (no. 2).

Coelho, Edmundo Campos (ed.). 1966. *Sociologia da burocracia.* Rio de Janeiro: Zahar.

_____. 1976. *Em busca de identidade: o exército e a política na sociedade brasileira.* Rio de Janeiro: Forense-Universitária.

_____. 1977. "Fixaçao e elaboraçao de papéis: uma contribuiçao à teoria." *Dados* 14: 48-59.

Coelho, Magda Prates. 1970. "Radicalismo político estudantil em quatro escolas superiores." Universidade Federal de Minas Gerais, M.A. dissertation.

Cohn, Gabriel. 1972. "Análise sociológica da comunicaçao de massa." Universidade de Sao Paulo, doctoral dissertation.

Concone, Maria Helena. 1973. "Uma religiao brasileira: umbanda." Universidade de Sao Paulo, mimeographed.

Costa, Flávio Simoes. 1970. "Antônio Conselheiro: uma reformulaçao à luz da psicologia social." Universidade Federal da Bahia, M.A. dissertation.

Costa, Emilia Viotti da. 1966. *Da senzala à colonia.* Sao Paulo: Difusao Européia do Livro.

Costa, Fernando José Leite. 1970. "Processo de diferenciaçao na sociedade colonial." *Dados* 7: 42-61.

Costa Pinto, L.A. 1963. "As classes sociais no Brasil." *Revista Brasileira de Ciências Sociais* 3:11-20.

———. 1963. "Estrutura de classe en processo de câmbio." *Desarrollo Económico* 3: 249-82.

———. 1963. *Sociologia e desenvolvimento.* Rio de Janeiro: civilizaçao Brasileira.

———. 1969. *Desarrollo económico y transición social.* Madrid: Editorial Revista de Occidente.

———. 1969. *Nacionalismo y Militarismo.* Mexico, D.F.: Siglo Veintiuno.

Dagnino, Eveline. 1970. "Sistema de valores: um modelo." Universidade Federal de Minas Gerais, M.A. dissertation.

Darós, Gildo. 1972. "Conscientizaçao de agricultores numa área de reforma agrária: Passo Real, Rio Grande do Sul." Universidade Federal do Rio Grande do Sul, M.A. dissertation.

Dias, Fernando C. 1971. *A imagem de minas: ensaios de sociologia regional.* Belo Horizonte: Imprensa Oficial.

———. 1973. "Presença de Max Weber na sociologia brasileira contemporânea." Universidade de Brasília, mimeographed.

Dieghes, Antônio Carlos Sant'Anna. 1973. "Pesca e marginalidade no litoral paulista." Universidade de Sao Paulo, mimeographed.

Diegues Júnior, Manuel. 1964. "Imigraçao, urbanizaçao, industrializaçao." Rio de Janeiro: Centro Brasileiro de Pesquisas Educacionais.

Diniz Cerqueira, Eli. 1970. "Status do funcionário no órgao e desenvolvimento na organizacao." Instituto Universitário de Pesquisas do Rio de Janeiro, M.A. dissertation.

Dinitz Cerqueira, Eli; and Soares de Lima, Maria Regina. 1971 "O Modêlo político de Oliveira Vianna." *Revista Brasileira de Estudos Políticos* 30.

Dinitz Cerqueira, Eli; and Boschi, Renato R. 1976. "Empresário nacional: ideologia e atuaçao política nos anos 70." Rio de Janeiro: IUPERJ, mimeographed.

———. 1977. "Magnitude das empresas e diferenciaçao da estrutura industrial: caracterizaçao da indústria paulista na década de 30." *Dados* 14: 60-84.

Durhan, Eunice Ribeiro. 1973. *A caminho da cidade.* Sao Paulo: Perspectiva.

Esterci, Neide. 1973. "O mito da democracia no País das bandeiras: análise simbólica dos discursos sobre migraçao e colonizaçao no Estado Novo." Museu Nacional da Universidade Federal do Rio de Janeiro, M.A. dissertation.

Faria, Luiz Castro. 1974. "Populaçóes meridionais do Brasil: ponto de partida para uma leitura de Oliveira Vianna." Museu Nacional da Universidade Federal do Rio de Janeiro, mimeographed.

Faria, Vilmar. 1971. "Dépendance et idéologie des dirigeants industriels brésiliens." *Sociologie du Travail.* 3 (July-September).

_____. 1974. "Tipologia empírica das cidades brasileiras." São Paulo: CEBRAP, mimeographed.

Fausto, Boris. 1970. *A Revoluçao de Trinta: historiografia e história.* Sao Paulo. Brasiliense.

Feet, Neiva T. 1969. "O papel da comunicaçao coletiva na modernizaçao dos agricultores." Universidade Federal do Rio Grande do Sul, M.A. dissertation.

Fernandes, Florestan. 1963. "Pattern and Rate of Development in Latin America." In E. Vries and J. Medina Echavarría (eds.), *Social Aspects of Economic Development.* Paris: UNESCO.

_____. 1965. *A integraçao do negro na sociedade de classes.* Sao Paulo: Dominus and USP.

_____. 1966. *Educaçao e sociedade no Brasil.* Sao Paulo. Dominus and USP.

_____. 1968. *Sociedade de classes e subdesenvolvimento.* Rio de Janeiro: Zahar.

_____. 1969. *The Negro in Brazilian Society.* New York: Columbia University Press.

_____. 1972. *O negro no mundo dos brancos.* Sao Paulo: Difusao Européia do Livro.

_____. 1975. *A revoluçao burguesa no Brasil.* Rio de Janeiro: Zahar.

_____. 1975. *A investigaçao etnológica no Brasil e outros ensaios.* Petrópolis: Vozes.

_____. 1976. *Circuito fechado.* Sao Paulo: Hucitec.

Freyre, Gilberto. 1963. *Mansions and Shanties: The Making of Modern Brazil.* New York: Alfred Knopf.

_____. 1969. *Masters and Slaves.* New York: Alfred Knopf.

Ferreira, José Carlos. 1970. "Empresa industrial e desenvolvimento econômico no Brasil após guerra." Universidade de Sao Paulo, mimeographed.

Figueiredo, Vilma. 1970. "A racionalidade do empresário brasileiro: um estudo sobre filantropia." Instituto Universitário de Pesquisas do Rio de Janeiro, M.A. dissertation.

Fleischer, David F. 1977. "A bancada federal mineira: trinta anos de recrutamento político, 1945-1975." Universidade de Brasília, mimeographed.

Fonseca, Elga M. Lemos. 1970. "Funçoes sociais da habitaçao do operário de origem rural no município de Porto Alegre." Universidade Federal do Rio Grande do Sul, M.A. dissertation.

Foracchi, Marialice. 1965. *O estudante e a transformaçao da realidade brasileira.* Sao Paulo: Cia. Editora Nacional.

_____. 1972. *A juventude na sociedade moderna.* Sao Paulo: Biblioteca Pioneira de Ciências Sociais.

Francisco, José Jeremias Oliveira. 1973. "A obra e a mensagem: representaçoes simbólicas e organizaçao burocratica na Igreja Adventista do Primeiro Dia.'' Universidade de Sao Paulo, doctoral dissertation.

Franco, Maria Sylvia de Carvalho. 1974. *Homens livres na ordem escravocrata.* Sao Paulo: Ática.

Frohlich, Egon R. 1970. ''Análise de conteúdo de assuntos agrícolas e suas relevâncias situacionais nos jornais do Rio Grande do Sul.'' Universidade Federal do Rio Grande do Sul, M.A. dissertation.

Fukui, Lia Freitas Garcia. n.d. ''Les rôles sexuels dans l'organization familiale des 'sitiantes' traditionels au Brésil.'' Universidade de Sao Paulo, mimeographed

―――――. 1969. ''Les Relations mère-enfants parmi les paysans de statut socio-économique indépendent au Brésil.'' *Carnets de l'Enfance* 10.

―――――. 1972. ''Parentesco e família entre sitiantes tradicionais.'' Universidade de Sao Paulo, doctoral dissertation.

―――――. 1974. ''Les Rôles sexuels dans l'organization familiale des paysans du Brésil.'' Universidade de Sao Paulo, mimeographed.

Furtado, Celso. 1964. *A Dialética do desenvolvimento.* Rio de Janeiro: Fundo de Cultura.

―――――. 1972. *Análise do modelo brasileiro.* Rio de Janeiro: Civilizaçao Brasileira.

Gaboardi, Luci de L. 1971. ''Aspiraçoes educacionais e ocupacionais na família rural: Garibaldi.'' Universidade Federal do Rio Grande do Sul, M.A. dissertation.

Galvao, Ximenes Raul. 1969. ''Avaliaçao histórica do planejamento sócio-econômico brasileiro.'' Universidade de Sao Paulo, mimeographed.

Giannotti, José Arthur. 1971. ''A sociedade como técnica da razao: um ensaio sobre Durkheim.'' *Estudos CEBRAP* 1: 47-98.

―――――. 1973. ''O ardil do trabalho.'' *Estudos CEBRAP* 4.

―――――. 1974. ''O que é fazer: Para a crítica da noçao de comportamento.'' Sao Paulo: CEBRAP, mimeographed.

―――――. 1974. ''O contexto e os intelectuais.'' *Argumento* 4.

―――――. 1976. ''Nota sobre a categoria 'modo de produçao' para uso e abuso dos sociólogos.'' *Estudos CEBRAP* 17: 161-68.

Giuglient, Bernardino. 1972. ''Influências de fatores sócio-econômicos no nível e estrutura de consumo em famílias de agricultores e operários urbanos.'' Universidade Federal do Rio Grande do Sul, M.A. dissertation.

Gnacarini, José Cesar. 1973. ''Estudo, ideologia e a açao empresarial na agro-indústria açucareira no Estado de Sao Paulo.'' Universidade de Sao Paulo, doctoral dissertation.

Goldwasser, Maria Julia. 1971. ''Cria fama e deita-te na cama: um estudo de estigmatizaçao numa instituiçao total.'' In Gilberto Velho (ed.), *Desvio e divergência.* Rio de Janeiro: Zahar.

―――――.1975. *O palácio do samba.* Rio de Janeiro: Zahar.

Gouveia, Aparecida Joly. 1962. O emprego público e o diploma de curso superior.'' *Revista Brasileira de Estudos Pedagógicos* 58: 359-77.

―――――. 1964. ''O nível de instruçao dos professores do ensino médio.'' *Pesquisa e Planejamento* 8: 23-65.

_____. 1965. "Desenvolvimento econômico e prestígio de certas ocupaçoes." *América Latina* 7 (October-December): 66-79.

_____. 1966. Educaçao e desenvolvimento: pontos de vista dos professores secundários." *Revista Brasileira de Estudos Pedagógicos* 46 (no. 103): 65-90.

_____. 1970. *Professoras de amanha: um estudo de escolha ocupacional.* Sao Paulo: Livraria Pioneira.

Gouveia, Aparecida Joly; and Havighurst, Robert J. 1969. *Ensino médio e desenvolvimento.* Sao Paulo: Melhoramentos.

Grabois, Gisélia Potengy. 1973. "Em busca da integraçao: a política da remoçao de favelas no Rio de Janeiro." Museu Nacional da Universidade Federal do Rio de Janeiro, M.A. dissertation.

Guimaraes, Alberto Passos. 1964. *Quatro séculos de latinfúndio.* Sao Paulo: Fulgor.

Guimaraes, Cesar. 1972. "The Authoritarian Regime in Marx's Political Theory." University of Chicago, M.A. dissertation.

_____. 1977. "Empresariado, tipos de capitalismo e ordem política." *Dados* 14: 34-47.

Guimaraes, Alba Zaluar. 1973. "Sobre a lógica do catolicismo popular." *Dados* 11: 173-93.

_____. (ed.). 1975. *Desvendando máscaras sociais.* Rio de Janeiro: Livraria Francisco Alves.

Guimaraes, Cláudio Maria Cavalcanti de Barros. 1973. "Posse e uso da terra, relaçoes de poder e conservadorismo camponês." Universidade Federal de Pernambuco, M.A. dissertation.

Gurrieri, Adolfo; Faletto, Enzo; and Rodrigues, Leôncio Martins. 1964. "Estudo comparativo do comportamento operário no Brasil e no Chile." *Sociologia* 2-3, (June-October).

Hasenbalg, Carlos Alfredo. 1968. "Empresários e desenvolvimento econômico." *Dados* 4: 5-31.

_____. 1970. "O setor financeiro e desenvolvimento econômico no Brasil." Documento de Trabalho 1. Rio de Janeiro: IUPERJ, mimeographed.

Hasenbalg, Carlos Alfredo; and Brigagao, C. 1971. "Formaçao do empresariado financeiro no Brasil." *Dados* 8: 79-103.

Hasenbalg, Carlos A. n.d. "Desigualdades raciais no Brasil." *Dados* 14: 7-33.

Hirano, Sedi. 1975. *Castas, estamentos e classes sociais.* Sao Paulo: Alfa-Omega.

Hoffman, Helga. 1972. "Desemprego e subemprego no Brasil." Universidade de Sao Paulo, doctoral dissertation.

Hutchinson, Bertram (ed.). 1960. *Mobilidade e trabalho.* Rio de Janeiro: INEP, CBPE.

Ianni, Otávio. 1965. *Estado e capitalismo: estrutura social e industrializaçao no Brasil.* Rio de Janeiro: Civilizaçâo Brasileira.

_____. 1968. *O colapso do populismo no Brasil. Rio de Janeiro: Civilizaçao Brasileira.*

_____. *1970. Imperialismo y cultura de la violencia en América Latina.* Mexico, D.F.: Siglo Veintiuno.

————. 1971. *Sociologia da sociologia latino-americana.* Rio de Janeiro: Civilizaçao Brasileira.

————. 1971. *Estado e planejamento econômico no Brasil, 1930-70.* Rio de Janeiro: Civilizaçao Brasileira.

————. 1972. *Sociología y dependencia en América Latina.* Asunción: Centro Paraguayo de Estudios Sociológicos.

————. 1972. "Estado nacional e organizaçoes multinacionais." Sao Paulo: CEBRAP.

————. 1973. "A criança, o adolescente, a cidade." Sao Paulo: Tribunal de Justiça de Sao Paulo.

————. 1973. "Populismo y relaciones de clase." In T.S. DiTella, G. Germani, and O. Ianni (eds.), *Populismo y contradicciones de clase en Latinoamérica.* Mexico D.F.: Era.

————. 1973. "Raça, etnia e mobilidade social." Sao Paulo: CEBRAP, mimeographed.

————. 1974. *Imperialismo na América Latina.* Rio de Janeiro: Civilizaçao Brasileira.

Iutaka, Sugiyma. 1962. "Estratificación social y oportunidades educacionales en tres metrópolis latinoamericanas: Buenos Aires, Montevideo y Sao Paulo." *América Latina* 5. 53-72.

————. 1963. "Mobilidade social e oportunidades educacionais em Buenos Aires e Montevideo: uma análise comparativa." *América Latina* 6 (no. 2): 21-50.

————. 1965. "A estratificaçao social e uso diferencial de métodos anticoncepcionais no Brasil urbano." *América Latina* 8: 101-20.

Ivelar, Sônia Maria. 1971. "Desenvolvimento e tensoes sócio-políticas. Universidade Federal de Minas Gerals, M.A. dissertation.

Jaguaribe, Hélio. 1968. *Economic and Political Development: A Theoretical Approach and a Brazilian Case Study.* Cambridge, Mass.: Harvard University Press.

————. 1969. *La dependencia política y económica de América Latina.* Mexico, D.F.: Siglo Veintiuno Editores.

————. 1971. *Ciencia y tecnología en el contexto socio-político de América Latina.* Tucumán (Argentina): Universidad Nacional de Tucumán.

————. 1972. *Desenvolvimento econômico e desenvolvimento político.* Rio de Janeiro: Paz e Terra.

————. 1974. *Brasil: crise e alternativas.* Rio de Janeiro: Zahar.

Javier, Enciso. 1972. "O professor de ensino médio no Estado de Goiás: estudo da conjuntura e da estrutura." Universidade de Sao Paulo, mimeographed.

Keller, Francisca Isabel Schurig Vieira. 1973. *O japonês e a frente de expansao paulista.* Sao Paulo: Livraria Pioneira.

Klein, Lucia Maria Gomes. 1973. "A nova ordem legal e suas repercussoes sobre a esfera política." *Dados* 10: 154-65.

Kowarick, Lúcio. 1971. "Estratégias do planejamento social no Brasil." *Cadernos CEBRAP* 2.

————. 1973. "Marginalidade urbana e desenvolvimento: aspectos teóricos do fenômeno da América Latina." Universidade de Sao Paulo, doctoral dissertation.

_____. 1974. *"Capitalismo, dependência e marginalidade urbana na América Latina: uma contribuiçao teorica."* Sao Paulo: CEBRAP, mimeographed.

Lacerda, Maria do Carmo de. 1973. "Universidade e processo de decisao." Universidade de Brasília, M.A. dissertation.

Lafer, Celso. 1970. *"The Planning Process and the Political System in Brazil: a Study of Kubitschek's Target Plan, 1956-1961."* Cornell University, Ph.D. dissertation.

_____. 1975. *O sistema político brasileiro.* Sao Paulo: Perspectiva.

Lamounier, Bolivar. 1974. "Ideology and Authoritarian Regime: Theoretical Perspective and a Study of the Brazilian Case." University of California at Los Angeles, Ph.D. dissertation.

_____. "Ideologias conservadoras e mundaças estruturais." *Dados* 5: 5-21.

_____. 1973. "Juan Linz on Ideology in Authoritarian Regimes." Law and Modernization Program, Yale University, mimeographed.

Lamounier, Bolivar; and Cardoso, Fernando Henrique (eds). 1975. *Os partidos e as eleiçoes no Brasil.* Rio de Janeiro and Sao Paulo: CEBRAP/Paz e Terra.

Lamounier, Bolivar. 1974. "Ideologia e regimes autoritários: crítica a Linz." *Estudos CEBRAP* 7: 67-92.

Landhal, Helene. 1967. "Problemas humanos do desenvolvimento econômico e social." Universidade de Sao Paulo.

Leopoldi, José Sávio. 1975. "Escola de samba, ritual e sociedade." Museu Nacional da Universidade Federal do Rio Janeiro, M.A. dissertation.

Lima, Vivaldo Costa. 1970. "A família de Santo nos candomblés gêgê-nagôs da Bahia. Universidade Federal da Bahia, M.A. dissertation.

Lima, Júnior, Olavo Brasil de; and Klein, Lucia Maria Gomes. 1970. "Os atores políticos no império." *Dados* 7: 62-88.

_____. 1971. "Intervençoes militares na América Latina." Instituto Universitário de Pesquisas do Rio de Janeiro, M.A. dissertation.

Lopes, José Sergio Leite. 1974. "Os operários do açucar." Museu Nacional da Universidade Federal do Rio de Janeiro, M.A. dissertation.

_____. 1976. *O vapor do diabo.* Rio de Janeiro: Paz e Terra.

Lopes, Juarez Rubens Brandão. 1965. "Etude de quelques changements fondamentaux dans la politique et la société brésilienne." *Sociologie du Travail* 7 (July-September).

_____. 1966. "Some Basic Developments in Brazilian Politics and Society." In Eric N. Baklanoff (ed.), *New Perspective of Brazil.* Nashville: Vanderbilt University Press.

_____. 1967. *Crise do Brasil arcaico.* Sao Paulo: Difusao Européia do Livro.

_____. 1974. "Desenvolvimento e migraçoes internas." *Estudos CEBRAP* 6.

Loyola, Maria Andrea Rios. 1972. "Trabalho e modernizaçao na indústria têxtil: um estudo de caso sobre atitudes operárias em Minas Gerais." Museu Nacional da Universidade Federal do Rio de Janeiro, M.A. dissertation.

Loureiro, Maria Rita Garcia. 1977. *Parceria e capitalismo.* Rio de Janeiro: Zahar.

Lustosa, José Rodrigues. 1970. "A topologia humana na trilogia clássica de Gilberto Freire." Universidade Federal da Bahia, M.A. dissertation.

Machado, Mario B. 1975. "On the Sources of Brazilian Student Politics, 1960-1964." University of Chicago, M.A. dissertation.

_____. 1975. *"Political Socialization in Authoritarian Systems."* University of Chicago, Ph.D. dissertation.

Machado Neto, A.L. 1960. *Educaçao para o desenvolvimento.* Salvador: Fundaçao Comissao de Planejamento Economico da Bahia.

Madeira, F.R.; and Hernandez, L. n.d. "a nupcialidade em Sao Paulo." Sao Paulo: CEBRAP, mimeographed.

Maranhao, Silvio Marcelo; and Motta, Roberto. n.d. "Ensaios críticos de teoria." *Cumunicaçoes PIMES* 1.

Maranhao, Tullio Persio. 1975. "O processo cognitivo da pesca artesanal em Icaraí, Ceará." Universidade de Brasília, M.A. dissertation.

Martins, Carlos Estevam. 1972. "Brasil-Estados Unidos: dos 60 aos 70." *Cadernos CEBRAP* 9.

_____. 1973. "Tecnocracia como modo de produçao." *Revista de Administraçao de Empresas* (July-September).

_____. 1974. *Tecnocracia e capitalismo: a política dos técnicos no Brasil.* Sao Paulo: Brasiliense.

Martins, Carlos Estevam; Martins, Almeida; and Martins, Maria Hermínia Tavares de. 1974. "Modus in rebus: partidos e classes na queda do Estado Novo." Sao Paulo, mimeographed.

Martins, Helena Campos. 1972. "Rangel: nível de vida e padrao sanitário em termos de associaçao: estudo de uma comunidade nordestina. Universidade de Sao Paulo, mimeographed.

Martins, José de Souza. 1972. "A proletarizaçao imigrante italiano: Sao Caetano." Universidade de Sao Paulo, mimeographed.

Martins, Luciano. 1968. *Industrializaçao, burguesia nacional e desenvolvimento."* Rio de Janeiro: Saga.

_____. 1973. "Politique et développement économique: structures de pouvoir et système de décisions au Brésil, 1930-1964." Université René Descartes, doctoral dissertation.

Mary, Ingrid H. 1971. "Marginalidade econômica e suas implicaçoes sociais: Candelária." Universidade Federal do Rio Grande do Sul, M.A. dissertation.

Matos, Florisvaldo. 1970. "A comunicaçao social na revoluçao dos alfaiates." Universidade Federal da Bahia, M.A. dissertation.

Matta, Roberto da. 1963. "Notas sobre o contato e a extinçao dos indios gavioes do Médio Rio Tocantins." *Revista do Museu Paulista* 14.

_____. 1967. "Grupos Gê do Tocantins." *Atos do Simpósio sobre a Biota Amazônica.* Rio de Janeiro: Conselho Nacional de Pesquisas.

_____. 1970. "Apinayé Social Structure." Harvard University, Ph.D. dissertation.

_____. 1970. 'Mito e antimito entre os timbira." *Mito e comunicaçao.* Rio de Janeiro: Tempo Brasileiro.

_____. 1971. "Les Presages apinayé." In J. Pouillon and P. Maranda (eds.), *Echanges et communications: mélanges offerts à Claude Lévi-Strauss.* The Hague: Mouton.

_____. 1973. *Ensaios de antropoligia estrutural.* Petrópolis: Vozes.

————. 1976. "Quanto custa ser índio no Brasil: consideraçoes sobre o problema da identidade étnica." *Dados* 13: 33-54.

————. 1976. *Um mundo dividido: a estrutura social dos índios apinayé.* Petrópolis: Vozes.

Mayeama, Takashi. 1967. "O migrante e a religiao: estudo de uma seita religiosa japonesa em Sao Paulo. Universidade de Sao Paulo, mimeographed.

Medina, Carlos Alberto de. 1963. "A favela como uma estrutura atomística: elementos descritivos e constitutivos." *América Latina* 12 (no. 3).

————. 1964. *A favela e o demogogo.* Sao Paulo: Imprensa Livre.

Melatti, Julio Cezar. 1963. "O mito e o xama." *Revista do Museu Paulista* 14.

————. 1967. "Indios e criadores: a situaçao dos krahó na área pastoril do Tocantins." *Monografias do Instituto de Ciências Sociais* 3.

————. 1970. *Indios do Brasil.* Brasília: Editora de Brasília.

————. 1970. "O sistema social krahó." Universidade de Sao Paulo, doctoral dissertation.

————. 1973. *O sistema de parentesco dos índios krahó.* Brazília: Fundaçao da Universidade de Brasília.

Melo, José Luiz Pereira de. 1973. "Brazilian Students in the U.S.: a study of Change in Political Orientation." Northwestern University, Ph.D. dissertation.

Mello, Wilmo. 1973. "A imigraçao italiana e a transformaçao da estrutura econômico-social do município de Sao Carlos." Universidade de Sao Paulo, M.A. dissertation.

Mello e Souza, Antônio Candido. 1964. *Os parceiros do Rio Bonito. Rio de Janeiro:* Livraria José Olympio.

Mendes, Candido. 1966. *Memento dos vivos.* Rio de Janeiro: Tempo Brasileiro.

————. 1966. "Sistema político e modelos de poder no Brasil." *Dados* 1.

————. 1967. "O governo Castelo Branco: paradigma e prognose." *Dados* 2-3: 63-111.

————. 1968. "Prospectiva do comportamento ideológico: o processo de reflexao na crise do desenvolvimento." *Dados* 4: 95-132.

————. 1969. "Elites de poder, democracia e desenvolvimento." *Dados* 6: 57-90.

————. 1974. *Después del populismo: impugnacion social y dessarrollo en América Latina.* Mexico D.F.: Fondo de Cultura Económica.

Mendes, Candido, et al. 1974. *Crise e mudança social na América Latina.* Rio de Janeiro: Eldorado.

————. 1974. *O outro desenvolvimento.* Rio de Janeiro: Arte Nova.

Menezes, Djacir. 1975. *Temas polemicos: capítulos da sociologia política.* Rio de Janeiro: Editora Rio.

Menezes, Eduardo Diatay Bezerra. 1974. "Fundamentos científicos da comunicaçao." Petrópolis: Vozes.

Mercadantes, Elizabeth Frohlich. 1973. "Orientaçao vulcrativa dos jovens judeus paulistanos para com a sociedade Nacional." Museu Nacional da Universidade Federal do Rio de Janeiro, M.A. dissertation.

Mercadante, Paulo, 1965. *A consciência conservadora no Brasil.* Rio de Janeiro: Saga.

Miceli, Sergio. 1972. *A noite da madrinha.* Sao Paulo: Perspectiva.

Monteiro, Douglas. 1973. "Os errantes do novo século milenarista: um estudo sobre o surto do Contestado." Universidade de Sao Paulo, mimeographed.

Monteiro, Douglas Teixeira. 1972. "Mundaças de relaçoes vicinais em áreas operárias de Sao Paulo." Universidade de Sao Paulo, mimeographed.

Moreira, Inaia Carvalho. 1969. "Atitudes operárias na Bahia." Universidade Federal da Bahia. M.A. dissertation.

Morel, Regina Lucia de Moraes. 1975. "Consideraçoes sobre a política científica no Brasil." Universidade de Brasília, M.A. dissertation.

Moura, Margarida Maria. 1973. "Os sitiantes e a herança." Museu Nacional da Universidade Federal do Rio de Janeiro, M.A. dissertation.

Mourao, Augusto A. Fernando. 1971. "Populaçoes do litoral sul do Estado de Sao Paulo." Universidade de Sao Paulo, mimeographed.

Negrao, Lígia. 1973. "O movimento messiânico urbano: messianismo e mudança social no Brasil." Universidade de Sao Paulo, mimeographed.

Neto, Paulo Elpidio de Menezes; and Paulson, Belden. 1970. "A classe de liderança no Ceará." *Revista de Ciências Sociais* 1 (no 1): 57-95.

Neves, Maria Cecília Baeta. 1973. "Greve dos sapateiros de 1906 no Rio de Janeiro: notas de pesquisa." *Revista de Administraçao de Empresas* 13 (July).

Noronha, Ronaldo de. 1971. "Orientaçoes políticas dos setores médios." Universidade Federal de Minas Gerais, M.A. dissertation.

Oliveira, Claudia Meneses Paes de. 1972. "A mudança: um estudo de migraçao interna." Museu Nacional da Universidade Federal do Rio de Janeiro, M.A. dissertation.

Oliveira, Francisco de, et al. 1971. "Emprego e força de trabalho na América Latina." Sao Paulo: CEBRAP.

Oliveira, Francisco de. 1972. "A economia brasileira: crítica à razô dualista." *Estudos CEBRAP* 2.

_____. 1973. "Projeçao da demanda de alimentos." Sao Paulo: CEBRAP, mimeographed.

Oliveira, Francisco de; and Reichstul, Henri-Philippe. 1973. "Mudanças na divisao regional do trabalho no Brasil." *Estudos CEBRAP* 4.

Oliveira, Lucia Lippi de. 1973. "O Partido Social Democrático: estudo do caso." Instituto Universitário de Pesquisas do Rio de Janeiro. M.A. dissertation.

Oliveira, Maria Colete F.A. 1972. "Família e reproduçao." Universidade de Sao Paulo, mimeographed.

_____. 1976. "Famílias múltiplas." Universidade de Sao Paulo, mimeographed.

Oliveira, Nei Roberto da Silva. 1974. "A juventude universitária: uma abordagem crítica." *Revista de Ciências Sociais* 5 (no. 2): 113-42.

Oliveira, Roberto Cardoso de. 1962. "Estudo de áreas de fricçao interétnica no Brasil." *América Latina* 5 (no. 3): 85-90.

_____. 1964. "O índio e o mundo dos brancos." Sao Paulo: DIFEL.

_____. 1967. "Problema e hipóteses relativos à fricçao interétnica: sugestoes para uma metodologia." *Revista do Instituto de Ciências Sociais* 4 (no. 1).

Oliveira, Roberto Cardoso de; and Castro Faria, L. 1971. "Interethnic Contact and the Study of Populations." In F.M. Salzuno (ed.), *The Ongoing Evolution of Latin America.* New York: Charles Thomas.

────. 1971. "Indentidad étnica, identificación y manipulación." *Américan Indígena* 31 (no. 4): 923-53.

────. 1972. *A sociologia do Brasil indígena.* Rio de Janeiro: Tempo Universitário.

────. 1973. "Povos indígenas e mudança sócio-cultural na Amazônia." Universidade de Brasília, mimeographed.

────. 1974. "Processos de articulaçao étnica." Universidade de Brasília, mimeographed.

────. 1974. "Um conceito antropológico de identidade." Universidade de Brasília, mimeographed.

────. 1976. *Identidade étnica e estrutura social.* Sao Paulo: Livraria Pioneira.

Palmeira, Moacir. 1971. "Latifundium et capitalisme: lecture critique d'un débat." Université René Descartes, doctoral dissertation.

────. 1966. "Nordeste: mudanças políticas no século XX." *Cadernos Brasileiros* 37 (September-October): 67-86.

────. 1972. "Feira e mudança econômica." Museu Nacional da Universidade Federal do Rio de Janeiro, mimeographed.

Parahyba, Maria Antonieta. 1970. "Abertura social e participaçao política no Brasil (1870 à 1920)." *Dados* 7:89-102.

Passos, Alaor. 1968. "Developmental Tensions and Political Stability." *Journal of Peace Research* 1.

────. 1968. "Transiçao e tensao nos estados Brasileiros." *Dados* 5: 57-81.

Pastore, José. 1963. Rendimento escolar em Sao Paulo: uma interpretaçao sociológica." Universidade de Sao Paulo, mimeographed.

────. 1968. "Satisfaction among Migrants to Brasília." University of Wisconsin at Madison, Ph.D. dissertation.

────. 1971. "Migraçao, mobilidade social e desenvolvimento." In Manoel Augusto da Costa (ed.), *Migraçoes internas no Brasil.* Rio de Janeiro: IPEA/INPES.

Patarra, Neide Lopes. 1972. "O estudo sobre reproduçao humana no Distrito de Sao Paulo: um enfoque sociológico." Sao Paulo: CEBRAP, mimeographed.

Pena, Maria Valéria Junho. 1971. "Setor empresarial e poder político em uma área dependente." Universidade Federal de Minas Gerais, M.A. dissertation.

Peirano, Marisa Gomes. S. 1975. "O simbolismo de uma colônia de pescadores no litoral do Ceará." Universidade de Brasília, M.A. dissertation.

Pereira, A. Wlademir. 1969. "O desenvolvimento industrial em Sao Paulo." Universidade de Sao Paulo, doctoral dissertation.

Pereira, Elisa Maria. 1972. "Política cafeeira e interesses de classe no Brasil." Instituto Universitário de Pesquisas do Rio de Janeiro, M.A. dissertation.

Pereira, Joao Baptista Borges. 1967. *Cor, profissao e mobilidade.* Sao Paulo: Livraria Pioneira Editora.

Pereira, José Carlos. 1966. "A estrutura do sistema industrial em Sao Paulo.' *Revista Brasileira de Ciências Sociais* 4 (no. 1): 7-116.

────. 1967. *Expansao e evoluçao da indústria em Sao Paulo.* Sao Paulo: Companhia Editora Nacional.

Pereira, Ligia Maria Leite. 1974. "Experimentaçao numérica com modelos de desenvolvimento nacional." Universidade Federal de Minas Gerais, M.A. dissertation.

Pereira, Luiz. 1965. *Trabalho e desenvolvimento no Brasil.* Sao Paulo: Difusao Européia do Livro.

Pereira, Vera Maria Candido. 1972. "Authoritarismo e preconceito. um estudo de ideologia política da classe média no Rio de Janeiro." Instituto Universitário de Pesquisas do Rio de Janeiro, M.A. dissertation.

Perrelberg, Rosine, 1976. "As fronteiras do silêncio." Museu Nacional da Universidade Federal do Rio de Janeiro, M.A. dissertation.

Perseu, Abramo. 1969. "Aspectos estruturais na Bahia." Salvador: Universidade Federal da Bahia, mimeographed.

Pillatti, Orlando. 1975. "O morar na cidade." Universidade de Brasília, mimeographed.

Pinheiro, Paulo Sérgio Moraes S. 1971. "La Fin de la Première Republique au Brésil: crise politique et revolution." Paris: Fondation Nationale des Sciences Politiques, mimeographed.

────. 1974. "Classes médias urbanas: formaçao, natureza, intervençao na vida política." Sao Paulo: UNICAMP, mimeographed.

────. 1975. *Política e trabalho no Brasil: dos anos vinte à 1930.* Rio de Janeiro: Paz e Terra.

Pinho, Carlos Marques. 1969. "Educaçao e desenvolvimento econômico." Universidade de Sao Paulo, doctoral dissertation.

Pinto, Agerson Tabosa. 1972. "Aspectos políticos da crise do modelo agro exportador e as relaçoes de classes no Brasil." *Revista de Ciências Sociais* 3 (no. 2): 123-46.

Pintagui, Cleonice. 1975. 'O contexto sócio-político do candomblé em Salvador-Bahia. " Universidade de Brasília, M.A. dissertation.

Pompermayer, Malori José. 1970. "Autoritarismo no Brasil." Universidade Federal de Minas Gerais, M.A. dissertation.

Prado, Caio Jr. 1966. *A Revoluçao Brasileira.* Sao Paulo: Ed. Brasiliense.

Prandi, J. Reginaldo; Berezovsky, Melanie; Souza, Beatriz Muniz de; and Nascimento, Renata Raffaelli. 1973. *Católicos, protestantes, espiritas.* Rio de Janeiro: Vozes.

Prandi, J. Reginaldo. n.d. "Mensagem católica e mudança social no Brasil: 1940-1971." Mimeographed.

Quadros, Consuelo Novaes Soares. 1970. "Os partidos políticos na Primeira República." Universidade Federal da Bahia, M.A. dissertation.

Queiroz, Maurício Vinhas de. 1966. "Messianismo e conflito social." Rio de Janeiro: Civilizaçao Brasileira.

────. 1973."Grupos econômicos e o modelo brasileiro." Universidade de Sao Paulo, doctoral dissertation.

Queiroz, Maria Izaura Pereira de. 1965. *O messianismo no Brasil e no mundo.* Sao Paulo: Dominus.

————. 1965. "Les Classes sociales dans le Brésil actuel." *Cahiers Internationaux de Sociologie* 39: 137-69.

————. 1967. *O mandonismo local na vida política brasileira.* Sao Paulo: Anhembi.

————. 1968. *Réforme et révolution dans les sociétés traditionnelles.* Paris: Anthropos.

————. 1972. *Images méssianiques du Brésil.* Cuernavaca (Mexico): Centro Intercultural de Documentación.

————. 1973. *Bairros rurais paulistas.* Sao Paulo: Livraria Duas Cidades.

————. 1973. *O campesinato brasileiro.* Petrópolis: Vozes.

————. 1976. *O mandonismo local na vida política brasileira e outros ensaios.* Sao Paulo: Alfa-Omega.

Quintas, Amaro. 1967. "O sentido social da revoluçao praireira." Rio de Janeiro: Civilizaçao Brasileira.

Quintela, Maria Helena Diégues. 1972. "Imagens da educaçao." Museu Nacional da Universidade Federal do Rio de Janeiro, M.A. dissertation.

Rabaçal, Alfredo Joao. 1963. "Embaixadas pacíficas." Universidade de Sao Paulo, mimeographed.

Rabello, Ophelia. 1965. *A rede sindical paulista.* Sao Paulo: Instituto Cultural do Trabalho.

Ramos, Alcida R. 1972. "The Social System of the Sanuma of Northern Brazil." University of Wisconsin, Ph.D. dissertation.

Ramos, Alcida R.; and Peirano M. 1973. "O simbolismo de caça em dois rituais de nominaçao." Universidade de Brasília, mimeographed.

Rattner, Heinrich. 1965. "A persistência de padroes tradicionais e problemas de integraçao na sociedade brasileira entre estudantes universitários judeus de Sao Paulo." *Sociologia* 27 (no. 2): 121-52.

Reis, Ana Maria B. 1969. "Integraçao do operário de origem rural na sociedade urbana industrial." Universidade Federal do Rio Grande do Sul, M.A. dissertation.

Reis, Fábio W. 1974. "Political Development and Social Class." Harvard University, Ph.D. dissertation.

————. 1974. "Solidariedade, interesses e desenvolvimento político." *Cadernos DCP* 1: 5-58.

————. 1974. "Brasil: estado e sociedade em Perspectiva." *Cadernos DCP* 2: 35-74.

————. 1975. "As eleiçoes em Minas Gerais." In Bolivar Lamounier and Fernando Henrique Cardoso (eds.), *Os partidos e as eleiçoes no Brasil.* Rio de Janeiro: Paz e Terra.

————. 1976. 'O institucional e o constitucional." *Cadernos DCP* 3: 107-122

Renner, C.H.O. 1971. " Migraçao rural-urbana e fertilidade em Sao Paulo." Sâo Paulo, mimeographed.

Ribeiro, Augusto Barbosa de Carvalho. 1965. "Contrato coletivo de trabalho: análise jurídico-sociológica da contrataçao coletiva e de alguns contratos realizados no Brasil." Universidade de Sao Paulo, doctoral dissertation.

Ribeiro, Boanerger. 1972. "Independência nacional e liberdade de culto (1822-1888): alguns aspectos culturais da introduçao do protestanismo no Brasil e do presbiterianismo em Sao Paulo." Universidade de Sao Paulo, doctoral dissertation.

Ribeiro, Darcy. 1970. *Os índios e a civilizaçao.* Rio de Janeiro: Civilizaçao Brasileira.

Ribeiro, René. 1971. "Messianismo e desenvolvimento." Recife: Universidade Federal de Pernambuco, mimeographed.

Riedli, Mario. 1969. "Estratigrafia social numa área de colonziçâo do Rio Grande do Sul. Universidade Federal do Rio Grande do Sul. M.A. dissertation.

Rios, José Arthur. 1961. "Estratificación y movilidad social en Río de Janeiro." *América Latina* 4: 377-79.

Rocha, Wagner Neves. 1972. "O sábado e o tempo." Museu Nacional da Universidade Federal do Rio de Janeiro, M.A. dissertation.

Rodrigues, Albatino José. 1963. "Estrutura sindical Brasileira." *Revista de Estudos Sócio-Econômicos* 1 (January).

――――. 1968. *Sindicato e desenvolvimento no Brasil.* Sao Paulo: DIFEL.

――――. 1972. "Estudo sobre as mulheres que geraram um nascido-vivo durante a pesquisa prospectiva de reproduçao humana no distrito de Sao Paulo." Universidade de Sao Paulo, doctoral dissertation.

Rodrigues, Leôncio Martins. 1965. "Consideraçoes preliminares sobre greves operárias em Sao Paulo." *Sociologia* 27 (September): 209-18.

――――. 1967. "Atitudes operárias na empresa automobilística." Faculdade de Filosofia, Ciências e Letras da Universidade de Sao Paulo, mimeographed.

――――. 1966. "Sindicalismo, classes sociais e subdesenvolvimento." *Revista do Instituto de Ciências Sociais* 2.

――――. 1966. "Sindicalismo y desarrollo en el Brasil." *Revista Latinoamericana de Sociologia* (March).

――――. 1966. *Conflito industrial e sindicalismo no Brasil.* Sao Paulo: Difusao Européia do Livro.

――――. 1968. "Classe operária e sindicalismo no Brasil." In Leôncio Martins Rodrigues (ed.), *Sindicalismo e Sociedade.* Sao Paulo: Difusao Européia do Livro.

――――. 1970. *Industrializaçao e atitudes operárias.* Sao Paulo: Editora Brasiliense.

――――. 1971. "O sindicalismo e os trabalhadores industriais no Brasil." *Cadernos do Centro de Estudos Rurais e Urbanos.*

――――. 1972. "Trabalhadores e sindicatos no processo de industrializaçao." Universidade de Sao Paulo, mimeographed.

Sá, Maria Auxiliadora Freitas de. 1973. "Relaçoes de poder em uma comunidade sertaneja." Universidade Federal de Pernambuco, M.A. dissertation.

Sader, Emir Simiao. 1967. "Conflito industrial e luta de classes." *Teoria e Pratica* 2. Sao Paulo.

――――. 1971. "A formaçao do estado nos países subdesenvolvidos." Universidade de Sao Paulo, mimeographed.

Saffioti, Heleieth I.B. 1968. "O trabalho como atividade diferencialmente alienadora para o homem e a mulher nas sociedades de classes." *Revista Ciência e Cultura* 20 (no. 123): 224-25.

————. 1968. "A condiçao de mulher nas sociedades de classes. *Revista Ciência e Cultura* 20 (no. 2): 225.

————. 1968. "Mulher: questao de Ciência." *Boletim da Cadeira de Sociologia e Fundamentos Sociológicos da Educaçâo* 1 (no. 4).

————. 1969. "Fertilidade e participaçao feminina na forca de trabalho." *Boletim da Cadeira de sociologia e Fundamentos Sociológicos da Educaçao* 1 (no. 4).

————. 1969. *A mulher na sociedade de classes: mito e realidade.* Sao Paulo: Quartro Artes.

————. 1969. "Profissionalizaçao feminina: professoras primárias e operárias." Sao Paulo: Universidade de Araraquara, mimeographed.

————. 1973. "Aspectos gerais do problema da mulher." *Cadernos do CERU* 6: 5-106.

————. 1975. Feminine Work under Capitalism. In Ruby R. (ed.) *Cross-Cultural Perspective in the Women's Movement and Women's Status.* Paris: Mouton.

Saito, Hiroshi. 1960. "Mobilidade de ocupaçao e de status de um grupo de imigrantes." *Sociologia* 22: 241-53.

Santos, Wanderley Guilherme dos. 1966. "Uma revisao da crise brasileira." *Cadernos Brasileiros* 8.

————. 1967. "Estudos sobre a teoria da demonstraçao (1) a teoria da agressao de Johan Galtung." *Dados* 2-3: 133-149.

————. 1967. "A imaginaçao político-social Brasileira." *Dados* 2-3: 182-193.

————. 1968. "Nota sobre conflito internacional." *Dados* 5: 162-65.

————. 1969. "Teoria política e prospectos democráticos." *Dados* 6: 5-23.

————. 1970. "Raízes da imaginaçâo político-social Brasileira." *Dados* 7: 137-61.

————. 1971. "Nuevas profesiones, nuevas academias: sugerencias para un debate pedagógico." *Desarollo Económico* 41 (April-June).

————. 1971. "Governadores políticos, governadores técnicos, governadores Militares." *Dados* 8:7-25.

————. 1971. "Eleiçoes, representaçao, política substantiva." *Dados* 8: 123-28.

————. 1973. "Paralisia de decisao e comportamento legislativo: a experiência brasileira, 1959-1966." *Revista de Administraçao de Empresas* 13 (April-June).

————. 1977. "As eleiçoes e a dinâmica do processo político brasileiro." *Dados* 14: 211-39.

Santos, Yolanda. 1972. "A imagem do índio na ficçao do paraíso." Universidade de Sao Paulo, mimeographed.

Saraiva, Hélcio N. 1965. "Information-Seeking Behavior as Related to Sociological Factors in a Rural Northeast Brazilian Município." University of Wisconsin. M.A. dissertation.

————. 1969. "The Variable Discrimination Hypothesis and the Measurement of Socioeconomic Status in an Isolated Brazilian Area." University of Wisconsin, Ph.D. dissertation.

Sarmento, Walney Moraes. 1970. "O nordeste como regiao subdesenvolvida." Universidade Federal da Bahia, M.A. dissertation.

Sarti, Ingrid. 1973. "Estiva e política: estudo de caso no Porto de Santos." Universidade de Sao Paulo, M.A. dissertation.

Schaden, Egon. 1972. "Problemas de aculturaçao no Brasil." Sao Paulo: Escola de Comunicaçao e Artes, mimeographed.

———. 1972. 'O estudo do ídio brasileiro." Sao Paulo: Escola de Comunicação e Artes, mimeographed.

Schmidt, Benício Viera. 1970. "Um teste de duas estratégicas políticas: a dependência e a autonomia." Universidade Federal de Minas Gerais, M.A. dissertation.

Schneider, Dorit W. 1973. "Classes esquecidas." Museu Nacional da Universidade Federal do Rio de Janeiro, M.A. disseration.

Schneider, Joao Elmo. 1970. "A influência de fatores sócio-culturais na inovabilidade e eficiência dos agricultores: municípios de Westphalen e Estrela." Universidade Federal do Rio Grande do Sul. M.A. dissertation.

Schwartzman, Simon. 1966. *Den politiske process in Lutin Amerika*. Oslo: Minerva's Kvartalsskrift.

———. 1968. "Desenvolvimento e abertura política." *Dados* 6: 24-56.

———. 1970. "Representaçao e cooptaçao política no Brasil." *Dados* 7; 9-41.

———. 1971. "Veinte años de democracia representativa en Brasil." *Revista Latinoamericana de Ciencias Políticas*.

———. 1972. "International Systems and Intra-National Tensions." In Peter Heintz (ed.), *A Macro-Sociological Theory of Societal Systems*. Hans Huber Publishers.

———. 1975. *Sao Paulo e o estado nacional*. Sao Paulo: DIFEL.

Senna, Ronaldo Sales. 1973. "Garimpo e religiao na chapada diamantina." Salvador: Universidade Federal da Bahia, mimeographed.

Seubert, Eva. B. 1975. "Estratificaçao social em fotografia aérea: Alegrete." Universidade Federal do Rio Grande do Sul, M.A. dissertation.

Seyferth, Ziralda. 1973. "A colonizaçao alema no Vale do Itajaí-Mirim." Museu Nacional da Universidade Federal do Rio de Janeiro, M.A. dissertation.

Sigaud, Lígia Maria. 1972. "A naçao dos homens: uma análise regional de ideologia." Museu Nacional da Universidade Federal do Rio de Janeiro, M.A. dissertation.

Silva, Armando Correia da. 1967. *Estrutura e mobilidade social do proletariado urbano em Sao Paulo*. Rio de Janeiro: Civilizaçao Brasileira.

Silva, Celso José da. 1972. "Marchas e contramarchas do mandonismo local em Caeté: um estudo de caso." Universidade Federal de Minas Gerais, M.A. dissertation.

Silva, Joao Saturnino da. 1973. "O sistema agro-industrial canavieiro do recôncavo." Universidade Federal da Bahia, M.A. dissertation.

Silva, José Fábio Barbosa da. 1970. "Juazeiro a Nova Jerusalém: estudo do movimento do Padre Cícero." Universidade de Sao Paulo, doctoral dissertation.

Silva, Luiz Antônio Machado da. 1967. "A vida política na favela." *Cadernos Brasileiros* 41.

Silva, Luiz Antônio Machado da. 1969. "Les Politiques d'intervention dans les Favelas." *Economie et Humanisme*.

_____. 1969. "O significado do botequim." *América Latina* 12 (July-September): 160-82.

_____. 1971. "Mercados metropolitanos de trabalho manual e marginalidade." Museu Nacional da Universidade Federal do Rio de Janeiro, M.A. dissertation.

_____. 1972. "O potencial de ruptura dos grupos marginais." *Cadernos do Centro de Estudos e Açao Social.*

Simao, Azis. 1962. "Industrializaçao e sindicalizaçao no Brasil." *Revista Brasileira de Estudos Políticos* 13 (January).

_____. 1966. *Sindicato e estado.* Sao Paulo: Dominus.

_____. 1968. "L'Industrialisation, la planification et les associations professionelles au Brésil." *Revue Internationale du Travail.* 98 (no. 2).

Singer, Paul I.; and Santos, J.L.F. 1971. "A dinâmica populacional de Salvador." Sao Paulo: CEBRAP, mimeographed.

Singer, Paul I. 1971. "Força de trabalho e emprego no Brasil, 1920-1969." *Cadernos CEBRAP* 3.

_____. 1972. "O milagre brasileiro: causas e conseqüências." *Cadernos CEBRAP.*

Singer, Paul I.; Kowarick, Lúcio; Camargo, Candido P. Joao; and Wilheim, Jorge. 1973. *Urbanización y recursos humanos: el caso de San Pablo.* Buenos Aires: SIAP.

Singer, Paul I.; and Madeira, Felícia R. 1973. "Estrutura de emprego e trabalho feminino no Brasil, 1920-1970." *Cadernos CEBRAP* 13.

Singer, Paul I. 1974. "Contradiçoes do milagre." *Estudos CEBRAP* 6.

Soares, Gláucio Ary Dillon; and Noronha, Amélia. 1960. "Urbanizaçao e dispersao eleitoral." *Revista de Direito Público e Ciência Política* (July-December): 258-70.

_____. 1961. "Interesse político, conflito de pressoes e indecisao eleitoral nas eleições de 1960 no Estado da Guarnabara." *Síntese Política, Econômica e Social* 9 (January-March): 5-34.

_____. 1961. "Classes sociais, strata sociais e as eleições presidenciais de 1960." *Sociologia* 23: 217-38.

Soares, Gláucio Ary Dillon. 1961. "Desenvolvimento econômico e radicalismo político." *Boletim do Centro Latino-Americano de Pesquisas em Ciências Sociais* 2 (May): 117-57.

_____. 1962. "Desenvolvimento econômico e radicalismo político: o teste de uma hipótese (Chile)." *América Latina* 5 (no. 3): 65-84.

_____. 1962. "El sistema electoral y la reforma agraria en el Brasil." *Ciencias Políticas y Sociales.*

_____. 1963. "Brasil: la política del desarrollo desigual." *Ciencias Políticas y Sociales* 32 (April-June): 159-95.

_____. 1964. "Economic Development and Political Radicalism." Washington University, Ph.D. dissertation.

_____. 1964. "The Political Sociology of Uneven Development in Brazil." In Irving Louis Horowitz (ed.) *Revolution in Brazil.* New York: E.P. Dutton.

_____. 1965. "As bases ideológicas do lacerdismo." *Revista Civilizaçao Brasileira* 1 (September).

_____. 1965 "Congruência e incongruência entre indicadores de desenvolvimento econômico." *América Latina* 8.

_____. 1966. "Classes sociais rurais e cooperativismo agrícola: nota de pesquisa." *Revista de Direito Público e Ciência Política* 9 (no. 1): 68-77.

_____. 1966. "Actitudes políticas de los intelectuales." *Revista Latinoamerica de Sociología* 2 (no. 1): 43-66.

Soares Gláucio A.D.; and Soares, Mireya S. de. 1966. "La fuga de los intelectuales." *Aportes* 2 (October); 53-66.

Soares, Gláucio, A.D. 1967. "Brasil: A política do desenvolvimento desigual." *Revista Brasileira de Estudos Políticos* 22 (January): 19-70.

_____. 1967 "A Nova Industrializaçao e o Sistema Político Brasileiro." *Dados* 2-3.

_____. Soares, Gláucio, A.D.; and Robert Hamblin. 1967. "Socio-Economic Variables and Voting for the Radical Left: Chile, 1952." *American Political Science Review* 61 (December).

Soares, Gláucio A.D. 1967. "The Politics of Uneven Development: The Case of Brazil." In Seymour Martin Lipset and Stein Rokkan (eds.), *Party Systems and Voters' Alignments.* New York: Free Press.

_____. 1971. "El sistema electoral y la representación de grupos sociales en el Brasil, 1945-62." *Revista Latinoamericana de Ciencia Política* 2 (no. 1): 3-21.

_____. 1973. *Sociedade e política no Brasil.* Sao Paulo: DIFEL.

_____. 1976. *A questao agrária na América Latina.* Rio de Janeiro: Zahar.

Sodré, Nelson Werneck. 1964. *História da burguesia brasileira.* Rio de Janeiro: Civilizaçao Brasileira.

_____. 1965. *História militar do Brasil.* Rio de Janeiro: Civilizaçao Brasileira.

Somarriba, Maria das Nerges Gomes. 1973. "O desenvolvimento como processo histórico: anatoçoes sobre o caso Brasileiro." Universidade de Brasília, M.A. dissertation.

Souto Mairo, Heraldo Pessoa. 1969. "Levantamento sociocultural de Caxangá." Recife: IBRA, mimeographed.

Souza, Amaury, 1966. "Março ou abril? uma bibliografia comentada sobre o movimento político de 1964 no Brasil." *Dados* 1.

_____. 1968. "Exposiçao aos meios de comunicaçao de massas no Rio de Janeiro: um estudo preliminar." *Dados* 4:145-68.

_____. 1969. "The Brazilian Communist Party and Its National Environment." Riverside: University of California, mimeographed.

_____. 1972. "Determinismo social, racionalidade e voto flutuante em 1960." *Dados* 9:135-45.

_____. 1973. "O cangaço e a política da violência no nordeste brasileiro." *Dados* 10:97-125.

_____. 1973. "Migraçâo, expectativas crescentes e a promessa de protesto coletivo." Rio de Janeiro: IUPERJ, mimeographed.

Souza, Beatriz Muniz de. 1969. *A experiência da salvaçao: pentecostais em Sao Paulo.* Sao Paulo: Livraria Duas Cidades.

Souza, Carlos Eduardo Baesse de. 1973. "A ciência política no Brasil: uma análise sociológica." Universidade de Brasília, M.A. dissertation.

Souza, Maria José. 1973. "Aspectos políticos do Ceará na Primeira República." Universidade Federal da Bahia, M.A. dissertation.

Souza Barros. 1969. *Contraste nas sociedades tradicionais.* Rio de Janeiro: Paralelo.

Talles, Célia Marques. 1972. "Tentativa de classificar a semântica do vocabulário de uma comunidade religiosa de Candomblé." Universidade Federal da Bahia, M.A. dissertation.

Tavares, Maria da Conceçâo. 1966. "Auge e declínio do processo de substituiçao de importaçoes." *Dados* 1.

_____.1972. *Da substituiçao de importaçoes ao capitalismo financeiro.* Rio de Janeiro: Zahar.

Tavares, Maria das Graças P. 1975. "Um estudo de tomada de decisoes em uma comunidade pescadora." Universidade de Brasília, M.A. dissertation.

Taylor, Kenneth, I. "Sanuma Food Prohibitions: The Multiple Classification of Society and Fauna." University of Wisconsin, Ph.D. dissertation.

Teixeira, Anísio. 1969. *Educaçao no Brasil.* Sao Paulo: Cia. Editora Nacional.

Toscano, Gabriela. 1972. "Urbanizaçao e desenvolvimento agrícola em Goiás." Universidade de Brasília, M.A. dissertation.

Tragtenberg, Maurício. 1974. *Burocracia e ideologia.* Sao Paulo: Atica.

Trindade, Hélgio. 1971. "L'Action intégraliste Brésilienne: un mouvement de type fasciste des années 30." Université de Paris, doctoral dissertation.

_____. 1974. *Integralismo: o fascismo brasileiro na década de 1930.* Sao Paulo: DIFEL.

_____. 1975. "Padroes eleitorais no Rio Grande do Sul." In B. Lamounier and F. H. Cardoso (eds.), *Os partidos e as eleiçoes no Brasil.* Rio de Janeiro: Paz e Terra.

Uribe, Rolando Arquimedes Perez. 1972. "Consideraçoes sociológicas do militarismo na América Latina." Universidade de Sao Paulo, doctoral dissertation.

Uricoechea, Fernando. 1976. "The Patrimonial Foundations of the Brazilian Bureaucratic State: Landlords, Princes, and Militias in the Nineteenth Century." University of California at Berkeley, Ph.D. dissertation.

_____. 1977. "A formaçao do estado brasileiro no século XX." *Dados* 14:85-109.

Velho, Gilberto C. A. (ed.). 1971. *Desvio e divergência.* Rio de Janeiro: Zahar.

_____. 1971. "A utopia urbana: um estudo de ideologia e urbanizaçao." Museu Nacional da Universidade Federal do Rio de Janeiro, M.A. dissertation.

_____. 1973. *A utopia urbana.* Rio de Janeiro: Zahar.

_____. 1975. "Nobres e anjos." Universidade de Sao Paulo, doctoral dissertation.

_____. 1976. "Accusations, Family Mobility, and Deviant Behavior." *Social Problems* 23 (February):268-75.

Velho, Ivonne. 1975. *Guerra de orixás.* Rio de Janeiro: Zahar.

Velho, Otávio G. 1969. "O conceito de camponês e sua aplicaçao à análise do meio rural brasileiro." *América Latina* 5 (no. 3).

_____. 1970. "Frentes de expansao e estrutura agrária." Museu Nacional da Universidade Federal do Rio de Janeiro, M.A. dissertation.

_____. 1972. *Frentes de expansao e estrutura agrária*. Rio de Janeiro: Zahar.

_____. 1973. "Modes of Capitalist Development, Peasantry, and the Moving Frontier." University of Manchester, Ph.D. dissertation.

_____. 1976. *Capitalismo Autoritário e campesinato*. Sao Paulo: DIFEL.

_____. 1976. "Modos de desenvolvimento capitalista, campesinato e fronteira em movimento." *Dados* 13.

Vianna, Luiz Werneck. 1976. *Liberalismo e sindicato no Brasil*. Sao Paulo: Paz e Terra

Vieira, Evaldo Amaro. 1972. "Um aspecto do trabalho bancário: sua correlaçao com a desordem mental." Universidade de Sao Paulo, mimeographed.

Vinhas, Maurício. 1970. *Estudo sobre o proletariado brasileiro*. Rio de Janciro: Civilizaçao Brasileira.

Walker, Roger Boyd. 1971. "Mao de obra e emprego urbano: a importância do setor terciário." Rio de Janeiro: SENAC, mimeographed.

Wanderley, Maria Nazareth Baudel. 1966. "Le Travail et les travailleurs dans les plantations de canne à sucre du Pernambuco." Paris: Institut des Sciences sociales du Travail, mimeographed.

Weffort, Francisco C. 1965. "Raízes sociais do populismo na Cidade de Sao Paulo." *Revista Civilizaçao Brasileira* 1 (May):39-60.

_____. 1967. "Le Populisme dans la politique brésilienne." *Temps Modernes* (October).

_____. 1971. "Sindicatos e política." Universidade de Sao Paulo, *Livre Docência* dissertation.

_____. 1972. "Participaçao e conflito industrial: Contagem e Osasco, 1968." *Cadernos CEBRAP* 5.

Willems, Emílio. 1961. *Uma vila brasileira*. Sao Paulo: DIFEL.

_____. 1966. *Followers of the New Faith: Cultural Change and the Rise of Protestantism in Brazil and Chile*. Nashville: Vanderbilt University Press.

Woortmann, Klaas. 1969. "Grupo doméstico e parentesco num vale da Amazônia." Salvador: Universidade Federal da Bahia, mimeographed.

Xansa, Leonidas; and Ferraz, Francisco. 1967. "As eleiçoes de 1966 no Rio Grande do Sul." *Revista Brasileira de Estudos Políticos* 23-24.

Zarur, George de Cerqueira Leite. 1972. "Parentesco, ritual e economia no Alto Xingu." Museu Nacional da Universidade Federal do Rio de Janeiro, M.A. dissertation.

Zekhry, Shlomo. 1970. "A recuperaçao do menor infrator." Universidade de Sâo Paulo, mimeographed.

Zevallos, Savien Espinosa. 1963. "Introducción al desarrollo humano Regional." Universidade de Sao Paulo, mimeographed.

GLOSSARY

Agreste	A geographic region of the Northeast. A transitional zone between the coast, where sugarcane grows, and the backlands.
AIB	National Integral Alliance, a profascist movement.
ANL	National Libertarian Alliance. A liberal movement active at the end of the Old Republic.
ARENA	National Renovating Alliance, a political party created after 1964.
Aroeira	A type of wood, hard and heavy.
Babaçu	A palm tree whose leaves are commonly used for covering houses.
Bandeira	Expeditions organized to move into the backlands, searching for treasures or other ways of making a fortune, and which resulted in frontier expansion.
Bandeirante	Participant in the expeditions to the backlands.
Bandeirismo	Ideology generated by the national colonization movement toward the frontier.
BNH	National Housing Bank.
Barraçao	The plantation store.
Brauna	A type of wood, hard and heavy
Braça	Local measure. Equivalent to 2.20 meters.
Brazilian States	Amazonas, Pará, Maranhao, Piauí, Ceará, Rio Grande do Norte, Paraíba, Pernambuco, Alagoas, Sergipe, Bahia, Minas Gerais, Espírito Santo, Rio de Janeiro, Sao Paulo, Paraná, Santa Catarina, Rio Grande do Sul, Acre, Amapá, Roraima, Rondonia, Mato Grosso, Campo Grande, Goiás, Distrito Federal.
Brazilian Forms of Government	Since independence from Portugal: First Kingdom or Empire (1822-31); Second Kingdom or Empire (1831-89); First Republic (1889-1930); New Republic (1930-45); Liberal

	Period (1945-64); Authoritarian Military Governments (from 1964 to present).
Brazilian Presidents	From 1889 to 1977: Deodoro da Fonseca (1889-91); Floriano Peixoto (1891-94); Prudente de Moraes (1894-98); Campos Sales (1898-1902); Rodrigues Alves (1902-09); Nilo Peçanha (1909-10); Hermes da Fonseca (1910-14); Venceslau Brás (1914-18); Delfim Moreira (1918-19); Epitácio Pessoa (1919-22); Artur Bernardes (1922-26); Getúlio Vargas (1930 — Head of Provisional Government; 1934-37 — president elected by the National Assembly; 1937-45 — head of the New State); Eurico Gaspar Dutra (1946-51); Getúlio Vargas (1951-54); Café Filho, Carlos Luz, and Nereu Ramos (1954-55); Juscelino Kubitschek de Oliveira (1956-61); Jânio Quadros (1961); Joao Goulart (1961-64); Castelo Branco (1964-67); Costa e Silva (1967-69); Garrastazu Medici (1969-74); Ernesto Geisel (1974-[79]).
Cabo	Corporal. Man in charge of measuring and responsible for groups of sugarcane plantation workers. He represents the next step above the mere laborer in the plantation hierarchy.
CAPES	Coordination for the Improvement of University Training, a government program for the improvement of graduate schooling and which operates primarily through grants.
Cambao	The obligation of working for the plantation a few days a year.
CEBRAP	Brazilian Center for Analysis and Planning.
Cento	One cento. In the text it refers to 120 or 130 stalks of sugarcane, cut and tied together by one worker.
Chas	Table lands in the state of Pernambuco which are useless for growing sugarcane, and where fruits, vegetables, and manioc are grown for the supply of urban centers.
CLACSO	Latin American Council for the Social Sciences.
Clandestino	Nonregistered laborer or clandestine worker.
CLT	Consolidated Labor Laws.
CNA	National Confederation of Landowners.
CNP	Brazilian Council of Science and Technology, a national agency which sponsors graduate research.
Condiçao	Worker obligation due to the plantation owner.
Conta	An area of sugarcane plantation measuring 22 by 22 meters and which must be weeded by laborers.
CONTAG	National Confederation of Agricultural Workers.
Coronel	Colonel. The word refers to the highest echelon of the Old

	National Guard. The wealthiest farmers could become members of the guard. Nowadays the term refers to local political bosses.
Coronelismo	Political system in which the *coronel* plays a major role.
Corte da Conta	Penalty assigned to laborers for not weeding the sugarcane according to the landowner representatives' criteria of duty. As a consequence, workers' credit is withdrawn from the plantation store where they receive their weekly supply of goods.
Cruzeiro	Brazilian currency.
Curral	Corral.
DNOCS	National Department of Works against Droughts.
Decimo	Thirteenth salary.
Empreiteiros	Labor contractors.
Empresa	Enterprise.
Engenho	Sugar mill complex of the past. At times the term refers to the sugar mill itself. It also means the plantation.
Engenhos Bangues	Primitive sugar mills.
Engenhos Centrais	Central sugar mills.
Engenho da Galiléia	Galiléia Sugar Mill, site where the first peasant league developed.
Estado Novo	Name given to the authoritarian government of President Getúlio Vargas. It means literally "New State" and could be understood as the Brazilian equivalent to the New Deal, mainly for the labor policies developed at the time. It lasted from 1937 to 1945.
Estância	Ranch.
Estatuto do Trabalhador Rural	Rural Labor Law.
Fazenda	Farm.
FAPESP	Research Protection Foundation of the State of Sao Paulo.
FETAPE	Pernambuco Agricultural Workers' Federation.
Fichados	Registered workers.
FINEP	Projects and Studies Financing Agency; a national agency which sponsors science and technology projects and which is part of the Ministry of Planning.

Florianismo	Name of a political movement which was active after the proclamation of the Republic.
Foreiros	Peasants who pay rent for the land they occupy.
Fornecedor	Sugarcane supplier, the present function of the *senhores de engenho.*
Fornecedor de Cana	The same as *fornecedor.*
Foro	Rental rate.
FUNRURAL	Rural Social Security Fund.
Gabao	The plantation store's special token which functions as currency within the plantation boundaries.
GERAN	Executive Group for the Rationalization of the Northeastern Agroindustry.
Granjismo	Movement of the population towards weekend resorts.
IAA	Institute for Sugar and Alcohol.
IBRA	Brazilian Institute for Agrarian Reform.
ICM	Sales tax.
INPS	National Institute for Social Security.
Interventores	Federal government-appointed trusted commissioners to replace state governors.
IUPERJ	University Research Institute of Rio de Janeiro.
Jagunços	Bandits.
Latifúndio	Large landholding.
Mamelucos	Individuals of mixed European and Brazilian Indian ethnic origin.
Minifúndio	Small landholding.
Morador	Plantation worker who lives in the plantation households.
Guarda Nacional	Local militia created in 1831, when the old militias were abolished. It had a peace-keeping function among local chieftains.
Pangola	Type of grass, appropriate for feeding cattle.
Pelego	Middleman. Labor elite which mediated between the Ministry of Labor and the labor unions.
PNAD	National Household Sampling Research.
Política dos Governadores	Political Coalition between local chieftains and the states' powers.
Ponto	The place where sugarcane is taken from the donkeys that carried it, to be picked up by the mill's trucks or engines.

PR	Republican Party
PROTERRA	Program for Land Redistribution and Incentives of the Northeastern Agroindustry.
PSD	Social Democratic party, political party created by Vargas during the Liberal Period.
PTB	Brazilian Labor Party
Quarta	Local measure, equivalent to 1.68 bushels or 88 liters.
Queremismo	A political movement in support of the continuation of the Vargas regime.
Recusa do Foro	Device by which landowners refuse to accept payment for the renting of land in the hope of having a legal claim for the renter's eviction.
Remunerado	Local term which means the paid weekly rest.
Rendeiros	People who rent the land for subsistence and commercial crops.
Repouso Semanal	Paid weekly rest to which the workers are entitled by federal law.
Roubo da Balança	Theft made in weighing of the sugarcane cut by workers by altering the plantation scales.
Senhor de Engenho	Owner of an *engenho*, also a sugarcane supplier.
Sertao	The west, the backlands, the dry region of the interior.
Sertanista	Man who knows the backlands well.
Sítio	A plot of land.
Sociedade Agrícola e Pecuária de Plantadores de Pernambuco	Agricultural and Cattle-Raising Society of Pernambuco Growers, the first peasant league.
SUDENE	Superintendency for the Development of the Northeast.
Tabela de Campo	Wage and labor equivalence table.
Taguá	Raw material used to mold bricks and tiles.
Tarefa	Local measure equivalent to 0.896 acres or 0.3 hectares.
Tarefa Exagerada	Work area assigned by landlords and which exceeds the usual measurement of one *tarefa*.
Tenentismo	Lieutenants' movement. A military rebellion which was decisive in bringing down the Old Republic.
Terreiros	Religious gathering grounds.

Tomba	The place where sugarcane is cut.
UDN	National Democratic Party, created to opose Vargas during the Liberal Period.
Usina	Sugar mill which besides receiving sugarcane from suppliers also has its own plantations. It refers to modern factories which replaced the old sugar mills or *engenhos*.
Usineiro	Owner of an *usina*.
Várzea	Lowland.
Vara de Medir	A measuring rod which should be equivalent to one *braça*.
Zona da Mata	The state of Pernambuco's sugarcane zone.

About the Contributors

Neuma Aguiar is associate professor of sociology at the Instituto Universitário de Pesquisas do Rio de Janeiro, where she has been the head of the Graduate Program in Political Science and Sociology. She has written widely on the sociology of development and published in journals such as *Revista Latinoamericana de Sociología, Desarrollo Económico, Studies in Comparative International Development,* and *Dados.* She has edited a book on Social Stratification in Portuguese entitled *Hierarchies within Social Classes.* She holds a Ph.D. from Washington University in St. Louis with a dissertation on "The Mobilization and Bureaucratization of the Working Class in Brazil from 1930 to 1964."

Manoel Tosta Berlinck has been director of the Institute of Philosophy and Human Sciences at the Universidade de Campinas in the state of Sao Paulo. He has recently published a book in Portuguese on *Social Marginality and Class Relationships in the City of Sao Paulo.* He has a Ph.D. in Sociology from Cornell University with a dissertation on "The Structure of the Brazilian Family in the City of Sao Paulo."

Aspásia Alcântara de Camargo is a research coordinator at the Center for Research and Documentation of Contemporary History, Getúlio Vargas Foundation, where she directs a research program on oral history. She has offered courses as a visiting professor at the Instituto Universitário de Pesquisas do Rio de Janeiro and at the National Museum of Universidade Federal do Rio Janeiro. She has accomplished her doctoral degree at the Ecole Pratique des Hautes Etudes in Paris with a dissertation on "Peasant Movements and Populist Crisis."

Antônio Otávio Cintra is president of the Joao Pinheiro Foundation, a modern planning agency which assesses the state of Minas Gerais. He teaches political science at the Federal University of Minas Gerais and has done his graduate work at the Massachusetts Institute of Technology

255

with a doctoral dissertation on "The Belo Horizonte Metropolitan Planning Experience."

Daniel J. Hogan is an American residing in Brazil since 1969, teaching sociology at the Graduate School of the Universidade de Campinas, Sao Paulo. He holds a Ph.D. in Sociology from Cornell University.

Olavo Brasil de Lima Júnior is associate professor of political science at the Instituto Universitário de Pesquisas do Rio de Janeiro where he has conducted research on public policy applied to education and the 1976 Brazilian elections. He has done his graduate work at the University of Michigan.

Moacir Palmeira is associate professor in the Graduate Program of Social Anthropology at the National Museum, Federal University of Rio de Janeiro. He has a doctoral degree in sociology from René Descartes University, Paris, with a dissertation on "Latifundium and Capitalism: Critical Readings of a Debate."

Otávio Guilherme Velho is head of the Graduate Program in Social Anthropology at the National Museum, Federal University of Rio de Janeiro. He has published two books in Portuguese on the Brazilian frontier: *Expansion Front and Agrarian Structure* (1972) and *Modes of Capitalist Development, Peasantry, and the Moving Frontier* (1976). The latter was also his doctoral dissertation presented at the University of Manchester, England, where he obtained his Ph.D.

Wanderley Guilherme dos Santos is executive director of the Instituto Universitário de Pesquisas do Rio de Janeiro. He has published on a wide variety of topics ranging from the Brazilian sociopolitical imagination, to liberalism and authoritarianism, and public policy. He has been a visiting professor of political science at the University of Wisconsin, and has done his graduate work at Stanford University.

Name Index